Praise for *Skippy Dies*

"If killing your protagonist with more than 600 pages to go sounds audacious, it's nothing compared with the literary feats Murray pulls off in this hilarious, moving and wise book . . . The exchanges between these boys are so profane and believable, they border on genius . . . The mixture of tones is the book's true triumph, oscillating the banal with the sublime, the silly with the terrifying, the sweet with the tragic. In short, it's like childhood. In shorter, like life."
—Jess Walter, *The Washington Post Book World*

"Skippy is so desperately, painfully alive that you hope the mere act of reading about him will save him . . . A virtuosic display you'd expect from a writer with the confidence to kill off his title character *in the title*."
—Radhika Jones, *Time*

"[Murray's] remarkable dialogue . . . captures the free-associative, sex-obsessed energy of teen-age conversation in all its coarse, riffing brilliance."
—*The New Yorker*

"An utterly engrossing read."
—*Elle*

"Darkly funny and wholly enjoyable . . . Murray will never once lose your attention, writing with wit and charm and making this tragicomedy both hilarious and effortlessly moving."
—*The Observer's Very Short List*

"[Murray] nails the ridiculousness of adolescence without ever losing sight of its deadly earnest and painfully raw aspects, and he brings equal honesty and empathy to his adult characters—except when he wants to make them cartoons, and then they're brilliant cartoons."
—Ron Hogan, Beatrice.com

ALSO BY PAUL MURRAY

An Evening of Long Goodbyes

PAUL MURRAY

Skippy Dies

Paul Murray was born in 1975. He studied English literature at Trinity College in Dublin and creative writing at the University of East Anglia. His first novel, *An Evening of Long Goodbyes*, was short-listed for the Whitbread Prize in 2003 and was nominated for the Kerry Irish Fiction Award.

Skippy Dies

PAUL MURRAY

FABER AND FABER, INC.
An affiliate of Farrar, Straus and Giroux
New York

Faber and Faber, Inc.
An affiliate of Farrar, Straus and Giroux
18 West 18th Street, New York 10011

Originally published in 2010 by Hamish Hamilton, an imprint of Penguin Books,
Great Britain
Published in the United States in 2010 by Faber and Faber, Inc.
First American single-volume paperback edition, 2011

Grateful acknowledgment is made for permission to reprint the following previously published material: Excerpts from *Goodbye to All That* by Robert Graves, reprinted by permission of Carcanet Press Ltd. "On Portents" from *Complete Poems* by Robert Graves, reprinted
by permission of Carcanet Press Ltd. "L'Amoureuse" from *Capitale de la douleur* by Paul
Éluard, copyright © Gallimard, reprinted by permission.

Library of Congress Control Number: 2010926173
Hardcover ISBN: 978-0-86547-943-2
Paperback Boxed Set ISBN: 978-0-86547-948-7
Single-Volume Paperback ISBN: 978-0-86547-861-9

www.fsgbooks.com

1   3   5   7   9   10   8   6   4   2

For Seán

Skippy Dies

Skippy and Ruprecht are having a doughnut-eating race one evening when Skippy turns purple and falls off his chair. It is a Friday in November, and Ed's is only half full; if Skippy makes a noise as he topples to the floor, no one pays any attention. Nor is Ruprecht, at first, overly concerned; rather he is pleased, because it means that he, Ruprecht, has won the race, his sixteenth in a row, bringing him one step closer to the all-time record held by Guido 'The Gland' LaManche, Seabrook College class of '93.

Apart from being a genius, which he is, Ruprecht does not have all that much going for him. A hamster-cheeked boy with a chronic weight problem, he is bad at sports and most other facets of life not involving complicated mathematical equations; that is why he savours his doughnut-eating victories so, and why, even though Skippy has been on the floor for almost a minute now, Ruprecht is still sitting there in his chair, chuckling to himself and saying, exultantly, under his breath, 'Yes, yes' – until the table jolts and his Coke goes flying, and he realizes that something is wrong.

On the chequered tiles beneath the table Skippy is writhing in silence. 'What's the matter?' Ruprecht says, but gets no answer. Skippy's eyes are bulging and a strange, sepulchral wheezing issues from his mouth; Ruprecht loosens his tie and unbuttons his collar, but that doesn't seem to help, in fact the breathing, the writhing, the pop-eyed stare only get worse, and Ruprecht feels a prickling climb up the back of his neck. 'What's wrong?' he repeats, raising his voice, as if Skippy were on the other side of a busy motorway. Everyone is looking now: the long table of Seabrook fourth-years and their girlfriends, the two St Brigid's girls, one fat, one thin, both still in their uniforms, the trio of shelf-stackers from the shopping mall up the road – they turn and watch as Skippy gasps and dry-heaves, for all the world as if he's drowning, though how could he be drowning here, Ruprecht thinks, indoors, with the sea way over on the other side of the park? It doesn't make any sense, and it's all happening too quickly, without giving him time to work out what to do –

At that moment a door opens and a young Asian man in an Ed's shirt and a badge on which is written, in mock-cursive, *Hi I'm*, and then, in an almost unreadable scrawl, **Zhang Xielin**, emerges behind the counter, carrying a tray of change. Confronted by the crowd, which has risen to its feet to get a better view, he halts; then he spies the body on the floor and, dropping the tray, vaults over the counter, pushes Ruprecht aside and prises open Skippy's mouth. He peers in, but it's too dark to see anything, so hoisting him to his feet, he fastens his arms around Skippy's midriff and begins to yank at his stomach.

Ruprecht's brain, meanwhile, has finally sparked into life: he's scrabbling through the doughnuts on the floor, thinking that if he can find out *which* doughnut Skippy is choking on, it might provide some sort of a key to the situation. As he casts about, however, he makes a startling discovery. Of the six doughnuts that were in Skippy's box at the start of the race, six still remain, none with so much as a bite gone. His mind churns. He hadn't been observing Skippy during the race – Ruprecht when eating competitively tends to enter a sort of a *zone* in which the rest of the world melts away into nothingness, this in fact is the secret of his record-nearing sixteen victories – but he'd assumed Skippy was eating too; after all, why would you enter a doughnut-eating race and not eat any doughnuts? And, more important, if he hasn't eaten anything, how can he be –

'Wait!' he exclaims, jumping up and waving his hands at Zhang. 'Wait!' Zhang Xielin looks at him, panting, Skippy lolling over his forearms like a sack of wheat. 'He hasn't eaten anything,' Ruprecht says. 'He isn't choking.' A rustle of intrigue passes through the body of spectators. Zhang Xielin glowers mistrustfully, but allows Ruprecht to extricate Skippy, who is surprisingly heavy, from his arms and lay him back down on the ground.

This entire sequence of events, from Skippy's initial fall to the present moment, has taken perhaps three minutes, during which time his purple colour has faded to an eerily delicate eggshell blue, and his wheezing breath receded to a whisper; his contortions too have ebbed towards stillness, and his eyes, though open, have taken on an oddly vacant air, so that even looking right at him Ruprecht's not a hundred per cent sure he's even actually conscious, and it seems all of a sudden as if around his own lungs Ruprecht can feel a pair of cold hands clutching as he realizes what's about to happen, though at the same time he can't quite believe it – *could* something like that really happen? Could it really happen *here*, in Ed's Doughnut House? Ed's, with its authentic jukebox and its fake leather and its black-and-white photographs of America; Ed's, with its fluorescent lights and its tiny plastic forks and its weird sterile air that should smell of doughnuts but doesn't; Ed's, where they come every day, where nothing ever happens, where nothing is *supposed* to happen, that's the whole point of it –

One of the girls in crinkly pants lets out a shriek. 'Look!' Jigging up and down on her tiptoes, she stabs at the air with her finger, and Ruprecht snaps out of the stupor he's fallen into and follows the line downwards to see that Skippy has raised his left hand. Relief courses through his body.

'That's it!' he cries.

The hand flexes, as if it has just woken from a deep sleep, and Skippy simultaneously expresses a long, rasping sigh.

'That's it!' Ruprecht says again, without knowing quite what he means. 'You can do it!'

Skippy makes a gurgling noise and blinks deliberately up at Ruprecht.

'The ambulance is going to be here in a second,' Ruprecht tells him. 'Everything's going to be fine.'

Gurgle, gurgle, goes Skippy.

3

'Just relax,' Ruprecht says.

But Skippy doesn't. Instead he keeps gurgling, like he's trying to tell Ruprecht something. He rolls his eyes feverishly, he stares up at the ceiling; then, as if inspired, his hand shoots out to search the tiled floor. It pads blindly amid the spilled Coke and melting ice cubes until it finds one of the fallen doughnuts; this it seizes on, like a clumsy spider grappling with its prey, crushing it between its fingers tighter and tighter.

'Just take it easy,' Ruprecht repeats, glancing over his shoulder at the window for a sign of the ambulance.

But Skippy keeps squeezing the doughnut till it has oozed raspberry syrup all over his hand; then, lowering a glistening red fingertip to the floor, he makes a line, and then another, perpendicular to the first.

T

'He's *writing*,' someone whispers.

He's writing. Painfully slowly – sweat dripping down his forehead, breath rattling like a trapped marble in his chest – Skippy traces out syrupy lines one by one onto the chequered floor. E, L – the lips of the onlookers move soundlessly as each character is completed; and while the traffic continues to roar by outside, a strange kind of silence, almost a serenity, falls over the Doughnut House, as if in here time had temporarily, so to speak, stopped moving forward; the moment, rather than ceding to the next, becoming elastic, attenuated, expanding to contain them, to give them a chance to prepare for what's coming –

TELL LORI

The overweight St Brigid's girl in the booth turns pale and whispers something in the ear of her companion. Skippy blinks up at Ruprecht imploringly. Clearing his throat, adjusting his glasses, Ruprecht examines the message crystallizing on the tiles.

'Tell Lori?' he says.

Skippy rolls his eyes and croaks.

'Tell her what?'

Skippy gasps.

'I don't know!' Ruprecht gabbles, 'I don't know, I'm sorry!' He bends down to squint again at the mysterious pink letters.

'Tell her he *loves* her!' the overweight or possibly even pregnant girl in the St Brigid's uniform exclaims. 'Tell Lori he loves her! Oh my God!'

'Tell Lori you love her?' Ruprecht repeats dubiously. 'Is that it?'

Skippy exhales – he smiles. Then he lies back on the tiles; and Ruprecht sees quite clearly the rise and fall of his breast gently come to a stop.

'Hey!' Ruprecht grabs him and shakes him by the shoulders. 'Hey, what are you doing?'

Skippy does not reply.

For a moment there is a cold, stark silence; then, almost as if from a united desire to fill it, the diner explodes in a clamour. *Air!* is the consensus. *Give him air!* The door is thrown open and the cold November night rushes greedily in. Ruprecht finds himself standing, looking down at his friend. 'Breathe!' he shouts at him, gesticulating meaninglessly like an angry teacher. 'Why won't you breathe?' But Skippy just lies there with a reposeful look on his face, placid as can be.

Around them the air jostles with shouts and suggestions, things people remember from hospital shows on TV. Ruprecht can't take this. He pushes through the bodies and out the door down to the roadside. Biting his thumb, he watches the traffic fleet by in dark, impersonal blurs, refusing to disclose an ambulance.

When he goes back inside, Zhang Xielin is kneeling, cradling Skippy's head on his lap. Doughnuts scatter the ground like little candied wreaths. In the silence, people peek at Ruprecht with moist, pitying eyes. Ruprecht glares back at them murderously. He is fizzing, he is quaking, he is incandescent with rage. He feels like stomping back to his room and leaving Skippy where he is. He feels like screaming out, 'What? What? What? What?' He goes back outside to look into the traffic, he is crying, and in that moment he feels all the hundreds and thousands of facts in his head turn to sludge.

5

Through the laurel trees, in an upper corner of Seabrook Tower, you can just make out the window of their dorm, where not half an hour ago Skippy challenged Ruprecht to the race. Above the lot, the great pink hoop of the Ed's Doughnut House sign broadcasts its frigid synthetic light into the night, a neon zero that outshines the moon and all the constellations of infinite space beyond it. Ruprecht is not looking in that direction. The universe at this moment appears to him as something horrific, thin and threadbare and empty; it seems to know this, and in shame to turn away.

I

Hopeland

These daydreams persisted like an alternate life . . .

Robert Graves

In winter months, from his seat in the middle desk of the middle row, Howard used to look out the window of the History Room and watch the whole school go up in flames. The rugby pitches, the basketball court, the car park and the trees beyond – for one beautiful instant everything would be engulfed; and though the spell was quickly broken – the light deepening and reddening and flattening out, leaving the school and its environs intact – you would know at least that the day was almost over.

Today he stands at the head of the class: the wrong angle and the wrong time of year to view the sunset. He knows, however, that fifteen minutes remain on the clock, and so, pinching his nose, sighing imperceptibly, he tries again. 'Come on, now. The main protagonists. Just the main ones. Anybody?'

The torpid silence remains undisturbed. The radiators are blazing, though it is not particularly cold outside: the heating system is elderly and erratic, like most things at this end of the school, and over the course of the day the heat builds to a swampy, malarial fug. Howard complains, of course, like the other teachers, but he is secretly not ungrateful; combined with the powerful soporific effects of history itself, it means the disorder levels of his later classes rarely extend beyond a low drone of chatter and the occasional paper aeroplane.

'Anyone?' he repeats, looking over the class, deliberately ignoring Ruprecht Van Doren's upstretched hand, beneath which the rest of Ruprecht strains breathlessly. The rest of the boys blink back at Howard as if to reproach him for disturbing their peace. In Howard's old seat, Daniel 'Skippy' Juster stares catatonically into space, for all the world as if he's been drugged; in the back-row suntrap, Henry Lafayette has made a little nest of his arms in which to lay his head. Even the clock sounds like it's half asleep.

'We've been talking about this for the last two days. Are you telling me no one can name a single one of the countries involved? Come on, you're not getting out of here till you've shown me that you know this.'

'Uruguay?' Bob Shambles incants vaguely, as if summoning the answer from magical vapours.

'No,' Howard says, glancing down at the book spread open on his lectern just to make sure. *'Known at the time as "the war to end all wars",'* the caption reads, below a picture of a vast, water-logged moonscape from which all signs of life, natural or man-made, have been comprehensively removed.

'The Jews?' Ultan O'Dowd says.

'The Jews are not a country. Mario?'

'What?' Mario Bianchi's head snaps up from whatever he is attending to, probably his phone, under the desk. 'Oh, it was . . . it was – ow, stop – sir, Dennis is feeling my leg! Stop feeling me, feeler!'

'Stop feeling his leg, Dennis.'

'I wasn't, sir!' Dennis Hoey, all wounded innocence.

On the blackboard, 'MAIN' – Militarism, Alliances, Industrialization, Nationalism – copied out of the textbook at the start of class, is slowly bleached out by the lowering sun. 'Yes, Mario?'

'Uh . . .' Mario prevaricates. 'Well, Italy . . .'

'Italy was in charge of the catering,' Niall Henaghan suggests.

'Hey,' Mario warns.

'Sir, Mario calls his wang *Il Duce*,' says Dennis.

'Sir!'

'Dennis.'

'But he does – you do, I've heard you. "Time to rise, Duce," you say. "Your people await you, Duce."'

'At least I have a wang, and am not a boy with . . . Instead of a wang, he has just a blank piece of . . .'

'I feel we're straying off the point here,' Howard intervenes.

'Come on, guys. The protagonists of the First World War. I'll give you a clue. Germany. Germany was involved. Who were Germany's allies – yes, Henry?' as Henry Lafayette, whatever he is dreaming of, emits a loud snort. Hearing his name, he raises his head and gazes at Howard with dizzy, bewildered eyes.

'Elves?' he ventures.

The classroom explodes into hysterics.

'Well, what was the question?' Henry asks, somewhat woundedly.

Howard is on the brink of accepting defeat and beginning the class all over again. A glance at the clock, however, absolves him from any further effort today, so instead he directs them back to the textbook, and has Geoff Sproke read out the poem reproduced there.

'"In Flanders Fields",' Geoff obliges. 'By Lieutenant John McCrae.'

'John McGay,' glosses John Reidy.

'That's enough.'

'"*In Flanders fields,*"' Geoff reads, '"*the poppies blow*":

'Between the crosses, row on row,
That mark our place; and in the sky
The larks, still bravely singing, fly
Scarce heard amid the guns below.

We are the Dead. Short days ago
We lived –'

At this point the bell rings. In a single motion the daydreaming and somnolent snap awake, grab their bags, stow their books and move as one for the door. 'For tomorrow, read the end of the chapter,' Howard calls over the melee. 'And while you're at it, read the stuff you were supposed to read for today.' But the class has already fizzed away, and Howard is left as he always is, wondering if anyone has been listening to a single thing he's said; he can practically see his words crumpled up on the floor. He packs away his own book, wipes clean the board and sets off to fight his way through the home-time throng to the staffroom.

In Our Lady's Hall, hormonal surges have made giants and midgets of the crowd. The tang of adolescence, impervious to deodorant or opened windows, hangs heavy, and the air tintinnabulates with bleeps, chimes and trebly shards of music as two hundred mobile phones, banned during the school day, are switched back on with the urgency of divers reconnecting to their oxygen supply. From her alcove a safe elevation above it, the plaster Madonna with the starred halo and the peaches-and-cream complexion pouts coquettishly at the rampaging maleness below.

'Hey, Flubber!' Dennis Hoey scampers across Howard's path to waylay William 'Flubber' Cooke. 'Hey, I just wanted to ask you a question?'

'What?' Flubber immediately suspicious.

'Uh, I was just wondering – are you a bummer tied to a tree?'

Brows creasing, Flubber – fourteen stone and on his third trip through second year – turns this over.

'It's not a trick or anything,' promises Dennis. 'I just wanted to know, you know, if you're a bummer tied to a tree.'

'No,' Flubber resolves, at which Dennis takes flight, declaring exuberantly, 'Bummer on the loose! Bummer on the loose!' Flubber lets out a roar and prepares to give chase, then stops abruptly and ducks off in the other direction as the crowd parts and a tall, cadaverous figure comes striding through.

Father Jerome Green: teacher of French, coordinator of Seabrook's charitable works, and by some stretch the school's most terrifying personage. Wherever he goes it is with two or three bodies' worth of empty space around him, as if he's accompanied by an invisible retinue of pitchfork-wielding goblins, ready to jab at anyone who happens to be harbouring an impure thought. As he passes, Howard musters a weak smile; the priest glares back at him the same way he does at everyone, with a kind of ready, impersonal disapproval, so adept at looking into man's soul and seeing sin, desire, ferment that he does it now like ticking a box.

Sometimes Howard feels dispiritedly as if not one thing has changed here in the ten years since he graduated. The priests in particular bring this out in him. The hale ones are still hale, the doddery ones still dodder; Father Green still collects canned food for Africa and terrorizes the boys, Father Laughton still gets teary-eyed when he presents the works of Bach to his unheeding classes, Father Foley still gives 'guidance' to troubled youngsters, invariably in the form of an admonition to play more rugby. On bad days Howard sees their endurance as a kind of personal rebuke – as if that almost-decade of life between matriculation and his ignominious return here had, because of his own ineptitude, been rolled back, struck from the record, deemed merely so much fudge.

Of course this is pure paranoia. The priests are not immortal. The Holy Paraclete Fathers are experiencing the same problem as every other Catholic order: they are dying out. Few of the priests in Seabrook are under sixty, and the newest recruit to the pastoral programme – one of an ever-dwindling number – is a young seminarian from somewhere outside Kinshasa; when the school principal, Father Desmond Furlong, fell ill at the beginning of September, it was a layman – economics teacher Gregory L. Costigan – who took the reins, for the first time in Seabrook's history.

Leaving behind the wood-panelled halls of the Old Building, Howard passes up the Annexe, climbs the stairs, and opens, with the usual frisson of weirdness, the door marked 'Staffroom'. Inside, a half-dozen of his colleagues are kvetching, marking homework or changing their nicotine patches. Without addressing anyone or otherwise signalling his presence, Howard goes to his locker and throws a couple of books and a pile of copies into his briefcase; then, moving crab-like to avoid eye contact, he steals out of the room again. He clatters back down the stairs and the now-deserted corridor, eyes fixed deter-minedly on the exit – when he is arrested by the sound of a young female voice.

It appears that, although the bell for the end of the school day rang a good five minutes ago, class in the Geography Room is still in full swing. Crouching slightly, Howard peers through the nar-row window set in the door. The boys inside show no sign of impatience; in fact, by their expressions, they are quite oblivious to the passage of time.

The reason for this stands at the head of the class. Her name is Miss McIntyre; she is a substitute. Howard has caught glimpses of her in the staffroom and on the corridor, but he hasn't yet managed to speak to her. In the cavernous depths of the Geography Room, she draws the eye like a flame. Her blonde hair has that cascading quality you normally see only in TV ads for shampoo, complemented by a sophisticated mag-nolia two-piece more suited to a boardroom than a transition-year class; her voice, while soft and melodious, has at the same time an ungainsayable quality, an undertone of command. In the crook of her arm she cradles a globe, which while she speaks she caresses absently as if it were a fat, spoiled housecat; it almost seems to purr as it revolves langorously under her fingertips.

'. . . just beneath the surface of the Earth,' she is saying, 'tem-peratures so high that the rock itself is molten – can anyone tell me what it's called, this molten rock?'

'Magma,' croak several boys at once.

'And what do you call it, when it bursts up onto the Earth's surface from a volcano?'

'Lava,' they respond tremulously.

'Excellent! And millions of years ago, there was an enormous amount of volcanic activity, with magma boiling up over the entire surface of the Earth non-stop. The landscape around us today –' she runs a lacquered fingernail down a swelling ridge of mountain '– is mostly the legacy of this era, when the whole

14

planet was experiencing dramatic physical changes. I suppose you could call it Earth's teenage years!'

The class blushes to its collective roots and stares down at its textbook. She laughs again, and spins the globe, snapping it under her fingertips like a musician plucking the strings of a double bass, then catches sight of her watch. 'Oh my gosh! Oh, you poor things, I should have let you out ten minutes ago! Why didn't someone say something?'

The class mumbles inaudibly, still looking at the book.

'Well, all right . . .' She turns to write their homework on the blackboard, reaching up so that her skirt rises to expose the back of her knees; moments later the door opens, and the boys troop reluctantly out. Howard, affecting to study the photographs on the noticeboard of the Hillwalking Club's recent outing to Djouce Mountain, watches from the corner of his eye until the flow of grey jumpers has ceased. When she fails to appear, he goes back to investi–

'Oh!'

'Oh my God, I'm so sorry.' He hunkers down beside her and helps her re-amass the pages that have fluttered all over the gritty corridor floor. 'I'm so sorry, I didn't see you. I was just rushing back to a . . . a meeting . . .'

'That's all right,' she says, 'thanks,' as he places a sheaf of Ordnance Survey maps on top of the stack she's gathered back in her arms. 'Thank you,' she repeats, looking directly into his eyes, and continuing to look into them as they rise in unison to their feet, so that Howard, finding himself unable to look away, feels a brief moment of panic, as if they have somehow become locked together, like those apocryphal stories you hear about the kids who get their braces stuck together while kissing and have to get the fire brigade to cut them out.

'Sorry,' he says again, reflexively.

'Stop apologizing,' she laughs.

He introduces himself. 'I'm Howard Fallon. I teach History. You're standing in for Finian Ó Dálaigh?'

'That's right,' she says. 'Apparently he's going to be out till Christmas, whatever happened to him.'

'Gallstones,' Howard says.

'Oh,' she says.

Howard wishes he could unsay *gallstones*. 'So,' he rebegins effortfully, 'I'm actually on my way home. Can I give you a lift?'

She cocks her head. 'Didn't you have a meeting?'

'Yes,' he remembers. 'But it isn't really that important.'

'I have my own car, thanks all the same,' she says. 'But I suppose you could carry my books, if you like.'

'Okay,' Howard says. Possibly the offer is ironic, but before she can retract it he removes the stack of binders and textbooks from her hands and, ignoring the homicidal looks from a small clump of her pupils still mooning about the corridor, walks alongside her towards the exit.

'So, how are you finding it?' he asks, attempting to haul the conversation to a more equilibrious state. 'Have you taught much before, or is this your first time?'

'Oh –' she blows upwards at a wayward strand of golden hair '– I'm not a teacher by profession. I'm just doing this as a favour for Greg, really. Mr Costigan, I mean. God, I'd forgotten about this Mister, Miss stuff. It's so funny. *Miss McIntyre*.'

'Staff are allowed to use first names, you know.'

'Mmm . . . Actually I'm quite enjoying being *Miss McIntyre*. Anyhow, Greg and I were talking one day and he was saying they were having problems finding a good substitute, and it so happens that once upon a time I had fantasies of being a teacher, and I was between contracts, so I thought why not?'

'What's your field normally?' He holds open the main door for her and they step out into the autumn air, which has grown cold and crisp.

'Investment banking?'

Howard receives this information with a studied neutrality, then says casually, 'I used to work in that area myself, actually. Spent about two years in the City. Futures, primarily.'

'What happened?'

He cracks a grin. 'Don't you read the papers? Not enough future to go around.'

She doesn't react, waiting for the correct answer.

'Well, I'll probably get back into it some day,' he blusters. 'This is just a temporary thing, really. I sort of fell into it. Although at the same time, it's nice, I think, to give something back? To feel like you're making a difference?' They make their way around the sixth-years' car park, a series of Lexuses and TTs – and Howard's heart sinks as his own car comes into view.

'What's with the feathers?'

'Oh, it's nothing.' He sweeps his hand along the car's roof, ploughing a mighty drift of white feathers over the side. They pluff to the ground, from where some float back up to adhere to his trousers. Miss McIntyre takes a step backwards. 'It's just a . . . ah, sort of a gag the boys play.'

'They call you Howard the Coward,' she remarks, like a tourist inquiring the meaning of a puzzling local idiom.

'Yes.' Howard laughs mirthlessly, shovelling more feathers from his windscreen and bonnet and not offering an explanation. 'You know, they're good kids, generally, in this place, but there's a few that can be a bit, ah, high-spirited.'

'I'll be on my guard,' she says.

'Well, like I say, it's just a small percentage. Most of them . . . I mean, generally speaking it's a wonderful place to work.'

'You're covered in feathers,' she says judiciously.

'Yes,' he harrumphs, swiping his trousers summarily, straightening his tie. Her eyes, which are a brilliant and dazzling shade of blue custom-made for sparkling mockingly, sparkle mockingly at him. Howard has had enough humiliation for one day; he is just about to bow out with the last shreds of his dignity, when she says, 'So what's it like, teaching History?'

'What's it like?' he repeats.

'I'm really liking doing Geography again.' She gazes dreamily around at the ice-blue sky, the yellowing trees. 'You know, these titanic battles between different forces that actually created the shape of the world we're walking around in today . . . it's so *dramatic* . . .' She squeezes her hands sensually, a goddess forging worlds out of raw matter, then fixes The Eyes on Howard again. 'And History – that must be so much fun!'

This isn't the first word that springs to mind, but Howard limits himself to a bland smile.

'What are you teaching at the moment?'

'Well, in my last class we were doing the First World War.'

'Oh!' She claps her hands. 'I *love* the First World War. The boys must be enjoying that.'

'You'd be surprised,' he says.

'You should read them Robert Graves,' she says.

'Who?'

'He was in the trenches,' she replies; then adds, after a pause, 'He was also one of the great love poets.'

'I'll take a look,' he scowls. 'Any other tips for me? Any other lessons you've gleaned from your five days in the profession?'

She laughs. 'If I have any more I'll be sure and pass them on. It sounds like you need them.' She lifts the books out of Howard's arms and aims her car key at the enormous white-gold SUV parked next door to Howard's dilapidated Bluebird. 'See you tomorrow,' she says.

'Right,' Howard says.

But she doesn't move, and neither does he: she holds him there a moment purely by the light of her spectacular eyes, looking him over with the tip of her tongue tucked in the corner of her mouth, as if she is deciding what to have for dinner. Then, smiling at him coyly with a row of pointed white teeth, she says, 'You know, I'm not going to sleep with you.'

At first Howard is sure he must have misheard her; and when he realizes that he has not, he is still too stunned to reply. So he just stands there, or perhaps totters, and the next thing he knows she's climbed into her jeep and pulled away, sending white feathers swirling about his ankles.

The door swings open with a creak and you step inside, into the Great Hall. Spiderwebs cover everything, drifting from floor to ceiling like veils from a thousand left-behind brides. You look at the map and go through a door on the far side of the hall. This room used to be the library; books cover the floor in dusty piles. On the table is a scroll, but before you can read it the grandfather clock bursts open and there are one, two, three zombies coming at you! You swipe at them with the torch and duck round the other side of the table, but more appear in the doorway, drawn by the smell of someone alive –

'Skippy, this is totally boring.'

'Yeah, Skip, do you think someone else could have a go, maybe?'

'I'll just be a second,' Skippy mumbles, as the zombies pursue him up a rickety staircase.

'What do you think these zombies do all day?' Geoff wonders. 'When there's no one around they want to eat?'

'They order pizza,' Dennis says. 'Which Mario's dad delivers.'

'I told you a thousand times, my father is not a pizza delivery-man, he is an important diplomat in the Italian embassy,' Mario snaps.

'Seriously, though, how often is anyone going to call into their creepy house? Like, what do they do, just wander around it all day long, moaning to each other?'

'They sound sort of like my parents,' Geoff realizes. He gets up and stretches out his arms and staggers around the room, saying in a sepulchral zombie voice, '*Geoff . . . put out the garbage . . . Geoff . . . I can't find my glasses . . . We've made great sacrifices to send you to that school, Geoff . . .*'

Skippy wishes they would stop talking. Heat coils round his

brain like a fat snake, tighter and tighter, making his eyelids heavy
. . . and now just for a second the screen blurs, enough time for a
raggy arm to fling itself around his neck – he shakes awake, he
tries to wriggle free, but it's too late, they're all over him, pulling
him to the ground, crowding around till he can't even see himself,
their long nails slashing down, their rotten teeth gnashing, and
the little spinning light that is his soul whirls up to the ceiling . . .

'*Game over, Skippy,*' Geoff says in the zombie voice, laying a
heavy hand on his shoulder.

'Finally,' Mario says. 'Now can we play something else?'

Skippy's dorm, like all the other dorms, is in the Tower, which
sits at the end of Our Lady's Hall and is the very oldest part of
Seabrook. In days of Yore, when the school was first built, the
entire student population ate, slept and sat through classes here;
nowadays, day boys form the majority of the pupils, and out of
each year of two hundred there are only twenty or thirty unlucky
souls who have to come back here after the bell has gone. Any
Harry Potter–type fantasies tend to get squashed pretty quickly:
life in the Tower, an ancient building composed mostly of
draughts, is a deeply unmagical experience, spent at the mercy
of lunatic teachers, bullies, athlete's foot epidemics, etc. There
are some small consolations. At a point in life in which the lovely
nurturing homes built for them by their parents have become
unendurable Guantánamos, and any time spent away from their
peers is experienced at best as a mind-numbing commercial
break for things no one wants to buy on some old person's TV
channel and at worst as a torture not incomparable to being
actually genuinely nailed to a cross, the boarders do enjoy a certain prestige among the boys. They have a sort of sheen of independence; they can cultivate mysterious personae without
having to worry about mums or dads showing up and blowing
the whole thing by telling people about amusing 'accidents' they
had when they were little or by publically admonishing them to
please stop walking around with their hands wedged in their
pockets like a pervert.

Unarguably the best thing about being a boarder, though, is that the Tower overlooks, in spite of the feverish tree-planting efforts of the priests, the yard of St Brigid's, the girls' school next door. Every morning, lunchtime and evening the air rings with high feminine voices like lovely secular bells, and at night-time, before they close the curtains, you can see without even needing to look through the telescope – which is a good thing, because Ruprecht is extremely particular about what his telescope is used for, and always keeps it pointed into the girl-less reaches of the sky above – your female counterparts walking around in the upper windows, talking, brushing their hair or even, if you believe Mario, doing naked aerobics. That's as close as you'll get, though, because, while it's the constant subject of plans and boasts and tall tales, no one has ever verifiably breached the wall between the two schools; nor has anyone conceived of a way past the St Brigid's janitor and his infamous dog, Nipper, not to mention the terrifying Ghost Nun who legend has it roams the grounds after dark wielding either a crucifix or pinking shears, depending on who you talk to.

Ruprecht Van Doren, owner of the telescope and Skippy's room-mate, is not like the other boys. He arrived at Seabrook in January, like a belated and non-returnable Christmas gift, after both his parents were lost on a kayaking expedition up the Amazon. Prior to their deaths, he had been schooled at home by tutors flown in from Oxford at the behest of his father, Baron Maximilian Van Doren, and consequently he has quite a different attitude to education from his peers. For Ruprecht, the world is a compendium of fascinating facts just waiting to be discovered, and a difficult maths problem is like sinking into a nice warm bath. A cursory glance around the room will give an idea of his current projects and interests. Maps of many kinds cover the walls – maps of the moon, of near and far-off constellations, a map of the world stuck with little pins marking recent UFO sightings – as well as a picture of Einstein and scoresheets commemorating notable Yahtzee victories. The telescope, bearing a sign that reads

21

in big black letters DO NOT TOUCH, points out the window; a French horn gleams pompously from the foot of the bed; on the desk, hidden beneath a sheaf of inscrutable printouts, his computer performs mysterious operations whose full nature is known only to its owner. Impressive as this may be, it represents only a fraction of Ruprecht's activity, most of which takes place in his 'lab', one of the dingy antechambers off the basement. Down here, surrounded by yet more computers and parts of computers, more towers of unfathomable papers and electrical arcana, Ruprecht constructs equations, conducts experiments and continues his pursuit of what he considers the Holy Grail of science: the secret of the origins of the universe.

'Newsflash, Ruprecht, they know about the origins of the universe. It's called the Big Bang?'

'Aha, but what happened *before* the Bang? What happened during it? What was it that banged?'

'How would I know?'

'Well, you see, that's the whole point. From the moments *after* the Bang until this moment right now, the universe makes sense – that is to say, it obeys observable laws, laws that can be written down in the language of mathematics. But when you go before that, to the very, very beginning, these laws no longer apply. The equations won't work out. If we could solve them, though, if we could understand what happened in those first few milliseconds, it would be like a master key, which would unlock all sorts of other doors. Professor Hideo Tamashi believes that the future of humanity could depend on our opening these doors.'

Spend twenty-four hours a day cooped up with Ruprecht and you will hear a lot about this Professor Hideo Tamashi and his groundbreaking attempts to solve the Big Bang using ten-dimensional string theory. You will also hear a lot about Stanford, the university where Professor Tamashi teaches, which from Ruprecht's descriptions of it sounds like a cross between an amusement arcade and Cloud City in *Star Wars*, a place where everyone wears jumpsuits and nothing bad ever happens. Ruprecht has had his heart set on studying under Professor Tama-shi more or less since he could walk, and whenever he mentions the Prof, or Stanford and its *really first-rate* lab facilities, his voice takes on a starry, yearning quality, like someone describing a beautiful land glimpsed once in a dream.

'Why don't you just *go* then,' Dennis says, 'if everything's so whoop-de-doo over there?'

'My dear Dennis,' Ruprecht chortles, 'one does not just "go" to somewhere like Stanford.'

Instead, it seems, you need something called an *academic résumé*, something that shows the *Dean of Admissions* that you are just that fraction smarter than all the other smart people applying there. Hence Ruprecht's various investigations, experiments and inventions – even the ones, his detractors, principally Dennis, argue, purportedly undertaken for the Future of Humanity.

'That tub of guts doesn't give two hoots about humanity,' Dennis says. 'All he wants is to ponce off to America and meet other dweebs who'll play Yahtzee with him and not make fun of his weight.'

'I suppose it must be hard for him,' Skippy says. 'You know, being a genius and everything, and being stuck here with us.'

'But he's not a genius!' Dennis rails. 'He's a total fraud!'

'Come on, Dennis, what about his equations?' Skippy says.

'Yeah, and his inventions?' adds Geoff.

'His *inventions*? The time machine, a tinfoil-lined wardrobe attached to an alarm clock? The X-ray glasses, that are just regular glasses glued onto the inside of a toaster? How could anyone take these for the work of a serious scientist?'

Dennis and Ruprecht don't get on. It's not hard to see why: two more different boys would be hard to imagine. Ruprecht is eternally fascinated by the world around him, loves to take part in class and throws himself into extra-curricular activities; Dennis, an arch-cynic whose very dreams are sarcastic, hates the world and everything in it, especially Ruprecht, and has never thrown himself into anything, with the exception of a largely successful

campaign last summer to efface the first letter from every manifestation of the word 'canal' in the Greater Dublin Area, viz. the
myriad street signs proclaiming ROYAL ANAL, WARNING! ANAL,
GRAND ANAL HOTEL. As far as Dennis is concerned, the entire
persona of Ruprecht Van Doren is nothing more than a grandilo-
quent concoction of foolish Internet theories and fancy talk lifted
from the Discovery Channel.

'But Dennis, why would he want to make up stuff like that?'

'Why does anyone do anything in this shithole? To make himself look like he's better than us. I'm telling you, he's no more a
genius than I am. And if you ask me, this stuff about him being
an orphan, that's a crock too.'

Well, that's where Dennis and his audience part company. Yes,
it's true that details of Ruprecht's ex-parents remain vague, apart
from an occasional passing reference to his father's skills as a
horseman, 'famed the length of the Rhine', or a fleeting mention
of his mother, 'a delicate woman with aesthetic hands'. And it's
true that although Ruprecht's present line is that they were bota-
nists, drowned while kayaking up the Amazon in search of a rare
medicinal plant, Martin Fennessy claims that Ruprecht, shortly
after his arrival, told him that they were professional kayakers,
drowned while competing in a round-the-world kayaking race.
But nobody believes he or anyone else, with the possible exception of Dennis himself, would do something as karmically
perilous as lie about the death of his parents.

That's not to say Ruprecht isn't annoying, or that he's not
poison to a body's street-cred. There are definite drawbacks to a
public association with Ruprecht. But the bottom line is that for
some inexplicable reason Skippy actually *likes* him, and so the
way it's panned out is that if you're friends with Skippy you now
get Ruprecht into the bargain, like a two-hundred-pound booby
prize.

And by now some of the others have become quite fond of
him. Maybe Dennis is right, and he is talking non-stop bollocks – it
still makes a change from everything else they're hearing these

days. You know, you spend your childhood watching TV, assuming that at some point in the future everything you see there will one day happen to you: that you too will win a Formula One race, hop a train, foil a group of terrorists, tell someone 'Give me the gun', etc. Then you start secondary school, and suddenly everyone's asking you about your *career plans* and your *long-term goals*, and by goals they don't mean the kind you are planning to score in the FA Cup. Gradually the awful truth dawns on you: that Santa Claus was just the tip of the iceberg – that your future will not be the rollercoaster ride you'd imagined, that the world occupied by your parents, the world of washing the dishes, going to the dentist, weekend trips to the DIY superstore to buy floor-tiles, is actually largely what people mean when they speak of 'life'. Now, with every day that passes, another door seems to close, the one marked PROFESSIONAL STUNTMAN, or FIGHT EVIL ROBOT, until as the weeks go by and the doors – GET BITTEN BY SNAKE, SAVE WORLD FROM ASTEROID, DISMANTLE BOMB WITH SECONDS TO SPARE – keep closing, you begin to hear the sound as a good thing, and start closing some yourself, even ones that didn't necessarily need to be closed . . .

At the onset of this process – looking down the barrel of this grim de-dreamification, which, even more than hyperactive glands and the discovery of girls, seems to be the actual stuff of growing up – to have Ruprecht telling you his crackpot theories comes to be oddly comforting.

'Imagine it,' he says, gazing out the window while the rest of you huddle around the Nintendo, 'everything that *is*, everything that has *ever been* – every grain of sand, every drop of water, every star, every planet, space and time themselves – all crammed into one dimensionless point where no rules or laws apply, waiting to fly out and become the future. When you think about it, the Big Bang's a bit like school, isn't it?'

'What?'

'Ruprecht, what the hell are you talking about?'

'Well, I mean to say, one day we'll all leave here and become scientists and bank clerks and diving instructors and hotel managers – the fabric of society, so to speak. But in the meantime, that fabric, that is to say, us, the *future*, is crowded into one tiny little point where none of the laws of society applies, viz., this school.'

Uncomprehending silence; and then, 'I tell you one difference between this school and the Big Bang, and that is in the Big Bang there is no particle quite like Mario. But you can be sure that if there is, he is the great stud particle, and he is boning the lucky lady particles all night long.'

'Yes,' Ruprecht responds, a little sadly; and he will fall silent, there at his window, eating a doughnut, contemplating the stars.

Howard the Coward: yes, that's what they call him. *Howard the Coward*. Feathers; eggs left on his seat; a yellow streak, executed in chalk, on his teacher's cape; once a whole frozen chicken there on the desk, trussed, dimpled, humiliated.

'It's because it rhymes with Howard, that's all,' Halley tells him. 'Like if your name was Ray, they'd call you Gay Ray. Or if it was Mary, they'd call you Scary Mary. It's just the way their brains work. It doesn't mean anything.'

'It means they *know*.'

'Oh God, Howard, one little bump, and it was years and years ago. How could they possibly know about that?'

'They just do.'

'Well, even if they do. *I* know you're not a coward. They're just kids, they can't see into your soul.'

But she is wrong. That is exactly what they can do. Old enough to have a decent mechanical understanding of how the world works, but young enough for their judgements to remain unfogged by anything like mercy or compassion or the realization that all this will one day happen to them, the boys – his students – are machines for seeing through the apparatus of worldliness that adulthood, as figured by their teachers, surrounds itself with, to the grinding emptiness at its heart. They find it hilarious. And the names they give the other teachers seem so unerringly *right*. Malco the Alco? Big Fat Johnson? Lurch?

Howard the Coward. Fuck! Who told her?

The car starts on the third try and putters past slow droves of boys babbling and throwing conkers at each other till it reaches the gate, where it joins a tailback waiting for a space to open up on the road. Years ago, on their very last day of school, Howard and his friends had paused beneath this same gate – SEABROOK COLLEGE arching above them in reversed gold letters – and turned to give what was now their alma mater the finger, before passing through and out into the exhilarating panorama of passion and adventure that would be the setting for their adult lives. Sometimes – often – he wonders if by that small gesture, in a life otherwise bare of gestures or dissent, he had doomed himself to return here, to spend the rest of his days scrubbing away at that solitary mark of rebellion. God loves these broad ironies.

He reaches the top of the line, indicating right. There's the ragged beginnings of a sunset visible over the city, a lush melange of magentas and crimsons; he sits there as witty responses crash belatedly into his mind, one after another.

Never say never.

That's what you think.

Better join the queue.

The car behind honks as a gap opens up. At the last second, Howard switches the indicator and turns left instead.

Halley is on the phone when he gets home; she swivels her chair around to him, rolling her eyes and making a *blah blah* shape with her hand. The air is dense with a day's smoke, and the ashtray piled high with crushed butts and frazzled matchsticks. He mouths *Hi* to her and goes into the bathroom. His own phone starts to ring as he's washing his hands. 'Farley?' he whispers.

'Howard?'

'I called you three times, where have you been?'

'I had to do some work with my third-years for the Science Fair. What's wrong? Is everything okay? I can't hear you very well.'

'Hold on' – Howard reaches in and turns on the shower. In his natural voice he says, 'Listen, something very –'

'Are you in the shower?'

'No, I'm standing outside it.'

'Maybe I should call you back.'

'No – listen, I wanted to – something very strange has just

happened. I was talking to the new girl, the substitute, you know, who teaches Geography –'

'Aurelie?'

'What?'

'Aurelie. It's her name.'

'How do you know?'

'What do you mean, how do I know?'

'I mean' – he feels his cheeks go crimson – 'I meant, what kind of name is Aurelie?'

'It's French. She's part-French.' Farley chuckles lasciviously. 'I wonder which part. Are you all right, Howard? You sound a bit off.'

'Well, okay, the point is, I was talking to her in the car park just now – just having a nice, normal conversation about work and how she's getting on, and then out of the blue she says to me –' he goes to the door and opens it a sliver. In the next room Halley is still nodding and making mm-hmm noises, the phone cradled between her jawbone and shoulder '– she tells me she isn't going to sleep with me!' He waits, and when no response is forthcoming, adds, 'What do you think of that?'

'That is strange,' Farley admits.

'It's *very* strange,' Howard affirms.

'And what did you say?'

'I didn't say anything. I was too surprised.'

'You hadn't been rubbing her thigh or anything like that?'

'That's just it, it was completely unprompted. We were standing there talking about schoolwork, and then out of nowhere she goes, "You know, I'm not going to sleep with you." What do you think it could mean?'

'Well, offhand I'd say it means she isn't going to sleep with you.'

'You don't just *say* to someone that you're not going to sleep with them, Farley. You don't introduce sex into the conversation, out of a clear blue sky, and then just banish it. Unless sex is what you really want to talk about.'

'Wait – you're suggesting that when she told you, "I'm not

going to sleep with you," what she actually meant was, "I *am* going to sleep with you"?'

'Doesn't it sound like she's laying down a challenge? Like she's saying, "I'm not going to sleep with you *now*, but I *might* sleep with you if certain circumstances change."'

Farley hums, then says reluctantly, 'I don't know, Howard.'

'Okay, I see, she's just trying to save me a little time and embarrassment, is that it? She's just trying to help me out? There couldn't possibly be any sexual element.'

'I don't know what she meant. But isn't this entirely academic? Don't you already have a girlfriend? And a mortgage? Howard?'

'Well obviously,' Howard says, simmering. 'I just thought it was a strange thing to say, that's all.'

'If I were you I wouldn't lose any sleep over it. She sounds like one of those flirty types. She's probably that way with everybody.'

'Right.' Howard agrees curtly. 'Here, I'd better go. See you tomorrow.' He hangs up the phone.

'Were you talking to someone in there?' Halley asks him when he comes out.

'Singing,' Howard mutters.

'Singing?' Her eyes narrow. 'Did you actually *have* a shower?'

'Hmm?' Howard realizes he's neglected a key element of his cover story. 'Oh yeah, I just didn't wash my hair. The water's cold.'

'It's cold? How come? It shouldn't be cold.'

'I was cold, I mean. In the shower. So I got out. It's not important.'

'Are you coming down with something?'

'I'm fine.' He sits down at the breakfast bar. Halley stands over him, examines him carefully. 'You do look a bit flushed.'

'I'm fine,' he repeats, more vehemently.

'All right, all right . . .' She walks away, puts on the kettle. He turns to the window, silently trying out the name *Aurelie*.

Their house lies several four-lane miles from Seabrook, on the front line of the suburbs' slow assault on the Dublin mountains. When Howard was growing up, he used to ride his bike around here in the summer with Farley, through fairy-tale woods ticking with grasshoppers and sunshine. Now it looks like a battlefield, mounds of sodden earth surrounding trenches waterlogged with rain. They're building a Science Park on the other side of the valley: every week the landscape has morphed a little more, the swell of a hill shorn off, a flat gashed open.

That's what they all say.

'What have you got there?' Halley comes back with two cups.

'Book.'

'No shit.' She takes it out of his hands. 'Robert Graves, *Goodbye to All That.*'

'Just something I picked up on the way home. First World War. I thought the boys might like it.'

'Robert Graves, didn't he write *I, Claudius*? That they made into a TV series?'

'I don't know.'

'He did.' She scans the back of the book. 'Looks interesting.'

Howard shrugs non-committally. Halley leans back against her chair, watching his eyes buzz restlessly over the counter surface. 'Why are you acting weird?'

He freezes. 'Me? I'm not acting weird.'

'You are.'

Interior pandemonium as he desperately tries to remember how he normally acts with her. 'It's just been a long day – oh God –' groaning involuntarily as she pulls a cigarette from her shirt pocket. 'Are you going to smoke another of those things?'

'Don't start . . .'

'They're *bad* for you. You said you were going to quit.'

'What can I tell you, Howard. I'm an addict. A hopeless, pathetic addict in the thrall of the tobacco companies.' Her shoulders slump as the tip glows in ignition. 'Anyway, it's not like I'm pregnant.'

Ah, right – this is how he normally acts with her. He remembers now. They seem to be going through a protracted phase in which they're able to speak to each other only in criticisms, needles, rebukes. Big things, little things, anything can spark an argument, even when neither of them wants to argue, even when he or she is trying to say something nice, or simply to state an innocuous fact. Their relationship is like a piece of malfunctioning equipment that when switched on will only buzz fractiously, and shocks you when you're trying to find out what's wrong. The simplest solution seems to be not to switch it on, to look instead for a new one; he is not quite ready to contemplate that eventuality, however.

'How was work?' he says conciliatorily.

'Oh . . .' She makes a gesture of insignificance, flicking the dust of the day from her fingers. 'This morning I wrote a review of a new laser printer. Then most of the afternoon I spent trying to get hold of someone in Epson to confirm the specs. Usual roller-coaster ride.'

'Any new gadgets?'

'Yeah, actually . . .' She fetches a small silver rectangle and presents it to him. Howard frowns and fumbles with it – card-thin and smaller than the palm of his hand.

'What is it?'

'It's a movie camera.'

'*This* is a camera?'

She takes it from him, slides back a panel and returns it. The camera issues an almost but not quite inaudible purr. He holds it up and aims it at her; a pristine image of her appears in the tiny screen, with a red light flashing in one corner. 'That's incredible,' he laughs. 'What else does it do?'

'*Make every day like summer!*' she reads from the press release. 'The Sony JLS9xr offers several significant improvements on the JLS700 model, as well as entirely new features, most notably Sony's new Intelligent Eye system, which gives not only unparalleled picture resolution but real-time image augmentation – meaning that your movies can be even more vivid than they are in real life.'

'More vivid than real life?'

'It corrects the image while you record. Compensates for weak light, boosts the colours, gives things a sheen, you know.'

'Wow.' He watches her head dip slightly as she extinguishes her cigarette, then lift again. Miniaturized on the screen she does indeed seem more lustrous, coherent, *resolved* – a bloom to her cheeks, a glint to her hair. When he glances experimentally away from it, the real-life Halley and the rest of their home suddenly appear underdefined, washed out. He turns his eye to it again, and zooms in on her own eyes, deep blue and finely striated with white; like thin ice, he always thinks. They look sad.

'And how about you?'

'Me?'

'You seem a bit down.' Somehow it's easier to talk to her like this, mediated by the camera viewer; he finds the buffer making him audacious, even though she's sitting close enough to touch.

She shrugs fatalistically. 'I don't know . . . it's just these PR people, God, they sound like they're turning into machines themselves, you know, ask them anything at all and they feed you the same pre-recorded answer . . .' She trails off. The backs of her fingers move across her forehead, barely touching it; the viewer picks up fine lines there that he has never noticed before. He pictures her here on her own, frowning at the computer screen in the alcove of the living room she has made her office, surrounded by magazines and prototypes, only smoke for company. 'I tried to write something,' she says thoughtfully.

'Something?'

'A story. I don't know. Something.' She seems happier too, with this arrangement, liberated by not having to look into his eyes; she gazes out the window, down at the ashtray, kneads her bracelet against the bones of her wrist. Howard suddenly finds himself desiring her. Maybe this is the answer to all of their problems! He could wear the camera all the time, mount it onto his head somehow. 'I sat down and told myself I wasn't getting up until I'd written something. So I stayed there for a full hour and God help me, all I could think of was printers. I've spent so long cooped up with this stuff that I've forgotten how actual human beings think and behave.' She slurps her tea disconsolately. 'Do you think there's a

33

market for that, Howard? Epic novels starring office equipment? *Modem Bovary. Less Than Xerox.*'

'Who knows? Technology's getting smarter every day. Maybe it's only a matter of time before computers start reading books. You could be on to something big.' He places his free hand on hers, sees it jump in Lilliputian form into the corner of the screen. 'I don't understand why you don't just quit,' he says. They have had this conversation so many times now, it is an effort to keep it from sounding mechanical. But maybe it will turn out differently this time? 'You've got a bit of money saved, why don't you take some time off and just write? Give yourself six months, say, see what you come up with. We could afford it, if we tightened our belts.'

'It's not that simple, Howard. You know how hard it is to find someone who'll give me a work permit. Futurlab's been good to me, it'd be stupid to quit there with things as they are.'

He ignores the implied accusation here, pretends that this really is about her writing. 'You'd find something. You're good at what you do. Anyway, why not worry about that when the time comes?'

She pulls a face and mutters something.

'Seriously, though, why don't you?'

'Oh, for Christ's sake – I don't know, Howard. Maybe this is all I'm good for. Maybe office equipment is all there is to write about.'

He withdraws his hand, exasperated. 'Well, if you won't do anything about it, then you've got to stop complaining.'

'I'm not complaining, if you ever actually listened to what I –'

'I do listen, that's the problem, I'm listening all the time to you telling me you're unhappy, but then when I try to encourage you to do something about it –'

'Just forget it, I don't want to talk about it.'

'Fine, but then don't tell me I'm not listening when the problem is you don't want to *talk* –'

34

'Can we just forget – Jesus, would you put that fucking thing down?' She stares at him, alight with wounded fury, until he slides the camera's panel shut. Right, right, this is how they act. She grabs another cigarette, lights and tugs at it in a single blur of antipathetic motion.

'Fine,' says Howard, picking up his book and getting to his feet. 'Fine, fine, fine, fine.'

He closets himself in the spare room and turns the pages of the Robert Graves book till he hears her get in the shower.

Halley and he have been together for three years, which, at twenty-eight, constitutes the longest relationship of his life so far. For a long time it coasted along, joshing and amicable. But now Halley wants to get married. She doesn't say it, but he knows. Marriage makes sense for her. As an American citizen, her right to work here currently depends on the benevolence of her employer, who must renew her permit every year. By marrying Howard, she would become, in the state's eyes, naturalized, and so free to go where she pleased. That isn't the only reason she desires it, of course. But it does bring the matter into focus rather sharply: suddenly the question becomes, why do they *not* get married right away? And it hangs above them like some hulking alien spacecraft, blocking out the sun.

So why don't they? It's not that Howard doesn't love her. He does, he would do anything for her, lay down his life if it came to it – if for example she were a princess menaced by a fire-breathing dragon, and he a knight on horseback, he would charge in with his lance without a second thought, stare the serpent right in its smouldering igneous eye, even if it meant getting barbecued there on the spot. But the fact is – the fact is that they live in a world of facts, one of which is that there are no dragons; there are only the pale torpid days, stringing by one like another, a clouded necklace of imitation pearls, and a love binding him to a life he never actually chose. Is this all it's ever going to be? A grey tapestry of okayness? Frozen in a moment he drifted into?

And so in short everything remains on hold, and everything remains unspoken, and Halley gets more confused about where they are going and what is wrong, even though technically nothing *is* wrong, and she gets angry with Howard, and Howard as a result feels even less like getting married. Actually, when the plates start flying, it feels like they've already been married for years.

After dinner (microwaved) a détente of sorts is reached, whereby he sits reading in the living room while she watches TV. When she rises to turn in at ten-thirty, he presents his cheek for her to kiss. The protocol that has emerged of late is that the first person to the bedroom is given a half-hour's grace, so he or she can be asleep by the time the second comes in. It is forty-five days, if you're asking, since they last had sex. Nothing has been explicitly said; it is something they have agreed on tacitly, indeed is one of the few things they do not, at present, disagree on. Eavesdropping on the pornographic conversations of the boys at school, Howard considers how inconceivable the idea of *not wanting* to have sex would have seemed to his younger self – remembers how his every atom hurled itself (mostly fruitlessly) after physical contact with the unthinking, unstoppable urgency of a wild salmon flapping up a waterfall. *There's a woman in your bed and you're not having sex with her?* He can practically hear the disappointment and confusion in that younger self's voice. He's not saying that he likes the present situation. But it is easier, at least in the short to middle term.

Often, as they lie side by side in the darkness, neither letting on to the other that they are still awake, he has long, candid conversations with her in his imagination, where he fearlessly lays everything out on the table. Sometimes these imaginary conversations end with the two of them breaking up, others with their realizing that they can't live apart; either way, it feels good to make a decision.

Tonight, though, he is not thinking about this. Instead he is sitting in the front row of a classroom, staring with the other boys at a globe that spins with luxurious, excruciating slowness under

36

slender fingers. And as he stares into it, the globe changes under the fingers from a map of the world into a crystal ball . . . a crystal ball–cum–lucky dip, where any future you want is there for the taking; and under his breath he is murmuring, *'We'll see about that. We'll see.'*

H O O O O O O O O O O O O O O O O O O O O O O O O
S S S S S S S S S S S S S S S S H H H H H H H
H H H!!

It's a lift going up your brain and right through into space! You can feel your eyes bulging like they're going to explode! Your head's full of elephants, cartoon elephants in a line, lifting their hooves and playing their trunks so music comes out! You're laughing and laughing, you laugh so much you can hardly stand!

But on the ground Morgan is crying. He is crying because Barry's kneeling on his arms, pinning him down. Above the skips the doughnut sign shines in the other direction like it doesn't want to see.

Behind Ed's is where things happen and if you know what is good for you you will stay the fuck away.

Almost as soon as they come the happy explosions start to drain away. Carl stops laughing and takes a step forward. Morgan shrinks back as far as he's able, his white feet waggling in the dark like little animals. Barry whispers in his ear, 'Just do yourself a favour and hand them over.'

'I don't have any,' Morgan pleads. 'I swear!'

'Then why did you come?' Barry's voice is gentle, like a mother's voice. 'Why did you come down here, you faggot?'

'Because you told me to,' Morgan says, between sobs.

'We also told you to bring something.' When Morgan says nothing, Barry slaps him on the cheek. 'We fucking told you to bring something, shithead.'

'I came to tell you I couldn't bring them.' Morgan's face is lifted up and back to look at Barry behind him, so the tears trickle backwards towards his ears.

'Why not?'

'My mum keeps them locked away! She keeps them locked away!'

Carl's head is now very heavy. The elephants have stopped dancing; one after the other they are crashing to the floor. From far away he hears Barry say, 'We asked you nicely.' He gives Carl the signal.

Carl shakes the can hard. He knows what he has to do. But first HOOOOSSHHHHHHH, the sky bounces and pops, he comes out from under his jacket, his face a ☺ drawn on with crayon – 'Do it,' Barry hisses. He lifts his cigarette lighter to the tip of the can –

'Oh God . . .' Morgan squeaks, 'oh God . . .'

'Don't be stupid, Morgan,' Barry says. 'Just give us what we want.'

'I can't!' His face is shiny-wet with crying. 'I can't, my mum will find out –'

'Okay, Morgan,' Barry says, like he is sad about it. 'Then you know what we have to do.'

Carl sinks to one knee and aims the can.

'No!' Morgan screams, but no one can hear him from here. 'No, wai–'

The flame roars, and for a second it swallows up everything. Then it goes, leaving a blue-white flash glowing in the dark. The air is full of the smell of burning.

'Have you something to give us now, Morgan?' Barry says.

Morgan is crying without making any noise. He rolls over onto his stomach, squirming around like a worm in the dirt.

'Have you changed your mind? Have you something to give us? Or do you want to have another talk with the Dragon here?'

Morgan shrivels up like he's been burned again. Then his hand appears, holding up an orange see-through tube. Barry grabs it. 'Why didn't you just give it to us when we asked? You could have saved all of us a lot of trouble, arsehole.'

Morgan is too busy crying to reply, this weird shaking crying that doesn't make any sound. His feet are all red, you can see it even in the dark. Barry turns to Carl. 'Let's get out of here.'

Carl nods. As he goes he sees Morgan's phone has fallen onto the ground. He picks it up and puts it in his pocket.

In the jacks of Burger King, Barry shakes out four pills from the orange tube onto the toilet lid. He mashes them up with his phone and makes the powder into two fat lines. It was his idea so he goes first. Then it's Carl's turn. He leans in with the Burger King straw and snorts. Powder charges up his nose. Instantly, with a metal noise *zing* like a sword being drawn, everything tightens to one sharp edge.

Now it all makes sense. Carl feels shivery-new, he feels ice-cold. Everything is great. It is great to be here with Barry, it was a good plan to get the pills from Morgan Bellamy. They leave the cubicle and walk out into the silver and white and glass of the mall like two G's in a hip-hop video. They ride up the down-escalator and down the up-escalator, they shout things at girls. They steal a cigarette lighter, a pack of cards, *Marbella Ireland* magazine. Then it starts getting boring.

'Let's go and visit the Gook,' Barry says.

On the way back they check on Morgan, but he is gone. Do you think he'll tell? No way because he knows what would happen to him then.

The Gook isn't in Ed's tonight, just Gookette. She looks up and when she sees them she goes stiff. They walk up to the counter real slow. In the background ᛒᛖᛏᚼᚨᚾᛁ is playing:

> I wish I was eighteen so you could photograph me
> We'd put it on the Internet so everyone could see
> How I make your love grow, the things you do to me
> When teacher isn't looking, when my parents are asleep

'Can I help you?' Gookette says like she doesn't want to help them. In her gook voice the words come out, 'Cah ah hep yo?' like she is retarded. Barry pretends to read the big lit-up menu behind her head.

'Yes, I would like an Agent Orange juice, please?'

'We doh have.'

'You doh have? Okay, then I will have a napalm sandwich.'

'We doh have.'

'You doh have napalm sandwiches either?'

'Only stuff on menu.'

Beside him Carl is laughing because he knows Agent Orange and napalm are things they dropped on the gooks to burn them in the Vietnam War. He knows because Barry told him. Barry knows everything about Vietnam, he has seen every film, *Platoon*, *Apocalypse Now*, *Hamburger Hill*, *Full Metal Jacket*, *Good Morning, Vietnam*, *Rambo First Blood* parts I and II, other ones as well, he has them at home on DVD.

I wish I was eighteen, it would be so fine –

BETHani sings –

> To show everybody how we pass the time
> And all the boys around the world could peek into my home
> So there's always someone watching and I never feel alone

Barry asks Gookette if she wants to make sexy. He licks his fingers and rubs them over his chest, going, 'Me so horny, me ruv you rongtime' to Gookette. Gookette stares at him like she wants to smack him, which is funny because she is about five feet tall and also because she probably doesn't even know what he's saying, all she knows in English are doughnut names.

Carl turns round to check the door and everyone who is watching quickly looks down at their doughnuts – except for two girls in a booth who look back at him.

'Me rikee bro-job,' Barry is saying now. 'Bro-job, bro-job.' He helps her out by sucking an imaginary dick using his curled hand and his tongue in his cheek. She stares at him with eyes like stones.

'You stupid bitch, he wants a blowjob,' Carl says. 'How much is a blowjob?'

He takes a five-euro note from his wallet and crumples it up and throws it at her. It hits her on the arm and bounces back to land on the counter. 'How much?' he says again. Now he balls up a twenty and throws it at her. This one hits her on the cheek. It annoys him that she doesn't scrabble after the money or even move at all. He takes out another twenty then sees Barry is staring at him.

'What the fuck are you doing?' Barry says.

'What?' Carl says.

'What are you doing with the fucking money?'

'Trying to get you a fucking blowjob, asshole,' Carl says.

Barry's face has flared up red. 'No, you spa, I mean why didn't you tell me you had all that money? What the fuck were we doing sniffing fucking furniture polish if you had money all along?'

'I forgot,' Carl says.

'You *forgot*? How did you *forget*?'

Carl does not know how he forgot. Suddenly he feels quite tired. Everything is starting to fizz away at the edges, like a pill in water. He wishes he had the orange tube but it is in Barry's pocket and Barry is looking way too angry to give it to him. But then hurray! here comes the Gook running out of the back room, waving his arms and shouting, 'You bah! You bah!'

'You bah! You bah!' they shout back at him. Carl knocks over the plastic straw holder and straws with different-colour stripes spill over the floor. The Gook rushes through the hatch in the counter. Carl raises his fists just to see what'll happen. Instantly the Gook clicks into this Jet Li–type martial arts pose and for a moment they both stay like that, no one moving, except the Gook's nostrils get bigger and smaller. Then Carl and Barry turn and run out of the shop, laughing and shouting, 'You bah! You bah!'

Across the road on the wall of the park, Barry is happy again so they can have more pills. Carl crushes them up with a key. In the big glass window of the Doughnut House, Gookette is crouched down picking up straws.

'Do you think he's riding her?' Barry says. 'Charlie?' Sometimes they call the Gook 'Charlie'.

Carl says, 'I don't know.' Above them there is a full moon in the sky and stars. The moon is a _____ of the Earth that the Earth orbits around.

'He wouldn't get anyone else to ride him,' Barry says. 'Those gooks have wormy little dicks.' He makes an imaginary rifle with his hands and points it at Gookette and fires two bullets into her. He discharges the shells and reloads. 'I'd ride her,' he says.

Carl doesn't say anything. The pills keep squirting out from under the key, twice he has to pick them up off the ground.

'It makes me sick to see gooks just walking around here like they own the place,' Barry says. 'After everything that happened.'

On eBay you can buy actual dog-tags from Marines that were in Vietnam, and even an old U.S. Army jeep. But Barry never has any money to buy anything because his dad is a major scab even though he is loaded. Half the time Carl has to loan him cash just to buy beer.

They inhale again, and Carl feels the pills burn at the top of his nose like pure glowing energy that wants to lift him up and throw him all around the sky! So for a second he doesn't realize that the door of the Doughnut House has opened. Then Barry says, 'Well well.' Carl looks up and sees two girls, the same two girls he noticed a minute ago. They are just standing there in the doorway, looking across the road at Carl and Barry. Then, when they see the boys staring back at them, they start walking away.

'Looks like they want to party,' Barry says. He hops down from the wall. Carl hops down too. Energy shoots through his arms, the pills make you feel like you are on a mission.

The girls are talking to each other in a loud, fake sort of way, like they know someone is listening. They are from St Brigid's, he has seen them before in the mall.

'Hey!' Barry calls after them. They ignore him.

'Oh my God, she is *such* a leper,' the shorter girl is saying.

'Hey!' Barry shouts again. This time the girls turn round and wait. 'How are you doing,' Barry says, catching up with them. The girls don't say anything. 'I'm Barry,' he says. 'This is Carl.'

'We're off our heads,' Carl says. The shorter girl leans up and whispers into the ear of the other one and both of them start giggling behind their hands. Barry glares at Carl.

'So, what are your names?' he asks them, which sets off another explosion of giggles, like this is the most spastic thing you could ever ask someone. Classic girl behaviour: Carl is not going to let it throw him off. He pictures Morgan sprawled out on the waste ground, thinks about standing above him with the furniture-polish flame-thrower.

'What have you guys been doing tonight?' Barry says.

'Uh . . . eating doughnuts?' the shorter girl says, with a *duh* expression. She's not actually short, it's more that the other girl is tall. Both are thin. The short girl has crinkly hair and glasses like someone on TV, Carl can't remember who. The other girl has long dark hair and pale skin. Her lips are a shiny lollipop-red. She is wearing mittens and looking at Carl.

'Did you know tonight is your lucky night?' Barry is saying.

'Why, because we get to meet you?' Crinkly-Hair says.

'Not just that,' Barry says. 'We have a once-in-a-lifetime offer to make you.'

Crinkly-Hair laughs a sarcastic laugh and looks at Lollipop-Lips. 'We have to go.'

'Don't you want to know what it is?'

'What is it?'

'We can't show you here.'

She laughs again. 'We *have* to go,' she says, and turns away. But they don't go anywhere, and a second later she turns back again and says, 'Okay, what is it?'

'Follow me.' Barry leads the girls up the road. Carl wonders where he is taking them and what the once-in-a-lifetime offer is. He wants to ask Barry but Barry has walked on ahead of him, down a long driveway belonging to one of the new apartment blocks. The girls are dawdling behind Carl, talking to each other about something completely else as though they don't care about what Barry has to show them and have almost forgotten about it. The pills are making Carl's hands shake and want to do things.

Barry has stopped under a lamppost and is waiting for them there. They catch up and Crinkly-Hair looks at Barry like she's saying, 'So?' Carl is looking at him too but Barry pretends not to see. Lollipop waits a little way back with a mysterious smile as if she is thinking of a secret joke. Now and then she flicks back her hair with a white hand so the light goes shooting through it.

Barry takes the orange tube from his pocket. Wait, what?

'Diet pills,' he says. 'The best you can get.'

The crinkly-haired girl's face goes dark. 'Are you saying we need to go on a diet?'

'You will soon if you keep eating doughnuts,' he says as a joke, but she doesn't laugh. 'Relax,' he says. 'I'm not saying that at all. These are designed so that you won't ever need to go on a diet. They're actual medical pills developed by doctors. Take one of these a day and you'll never have to worry about your weight again.'

Crinkly-Hair takes the tube from his hand and examines it. 'Ritalin,' she reads. 'That's the stuff they prescribe for ADHD.' She turns to Lollipop. 'It's what they gave Amy Cassidy after she smashed up the nature table.'

'You can take it for different things,' Barry says.

'If you snort it you can get really high,' Carl says, looking at Barry. But Barry acts like he doesn't hear. What is he doing? Is he trying to sell the pills to these girls? They are supposed to be for him and Carl, they have been planning to get them all week! Carl starts to get angry, but he keeps it hidden for now. Maybe Barry has a plan, like he is planning for them to fuck the girls.

'Morgan Bellamy,' Crinkly-Hair is reading from the label. 'I thought you said your name was Barry.' She lifts her eyes to Barry challengingly. Lollipop is hotter but Crinkly-Hair is sexy too, Carl thinks, he would ride her if the other one wouldn't do it.

'Barry is my middle name,' Barry tells her. 'Nobody calls me Morgan except my grandparents.'

45

'Where did you get these?'

'The doctor prescribed them for me. But now I don't need them any more.'

'Oh, you're cured, are you?'

'That's right,' Barry says, smiling at her. She tries to stop herself smiling back at him but she can't. 'So what do you think? I'll give you this entire bottle for thirty euro. That's only fifteen each,' he says to Lollipop, trying to bring her into it. But she hangs back and doesn't speak.

'We don't have any money,' Crinkly-Hair says.

'Or I'll give you five for five,' Barry says, deliberately not looking at Carl while he is saying this. 'This really is a great offer, ladies. Normally you can't get this stuff without a prescription. Here, take a look.' He takes the tube back from Crinkly-Hair and pours some of the little skin-coloured discs out onto his palm and holds it out. Crinkly-Hair hovers over it, like she's breathing in the smell of the pills, though they don't smell of anything. Then suddenly light flashes over them. Barry folds up his hand. A car comes up the driveway, a grown-up face suspicious in the window as it goes past.

Lollipop tweaks her friend's elbow. 'We should go,' she murmurs. Her voice is low and soft like cat's fur.

Crinkly-Hair nods. 'It's getting late,' she says, and steps back.

'Wait,' Barry says. 'Why don't you take a couple of these, as free samples? I'll give you my number, and if you like them I can get you some more.' He holds out the pills. The girls look at him, swaying slightly from side to side.

'Or, okay, why don't you give me your numbers, and I can call you to see if you changed your mind?' He takes out his phone. Carl takes out Morgan Bellamy's phone and flips it open too. He points it at Lollipop but doesn't speak. She gazes back at him, biting her bottom lip gently.

'Okay.' Barry shuts his phone without stopping smiling. 'How about this, how about we just come and meet you tomorrow? You two are in St Brigid's, aren't you?'

The two of them look sideways at each other then back at Barry.

'How about we come and meet you after school, and we can talk about it some more. Maybe we can work out a better deal. Like if you don't have enough money right this second, we can work something out. How about behind Ed's, say we meet you there, at four o'clock?'

The girls swap glances again and shrug their shoulders.

'So see you tomorrow?' Barry calls after them as they walk off down the driveway.

'Definitely,' Crinkly-Hair says, without looking back. Then she and Lollipop burst into giggles again.

'Fucking St Frigid's bitches,' Barry says, when they have passed out of sight.

What the fuck are you doing? Why were you trying to give away our drugs? Carl wants to shout. But instead he just says, 'Is that stuff true? About diets?'

'I read about it on the Internet,' Barry says. As they walk down the driveway back to the road, he starts telling Carl how in this thing he read these lads were dealing it and making serious cash. 'Think about it, dude. All birds ever talk about is their fucking weight. They'll go mental for this shit. Those two totally would have bought some, if that bloke hadn't driven past. I'll bet you anything they'll be there tomorrow. And say they bring their friends, I bet we could sell all of these and more.'

But why does he want to sell them? Why doesn't he just want to snort them with Carl? Wasn't that the plan? This is the way Barry's brain works though, new ideas are coming all the time, turning into plans. Carl has no ideas, no plans; he is just carried along on Barry's like a piece of plastic on the sea.

'I wonder if we could get more from Morgan,' Barry is saying. 'Like we could offer him a cut. Or there must be other people in school – or shit, junior school! I bet there's loads of kids with prescriptions down there that . . .'

Carl tunes him out. He flips open Morgan's phone and presses a button. Lollipop-Lips appears and gazes darkly, velvetly, out at him, biting her bottom lip, swaying from side to side. Then she freezes. Then she is there again, gazing, biting, swaying.

Now they have left the village behind, the shopping malls and pubs and restaurants, to go up a sleeping avenue with neat trimmed hedges and black SUVs. Carl feels the night become heavy again and knows that this time there will be no fighting it, it will keep getting heavier and heavier as he gets nearer to the house that is his house until it has dragged him all the way into tomorrow.

'. . . genius of diet pills,' Barry is saying very quickly beside him. He is excited: maybe he is thinking about the U.S. Army jeep on eBay. 'You don't just buy them for a night out. You take them every day. And also, it's *girls*. When do you ever see girls down in the park, buying drugs off knackers? Never. It's a totally untapped market. I swear to God, we're going to be rich! Fucking *rich*!' He grins at Carl, and waits for Carl to grin back.

'Show us them a second,' Carl says. Barry hands him the tube, chuckling some more. Carl opens it and pours the pills into his palm. Then, as hard as he can, he flings them away into the air. Pills skitter along the road, bounce off car roofs, pelt softly into the grass.

Barry is stunned. For a minute he can't even speak. Then he says, 'What the fuck did you do that for?'

Carl keeps walking. There is a sour fire burning in him the colour of dried blood.

'You fucking *twat*,' Barry says, 'you spa, now what are we going to say to those girls tomorrow?'

Carl raises his palm and smacks Barry flat on the ear. Barry gasps and staggers sideways. 'What's the matter with you, you psycho?' he cries, clutching his head. 'What the fuck is wrong with you?'

It's tomorrow. Skippy's bare-legged at the edge of the pool, chlorine and earliness stinging his eyes. Outside the morning is a grey fuzz, the first shapes just beginning to emerge from it. On either side of Skippy, boys are lined up, their white Seabrook College swimming caps making them look like clones with the school crest stamped on their bald heads. Then the whistle, and before his mind even realizes, his body's thrown itself forward and into the water. Instantly a thousand blue hands reach for him, seize him, pulling him down – he catches his breath, fights them off, scrabbles his way to the surface –

Breaking through, he emerges into a commotion of colour and noise – the yellow plastic roof, the crash and foam of the other swimmers, an arm, a goggled head thrown sideways, Coach like a gnarled tree trunk bending over the water, clapping his hands and shouting, *Let's go let's go* and in the lanes around Skippy the boys like disobedient reflections stealing ahead, disappearing behind their wakes. Everyone hurtling for the wall! But the water grapples against him, the bottom of the pool is magnetic and it's tugging him down again, down to where . . .

The whistle goes. Garret Dennehy comes in first, right behind him Siddartha Niland. In the seconds after, the others slide up alongside them, lean back against the wall, gasping, lifting off their goggles. Skippy's still back in the middle of the pool.

'Come on, Daniel, for Christ's sake, you're like an old granny walking in the park!'

Three times a week, at 7 a.m., training for one hour. Count yourself lucky, the Senior team trains every morning and Saturdays too. Breaststroke, backstroke, butterfly, crawl, back and forth through the blue chemicals; repetitions on the tiles, crunches and squats, till every muscle is burning.

'Being a great athlete is not just about natural ability,' Coach likes to shout, pacing up and down along the poolside as you squirm through your sets. 'It's about discipline, and it's about commitment.' So if you miss a session, you'd better have a good excuse.

Afterwards, the team huddles shivering by the doorway of the changing room, hands pressed under armpits. When you get out of the water the air feels cold and nothingy. Your arm moves and it moves against nothing. You speak and the words disappear instantly.

Coach wraps and unwraps the cord of the whistle around his hand, everyone gathered round him like the Apostles with Jesus in old paintings. If you look closely you can see how his body's all twisted up even when he's standing still. 'You lads did good work on Saturday. But we can't afford to rest on our laurels. The next meet is on 15 November. That might sound like a long way away. All the more reason for us to work hard and keep our momentum going. I want to see us in the semi-finals.' He tosses his head towards the changing room. 'Okay, off you go.'

The showers never feel like they're making you clean. The tiles are lined with scuzz, the footbath half-full of brackish water; hair shivers in grey clumps in the grating, like drowned mermaids.

'You swam like a turd today, Juster,' Siddartha says. 'What's the story? Were you up late last night bumming Van Doren?'

Skippy mumbles something about pulling a muscle at the meet.

Siddartha wrinkles up his nose, sticks his upper teeth over his lip and makes the kangaroo noise: *Tcch-tcch-tcch, I think I pulled a muscle at the meet.* Well, you'd better speed up. Just because you fluked through on Saturday doesn't mean you've got a right to a permanent place on the team.'

'Don't mind him,' Ronan Joyce says, when Siddartha turns round. 'Dickhead.'

But Skippy doesn't mind him: the pill he took when he woke

up takes care of that. The sleepy feeling threads through him, wrapping around him like a blanket. Noises, images, the things people say, come to him all broken up and slowed down; the needly water of the shower, hitting his body, turning from cold to hot, he hardly notices, nor when he steps out again into the freezing changing room.

Ruprecht and the others are already eating by the time he gets to the Refectory. Monstro is behind the counter, ladling scrambled eggs like some kind of giant infection from a steel vat. The food in the Ref is always gross, the cheapest stuff they can get. Today even the toast is burnt.

Crowd-cheering noises from Geoff as he sits down. 'This is very exciting, sports fans – we've just been joined by champion swimmer Daniel Juster, direct from his gruelling training regime! How are you feeling today, champ?'

'Sleepy.'

A chorus of baa's proceeds from a far corner as Muiris de Bhaldraithe, Seabrook's biggest bogger and self-alleged lynchpin of the clandestine Real IRA Juniors, Dublin Brigade, enters the room. *Scccrrrrcccchh, scccrrrrcccchh*, Ruprecht meticulously scrapes the burnt from his toast.

'"Sleepy." That's top athlete Daniel "Skippy" Juster, ladies and gentlemen.'

Scccrrrrcccchh, scccrrrrcccchh, scccrrrrcccchh, goes Ruprecht's toast. Skippy stares into his breakfast as if it's appeared out of nowhere.

'I could probably be a top athlete if I wanted to,' Mario puts in carelessly. 'It's just that I don't want to.'

'Oh yeah, Mario, that's why,' Dennis says.

'Up yours, Hoey, that *is* why. For your information, this summer two different Premiership teams rang me up to offer me trials.'

'The Premiership of masturbating,' Dennis says.

'If there was a Premiership of masturbating, you would be David Beckham,' Niall adds.

Seizing an imaginary microphone, Dennis adopts a limp

Estuary accent: 'Masturbating's changed a lot since I were a lad, Brian. In my day, we masturbated for the sheer love of it. Day and night we did it, all the kids on our estate, masturbating on the old waste ground, masturbating up against the wall of the house . . . I remember me mam coming out and shouting, "Stop that masturbating and come in for your tea! You'll never amount to anything if all you think about is masturbating!" Masturbating crazy we were. Your young masturbators today, though, it's all about the money, it's all about agents and endorsements. Sometimes I worry that the masturbating's in danger of being squeezed out altogether.'

'Hey, Skip, what was the hotel like on Saturday?' Geoff asks. 'Did you have a minibar?'

'No.'

'Was there a hot tub?'

Scccrrrrcccchh! Scccrrrrcccchhh! Scccrrrrcccchhh!

'Jesus, Ruprecht, what the hell are you doing?' Skippy rounds on him.

'Burnt toast is a carcinogen,' Ruprecht replies placidly, continuing his excoriation.

'A what?' says Geoff.

'It gives you cancer.'

'Toast gives you cancer?' Mario says.

'Giving us cancer would actually be a step up for this place,' Dennis says, looking around splenetically at the Ref.

'Car-SIN-oh-jen,' Geoff repeats slowly.

Scccrrrrccccccrrrrcccchhh, goes the knife on the bread, then Skippy grabs Ruprecht's plump wrist. He looks up in surprise.

'It's annoying,' Skippy says, embarrassed.

The bell goes. Potato-Head Tomms rises and claps his hands for them all to carry their trays over to the trolleys. 'I just have to get something from my locker,' Skippy tells the others. It's 8:42, the corridors are full of puffy-eyed boys in coats, hurrying to check-in. News of Saturday's swim meet has spread: as he makes his way against the tide to the basement steps, people he's never spoken to are nodding to him in acknowledgement; others punch him on the arm or stop to say congratulations.

'Hey, well done on the other night, Juster.'

'Here, heard about your race. Nice one, man.'

'Good job, Juster, when's the semi-final?'

If you're used to people looking past or through or most often over you then the attention is pretty strange. Now two guys from the low streams, Darren Boyce and someone else whose name Skippy isn't even sure of, break free from the shoals to approach him. Darren is smiling and holding out his arms – then at the last minute he shoves his friend so he clatters into Skippy and sends him crashing into the wall; they laugh and move off in the other direction.

He picks himself up. The toast-sound echoing through his head again, *Scccrrrcccchh, scccrrrrcccchhh, scccrrrrcccchhh*. The pill's already wearing off! Shh, I know, calm down!

Down the steps through the waves of bodies. When he came back from summer holidays this year the boys had changed. Suddenly everyone was tall and gangling and talking about drinking and sperm. Walking among them is like being in a BO-smelling forest.

The basement is crammed with narrow aisles of lockers. They remind Skippy of coffins, cheap wooden coffins with combination locks. To one side there's a patched pool table, on which Gary Toolan is crisply, blondly annihilating Edward 'Hutch' Hutchinson, while Noddy the janitor looks on, leaning on his broom, cackling approvingly. A few doors up from Skippy, a small group has gathered furtively around Simon Mooney's locker, indicating the presence of contraband.

'Atomizers. Black Holes. Fifth Dimensions. Sizzlers,' Simon Mooney is reciting, poring over a plastic bag. 'Then we have rockets, bangers – these are like the loudest bangers you've ever heard.'

'What's this one?' Diarmuid Coveney points.

'Don't touch.' Simon whisks the bag primly out of reach and reopens it at a safer distance. 'That, my friend, is the infamous Spider Bomb. Eight individual fireworks in one.'

There is a murmur of awe and appreciation. 'Where d'you get them?' Dewey Fortune asks.

'My dad bought them in the North. He goes up there all the time on business.'

'Wow – do you think he could get me some?' Vaughan Brady suggests breathlessly.

Simon considers this with a drawn-together mouth, like he's sucking a sweet. 'No,' he says.

'Well – how about you sell us some of yours?'

'Hmm . . .' Simon does the sweet face again. 'No.'

'Why not? You've got loads.'

'Can we at least set a couple of them off now?'

'Come on, think of what Connie'd do if you let off a banger under his chair.'

'No.'

'Well, what did you bring them in for, if you're not going to set one off?'

Simon shrugs, and then, noticing Carl Cullen and Barry Barnes lurking in the vicinity, hastily stuffs the fireworks back in his locker and snaps shut the lock. The circle reluctantly disband, and head towards the stairs as the final bell goes.

Skippy closes the door of his locker and leans back against the door.

SCRRRRCCCHHHH, SCRRRRRCCCHHH, SCRRRRRC-CCHHHHH!

Hot tub? Minibar? Sweat drips down his back, everything's moving in jumps and rushes, like the moments are connected by waterslides and each time he blinks he's hurtled out into a new one not knowing where he is –

Shh, take it easy.

– and little particles of memory appearing out of nothing and exploding like fireworks against the inside of his eye, little sparks of images that are gone too quick to see, like dreams are gone the second you realize they're dreams – but dreams of *what*? Memories of *what*?

Shh. Deep breaths.

He takes out the amber tube and swallows a pill with some flat Sprite. Okay. Slowly and calmly he takes the books he will need for the morning's classes from his locker, and places them in his bag. He is late for Science but he does not hurry. Already things are feeling more normal again, see? The pills moving through you like sleep, like eating ice and feeling your insides freeze. Weird that the cure should just appear like that at the same time as the sickness –

'Hold it right there!' Mr Farley exclaims as Skippy comes through the door. He turns to the class. 'Which of the seven characteristics of life can we see Daniel exhibiting right now?'

Thirty grinning eyes swivel onto him. Skippy stands there like an idiot with his hand on the door. There is some snickering, and some shouted suggestions from the back of the room ('Excretion?' 'Gayness?') before Mr Farley steps back in. '"Breathing" is the answer. Oh yes, now you all know it. Breathing, or as it's known scientifically, respiration, is one of the seven characteristics of life. Thank you, Mr Juster, for that very elegant demonstration. You can take a seat now.' Skippy, blushing, hurries down to his desk beside Ruprecht. 'Every living thing on the planet breathes,' Mr Farley continues. 'However, not everything breathes the same thing, or in the same way. For example, humans breathe *in* oxygen and breathe *out* carbon dioxide, but plants do the opposite. That's why they're so important in combating global warming. Aquatic organisms breathe oxygen the same as humans, but they extract it from the water, through gills. Some organisms have both gills and lungs – can anyone tell me what these are called?'

Flubber Cooke puts up his hand. 'Mermaids?'

'No,' Mr Farley says. 'Anyone else – thank you, Ruprecht, the correct answer is *amphibians*.' He turns to chalk it up on the board. 'The word comes from the Greek *amphibios*, meaning "double life". Amphibians, for instance frogs, are organisms that can breathe on land and in water. They're important in evolution-ary terms, because life on Earth began in the sea, so the first ver-tebrates to crawl out onto the land must have had amphibious tendencies. And each of you has a more recent amphibious past, because babies, when they are in the womb, actually breathe liquid oxygen through gills, just like fish. The presence of gill slits on the foetus, furthermore, is taken by some to be evidence of our aquatic prehistory . . .'

'I wonder why they don't just let you stay amphibious,' Ru-precht ponders as they rejoin the throng in the corridor after class. 'So that it's up to the individual to choose where he wants to live, on the land or in the water.'

'Regarding the whole mermaids issue, being amphibious would certainly make it easier to have sex with them,' Mario says.

'Mermaids don't have beavers, you clown. Even if you were amphibious you couldn't have sex with them,' snaps Dennis.

'What's the point of mermaids if you can't have sex with them?'

'Well, I suppose the key thing to remember is that mermaids are imaginary,' Ruprecht notes. 'Although, interestingly, some marine biologists speculate that the legend may have arisen from large aquatic mammals of the sirenian class like dugongs and manatees, which have fish-like bodies but human-like breasts, and nurse their pups on the water's surface.'

'Von Blowjob, find a dictionary and look up "interesting".'

'What I don't understand,' Geoff says, 'is *why* did the first fish, like the one who started land animals, suddenly decide one day to just leave the sea? Like, to leave everything he *knew*, to go flop-ping around on a land where no one had even evolved yet for him to talk to?' He shakes his head. 'He was a brave fish, definitely, and we owe him a lot, for starting life on land and everything? But I think he must have been very depressed.'

Skippy doesn't contribute to this. That second pill is beginning to seem like a really bad idea. He's getting a weird feeling, a sort of sleepiness, but not nice sleepiness like earlier – this time it's pricklier, hotter, with a taste in his mouth. Then he remembers he's got Religion next, and he feels even worse.

Religion class is chaotic at the best of times, but Brother Jonas's is like a circus where the animals have taken over. The brother is from Africa and has never quite caught on to how things work here; on Dennis's Nervous Breakdown Leaderboard he's usually near the top, along with Ms Twanky (Bus. Org.) and Father Laughton, the music teacher. Taking his seat, Skippy notices that Morgan Bellamy, who usually sits at the next desk, is out today. Why does this feel like a bad sign?

'Who does the world belong to?' Brother Jonas is asking. He has a voice that is soft and dark and rough like the pads on a dog's paw, and his sentences go up and down tropically, like music: difficult to understand and easy to make fun of. 'To whom has God promised the world?'

No answer; the hum of conversation continues as before, but the instant the brother turns to drag the chalk shrieking across the blackboard, everyone jumps out from behind their desks and starts hopping about and flailing their arms. This is a new routine – a kind of a rain dance, performed in absolute silence, at the end of which, when Brother Jonas begins to turn round again, you jump into somebody else's desk, so that he's confronted with thirty serene and attentive faces patiently awaiting his words, but all in different places from before. The chalk scrapes and squeaks. Around Skippy, bodies whirl and jig. Skippy, however, stays where he is. Suddenly he is certain jumping around would not be a good plan. Even watching the others makes his stomach lurch.

Now the brother has finished writing and everybody's scrambling into their seats.

'Juster!' Lionel Bollard, 140 pounds of creatine and ski-tan, is trying to shove him out of his chair. 'Juster! Move!'

Doggedly, Skippy hangs on. Brother Jonas faces the class again. He begins to speak, then pauses, aware that something is amiss, but not sure what. Lionel has ducked into a desk behind and to the right; Skippy can feel his eyes crawling over him.

'The Meek Shall Inherit the Earth,' Brother Jonas pronounces, pointing to the words written on a gradually sloping incline on the blackboard, a caravan of letters going down a hill. 'We may believe that the world belongs to the merchants, who can purchase it with their wealth. Or to the politicians and the judges, who decide men's fates. But Jesus tells us that in the end . . .'

'Dan-iellll . . .' Lionel starts to sing, ever so softly. 'DAN-iellll . . .'

Skippy ignores him. Ignoring is what you are supposed to do with bullies, so they get bored and leave you alone. But the problem in school is they don't get bored, because whatever else there is to do is more boring still. The chalk squeals over the board again, and boys leap up and cavort like they're possessed. Skippy's head spins like a top. Lights are flashing on and off in the corners of his vision. Now Lionel's right beside him. 'Daniel,' he whispers, so low it can barely be heard, like it might just be happening in his imagination. 'Daniel . . .'

His eyelids are so heavy, but he knows that if he closes them he'll get those whirling pits that make you feel even worse.

'So we must ask ourselves: what is it to be meek? Jesus tells us that whosoever shall smite thee on thy right cheek, turn to him the other also. The meek man – yes, Dennis?'

'Yes, I was wondering . . . roughly how big would a soul be, roughly? I'm thinking, bigger than a contact lens but smaller than a golf ball, would that be about right?'

'The soul does not have a weight or a size. It is a bodiless manifestation of the eternal world and a most precious gift from the Almighty Father. Now, everyone, please open your books to page thirty-seven – am I meek in my own life?'

'Daniel . . . I've got a present for you, Daniel . . .' Lionel starts hacking up phlegm from the depths of his throat and gurgling it in his mouth.

'Am I meek in my own life? Do I listen to my teachers, my parents and my spiritual advisors? Am I a – Dennis, is your question about how to be more meek?'

'Would it be fair to say that Jesus was a zombie? I mean, he came back from the dead, right? So technically, couldn't you say he was a zombie? I mean, wouldn't that be the correct term, technically?'

Sweat breaks in waves over Skippy's zombie flesh. It doesn't seem to make any difference how often he wipes it away. Every noise in the classroom is amplified: Jason Rycroft's syncopated pencil-tattoo, Neville Nelligan's snuffling nose, the escalating, bee-like *hummmmmm* arising from Martin Anderson, Trevor Hickey and unidentified others, the hideous gurgling of Lionel and above it all inside your head the terrible carcinogenic *SCRRRRCCCH-HHH, SCRRRRRCCCHHH, SCRRRRRCCCHHHHH* –

The first thing that strikes a visitor to the Seabrook staffroom is the predominance of beige. Beige armchairs, beige curtains, beige walls; where it's not beige it's buff, or fawn, or tan, or manila. Isn't beige the Greeks' or someone's colour of death? Howard is fairly certain it is, or if it isn't it ought to be.

Three years have passed since he could accurately describe himself as a visitor to the staffroom, but the surreality of being here, amidst these figures of terror or hilarity from his youth – these imagos, these caricatures, now ambling around him, saying good morning, making tea, acting as if they were *normal people* – still descends on him from time to time. For a long while he found himself expecting them to give him homework, and being surprised, unpleasantly, when instead they would tell him about their lives. But every day it feels more ordinary, which he finds more unpleasant still.

Before he started teaching, he never would have guessed how much the staffroom resembled the rest of the school. The same cliquishness applies in here as it does among the boys, the same territoriality: that divan belongs to Miss Davy, Ms Ni Riain and the witch-faced German instructor; that table to Mr Ó Dálaigh and his Gaelgoir cronies; the high chairs by the window are reserved for Miss Birchall and Miss McSorley, the bluestocking spinsters, currently slumming it over a women's magazine; God help you if you use someone else's mug, or mistakenly take a yoghurt that isn't yours from the fridge.

A good portion of the staff are old boys. Policy is to hire alumni whenever possible, even at the expense of more talented teachers, in order to 'protect the ethos' of the school, whatever that may be. It seems to Howard like a raw deal for the students, but it's the only reason he got the job, so he doesn't complain. For some teachers, Seabrook is the only world they have known; the female staff can only partially offset the atmosphere of clubbiness, if not downright infantilism, that this creates.

As for that female staff. A stringent policy is in effect here too. The Paraclete Fathers view women and womankind with a certain amount of unease. While recognizing their great contribution to society and the furtherance of the species generally, the order would be quite happy for the fairer sex to continue to do so elsewhere; the presence of a girls' school right next door has long been lamented by the order as a particularly cruel twist of fate. Of course, the profession being mostly composed of women, some incidence of female teachers at Seabrook is inevitable; it is only by a painstaking filtering process that Father Furlong, the school principal, has mitigated the inherent dangers of this tendency, assembling a staff that even a fourteen-year-old boy would have difficulty construing as sexual entities. Most are comfortably into their fifties, and it is debatable whether they were setting hearts alight even in their heyday, if they had a heyday.

The dearth of eye candy in the staffroom doesn't do much to brighten the atmosphere, which on a rainy morning, after a fight with your significant other, can seem singularly lethargic, or even, why not, deathly. Ambitious teachers go on to deanships – each year has its own dean, and each dean his own office; the denizens of the staffroom are the career mid-rankers, doing the same thing for twenty years, happy to run out the clock. How dismal and old they seem, even the ones who are not old; how hidebound, how cut off from the world.

'Good morning, Howard,' Farley chimes, crashing through the door.

'Morning.' Howard looks up grudgingly from his essays.

'Good morning, Farley,' chirrup Misses Birchall and McSorley from their perch by the window.

'Good morning, ladies,' Farley returns.

'Ooh, ask him,' Miss McSorley prompts her companion.

'Ask me what?' Farley says.

'We're doing a questionnaire,' Miss Birchall informs him. '"Are you a kidult?"'

'Am I a what?'

She tilts back her head and peers down through her glasses at the magazine. '"The twenty-first century is the age of the kidult – adults who shun responsibility, and instead spend their lives in the pursuit of expensive thrills."'

'I'm flattered you should ask me,' Farley says. 'No, really.'

'"Question one,"' Miss Birchall reads. '"Are you single? If in a relationship, do you have children?" You're not in a relationship, are you, Farley?'

'He's never in a relationship,' Miss McSorley contributes. 'He only likes *one-night stands.*'

'"Question two,"' Miss Birchall reads over Farley's protests. '"Which of the following do you own: Sony PSP, Nintendo Game-boy, iPod, Vespa or other classic scooter –"'

'I don't own any of those things,' Farley says.

'But you'd like to,' Miss McSorley suggests.

'Oh sure, I'd like to,' Farley says. 'If I had any money I'd own them.'

'The problem is that we don't get paid enough to be kidults,' Howard says.

'We aspire to be kidults,' Farley says. 'How's that?'

He excuses himself from the rest of the questionnaire on the grounds that he is in urgent need of a cup of coffee after his second-year Biology class. Since September, Farley's been teaching the seven characteristics of life, and as they approach the class on reproduction, the boys have become increasingly agitated. 'They're concentrating so hard I can practically hear it. Today I accidentally mentioned *wombs*. It was like letting a drop of blood fall into a tank of piranhas.'

'You could feed my entire second-year class to a tank of piranhas and they wouldn't even notice,' Howard says morosely. 'They'd snooze right through.'

62

'That's History. This is Biology. These kids are fourteen. Biology courses through their veins. Biology and marketing.' Farley shunts a pile of newspapers off the couch and sits down. 'I'm not exaggerating. They've been like this since the first day of term.'

'Surely they know all of that stuff already. They've got broadband at home. They probably know more about sex than I do.'

'They want to hear it from an adult.' Farley picks up a photocopy of today's crossword from the table and with a biro begins meticulously blacking out the white squares. 'They want to hear it confirmed officially that for all our talk, the adult world and their subterranean sex-obsessed porno-world are basically the same, and no matter what else we try to teach them about kings or molecules or trade models or whatever, civilization ultimately boils down to the same frenzied attempt to hump people. That the world, in short, is teenaged. It's quite a frightening admission to have to make. It feels like a capitulation into anarchy, frankly.'

He returns the crossword, now a single square of blackness, to the table, and leans back Byronically on the couch. 'This isn't how I imagined the teaching life, Howard. I saw myself naming the planets for apple-cheeked sixteen-year-old girls. Watching their hearts awaken, taking them aside and gently talking them out of the crushes they have on me. "The boys my age are such dorks, Mr Farley." "I know it seems like that now. But you're young and you're going to meet some wonderful, wonderful men." Finding poems on my desk every morning. And underwear. Poems and underwear. That's what I thought life was all about. Look at me now. A failed kidult.'

Farley likes to make lugubrious speeches of this nature, but he does not in reality share Howard's sentiments vis-à-vis deathliness; on the contrary, he genuinely seems to enjoy 'the teaching life' – enjoys the noisy egoism of the boys, the cut and thrust of the classroom. Howard finds this baffling. Working in a secondary school is like being trapped with a thousand billboards, each one shouting for your attention, but, when you look, with no idea what it is they want to tell you. Still, it could be worse. The state-run school not half a mile away caters to the children of St Patrick's Villas, the run-down complex of flats behind the more easterly of the shopping malls; horror stories regularly emerge about teachers pelted with eggs, threatened with sawn-off shotguns, coming into class to find the blackboard covered in spit, or shit, or jism. 'At least we're not in Anthony's,' the Seabrook staff console each other on bad days. 'There are always vacancies at St Anthony's,' the management jokingly-but-not-really tell staff when they complain.

The door opens and Jim Slattery, the English teacher, bustles in to a flurry of good-mornings.

'Good morning, Jim,' chime Misses Birchall and McSorley.

'Good morning, ladies.' Slattery shakes rain from his anorak and removes his bicycle clips. 'Good morning, Farley. Good morning, Howard.'

'Good morning, Jim,' Farley returns. Howard grunts perfunctorily.

'Pleasant enough day out there,' Slattery remarks, as he does every morning it's not actually raining fire, and makes a beeline for the kettle.

'Kipper' Slattery: as re deathliness, Exhibit A. Another old boy, he has taught at Seabrook for decades – in fact he is wearing the same jacket this morning that he did in Farley and Howard's schooldays, an eye-searing, headache-inducing houndstooth that reminds Howard of a Bridget Riley painting. He is an amiable, shambling man, with shaggy eyebrows that bristle from his forehead like two Yetis about to hurl themselves from a cliff, and has never lacked enthusiasm for his subject, which he communicates in long, rambling sentences that very few of his students have ever had the tenacity or will to disentangle; instead, by and large, they take the opportunity to sleep – hence his nickname.

'Speaking of frenzied attempts to hump people,' Farley remembers, 'did you decide what you're going to do about Aurelie?'

Howard frowns at him, then glances about in case anyone has heard. The Misses, however, are occupied in their horoscopes; Slattery is drying his feet with a paper towel while waiting for his tea to draw. 'Well, I wasn't planning on "doing" anything,' he says, in a low voice.

'Really? Because yesterday you sounded quite het up.'

'I just thought it was a very unprofessional thing to say on her part, that's all.' Howard scowls at his shoes.

'Right.'

'It's just not the way you speak to a work colleague. And this whole business of not telling me her name, it's so *juvenile*. It's not like she's even all that hot. She's got a highly inflated sense of her own worth, if you ask me.'

'Good morning, Aurelie,' the Misses chant; Howard's head snaps up to see her at the coat-rack, divesting herself of a modish olive-green raincoat.

'We were just talking about you,' Farley says.

'I know,' she says. Beneath the raincoat is a pencil-line tweed skirt and a delicate cream sweater that exposes clavicles like parts of some impossibly graceful musical instrument. Howard can't help staring: it's as if she's walked into his memory and chosen her outfit from the wardrobe of all the preppy golden-haired princesses he yearned for hopelessly across the malls and churches of his youth.

'Howard here is wondering why you won't let him know your first name,' Farley says, intuitively dodging to one side so that Howard's sharp elbow finds only the back of the couch.

Miss McIntyre dips her little finger into a small pot of lip-balm and gazes down appraisingly at Howard. 'He's just not allowed,' she says, smearing translucent gunk on her lips. Howard is embarrassed at how erotic he finds this.

'That's ridiculous,' he retorts gruffly. 'Anyway, I know your name.'

She shrugs.

'Well, what if I decide that's what I'm going to call you? What are you going to do then?'

'I'll throw you out of class,' she says expressionlessly. 'You don't want that, do you? Not when you're doing so well.'

Howard, feeling all of thirteen years old, is lost for words. Fortunately the door opens, and her attention is diverted. You can always hear Tom Roche coming: since his accident, his right leg barely moves, so he uses a cane, and with every second step must heft forward his full weight, making his passage sound like a body being dragged. It's said he's in constant pain, though he never mentions it.

'Tombo!' Farley raises a hand for a high-five that does not arrive.

'Good morning,' Tom responds, with deliberate stiffness.

As he passes the sofa, Howard gets a faint whiff of alcohol. 'Hey, ah, congratulations on the swimming race the other night,' he calls after him, hearing his own voice girlish and obsequious. 'Sounds like you really cleaned the place out.'

'It was a good team performance,' the taciturn response.

'Tom's taken over as coach of the swimming team,' Howard explains woodenly to Miss McIntyre. 'There was a big race at the weekend and they swept the boards. First time the team ever won anything.'

'Tombo's inspirational,' Farley adds. 'The kids'd follow him to the ends of the Earth. Like the Moonies.'

'It makes such a difference to have someone who inspires you,' Miss McIntyre says. 'Like a genuine leader? It's so rare these days.'

'Unless he just slipped a little something into their food the night before,' Farley says. 'Maybe that's his secret.'

'We worked damn hard for that race,' Tom rejoins from his locker. 'The boys take it seriously, and we work damn hard.'

'I know that, Tom. I was joking.'

'Well, I don't think it shows a very responsible attitude for a teacher to talk about drug abuse in such a frivolous way.'

'Would you relax? It was just a joke. Jesus.'

'Some people around here joke far too much. Excuse me, I have work to do.' Gritting his teeth, Tom jerks himself forward and lurches out the door.

After a moment has elapsed, Miss McIntyre observes, 'What an interesting man.'

'Fascinating,' agrees Farley.

'He doesn't seem too fond of you two.'

'It's historical,' Howard says.

'Howard and Tom and I were in school together,' Farley says, 'and it so happened that the two of us were there the night of his accident – he had this terrible accident, I'm sure you must have heard about it?'

She nods slowly. 'He had some kind of a fall?'

'It was a bungee jump. Up in Dalkey Quarry, on a Saturday night in November – just this time of year, actually. We were in our final year. Tom was the big sports star – tipped for greatness, just waiting for the call-up to the national team, the rugby team, although tennis, athletics, he was no slouch at those either. The jump ended everything. It took him a year just to walk again.'

'God,' Miss McIntyre says softly, her head swinging back to the door he just left through. 'That's so sad. And does he . . . have anyone? To take care of him? Is he married?'

'No,' Howard says reluctantly.

'He's sort of married to the school,' Farley says. 'He's been here ever since. Teaching Civics, helping out with the track and tennis teams. Now he's coaching swimming.'

'I see,' Miss McIntyre says obscurely, still studying the door. Then she rouses, issues them both a brief summary smile. 'Well. I should get some work done too. I'll catch you boys later.'

She whisks away, leaving a tantalizing spell of perfume that lingers to torment Howard as the ambient lethargy redescends.

'Minus fourteen in Minsk yesterday,' Farley reads from the newspaper. 'Thirty-three in London . . . Wow, sixty-seven in Corsica. Maybe we should move to Corsica – what do you say, Howard?'

'You don't think she's into Tom, do you?' is what Howard says.

'Who, Aurelie? She just met him.'

'She seemed *interested* by him.'

'I thought you decided she had a highly inflated sense of her own worth. What do you care if she's interested?'

'I don't,' Howard remembers hurriedly.

'Are you worried she'll tell him she doesn't want to sleep with him too?' Farley says slyly.

'No, it's just . . .'

'Maybe she's planning not to sleep with the whole faculty!'

'Just let it go, would you?' Howard snaps.

'Not-to-be-taken Aurelie,' Farley chuckles, returning to the weather report.

'Hey, Von Blowjob, let me see your homework.'

'No way, there isn't time.'

'I just want to *see* it, that's all. Come on, Cujo won't be here for – hey, Skippy, let me see your homework . . . hey! Skippy?'

'Earth to Skippy!'

'Hmm? What?'

'Whoa, are you feeling okay? You look sort of green.'

'I'm fine.'

'Like you're actually green, like frog-coloured?'

'I'm just a bit –'

'Hey, everyone, look at Skippy!'

'Shut up, Geoff.'

'He's turning amphibious!'

'Hey, maybe if you turn into a frog you'll be able to speak French better. Hey, everyone, Skippy thinks if he turns – ow!'

Max Brady, waiting to get his homework back from Dennis, scans the doorway. 'Where is the old bastard?'

'Maybe he's feeding his snakes.'

'Maybe he had a meeting with Satan.'

'Or he's off delivering lard to the poor.'

'"What is this, lard?" "You'll eat it and like it!"'

Turning in his desk, Vincent Bailey says *sotto voce* that he heard Cujo's in one of his bad moods today. Yeah, Mitchell Gogan says, he heard that in Cujo's fifth-year class this morning the priest caught someone playing a game on his phone under his desk and he put the boy's head inside the desk and whacked the lid closed on top of him so hard he had to get stitches.

'That's bollocks, Gogan.'

'Yeah, the fifth-year desks don't even have lids.'

'I'm just saying that's what I heard.'

'I heard that once he hit a guy so hard he nearly died.'

'Well, he's not allowed to hit people any more,' Simon Mooney interjects. 'My dad's a lawyer and he says that the law is, teachers aren't allowed –'

'Shh! Shut up! Here he comes!'

Instantly all conversation vanishes, and the class dutifully rise to their feet. The priest enters and crosses to the lectern. In the prevailing silence his black eyes scour the room, and although the boys do not move, interiorly they huddle together, as if caught in the midst of some icy wind.

'*Asseyez-vous.*'

Father Green: previous generations took some clandestine solace in the fact that this translates neatly as Père Vert. Mention him to your dad and he'll definitely remember him, and most probably chuckle at the terror he inspired – that is the way dads' memories seem to work, like nothing they felt when they were this age was really real! Nowadays, whether it's another instance of dumbing-down, or that the priest's mood swings have grown more extreme with the years, the linguistic esprit has been jettisoned in favour of the more direct Cujo; because that's what his French class is like, being trapped in a small room with a rabid animal. Rail-thin, a head taller than the tallest of the boys, on his best days the priest looks like the end of the world; his presence itself is like smouldering kindling, or knuckles cracking over and over.

On paper, though, Father Green is close to sainthood. As well as his various campaigns for Africa – the Seabrook Spinners Sponsored Cycle, the Seabrook Telethon featuring Miss Ireland runner-up Sophie Bienvenue, the Lucky Shamrock pins the boys go out and sell on St Patrick's Day – he makes regular trips to deprived areas of Dublin, delivering clothes and food. Sooner or later, most of the boys will end up 'volunteering' on one of these runs – travelling in the priest's lumbering estate to wastelands of glass and dogshit, carrying black bags and boxes into tiny houses with boarded-up windows while youths their own age collect in scabby

70

gangs to jeer at them every time they come out to the car, and the priest glowers terrifyingly at pupil and hoodlum alike, in his black raiment looking like a single downward stroke of a pen, a peremptory, unforgiving slash through the error-strewn copybook that is the world. You've got to wonder just how glad the Poor are to see him, rapping on the door with his false smile and his troop of trembling helpers. They should count their blessings they're not cooped up in French class with him four days a week, waiting for him to explode.

It's no secret that Father Green hates teaching, and he especially hates teaching French. Lessons are frequently suspended for tirades – usually directed at Gaspard Delacroix, the unfortunate exchange student – on the subject of France's decadence. He seems to believe the language itself to be morally corrosive, and most of the class is spent doing grammar, where its grossness can be partly contained; even then, those languorous elisions, those turbid glottals, enrage him. But what doesn't enrage him? Air particles enrage him. And the boys, with their expensive haircuts and bright futures, enrage him even more. The best they can do is stay quiet and try not to set him off.

Today, however – *pace* the stories of V. Bailey and M. Gogan – the priest seems in uncharacteristically jovial spirits, full of bonhomie and playfulness. He collects the copybooks and breezes through yesterday's homework, commenting, accurately, on how dull it is, and apologizing for putting such clever young men to such uninspiring work, which, although he's probably being sarcastic, they giggle at obediently; he pokes gentle fun at Sylvain, the anti-hero of the French textbook, who in today's exercise is discussing with his dweeby French friends all the lame places they have been that day using the past tense of the verb *aller*, before he sets them to work on an introductory letter to a fictitious pen pal while he checks through their copybooks.

Gradually, the oppressive mood in the classroom lifts. In the distance, there is birdsong, and a shaky ascending scale from Father Laughton's music class. Behind Skippy, Mario very quietly begins to tell Kevin 'What's' Wong how he had sex with his French pen pal's hot sister last summer. As he elaborates, he starts unconsciously kicking the back of Skippy's chair. Thin pages flap through the priest's bony fingers. Skippy, who is still decidedly green about the gills, turns round and stares meaningfully at Mario, but Mario doesn't notice, being involved in an impressively detailed account of the sexual predilections of the French pen pal's sister, who he is now claiming is a famous actress.

Kick, kick, kick, goes his foot against the chair. Skippy pulls at his hair, flushing.

'What's she been in?' Kevin 'What's' Wong asks.

'French things,' Mario says. 'She's very famous, in France.'

'Stop kicking my seat!' Skippy hisses.

Keeping his head craned close to the copybook he's marking, Father Green lilts to himself, *'I'm so piiiiimmmmp it's ri-dick-i-less.'*

Instantly everyone stops what they're doing. Did he just say what they think he said? Father Green, as if becoming aware of this shift of attention, looks up.

'Stand up, please, Mr Juster,' he says pleasantly.

Skippy rises uncertainly to his feet.

'What were you talking about there, Mr Juster?'

'I wasn't talking,' Skippy stammers.

'I distinctly heard talking. Who was talking?'

'Uhh . . .'

'I see, no one was talking, is that correct?'

Skippy doesn't reply.

'Lying,' Father Green counts on his fingers. 'Talking during class. Obscenity – do you know the meaning of obscenity, Mr Juster?'

Skippy – who's rapidly paling, becoming a ghost-frog – hoists a shoulder indeterminately.

'We live in an age of obscenity,' Father Green announces, quitting his lectern and addressing the class as if this were a new area of French grammar. 'Profanity of language. Profaning of the divine temple that is the body. Lustful images. We are immersed in it, we learn to love it, like pigs in excrement, is that not so, Mr Juster?'

Skippy stares back at him queasily. One hand grips the desk, as if that's all that's propping him up.

'*I'm so piiiiimmmmp it's ri-dick-i-less,*' the priest repeats, louder now, in an excruciating American drawl. Nobody laughs. 'Today while driving in my car,' he explains in a mock-conversational tone, 'I chanced to turn on the radio, and this is what I heard.' He pauses, screws up his face and then relays, '*Oh baby, I like to play rough, and when I'm pumpin' my stuff you just can't get enough . . .*'

Heads sink leadenly into arms: they can begin to see what's coming up next.

'I confess to finding myself a little confused –' Father Green scratches his head in a caricature of puzzlement '– as to what the fellow meant, and I made a note to myself to ask one of you boys. What stuff is he pumping, Mr Juster?'

Skippy just gulps.

'*Puuuummmmpin'* it,' the priest hums to himself. '*Pummmpin'* it real good . . . Could it be petrol? Is he perhaps a petrol attendant? Or perhaps he is referring to his bicycle? Is that what the song is about, in your opinion, Mr Juster? Is he referring to his bicycle?'

Skippy quails, his nostrils flare in and out, deep breaths –

'IS HE REFERRING TO HIS BICYCLE?'

Clearing his throat, Skippy replies in a faint high voice, 'Maybe?'

The priest's hand slams on 'Jeekers' Prendergast's desk like a thunderclap; everybody jumps in their seats. 'Liar!' he roars. The last of his earlier jollity and good humour has fallen away now, and they realize that it was phony all along, or rather a darker manifestation of his ordinary rage, waiting for its inevitable moment.

'Do you know what happens to sinful boys, Mr Juster?' Father Green sweeps his blazing eyes about the room. 'All of you, are you aware of the fate that befalls impure hearts? Of hell, the endless torments of hell that await the lustful?'

Eyes study folded hands, evading his fervid gaze. Father Green pauses a moment, then changes tack. 'Do you enjoy pumping your stuff, Mr Juster? Do you like pumping it rough?'

A couple of people snicker in spite of themselves. The boy does not reply; he is gazing at the priest open-mouthed as if he can't believe this is happening. Geoff Sproke puts his hands over his eyes. The priest, enjoying himself, pacing the boards in front of the blackboard like a barrister, says, 'Are you a virgin, Mr Juster?'

This, class, is what's called a double-bind. Note the formal perfection of its construction, the work of a real expert. Obviously Skippy's a virgin – Skippy's about as virginal as they come, and will probably stay that way till he's at least thirty-five. But he can't admit it, not with a classroom of boys looking at him, even if ninety-five per cent of them are virgins also. Neither, though, can he deny it, because the person asking is a priest, who expects all good Catholics to remain virgins until they are married, or at least is pretending to expect this for the purposes of his little game here. So Skippy merely wriggles and shivers and breathes noisily as his interrogator advances a step or two down the aisle.

'Well?' Father Green's eyes twinkle at him merrily.

Through clenched teeth, Skippy says, 'I don't know.'

'You don't know?' Father Green, in performer mode now, repeats incredulously, with a comical wink for his audience. 'What do you mean, you don't know?'

'I don't know.' Skippy stares back at him, his jaw wobbling, trying not to cry.

'You don't know what you mean when you say you don't know?'

'I don't know.'

'Mr Juster, God hates a liar, and so do I. You are among friends here. Why not tell us the truth? Are you a virgin?'

Skippy's face is shaking and sore-looking now. Five minutes remaining on the clock. Geoff shoots a desperate look at Ruprecht as if he might know what to do, but the light has fallen to make opaque blanks of his glasses.

'I don't know.'

The indulgent smile fades from the priest's lips, and the thunderclouds regather in the room. 'Tell me the truth!'

Actual tears roll down Skippy's cheeks. No one is snickering any more. Why can't he just give Father Green what he wants? But Skippy keeps saying, 'I don't know,' like a halfwit, turning greener and greener, making the priest angrier and angrier, until he says, 'Mr Juster, I am giving you one last chance.' And they see his bony hand curled up into a fist on Jeekers's desk, and they think of the fifth-year with the stitches and all of the other dark legends that swirl serpentine around the priest, and in their heads they scream at him, 'SKIPPY, FOR FUCK'S SAKE! JUST TELL HIM WHAT HE WANTS TO HEAR!', but Skippy is clammily, woozily silent and around him the air is full of sparks and the priest's eyes glitter at him hungrily like wolf eyes, and nobody knows what is going to happen, and then the priest steps forward, and Skippy, who is swaying slightly in place, abruptly straightens, bolt upright, opens his mouth and vomits all over Kevin 'What's' Wong.

The first time Halley set eyes on Howard was at a showing of *The Towering Inferno*. When she heard about him, her sister had wondered aloud how much of a future you could have with someone you'd met at a disaster movie. But at that point Halley wasn't feeling picky. She had been in Dublin just over three weeks – not so long that she didn't still get lost all the time on the infuriating streets that kept changing their names, but enough to disabuse her of most of her illusions about the place; enough too, with the deposit and first month's rent for her new apartment, to separate her from most of the money she'd brought, and cut the time available for soul-searching and self-finding quite drastically. That afternoon she'd spent in an Internet café, reluctantly updating her résumé; she hadn't had a conversation since the night before, a stilted exchange with the Chinese pizza delivery boy about his native Yunan province. When she spotted the poster for *The Towering Inferno*, which she and Zephyr must have watched twenty times together, it was like catching sight of an old friend. She went in and for three hours warmed herself in the familiar blaze of collapsing architecture and suffocating hotel guests; she stayed in her seat until the ushers started sweeping round her feet.

Standing on the kerb outside the cinema she unfolded her map of the city, and was scouring it for any place that might serve to use up the next couple of hours when a taxicab hurtled by and whipped it out of her hands. The map flapped madly up into the air, then swooped back down to spread itself over the chest of a man who'd just come out the cinema door. Halley crimsoned with embarrassment, then noticed that the man – bewilderedly unwrapping himself from the two-dimensional image of the city, so it looked almost as if he'd popped out of the map himself – was kind of cute.

('Cute how?' Zephyr asked her. 'Irish-looking,' Halley said, by which she meant a collection of indistinct features – pale skin, mousy hair, general air of ill-health – that combine to mysteriously powerful romantic effect.)

The man looked right and left, then saw her cringing on the far side of the cobbled street. 'I believe this is yours,' he said, presenting her with the incorrectly folded map.

'Thanks,' she said. 'Sorry.'

'Didn't I see you inside at the film?'

She nodded vaguely, pulling at her hair.

'I noticed because you stayed right to the end. Most people leap out of their seats the instant they see the credits appear. I always wonder what they're in such a hurry to get back to.'

'It's hard to comprehend,' she agreed.

'Yeah,' the man said, pursing his lips reflectively. The conversation had reached its natural conclusion and she knew he was considering whether he should leave it there in its brief, formal perfection or risk ruining that perfection by attempting to bring it a stage further; she found herself hoping he would take the chance. 'You're not from Dublin, are you?' he said.

'Hence the map,' she said, and then, realizing this sounded acerbic, 'I'm from the United States. California originally. But I've come from New York. What about you?'

'Here,' he said, gesturing at the surrounding streets. 'So – where was it you were looking for?'

'Oh,' she said. Not wanting to admit the dismal truth, that she had been looking merely for a destination, any destination, she squeezed her eyes tight shut and tried to remember one of the little triangles on the tourist map. 'Uh, the museum?' There was bound to be a museum.

'Ah right,' he said. 'You know, I've never been there since it moved. But I can show you where it is. It's not far.' With a shall-we gesture, he turned, and she followed him downhill to the quays, a fracas of trucks and bus stops and seagulls. He pointed upriver at the far bank. 'It's about half an hour's walk,' he said. 'Although, actually, I'd imagine it must be closing soon.'

'Oh.' She weighed her options. He was around her age and didn't seem psychotic; it would be nice to have a conversation not predicated on pizza delivery. 'Well, is there anywhere nearby I could get a drink?'

'Never a problem in this town,' he said.

Halley had left New York, her job and her friends and come to Ireland without any real plan, other than to be elsewhere, and vague notions of plumbing her own depths and writing some as-yet unconceived masterpiece; now, as she took a seat in the warm, dim, hops-scented snug, she already wondered if her true reason had been to fall in love. She'd grown so sick of the life she'd been living; what better way to forget all that than to lose yourself in someone new? To literally bump into someone, a stranger amid millions of other strangers, and let yourself discover him: that he has a name (Howard) and an age (twenty-five), a profession (history teacher) and a past (finance, murky) – every hour revealing more of him, like a magical pocket map that, once opened, will keep unfolding until it has covered the whole of your living-room floor with places you have never been?

('Just be careful,' Zephyr said. 'You're so bad at these things.' 'Well it doesn't have to be anything serious,' she said, and didn't mention that she'd already kissed him, on a bridge over some body of water she didn't know the name of, before exchanging phone numbers and parting for the night, to walk around in the maze of heteronymous streets till she found a policeman who could tell her where she was; because Halley believed that a kiss was the beginning of a story, the story, good or bad, short or long, of an us, and once begun, you had to follow it through to the end.)

In the following weeks they returned to the little cinema in Temple Bar and saw many more disaster movies together – *The Poseidon Adventure*, *Airport*, *The Swarm* – always staying right to the end; afterwards he led her through the boozy city, its rusting, dusty charms, its rain. Working out of her guidebook, they saw the bullet holes in the walls of the GPO, the forlorn, childlike skeletons in the catacombs of St Michan's, the relics of St Valentine. As they made their way, she imagined her great-grandfather walking down the same streets, cross-referencing the landmarks with tipsy yarns her father used to tell at the Christmas table, even while she laughed with embarrassment at the obese lines of her compatriots at the genealogy stand in Trinity College, where family trees were sold on elaborate parchment scrolls that looked like university degrees, as though conferring on their buyers an official place in history.

Later, sitting in the pub, Howard would make her tell stories about home. He appeared to have spent his childhood watching bad American TV shows, and when she described the suburb she'd grown up in, or the high school she'd attended, his eyes would iridesce, assimilating these details into the mythical country that invested the CDs and books and movies stacked around his bed. Much as she appreciated whatever mystique her foreignness gave her in his eyes, she did try to convey the mundane truth. 'It's really not much different from here,' she'd tell him.

'It is,' he'd insist, solemnly. He told her that he'd once thought of applying for the green card and moving over there. 'You know, doing something . . .'

'So? What happened?'

'What happens to anyone? I got a job.' He'd drifted into a position in a prestigious brokerage in London – *drifted* was his word, and when Halley challenged it he told her that most of his class at Seabrook had ended up working in the City, or in corresponding high-finance positions in Dublin or New York: 'There's a kind of a network,' he said. Salaries were lavish, and he would in all probability have been there still, neither loving nor hating it, if it hadn't been for the cataclysm he'd brought down on himself. *Cataclysm* was his word too; he also referred to it as a *blowup* and a *wipeout*.

After this cataclysm, whatever it was, he'd returned to Dublin and for the last couple of months had been teaching History at his old school. It was plain when she met them that Howard's parents – although, he said, they had enrolled his younger self in Seabrook as a conscious effort to bump the family a few rungs up the ladder – regarded *teaching* there as an unambiguously downward move. Dinner *chez* Fallon was a riot of cutlery on good china amidst long lakes of silence, like some unlistenable modernist symphony; beneath the prevailing veneer of politeness, a seething cauldron of disappointment and blame. It was like eating with some Waspy clan in New Hampshire; Halley was surprised at how un-Irish they seemed, but then most things in Dublin she found to be un-Irish.

She'd always suspected his relationship with Seabrook to be more complicated than he made out; it wasn't until they'd been together almost a year that he told her about the accident at Dalkey Quarry. To her it sounded like the kind of drunken disaster so typical of the lives of teenage boys, but for Howard, it became clear, everything that happened before and after was cast in its light. She began to wonder why he had gone back to the school – was it to punish himself? Some kind of atonement? It was as if, she thought, he were trying to deny the past and embed himself in it at the same time; or deny it *by* embedding himself in it. She didn't know how healthy a situation this was; whenever she tried to talk about it, though, he'd get irritable and change the subject.

That didn't matter; there were other things to talk about. Around that time Halley found out about the severance package from the brokerage. It was three times Howard's salary as a teacher; he had left it sitting in the bank.

She didn't push him into buying a house. She just told him it was dumb to leave so much money lying dormant. 'That's simple economics,' she said. Howard was the one person in Ireland who wasn't obsessed with property. The rest of the country talked of nothing else – house prices, stamp duty, tracker mortgages, throwing around the terminology like realtors at a convention – but the concept of actually owning a place had evidently never occurred to him. He needed someone to force him to pay attention to his own life, she told him. 'Otherwise you're going to drift right off the face of the Earth.'

And so a few months later they'd moved into a house on the outskirts of the suburbs, looking across a shallow valley onto spinneys of wayward, Seussian trees. Though the neighbourhood was not fancy – she doubted anyone around here was sending their kids to Seabrook – the house was well beyond their means. But the sheer profligacy of it became for her part of the point, the quixotic bravado of the two of them actually taking on life, going up to its doors and yelling, 'Let us in!' though they had neither invitation nor evening attire; it made her smile to herself as she dried her first dish, in their first evening in the new house. And the absurdity of compounding the debt by some day – not right away of course, but some day – filling the empty bedrooms, this made her smile too. She hadn't written so much as a word of a story, but for the first time in a long time she felt she was inside a story of her own, and surely that was better yet.

Only a year and a half has passed since then; still it feels like someone else's life. Through the window the pretty spinneys of trees have been uprooted, and the estate teeters on the brink of a vast tract of mud. Some day, they are promised, it will be a Science Park; right now there are only great weals and gashes, each one pinned with dozens of tiny stakes, as if some kind of acupuncture, or torture maybe, is being performed on the flayed skin of the Earth; all day long you can hear the bulldozers claw, the circular saws slice into concrete, the last of the tree roots being wrenched up and dismembered.

'I guess we should have read the fine print,' is all Howard will say on the subject: he doesn't have to spend every day here, listening to it. In recent weeks the racket has been augmented by a nightly apocalypse of fireworks, attended by car alarms and barking dogs, as well as regular power cuts, as the diggers in the nascent Science Park accidentally cut through cables.

She lights a cigarette and stares at the cursor blinking implacably at her from the screen. Then, as if in retaliation, she leans in and hammers:

If memory technology continues to expand at the current rate, data equivalent to the collected experience of an entire human life will soon be storable on a single chip.

Slumping back she gazes at what she's written, streels of smoke spreading lazily over her shoulder.

What with the phony war going on in Iraq, it's not a great time to be an American abroad. Hearing her accent, people, strangers, have actually stopped Halley in the street – or the supermarket, or the cinema box-office – to upbraid her on her country's latest outrage. When it came to looking for a job though, she found that her ethnicity wasn't a problem. Quite the opposite: to the business and technology community here, an American accent was literally the Voice of Authority, and anything it said treated as dispatches from the mother ship. Another surprise: Irish people are crazy for technology. She'd thought that a country with such a weight of history might be prone to looking backward. In fact, the opposite is true. The past is considered dead weight – at best something to reel in tourists, at worst an embarrassment, an albatross, a raving, incontinent old relative that refuses to die. The Irish are all about the future – had not their own premier even said he *lived* in the future? – and every new gadget that emerges is written up as further evidence of the country's vertiginous modernity, seized upon as a stick to beat the past and the yokels of yesteryear barely recognizable as themselves.

There was a time when Halley too had thrilled at the unstoppable march of science. As a cub reporter in New York, seduced away from her 'real' stories by the energy of the Internet boom, she'd had the sense of standing right at the heart of a Big Bang – of a new universe exploding into being, transfiguring all that it touched. The things they could do! The great leaps into the unthinkable that were happening every single day! Now in the face of these relentless, self-advertising wonders she feels more and more of an interloper – clumsy, incompatible, obsolete, like a parent whose kids don't include her in their games any more. And sitting at her desk in her house in the suburbs, it strikes her that in spite of all the changes she has dutifully transcribed, there is really very little difference between her life and her mother's, twenty-five years before – except that her mother spent the day looking after her children, while Halley's is passed in the company of little silver machines, in the service of an insatiable mortgage. So this anger she finds boiling up in her, the irrational, unfair anger she feels when Howard comes home, for all the hours he spent away from her, is that then the same anger her mother was always so full of?

Her sister tells her she's depressed. 'Worrying that you're turning into Mom is like the textbook definition of depression. The depression textbooks all have pictures of our mom in them. Quit that fucking job, already. I don't understand why you don't.'

'I've told you a hundred times, it's this visa thing. I can't just quit and find something else. No one's going to sponsor me for a job I have no experience in. It's this or wait tables.'

'Waiting tables isn't so bad.'

'It's bad when you have a mortgage. You'll see when you're older. Things get complicated.'

'Right,' Zephyr says. There is a combative silence of a kind that keeps breaking into their conversations these days. Zephyr is five years younger, and has just begun studying art in Providence, Rhode Island. Every day over there seems richer with ideas, fun, adventure than the one before; every day Halley seems to have less to tell in response. Pretending to herself that she doesn't notice costs her no little effort, and often she'll find herself spinning off mid-conversation into private fugues of jealousy –

'What?' realizing Zephyr has asked her a question. 'Sorry, it's a bad line.'

'I just wondered if you'd been writing anything.'

'Oh . . . no. Not at the moment.'

'Oh,' Zephyr says sympathetically.

'It's not a big deal,' Halley tells her. 'When something inspires me, then I'll do it.'

'Of course you will!' Zephyr's voice crackles enthusiastically; Halley winces, hearing echoes of her own past efforts at sisterly bucking-up.

She goes to the window to let the smoke out. Across the street she sees her neighbour's two golden retrievers bounce anticipatorily about their front garden; a moment later her neighbour's car pulls up. He unlatches the gate, bends to bury his face in their blond flyaway fur; his wife opens the door to greet him, new baby in her arms, pretty daughter peeping out from behind her. The dogs leap around like this is the greatest thing that's ever happened. Everyone looks so happy.

Standing there unseen, Halley thinks of the way that Howard braces himself when he comes through the door these days, the cloaked expression of weariness as he asks about her day. He is bored: he is in the grip of some massive boredom. Does it emanate from her? Is she leaking boredom into his life, like a radiating atom, the dull, decaying isotope of a lover? She recalls her parents, how they'd morphed with the decades of recession from the hippie fellow-travellers who'd given her and Zephyr their absurd names into dyspeptic fiftysomethings, walling themselves in with investments as they waited for the sky to fall. She wonders if that's all that lies ahead, an incremental process of distancing, from the world and from each other. Maybe that was why her parents fought; maybe the fights were misguided attempts to find a way back, to recover the why of things that they had lost.

She waits for the sound of Howard's car and resolves that tonight she will make herself airy, lightsome, that tonight they will not fight. But already she can feel the anger surge upward through her, bubbling out of her core, because already she can see him coming in, asking her how she is, trying not to be bored as she tells him; trying to keep himself interested, as if this is a project he's set for his class – trying to be good, trying to make himself love her.

'Howard? You busy, Howard?'

'Well, actually, I was just about to –'

'I won't keep you. Just walk with me a moment, little matter I want to discuss with you. How is everything, Howard? How's . . . is it Sally?'

'Halley.' Howard glances forlornly at the exit as the Automator leads him away in the opposite direction.

'Halley, of course. You made an honest woman of her yet? I'm joking, obviously. No pressure from this end. It's the twenty-first century, school's not going to judge you for your personal living arrangements. How about work, Howard, how's that end of things? Into your third year of it now, probably got it pretty well taped at this stage, am I right?'

'Well –'

'Fascinating subject, History. Know what I like about it? It's all written down right there in front of you. Not like Science, where they turn everything on its head every two years. Up is now down. Black is now white. Bananas, that we've been saying are good for you, actually give you cancer. History won't do that. All done and dusted. Case closed. Might not be quite what it used to be, in terms of kids moving to Media Studies, Computer Studies, subjects with more obvious relevance to today. And what is it they say, history teaches us that history teaches us nothing? Makes you wonder what the point of history teachers is, doesn't it? Ha ha! That's not my view, though, Howard, don't look so alarmed. No, as far as I'm concerned, only a fool would write history off, and history teachers like yourself, barring some really major unforeseen circumstances, will always be key members of our faculty here at Seabrook.'

'Great,' Howard says. Talking with the Automator has been likened to trying to read a ticker-tape parade; the margin for confusion is not helped by the high velocity at which the Acting Principal is presently moving, forcing Howard into an ignominious trot.

'History, Howard, that's what this school was built on, as well as your more obvious foundations, of course – clay, rock, what have you.' He stops abruptly, so that Howard very nearly crashes into him. 'Howard, take a look around you. What do you see?'

Dazedly, Howard does as he is told. They are standing in Our Lady's Hall. There is the Virgin with the starry halo; there are the rugby photographs, the noticeboards, the fluorescent lights. Try as he might, he can perceive nothing out of the ordinary, and at last is forced to answer feebly, 'Our Lady's . . . Hall?'

'Exactly,' the Automator says approvingly.

Howard is ashamed to feel a glow of pride.

'Know when this hall was built? Silly question, you're the history man, of course you do. Eighteen sixty-five, two years after the school was founded. Another question, Howard. Does this corridor say *excellence* to you? Does it say, *Ireland's top secondary school for boys?*'

Howard takes another look at the hall. The blue-and-white tiles are scuffed and dull, the grubby walls pocked and crumbling, the window-sashes rotted and knotted with generations of cobwebs. On a winter's day, it could double for a Victorian orphanage. 'Well . . .' he begins, then realizes the Automator has turned on his heel and is power-walking back the way they came. He scurries after him; as he strides, the Automator continues his address, interspersing it with loud directives for the benefit of passing students – 'Haircut! No running! Are those white socks?' – more or less indiscriminately, like a Tannoy in some totalitarian state.

'Once upon a time, Howard, that building was state of the art. Envy of every school in the country. Nowadays it's an anachronism. Damp classrooms, inadequate light, poor heating. As for the Tower, to call it a death-trap would be paying it a compliment. Times change, that's the overall point I'm trying to make here. Times change, and you can't rest on your laurels. Teaching's a premium service these days. Parents don't just hand over their children and let you do what you like. They're looking over your shoulder all the time, and if they suspect they're not getting full value for money, they'll whip little Johnny out of here and plonk him into Clongowes before you can say Brian O'Driscoll.' They have come back through the Annexe, the modern wing of the school, and up the stairs, and are paused now at the open door of the Principal's office, occupied until recently by Father Furlong. 'Come on in for a minute, Howard.' The Automator waves him through. 'You'll have to excuse the mess, we're just doing a little rearranging.'

'So I see . . .' Cardboard boxes cover the floor of the old priest's sanctum sanctorum, some filled with Father Furlong's possessions, late of these shelves, others with the Automator's, transported up from his Dean's office in the old building. 'Does this mean . . . ?'

''Fraid so, Howard, 'fraid so,' the Automator sighs. 'Try to keep it under your hat for now, but the prognosis isn't good.'

Desmond Furlong's heart attack in September had taken everyone by surprise. A diminutive, parchment-yellow man, he had cultivated an air of rarefaction that teetered on the brink of actual incorporeality, as if at any moment he might evaporate into a cloud of pure knowledge; physical ailments had always seemed decidedly beneath him. But now he lies in hospital, mortally ill; and while his orrery still rests on the grand cherrywood desk, his photograph still hangs on the office wall (smiling mirthlessly, like a king who has wearied of his crown) and his iridescent fish still shimmer through the gloom of the aquarium on the dresser, his many bookcases today are empty, save for dust and a single stress-busting executive toy like a hastily planted flag.

'It's tough,' the Automator says, placing a consolatory hand on Howard's shoulder and gazing meditatively into a crate full of Post-its, then stepping aside as a woman staggers in bearing a fresh batch of boxes, which she deposits heavily by the waste-paper basket.

'Hello, Trudy,' Howard says.

'Hello, Howard,' Trudy replies. Trudy Costigan is the Automator's wife, a compact blonde who in her St Brigid's days was voted Best-Looking Girl and Girl Most Likely To, and who shows traces still of her former splendour amid the ravages incurred by the demands of her husband and the five children he has fathered by her (all boys, one a year, as though there is no time to spare – as though, his more paranoid observers whisper, he is raising some sort of *army*). Since his appointment to Acting Principal, she has also served as the Automator's unofficial PA, organizing his diary, arranging meetings, answering the phone. She drops things a lot and blushes when he speaks to her, like a secretary fostering a secret crush on her boss; he in turn treats her like a well-meaning but cerebrally ungifted pupil, hustling her, harrying, snapping his fingers.

'It's tough,' he repeats now, directing Howard into a high-backed African chair, another of the sparse group of survivors from the *ancien régime*, then sitting down on the other side of the desk and making a steeple of his fingers, as Trudy briskly removes from a box and arranges around him a bonsai tree, a pen-set and a framed photograph of their boys in rugby strip. 'But we can't let it get us down. That's not what the Old Man'd want. Got to keep moving forward.' He leans back in his chair, nodding to himself rhythmically.

A strangely solicitous silence fills the room, which Howard has the growing impression he is expected to fill. 'Any word on who might take over?' he obliges.

'Well, it hasn't been discussed in any kind of detail yet. Naturally what we're hoping is that he'll make a full recovery and get right back in the driving seat. But if he doesn't . . .' The Automator sighs. 'If he doesn't, the fear is there simply may not be a Paraclete to fill the position. Numbers are down. The order is ageing. There just aren't enough priests to go around.' He lifts the photograph of his children and studies it intently. 'Lay principal would be a sea change, no question about it. Divisive. Paracletes are going to

89

want one of their own in charge, even if they have to ship him in from Timbuktu. Some of the faculty too, the old guard. But they may not have that option.' His glance slips sidelong from the photograph to Howard. 'What about you, Howard? How would you feel about a principal drawn from the ranks? Is that something you could see yourself supporting? Hypothetically?'

Behind him Howard can sense Trudy holding her breath; it dawns on him that the Automator's esoteric remarks regarding the teaching of History earlier were blandishments, or possibly threats, intended to win Howard's backing in some upcoming, non-hypothetical clash. 'I'd be in favour of it,' he returns, in a strained voice.

'Thought you would,' says the Automator with satisfaction, replacing the photograph. 'Said to myself, Howard's part of the new generation. He wants what's best for the school. That's the attitude I like to see in my staff, my fellow staff I mean.' He swivels round in his chair, addressing the mournful picture of the Old Man. 'Yes, it'll be a sad day when the Holy Paraclete Fathers hand over the reins. At the same time, it's not totally impossible there could be benefits. Country's not what it used to be, Howard. We're not just some little Third World backwater any more. These kids coming through now have the confidence to get up there on the world stage and duke it out with the best of them. Our role is to give them the best possible training to do that. And we must ask ourselves, is a clergyman in his sixties or seventies absolutely the right man for that job?' Emerging from behind the desk and manoeuvring round his wife as if she were another of the cardboard boxes, he begins to pace militaristically about the room, so that Howard has to jog his chair round to face him. 'Don't get me wrong. The Paraclete Fathers are extraordinary men, great educators. But they're *spiritual* men, first and foremost. Their minds are on loftier matters than the here and now. In a competitive market economy – to be perfectly frank, Howard, you've got to wonder whether some of our older priests are even aware what that *is*. And that puts us in a dangerous position, because we're competing with Blackrock, Gonzaga, King's Hospital, any number of top secondary schools. We've got to have a strategy. We've got to be ready to move with the times. Change is not a dirty word. Neither for that matter is profit. Profit is what enables change, positive change that helps everyone, such as for example demolishing the 1865 building and constructing an entirely new twenty-first-century wing in its place.'

'The Costigan wing!' pipes up Trudy.

'Yes, well –' the Automator tugs his ear '– I don't know what it would be called. We'll cross that bridge when we come to it. My point is, we've got to start playing to our strengths, and there's one strength we have that's stronger than every other school. Know what that is?'

'Um . . .'

'Exactly, Howard. History. This is the oldest Catholic boys' school in the country. That gives the name of Seabrook College a certain resonance. Seabrook *means* something. It stands for a particular set of values, values like heart and discipline. A marketing man might say that what we have here is a product with a strong brand identity.' He leans against the denuded bookcase, wags his finger at Howard pedagogically. 'Brands, Howard. Brands rule the world today. People like them. They trust them. And yet, branding is something that this administration has neglected. I'll give you an example. This year is the school's 140th anniversary. Perfect opportunity to raise a hoo-ha, get people's attention. Instead it's barely been registered.'

'Maybe they're waiting for the 150th,' Howard says.

'What?'

'I mean, maybe they want to wait till the 150th anniversary to raise a hoo-ha. You know, as most people would regard it as a bigger deal.'

'The 150th's ten years away, Howard. Can't afford to sit around ten years, not in this game. Anyway, 140 years is just as big a deal as 150. Numerical difference, that's all. Point is, this is a significant opportunity for brand reinforcement and we've almost missed the boat on it. Almost but not completely. We still have the Christmas concert. What I'm thinking is, this year we turn it into a special 140th-anniversary spectacular. Make a real fuss over it. Media coverage, maybe even a live broadcast.'

'Sounds great,' Howard agrees dutifully.

'Doesn't it? And what I want to do is include some kind of historical overview of the school. Put it in the programme notes, even incorporate it into the show somehow. "140 Years of Triumph", "Victory through the Ages", something like that. With, you know, amusing anecdotes from yesteryear, first use of an electric light switch, so forth. People like that sort of thing, Howard, gives them a feeling of oneness with the past.'

'Sounds great,' Howard repeats.

'Great! So you'll do it?'

'What? Me?'

'Outstanding – Trudy, make a note that Howard's agreed to be our "brand historian" for the concert.' Restoring himself to his position at the desk, the Automator straightens a sheaf of papers summatively. 'Well, thanks for stopping by, Howard, I – oh,' as Trudy leans in and whisperingly points to something on her clipboard. 'One other thing, Howard. You have a Juster in your second-year class, a Daniel Juster?'

'That's right.'

'Wanted to sound you out about him. He was involved in an incident today in Father Green's French class, an incident of vomiting.'

'I heard something about that.'

'Who is this kid, Howard? Priest asks him a question, he vomits all over the place?'

'He's – well, he's . . .' Howard deliberates, summoning Juster's from an image of thirty bored faces.

'Apparently he likes to call himself "Slippy". What's that about? He a slippery customer, that it?'

'Actually I think it's "Skippy".'

'"Skippy"!' the Automator says derisively. 'Well, that makes even less sense!'

'I believe it comes from the, uh, television kangaroo?'

'Kangaroo?' the Automator repeats.

'Yes, you see the boy, ah, Juster, has these buck teeth, and when he speaks he sometimes makes a noise which some of the boys find similar to the noise the kangaroo makes. When it's talking to humans.'

The Automator is looking at him like he's speaking in tongues. 'Okay, Howard. Let's leave the kangaroos for the minute. What's his story? Ever had any trouble with him?'

'No, generally he's an excellent student. Why? You don't think he got sick deliberately?'

'Don't think anything, Howard. Just want to make sure we've got the angles covered. Juster's rooming with Ruprecht Van Doren. I don't need to tell you he's one of our top students. Single-handedly raises the grade average for the year by about six per cent. We don't want anything happening to him, mixing with the wrong element, what have you.'

'I don't think you have anything to worry about as far as Juster's concerned. Maybe he's a bit of a dreamer, but . . .'

'Dreaming's not something we encourage here either, Howard. Reality, that's what we're all about. Reality; objective, empirical truths. That's what's on the exam papers. You go into an exam hall, they don't want to know what crazy mess of nonsense you dreamed last night. They want hard facts.'

'I meant,' Howard struggles, 'I don't think he's any kind of a subversive. If that's what you're worried about.'

The Automator relents. 'You're probably right, Howard. Probably just ate a bad burger. Still, no point taking chances. That's why I'd like you to have a word with him.'

'Me?' Howard's heart sinks for the second time in five minutes.

'Ordinarily, I'd send him for a session with the guidance counsellor, but Father Foley's out this week having his ears drained. It sounds like you've got a pretty good handle on him, and I know the boys relate to you –'

'I don't think they do,' Howard interjects quickly.

'Of course they do. Young man like you, they see you as some-one they can confide in, sort of a big brother figure. It doesn't have to be anything formal. Just a quick chat. Take his tempera-ture. If he's got some sort of issue, set him straight. Probably nothing. Still, best to make sure. Vomiting in the classroom is definitely not something we want catching on. Time and a place for vomiting, and the classroom is not it. Think you could teach a class, Howard, with kids vomiting everywhere?'

'No,' Howard admits sullenly. 'Though the way I hear it, it's Father Green you should be talking to, not Juster.'

'Mmm.' The Automator withdraws into his thoughts a moment, spinning a fountain pen through his fingers. 'Things can get a little close to the knuckle in Jerome's classes, it's true.' Again he pauses, the chair creaking as he shifts his weight backwards; addressing himself to the portrait of his predecessor, he says, 'To be frank, Howard, could be the best thing for everyone if the Paracletes started taking more of a back seat. No disrespect to any of them, but the truth is that in educational terms they're outmoded tech-nology. And having them around makes the parents anxious. Not their fault, of course. But pick up a newspaper, every day you see some new horror story, and mud sticks, that's the tragedy of it.'

It's true: for ten years or more, a relentless stream of scan-dals – secret mistresses, embezzlement and, to a degree still almost incomprehensible, child abuse – has eroded the power the Church once wielded over the country almost to nothing. The Paraclete Fathers remain one of the few orders to remain untouched by disgrace – in fact, thanks to their role in one of the top private schools at a time of spectacular wealth creation and even more spectacular conspicuous consumption, they have retained a cer-tain cachet. Nonetheless, once-simple things, such as dropping a child home from choir practice, have been thoroughly removed from the priests' gift.

'Flipside of a strong brand is that you have to protect it,' the Automator says, swivelling back to Howard. 'You have to be vigi-lant against ideas or values that are contrary to what the brand is about. This is a precarious time for Seabrook, Howard. That's why I want to be certain everyone's singing from the same hymn sheet. We need to make sure, now more than ever, that everything we do, down to the last detail, is being done the Seabrook way.'

'Okay,' Howard stammers.

'Look forward to hearing your feedback on our friend, Howard. And I'm glad we had this little talk. If things pan out the way I think they will, I'm seeing big things for you here.'

'Thanks,' Howard says, getting to his feet. He wonders if he's supposed to shake hands; but the Automator has already directed his attention elsewhere.

'Bye, Howard.' Trudy looks up at him for one demure moment as he trudges out of the office, and makes a tick on her clipboard.

Carl and Barry spend their whole lunchtime down in the junior school playground, trying to find more pills. It is total bullshit. You ask the kids a question and they just look at you, it's like they speak a different language down here that over the summer Carl and Barry have forgotten. And all of them act mental, so you can't tell which ones might have prescriptions. After half an hour, Barry's got exactly one pill, which might just be a mint. He's really angry. Carl wishes he had not thrown away their pills! He doesn't remember now why he did it, he doesn't know why he does things sometimes. He thinks about Lollipop waiting for him this evening and him not coming.

Now the bell goes and the kids run back inside in one big swarmy yell. 'Fuck it,' Barry says, and he and Carl begin the trudge back over the rugby pitches towards the senior school. But then they see something.

The boy's name is Oscar. Last year he was in third class, four below Carl and Barry, but he was already famous for the trouble he got into. Not just messing in class – weird shit, like getting stuck in ventilation shafts, eating chalk, pretending he was an animal and yelping down the corridors. Now, walking along with his bag trailing in the grass behind him, you can see him talking to himself, the fingers of his hands flashing out again and again like little pink explosions. Then he stops, and looks up, and gulps. That's because Carl and Barry are blocking his way.

'Hello there,' Barry says.

'Hello,' Oscar answers in a small voice.

Barry tells Oscar politely that he and Carl are doing a science experiment in the senior school using these pills. But they have run out! He shows Oscar the sweets they have brought for anyone who can help them find new pills. Even before he can finish, Oscar is jumping up and down, shouting, 'Oh! Oh! Oh!'

'Shh,' Barry says, looking over his shoulder. 'Come this way a second.' They bring Oscar behind one of the big trees. 'Do you have them with you?' Barry says. 'In your schoolbag?'

'No,' Oscar says. 'My mum gives me them in the morning.'

'In the morning?' Barry asks.

'After my Shreddies,' Oscar says. 'But I know where she keeps them! I can reach them if I stand on a chair.'

He is all ready to run off and get them right now! But Barry tells him to wait till after school. 'You go home and bring us back as many pills as you can. Don't take them all or your mum will notice. We'll wait for you over there in the mud-piles, okay? And we'll give you this whole bag of sweets.'

Oscar nods in excitement. Then he says, 'I have a friend who gets pills too.'

'That's brilliant,' Barry says. 'Bring him too. But make sure you come as quick as you can. It's urgent.'

The kid runs off, his schoolbag bumping along the ground after him. Barry's eyes are shining with cleverness. 'Back in business,' he says.

At 3:45 Carl and Barry go down to the mud-piles, through the trees along the side of the pitches so no one sees them. Trucks dumped the piles here two summers ago, a whole string of them from the long-jump sandpit right up to the back wall of the school. Carl and Barry's class used to play War on Terror on them every lunchtime until a boy from fifth class split his head open and his parents took the school to court. Now no one is allowed to play on them, or even run in the yard any more.

Oscar waits for them in the very last of the mounds. Another even twitchier boy is with him. Oscar says his name is Rory, his face is a weird fizzy white that reminds Carl of the drink his mom drinks for her stomach. Between them they have twenty-four pills. But there is a problem.

'We don't want sweets,' Oscar says.

97

'What?' Barry says.

'We don't want them,' Oscar says.

'But you made a deal,' Barry says.

Oscar just shrugs. Behind him the chalky sick-looking kid folds his arms.

'Look,' Barry says, 'look at all the sweets we have.' He holds the bag open for them to see. 'Mars Bars, Sugar Bombs, Gorgo Bars, Stingrays, Milky Moos, Cola Bottles . . .'

The kids don't say anything. They know it's a shit deal. In junior school all anyone does is make trades, for football stickers, lunches, computer games, whatever, you know when someone's trying to rip you off. Above the black ridge, light is bleeding out of the sky. Carl thinks they should just grab the kids and take the pills from them. But Barry has explained to him already that what they want to establish here is an ONGOING RELATIONSHIP. If you TAKE the pills today, what will you do tomorrow? (Ever since last night when Carl threw away the pills, Barry's been speaking to him in a SLOW, CAREFUL voice, the same way Carl's remedial maths teacher does when she's telling him, Now say if you want to save for a new bike that costs two hundred euro, and you put a hundred euro in the bank, and the RATE OF INTEREST is ten per cent, then it would take you . . . Carl, it would take you . . . ?)

Barry stomps down to one end of the dugout, then comes back again and takes out his wallet. There is a twenty-euro note in there. He waves it under Oscar's nose. 'Twenty euro, and the sweets.' Oscar doesn't even look at the money. Across the pitches the clock strikes four. The girls will be arriving soon. 'What is it you want?' Barry shouts. 'How can we do a deal if you won't say what you want?'

The two small boys look at each other. Then in the distance a banger goes off. Oscar's face lights up. 'Fireworks!' he says.

'You just thought of that now!' Barry says.

'Fireworks!' The white-faced kid speaks for the first time.

'Where the fuck are we supposed to get fireworks?' Barry says.

But now the two boys are yapping away about what kind and how many – 'Bangers – rockets – quartersticks!'

'Okay, okay,' Barry says. 'You win. If you want fireworks, fair enough. But we can't get them to you till tomorrow. So here's what we'll do. You give us the pills now for our experiment, and then tomorrow we'll meet you here again, same time, same place, with the fireworks.'

'Ha ha!' Oscar laughs – actually laughs! 'No way.'

Barry makes a noise like *Gnnnhhhh* through his teeth, and Carl can tell he is thinking, Fuck the deal, let's teach these faggots some respect. But then he turns to Carl and says, 'Watch them,' and he pegs it off across the rugby pitches.

'Where's your friend gone?' Oscar asks. Carl says nothing, just folds his arms and tries to look like he knows what's happening.

'What's your science project about?' the white-faced kid Rory asks.

'Shut the fuck up,' Carl says. He looks out into the going-dark evening. Maybe Barry won't come back. Maybe he's gone to meet Lollipop on his own! This is all a trick, he arranged it with the kids, and –

Panting, Barry clambers back into the dugout. In his hand is a plastic bag. 'Fireworks,' he says.

Every kind: Black Holes, Sailor Boys, Spider Bombs and others. Barry fans them out on the ground. 'You can't have all of them,' he says, like a dad in a shop. 'Pick out three each.' The boys stare, whispering the names to each other. 'Today, arseholes. And give me those pills first.'

They hand over the pills without even thinking – the white-faced kid's in a Smarties box, Oscar's wrapped in old clingfilm that smells like sandwiches. Barry counts them into Morgan Bellamy's tube. Then he nods, and the two kids snatch up the fireworks before he can change his mind.

Now Carl and Barry are hurrying back over the pitches. The squishy ground is going hard with cold, the grass and trees are dark like night is spreading up from below.

'Where did you get all that stuff?' Carl asks.

'Firework fairy.' Barry smiles mysteriously. He is happy again now. As they walk he tells Carl how it just goes to show, everybody has a price, and often it's a lot less than you expect. But he does not let Carl carry the pills or even touch them.

There are no lights behind Ed's. First all Carl sees are the glowing tips of their cigarettes. Then the faces come out of the dark. Five of them: Lollipop, Crinkly-Hair and three others, talking in American-girl accents, waving around their Marlboro Lights. It is strange seeing them here, among the weeds and the cans and the bashed-up supermarket trolleys. The Tower stares over the scraggly trees and bushes like a giant stone face. But no one real is watching.

'Hey, ladies,' Barry says, like this is all totally normal, like he has just wandered over to their table at LA Nites. They look back at him without speaking, and as the boys come closer, the three new girls huddle together, their eyes flicking from Barry to Carl and back again.

'Weren't you supposed to be here a half-hour ago?' Crinkly-Hair sounds pissed off.

Rising above the others, Lollipop gazing right at him. Carl feels his dick wake and stir in his pants.

'We had some trouble with our connection,' Barry tells her.

'I thought that was your own personal prescription,' Crinkly-Hair says.

Barry can't think of an answer, so he just smiles. The new girls are looking really unhappy now, like Carl and Barry are two total scumbags. 'Well, are we going to do business or not?' Barry says. He takes out the orange see-through tube and holds it out, the way you'd hold out food to a stray cat. With a shrug, Crinkly-Hair comes over to him, and one by one the other girls follow. But Lollipop stays at the edge, looking over to where Carl is standing guard by the gap leading back to the road.

'They're medically developed by scientists,' Barry is explaining to the new girls.

'I read about them in *Marie Claire*,' one of the girls says. 'They stop you getting hungry.'

'That's right,' Barry says. 'In Hollywood everyone takes them.'

'How much do they cost?' another girl asks.

'Three euro each,' Barry says. 'Or ten for twenty.'

'Yesterday you were going to give us five for five,' Crinkly-Hair says.

Barry shrugs. 'Supply and demand,' he says. 'I don't control the market. If you don't want them there are some girls from Alex's who said they'd take the lot.'

'I'd say,' Crinkly-Hair says sarcastically, but the other girls are reaching into bags for purses decorated with slinky cartoon cats and glittery flowers. Carl turns to watch the entrance while the deal goes through. Behind him he hears their voices counting, first coins, then pills. Every second it gets darker, like the air is filling up with particles. He realizes someone is standing beside him. It is Lollipop. She is looking at Carl. 'I have a problem,' she says.

It is only the second thing he has ever heard her say. He makes a sound somewhere between 'Huh?' and 'What?'

'I want to buy some diet pills,' she says. 'But I don't have any money.'

'You don't have any money?'

'No.'

'You don't have any?'

'No.'

She looks at him with expressionless green eyes. This close he can almost taste how red her lips are. The others are talking among themselves. 'Last night your friend said that you might be able to work something out?' she says. She raises an eyebrow. Her school blouse is two buttons open and if he leans forward Carl can make out the top half of a white tit.

'What do you mean?' he says.

'I don't know.' She noses the toe of her shoe against the ashy black ground. Carl lunges for her with his mouth. She pulls back, but takes his hand and leads him across the clearing and into the trees.

In here the air tastes of wet leaves and through the weeds he can see old initials graffitied on the wall. She is standing right up against him, an inch away, he smells the smell of her, it is sweet like strawberries. She pushes her hair back with her hand. The other voices seem far away. She leans in and upwards and her mouth is on his, her tongue strokes through it, deeper and deeper, like an oar through the water . . . She stops. 'Are you Carl or Barry,' she says.

'Carl.'

'My name is Lori,' she says. 'Short for Lorelei.'

'Lollipop,' he mumbles.

'What?'

'Nothing.'

Then she's kissing him again. The smell of her hair and skin swirl all around him. He sticks a hand on her left tit. She lifts it off but doesn't take her mouth away. For another twenty seconds, thirty, her thin body crushes up tighter and tighter against him, as if she's screwing herself into place with her tongue. Then, like the claw in the fairground when the money runs out, she separates herself from him and steps backwards. She gazes at him with her expression of expressionlessness.

'Um, Lori, what are you *doing* in there?' goes Crinkly-Hair from outside.

Lori moves him aside with her hand and walks back into the clearing. A second later Carl limps out after her, pulling his jacket down over his boner. Going up to Barry, he says, 'Ten.'

At first Barry doesn't get it, but then he clicks and without a word counts out the ten pills. Lori stands beside Carl not looking at him and holds her hands cupped for Barry to pour the pills into, like she's waiting for communion. And the pills do look like little communions. Then she puts them in the pocket of her coat and goes back to her friends.

It is completely dark now. Before they go Barry tries to make each of the girls take his number, but they are chattering to each other like he isn't there, like this is all over and they are already far away. They leave without saying goodbye.

When they are out of sight, Barry lets out a whoop. 'Our first score! Check it out, dude!' He opens his fist on a nest of notes and coins. Then he hugs Carl. 'This is just the beginning, hombre. We are going to fucking *rule* this neighbourhood!' Holding his hands up to the sky, he turns to the traffic going by and shouts into the headlights, 'We are the men! We are the fucking men!'

They start walking towards Burger King. Barry looks at Carl slyly. 'She sucked your dick, didn't she?'

Carl says nothing, then slowly nods with a half-smile.

'*Damn!*' Barry laughs, and strikes his thigh. 'Why didn't I think of that?'

Carl laughs too, then he looks back – but the girls are gone, of course. They are long gone.

The door opens, the priest's blackness disappears into the deeper black of the shadows like he's never been there. Except for the smell of incense that still twists itself through the air. You go to the window to chase it away, cold blasts in to clash against the sick-sweat on your arms and chest and back. The wrinkled sheets thrown back on the bed like shed skin, the taste of pills still in your mouth like you are made of pills.

The five imprints of his fingertips still burning on your cheek.

'Hello?' the voice that answers the phone is clipped, hiding, like a spy's voice.

'Dad?'

'Hey there, sport.' The voice relaxes a little bit, or pretends to. 'Wasn't expecting to hear from you tonight. How's things?'

'Well, not so good, actually.'

'Oh no? What's bugging you, sport?'

Lately Dad's started doing this thing of calling you 'sport'. You know he does it to make you feel like everything's okay. But it doesn't work. Instead it's like he's forgotten who he is, and he's trying to cover it up with pieces of dads from TV, sunny American dads in sitcoms who go out with you to the yard to throw a baseball back and forth.

'I got sick today,' you say.

'Sick sick?'

'Yeah, in class.'

'Did you eat something?'

'I don't think so.'

'Must be a tummy bug. How're you feeling now?'

'Okay.'

'You don't sound great.'

'I had to go to the nurse.'

'What did she say?'

'She just sent me to bed. She said I shouldn't go to training tomorrow.'

'You're going to miss training?'

'Yeah.'

'Hmm.' Behind the patchwork of TV dads you can hear him not knowing what to say. Dad doesn't like talking on the phone: it's like the longer he talks the thinner the patchwork is stretched, the more the things they aren't saying come gusting through. 'That sounds like a bad dose, all right. Well, keep an eye on it, sport, and let's see how it goes.'

'Okay.' You wait a second and then, like you've just thought of it, 'Is Mum around?'

'Mum?' Dad repeats, like she's a neighbour who moved away long ago.

'Yeah.'

There is another delay, and then, 'You know I think she might be taking a nap, slugger. But let me just check.' He lays down the phone and you listen to him going to check: opening the door of the kitchen, shooing Dogley off the step, calling Mum's name, then clomping back to the phone to give you the answer you expected. 'Yeah, she's just this minute lain down for a rest, Danny. Better not wake her. Maybe she'll give you a ring tomorrow.' With this promise he falls silent, waiting for you to wrap up the conversation.

You and Dad are playing a game. There are many rules to the game, maybe an infinite number of rules, all around you like tiny fish-bones or infra-red beams. The most important rule though is that you never ever talk about the game: you act like there is no game, even though both of you know the other person is playing it; you keep yourself very still, you act like everything is normal, and if you can't remember what normal is you turn yourself into TV Dad and TV Son.

Or that's what you're supposed to do. Tonight something has gone wrong and you can't play it right. 'I was wondering . . .'

'What?'

You know you shouldn't say it. So you change it. 'I was wondering what you decided about mid-term.'

'Oh – you know we haven't had much of a chance yet to talk about it, buddy. Things have been a bit topsy-turvy lately. But I'm fairly sure it'll be okay. Fingers crossed.'

'Oh,' you say. You go to the window, touch the curtain, like it might have magical powers. 'Erm,' you say. You take a deep breath. Are you actually going to say it? Are you? 'Do you think I could come home this weekend?'

'This weekend?' Dad doesn't understand. 'What do you mean, sport?'

'I just thought . . .' You are ashamed to hear your voice cracking – this is totally against the rules! 'Like, because I was sick, it might be good to come home for the weekend . . .'

'Hmm . . .' Behind his patchwork voice Dad is screaming, *What are you doing?* 'Well, sport, we'd both love to see you, but like I say things have been a bit, ah, a bit crazy here lately . . .'

'I know, but . . .' Your throat is filling up with ashes, sawdust.

'Obviously if you're sick, but . . . you know, I'm just wondering if it would be such a good idea.'

'Please?' You are sobbing, great big jags of mucous and tears.

'I think it'd probably be best to stick to the original plan, sport,' Dad pretends not to hear, 'we're both really looking forward to seeing you at mid-term and I'm certain, I'm nearly ninety per cent certain, that if we stick to that original plan it'll all be fine. And mid-term, it's only two weeks away, right? Isn't that right?'

You aren't able to reply. So Dad talks instead. 'Your mum'll be kicking herself she missed you tonight. She's so excited about your next race, we were both so sorry we couldn't be there on Saturday, but this next one, she's determined, and Dr Gulbenkian thinks we're really about to turn a corner here, so you keep your fingers crossed, and keep up the training, and come November we'll, ah, we'll . . .' He runs out of words and can only wait there for your sobs to burn themselves out. 'Okay there, Danny?'

'Yeah,' you manage to stammer.

'Okay,' Dad says. 'Well, I suppose I should let you get back to it, right?'

'I suppose so.'

'Okay. Talk to you soon, sport, all right? We miss you.'

You hang up, wipe your eyes and nose on your sleeve, hover a long time by the window taking long shuddery breaths. Autumn leaves are curled in the casement, tangled up in a fuzz of cobwebs. Ruprecht's moon map flickers in the draught, the mountains and craters and marshes, the seas that are not seas, Sea of Rains, Sea of Snakes, Sea of Crises, stiff and grey and unmoving like icing on a birthday cake left behind a thousand years ago.

How can they know what it looks like way off in space, when they can't tell what's happening inside a body of a person that's right there in front of them?!!

Oh boo hoo, are you going to cry some more, Skippy? Are you going to take a pill and fall asleep again? Or switch on your Nintendo and play your little game?

Do you feel like you're caught in the mouth of something huge?

The fingers burning into your cheek. Answer me, Mr Juster!

Back at the foot of the crumbling steps. In the leafless trees the things that have replaced the birds. The door swings open with a creak and you step inside the Great Hall. Make your way through the whispering stone, through shafts of grey light trapped in the spiderwebs. Weave past the zombies that burst from the library clock, clamber into the dumbwaiter. You've done this part so many times it's stopped being scary, become just a pattern that you follow without thinking.

Once upon a time the Realm was ruled by a beautiful princess. You'll see her on the title screen, *Hopeland* written above her in medieval-type writing: blue eyes, hair the colour of honey, frost making her sparkle like a far-off star. In her frozen hands she holds a little harp – that's the one she would play each morning from the Palace ramparts to bring up the sun. But then Mindelore stole it, and used it to summon three ancient Demons, who have laid waste to the Realm and imprisoned the princess in ice! The elders have chosen you, Djed, an ordinary elf from the forest, to find the magical weapons, save the princess and free the Realm from the Demons' grip. You've got the Sword of Songs and the Arrows of Light – all you need now is the Cloak of Invisibility, then you'll be ready to fight the Demons. But you keep getting stuck here, in the House of the Dead –

'Are you still playing that thing?' The door flies open and Ruprecht comes bustling into the room. Without waiting for a reply he sits down at his computer, drumming his fingers anticipatorily on his thigh as it wakes itself up. 'Father Green was looking for you,' he says over his shoulder.

'I know.'

'What did he want?'

'Just to see if I was feeling better.'

'Oh.' Ruprecht's stopped listening – frowns into the screen as his inbox loads.

Earlier this month, Ruprecht wrote the following e-mail, which was transmitted by satellite into space:

Greetings, fellow intelligent life-forms! I am Ruprecht Van Doren, a fourteen-year-old human boy from planet Earth. My favourite food is pizza. My favourite large animal is the hippo. Hippos are excellent swimmers despite their bulk. However, they can be more aggressive than their sleepy demeanour might suggest. Approach with caution!!! When I finish school, I intend to do my PhD at Stanford University. A keen sportsman, my hobbies include programming my computer and Yahtzee, a game of skill and chance played with dice.

By logging on to the METI website, you can chart the message's progress. It hasn't even got as far as Mars yet; still, every night Ruprecht checks his computer to see if any extraterrestrials have mailed him back.

'Who the hell's going to want to reply to *that*? It's the gayest e-mail I ever heard,' Dennis says. 'And furthermore, that's a total lie about you being a keen sportsman, unless you count eating doughnuts as a sport.'

'It's quite possible that doughnut-eating is considered a sport in distant galaxies,' Ruprecht says.

'Yeah, well, even if it is, and even if there are a bunch of fat lame Yahtzee-playing aliens out there, they're still not going to get your gay message for like a hundred years. So you'll totally be dead by the time they get back to you.'

'Maybe I will, and maybe I won't,' is Ruprecht's somewhat mysterious response to this.

METI stands for Message to Extra-Terrestrial Intelligence, and is an offshoot of SETI, the Search for same. This Search, a collaborative effort involving nerds from all over the world, concentrates primarily on the random transmissions that bombard the

Earth from space every day. These transmissions are picked up by the SETI radio observatory in Puerto Rico, divided up into little parcels of data and sent out to the PCs of Ruprecht and others like him, which will trawl through them with the aim of finding, amid the mass of unintelligible static thrown out by the stars, a sequence or pattern or repetition that might intimate the presence of intelligent communicating life.

Behind the emergence of METI is none other than Professor Hideo Tamashi, the celebrated string theorist and cosmologist. It was he who organized the space-mail; on another occasion, he and a group of schoolchildren broadcast a performance of Pachelbel's Canon in D Major. According to Professor Tamashi, the existence of extraterrestrial life is, statistically, more likely than not; moreover, the future of humanity could depend on making contact. 'In the next thirty or forty years, ecological collapse may well make Earth unliveable,' Ruprecht explains. 'If that happens, the only way we'll survive is by colonizing a new planet, which realistically we could only do by travelling through hyperspace.' Travelling through hyperspace requires unlocking the secrets of the Big Bang; however, the ten-dimensional theory the Prof maintains holds the key is itself so fiendishly difficult that he believes the only way to solve it in time is if some kindly superior alien civilization takes us under its wing.

Tonight, though, the ETs are keeping their counsel. Ruprecht, with a little sigh, shuts down the computer and rises from his chair.

'Nothing?'

'No.'

'But you think they will come some day? Like to Earth?'

'They have to,' Ruprecht responds grimly. 'It's as simple as that.'

He makes a couple of adjustments to his Global UFO Sightings Map, then fishes his toothbrush from his washbag and pads out to the bathroom.

Outside, the laurels swoosh in the cold air, and the darkness is tinged with the pink glow of the neon Doughnut House sign, like sugar on the night. Alone in the room, Skippy runs for cover as zombies crash through the floorboards and stretch after him with sinewy arms and splintered nails. Once upon a time they were people, maybe a family even, and when you look into their decaying faces it's like you can still see a sad spark of who they were . . .

Later, with the lights out: 'Hey, Ruprecht.'

'Yes?'

'Say if you could travel in time –'

The sound of Ruprecht propping himself on his elbows in the opposite bed. 'It's quite consistent with Professor Tamashi's theories,' he says. 'Merely a case of sufficient energy, really.'

'Okay, well – does that mean you could stop the future?'

'Stop the future?'

'Well, like, say if we started going back in time tonight, could we just keep going back for as long as we wanted? So we'd never actually get to tomorrow?'

'I imagine so,' Ruprecht says, pondering this. 'Or if you travelled at the speed of light, time would stop, so it would always be today.'

'Huh,' Skippy says thoughtfully.

'The problem in either case is energy. Travelling in time would require gaining access to hyperspace, which costs an enormous amount of power. And the closer you approach the speed of light, the more your weight increases and prevents you from reaching it.'

'Wow, sort of like the universe is holding on to you?'

'You might put it that way, yes. But anyway, you hardly want to stop time now, not with mid-term coming up!'

'Ha ha, right . . .'

Silence resettles like a fresh snowfall that covers the room. Soon Ruprecht's breathing turns into murmurous snores and little chomping noises; he's having the dream where he's being given the Nobel Prize, which he imagines as a large silver trophy filled with fudge . . . Ghostly grey-black moonlight creeps through the window; Skippy watches it gleam on his swimming trophy, the photo of Mum and Dad.

III

And once they're sure he is asleep, they file into the room and gather round his bed, their long wasting limbs hanging limp by their sides, their rotting breath breathing WE ARE THE DEAD as they grab his hand and pull him up the stairs to a room and a Shape in a bed that lifts its head and draws aside the covers to reveal its body to him, skin faded to the same colour as the bedsheets it rises out of, reaching for him with hands that turn into hands that grip him freezing tight, and its mouth closes on his so he can't scream or even breathe or wake up Ruprecht, he stretches under the pillow for the pills but they are gone! someone must have come in and taken them! and now the room fills with water and he starts drowning, the hands pulling him down below the surface –

He pulls his eyes open. There is no water, no one in the room except him and Ruprecht. The pills are where they always are. The ghostly almost-light hangs in the room like somebody there. He turns away from it, his hand wrapped around the little amber tube.

It is late when Father Green descends from the Tower. The lights are out in Our Lady's Hall, but there is moon enough in the windows for him to make his way; although by now, no doubt, he could make it in his sleep, if he were the kind to sleep. This is his favourite time, when the school has gone to bed, and he may finally get to work! The poor will always be with us, says the Lord, so there is always work to be done; he may no longer be a young man, but Father Green has no intention of shirking his duties – and tonight, for the first time in a long time, he feels a tingle of the old vigour! The old sap, rising in his –

What?

He thought he heard footsteps. When he turns round, though, the hall is empty. Of course it's empty, who would be there, at this hour? Lately his mind has grown fond of tricks like this – shapes coming out of the shadows, strange echoes, as of someone behind him. Perhaps he should speak to the nurse, have her check him over . . . oh, but think how 'Greg' would love that! No, he'll wait, it will fade away in due course, *Deo volente*.

Passing beneath the Virgin he crosses himself, then walks down the steps to the basement. His office used to be on the top floor. Now that is a 'computer room', and his charitable work is consigned to the underworld. Progress. Father Green hears rumours that if Desmond Furlong does not return, Acting Principal Costigan – 'Greg' – intends to demolish the Old Building altogether – that's right, this same one whose construction Père Lequintrec oversaw, brick by brick, back when there was not a school in the country worthy of the name as far as Catholic boys were concerned. Back when the order was strong, when they had that zeal! Instead of being content to serve merely as window-dressing, at a finishing school for young financiers.

'Greg'. 'Call me Greg, please.' And he, of course, is 'Jerome'. 'Jerome, I don't know how you do it.' 'Jerome, you're an inspiration to us all.'

He turns on the light of the dingy office, opens a draft of a request for donations from corporate friends of the school. How many times has he written this same letter? Tonight though he can't bring his mind to focus on it.

'Jerome, just a quick word if I may . . .'

Father Green had been on his way to the Residence for dinner; he had barely noticed the Acting Principal approach. Typically, 'Greg' steers clear of him – one of the old dinosaurs, nothing to be done with him except wait for him to die. And yet here he was – was he? Yes, he was! – interrogating the priest about this business with the boy getting sick in his morning French class! 'Gather you had a little dust-up with one of your second-years,' he said.

Well! Father Green had been so surprised he hadn't managed to reply; and it must have looked like an admission of guilt, because the Acting Principal proceeded directly into a telling-off – couched, albeit, in all sorts of patronizing flannel: 'Times have changed, Jerome . . . sometimes I myself . . . bear in mind these boys aren't quite as robust as in our day . . .' (In *our* day! Did he take 'Jerome' for such a fool?) 'Might be more productive in the long run, Jerome, if you went a little easier on them.'

Ah yes. Go easy: the motto of the age. For these children, as for their parents, everything must be easy. It is their entitlement, it is their *right*, and anything that infringes on it, anything that requires them to lift themselves even momentarily from their cosy stupor, is *wrong*. They will live their lives without ever knowing want or hardship, and they will take this as no more than their due, sanctioned, somewhere in the vaporous satellite-strewn heavens, by the same amorphous God who brings them Swedish furniture and four-wheel-drive jeeps, who appears when summoned for weddings and christenings. A kindly, twinkle-eyed God. An *easy* God.

Go easy. Well, that got his blood up, all right! He was within an inch of grabbing 'Greg' by the lapels! Damn it, man, do you think that God no longer keeps the books? Look around you! Sin is everywhere! It is more powerful than ever before, polluting, poisoning, corroding like a cancer! The boys *need* someone to frighten them! They need someone to tell them the *truth*! That their souls are in peril, that their only hope is to prostrate themselves before God, beg Him for the divine grace to be freed of their wickedness!

But he did not grab 'Greg's' lapels, and he did not say any of this; he merely smiled, promised to mind his temper in future, and to apologize to the boy whose feelings were hurt. It was no great surrender; he is all too aware of the impotence of his efforts. The torments of Hell mean nothing to these boys. *Souls, God, sin*, these are words from another time. The superstitious ravings of an old scarecrow.

For a long time now Father Green has wondered what he is doing here. The thought of retirement appals him: he has watched too many of his colleagues deliquesce into inertia – men he worked with side by side on the missions, in the heathen wilderness with nothing but their faith to guide them, now pottering about the Residence like gummy smiling zombies, pacifically awaiting death. And yet work – which had always been his salvation – work too has lost its savour. He does not mean teaching: that has never interested him, and today's boys are worse than ever before, steeped in licentiousness, an orchard of apples rotting on the branch. But in the council flats, on the estates, where he used to see, in the first years after they recalled him from Africa, a kind of promise amidst the desolation – a hopefulness, an honesty, a capacity for change – now the desolation is all he sees. The same problems of twenty years ago: mildewed rooms, sinks full of bottles, children running around half-wild over ground littered with syringes; the same easy capitulations, the same weakness, the same abrogation of responsibility. And here in his office, the same endless scrabbling after pennies, the endless, ignominious banging of the drum.

Perhaps everything he believed for so many years is simply

wrong? Perhaps there simply is no grain of goodness in the heart of man, waiting to be brought to the light, perhaps man is base to the core, any flicker of virtue merely a trick of the light, a – what is the word? – a corposant. On his darker nights (and most nights, now, seem dark) he has wondered if he has not spent forty-four years toiling after a myth.

Is it not strange how a single chance encounter may throw an entirely new light on one's situation? How an exchange so brief as to appear quite without significance may reveal a way forward, a new path where before there was none? This evening Father Green had acceded to 'Greg's' request and mounted the stairs to the Tower to apologize to the boy whose feelings he had allegedly hurt. It was a nonsense of course – he had been caught speaking obscenely in class for one, and for another these boys had no feelings, they were the very embodiment of the modern age, insensate to the core, and Father Green made his little pilgrimage in the same spirit of indifference and defeat with which he has carried out so many of his duties in recent times. But the moment the boy opened the door – well, too much to call it a Damascene conversion; too much, of course, absurd. And yet it was clear in the instant, that silvered instant on the threshold, the priest had made a mistake. He had made a mistake about this boy, and the shock of it echoed back through him, causing him to ask himself what other mistakes he might have made in the recent past. Because you could see – impossible to describe in retrospect the clarity, the vividness of it – you could *see* the innocence in this boy's face. He was *different* – how had Father Green never noticed it before? Younger than his peers, for one: not yet slipped down the sinkhole of pubescence, still retaining the miniature perfection of the child, his roseate skin unblemished, his gaze bright and unclouded. But that accounted only for part of it. There was a fragility to him, an unworldliness, a purity that verged almost on a kind of anticipatory pain, as of a fruit that if it is touched at all must bruise; and a shadow of grief, perhaps at the iniquity of the world he found himself in, beholding which Father Green had felt moved to a spontaneous tenderness such as he had not experienced in a long time, and reached out to console the boy (recalling it now, he feels this sensation pass through him once more, and in the lonely office his hand unfolds to caress the empty air).

The conversation that followed was desultory: was the boy feeling better? He was. Did he accept Father Green's apology for losing his temper? He did. But Father Green had already learned a profound lesson: that despair too is a sin, and a most insidious one, because it obscures those instances of God's grace that are among us, and leads us into solipsism and hardness of heart. He had allowed himself to be clouded by pessimism, curdled by rage, but God in his mercy had given him a chance to atone. And the nature of his penance is clear: he must help this boy. For here is one who may be helped, who may yet be saved from the depredations of his time – subtly, of course, obliquely, an invisible hand gently steering him towards goodness. One could still do that, couldn't one, one could still take a boy under one's wing? And in saving him – Father Green's mind is racing now – might he not thereby rediscover his own lost path? Might this boy not be the Lot who saves, for Father Green, the profaned city in which he is lost? Even as he asks the question, he hears his heart respond unequivocally, yes! Yes, Jerome, yes!

Was that a – laugh? Did he hear someone laughing, out there in the dark? One of the boys, no doubt – he leaps for the door. But outside there is nothing; only a prickling silence that mocks his paranoia. He holds his head. Late, Jerome, it is late. At this hour one labours merely under illusions.

He turns out the light, sets off back through the school towards the Residence. As he goes he imagines the trials that might afflict a youngster, and how best a concerned friend might help to tease these out. He ignores the curious sense he has that someone is following him. Just another of these irritating tics that have plagued him these last few weeks.

But he knows who it is.

Next morning Skippy's recovered from his mystery illness, and though initially he's followed wherever he goes by a chorus of fake barfing, it's not long before he's bumped from the limelight by new and bigger stories. It appears that at some point after the final bell yesterday, someone broke into Simon Mooney's locker and took all his fireworks from inside it. Simon Mooney is staggering white-faced from group to group, asking people if they have any information, but no one does; after all his gloating yesterday it's debatable whether they'd give it to him even if they did.

The other big news is Miss McIntyre's announcement in Geography class today of a possible field trip to Glendalough to see the U-shaped valley. This causes quite a stir. A U-shaped valley, made by a glacier! With *her*!

There was a time not so long ago when few people would have been much moved by the prospect of a U or any other shape of valley. Prior to Mr Ó Dálaigh's departure for a gallstone operation, the only fact of interest anyone can remember learning in Geography is that there is a town in Turkey called Batman (pop. 131,986; chief industries: oil, food production). But all that changed when Miss McIntyre arrived on the scene. It's like simply by pointing to things she can make them come alive – make them dance and sparkle, like the brooms and cups and so on in *The Sorcerer's Apprentice* – and now the boys can't understand how they ever found geographical features boring. This new-found interest in the world around them isn't confined to the classroom either. Under her tutelage, previously non-committal boys, boys who could barely be brought to look at anything unmediated by an electronic screen, have been transformed into Taliban-like ecological zealots. They write furious letters to the directors of polluting companies; they excoriate mothers for driving the half-mile to the shops to buy one (solitary) filo pastry roll; they ruthlessly make away with anything recyclable that is left out of sight for even a moment (unopened cans of Coke, homework) and berate comrades over inefficient use of deodorant spray. Ruprecht, of course, says that these kind of piecemeal measures won't have any effect, and that even if much more drastic action were taken, which it probably won't be, Earth has more than likely gone past the point at which the environmental devastation of the last two centuries can still be reversed. But this falls on deaf ears.

'M-maybe she'll take us to the U-shaped valley and then we'll never come back here,' flushes Victor Hero.

'She can make *ice* seem warm,' Bob Shambles says dreamily.

But the biggest news of all comes just before lunchtime, when the boys emerge from History class to find that a rash of posters has appeared all over Our Lady's Hall.

'HALLOWE'EN HOP'
END OF TERM SECOND-YEAR MIXER WITH ST BRIGID'S
SOFT-DRINK REFRESHMENTS
ALL PROCEEDS TO CHARITY

Beneath these words is a crudely executed graphic of a Frankenstein's monster jiving, soft drink in hand, beside an old record-player.

'What the hell is a Hop?' Mario says.

'I think it's like a dance,' Niall says, frowning. 'A kind of dance, from days of Yore?'

'Or a dance for one-legged people?' Geoff surmises.

'It's a Hallowe'en disco for the second-years from the two schools,' Dennis says. 'My brother told me about it.'

'A disco?' Skippy says.

'They do it every year,' Dennis says. 'Everyone dresses up.'

'Holy shit,' Mario says.

'This is excellent!' says Niall.

'A *ghoul* for every boy,' Geoff says in his zombie voice.

Up and down the corridor boys are excitably making the same discovery, much to the chagrin of the Automator, who snaps at them to quit stalling and get to class, then realizes it's lunchtime.

'I'd better buy some condoms,' Mario says. 'This Hop will be a serious beavershoot.'

'It's going to be *spook*-tacular!' Geoff says in the voice.

'Will you stop that?' says Dennis.

'Juster!' Someone's calling Skippy. It's Howard the Coward, hailing him from across the hall. What can he want?

'I wonder how many condoms I will need?' Mario ponders as Skippy trudges away. 'Probably I should get a couple of boxes, to be on the safe side.'

'Make no *bones* about it –'

'God damn it, Geoff –'

'We're going to have a *wail* of a time!'

Leaving the Automator's office yesterday evening, Howard had little intention of following through on his promise to talk to Daniel Juster. The Acting Principal loved to issue orders, but that was usually as far as his interest extended, meaning that if Howard could just keep out of his way for the next couple of days, there was a good chance he'd forget their entire conversation. This seemed to Howard, who didn't see why he should be lumbered with extra work, to be the best course of action – until this morning, when a very strange thing had happened.

He'd stayed up late the night before to finish *Goodbye to All That*, and in his second-year class today he decided to begin with a brief excerpt from the book before wrapping up the First World War and moving on to the Easter Rising. Graves's account bore little resemblance to the barren history textbook. It fluoresced with imagery – the skeletons in the craters in no man's land, picked clean by the rats; a wood full of German corpses, whose overcoats Graves brings back to his trench for blankets; the officers-vs-sergeants cricket game, with a rafter for a bat, a rag tied with string for a ball, and as a wicket, a parrot's cage, 'with the clean, dry corpse of a parrot inside': every page contained some nightblack gem.

After reading aloud for a couple of minutes, Howard became aware of an unusual silence. Instantly he was on his guard. A silent classroom, in his experience, meant one of two things: either everyone had fallen asleep, or they had planned some sort of a trap and were waiting for him to stumble into it. When he scanned the desks, though, the boys appeared fully conscious, and there was no hint of impending attack. It dawned on him that this must be what is known as an *attentive* silence. Attempting to conceal his surprise, fearful of breaking the spell, he continued reading.

The book held their attention right up to the end; when the bell went, Howard had the giddying sensation of actually having *imparted knowledge*. It was an unexpectedly replete and heartening sort of feeling – so much so that when he spies Juster now, examining a poster for the Hallowe'en Hop, instead of turning in the other direction he decides to call him over. He watches the boy shuffle across the hall, and readies an avuncular smile.

'I just wanted a quick chat,' he reassures him. 'You don't need to look so freaked out.' As he speaks the words, it strikes Howard that the Automator made a shrewd move, picking him to talk to the youngster; certainly he's going to be more on his wavelength than some septuagenarian priest. 'I hear you tossed your cookies in French class yesterday,' he says.

'I what?' Juster says.

'You threw up. You got sick.'

The ends of the boy's mouth turn down.

'I just wanted to see if you were feeling better.'

'Yes, sir.'

'Yes, you're feeling better?'

'Yes, sir.'

'You and Father Green have buried the hatchet?'

Juster nods.

'He can be a tough old buzzard, but I wouldn't take anything he says to heart,' Howard says. The boy makes no response. Frankly he does not seem to Howard all that appreciative of his interest – but kids often hide their vulnerability behind this kind of attitude, he reminds himself, you have to give them space, let them come to you. 'And how are things generally? How are you doing?'

'Fine.' Juster suddenly looks wary, as if Howard is trying to catch him out somehow.

'Your schoolwork going okay? Not finding it too hard this year?' The boy shakes his head. 'Your family's doing well? Your parents?' He nods. Howard searches around for another question. 'How about swimming? I hear that's going great.' The boy nods again, pale brows furrowed apprehensively like he's playing chess with Death for his soul. Howard begins to get exasperated. This is like pulling hen's teeth. Still, he ought to put in another minute, just in case Greg does ask about it. 'You know, I was talking to your swimming coach yesterday,' he says. 'He told me some really –'

But the words die away on his lips, as he is caught in a smile as sudden and bright and paralysing as a prison searchlight . . . Miss McIntyre has appeared beside them; the smile is, evidently, for him. He hears himself speak to her, without knowing what he says. God, those eyes! Just looking into them is like being kissed – or, no, like being magicked off to another world, where it's just the two of them alone, the rest of the universe mere tinselled scenery, orbiting in a slow waltz around them –

'Uh, sir?' Howard is returned to reality by a small voice tugging at him. He turns and stares at the owner as though he's never seen him before in his life.

'Oh – I'm so sorry!' Miss McIntyre brings a hand to her mouth. 'I didn't realize you boys were in the middle of something.'

'No, no, it's fine,' he assures her hastily, then returns to address Juster. 'Daniel, you'd better head off to your next class.'

'It's lunchtime.'

'Well, to your lunch, then. We can finish this later in the week.'

'Right,' Juster says dubiously.

'Good man,' Howard says. 'Okay, well, off you go so.' Juster obligingly stumps off down the corridor. 'We'll catch up later in the week,' Howard calls after him. 'And have a good talk, okay?' He turns back to bask in the lovely light of Aurelie McIntyre.

'Sorry,' she repeats gaily. 'I didn't see him there, or I wouldn't have interrupted you.'

'No no, don't worry, it was nothing,' Howard assures her. 'He had a little run-in with Jerome Green yesterday. Greg asked me to have a word with him, make sure he was all right.'

'I think he's in my Geography class,' she comments, adding, 'He's so *small*!'

'Usually he'd be sent to the guidance counsellor, but Greg thought he'd prefer to speak to someone younger,' Howard elaborates. 'You know, that he could relate to.'

She absorbs this thoughtfully, or mock-thoughtfully: many of her gestures, he's noticed, have this disconcerting hint of unseriousness, of artificiality, as though she has lifted them for her own amusement from some antiquated sitcom. How to get to the real Aurelie?

'Oh, here, I meant to say to you –' he chucks her arm '– I took your advice and got that Robert Graves book. I was reading it to my class just now. You were right, they loved it!'

'I told you.' She smiles.

'It gives the war a whole new dimension, you know, hearing from someone right there in the thick of it. They really connected with it.'

'Maybe it reminds them of school,' she suggests. 'Didn't someone describe the trenches as ninety-nine per cent boredom and one per cent terror?'

'I don't know about boredom. God, the chaos of it, the brutality. And it's so *vivid*. I'd definitely be interested in reading his poetry, if only to see how he can go from describing, you know, people getting their guts blown out, to writing about love.'

'Maybe it's not that much of a leap,' she says.

'You don't think?'

'Have you ever actually *been* in love?' she says teasingly.

'Yes, of course,' Howard professes, flustered. 'I just meant, in terms of *writing*, that stylistically it must be quite a, a jump from one to the other . . .'

'Mm-hmm.' She is doing the thing with her tongue, examining her upper lip with the very tip.

'Listen,' he says, 'we sort of got off on the wrong foot the other day.'

'Did we?'

'Well, I mean . . .' He is dimly conscious of boys streaming by them on either side. 'You know you told me you weren't going to, ah, to do a certain thing with me?'

'I told you I wasn't going to sleep with you.'

'Yes, that's right . . .' feeling himself flushing deeply. 'Well, I just wanted . . . I hoped I hadn't given the impression – I mean, I just wanted to tell you that I wasn't, you know, I wasn't intending to, ah, do that with you either.'

She takes a moment to digest this, then says: 'That's all you could come up with, after two whole days?'

'Yes,' he says reluctantly.

'Now I'm *definitely* not going to sleep with you,' she says with a laugh, and turns on her heel.

'Look,' he puts in desperately, 'when you say that – what is it that you mean?'

'See you later, Howard,' she calls over her shoulder.

'Wait!' But the enchantment is over: as he hurries after her, he is aware once more of existing in a world of objects, of *obstacles*, coming betw–

'I do beg your pardon, Howard, I didn't see you . . .'

Howard, winded, can only gasp.

'Ah, Robert Graves!' Jim Slattery lifts the book from the floor where it has fallen. 'Are you reading this to the boys?'

Hopelessly, Howard stares after her receding form, which even seen from behind seems to mock him.

'Remarkably versatile writer, Graves,' Slattery continues oblivious. 'One doesn't come across his sort too often these days. Poetry, novels, classical mythology . . . I wonder, have you ever looked at his *White Goddess*? Barmy sort of a thing, but quite intriguing . . .'

Howard knows there is no escape now. For five years he sat in a classroom and listened to these rambles. Once Jim Slattery starts on a topic that interests him, only an act of God can divert him.

'. . . delves into various pre-Christian societies – Europe, Africa, Asia – and keeps finding this same figure, this White Goddess, with long fair hair, blue eyes and a blood-red mouth. Right back to the Babylonians, it goes. His theory is that poetry as we know it grew out of this goddess-worship. All poetry, or rather all true poetry, tells the same story – a fertility myth, I suppose you'd call it . . .'

Blue eyes, a blood-red mouth.

'. . . battle between the poet, who represents the coming spring, and as it were his supernatural double or negative self, who represents the past, winter, darkness, stasis, so forth, for the love of this White Goddess . . .'

Definitely not going to sleep with you.

'Ended up in Mallorca, of all places – Graves, that is. Moved there with a woman, a poet. Deya. Went there ourselves, actually, a couple of years ago, my wife and I. Delightful place, once you get away from the resorts. Astonishing scenery. And the seafood! I remember my wife turning to me one night, she was having the shrimp . . .'

Howard nods vacantly. In the distance, he imagines he can see her white scarf whisk into the thicket of the Annexe, like the tip of a fox's tail.

As soon as Skippy's out of sight he starts to run. He keeps running until he finds himself in his room, his head full of flying sparks, almost too thick to see through.

Talk to you? What does he want to talk to you about?

Oh fuck!

Panic crackles down his nerves to spark painfully in his fingertips, thoughts crash into each other like bumper cars, and the worst thing about it is *he doesn't know why*! He doesn't know what's pushing against the door of his brain, he doesn't know why his heart's beating so fast, he doesn't know why it's so important he doesn't talk to Howard the Coward – and now he doesn't know why he's standing on a chair and hauling his bag from the wardrobe, tugging open drawers and flinging the contents over his shoulder onto the bed, underwear, socks, T-shirts, jumpers, runners –

And then something flickers past the window.

A moment later, he hears Edward 'Hutch' Hutchinson's stereo come on full volume through the wall, though he knows Hutch is downstairs in the Ref. Beside the bed, Skippy's radio alarm clock is flashing 00:00. He puts down his bag, and slowly turns to face the window. The room feels wobbly and floating off at the edges.

It went by almost too quickly to see; at the same time, somehow, he saw it. As he moves towards the window he hears a sudden clash of TVs, radios, computers babbling from the corridor, voices opening doors and asking each other what's going on. He steps softly like it's not him doing it, not daring to believe he saw what he thinks he saw; he pretends in fact this is not what he's thinking, he pretends as he puts his eye to Ruprecht's telescope that he is just having a casual look-around . . .

But all he sees are clouds and birds. Oh wow, what a surprise.

126

Did he really expect that aliens were going to choose just this exact moment to arrive? Like they've come the whole way across space just to rescue – wait, there it is! Out of nowhere it appears in his viewer and is gone again. He scrambles around the sky, chasing after it, his heart pounding like it's going to come right through his chest. Can this really be happening? Is he hallucinating? But no, now he gets a fix on it at last: a SAUCER-LIKE CRAFT, gliding through the air!

Ruprecht meanwhile is down in his laboratory, working on his Wave Oscillator. To a mind not quite so brilliant as his, the lab might come across as a little *unheimlich*. It is a cramped and windowless room deep in the bowels of the basement, lit by a single naked bulb; damp seeps up the walls, drips drip from the ceiling, and husks of previous inventions – the Clone-o-matic, the Weather Machine, the Invisibility Gun, the Protectron 3000 – loom from the shadows, each one aborted and cannibalized for other projects, so that now they resemble casualties from some awful mechanical war. For Ruprecht, though, the laboratory is a refuge, an oasis of order and rational thought. The heat from the computers means that the room is always toasty-warm, and it is sufficiently removed from the rest of the building that one can play one's French horn at any time, day or night; there is even a television, for when one would rather watch the National Geographic channel without 'humorous' commentary about beavers, etc. from other parties.

The Van Doren Wave Oscillator is a METI instrument of Ruprecht's own devising. The idea is quite simple: the VDWO takes sounds (for example the main theme of Pachelbel's Canon, played on French horn) and translates them into the full spectrum of frequencies, including those outside human – but perhaps not extraterrestrial – hearing, and broadcasts them into space.

'Blowjob, what's the point of playing a load of boring music into space? You want them to think that everyone on Earth is like a hundred years old?'

'As a matter of fact, classical music has much to recommend it as a means of communication. On the one hand, it's a mathematical system, which any intelligent being will be able to understand; on the other, it gives an insight into the physiological nature of humans, musical features such as drone, repetition, percussion, being based on heartbeats, breathing, and so forth. Professor Tamashi has a very interesting paper on the subject.'

'Oh right, I must have missed that somehow.'

The Wave Oscillator has had its fair share of teething problems; however, today Ruprecht thinks he might finally have these sorted out. Taking it from the worktop – the VDWO is an innocuous rectangular affair about the size of a mid-range box of chocolates – he plugs it gingerly into the mains and steps back. Nothing explodes or catches fire. Good. He switches it on. A red light comes on and an efficient-sounding hum. Ruprecht seats himself in a chair and takes his French horn from its case. He pauses momentarily before beginning, eyeing the door. He usually likes to have Skippy around when doing test runs, but he disappeared after History class and hasn't replied to any of Ruprecht's texts. Well, if he wants to miss out on the scientific event of the century, that's his lookout.

Today's performance is a personal favourite, the opening movement of Bach's Concerto for French Horn. As he plays, Ruprecht imagines two elegant beings on the other side of the universe putting down the books they are reading and beaming in delight as the lovely music unspools through their futuristic radio; one makes a *shall we?* face to the other, then they hop into their spaceship – cut to New York, a podium, on which the polite aliens and the enterprising youngster who brought them here are celebrated by the worl–

The scream of static is so unbelievably loud it knocks Ruprecht clear off his chair. For a moment he remains there, pinned to the ground by the sheer noise of it – then, with some difficulty, as his fingers are in his ears, he begins to crawl towards the Oscillator, from which a German voice now issues, declaring, at the same insane volume, something about Bockwurst? Until, mercifully, the power cuts out.

Silence: Ruprecht pants on the floor, curled up like a foetus in the darkness. A moment later, the lights come back on, and with them the TV, the computers and every other appliance in the room – though not the Oscillator, which is now smoking guiltily. Ruprecht bends down to examine it, then drops it with a cry, nursing his burned fingers. A wave of frustration surges through him. What is wrong with it? Why won't it work? Useless, it's all useless: or rather *he* is useless – stupid, useless and dull, so what's the point of even trying? He kicks the Van Doren Wave Oscillator across the room, where it comes to rest, still smouldering, against the foot-unit of Protectron 3000, then throws himself despairingly into his chair.

'Sometimes the reason we do not see the answer is that we are looking too closely at the question,' a voice says.

Ruprecht looks up with a start. On the TV, which has come on by itself, is a familiar face – wrinkled and brown like a nut, possessed of eyes of an extraordinary opalescence, whose irises seem to glitter as though performing some labyrinthine calculation.

'All this time, I realized, the complexities of the problem had distracted me from what lay behind it,' the face says. 'The addition of a further dimension makes everything clear once again. It presents us with a reality that is at once simple, and of an almost impossible beauty.'

'Holy shit,' says Ruprecht.

An almost impossible beauty. Dancing back and forth, glittering like a runaway star through the dowdy greys of autumn – Skippy can't tear himself away, even as a series of loudening clumps, thumps and pants, as of someone overweight making his way up a staircase two steps at a time, issue from outside, until finally Ruprecht, burnished with sweat, bursts in and blurts, somewhat opaquely, 'Multiverse' – before realizing what Skippy is doing: 'My *telescope!*' he cries.

'Sorry –'

'It's not supposed to be moved.' Ruprecht fusses him away, jealously seizing the barrel.

'I thought I saw a UFO,' Skippy says.

'It's not even pointed at the *sky*,' Ruprecht rebukes. He addresses himself to the eyepiece to make sure; there is nothing to be seen at the far end except a St Brigid's girl with a frisbee in the yard over the wall. 'Anyway –' he retracts himself, remembering why he ran up here all the way from the basement '– that's not important. What's important is this. It appears that *our universe may not be the only universe there is.* We may be just one of an *infinite number* of universes, drifting through the eleventh dimension!'

'Wow,' says Skippy.

'I know!' Ruprecht says excitably. '*Eleven* dimensions! When everyone thought there were only ten!'

He goes on in this vein, circling and recircling between the beds, smacking his forehead and exclaiming things like *watershed* and *stupendous*. But Skippy doesn't hear him. Looking through the telescope, he is watching the frisbee girl again as she runs back and forth over the gravel, jumping and twisting mid-air, upstretching her arm to catch the disc and spinning it off again before her feet even touch the ground, laughing as she scoops strands of dark hair out of her mouth . . . She seems so much brighter than everything around her, a fragment of summer that's somehow found its way into October; at the same time, she makes everything around her brighter too – she makes it all fit together somehow, like in a musical where someone bursts into song and everyone else starts singing as well – not just the other girls but the trees, the walls, the gravel of the yard, Ruprecht, even Skippy himself at the telescope –

A howl from behind shatters his reverie. Dennis and Mario have sneaked in and wedgied Ruprecht; discussion of the eleventh dimension is suspended as its main proponent in the room rolls around the floor scrabbling at his underpants.

'Whatcha lookin' at, there, Skipford?' Before Skippy can re-direct the telescope, he finds he's been shouldered out of the way; Dennis, with his eye to the glass, launches into a series of bell-ringing, steam-whistling-from-ears-type noises. 'Whoo-ee, sexy lady!'

'What, let me look,' and now Mario is in on the action. 'Hubba hubba, that is a nice piece of ass.'

'Wait till you see her bazoongas – hey look, Skippy's blushing! What's the matter, Skippy? Is she your *girlfriend*?'

'What are you talking about,' Skippy says disgustedly, although this is not very convincing as he's turned bright red.

'Look, Mario, look, Ruprecht, Skippy doesn't like it when you talk about his *girlfriend* – is that because you *love* her, Skippy? Because you *love* her, and want to *marry* her, and kiss her and hug her and hold her hand, and say, "I wuv woo, woo are my girlfriend –"'

'I have no idea what you're on about.'

'I wonder if this smoking-hot girl will be going to the Hop,' Mario ponders.

'You think she'll be at the Hop?' Skippy lighting up like a Christmas tree.

'There will be no shortage of hot bitches at this Hop,' Mario says. 'Furthermore, the girls of St Brigid's are famed for their slutty ways. They will be like skittles, waiting to be bowled over by Mario's big balls.'

'I wonder if she'll be there,' Skippy says.

'Skippy, you're dreaming if you think a girl like that'll go any-where near a loser like you.' Dennis has got Mario in a headlock and is bouncing up and down.

'Let go of me, you bummer,' gurgles Mario.

'What's that, Mario? I can't hear you, speak a little louder?'

'Who's TR Roche?' Ruprecht has risen from the floor and is peering at the label on an amber tube in his hand.

'Yeah, and why are there clothes thrown all over the bed?'

Mario says, belatedly noticing the chaotic state of the room. 'And this big bag?'

'Yeah, Skip, what's with the bag? Mid-term is next week.'

'Are you planning a trip somewhere?'

Skippy regards tube and bag in apparent mystification. 'No,' he says. 'I'm not going anywhere.'

Friday at last. Within an hour of the final bell, the halls of the school are bare: the boys gone home, the teachers relocated to the Ferry, a small pub in the lee of the school that has long been the local for Seabrook faculty – to the perpetual dismay of the proprietor, who has seen the lucrative underage market decamp elsewhere.

Howard finds these staff drinking sessions hard work. 'I just have nothing to say to these people. I have nothing to say to them on a Monday morning. What am I going to have to say to them at the end of the week?'

'Howard, you are "these people",' Farley tells him. 'Stop living in denial. You're a teacher, accept it.'

He can accept it, just, when someone is paying him for his trouble; but to give up the first precious hours of his weekend in the name of *esprit de corps* – that, most Fridays, is too much.

But not this Friday. Tonight he comes down to the pub directly, and sits watching the door with a grim expression while Jim Slattery pours hurling anecdotes into his unhearing ear and Tom Roche lours at him from the bar like a soured and crippled Peter Pan. The door, however, fails to deliver what he hopes for.

'I was sure she'd be here,' he says dolefully.

'She didn't come last week,' Farley says, through chattering teeth. They have come out to the canopied smoking deck to scan the side-gate of the school; the outdoor heater does not work and the temperature is merrily plummeting towards zero.

'She said she would today. She said so.'

Since their brief encounter after class on Wednesday, and her mysterious parting joke/threat, Howard has made repeated attempts to get Aurelie McIntyre on her own. It's infuriating, like

133

trying to romance a will-o-the-wisp. Everything about her remains defiantly ambiguous, including the question of whether or not she wants to be romanced; yet the more elusive she is, the more impossible and pointless and not-worth-doing it seems to pursue her, the more inextricably Howard finds himself bound to her; the more he thinks about her, the more he craves just a word, just a moment of her time. He'd been looking forward to tonight for two whole days: even if she didn't talk to him, he thought, at least he'd have an hour or two to look at her, to take in her unearthly beauty from across the crowded bar.

'Obviously I can't help wondering how Halley fits into all this,' Farley says.

'Mmm,' Howard says.

'Because doesn't she think you love her? And you're going to marry her?'

Howard mumbles indistinctly.

'Then what are you doing chasing around after Aurelie? I mean, like I say, I'm just wondering.'

Howard sighs testily. 'I'm not *chasing* her. I've barely even spoken to her. I don't know if there's anything real about this at all.'

'But you want it to be real.'

Howard sighs again, watching the crystalline sparkles that twinkle in his breath. 'I do love Halley,' he says. 'And I know I have a great life with her. It's just that . . . it sometimes feels kind of bitty. You know?'

'Not really.'

'I mean, we go to a film, we eat dinner, we fight, we joke, we go out with friends – sometimes it seems like none of it really adds *up* to anything. It's just one thing after another. And twenty-four hours later I've forgotten it all.' He takes a swig from his beer. 'I'm not saying it's bad. It's just not how I expected my life would be.'

'What did you expect?'

Howard ponders this. 'I suppose – this sounds stupid, but I suppose I thought there'd be more of a *narrative arc*.' Seeing Farley's blank look, he elaborates: 'A direction. A point. A sense that it's not just a bunch of days piling up on top of each other. Like, for instance, this book I'm reading, this Robert Graves book –'

'This is the book that Aurelie recommended to you?'

'What's that got to do with it?'

'Nothing, nothing.' Farley raises his hands placatingly. 'Carry on.'

'Well, he's just so *brave*. Like, he's leading his regiment into battle, he's going into no man's land in the middle of the night to rescue his comrades – this is before he even turns twenty-one.'

'So what, you're going to leave Halley and go off and live in a trench with Aurelie, is that it? And wait for the Germans?'

'No,' Howard says irritably, 'I just . . .'

At that moment the door opens, and Jim Slattery bustles out. 'Aha,' he salutes the two of them. 'Cassius and Brutus.'

'Heading off?' Farley returns. Jim leaves at precisely this time every Friday.

'Hell hath no fury like a woman watching the dinner go cold,' the older man chuckles. 'You lads will find out about that some day.' He looks along the deck and into the night sky. 'Chilly out here.' He rubs his hands together. 'Or maybe it's just age. Anyhow. I'll leave you young bucks to it. As you were, gentlemen . . .'

He ambles off, his tuneless whistle fading into the traffic.

'I just don't want to end up like *him*,' Howard says, when he's out of sight. 'Thirty-five years' work and what's he got to show for it? Colleagues who ignore him, students who laugh at him, a wife who makes his lunch every day so he won't God forbid eat a pub sandwich. Teaching the same damn thing over and over and over, *King Lear* and "The Road Not Taken" . . .'

'He doesn't seem to mind,' Farley says. 'In fact I bet he still gets misty-eyed when he reads out "The Road Not Taken."'

'You know what I'm saying, though? I mean, some day we're going to be *dead*.'

Farley laughs. 'Howard, you're the only person I know who went directly from losing his virginity to a mid-life crisis.'

'Mmm.'

The door opens again; Howard hears Tom's voice from inside, loud with alcohol. Two young women from the building society down the street have emerged onto the deck to light cigarettes. Their eyes flick cursorily over Howard and Farley. 'Howdy,' Farley says. They smile through their shivers. He goes over to bum a cigarette.

'If it's any comfort to you,' he says, returning to Howard, 'what you were saying about lacking a sense of an overarching structure – about life feeling *bitty* – scientifically speaking, that does happen to be one of the big questions of our time.'

Howard takes a wary slug from his beer.

'How to reconcile the macro and micro. See, there are two big theories of how the universe works. On the one hand you have the quantum mechanical explanation, the Standard Model as it's called, which says that everything is made of very small things – particles. There are hundreds of different kinds of particle, it's all very frenetic and weird and disparate – bitty, as you say. Then, on the other hand, there's Einstein's relativistic account, which is very geometric and elegant and deals with the universe on a grand scale. Light and gravity are caused by ripples in spacetime, everything's ruled by these very simple laws – it's nothing *but* overarching structure, in short.'

He pauses to pull on his cigarette, exhaling a luxurious torrent of smoke.

'The thing is, though both explanations are, as far as we can work out, right, neither one works on its own. The curved space account goes to pieces when it runs into subatomic particles. The Standard Model is too chaotic and confused to get us to the big elegant symmetries of spacetime. So neither one is complete, and when you need to use both at the same time, like when you're trying to describe the Big Bang, they won't fit together. It's the same thing you're talking about – you know, on a quotidian level, it's difficult to find any evidence of a narrative arc or a larger meaning in your life, but at the same time, if you try and *give* your life a meaning – like live according to a principle or a mission or an ideal or whatever – then inevitably you distort the details. The small things keep agitating against it and popping out of place.' Another pull, pearl smoke rushing the twilight. 'Every couple of years some scientist comes along with the grand unified theory that supposedly ties everything together. String theory, supergravity. M-theory is the latest. But when you look closer they always fall to pieces.'

Howard gazes at him deadpan. 'That's not actually very comforting, Farley.'

'I know,' Farley sighs. He takes a last drag on his cigarette and dashes it under his heel. 'Look, if I tell you something, can we go back inside?'

'Tell me what?'

'Seriously, I feel bad about telling you, but I think I'm getting frostbite out here.'

'Just tell me.'

'Well –' Farley makes a play of adjusting his shirt-cuffs '– it seems a certain someone has volunteered to supervise this Hallowe'en Hop.'

'Aurelie?'

'I heard her talking to Greg yesterday.'

'Why?' The Hop, coming as it does on the first night of the mid-term holidays, is always drastically undersubscribed in terms of supervision.

'Beats me.' Farley shrugs. 'Maybe she sees it as a novelty.' He skates his fingertips in a figure-8 over the railing, then adds nonchalantly, 'They're going to need at least one other chaperone . . .'

'Huh,' Howard says, and for a moment they silently watch colluding clouds and evening darken the sky.

Then Farley stretches his back. 'Okay, I'm going to get a drink,' he says. 'Are you coming in?'

'I'll be in now,' Howard says distractedly.

'You ladies care for anything at the bar?' he hears Farley say to the building-society girls. 'They do a mean pint of snakebite here.'

The girls titter; the door swings closed. Howard watches his fingers blueing on the glass neck of the beer bottle. He thinks of Halley, at her computer in their little house, wrapping up work for the week, starting to make the dinner. If he could just be certain that this was the life he wanted, and not just the life he'd ended up with because he was afraid to go after the one he wanted. If he could just be sure he wasn't going to end up a fubsy old duffer in a jacket from thirty years ago, so hopelessly failed he no longer even realizes what might have been . . .

When Howard and Farley were in their final year of school, Jim Slattery's wife left him. The boys weren't told, of course, but it was obvious almost immediately. The teacher started turning up to school in odd socks, unshaven, his hair awry. The back seat of his car filled up with takeaway boxes. His classes, never what could be called linear, grew more rambling than ever; sometimes he would break off for minutes on end, arrested by some mysterious detail in the window. One afternoon, in the middle of another of these strange hiatuses, Guido LaManche had called out from the back row, 'Where's your wife, Jim?'

Slattery's expression gave him away at once. He was too shocked to feign incomprehension or to cover up; he just stood there, open-mouthed. Gleefully, Steve Reece repeated the question: 'Where's your wife, Jim?' And in a flash it had been taken up by the whole class, who chanted it over and over: 'Where's your wife, Jim? Where's your wife, Jim?'

Slattery tried to ignore it, began to burble something about the poem they had just been reading, but the chanting grew louder, drowning him out, and finally, to jeers, he fled the classroom.

The next day the takeaway-littered car was missing from the car park, and instead of English class, at a special assembly, the sixth-years got a lecture from Father Furlong, typically abstruse, on the subject of *compassion*. This was followed by a more direct address from the Dean that suspended lunchtime exit privileges for the remainder of the week. Neither mentioned Jim Slattery's name, nor what had happened in that classroom.

Nobody expected to see the English teacher for some time, but the very next day he returned to work. He made no reference to what had happened, simply picked up where he had left off. There were sniggers, catcalls, double-entendres, but these remained isolated. A few weeks later they heard that his wife was back.

Howard remembers that afternoon as if it were yesterday: the page of the book on his desk, the weather outside, the faces around him, and most of all Slattery's own face – at first confused, as though they had broken into a patois he didn't understand, and then, understanding, not so much upset for himself as shocked, shocked at the discovery of how cruel his boys could be. It was the first time Howard had seen a grown-up look like that: frangible, as if he would fall to pieces if you touched him.

The funny thing is, although every other element of that class is etched into his memory, Howard can't seem to recall whether he had taken up the chant. Try as he might, he cannot lay hold of that one detail; his mind has smeared it over, like the face of an informer in a TV documentary. Had he sat back, arms folded in disgust, refusing to open his mouth? Had he kept his head down, so no one could see if he was chanting or not? Or had he – there in the middle aisle, middle row, hiding out in the mainstream – had he joined in the chant, loud as anyone? Smiling at the others to show what a laugh he thought it was? He has no idea, he can't even hazard a guess; now isn't that strange?

These lucky dog is fucking loevly Russan virgin
She is drunked and to be fucked by bottel
Bitches screames as she fucked evry hole by five studs
Vozhnogy btzhaga child-rape ltazoy drastilnje
These granny has not forgot how to fucking!

Each picture is a doorway to a little world that in his head Carl sees them float like bubbles somewhere far away in space, attached to his computer by tiny invisible threads. Each bubble has a girl inside, or maybe two girls, and dildos or studs or a dog, and they are waiting for you to call them to click on them and bring them out of space into your computer. You never know exactly what is in each one till you open it. Maybe the girl will only show her tits not her gee or she could even be a shemale. The picture-doorways are like wrappers like fireworks have or sweets and inside the worlds wait like secrets.

'I'm not talking about *love!*' Downstairs Carl's mom shouts at Carl's dad. 'I'm not even talking about that. I'm talking about just simple decent respect for me as a person who is your *wife*. Your *wife!*'

'Why are you saying this like it's news to me?' Dad shouts back. 'Who do you think pays your credit card bills that arrive on my desk every –'

If you get bored with humans there are cartoon characters. There is Ariel from *The Little Mermaid* licking out Belle from *Beauty and the Beast* or Pocahontas from *Pocahontas* getting fucked by the horse from *Mulan*. There are characters from computer games like *Hopeland* and *Final Fantasy* having sex. There are also old-fashioned ones like animals from *Jungle Book* which is a film or

Donald Duck fucking Minnie Mouse or Yogi Bear fucking Boo-Boo which is a smaller bear.

'– question of *buying* your way out of it, David, it's – look at me, David. I am, I am a woman. I deserve to be treated like a –'

'I know you're a woman. I *know* you're a woman because you're being *totally irrational*.'

'Oh, it's irrational, when the phone rings at two in the morning and when I answer they hang up? It's irrational, the phone ringing at two a.m. four nights running?'

Jessica Rabbitt, also the good-looking bird from *Scooby-Doo* riding Fred or sometimes Scooby. A lot of Smurfs gang-banging Smurfette. The Simpsons, mostly Homer or Bart fucking Lisa, though there's one Carl saw of Homer going into Maggie's room to fuck Maggie, his dick is out and his face is all scary the way it never is in the show, like his eyes are slits and his teeth are fangs and his hand is stretched out like a claw into the crib.

'Eileen saw you, David. So she must be being irrational too.'

'Eileen – listen, we both know Eileen is a deeply disturbed person, a deeply unwell person with serious personal issues –'

'She saw you, David, she saw you having dinner with a *teenaged girl*. A teenaged girl! Not much older than *Carl*!'

'Would you like to know who that was, Lucia? Would you like to stop screaming for five seconds so I can tell you who that was? That was my fucking *tennis coach*.'

'Oh, I see, was she helping you with your serve, in the restaurant? Were you having a few rallies together, sitting there in the fucking Four Seasons, you and your whore?'

In his room Carl turns up the stereo. He looks down at the book on the table. The economic success of the Netherlands was due in part to the man-made geographical structure called the _____.

Behind the right-hand speaker are he doesn't know how many fives and tens and twenties. Behind the left-hand speaker are fireworks. Barry can't keep them in his house because his mom searches his room. The last few days are like the part of the movie where the talking stops and over the music you see the money rolling in and the gangsters making deals and buying limos and doing coke. The kids are mad for fireworks, no matter how many Carl and Barry bring down to the mud-piles, it's never enough. Every day there are more kids with their prescriptions, some of them aren't even from Seabrook. Meanwhile, like in a mirror, the same thing is happening with the St Brigid's girls. The first five told other girls, who told other girls, and now there are so many girls looking for pills that Carl and Barry have to split up.

So they go back and forth from the mud-piles to the girls, turning fireworks into pills and pills into money, so much money. Barry has already bought a new pair of Nikes (Vendettas) and a digital camera. Now he is talking about a scooter, he thinks he and Carl should buy matching Vespas, silver ones. He wonders if they should invest in just a little bit of coke, just to see if it sold. Now that we've developed a customer base, he says to Carl, that's the hardest part of any business.

Carl is glad Barry is happy and trusts Carl again. But sometimes he gets worried. He keeps thinking of the scene in the movie where the gangsters get machine-gunned by the other gang.

What other gang? Barry says. Those fucking knackers that deal in the park?

Carl and Barry always buy their gear from these knackers in the park. Near the laneway to the train station there is a bench where one of them will always be. They wear tracksuits and have tattoos on their hands and one night last year they beat up Casey Ellington when he went to buy hash just because they didn't like the look of him, so bad he had to get his jaw wired. On Thursday the one with the greasy hair said, Youse lads are buyin a fair amount of coke these days.

Carl didn't say anything. Barry told him it was for mid-term break.

Don't be a bender, Barry says to Carl now. How would those scumbags even know about us?

He puts his arm around Carl. Look, he says, what we have here is a once-in-a-lifetime opportunity. All of these individual events have come together, and we are in the exact perfect place to take advantage of them. It's Hallowe'en, the kids want fireworks. There's a school dance with St Brigid's and all the girls are freaking out about fitting into their costumes. It's like a slot-machine ready to pay out, see? And we're the guys with the coin, Carl. We just happened to be in the right place at the right time. So we collect the money.

Carl has never been in the right place at the right time before. Maybe that is why it feels weird.

I'm not saying we have to do it for ever, Barry says. But we should keep going until the Hop at least. We'd be crazy to stop before then. Anyway, you wouldn't want to lose your favourite little customer, would you?

Lollipop-Lips has bought pills from Carl every night this week. He doesn't meet her with the others, not since that first time behind Ed's. Instead she will text him and say she wants to meet up in an hour and he will head out with the pills. Or sometimes she doesn't text him, he just goes out and finds her. There are not that many places to go, if you are not in Ed's or one of the malls you are probably in the Leisureplex or LA Nites or hanging around outside Texaco. When she sees him she will smile secretly, like she has magically brought him there. Then they go somewhere quiet and measure out the pills.

This slut so hungry for cock she must apease her cunt with the fist!

Barry says if she was paying money for all the pills she takes he and Carl would both be millionaires. I don't know how she gets through them so quick, he says, it's not like she was even fat in the first place. He keeps asking Carl if he has fucked her. She must be fucking you ten times a day for that many pills! Ha ha, Carl laughs. But she won't fuck him. She will only give him handjobs and let him feel her tits. Sometimes he tells her, you fuck me or else you pay cash like everyone else. But she just laughs and takes his hand and slips it under her shirt. In the cold damp leaves behind Ed's, her body a tiny pocket of heat, her breath in his ear, the tips of her black hair tickling his neck, he forgets everything else.

In his room he turns up the stereo, unzips his trousers. Here on the screen is a little world of a black-haired girl on the stairs in a house. There are about twenty pictures to tell the story, which is, she takes off her top, she lifts her skirt to show her stockings and black see-through knickers, she unbuttons her shirt and slides the skirt up over her thighs –

Last night in LA Nites he met her with Crinkly-Hair and their friend the fat girl and the two of them went into the alcove beside the cigarette machine. He had his hand on her tummy with his fingertips just under the waistband of her jeans, he was slipping them downwards so slowly she didn't seem to notice, he thought his boner was going to rip right through his trousers like the Incredible Hulk, down and down, was she going to let him? but then she said, Let's go for a walk.

Maybe she wanted to go somewhere quieter to have sex he thought so he said okay. They walked along the dual carriageway under the orange lights. Cars shocked past them or waited behind the traffic lights growling smoke from under their wheels. Show me where you live, she said. He led her down the dark straight avenue. The ends of rain dripped from the trees. Dad's Jag was back pulled up outside his house. Maybe there would be some way to get her inside without his parents seeing her. Or maybe Dad would just let him bring her in to fuck her. Do you want to go inside? he said. It's okay, she said. He didn't know if she meant yes or no but when he moved for the door and she did not he knew she meant no. Why not? he said. She didn't say anything. Then he said, I will give you this whole tube of pills if you fuck me. She just looked at him. It was a week's supply at least. Even a blowjob, he said.

The girl on the stairs pushes her tit up and bends her head down to lick her nipple. Carl's balls are boiling, his cock is rock-hard, he would almost get up and stick it through the computer screen!

Instead they went to Ed's. She wanted to go inside but he could not because he is barred. So he brought her around the back and showed her how to climb from the ledge of the skip up the drainpipe and onto the roof. The material of the rooftop is rough under your fingers, rippled like frozen waves, in the night in the pink light of the sign the flat grey rectangle looks like skin. There are empty beer cans, a johnny, a copybook someone threw up here with homework smeared into nothing by rain. She was looking up at the windows of the Tower. Who lives in there? she asked. Faggots, he said. Boarders. It looks like it's from a fairy-tale, she said. Then she said, are you going to the Hallowe'en Hop?

He just shrugged. He wished he had some beer. He waited for her to lie down but she didn't. Why are you barred? she said. He told her about the Gook. The Gook? she said, so he told her as well what Barry told him about the war and the Marines who died getting ambushed in the jungle by gooks and when they went home to their own country, America, instead of a hero's welcome people spat on them. That's terrible, she said. We should teach this Gook a lesson.

Like what?

Like a reminder of home, she said.

They took the staples out of the old copybook and started folding the pages into aeroplanes. When there were enough planes they poured lighter fluid over them. Then Carl shinned down the drainpipe and emptied the rest of the lighter into the bin outside the Doughnut House doors. He lit a piece of paper and threw it in. The bin went *foom!* the heat whacked his eyes, he pegged it back around and hoisted himself up onto the roof, and they both looked down over the edge as the doors burst open and the Gook charged out with a fire extinguisher in one hand and a blanket in the other that he flapped at the burning bin. That's when they lit the first plane and sent it swirling and flaming down on top of him. The Gook let out a little shriek, covering his head. They lit another one and launched it, he hopped out of the way, but then there was another, and another and another, until the sky was filled with pieces of falling fire, sailing down around the

Gook, and he just stood there in the middle of it with his mouth open, not moving at all – then he realized what was going on, and he started to jump up and down, a hoppity Rumpelstiltskin dance of rage, jabbering in Gook and shaking his fist at the rooftop, where the two of them were holding their hands over their mouths, about to explode from laughing.

But he had to go back inside to call the police, so they could jump down and hide in the park. But when the police had driven on they came out again and climbed back up there. The sky was dark blue, the doughnut sign was a big wide-open mouth, a mouth with no face around it or whose face was the whole world. Underneath it half of Lori was pink. The trees almost out of sight in the dark. Her wide-open mouth, her white bra. The pills in her coat pocket, her mouth swallowing his, she forgot to stop his fingers unbuttoning her jeans and sliding down into . . . Then her phone rang, the ringtone was that BETHani song, the one where she's in the changing room and the teacher is watching her through the hole in the wall. She put a hand on Carl's wrist.

Hi Dad. No I'm in Janine's. No watching TV. Just me and Janine.

The outline of his knuckles against the zip of her jeans. Carl did not breathe.

No! *Dad*. No there are no boys. No it's okay Janine's mom will drive me home I love you bye.

She fished out his hand and gave it back to him with a fake smile like an air hostess handing you your complimentary meal. I'd better go home, she said.

Okay, he said.

Loreliar.

The girl on the stairs is naked except for her stockings and she slides shiny wet fingers between her legs and looks out at Carl. Beside her not-naked Lori appears and disappears like a wave on Morgan Bellamy's phone. If you knew how you could move her face from the phone onto the girl on the computer. A nerd would

146

know how to do it. But Carl does not know how, so he has to switch back and forth from the computer to the phone, like he's carrying the face in his mind and imagining it onto the body, so the waves of black hair melt into each other, and Lori's lollipop lips turn into the wet shine on the girl on the stairs' fingers – as Carl stands over her, You better do what I say!!! No no Carl! Hiding her face with her wet hand. Carl's fist raised up. Oh so you like fists??!!!

'– a divorce!' Carl's mom screams, clattering up the stairs. Carl stuffs his boner back in his pants, zips himself up, flips the computer screen to FUN FACTS ABOUT THE NETHERLANDS! 'I'll get a divorce, mister, and I'll clean you out!' She has stopped outside Carl's door to shriek down, it is like nails going over a blackboard. 'So I hope your little floozies have . . . have good career prospects!'

'I'll get you fucking committed first!' Dad's voice bounces up from below. 'There's not a judge in the land who'd take your side, you bloody mad bint –'

The sound of Mom sinking to the floor on the landing: this is usually where she ends up when they are fighting. 'Why don't you go,' she sobs, the words mixed with the snick of the flint as she tries to light a cigarette. 'Why don't you just go, and leave my son and me in peace? Why don't you go once and for all, so we can live our lives with some semblance of dignity?'

'I'll tell you why, because I'm afraid you'll burn my fucking house down! Dignity, if you had even the smallest conception of what that meant you'd take one look at yourself and –'

Carl in his room, his head filling up with hotness, stares at the textbook. The fusion of two cities into a single urbanized mass known as a _____.

Mom lets out a scream and there is the sound of something hitting something else, probably she threw her shoe at him. 'You're a lunatic!' Dad shouts. 'A lunatic!' Her bedroom door bangs, and at the same moment Carl's phone jingles with a new message.

HEY WAT YOU DOIN

Fuck you, bitch.

NOTHIG HOMWORK

Because of a lack of natural resources, the Netherlands must import ✿✝#$♦℘&^@% and ☹*!!♦☀♝℘▱€ from ~~XXXXXXXXX~~.

IM SO BORD!!!!

Downstairs the front door slams, Dad's Jag starts up. The sound of the bathroom door locking and Mom crying behind it.

I NED SUM XITMENT . . .

The black-haired girl's eyes roll back in her head, as her hand plunges between her legs right up to the wrist.

The chief exports of the Netherlands are *pull your panties down bitch* and *if you say another word I will break your skull.*

Carl writes back,

OK.

Skippy and the telescope have become almost inseparable. Mornings, lunchtimes, at the end of every schoolday he dashes upstairs and attaches himself to the eyepiece, and for the hours that follow he will be either euphorically happy or speechless with despair, depending on whether or not he has caught a glimpse of Frisbee Girl. In less than a week, Ruprecht has seen him transformed from his usual amiable Ruprecht-helping self to a moon-eyed somnambulant who doesn't want to do anything except look out the window and ask over and over whether Ruprecht, or whoever else happens to be in the room, thinks this girl, whom he has never spoken to, will be at the Hop or not.

Ruprecht might have found all this quite annoying, but by a strange coincidence, he too has a new fascination. For the last five nights, he has been pulled deeper and deeper into its mysterious involutions; the more he investigates it, the more shadowy it becomes, and the more shadowy, the deeper it draws him in.

'They call it M-theory.' Monday evening: outside, a damasked sunset is crashing tremulously through a pale blue sky, gilding church steeples and phone masts, the tiled roofs of houses and the scaffolding of new apartments.

'What does the M stand for, Ruprecht?'

'No one knows.'

'No one *knows*?'

'The theory's so complicated that they're only beginning to understand it. So no one can agree what the M is for.' This, for Ruprecht, is one of its chief attractions. Who could resist a theory so obscure they don't even understand the name of it? 'Some people say it's for Multiverse. Others say it's for Magic. Matrix. Mystery. Mother.'

'Wow,' Victor Hero says huskily.

'It's all at a very early stage, obviously,' Ruprecht says, 'but what they *think* is that everything is made up of *membranes*. There are different kinds of membrane. Some are tiny particles. Others are huge universes. All of them floating around in eleven dimensions.'

'Eleven?' Geoff says.

'That's right,' says Ruprecht. Geoff does some counting on his fingers and looks confused.

'I know what you're thinking. Where are these seven extra dimensions? Good question. The answer is, all around us. You see –' Ruprecht takes off his glasses, getting into his stride now '– cosmologists believe that in our universe's original state, at the moment of creation, it existed as one pure, symmetrical, ten-dimensional structure. All stuff, all forces, were united as one into this structure. However, with the Big Bang, this "higher" universe, as we might call it, broke down. "Our" universe, that is, the dimensions we can see, expanded into spacetime. The higher dimensions, meanwhile, curled up to become very, very tiny. But although we can't see them, they're still *here*. In fact, the extra dimensions exist at every single point in space.'

Head-scratching from Geoff and Victor.

'It's a tricky idea to grasp,' Ruprecht says. 'By way of illustration, try thinking of a very narrow cylinder.'

'A hair,' Victor says.

'Mario's dick,' Dennis says, from Ruprecht's bed.

'Hey!' Mario exclaims.

'Okay –' Ruprecht determined not to be steered off-course '– to us, the very narrow cylinder of Mario's dick looks like a line, that is to say it looks one-dimensional. But to a very small creature, say an ant, that's walking along Mario's dick, he'll realize that as well as going lengthways he can go in a *circular* direction too. Even though *we* might not be able to perceive it, that very small ant is aware that Mario's dick has two dimensions, i.e. girth as well as length.'

'You're damn right it has girth!' Mario shouts. 'I don't need an ant to tell me it has girth!'

'According to string theory, which Professor Tamashi and other scientists have been using to try to solve the Big Bang, in addition to the four dimensions of spacetime we know, there are six of these very small, curled-up dimensions, making ten all told. And the strings, which are little strands of energy, wiggle around vibrating in these ten dimensions.'

'Like Dennis's mother,' Mario, seeking vengeance for the ant slur, interjects, 'wiggling around vibrating with her vibrator, because she is a famous slut, and also, she has ten dimensions because she is a fat bitch.'

'That about sums her up,' Dennis says coolly; gah, Mario's forgotten that Dennis hates his stepmother and so is immune to insults on that front –

'Wait, what are these strings again?' Geoff asks.

Ruprecht's eyebrow beginning to twitch just a little – 'Well, if you remember, I told you about it two minutes ago.'

'Oh, right, they're little bits of energy that everything's made out of?'

'That's the one.'

'But, uh, Ruprecht, things aren't made out of strings, they're made out of atoms. We did that in science class.'

'Yes, but what are atoms made out of?'

'How should I know what they're made out of?'

'Well, I'm telling you, they're made out of these little strings.'

'But didn't you say the strings were in another dimension?'

'Yeah, Ruprecht, how can they be here if they're actually in another dimension?'

Ruprecht coughs loudly. 'They exist in *ten* dimensions. Because ten is the number required mathematically for the theory to make sense. They vibrate at different frequencies, and according to the frequency they vibrate at, you get different kinds of particle. The same way that if you pluck a violin string you can get different notes, C, D, E –'

'F,' contributes Geoff.

'F, yes –'

'G –'

'*Similarly*, a string vibrating at one frequency will give you a quark, say, and a string vibrating at another frequency will give you a photon. That's a particle of light. Nature is made of all the musical notes that are played on this superstring, so the universe is like a kind of a symphony.'

'Wow . . .' Geoff looks in wonderment at his own arm, as if half-expecting it, now its cover's blown, to start chiming and tootling.

'But didn't you say there were *eleven* dimensions?' Victor Hero remembers.

'That's right. The major stumbling block of string theory was the Big Bang. Like all the other theories before it, string theory broke down when it came to the first moments of the universe. What use is a new theory if it can't solve the old problems?'

Geoff and Victor agree, not much use.

'When they added the *eleventh* dimension, though, everything changed. The theory didn't break down any more. But instead of just giving an account of *our* universe, scientists found themselves looking at a model of a whole *sea* of universes.'

'Holy smoke,' Geoff says.

'I wish *I* was in the eleventh dimension,' Dennis comments dolefully. 'With some porn.'

'Describe her to me again?' Skippy, meanwhile, is at the telescope with Titch Fitzpatrick. As Ruprecht makes his exposition, Skippy reels off the vast treasure of detail he has garnered from his few brief sightings of Frisbee Girl. Detaching himself from the eyepiece, Titch looks off to the left, one finger on his jaw, frowning and nodding. 'Hmm . . .'

When it comes to the ladies, Titch is the undisputed expert. He has got off with more or less every girl worth getting off with in the Seabrook area, his strike rate dwarfing even that of sporting stars like Calvin Fleet and Beauregard 'The Panzer' Fanning; it is widely held that at the end of last summer, at a party in Adam O'Brien's house, he had full actual sex with KellyAnn Doheny, a second-year from St Brigid's. Non-teenagers might find his appeal difficult to understand, as he isn't especially handsome, or big, or even funny; his features are striking only in their regularity, the overall effect being one of solidity, steadiness, the quiet self-assurance one might associate with, for instance, a long-established and successful bank. But that, in fact, is the whole point. One look at Titch, in his regulation Dubarrys, Ireland jersey and freshly topped-up salon tan, and you can see his whole future stretched out before him: you can tell that he will, when he leaves this place, go on to get a good job (banking/insurance/consultancy), marry a nice girl (probably from the Dublin 18 area), settle down in a decent neighbourhood (see above) and about fifteen years from now produce a Titch Version 2.0 who will think his old man is a bit of a knob sometimes but basically all right. The danger of him ever drastically changing – like some day joining a cult, or having a nervous breakdown, or developing out of nowhere a sudden burning need to *express himself* and taking up some ruinously expensive and embarrassing-to-all-that-know-him discipline, like modern dance, or interpreting the songs of Joni Mitchell in a voice that, after all these years, is revealed to be disquietingly feminine – is negligible. Titch, in short, is so remarkably unremarkable that he has become a kind of embodiment of his socioeconomic class; a friendship/sexual liaison with Titch has therefore come to be seen as a kind of self-endorsement, a badge of Normality, which at this point in life is a highly prized commodity.

'All right so,' he says as Skippy finally, breathlessly, wraps up his paean. 'Black hair, medium height, wide mouth, pale. That could be a few different people – Yolanda Pringle, maybe, or Mirabelle Zaoum. What're her kegs like?'

'Her kegs?'

'Medium small,' Dennis says from the bed.

'I would say about a 30B,' Mario estimates.

'Um,' Skippy says.

'What she does have is an ass,' Dennis says.

'Yes, this is one smoking hot ass,' Mario says. 'It is the kind of ass a man will not forget in a hurry.'

'Hmm,' Titch muses, and then, relinquishing the telescope, 'well, I'll have a think about it. But it doesn't look like she's going to show today.'

'No,' Skippy says mournfully.

'Don't worry about it, T-man,' Dennis chips in cheerfully from the bed. 'This girl's about a trillion miles out of Skippy's league anyway.'

Titch receives this expressionlessly, then turns back to Skippy. 'Give me a call next time you see her,' he says, and wanders out of the room without goodbye, like he's exiting a lift full of strangers in a department store.

'The eleventh dimension is infinitely long, but only a very small distance across,' Ruprecht is telling Geoff and Victor, 'maybe no more than a trillionth of a millimetre. That means it exists only a trillionth of a millimetre from every point in our three-dimensional world. It's closer to your body than your own clothes. And on the other side of it – who knows? There could be another universe just one millimetre away, only we can't see it because it's in another dimension. There could be an infinite number of them, floating all around us.' His voice lofts rapturously. 'Imagine it! An infinite number of universes, whose qualities we can't even begin to guess at! With totally different laws of physics! Shaped like cylinders or prisms or doughnuts!'

'Doughnuts?' The word lights a synapse in Geoff's brain, which for the last few minutes has been playing a counting game with the clouds ambling by outside.

'Why not? Or, or shapes that are entirely new –'

'Or banana-shaped,' Geoff, who has realized he is feeling a little peckish, suggests.

'Or shaped like the Formula One track at Silverstone?' Victor adds.

'Maybe,' Ruprecht says. 'Maybe.'

'Could there be,' it suddenly strikes Geoff, 'a universe that's full of beer?'

'Theoretically, I suppose, yes.'

'And how would you get,' Geoff says slowly, 'from *this* universe, into the one that's full of beer?'

'That's one of the things we're hoping to find out,' Ruprecht informs him grandly. 'Professor Tamashi's holding an online round-table on Friday night to discuss that very issue, among others.'

'Hmm. Uh, Ruprecht, Friday night is the Hop?'

'The Hop?' Ruprecht repeats vaguely. 'Oh yes, that's right, so it is.'

'In that case, I have a feeling this online round-table will have to go ahead without Mario,' Mario says from the bed. 'I don't know about you guys, but I am planning to score a lot of bitches at this Hop. Probably I will start with one really hot girl, straight sex, no frills. Then I will have a sixty-nine. Then it will be time for a threesome.'

'Mario –' Dennis sits up '– what makes you think any girl is going to go anywhere near you? Let alone like fifteen different girls.'

Mario hesitates, then says conspiratorially, 'I have a secret weapon.'

'You do?'

'You bet, mister.' He flips open his wallet. 'Read it and weep, boys. It is my lucky condom, which never fails.'

A silence, as Mario smugly returns his wallet to his pocket, and then, clearing his throat, Dennis says, 'Uh, Mario, in what way exactly is there anything *lucky* about that condom?'

'Never fails,' Mario repeats, a little defensively.

'But –' Dennis pinches his fingers to his nose, brow furrowed '– I mean, if it was really a lucky condom, wouldn't you have used it by now?'

'How long have you had it in there, Mario?' Geoff says.

'Three years,' Mario says.

'Three *years*?'

'Without using it?'

'Doesn't that sound more like an *unlucky* condom?'

Mario looks troubled as his unshakeable faith in the luckiness of the lucky condom begins to show cracks.

'It was definitely pretty unlucky for the condom, to wind up in your wallet!'

'Yeah, Mario, your wallet is like the Alcatraz of condoms.'

'It's like the condom Bermuda Triangle!'

'Condoms tell each other stories about your wallet, "Oh, he disappeared into Mario Bianchi's wallet, and he was never seen again."'

'Yeah, I bet right this very second your lucky condom is in there whistling the theme from *The Great Escape* and digging a tunnel out of your wallet with a plastic coffee stirrer –'

'What do you know about it?' Mario rounds on them. 'Eh, you silly nerds, all you know about is this foolish business of the theory of many dimensions. Well, I tell you about something that is happening in *this* dimension, and that is this Friday I will be boning countless ladies. And that, which I call Mario-theory, is something that you can see with your own eyes, and not just some equations that only gays can understand! So don't come crawling to me looking for one of my many bitches in the sex orgy I am having, after you have struck out with every girl at the Hop!'

Autumn deepens. A fresh chaos of yellow leaves covers the lane up to the school each morning, as if it's been visited overnight by woodland poltergeists; after school, you make the return journey through a strange, season-specific gloaming, a pale darkness, spooked and paradoxical, which makes your classmates up ahead seem to fade in and out of existence. The hobgoblin shadow of Hallowe'en, meanwhile, is everywhere. The shopping malls bristle with pumpkins and skeletons; houses lie swathed in cotton-wool cobwebs; the sky cracks and fizzes with firework-tests of increasing rigour. Even teachers fall under the spell. Classes take odd detours, routines slowly vaporize, until by the late stages of the week, the rigid precepts of everyday termtime seem no more real, or even slightly less real, than the fluorescent ghosts glowing from the windows of Ed's Doughnuts next door . . .

It's crossed Skippy's mind – though he knows it makes no sense, given that other people have seen her too – that Frisbee Girl herself might not be real: that she too may be a kind of Hallowe'en emanation, a dark mirage of smoke and wishes who exists only in the far end of the telescope and will, if he tries to get any closer to her, vanish entirely. And so, while half of him is dying for it to be Friday, can scarcely comprehend how he can possibly make it till Friday – the other half hopes that Friday will never come.

Time, however, has no such reservations; and now he wakes up in the pitch-darkness of the last morning of term.

For the last quarter of the swimming team's final training session Coach reels in the laneway markers and brings out the net so they can play water polo. With a *whap!* the ball sails into the air; white and gold and brown bodies leap and splash, yells and hoots clang and rebound from the yellow roof, steam wafts across the water like poison gas over a gaudy blue battlefield. Skippy's floating near the back where there's not much happening. Come over here a minute, Daniel, Coach says.

He crouches down as Skippy swims up to him. It hurts him to bend like this, you can see it in the way his eyes screw up.

You've missed a lot of training lately.

Sorry, Coach, I was sick. I have a note.

Notes are all well and good, but you'll need to make that work up somehow. The meet's only two weeks after we come back from break, you know. There are going to be some good schools there. And your times lately have not been great.

Yes, Coach.

I really want to include you on the team, Daniel, but I'll need to see a marked improvement when you come back.

Okay, Coach.

You're going home for mid-term?

Yes.

There's a pool up there – where are you again, Rush?

Yeah, there's a pool and also I swim in the sea too.

I see. That's good. Well, try and get as much practice as you can over the holiday, all right?

Yes, Coach.

Good. Coach's mouth tightens. The skin of his face is wrinkly but his eyes are clear blue, like a swimming pool waiting for someone to dive in. Daniel, is everything all right with you? Lately I've been getting the impression that there's something on your mind.

No, Coach, not at all.

You're sure? This . . . this illness of yours, you're over that?

Oh yeah, totally.

Okay. The eyes monitor his unblinkingly. I just want you to know that if there is something bothering you, you can come to me and talk about it. That's what I'm here for. Everything private and confidential.

Thanks, Coach.

I'm not some old teacher. I'm your coach. I take care of my boys.

I know that, Coach. Everything's fine though.

That's good. You're looking forward to seeing your parents, I bet?

Sure.

How are they doing?

Fine.

Your mum?

She's fine.

Coach's hand on his shoulder. You give them my very best, okay? They should be very proud of you. You say that to them from me. He stands up.

Okay I will.

And remember, train hard! I want you on that bus to Galway.

Okay.

But Coach has turned away and is blowing his whistle at Siddartha Niland, who is jumping around waving a pair of swimming togs. In the shallow end Duane Grehan is crying out, My shorts! My shorts!

Steam rolls around the water in swaggering piles. But to your skin it is freezing cold.

Very last class before mid-term. Until recently, the Irish teacher, Ms Ni Riain, in spite of her advanced years, strangely conical breasts, and appearance, thanks to whatever brand of foundation she uses, of being made out of toffee, was widely considered Seabrook's number one babe, and the object of more than a few fixations – which no doubt says something about the nature of desire and its surprising willingness to work with the materials at hand. Since the arrival of Miss McIntyre, however, that particular illusion has been shattered, and Irish is now just another dull class to be struggled through.

There are ways of easing that struggle, though. In the middle of a boring sequence of interchanges on the Modh Coinníollach, Gaelic's infamously difficult conditional mood, Casey Ellington raises his hand. 'Miss?'

'Yes, Casey?'

'Someone told me that Hallowe'en actually started in Ireland,' Casey says with a furrowed brow. 'That can't be true . . . can it?'

The name of the boy who first discovered Ms Ni Riain's undergraduate degree in Irish folklore is lost to time, but the proud work he began lives on to this day. Angle it in the right way and a single well-placed question can sometimes burn up an entire class.

Hallowe'en, Casey Ellington learns, is a direct descendant of the Celtic rite of Samhain. In days of Yore, Samhain – also known as Féile Moingfhinne, or the Feast of the White Goddess – was one of the most important festivals. Held at the end of October, it marked the end of one pastoral year and the beginning of the next: an enchanted time, when the gates between this world and the Otherworld were opened, and ancient forces were let loose on the land.

'Otherworld?' Mitchell Gogan raising his hand this time.

'Irish folklore is dominated by tales of a mysterious supernatural race called the Sidhe,' Ms Ni Riain says. 'The Sidhe inhabited another world which shared the same space as ours but could not be seen by humans. *Sidhe* is usually translated as *fairies*' – any giggling here is vigorously stifled in the interests of keeping the digression in the air – 'but these fairies didn't have pretty wings or little pink frocks or hang around flower petals. They were taller than humans, and famous for their cruelty. They'd turn men blind, steal newborn babies, cast spells on whole herds of cattle so that they wouldn't eat and pined away, just for fun. It was considered bad luck even to speak their name. On the night of Samhain, all fires were extinguished, and the entrances to the burial mounds where they were believed to live left open until cockcrow next morning.'

'They lived in *burial mounds*?' says Neville Nelligan, no longer sure whether he's time-wasting or actually interested.

'They lived in earthworks, beside rivers, beneath particular trees, in underwater caves. They also lived in burial mounds that dotted the countryside. Originally, the word *sidhe* referred to these mounds, which were built by an older civilization, thousands of years before. Later on, people came to think of them as palaces that belonged to the fairies and connected their world to ours. There were folk-tales about men who fell asleep near one of these mounds and woke up with the gift of poetry or storytelling, or who discovered a door in the hillside and found their way into a feast underground – always with lovely harp music, sumptuous food, beautiful maidens – only to wake up next morning on the hillside, with no sign of the doorway, and go into the village to find that hundreds of years had passed and everyone they knew was dead.'

Perhaps it's the sombre weather, the gaunt wind and skeletal rattling of the fallen leaves outside, or maybe it's heightened sensibilities from the incipient Hop, but these stories take on a weird palpability – you can *feel* them, a shivery, mournful fog that weaves its way through the air. 'So if they lived in burial mounds –' Geoff barely daring to believe it '– does that mean the fairies were . . . *undead*?'

'Gods, fairies, ghosts, these were all mixed together as inhabitants of the Otherworld,' the teacher says. 'Initially the fairy legends may have started off as stories of the dead living on, feasting in their chambers. Or as a way of explaining what happened to this previous, pre-Celtic civilization that had now disappeared. But the point is that at Samhain, all of these strange beings, who lived side by side with us but who for the most part we didn't see, became visible and went roaming the land.'

'And where did they go, then?' Vince Bailey asks.

'Where did who go?'

'The gods, or the fairies, or whoever they were?'

'Well, I don't know . . .' Ms Ni Riain hasn't considered this.

'Maybe they were hit by a meteor,' Niall Henaghan interjects eagerly. 'Like the dinosaurs?'

'*Maybe they're still there . . .*' a zombified voice suggests.

'Geoff, I've told you a hundred times about that voice.'

'*Sorry.*'

'Anyway, none of this is getting us any closer to understanding the Modh Coinníollach. Where were we?' Ms Ni Riain settles her attention on the textbook – but at that moment the bell goes. School's out! The boys leap out of their seats; she smiles ruefully, realizing she's been had. 'All right. Have a good holiday, boys. Enjoy the dance tonight.'

'Happy Hallowe'en, Miss!'

'Happy Hallowe'en!'

'*Happy Hallowe'en . . .*'

'Oh, Geoff, for the last time . . .' She trails off; Geoff has already left the room . . .

By four o'clock – except for the small gaggle that scurries back and forth between the Art Room and the Sports Hall, arms heaped with dyed-black netting, papier-mâché skulls, partially eviscerated pumpkins with craft knives still jutting from their flanks – the school is utterly deserted. Or so it appears; beneath the superficial emptiness, the air groans with the freight of anticipation: the silence shrieks, the space trembles, crammed with previsions so feverish and intense that they begin to threaten to flicker into being, there in the depopulated hallways. Meanwhile, above the old stone campus, sombre grey clouds gather, laden and growling with pent-up energies of their own.

Upstairs, although the sun has not yet quite set – and although, of course, for the rest of the world it does not officially fall for another five days – Hallowe'en is in full swing. The Gothic environs of the Junior Rec Room abound with bedsheet ghosts, plastic-fanged vampires, rubicund Osama bin Ladens and robed Jedi. Frankenstein's Monster applies contusions to Victor Hero (deceased); two incompletely wrapped mummies quarrel over the last roll of toilet paper; the Scarlet Pimpernel hatches a plan with the Green Goblin to buy drink with the Goblin's big brother's fake ID. Here and there older boarders from the higher years, still waiting around for lifts home, look on scornfully and make sarcastic remarks. But the boys barely hear, being too caught up in the moment, and in their costumes, where they feel curiously at home – seeming to *inhabit* them in a way quite different to the awkward relationships they have with their school uniforms.

Now, as the sun's last rays glimmer out, the air momentarily shivers – tightening, drawing in on itself, as though experiencing a chill. Through the window the first car-headlights sweep up the avenue; a caravan of others wink in the distance beyond the tennis courts. An elf and what looks like a pint-sized science teacher bustle out of their dorm room to call on another three doors down.

'Yes?' Dennis quarter-opening the door.

'Are you nearly ready?'

'*I* am, but I'm waiting for Niall.'

Strolling up the corridor, clicking his fingers, Mario appears in a dark brown leather jacket, a pair of impenetrably black sunglasses and a glistening patina of hairgel.

'Are you bitches hot to trot? It's about to start.'

'Who are you supposed to be, the Fonz?'

'I am going as the famous stud, Mario Bianchi,' Mario says, with a snap of his gum.

Dennis just rolls his eyes.

'What in God's name is that *smell*?' Ruprecht covers his nose with a tweedy sleeve.

'That, my friend, is aftershave. Some day, if you ever start shaving and you stop being a gay, you will maybe use it yourself.'

'It smells like you've been pickled,' Ruprecht says.

Mario chews his gum, unperturbed, runs a hand through his slimy hair. 'So what are we waiting for?'

'Niall,' Dennis says, still keeping himself semi-concealed behind the door.

Mario turns his attention to Skippy, panning slowly up from his runners, fitted out with tiny wings, to his crepe-paper hunting hat, which sports a long speckled feather. 'Who are you? Wait, let me guess . . . you're that faggy elf, from that gay game of yours?'

Skippy's been working on his costume for the last three nights, and it does look impressively elvish. Over a green tanktop (one of several) of Ruprecht's that has shrunk in the wash, he's slung a quiver of glo-stick Arrows of Light; a plywood-and-tinfoil Sword of Songs hangs from his belt in a scabbard made from tennis-racket grip, alongside a rolled-up map of Hopeland (authentic parchment effect: soak an ordinary sheet of paper in strong coffee, then put it in the oven at 200 degrees).

Ruprecht's outfit is decidedly more prosaic – slacks, tie, horn-rimmed spectacles and a brown tweed jacket with leather elbow patches that is too long and insufficiently wide.

'Uh, Von Boring, did anyone explain to you that you're supposed to wear a costume . . . ?'

Ruprecht blinks in surprise. 'I'm Hideo Tamashi,' he says.

Mario looks blank.

'Professor Emeritus of Physics at Stanford? Revolutionized the entire field of cosmology? Probably the most important scientist since Einstein?'

'Oh, that Hideo Tamashi,' Mario says.

Dennis shakes his head. 'I have to hand it to you, Skippy, Blowjob, I didn't think you could possibly look any nerdier than you already are. But this is something really special.'

'What about you, Dennis?' Skippy says. 'Who are you going as?'

Without replying, Dennis steps out into the hall and perfoms a 360 in a rumpled charcoal-grey suit. A neat row of ballpoint pens pokes from his shirt pocket and a Seabrook pin from his tie. 'Can't you tell? Let me give you a clue . . .' With two hands he rubs vigorously at his face and hair, emerging flushed and bellicose, and in a stentorian voice bellows, 'Come on, you slackjaws, show some moxie! I'm not running a kindergarten here! Ship up or shape out! My way or the highway!' His eyes flick eagerly over the faces of the others, in whom realization is just beginning to twitch . . . 'Well, actually, the costume's not quite finished – I mean it's only half of the costume,' he says cryptically, then, craning his neck, calls into the room behind him, 'are you nearly ready in there?'

'I'm ready,' Niall's voice, sounding singularly dejected, returns.

'Behold, gentlemen . . .' The door at last swings open, and Dennis steps aside with a ringmasterly bow to reveal, in the middle of the room, Niall in a disastrous floral pinafore, a blonde wig and high heels. The dress has been enhanced by two balloons up top and a cushion in the belly area; Niall, underneath a lurid layer of enthusiastically applied make-up, wears an expression of profound suffering and humiliation.

It takes a moment for the others to realize the full genius of this double-act, then the first giggles emerge, transmuting swiftly into guffaws.

'What are you clowns laughing at?' Dennis barks. 'Laughing's for chumps! Take a note, Trudy –' Resignedly, Niall reaches into his handbag and produces a clipboard. 'Van Doren – suspension! Juster – expulsion! The wop I want served up on a pizza! No, wait – a calzone! God damn it, Trudy, why the hell are you writing so slowly, you're not pregnant again, are you?'

'No master, sorry master,' Niall cringes in falsetto.

'That's the spirit.' Dennis claps him on the back, sending a rugby ball tumbling from between Niall's legs, swaddled in a blue and gold Seabrook jersey.

'If he finds out about this you are so dead,' Skippy says. 'You're deader than dead.'

'Juster, when I want your opinion I'll ask for it,' Dennis continues, then turns to the band of masquers who've halted on their way downstairs to mill around the doorway. 'Fix that hair! Close that mind! Repeat after me! Page me the second the old man croaks it! Now, are you boys ready? A Seabrook boy is always ready. Ready to work. Ready to play. Ready to listen to his teachers, especially the greatest educator of them all, Jesus. As Jesus said to me once, Greg, what's your secret? And I said, Jesus – study your notes! Get to class! Shave that beard! You show up to your first day on the job dressed like a hippie, of course they're going to crucify you, I don't care whose son you are . . .'

In this fashion, the faux Acting Principal and his ersatz wife leave the room and are ushered to the head of the crowd to lead the procession downstairs, the laughter of the other boys ringing around them and split more or less equally between admiration of their bravado and gleeful anticipation of the moment they get caught.

'Wait – I just have to get something –' The cavalcade's already tripped away unhearing, down the spiral staircase. Back in his room, Skippy flips over the pillow and hovers there.

He hasn't taken a pill in days and days. It's partly because the last time he took one he threw up on Kevin Wong; but it's mostly because of seeing her, because the feelings he's had ever since he saw her have chased away the feelings he was having before – maybe not chased them away entirely, but to somewhere deep underground, where you can barely hear them whispering and growling. He's still freaking out – today, especially, he hasn't been able to eat and every time he thinks of Frisbee Girl, which is every second, his heart starts going a trillion miles an hour – but it's a different kind of freaking out. It's not like being attacked by his own brain, joined forces with the stuff around him so he has to cover his head. It's not the moments gathered against him, throwing him from one to the other. Instead everything follows on from everything else, the way it does in a story, and the air around him is turbulent and pure and cold, like standing under a waterfall. Can there be such a thing as happy terror? All Skippy knows is that he doesn't feel like blocking it out. Just to be on the safe side, though, he slips the tube into his quiver; then he runs off after the others, as they twist through the narrow, dark-panelled corridors of the Tower and out into the Quad, where they stop and catch their breath . . .

Night has fallen, utterly black, moon and stars inked out by storm-clouds that seem, even now, still to be arriving on the scene; the air is full of staticky rain that doesn't fall but hangs, tingling, waiting for you to walk into it. That's not all it's full of. From the leaf-strewn laneway leading down to Ed's Doughnut House, from the avenue that snakes past the priests' residence to the back gate by St Brigid's, from the road by the tennis court that goes to the main entrance, costumed forms are arriving, many of them – among the cowboys, devils, giant spiders, rugby internationals, Jasons and Freddys, corpses in various states of decay – costumed *female* forms. The car park is a riot of bare legs, flashing silver in headlights as they debouch from Saabs, Audis, SUVs; and as soon as these latter have gone, coats are shrugged off to reveal equally bare arms, bare midriffs and as much cleavage as they can get away with.

It seems the girls have by and large played down creativity in favour of the opportunity to dress slutty. Naughty nurses sashay up with kinky cowgirls; a pneumatic Lara Croft in thigh-high boots carries the nacreous tail-fin of a mermaid who for one heart-stopping moment appears naked from the waist up, till you realize she's wearing a fleshtone leotard; S&M cop, porno-Cleopatra, four woozy princesses tripping arm-in-arm in princess heels up the bumpy laneway; two Catwomen, already arching their backs at each other, a host of BETHanis in various guises familiar from the videos – all flocking to join the line that extends down the steps from the doors of the Sports Hall through which music swirls and colours glint like promises . . .

The boarders, attempting to take this in, are for a moment reluctant to move: it's as though they've stumbled upon Xanadu, right here in their own school, and they fear they might somehow shatter the illusion, scatter this heady dream to the four winds . . . Then, as a man, they think better of it, and hurry down to join the queue.

At the top of the steps the Automator is delivering his last-minute instructions to Howard the Coward and Miss McIntyre: 'It is now seven forty-five. At eight-thirty I want these doors *closed*. There is to be ABSOLUTELY NO ADMITTANCE after eight-thirty, under any circumstances. Prior to ten-thirty p.m., no one is to leave except with your permission. Once they leave, there is NO READMITTANCE. Anyone behaving in a disruptive or inappropriate fashion, I want their parents called immediately. And anyone –' he raises his voice here '– found to be in possession or under the influence of alcohol or controlled substances of any kind is to be punished with immediate suspension, pending full investigation by the School Board.'

He casts a searing gaze over the line of suddenly terrified-looking youngsters frozen silently on the hall steps, holding their alcoholic breath.

'Good,' he pronounces. Already late for his fundraising dinner at Seabrook Rugby Club, he takes his leave of the chaperones and strides down the line in the direction of the car park; then, a little distance past the tail of the queue, he stops. Scratching his head, he turns and slowly retraces his steps, as if he is not quite sure what he is looking for, until he arrives at Dennis and Niall.

A silence falls over the assembled masquers. Smoothing down his red tie, adjusting his charcoal blazer, the Automator stares at Dennis through narrowed eyes. Dennis, identically attired, hums nervously to himself, keeping his eyes fixed on the reptilian neck of Max Brady in front of him. Giggles begin to escape up and down the line. The effect, for anyone looking on, which everyone is, is akin to that of the Automator staring into a fairground mirror. His gaze flicks over to Niall, then back to Dennis. He begins to say something, then stops; after a full minute of naked staring, in which Dennis comes close to tears, he grunts, turns on his heel and continues on his way.

They listen to his footsteps echo off to the car park, the car door *chunks* open and closed and the motor starts; and then, as it revs off into the night, there is a mighty cheer.

'You are all suspended!' Acting Principal Dennis Hoey cries. 'Hallowe'en is banned! Study your navels! Cut those notes!' Niall shakes his head and silently thanks God, whom he has promised never to listen to Dennis again.

The doors are opened, and the line progresses swiftly forward. But before the party can begin, there remains one last trial to get through – the Sports Hall antechamber, where, seated alone at a table, Father Green is taking entrance money. The light here is sterile and unforgivingly bright, reducing them, no matter how glamorous or outlandish their attire, once more to children; as they shuffle by him to drop their crumpled fives into the bucket, the priest thanks them in an impersonal, excessively courteous tone, keeping his eyes firmly averted from the almost universally sacrilegious costumes, not to mention the acres of goosepimpled flesh – still, the transaction leaves them with a strange chill of ignominy, and they hurry away as quickly as they –

'Oh, Mr Juster . . .'

Skippy reluctantly turns back from the door. What is the problem? Didn't he see him put in his money? The priest's lashes, long and surprisingly feminine, waft upwards, uncloaking the coal-black stare.

'You appear to be losing a wing . . . ?' He extends a knotted finger.

Looking down, Skippy sees that the feathers have come unpinned from the ankle of one dragonskin boot. He bends quickly and adjusts it, then mumbling his thanks hastens into the hall.

The others have disappeared; everything is dark, and Skippy stumbles around for what seems like an age, bumping his way through witches, mutants, trolls and terrorists, unable to make out anyone he knows. Every available inch of space has been covered with black cloth, decorated in turn with crescents, stars, mystical runes. Black balloons float overhead like lost souls, ropey black webs drip from the eaves, mutilated mannequins climb out of the walls, and over the DJ booth, where Wallace Willis – lead guitarist with Shadowfax, Seabrook College's number one rock band – is spinning the discs, a gap-toothed pumpkin exults as though presiding over the bacchanal. When his eyes have adjusted to the darkness, Skippy finds he can identify most of the male half of the revellers. That Zeus over there, in cotton-wool beard and bathrobe, is Odysseas Antopopopolous; the IRA man in camouflage gear and balaclava can only be Muiris de Bhaldraithe. But some of them still defy him. That eerie Death, for instance, face lost beneath the hood of his robe, standing six and a half feet tall at least, who is he? And eerier still, the pink rabbit jitterbugging feverishly over beside Vincent Bailey and Hector O'Looney? And these *girls* – can they really be the same ones he sees every day, queuing up in Texaco for cigarettes and phone credit? Have they secretly, all this time, been *this*? If it weren't for the worn-down lines of the basketball court underfoot, the only trace of the hall's previous incarnation, Skippy'd think he'd somehow wandered into the wrong place . . .

'Hallo, Skippy,' a sepulchral voice says. 'Happy Holiday of the Dead.'

'Thanks, Geoff.'

'Isn't this incredible?'

'It's pretty amazing . . .'

'Would you like some fruit punch?'

'Okay.'

Elf follows zombie to the table where 'Jeekers' Prendergast is ladling punch from a huge vat prepared by Monstro from the ends of various cans of fruit concentrate. Dennis is there too, with Ruprecht; the former has just suspended Jeekers for his gay costume (eighties tennis ace Mats Wilander) and then expelled him for not ensuring there is booze in the punch. A moment later Niall bursts onto them. 'Hey everybody, Mario just got turned down by a girl!'

'I was not turned down, you faggot who is dressed as a woman,' Mario snaps, arriving behind him. 'I told you, she is a diabetic and she must go and take her insulin.'

'I saw the whole thing!' says Niall with an unrepentant air of jubilation. 'Wiiiipeouuuuut.'

'Keep laughing, Mr Funny, and when this bitch comes back from taking her insulin you are going to look pretty silly.'

'Well, even if she doesn't . . .' Geoff begins consolingly.

'She will.'

'Yes, but even if she doesn't, there are plenty of other ladies here anyway.'

'And most of them are drunk,' Dennis adds.

'Fascinating,' Ruprecht muses to Skippy. 'The whole thing seems to work on a similar principle to a supercollider. You know, two streams of opposingly charged particles accelerated till they're just under the speed of light, and then crashed into each other? Only here alcohol, accentuated secondary sexual characteristics and primitive "rock and roll" beats take the place of velocity.'

Skippy has gone to replenish his punch. Ruprecht sighs quietly, and looks at his watch.

Patrick 'Da Knowledge' Noonan and Eoin 'MC Sexecutioner' Flynn pimp-roll by, plastic Uzis tucked under their arms, the faint frisson of tension still detectable between them, the aftermath of a heated debate earlier today over who was going to come as Tupac, which debate Patrick won, meaning Eoin is now waddling along in a fat suit, dressed as Biggie Smalls. The squalling riff from Cream's 'Layla' blasts from the speakers; in the DJ booth, Wallace Willis nods to himself: oh yes. 'Flubber' Cooke, who has come in his supermarket shelf-stacking uniform, explains to a sexy nun that while it's part of his costume, the trolley is actually company property, so although he'd like to let her ride in it, he can't. Mr Fallon, the history teacher, drifts along the periphery with his hands in his pockets and a melancholy air.

'I'd like to say a few words about bullying,' Dennis, in an authentic sheen of perspiration, is declaiming to anyone who'll listen. 'Here at Seabrook, we simply will not tolerate bullying of a second-rate nature. Bullying must meet the same standards of excellence we expect everywhere else. If you need help with your bullying, please do not hesitate to speak to me or Father Green or Mrs Timony or Mr Kilduff or . . .'

And then, grabbing his arm, Geoff Sproke says, 'Hey, Skippy, look! Isn't that your girlfriend over there?'

'Skippy?'

'. . . uh, Skippy?'

'Hey, we're going to need a new Skippy over here!'

It's just like in a film. The music dims to nothing, voices fade out, everything melts away, leaving only her. She is talking with her friends, dressed in a long white dress, a slender tiara woven into her dark hair. She seems to glow like she is lit from within, and even though he is looking right at her, Skippy can't believe how beautiful she is. He looks right at her, and he still can't believe it.

'Hubba hubba,' Mario says. 'Like a steak on a barbecue, this bitch is smokin'. It is lucky for you that you have first dibs, Juster, otherwise she would be the prime candidate for some of Mario's Special Sauce.'

'Keep an eye on him, Skip,' says Dennis. 'Never trust an Italian. The Nazis did that, and look where it got them.'

'You're not going to throw up again, are you?' Ruprecht asks.

'I can't believe she's *here*,' Skippy whispers dazedly.

'Skippy, old pal.' Dennis claps a hand on his shoulder. 'It doesn't make any difference whether she's here or not. As far as you're concerned, she's on the North Pole. She's on the *moon*.'

'What's the deal with her costume?' Niall wonders. 'She looks sort of like one of the elves from *Lord of the Rings*.'

'Or the girl from *Labyrinth*?'

'You clowns, she's obviously Queen Amidala from *Phantom Menace*.'

'Oh, right, you mean in that scene in *Phantom Menace* where she wears a tiara in her hair? The special magical scene that doesn't exist? That scene?'

But Skippy doesn't think she looks like Queen Amidala, or the girl from *Labyrinth*, or anyone else. He has seen beautiful girls before, in films, on the Internet, in pictures pinned to locker doors and dorm rooms; but the beauty this girl has is something bigger, something beyond, with infinitely more sides to it – it's like a mountain with an impossible shape that he keeps trying to climb and falling off, finding himself lying on his back in the snow . . .

'Ladies and gentlemen . . .' Geoff announces, arriving back on the scene with Titch Fitzpatrick. 'Frisbee Girl's true identity is about to be revealed!'

Titch, in a red Formula One jumpsuit crowded with company logos, clearly has other fish to fry tonight: from every side, girls wave and pout and send him amorous gazes. 'Where is she, then?' he says impatiently.

'Over there,' Geoff points with a decomposing finger. 'Near the DJ booth?'

Titch presses his lips together, and rising onto his tiptoes cranes his head over in the direction Geoff is pointing. Inside, Skippy squirms. Finding out her name! This is becoming real! Is that what he wants? He can't even tell –

She is with three other girls – a GI Jane with sharp, intelligent features and bouncy curls, a scuba-diver in a tight-fitting wetsuit and an overweight girl in some kind of incredibly voluminous Victorian-type ballgown that keeps slipping down her shoulders. The four of them are huddled together, conferring, Frisbee Girl's eyes darting repeatedly from the dancefloor to the door, like she's watching out for someone.

'Lori Wakeham, Janine Forrest, Shannan Fitzpatrick, KellyAnn Doheny,' Titch reels off the names in a bored voice. 'I presume you're talking about Lori Wakeham, she's the one in the white dress.'

Lori.

'Who is she?' Geoff asks.

'Uh, Lori Wakeham? Did I not just say that?'

'No, I mean, you know, what's her story?'

Titch shrugs. 'Just your typical Foxrock princess.'

'She going out with anybody?' Mario says.

'Dunno,' Titch says indifferently. 'I've seen her with people at LA Nites. I don't know if she's got a boyfriend. She acts a bit like no one's good enough for her.'

'Frigid,' Mario comments.

'So basically you're saying Skipford here is wasting his time, right, T-dog?' Dennis interprets. 'You're saying that Skippy fancying her is like some kind of slime or ooze fancying, you know, Gisele. It's like some sort of disgusting slime or algae seeping over to Gisele and telling her to get her coat.'

'That's not what he's saying,' Geoff objects. 'He's just saying she acts like no one's good enough for her. But that's because she hasn't met Skippy yet.'

'What's so great about Skippy? No offence, Skippy.'

'Well, okay, he's a very good swimmer? And he's – he's nearly finished *Hopeland*?'

'Actually,' Titch remembers, 'I did see her with Carl a couple of times last week.'

Instantly, as if it's been sucked into some awful vacuum, all conversation ceases.

'I saw them together in the mall,' Titch says obliviously, 'and once outside Texaco. I don't know if they're going out. I can ask around if you want.'

'Good idea, you ask Carl, and if he comes over and smashes Skippy's face in, we'll know she's spoken for.' Just then, as though sensing the eyes on her, the fat girl in the unfortunate dress turns and squints in their direction; next thing they know, Titch has bolted into the crowd.

'Sorry, dude,' Niall commiserates. Skippy is gazing at the floor as if counting the fragments of his shattered life.

'I think you should go and talk to her anyway,' counsels Ruprecht.

'You fat moron, didn't you hear what he said?' Dennis rebuts. 'He said he'd seen her with *Carl*. *Carl* is the key word there. It means get the hell out of the way, or start digging your own grave.'

'He only said he'd *seen* her with Carl,' Ruprecht corrects him. 'There could be any number of explanations for that.'

'Oh sure, maybe they're in Stamp Club together.'

'Let's just stop talking about it,' Skippy says desolately.

'But *Carl*,' Ruprecht says. 'Why would anybody want to go out with Carl?'

'Because that's what girls do, you idiot,' Dennis returns. 'The more of an asshole a guy is, the more girls he's got lining up to give him blowjobs. That is a scientific fact.'

'You can't just *say* something is a scientific fact,' Ruprecht rejoins.

'I just did, fatass. And what do you know about it anyway? Who the hell ever gave you a blowjob?'

'Your mother,' Geoff prompts *sotto voce*.

'Your mother,' Ruprecht says to Dennis.

'*Step*mother,' Dennis corrects sulkily.

'Ruprecht has a point though,' Niall says. 'Like, is Carl even here?'

'Can we just stop talking about it?' Skippy remonstrates.

'No, but, if they were together, he'd be here, wouldn't he?'

'It seems to me that the only way of establishing the truth is for Skippy to go and talk to this girl,' Ruprecht repeats.

'Would you all just fucking shut up?' Skippy interjects. 'Just fucking shut up about it, why can't you.'

Surprised, they fall silent, and remain so a moment. Then Mario, with some remark about beavers, turns and plunges quixotically into the dancefloor; Dennis and Niall follow after him, already chuckling. Ruprecht pats Skippy on the shoulder, and directs another surreptitious glance at his watch. Skippy looks over at Lori. The other two girls are both speaking to her; she nods without seeming to be listening, thumb jabbing frenetically at her phone. He wishes he'd never told anyone about her, never found out anything about her, that he could have gone on just watching her through the telescope. Now, just like Dennis said, even though she's right here, she's on the other side of the world. *Don't give up yet, Skippy,* Geoff's voice sounds in his ear. *'Strange things happen at Hallowe'en . . .'* And at that very moment, in the middle of the twin lead-guitar break in 'Hotel California', one of Wallace Willis's all-time favourite solos, the music cuts out and the lights too, and in the interregnum of darkness there is a fierce peal of thunder, like some huge, amorphous black animal snarling right over their heads. Everybody cheers. Skippy's hand tightens on his sword.

Lightning flashes outside his window. In his imagination Carl hears cheers and laughing. His (Morgan's) phone says 19:49, which means 7:49. He is late. Liarliar has been texting him all night.

RU GOIN TO HP?U SHD ITL B FN

and

WE R GON DRNKN B4 BHND CHRCH U CMN

The lightning goes again, now he imagines the Sports Hall on fire, everybody inside screaming and burning.

He was ready to go, at 19:20 he put on his coat and took the pills from behind the stereo. In the lonely church parking lot he would make her beg for them. All her friends are gone, tears are rolling down her cheeks. Sorry, the price has gone up. She has no choice. She turns over, her belt clinks open, she pulls down her jeans, he fucks her right there on the rainy steps, while God peeps out through the stained-glass window at him.

But then at the door of his room he stopped, and he is still stopped. On the TV at the end of his bed a faggot sings a faggot song to a table of faggots.

Downstairs through the rain Carl's mom is on the phone.

'I just don't understand why a sixty-eight-thousand-euro car keeps breaking down! That's what I don't understand! I mean, isn't it odd that it's breaking down all the time, this wonderful sixty-eight-thousand-euro car?'

She has been on the phone for half an hour, saying the same things over and over. Or sometimes she will just cry, or scream something but cry at the same time so you can't understand what she's saying.

'Well, you get the train back, so, you get the train back, and they, I imagine they will be able to deliver it back to Dublin for you, I imagine that must be part of the service they prov– well, why wouldn't they? It's a perfectly reasonable – well, what about the expense of staying there? What about the expense of staying in a hotel?'

AT HOP NW OMG WE R SO SHTFCD WER R U

'Because it would be *nice* – because it would be! Because that is where your place is, in your home, with your wife and child! Look – no, don't give me the name of the – what am I supposed to do with the name of the ho– what's the point if you never answer your – David!'

He listens to her voice turning into a kind of shrieky growl, sort of like the pig on that Muppet show.

'No, well, why don't you stay there, in that case! Why don't you stay in your hotel, with your tennis coach, or your dental hygienist, or your – no, you're irrational! You're irrational, not to understand what you have here, which is love! So why don't you – no – no, David, it's too late for that – no, it's too late, so don't bother because – no it is *not*, because you forfeited that right when you put a, a dental hygienist before the happiness of your own – well, tell that to my solicitor because – no, I'm locking the doors now –'

THER CLSN DE DORS SOON!!!

The sound of keys jingling and locks turning and the chain rattling and windows slamming then Mom running back to the phone to shout, 'Do you hear that?' Then she stamps back into the living room and there is a loud scuffing dragging noise then a thud and she starts bawling like a baby.

On the TV three men are whipping another man with nettles, his back is all fiery red like he's been burned and he is screaming and laughing in between the screams. Carl turns up the sound, then he turns up the stereo too so the music from the show and the music from the stereo crash into each other and scramble together so there is no room for anything else in his brain. He lies in his bed, a man is hit on the toes with a sledgehammer, everyone is laughing.

RNT U CMNG IN ITS CLSN IN 15 MINS????!!!!!

Fuck you bitch you will have to get your pills somewhere else tonight. Carl is so bored, he takes a thumbtack from the wall and makes a line on his arm then pulls down his sleeve fast because the door has creaked open and Mom is standing there. Her face is invisible in the shadows. He can hear her snuffling even with the TV and the stereo.

'Carl, baby?'

He does not answer.

'Carl, turn off your music for a second, angel.'

He snorts with anger then points the stereo remote at the stereo then the TV remote at the TV. He is so sick of having to use two remotes! But he leaves the picture on and looks at it not Mom, the guys with the hammer laughing and the guy who is rolling around with his eyes closed and his mouth open.

'Oh, Carl . . .' Mom stands at the window a minute with the curtain held between her finger and thumb. 'Oh, honey . . .' Then she tumbles down sideways on the bed beside Carl's knees with her hands over her nose and mouth, and little mewly sounds squirm out of her. Her nails are long and gold and pointed like the claws of some gold animal and around her neck she is wearing a necklace with big shining diamonds like she's just come from having dinner in a fancy restaurant with someone important, instead of a microwave WeightWatchers that she ate on her own in the kitchen. 'Sometimes –' she lifts herself up and wipes snot from under her nose '– even though two people love each other very, very much, there comes a point in their lives . . .'

The phone chirps with a new message. It's from Barry.

DUDE UR FRNDS LUKN DAM FIN IL HAU 2 GIU HER 1 IF U RNT HEER!!

Carl's blood goes cold.

'For a while now your father and I haven't been seeing eye to eye. It's not, it's not anybody's fault, it's just the way relationships sometimes go . . .'

Barry giving her pills. Barry making jokes. Barry telling her clever things.

'. . . and God knows we've sat down so many times, and tried to, to hash it out, but in the end . . .'

Barry's hands sliding into her jeans. Barry fucking her in a toilet cubicle – her tits in Barry's hands, Barry's eyes all twisted up as he shoots his load all over her face!

'. . . out of options.' Carl's mom is looking at him with trembling shining eyes and her voice wobbles when she speaks: 'But your dad and I, we both want you to know that . . . that doesn't mean we love you any less, okay? Okay, honey?'

Barry's white cum rolling slowly down her cheek.

'No!' Carl shouts.

'Oh, my poor baby!' Carl's mom explodes into sobs. 'My poor baby,' and she scoops her hand under his neck and more strongly than you would expect tugs his head into her chest. 'Oh baby, we'll be okay, I promise, I love you so much, Carly, I always will, more than anything in the world, more than anything . . .' He is crushed up against her tit, he can hear the saline inside it sloshing around, it's like holding a seashell to your ear and hearing the sea, a fake sea . . . Above him she keeps talking and crying, against the window the rain beats, Carl feels his eyes close. But then he sees bitch-face on her knees sucking Barry's dick! He opens them again and checks the clock. 20:30. He struggles free of Mom and sits up.

'I have to go. I'm going to be late for the Hop.'

'Of course, darling. I don't want you to let this affect your life.' Mom wipes her cheek with the back of her hand and gives him a fake smile. 'We're going to stay strong for each other, aren't we?'

'I'm really late,' Carl says again. He stands up, zips his coat, not looking at her though he can feel her looking at him.

'You're going to be the cutest thing there,' she says. She starts to cry again.

Carl rushes out of the room and down the stairs. Two chairs are stacked up against the front door and the couch is poking halfway out the living-room door. He carries the chairs back into the kitchen.

IL HAV 2 GIV HR 1 IF U RNT HEER!!

He pushes the couch back into its place, then goes to open the front door. But the front door is locked. He unhooks the chain and slides back the bolt and turns the key in the latch. But it is still locked. Fuck it! Blood thumps in his head. Lori takes down her knickers, Barry sticks his fingers into her. 'Mom!' Carl roars. She doesn't reply. 'MOM!' even louder, charging back up the stairs.

'In here, darling,' her voice calls weakly from her own bedroom. He pushes through the door. Everything in here is gold and red. Mom is sitting at the end of her bed, watching TV. She has a glass in her hand and between her fingers is a white plastic tube, a fake cigarette you smoke to help you stop real cigarettes.

'The fucking door is locked,' Carl says.

'Oh sweetheart, I'm so sorry, I forgot . . .' She reaches for her bag and starts fishing in it for her keys. She flicks through them till she finds the right one, then hands the bunch to Carl. 'You can hang on to them for tonight, petal. Leave them on the breakfast bar when you come in. I've taken a sleeping pill so I won't be going anywhere.' Carl grabs the keys with a grunt of disgust. 'Have a good time, honey,' she calls after him. Tears are creeping back into her voice. 'Don't worry about me.'

Carl unlocks the front door and steps out into the cold rainy porch – and that's when the idea comes. At first he doesn't know it's an idea. It's just the words reappearing in his brain, KEY and PILL. He doesn't know why they are there. He stops on the step, frowning to himself, one hand on the doorknob about to pull it closed. KEY PILL KEY PILL, the words stare at him like the eyes of a painting. Carl's brain is not used to KEY PILL ideas, and in the KEY beginning it refuses to PILL fit them together – then all at once, all by themselves, they fall into place and the idea is there, where a second ago there was nothing. This must be what happens to Barry all the time! With the idea fizzing up his arms, Carl slips back into the house! Inside, he slams the door. He waits a moment to make sure his mom is still in bed. Then he creeps up the stairs and into her bathroom.

In the mirror over the sink he sees himself. The idea is written like a smirk across his face. Carefully, he lifts the keys to the light and prods through them. He picks out a tiny silver wand and puts it into the tiny silver lock in the mirror. The key turns silently. He screws up his eyes and pulls the handle. The door swings open without a sound.

Every inch of the cabinet has been filled. Tubes, jars, boxes, pills of every colour and size and shape, all with white labels with Carl's mom's name written on them. If Barry was here he could probably tell you which ones do what. But Carl is only looking for one thing.

They call it the date-rape drug, Barry said. It's this pill that they invented that if you put it in a girl's drink it makes her really horny and she'll do whatever you want. But then the next day she won't remember anything.

They invented a pill to make girls do that? Carl was surprised.

No, they invented it to be a sleeping pill but then someone else found out it did all this other stuff too when you mixed it with alcohol.

Sleeping pill.

OMG WE R SO SHTFCD.

Then she would do whatever you wanted.

That is Carl's idea for Lori.

But there is a problem. The labels on the little bottles and boxes do not tell you which one is the sleeping pill. Instead they have names, long strange names that slide out of shape while you are reading them. They sound like kings from history or alien planets. There are hundreds of them. He thinks of ringing Barry to ask him which pill he was talking about. But then he would have to tell Barry his idea, which he doesn't want to do while Barry is alone with the girl, in case it gives Barry an idea as well. Then he has another idea – put *all* the bottles and boxes in his bag and bring them to the Hop so that Barry can pick out the right ones! He is just lifting his hand to grab the bottles on the bottom shelf when he hears his mom in the next room. He freezes, then runs over to the shower door to hide, but nothing happens. Maybe it was just the TV. From here behind the shower door though he notices something he didn't see before, a white box on the window sill, beside her Ladyshave, with a pack of pills sticking out like a silver tongue.

The label tells him nothing, just another weird alien name. But inside the box he finds instructions, folded up like a map:

ZENOHYPNOTAN is a hypnotic designed to help you sleep. ZENOHYPNO-TAN is a benzodiazepine-like agent, a member of the cyclopyrrolone group of compounds. When experiencing sleeplessness, take one tablet of ZENOHYPNOTAN one hour before going to bed. DO NOT CONSUME WITH ALCOHOL. Do not operate heavy machinery. NEVER EXCEED THE RECOMMENDED DOSAGE. You may experience some or all of the follow-ing side-effects during or after use of ZENOHYPNOTAN: drowsiness, vomiting, sweating, fatigue, dizziness, changes in libido, loss of vision, anterograde amnesia, disorientation, numbed emotions, depression, anxiety, inability to sleep. Other reactions like restlessness, agitation, aggressiveness, delusion, rages, nightmares, psychoses, inappropriate behaviour and other behavioural effects have been known to occur with benzodiazepines and benzodiazepine-like agents. Should this occur, use of the drug should be discontinued. Termination of use may cause headaches, muscle pain, confusion, extreme anxiety, hypersensitivity to light, hallucinations, epileptic seizures, derealization, depersonalization, suicide. In the case of negative side-effects, please consult your doctor.

Here you are Lori, I got you a drink. Oh thank you. Smiling at her the way Barry would smile, in his imagination he is wearing a James Bond tuxedo. Why don't you drink it? he says.

In a little while, she says.

He smiles. He is not sure what is happening. Why don't you drink it now? he says.

I'm not thirsty now, she says. Her eyes are like two pills.

Drink it, he says. She backs away. What is going on? He grabs her wrist. Drink it! She won't, she fights him. He gets angrier and angrier. Her eyes fill with tears as he forces her wrist up to her mouth – and now she drops the cup, and it spills away into the grey fog of his imagination. I will never fuck you! she shouts. Carl begins to roar, not words, just a raggedy animal roar, and he folds his hands into clubs, and raises them against the shrinking girl –

'Carl?'

He freezes. Did he make a noise out loud? Did he imagine the knock at the door?

'Carl?' Mom is outside the door. 'Is that you, honey?'

Fuck shit fuck. He stuffs the box of pills into his back pocket. He opens the door. Mom is there in her robe. She looks at him not-understanding. 'I thought you'd gone,' she says.

'No,' Carl says. 'I forgot something.'

'Why are you in my bathroom? Why is the medicine cabinet open?'

Her breath smells of alcohol. He imagines the pill dissolving through her blood. She will not remember anything. Slowly he reaches out his hand to touch her arm. The dressing gown is silky-soft.

'You're dreaming,' he says.

184

She blinks at him.

'You're having a dream,' he says.

She closes her eyes and puts her hand on her forehead. Then she says, in not much more than a whisper, 'I remembered . . . you weren't wearing a costume.'

'A what?'

'A costume. For the dance? A costume?'

A costume. Fuck! Shit!

The Seabrook RFC clubhouse – a haven for old boys of all ages, where business and drinking can be done without the interference of yahoos or women – is located, like a frontier outpost, a couple of miles from the school: close enough for the Automator to be summoned from should anything – *anything* – go awry at the school dance. The Acting Principal made no secret of his unhappiness at leaving the Hop in the hands of two greenhorns, or one greenhorn and Howard. At first Howard wondered if it was only their lack of experience that concerned him. Could it be he detected a frisson? Did he suspect the chaperones needed a chaperone?

On the evidence of the night so far, Greg has little cause for worry. Everything is unfolding with all due propriety. After the vertiginous giddiness of the first half-hour, the students have settled down into a manageable medium-level hysteria. As for their chaperones, they have barely spoken a word to each other. Seeing that it was just the two of them, Miss McIntyre said at the outset, the most sensible thing would be to split up, didn't Howard think? Of course, he'd agreed vigorously, of course. Since then, they've worked opposite sides of the room. From time to time he'll catch a glimpse of her, sailing through the three-quarter-scale melee; she will flutter her fingers at him, and he'll hustle his features into a brief efficient smile, before she sails on again, the luminescent flagship of some invading army of beauty. Other than that, not so much as a whisper of frisson.

As he meanders around the room, he asks himself what exactly he'd hoped for from tonight. Up to now, he'd been pretending that he wasn't hoping for anything; he'd volunteered for this detail in a kind of deliberate trance, turning as it were a blind eye to himself, all self-critical faculties switched off. Even tonight, his grousing to Halley about what a chore and an imposition it was had been on one level quite sincere. It's only now, when it's crystal clear nothing is going to happen, that his hopes become unavoidable, materializing in the form of jags of disappointment at the same time that they appear, in the cold light of day, preposterous, fantastical, naive. How had he let himself get so carried away by a couple of flirtatious remarks? Was that all it took for him to be ready to betray Halley? Is that the kind of man he is? Is that really what he *wants*?

David Bowie's 'Young Americans' comes on over the sound system; Howard experiences a fresh pang, this one of homesickness for the house he left less than two hours ago. No, that isn't what he wants. He's not going to throw his life away for the sake of a cheap office affair. Tonight has been both a wake-up call and a reprieve. When he goes home, he can begin to put right all the things he's let slide; he can also thank God he didn't get close enough to Aurelie to embarrass himself further.

First, though, he may devote himself without distraction to his supervisory duties, although aside from judiciously coughing at couples whose petting is straying towards heaviness, there is not much to do but work his way tortuously from one end of the room to the other and back again, a supernumary presence swigging aimlessly at his punch, which is exactly as awful as the punch at his own Mid-term Mixer fourteen years ago. Fourteen years! he thinks. Half his life! As he makes his invisible way he entertains himself by superimposing onto the crowd faces from his own past, as if he's walking through it again, a ghost from the future . . . There's Tom Roche as a gladiator, intact, unbroken, ignoring the girls that flutter about him like hummingbirds to talk rugby with a young Automator, who's chaperoning with Kipper Slattery and Dopey Dean. There's Farley, two heads taller than everyone else, his Mr T costume making him look even skinnier than he already is, and Guido LaManche, sleeves of his sports coat rolled up à la Crockett from *Miami Vice*, dealing out lines to softly agape girls like a magician doing card tricks. And there's Howard himself, a cowboy, as generic and uncontroversial an outfit as he could think of, though now he sees within it a telltale pun inserted by fate (Howard the Cowherd). But then that nickname still awaited him; he was fourteen, half-grown, with no lines of destiny to thread him to anyone, or at least not that he could see; none of them knew yet what their lives were to be, they thought the future was a blank page on which you could write what you wanted.

He's woken from these thoughts by a noise at the main doors. It sets up just as he is walking by, a din of disconnected blows too violent and disorderly to be called *knocking* – more like punching, like someone is punching the door. Howard glances about him. No one else seems to have heard: the doors are on the other side of the cloakroom, and the music drowns out all but the loudest exterior noise. But he hears it, as it starts up again: an intensifying flurry of hammering and pounding, as if some furious non-human agency were trying to force its way into the hall.

Howard shut these doors, as per the Automator's instructions, at half past eight exactly. Another door at the far end of the hall leads to the toilets, the basement lockers and the Annexe; but all the main entrances are locked, and the only way in or out of the school is here, through these doors, which cannot be opened from the outside – unless, that is, they are broken down.

While he is standing there, the hammering stops: in its place, after a few seconds' prickling silence, comes a single, heavy thud. A moment's pause, and then another. This time the boys and girls in the vicinity hear it too, and seek out Howard's eye in alarm. His mind spins. Who is out there? All kinds of grisly thoughts flash through his head: gangs of marauders, haters of the school, come to terrorize them at knifepoint, at gunpoint, a Hallowe'en massacre . . . The thuds get louder: the doors shake, the bolt rattles. Although the majority still do not know its source, the disquiet seeps inwards, through the dancefloor; bodies become still, conversations fall silent. Should he call the Automator? Or the police? There isn't time. Swallowing, he enters the shady cloakroom and brings himself close to the door. 'Who's there?' he barks. He half-expects an axe or a tentacle or a metal claw to come crashing through the wood. But there is nothing. And then, just at the moment he begins to relax, the wood bulges under another blow. Howard curses, jumping back, then presses down the safety lock and pushes open the doors.

Awaiting him outside is a stormy, packed darkness, as though all space from the ground up has been usurped by the ominous thunderclouds. Wrapped within it, tensed for another charge, stands a lone figure. Howard can't make out who it is; groping around behind him, he finds the light switch and flicks it on.

'Carl?' He squints into the blacked-out face. The boy is wearing his everyday clothes – jeans, shirt, shoes – but has smeared his features with soot. A pretty impoverished costume; somehow that makes it all the more frightening.

'Can I come in?' the boy says. His clothes are wet – it must have been raining. He peers over and under Howard's arm, stretched protectively across the portal.

'The doors closed half an hour ago, Carl. I can't let anyone else in now.'

Carl doesn't seem to hear him – he's craning and ducking, stretching and shrinking his frame, in his effort to spy into the dance. Then abruptly he turns his attention back to Howard. 'Please?'

From his lips, the word comes as a shock. For a moment Howard wavers. It's the start of the holidays, after all, and the Automator isn't here to see. But something about the boy unnerves him. 'Sorry,' he says.

'What?' Carl opens his hands at his sides.

He seems to be getting bigger every second, as if he's partaken of some Alice-in-Wonderland potion. Involuntarily Howard takes a step backward. 'You know the rules,' he says.

For a long moment, Carl looms over him, eyes staring whitely out of the black mask. Howard looks back at him neutrally through the fissile air, not breathing, waiting to dodge a flying fist. But it does not come; instead the hulking boy revolves and slowly descends the steps.

Instantly Howard's resolve is pierced by guilt. 'Carl,' he calls. 'Take this.' Howard extends the umbrella Father Green left under the table. 'In case it rains again,' he says. Carl gawps at the hooked black handle under his nose. 'Don't worry,' Howard adds uselessly. 'You can return it after the holidays. I'll explain.'

The boy takes it without a word. Howard watches him pass down the rain-slicked avenue, through the intervals of light cast by the lamps, a row of white moons against the starless sky. With a sigh he closes the door and slides down the bolt.

Re-entering the hall proper, he finds the party in full swing again. From a corner of it, Miss McIntyre observes him with folded arms; he smiles wanly, then hastily removes himself from the dancefloor as DJ Wallace Willis puts on a record sufficiently slow in tempo for the kids, hitherto an amiably bouncing mass, to redistribute themselves into soulfully intertwined couples, kissing each other with varying degrees of accomplishment and Frenchness.

Taking refuge at the punch stand, he rubs his eyes and checks his watch. Two more hours to go. All around him, everyone who has not been asked or has not the courage to ask someone to dance is vigorously conversing in an effort not to notice the slow-motion epic of desire unfolding on the dancefloor. The soundtrack is 'With or Without You', by U2; as he listens, Howard is seized by the unshakeable certainty that he sat out this very song at this very punchbowl, fourteen years before. God, this job! These days he can hardly take a step without falling down a trapdoor into his own past.

Five months ago, Howard had attended his Class of '93 Ten Year Reunion in this same hall. Long dreaded, it had proved an unexpectedly pleasant affair. A three-course meal, full bar, partners left at home until the Alumni and Spouses Golf Outing the following day; unflattering nicknames left unspoken, enmities of the past carefully let lie. Everyone was eager to appear socialized, to present his adult self, successfully emerged from its chrysalis. They pressed business cards into Howard's palm; they took photos of babies from wallets; they waggled wedding rings and sighed tragicomically. Each reintroduction repeated a truth at once shocking and totally banal: people grow up and became orthodontists.

And yet none of them had been quite convincing. Once you've seen someone firing peas out of his nostril, or trying and failing, for a full fifteen minutes, to climb over a gym horse, it's difficult to take him seriously as a top legislator for the UN or a hedge-fund manager at a private bank, no matter how many years have passed. The hall had seemed to Howard no less full of burlesques and pastiches than it does tonight. And he was the pastiche poster-boy, for he had actually switched sides from being one of the students to being one of the teachers, from child, as it were, to grown-up – and it had *just happened*, one event in a long muddled train of events, without any great catharsis or epiphany on his part, without any interior transformation or evolution whereby he might have known anything worth teaching; instead it was like calling one of the kids from the middle row of his History class and asking him to take over, and while he was at it pay a mort-gage, and fret over whether or not to get married.

He looks out over the sea of slowly bobbing heads, imagines his boys in twenty years' time, with thinning hair, beer guts, pho-tos in their wallets of children of their own. Is everyone in the world at the same game, trying to pass himself off as something he is not? Could the dark truth be that the system is composed of individual units *none of whom really knows what he is doing*, who emerge from school and slide into the templates offered to them by accident of birth – banker, doctor, hotelier, salesman – just as tonight they'd separated according to prearranged, invisible sym-metries, nerds and jocks, skanks and studs –

'Penny for 'em,' a female voice speaks directly into his ear.

He jumps. Miss McIntyre smiles at him. 'How are you getting on?'

'Fine,' he recovers. 'Bored.'

'Who was that banging on the door?'

'Carl Cullen. He wanted to come in.'

'You didn't let him?'

'He was either drunk or on something,' Howard responds laconically. 'Anyway, he knew what time the doors closed.'

'I'm glad it wasn't me who had to speak to him,' she says, in a rare tone of respect.

'Yeah, well . . .' he shrugs it off. 'What have you got there?'

'I raided the girls' toilets.' She holds up two carrier bags crammed with clinking bottles. 'You should have seen their little faces.'

'Did you kick them out?'

'No . . . I felt sorry for them. It was bad luck. I'd just gone down to use the loo.' She sets the bags down on the table and rummages through them. 'Look at all this stuff. I feel like Eliot Ness.' She raises her head again. 'So what were you thinking about?'

'Thinking?' Howard repeats, as if the word is unfamiliar.

'Just now. You were away off somewhere.'

'I was wondering why the DJ is playing all these old songs.'

'You looked sad,' she says. She lays a finger on his chest and gazes at it, like an electrician into a nest of wiring. 'I bet,' she says slowly, 'you were thinking of the dances you went to, when you were young, and wondering where all the time went, and what happened to all the dreams you had then, and if this life is anything like the one you wanted.'

Howard laughs. 'Bingo.'

'Me too,' she says ruefully. 'I suppose it's inevitable.' She turns her gaze over the hall, where two-personned silhouettes are swaying almost motionlessly to 'Wild Horses' by the Rolling Stones. 'So how did you do, at your Hop?'

'What do you mean?'

'Howard, eventually this playing-dumb routine is going to stop seeming charming. Did you score? Did you dance a slow-set? Or were you one of the losers watching from the sidelines?'

Howard considers lying, then comes clean. 'Loser,' he says.

'Same here,' she nods dolefully. Howard rounds on her in disbelief. 'You? You're telling me no one wanted to kiss you?'

'What can I say? I was your classic ugly duckling.' She looks away. 'So do you feel like making up for lost time?'

He starts. 'What?'

She shrugs, inclines her head towards the crowd. 'I don't know. Take home one of those little nymphets. I'm sure they'd love some extra lessons from a handsome teacher. They're all so gorgeous, aren't they? And *skinny* – God, none of them must have eaten for a week.'

'They're a little young for me.'

'Take two. Fourteen plus fourteen is twenty-eight.'

'I have a girlfriend who might object.'

'That's a shame,' she says ambiguously. She clams up, addresses herself to the music, leaving Howard to wonder just what has passed him by. 'This is such a great song,' she remarks, and then, forthrightly, to Howard, 'Would you like to dance?'

Only by a miracle does Howard manage not to drop his paper cup of punch. 'Here? Now? With you?'

She arches a gamine eyebrow. Howard's mind is a sea of flying chicken feathers. 'We can't,' he stammers, then adds hurriedly, 'It's not that I don't *want* to . . . but, you know, in front of the kids, and everything?'

'Then let's sneak out!' she whispers.

'Out?' he repeats.

'Somewhere no one will see us. For five minutes.' Her eyes glitter at him like mirrorballs.

'But what about the . . . didn't Greg say . . . ?' He gestures weakly at the costumed teenagers.

'Five *minutes*, Howard, what's the worst that can happen? Just till the end of this song, it's practically over anyway . . . we'll just go out into the corridor . . . ooh, we can make Cosmopolitans!' She views his expression of agonized vacillation, cringing at her like an animal begging to be put out of its misery, and takes his hand. 'You owe it to yourself, Howard,' she says. 'You have to dance at least one slow-set in your life.'

The lights are low and he doesn't think anyone sees them leave.

'Wild Horses' fades into REM's 'Everybody Hurts', extending the mass kissing for another three minutes. To a dark corner where a boy in a red Formula One outfit is welded to the mouth of a sexy secretary, a girl in a dress unfortunately resembling an exploding wedding cake totters up. In a trembling voice, she says, 'Titch?' Formula One ignores her. She waits a moment, unsure, then taps him on the back. 'Titch?'

He breaks off and turns round, exasperated. Sexy Secretary, looking daggers at Wedding Cake, wipes a damp chin with her sleeve.

'Titch, we need to talk,' Wedding Cake says.

Elsewhere, a thirties gangster with a pencil-moustache adorning her upper lip approaches a sexy GI and a princess. 'Hey, Alison? – Oh my God, sorry Janine, you look just like Alison from behind!'

'That's okay, Fiona! I think Alison's over there with Max Brady?'

'Thanks!' Thirties Gangster moves off. Sexy GI's smile vanishes instantly, and she says to the princess, 'That bitch, there's no *way* I look like fucking Alison Cummins from behind. Her arse is like three times the size of mine!'

'Fiona looks like a lesbian in that suit,' the princess says.

'She's such a stupid cunt,' the sexy GI says.

The princess, the GI, the scuba-diver and the Victorian-lady-who-looks-like-a-wedding-cake knew it would be dodgy trying to sneak drink inside so they had three Breezers and a naggin of vodka each before they came in – well, no one actually finished the naggin except Victorian Lady and then she kept falling over on the way up here and they practically had to carry her past the pervy old priest. Still, the princess is quite locked, and the GI is even more locked. In the car park she took two of the pills, and now she's talking really fast and loud and not making that much sense.

'Looks like KellyAnn's finally hunted down Titch,' the princess says, looking at the scene unfolding in the corner.

'Oh my God, she's not going to tell him *now*?' the scuba-diver says.

'What does she think he's going to do,' the GI says, 'stop kissing Ammery Fox and get down on one knee right here in the fucking Seabrook gym hall and say, Oh, KellyAnn, please marry me? I mean, hello?'

'He's *quite* good-looking,' the princess judges.

'He's nothing special,' the GI says dismissively. 'He's a *boy*, you know?'

A strongman with a handlebar moustache and leopardskin leotard interposes himself between the girls and glances from one to the other, smiling. They gaze back at him with expressions of naked disgust of the kind ordinarily reserved for, say, sex offenders. The strongman withdraws, looking significantly less strong.

'God, I'm so sick of these fucking *boys*,' the GI declares. 'I need a *man*.'

'Me too,' the princess says.

'Oh Jesus – Lori, don't look but that weird fucking Robin Hood thing is completely staring at you again,' the scuba-diver says.

'Oh my God, what is his problem?'

'Maybe I should go over and tell him to stop freaking you out.'

'Don't waste the oxygen.'

'Did you hear anything from Prince Charming?' the GI asks.

The princess's face falls.

'Oh, Lori . . .' The GI reaches out and lays a hand on the princess's shoulder. 'Don't let him ruin your night. Switch off your phone and stop thinking about him.'

'I'm not thinking about him,' the princess mumbles, hair falling over her face.

'I suppose he at least might have had some drugs,' the GI says. 'God, this thing is *so* fucking boring. Seabrook boys are such invertebrates.' She withdraws her hand, wraps her bare arms around herself. 'I need a shag so badly.'

Near the heart of the dancefloor, Niall/Trudy has been arrested on his way back from the toilets by a heartstoppingly lovely girl dressed as Natasha Fatale, arch-enemy of Bullwinkle the Moose. The girl wants to know where he got his lipstick. Niall, sweating profusely, is not sure how to proceed. Should he tell her he got it from his sister and he doesn't know the name? Or should he tell her the truth, that he fell in love with it in a little boutique in Sandy-cove village? The heartstopping girl waits expectantly. Niall feels one of his breasts slide inexorably out of his corset.

Dennis and Skippy, meanwhile, are over by the punchbowl watching Ruprecht, who has somehow got talking to a girl.

'Is he the guy from *The Karate Kid*?' the girl is shouting over the music.

'He's Professor Emeritus of Physics at Stanford,' Ruprecht shouts back.

The girl looks utterly lost for a reply; after a few moments, she simply gives up and walks away. Ruprecht, who initiated the conversation only because the girl, dressed as a saucy waitress, was carrying a chocolate cake, which turned out to be fake, is un-fazed, and rejoins the others just as Mario trudges over with a grim expression.

'How's it going, Mario?' Dennis asks innocently.

'Pff, fuck these school-going girls.' Mario makes a dismissive gesture. 'In Italy, I prefer to date the girls who are in college – those who are nineteen, twenty, and have a good knowledge of sexual techniques. These girls, who are repressed and frigid, do not know which way is up.'

'They don't know much about science either,' Ruprecht adds.

'Also, what is with this music from days of Yore, that is badly cramping my style?'

Mario's not the only one asking. Over in the DJ booth, Wallace Willis has just segued from Led Zeppelin into 'All Right Now' and is so engrossed in Paul Kossoff's classic riff that at first he pays no attention to the irate voices emanating from somewhere below: 'Yo, cracker!' 'Hey, honky – yo, you jus' gonna ignore me?' Finally he realizes that the voices are addressing him, and peers over the side of the booth to see two smallish, disputatious-looking boys in trousers the size of refrigerators making inscrutable hand-gestures at him. 'That's right, nigga, we be talkin' to you!'

'Dang, G, what up wid dis music y'all playin?'

Wallace, who's dressed in a pristine white sailor-suit and holding an enormous lollipop, slides off his headphones. 'What?' he says.

'Nigga, this be the shit my dad listens to!' one of them says.

'Yeah, homes, what is it, *One Hundred Greatest Jeans Commercials*?' the other adds, waving a plastic machine-gun at him.

'This is Free,' he informs them.

'G, I don't care if it cost you fifty fuckin' dollars, put on som'in wi' *bass*!'

'Yeah, motherfucker, this ain't yo' Aunt Mabel's birthday party, play some hip-hop, dawg!'

'No requests,' Wallace says.

'You makin' a mistake,' one of the voices warns.

'The Acting Principal asked *me* to be the DJ,' Wallace replies primly, and replaces the headphones over his ears. The two bad-tempered gangstas, both of whom are, incontestably and in spite of their best efforts, white, lour at him a moment longer, and then abruptly disappear.

Midway through the next song – 'Hold the Line' by Toto – the sound cuts out. The crowd shuffles to a halt, and the hall is filled with a frazzle of consternation. It can't be the storm that's to blame this time, because the turntables are still lit up, and the disco lights still skirling over the now-static heads. There must be a connection loose somewhere. Wallace Willis casts about for grown-up assistance, but can't seem to locate Mr Fallon and Miss McIntyre. He unlatches the half-door to his booth, descends the steps and is stooping to examine the jumble of cables beneath it when the music starts up again. Everybody cheers and resumes dancing. But the song that is playing now is not the song that was playing a moment ago; in fact it is not a song that features in Wallace's music collection at all. Wait, he shouts, stop dancing, this is the wrong song! This is the wrong song! But nobody appears to hear him – they are too busy throwing gangsterish shapes and shaking their booty to the interloping song's extremely loud bass line . . .

Bass. It's only now that Wallace realizes what has happened. This is not a programming error, or a crossed wire, or a freak occurrence brought about by the storm. His sound system has been hijacked! By the boys with the giant trousers!

I'm a case of champagne and she's falled off the wagon / I'm slayin the ho like St George slayed the dragon . . .

Hunched over, he follows the wires in the hope of finding the point where the takeover has occurred. But it's so *dark*, and behaviour on the dancefloor is getting increasingly raucous, and after he has been bumped three or four times Wallace decides to concentrate instead on finding the teachers. Even after a full circuit of the hall, though, they are nowhere to be seen. Wallace begins to get worried. The unauthorized music is having a strange effect on people, making them shoutier, jumpier, and their dance moves decidedly more provocative. Things are in danger of getting out of hand. Where are the teachers? A terrible thought hits him. Are the wide-trousered boys behind this disappearance too? He remembers those Uzis slung around their necks – is the whole party now under the control of gun-toting, rap-loving gangstas?

'But it's for charity!' Wallace squeaks, out loud. No one hears. Picturing the two unfortunate teachers tied up in a closet somewhere, he hurries towards the back door, fighting his way through writhing bodies that, a moment ago, belonged to titchy piffling second-years, but now, as if bathed in some new colour of light, appear quite unfamiliar . . .

A group of boys has managed to fish down some of the black lost-soul-like balloons, unknotted their umbilici and sucked in their contents; now they are rapping over the bassline in voices squeaky with helium, like a chorus of gangsta rats. One of them, a Colonel Kilgore with a cheroot between his teeth and cheeks daubed with axle-grease, reaches into his fatigues and pulls out his phone: pressing a button to call up a message that reads:

LET ME IN

Strafing the dancers with his machine-gun, he moves towards the double-doors . . .

She gots the assitude / And I gots the latitude / We in-ex-tric-er-ab-ly linked, like heart attacks and fatty food . . .

The floor quivers with bass; the staticky, alien energy that had been buzzing about the edges of everything earlier in the night seems now to converge, infiltrating the space like an invisible gas.

'Hey, Skipford, look, your girlfriend is on her own!'

'Her friend ran off to get sick, you should go and talk to – hey, she's looking at us! Hallo there! Hey! That's right, over he– ow! What?'

'What the hell are you doing?'

'What's the problem? You want to talk to her, right? Do you want to talk to her or don't you?'

'Well, yeah, but not right this second . . .'

'Skippy, if you want to talk to her, I can now reveal to you a chat-up line that is one hundred per cent foolproof and fail-safe. It is something I have been developing for several months for personal use, but I will tell it to you because you are my friend, and I would rather see you nailing this hot bitch than Carl, who has spat in my lunch more times than I can count. So here it is: when I see a chick I want to score, I go up to her and say, Pardon me, you are stepping on my dick.'

Quizzical looks.

'Because my dick is so long, you see, that it comes all the way down my trousers and out onto the floor.'

Silence, and then: 'Let *me* give you some advice, Skippy – never, ever do anything Mario tells you. Ever.'

'Yeah, Skip, just go over and say hi, that's all you need to do.'

'Okay, well, maybe I'll just wait a little while and then . . .'

'Do it *now*, her friends will be back in a minute.'

'Yeah, or someone else'll make a move on her.'

'I feel nauseous . . .'

'True love,' Geoff says cheerfully.

'Come on, Skip, Carl's not here.'

'Juster, as your Acting Principal I order you to go over there and hit on that girl,' Dennis commands. 'That's more – hey, where's he going? Hey, she's over that way!'

Ruprecht waddles after his friend. 'What's wrong?'

'Get them to leave me alone. I don't want to talk to her now.'

'Why not?'

'I don't feel well. I can't breathe.'

'Hmm . . .' Ruprecht strokes his chin. He may never have been in love, but he knows all about not breathing. 'Perhaps you might find this helpful.' He presses something into his hand. Skippy looks down and just has time to recognize the blue tube of Ruprecht's asthma inhaler, before Dennis sneaks up behind him and shoves him with both hands, sending him careering into Frisbee Girl.

'Someone had to do something,' Dennis says querulously, in response to the accusing looks the others are giving him. 'He could have gone on mooning over this bimbo for ever.'

'I wonder if he's using my line,' Mario cranes his neck.

'I'm not sure he's saying *anything*,' Ruprecht bites his thumb pensively.

'It doesn't matter what he says to her,' Dennis says. 'Skippy and that girl are from two different worlds. It's like a fish trying to hit on a supermodel. That fish could have the best lines in the world, it wouldn't make any difference. It's still a fish, with, you know, scales and stuff.'

'So why did you push him into her?' Geoff demands.

'To bring him back to reality,' Dennis says self-righteously. 'The sooner he finds out the truth, the better. Hot girls like her don't go out with weedy losers. They just don't. That's the way it works.'

There is a meditative silence, then Geoff says, 'That's how it *usually* works. But maybe tonight is different.'

'Why the hell would tonight be any different, you anus?'

'Because of Hallowe'en.' Geoff turns his festering, Play-Doh visage to Dennis, and in his beyond-the-grave basso expands, '*The ancient feast of Samhain, when the gates between our world and the Otherworld are opened, and unholy spirits march unchecked through the land. All laws are suspended, and nothing is as it seems . . .*'

'Sure,' Dennis says, 'except tonight's not Hallowe'en, it's Friday 26 October.'

With a gasp, Ruprecht checks his watch and then, without a word of explanation, sprints for the side-door out to the corridor. Dennis, Mario and Geoff look at each other incredulously. No one has ever seen Ruprecht sprint before.

'Hmm,' Dennis says thoughtfully, 'I see what you mean,' and they return to observing Skippy with renewed interest.

So far, things have gone predictably badly. He crashed right into her, spilling half her drink, and now she's looking at him with a mixture of terror and contempt, the latter gaining the upper hand with every second he stands here twitching and blinking and not saying anything. But it's impossible to think! Up close she's even more beautiful, and every time she looks at him he feels like he's been hit by lightning.

'Uh, sorry,' he manages to croak at last.

'That's okay,' the girl says in a deeply ironic tone. She makes to move past him. Impulsively, he sidesteps into her path.

'Daniel,' he blurts. 'Uh, that's who I am.'

'O-*kay*,' the girl responds, and then when he doesn't get out of the way, with obvious reluctance, she says, 'Lori.'

'Lori,' he repeats, then falls back into the twitching, blinking silence. Behind the scenes, his brain, dashing around trying to put out the fires that have sprung up all over the place, shouts at him, *Say something else! Say something else!* But it does not tell him what, so he opens his mouth with no idea what's going to come out until he hears himself speak the words, 'Do you like . . . Yahtzee?'

'What's "Yahtzee"?' pronounced in a tone of pre-emptive disgust that could burn through metal.

'It's a game of skill and chance,' Skippy says miserably. 'Played with dice.'

The girl looks like if she were any more bored she would actually be dead. 'Do you have any drugs?' she says.

'I have an asthma inhaler,' he replies eagerly.

The girl just looks at him. 'Um,' he says. Inside his whole body groans in agony. He couldn't help it, it was right there in his hand! Now he stares at his shoes, from which one of the wings is coming off again, wishing the ground would swallow him up – when something else hits him. Scrambling off his quiver, he fishes down past the Arrows of Light – 'I have these.' He produces the tube breathlessly.

'What are they,' she says, without seeming too enthusiastic.

'They're, um, travel-sickness pills.'

'Travel-sickness pills?'

Skippy's head bobs mutely. She gazes at him as if urging him to complete the thought. 'But you're not going anywhere,' she says finally.

'No, but . . .' He wants to explain about the pills and how they take you away from where you are even though you're still there; but it sounds stupid even before he says it, and he tails off, sinking under the weight of his own foolishness. She is right, he isn't going anywhere. He has ruined everything for ever, there is no way he'll be able to wipe this from her memory. Now he just wants it to be over. 'No,' he says.

The girl is frowning, as though she's doing maths in her head. Then she says, 'What happens if you mix travel pills and asthma inhaler.'

'I don't know,' Skippy says. Glancing over his shoulder, her eyes suddenly fix and widen. Skippy turns too, and sees that the main doors have been opened. He's surprised, because when he checks his watch it's still only 9.45.

'This thing is totally lame,' the girl decides. 'I'm getting out of here.' And before Skippy can say anything, she is walking away, every step she takes a sledgehammer whomping his heart into little tiny pieces. Then she pauses, and over her shoulder, in the careless way you might speak to a stray dog you'd met in the park, she says, 'Coming?'

For some reason he starts babbling about how he thinks you have to ask permission before you can leave. But she's already halfway across the hall.

'Hey, wait up!' He comes to and chases after her, catching up with her as she enters the cloakroom; and side by side they step out into the night.

'Holy shit,' Dennis says.

'This Hallowe'en is powerful stuff,' Mario says. He reflects a moment. 'Perhaps these supernatural forces are also behind the mystery of my failure with the ladies tonight. If a born loser like Skippy can score a hottie-to-the-max like that, you know that some crazy shit is going down.'

Meanwhile, a long-limbed shadow is pushing through the crowd. Another reversal – this is a shadow for which people get out of the way. It rolls its eyes and gnashes its teeth, it seizes girls as it moves through the hall, pulling off masks and boring into their eyes before casting them aside – and now it catches sight of someone, blundering in tears in the opposite direction, her volu-minous dress slipping down her arms so it looks like she's escap-ing from an enormous pink-and-white jellyfish. It makes for her, grabs her wrist and pulls her into it. 'Where's your friend?' it demands. 'Lori, where is she?'

But the weeping girl just bursts out into fresh wailing. The shadow swears and goes back the way it came, shouldering people left and right in spite of the path that has opened up in front of it.

Howard and Miss McIntyre do not make it back to the Sports Hall by the end of the song. As soon as they pass through the door, they find themselves bewitched by the strangeness of the school at night. Its inky silence, its somnolence, make the familiar corridors feel like the underground chambers of a mausoleum, untrodden for centuries; Howard has to resist the temptation to yawp! hoot, jump around, shatter the echoey hush. Every step promises to take them deeper into uncharted terrain. Soon the music is only a distant murmur.

At last they shore up in the Geography Room. Overhead, thunder roars continuously, as though they are in the foundations of some celestial interchange, into which bodiless locomotives come crashing every instant. 'We'll have one quick drink and then we'll go back,' Miss McIntyre says. She searches through the carrier bags for the ingredients – apparently she was serious about the Cosmopolitans – while Howard, hands in his pockets, looks at the pictures on the walls. The Geography Room is covered from floor to ceiling with photographs, charts and illustrations. One wall is devoted to aerial shots of the Earth, wild weaves of colour that reveal themselves, when you read the text below, to be clouds around Everest, a rainbowed view of Patagonian ice-sheets, a hundred thousand flamingos in flight over a lake in Kenya, a blue faro of the Maldives. On another, pictures of happy banana-pickers in South America, happy miners in the Rhine-Ruhr Valley, happy tribes in their rainforests, rub shoulders with graphs depicting the CHIEF EXPORTS OF EUROPE, MINERALS AND THEIR USES, COLTAN – FROM THE CONGO TO YOUR PHONE! The room is like a shrine to the harmonious working of the world: a panoply of facts and processes, natural, scientific, agricultural, economic, all coexisting peacefully on its walls, while the human fallout from these interactions, the corollary of coercion, torture, enslavement that accompanies every dollar earned, every step towards alleged progress, is left for his class: History, the dark twin, the blood-shadow.

'I really like these volcanoes,' he says, stopping at the pictures by the door. 'You don't see enough volcanoes these days.'

'Vodka . . . cranberry juice . . . damn, there's something else . . .' Miss McIntyre says to herself. 'Sorry, what was that?'

'I was just remembering what you said before, about the Earth being forged out of all these grand forces . . . It's true, you look at these pictures and you realize we're walking through the set of this incredible epic they stopped filming a hundred million years ago . . .'

'Cointreau!' she exclaims and returns to the carrier bags. 'Cointreau, Cointreau . . . oh, to hell with it.' She takes a swig from the vodka bottle, and passes it to him. 'Come on, it'll warm you up.'

'Cheers, so,' he says. She makes a fist and playfully punches the base of the bottle. He drinks. The vodka burns all the way down to his stomach. 'I can't hear the music at all now,' he says to distract himself from the discomfort.

'We'll go back in a minute,' she says. She hops up on the teacher's desk and crosses her legs beneath her; from here she regards Howard mockingly, like an imp on a toadstool. 'So you're nostalgic for the Palaeozoic now, is that it?'

'Definitely quieter, these days. No new mountains, same old continents and oceans. Occasional earthquake kills a few thousand, that's as much drama as we get.'

She receives this with an amused smile, like someone holding a royal flush in a poker game for matchsticks. 'Dramatic things can still happen,' she says. 'All this, for a start.' She gestures behind her, at the blackboard, on which is written:

GLOBAL WARMING:

DEFORESTATION -> DESERTIFICATION
LOSS OF HABITATS -> DECREASE IN BIODIVERSITY ->
MASS EXTINCTION
RISING TEMPERATURES -> DROUGHT -> CROP FAILURE
POLAR ICE CAPS MELTING -> RISING SEAS -> FLOODING
DIVERSION OF GULF STREAM -> GLACIATION -> ICE AGE

'An ice age, that would be dramatic enough for most people, no? Or Dublin, London, New York being underwater?'

'That's true,' Howard says.

'Some scientists think we're already past the point of no return. They give the world as we know it another fifteen years. We could be the very last generations of the species.' She reels this off in a conversational tone, the same mischievous light flickering in her eyes, as if it's some rambling shaggy-dog joke, not for young ears. 'The boys take it *very* seriously. Recycling their Coke cans, using energy-efficient lightbulbs. Yesterday, they were all writing letters to the Chinese ambassador. The Chinese government want to build a dam in a UNESCO Heritage Site, it's going to destroy the homes of millions of people, including the Naxi – they're one of the world's last surviving matriarchies, Howard, did you know that? The boys were so angry! But most people seem to be able to let that stuff just slide over them.'

'They don't have you to inspire them,' Howard says.

'I suppose we can't really conceive of our way of life ever changing,' she says, ignoring his clunky flattery. 'Let alone coming to an end. It's just like the boys here doing stupid things – you know, climbing electricity pylons, jumping their skateboards off ten-foot walls – because they can't imagine getting hurt. They think they'll go on for ever. So do we. But nothing goes on for ever. Civilization ends, everything ends, that's what you teach them in History class, isn't it?'

She utters these words softly, like a lullaby. Her stockinged knee is rested against his thigh. The air seems to shoot with sparks.

'History teaches us that history teaches us nothing,' Howard remembers.

'That doesn't say much for history teachers, does it,' she whispers up at him.

Standing before her at the top of the class, Howard is aware, suddenly, of the empty rows of pupils' desks behind him, that nobody in the entire world knows where they are. 'You teach me something, so,' he goads her gently. 'Educate me.'

Her eyes wander ceilingward, as she makes a play of scaring up a thought; then, leaning forward, she confides in a whisper, 'I don't think you're in love with your girlfriend any more.'

This stings, but he keeps smiling. 'You can see into my heart now?'

'You're easy to read,' she says, tracing a fingertip over his face. 'It's all right here.'

'Well, maybe I can see into your heart too,' he retorts.

'Oh yeah? What do you see there?'

'I can see you want me to kiss you.'

She laughs coyly, and swings her legs off the desk. 'That's not what you see,' she says. She retreats to the far side of the room, smoothing down her dress. Then, in an amicable, impersonal voice, like a television interviewer putting a fresh question to her guest, she says, 'Tell me why you left the stock market to become a teacher. Did you suddenly feel the urge to do something meaningful? Had you become disillusioned with the pursuit of wealth?'

Howard understands that this is a hoop he must jump through; he has erred, and this conversation, artificial as it is, is now the only possible route back to what those lips seemed to promise a few seconds ago. He takes a moment to draw breath, consider his tactics, then, keeping his position by the desk, responds in the same pleasantly neutral tone, 'It was more that the pursuit of wealth became disillusioned with me.'

'Burnout,' she says expressionlessly.

Howard shrugs. He is realizing that this is still too sensitive for him to be ironic and offhand about.

'It happens,' she says. 'It's a stressful job. It's not for everybody.'

'The people whose money it was weren't so philosophical.'

'Is that why they call you Howard the Coward?'

'No.'

'Was it something to do with what happened in Dalkey Quarry?' Her eyes narrow in on him predatorily. 'The bungee jump? Where your friend got hurt?'

He just smiles.

'Were you the one who was supposed to jump, is that it?' She turns away, and continues, in the same bland TV interviewer voice, 'Haunted by your reputation, you failed at your job in London and came home, resolving to live a worthy but risk-free life. And so you became a history teacher.' She leans up against the door, her eyes gleaming at him through the shadows. 'Where you always know the ending, and nothing's ever going to jump out at you. Like walking through a set from an incredible epic that finished shooting years and years ago.'

It flashes through his mind that she might hate him; this doesn't seem an impediment to what they are about here. 'Different jobs suit different people,' he says amiably. 'You thought about being a teacher once.'

'I thought about being a lot of things,' she agrees. 'But I never had any vocation. You have to actively want to be a teacher. You don't have to actively want to be a consultant, because they pay you so much. They provide the motivation for you. It's much easier.'

'And yet here you are.'

She laughs. 'Yeah, well . . . I needed a change. Change is stimulating, don't you agree?' She has folded her hands behind her back, and angles her chin away from him. He takes a step towards her, as towards a dark precipice; his movements seem automatic, as if he is a character he is reading about in a story. 'Didn't someone say once,' she continues, 'that being bored is the one unforgivable sin?'

'I think it was being boring.'

'Same difference,' she says, resting her head back against the door. 'The world is so huge, so many things to do and see . . . And for us, in the West, with more money and power and freedom than any other people in *history* . . .' She shakes her head. 'To be bored is really a crime. It's an insult to everyone who doesn't have money and power and freedom.' She looks at him again. 'Don't you think we have a duty to do whatever it takes not to be bored?'

The last of these words are uttered into, and the rest of her philosophy lost inside, Howard's mouth. Her body twines around him; he pushes her against the blackboard, her pelvis mashing into his, the words WARMING DESERTIFICATION FLOODING EXTINCTION smeared into illegibility by her back. She bites his lips, her hands glide up his chest to grip his shoulders; she exhales involuntarily, a deep grunt, surprisingly masculine, as the heel of his hand grinds momentarily between her legs, then propels him backwards until he hits the teacher's desk. He climbs up on it, she climbs onto him. Outside, the storm has finally blossomed: it roars, howls, thrashes against the window like something out of the Palaeozoic, or an epic movie; and as the demonic machinery of hands, mouths, hips takes over, Howard, perhaps not quite at the level of consciousness, but some substratum just below it, finds himself back again, as he has been on so many days and nights, at the edge of a windswept rockface, in a half-ring of shadowed faces, a hand holding out to him a slip of paper on which is written his own name, like a scales weighing up his soul –

http://www.bbc.co.uk/science/goodmorningtomorrow.htm

We're very pleased to have PROFESSOR HIDEO TAMASHI *of Stanford University with us to answer your questions on parallel universes and the stranger-than-fiction world of M-theory . . .*

KRYSTAL: **You talk a lot about other dimensions that are too small for us to see. That doesn't make much sense.**

PROF TAMASHI: You're right, Krystal, it doesn't. Higher dimensions are counter-intuitive because our brains are biologically hard-wired to perceive the world around us as three dimensions of space plus one of time. However, four dimensions of space-time are not enough to explain the creation and make-up of the universe. We may not be able to see them, but higher dimensions, or hyperspace, allow us to explain phenomena that would otherwise remain a mystery. M-theory describes the movement of membranes through these dimensions, some very small, like particles, some very large, like universes. In this way it presents the possibility of a bridge between the subatomic world and the macro world.

BUSTA MOVE: **Where do these membranes come from?**

PROF TAMASHI: That's a good question, Busta. M-theory maintains that a multiverse consists of membrane-universes floating like bubbles in Nothing. Each bubble forms for free as a quantum fluctuation in Nothing. Universes may be created all the time in this way.

STANFORD BOUND: **Tamashi-san, it is a great honour to speak to you. My question is this: is it possible for a human being to travel through hyperspace to one of these proximate universes?**

PROF TAMASHI: Well, Stanford, Einstein's equations do permit the possibility of jumping into hyperspace through a wormhole to reach another universe. However, our present technology does not supply enough energy to open up such a wormhole.

STANFORD BOUND: **What about pre-existing gateways, e.g. black holes?**

PROF TAMASHI: According to the solutions we have for black holes at present, this is certainly a theory. The short answer is that we just don't know whether or not this would be possible. Perhaps it would lead into another universe. Alternatively, it might lead to a far-off region of this universe, or back into the past. Most likely you would not survive the journey, or if you did you would encounter serious problems getting back.

SKIPPY AND LORI: **What happens when you take asthma inhaler and travel pills?**

What happens is nothing for a little bit and then everything starts moving in slow motion e.g. when you step forward it takes for ever for your foot to touch the ground again and it feels like you might keep on continuing upwards and not come down at all like being on the moon! One great leap for man! you shout. Lori is behind you, she is laughing and laughing, everything has become very funny, the names of the chocolate bars stacked beside the checkout in Texaco, a man with a big nose walking his dog that also has a big nose, even the knackers in the village that stare at you in your costumes, it's like you've stepped out of a spacecraft from thousands of years in the future and you are walking around looking at arrow-heads and woolly mammoths. The feeling is like having a fuzzy forcefield round you that keeps you warm and also makes you laugh and you wonder is it the pills or the inhaler or is it her because she's there? Or is this really happening?

The park gates are closed so you jump over the wall and go down to the lake and sit on the swings there, you hoosh some more of Ruprecht's Ventalin, it feels so weird like doing a reverse sneeze! Then you push Lori on the swing then she pushes you because otherwise it wouldn't be fair she says then it starts to rain again and you both jam into one swing under one umbrella a black one that you found thrown into the bushes right outside the Sports Hall am I squashing you? she says it's okay you say. Lori's phone starts ringing, she takes it out and presses Ignore. It stops then immediately it starts again. Who is it? No one she says, she switches it off and then she digs around in her pockets and says we should try these too. All around the rain going ksssshhhhhhh-hccchhhhhhhhhhhhhboooom.

What are they?

They're called Ritalin?

What do they do?

I don't know.

Though she's got a whole pocket full of them. So you take one then two then three then you don't know but your head is going frrrrssshhhh every time you turn it like skis turning on snow like every time you blink it becomes this long voyage eighty days around the world and every time you open your eyes it's like in a different place only with Lori beside you every time you keep floating off into space and she keeps bringing you back let's have a rolling race she says but the grass is wet but anyway you roll down the hill you win no I win she says okay we both win you stand up but your head does not stop spinning you pull bits of grass off each other her hand stops in your hair your hand stops in her hair

and then you both run, you run and run, and then you are outside Ed's, you go inside and buy doughnuts and Cokes and sit down across the table from each other. What happens is that Lori is the most beautiful girl in the world, she is the most beautiful anything anywhere, more beautiful than the most beautiful painting, more beautiful than oceans sunsets dolphins glaciers. You want to tell her this but she is already trying not to giggle. Do you believe in flying saucers? she says. You go, Yes.

Because there is one . . . hovering . . . right . . . above . . . your . . . head . . . then she drops the doughnut on your head and you throw it at her and she throws it back at you and now you are throwing all your doughnuts at each other

Oh no they are invading Earth!

Resistance is useless!

and then the Chinese guy comes over and starts shouting and you realize everyone is looking at you and there are doughnuts everywhere but then outside the storm has stopped and patches of clear sky appear, great big holes of dark blue in the clouds like someone is tearing wrapping paper off a Christmas present and Lori says let's go for a walk so you walk up the road to the dual carriageway. Cars zip by you and electricity too invisibly to light up each of the lights and houses. Lori keeps trying to tell you this story about a friend of hers but then forgetting where she is and going back to the start. This is the best night of your life. Outside LA Nites bouncers in black jackets stare hard at IDs or bend down to kiss girls with stringy tops and thin legs. Up above the clouds are mostly gone, you notice one star twinkling right at you, when you see a star suddenly get bright like that it means it's a satellite and it's located you with its tracker beam. Lori goes, So what's with that costume anyway and you start telling her about *Hopeland* and Princess Hope and the three Demons Fire Ice and the one no one's ever seen and you're this guy Djed who's trying to find the magic weapons and save the Realm.

O-*kay* . . . she says. Do you like video games you say. No, she says. Hmm maybe shut up about that stuff for a little while. What about your costume? you ask her. Oh this is just something my mum picked up for me in New York? It's the dress ΒΕΤΉΑΝΙ wore to the Grammies. Wow, you mean the actual one she wore? She gives you a look like Hello? Um, no? It's just like a Marc Jacobs dress that costs eight hundred dollars. Oh right. Shit, Skippy, stop being such a spa! Do you like 𝔅𝔈𝔗ℌ𝔞𝔫𝔦? she says. Yes, you say. I *love* her, Lori says. You look quite like her, you say. Do you think so? Lori seems pleased. Definitely, you say, although 𝔅𝔈𝔗ℌ𝔞𝔫𝔦 is blonde and sort of a ho and Lori is five million times hotter. Some of my friends say that, she is saying. But my mom won't let me bleach my hair. What are your parents like? Are they on your case the whole time? Um. Out of nowhere the Game shrieks up at you! Well, sometimes. I don't see them that often, because I'm board-ing? Oh, right. That must be pretty shit, being stuck in school the whole time. Like what do you do for fun? Well, there's this guy Ruprecht. You start telling her about Ruprecht and his inventions. She likes this, she thinks it's funny. Okay so, crazy room-mate, she counts on her fingers, weird video games . . . do you ever do any-thing *normal*? Hmm. Do you? Swimming? you say. Oh yeah? Yeah and you tell her about the swim team and the races and the trophy you won. You won a trophy? she says. Yeah at this meet down in the country and after mid-term there's another meet somewhere else. That's amazing, she says. That's so cool. Yeah but I'm think-ing of quitting. Really, why would you want to quit? You shrug. Because I hate it. Suddenly you notice the sky is dark blue and waving and rushing and streaming like water, what's wrong with it? Wait a second it's you, you dope – quick turn your face in the other direction so she can't see. But she doesn't see, instead she says, I would love to be good at something like that. You brush your cheeks clear so you can turn to look at her. Why? Just to be really good at something, she says, I just think it would feel great. You're thinking, Why would she want to be good at something when she is *her*? When she is the most perfect thing that exists? But instead you say, You're good at frisbee.

How do you know that?

Everything freezes – the sky, the cars – You just . . . look like you would be?

I like frisbee, she agrees. But I'd love to be a singer, like a really brilliant singer. Maybe you should go on one of those shows? you say. I always get stage-fright, she says. She holds her arms, she looks up into the sky. It would just be nice to do something that made me feel special. You stop, you stare at her. You don't feel special?

Now she looks back at you. She smiles. *Most* of the time I don't feel special.

Your brain goes, *Holy shit You have to kiss her!!!*

I should probably go home, she says.

PROF TAMASHI: Our initial concept of the eleventh dimension was as a tranquil place, through which these membranes, these universes, floated gently, like clouds on a summer's day. It was a mystery to us how something like the Big Bang might have occurred from that scenario. And then one day I was speaking to my brother on the phone. We were recalling how as boys our father would take us to the harbour in Yokohama. My brother was very interested in ships at that time and it was common for US destroyers to dock there. These ships were huge, perhaps two hundred feet tall and in length equivalent to two or three city-blocks. But on one occasion we visited the docks and we saw a destroyer that had itself been half-destroyed. The whole front of the ship had been completely crushed, like a car that has hit a telegraph pole at high speed. What could have done that on the open seas? When we asked, we were told that it had been hit by a wave – one wave, which came out of nowhere, crushed in the bow and smashed everything right back to the bridge, causing more damage than all the weapons on the ship fired at once. At sea, rogue waves like that are known as 'white waves'. I asked myself, what if these 'white waves' exist in the higher dimensions too? What if the eleventh dimension was not a serene place, but a place of storms, with entire universes ripping through it like huge turbulent waves? Imagine the kind of cataclysm you'd have if one of these white-wave universes collided into another universe. I believe that the Big Bang is the aftermath of just such an encounter. Two membranes, two universes, smash into each other; the energy released is the Big Bang, which produces our universe. In this model, the problem of the singularity disappears. Universes may be colliding all the time, producing an infinite number of Big Bangs.

You are walking up the woodland avenue hand-in-hand. Above you the galaxies explode like slow fireworks. Beside you Lori is singing, a BETHani song, *If I had three wishes I would give away two, Cos I only need one, cos I only want you*, her voice sweet and fragile like a bird's. You turn up one road and down another, each one quieter and darker than the one before, the houses hidden behind walls and ivy. You are silent, listening to her sing, trying to think of something to make her not go home.

Tell me something, Daniel, she says after a while. Why are guys such assholes?

You think for a little bit. I don't know, you say.

I don't mean you, she says. You're not an asshole.

Thanks, you say. No, really.

I mean it, she says.

You stop outside a tall arched gate. Through the railings you can see a light set back among the trees. This is my house, she says.

Right, you say.

Do I look all right? she says. Like I don't look . . . ?

You look perfect, you say.

Will you be okay getting back?

Sure.

Okay. She taps a code into the intercom and the gates glide open to receive her. The moon is out, everything is silver, the cars in the distance go down the dual carriageway like breaths. You have no idea how to get from here to where you are kissing her, it is a chasm with no bridge across. Goodnight, then, she says.

Goodnight, you say with a dry mouth. With every second the chasm grows wider and your heart sinks lower as slowly you wake from her spell to the reality that this is over and soon everything that happened, her hand in your hand, the swings the park the doughnuts, all of it will be gone into the past and

and then she is kissing you, her arms are wrapped around you, her mouth minty and soft. You are so stunned that it takes you a moment to remember to kiss her back. You put your arms around her waist and push your lips against hers.

Have you ever kissed anyone before? she says.

Yes, you say, though only your mother and various aunts and not like this at all, but it doesn't seem to matter, because she is kissing you again, the tip of her tongue tracing sideways-8s on the tip of yours, sending you spinning and the whole sky and universe with you, and when she pulls away everything is still swimming, everywhere you look there are stars.

Okay, she says again.

Okay, you say through the dizziness and smiles and stars. So many stars, everywhere you look! They are coming from her, that's what's happening, swarming up out of her like friendly silver hornets, like they must have come spilling out of nothing when the Big Bang banged. Goodnight, Daniel, Lori says, as the gates close like arms around her, scooping her into them.

Goodnight, you say, not moving, smiling at the stars everywhere

      stars in her hair

                                  stars in her eyes

stars

             stars

  ★

                          ★

                  ★

II

Heartland

*People like us, who believe in physics, know that the distinction
between past, present and future is only a stubbornly persistent illusion.*

Albert Einstein

The phone rings shortly after dawn, the bland electronic tinkle exploding the quiet of the bedroom like a bomb blast. Howard, though he's been waiting for it all night, doesn't move; instead, deferring the moment until there is absolutely no way out, he lies with his eyes closed, listening to Halley's murmurous protest, the rustling crash of the sheets as she reaches over to the dresser. 'Hello . . . yes, Greg . . .' Her voice burrs with sleep, like her mouth is full of leaves. 'No, that's fine . . . no, sure, I'll just get him for you . . .' The bed creaks as she rolls back to him. 'It's for you,' she says. He opens his eyes to meet hers, just awoken, incandescently blue and bright, quizzing him.

'Thanks,' he says, taking the phone from her and turning away with it. 'Hello?'

'Howard?' the voice crackles tersely in his ear.

'Greg!' He tries to sound like this is a pleasant surprise.

'Howard, I want you in my office in exactly one hour.'

'Of course,' Howard says smilingly, and continues to smile as the line goes dead in his ear. 'See you then.' He swings his legs out of the bed and begins to put on his clothes, attempting to comport himself as though nothing is out of the ordinary. Halley props herself on her elbows, squinting against the day.

'Are you going *out*?' she says. In the morning light her bare breasts are like silver apples, the fruit of a fairy-tale land already disappearing out of his reach . . .

'Oh, yeah, did I not say? I promised I'd go and talk to Greg about the programme notes for this concert of his.'

'But it's Saturday.' She rubs her nose. 'And it's the *holidays*.'

Howard shrugs woodenly. 'You know what he's like. Everything has to be just right.'

'Okay,' she yawns, drawing the covers back up over her, claiming his abandoned share too. Her voice is muffled by eiderdown: 'I think it's good the way you're taking part in school activities more.'

'Yeah, well, you get out what you put in, don't you.' Howard buttons up his coat. 'I shouldn't be too long. Keep a spot for me.' He winks at her as he passes through the door, realizing as he does so that this is the first time he has winked in the whole span of their relationship.

The roads are eerily deserted, as though they have been cleared by decree to hasten his journey. A single car – Greg's – waits in the school car park; inside, the empty classrooms and corridors seem nothing more than an elaborate façade, a huge, byzantine foyer to the single occupied room. Mounting the stairs, every footstep clangorously echoing, Howard feels like some unfortunate in a Greek myth sent to do battle with the Minotaur.

Outside the Principal's office, on the bench known to generations as Death Row, Howard finds the lone figure of Brian 'Jeekers' Prendergast. He is chewing his nails and has a stranded look about him, as though he's been here for centuries, some minor fixture in a legend.

'Mr Costigan in there?' Howard points to the door; but before the boy can even reply, a voice comes booming from within, 'Get in here, Howard.'

Howard finds the Automator poised pugilistically in the dead centre of the room, as though ready to defend it against all comers. He is in his weekend wear – pale blue cotton shirt with a yellow sweater slung over the shoulders, beige slacks and brown Hush Puppies; it looks totally incongruous, like Godzilla in sweatpants.

'I'm afraid he's in a meeting at the moment, may I take a message?' Trudy, phone trapped between cheek and shoulder, leans and writes a name at the end of a list of names on the desk. 'Yes . . . we think a tummy bug is going round . . . Thank you, he'll call you later this morning . . .'

'Damn it,' the Automator mutters, pacing back and forth, scratching his jaw, and then, raising his voice, 'Well, damn it, Howard, sit down, man.'

Obediently, Howard seats himself on the other side of the desk from Trudy. The transformation in train on his last visit is now nearly complete: the high-backed African chairs have been replaced by ergonomic office models, and the aquarium by the door, where the multicoloured fish continue serenely to drift, oblivious to the changes, is now the only reminder of the room's previous incumbent.

'Would you like anything, Howard?' Trudy whispers solicitously. 'Tea? Coffee? Juice?'

'Damn it, Trudy, don't offer him juice! We have a very serious situation here!'

'Yes, dear,' she apologizes, setting down the phone, which immediately begins to ring again. 'Hello, Acting Principal's office?'

'Damn it,' the Automator repeats preparatorily, like a chainsaw warming up, and then, in a louder voice, 'Howard, what the hell? I mean – what in the name of God?'

'I –' Howard begins.

'In all my days as an educator, never once, not *once* have I witnessed anything that comes *close* to what I saw last night. Not *once*. Damn it – damn it, I put you in *charge*! Didn't I give you strict instructions as to – I mean, correct me if I'm wrong, one of those instructions wasn't to let the thing descend into a Roman orgy, was it?'

'N–'

'You're damn right it wasn't! And yet here we are with *this* on our hands –' he points to the phone '– parents ringing me all morning, wanting to know why little Johnny came home from an official supervised school Hop covered in puke and even more slack-jawed than usual! What do you think I should tell them, Howard? "You should have seen the shape he was in a half-hour before?" God damn it, do you have any clue what kind of a mess you've dropped us into here? I mean, what the hell happened in there?'

'I . . .'

'You don't know, of course, nobody knows, it's the Bermuda Triangle. Well, let me tell you something, Howard, *some*body knows, and when I find out, believe me, heads are going to roll. Because if those people –' pointing to the phone again '– my God, if they had any idea what actually happened . . .' He grasps at his hair, pacing back and forth distractedly like a deranged pastel-clad robot, then, taking a deep breath, comes to a stop in front of Howard. 'Okay,' he says. 'I suppose we're not going to get anywhere by flying off the handle. I'm not trying to pin this whole thing on you. All I'm looking for is an explanation. So you just tell me, in your own words, exactly what you saw last night.' He folds his arms and settles back against the sideboard, a vein twitching furiously in his forehead.

Twelve hours ago, Howard was lying supine on the teacher's desk in the Geography Room. From the wall the happy miners of the Rhine-Ruhr Valley grinned down at him, and looking back up at them, his head tilting back into empty space, Howard was half-dreaming he'd fallen down a mineshaft – or was it a trench, could they be soldiers, faces blackened for night-patrol . . . ? On top of him lay Miss McIntyre, her hands folded into him, her hair spilling over the floodplain of his chest, the borders of their bodies porous, liquid, indeterminate. The storm thundered at the window; intermittently, the room lit up with flashes of lightning so quick you couldn't be sure you hadn't imagined them; the last dregs of satiety buzzed through his blood like fortified wine. And then, with a sharp intake of breath, he felt her body stiffen against his, and before he could ask her what was wrong, he felt it too, the same irrefutable chill.

The drumbeat hit them as soon as they left the room, still scrabbling for buttons and zippers, and grew louder with every breathless hastening step down the deserted halls. Outside the door to the gym they found Wallace Willis, the Hop DJ, trembling from head to foot, with a look of grubby tearstained distress, like he'd spent three days locked in a drain. 'They're playing the wrong *songs*,' was all that he would say.

When they opened the gym door, the music was so deafening that for a moment it precluded any other sensation; but only for a moment, and then the full horror of the situation was upon them.

Discarded costumes strewed the floor. A Viking helmet, a gilt-trimmed bustier, a pirate's eyepatch, a pair of butterfly wings, as well as more conventional items such as trousers, T-shirts, stockings and undergarments – all lay blithely crushed beneath the feet of former wearers as they rocked in the bare flesh of each other's arms. Somehow, the invisible barriers separating them at the start of the night had come crashing down. Goths were with jocks, dweebs with bimbos, studs with skanks, blimps with waifs – everyone was with everyone, indistinguishable, propping each other up or collapsed in nearly naked heaps; as if the germ of Howard and Aurelie's secret moment in the Geography Room had been caught by an internal breeze and, as in some nightmar-ish morality tale, blown down here, where in the hothouse atmo-sphere it had grown ten feet tall and spread like a weed over everything, so that now wherever they looked they saw it repro-duced in monstrous, magnified form, stripped, in the lurid circus colours of the lights, of everything but mindless carnality.

'Oh my God,' Miss McIntyre crooned, in a voice cracking with self-disgust; Howard tried to think of something comforting or exculpating or purposeful to say, but found nothing.

The two of them did their best to restore order. But the kids simply didn't listen. It wasn't defiance; rather they seemed in a kind of erotic trance. They would stare, moon-eyed, at Howard, as he wagged his finger in their faces, threatened them with sus-pension, letters home, police, and then as soon as he had turned his back resume whatever it was he had interrupted.

'This is hopeless!' Miss McIntyre exclaimed, at the brink of tears.

'Well, what do you suggest we do?' Howard said, feverishly

gathering up a long coil of toilet paper at the end of which a priapic mummy was groping the breasts of a girl who, although standing upright, appeared to be asleep, a rainbowed shiver of fabric, once a mermaid's tail, lying balled at her feet. '*Stop* that!' He bundled the toilet paper into the mummy's hands. 'Here, cover yourself up, for God's sake!'

'We have to call Greg,' Miss McIntyre said.

'Are you out of your *mind*?'

'We have to – get *away* from me!' leaping, with a wail, from the extended paws of a mysterious pink rabbit.

'Surely we don't need to involve him . . . ?' Howard pleaded, though all the evidence pointed to the opposite.

But it was academic, because somehow the Automator was already there in the doorway. For a moment he did not move from it – looking on stony-faced as Dennis Hoey, shirt unbuttoned, tie flung back over his shoulder, staggered by him flapping his arms and raving hoarsely, 'Study your shirtsleeves! Tuck in those notes!' and over the PA a gangsta rapped:

I chop off your head bitch
And jizz on your grave –

Then he swung into action. Striding onto the dancefloor, sundering any couples he encountered by grabbing both parties by the neck and literally flinging them in opposite directions, the Acting Principal cut a path to the wall-mounted fusebox – of course, why hadn't Howard thought of that? Abruptly the music ceased; a moment later, the house-lights came up, and all but the most abandoned of the revellers paused, blinked, murmured to themselves uncertainly.

'All right!' the Automator bellowed over their heads. 'I want everyone lined up against that wall, this minute!'

The effect was not immediate, but some dim ember in their minds recognized his voice, and gradually they began to obey, stumbling and ragged in the bright light. In five minutes they were marshalled into a row, those not capable of standing kneeling or squatting on the floor, all gazing at the Automator with stuporous, unfocussed eyes. For a time he did nothing but stare, as if his fury was such he could not trust himself to speak. Then finally he said, 'I don't know what's got into you people tonight. But let me assure you of this, there are going to be repercussions. *Serious* repercussions.' Standing at his left hand, Howard cringed interiorly. 'It is now –' the Automator flourished his watch '– exactly twenty-two thirty-three and thirty seconds. In twenty-six and a half minutes, at twenty-three hundred hours, I am going to open those double-doors, and you are going to proceed directly to your parent or guardian. None of you will mention any aspect of what transpired here. If they ask, you will say that you had fun, but now you are feeling tired and would like to go to bed, good-night. What will you say?'

'Hahfuhhhtiguhnight,' the zombified horde mumbled piteously.

'Good. In a moment, I am going to direct you to put on your clothes. At my word, I want you in blocks of ten, starting at this end with you, giant ant, to make your way in an orderly fashion to your costume. In the event that you cannot find your –'

He stopped. Near the door a very thin girl dressed only in an olive-drab brassiere and khaki cut-offs had stumbled out of the line, clutching her stomach.

'*At my word*, missy,' the Automator said. But the girl paid no attention: instead, doubled up, she emitted a long, painful moan. There was a loud shuffling noise as her two hundred peers adjusted their position to get a better look. The girl coughed delicately, as though about to make an announcement, and then – after a moment at once infinitely prolonged and inexorably doomed – the inevitable multicoloured torrent came gushing from her mouth.

'*Eeeeewwwwwwww!*' the zombies exclaimed in revulsion.

'Stop that!' the Automator commanded. But she could not stop, and the hall filled instantly with the acrid miasma of stomach acid and alcohol and too-sweet fruit punch. Along the line, mouths bulged; chests lurched. 'All right, maybe we should get some fresh air,' the Automator said hurriedly. 'Howard, open the –'

But it was too late. First at intervals, then, in seconds, en masse, with a noise like nothing Howard had ever heard before, what seemed like all two hundred teenagers were throwing up: pale, half-naked bodies in various attitudes of expulsion, a vast and hellish deluge washing over the floor . . .

'So much vomit,' the Automator recollects now, from the safety of his office.

'Yeah,' Howard says miserably. He was the one who mopped most of it up: two hours with an aching back, the Automator grim and unspeaking at the other end of the hall, a solitary black balloon the only other company, Miss McIntyre having gone home ashen-faced and wordless shortly after they'd discharged the kids, leaving him, as the clock tower tolled one, to climb into his car alone and drive in complicated elaborations of circles through the darkened suburbs for another hour, till he could be absolutely sure that Halley would be gone to bed, and then sit in the kitchen reeking of disinfectant in front of an undrunk glass of water as the panelled surroundings, at once familiar and secretly changed, sparkled at him complicitly; he lowered his head like he didn't know what they meant.

'I don't know what happened, Greg,' he says as sincerely as he can. 'They just suddenly seemed to . . . transform. I can't explain it. I don't know if there even is an explanation.'

'There's always an explanation, Howard. In this case the explanation is that the punch was spiked.'

'Spiked?'

'Punch'd turned blue, meaning probably sleeping pills of some kind, your standard date-rape set-up.' The Automator examines his nails thoughtfully. 'The results aren't back from the lab yet, but from the symptoms – loss of inhibitions and motor control followed by acute nausea – my guess is a large quantity of benzo-diazepine.'

'Back from the . . . ?'

'Couple of old boys working on the force, Howard. Simon Stevens, class of '85, Tom Smith, class of '91 – you might remember Smithy, couple of years ahead of you, decent prop-forward, lot of potential but never quite made the cut. Got them on the case this morning. Had to. All it takes is for one parent to figure out what happened in there and it'll be raining lawsuits. And when it does we'd better be ready.' He turns on his heel and circumnavigates the room, tapping thoughtfully at his lower lip. 'I've spoken to the boy in charge of the punchbowl but I don't think he has anything to do with it. Most likely someone distracted him while his partner slipped the mickey into the vat. What with the disco lights the colour-change wouldn't have been noticed. Though frankly some of these kids, first whiff they got the punch wasn't kosher they'd be queuing round the block for it. That doesn't explain how, with two supervisors in the room, the situation escalated to the level it did.' He wheels round: his gimlet eyes, and Trudy's doe-like ones, fix on Howard. 'How was that possible, Howard,' he says.

'It just seemed to . . . happen,' Howard says in a strangulated voice. The Automator waits without responding, and then says, 'When Wallace Willis called me, he said that you and Miss McIntyre did not appear to be in the hall.'

'Oh yes . . . that is . . .' Howard stutters, and then, as though it has just occurred to him, 'well, Miss McIntyre and I did both briefly leave the hall at one point.'

'You did?'

'Yes, we did, briefly.'

'Uh-huh.' The Automator scratches his ear, and then roars, 'God damn it, Howard, what the hell were you thinking? Rule one of education: never leave the kids unattended for a second, not for a *second*! I specifically told you, someone in the room at all times – damn it, there's your lawsuit right there! Flagrant neglect of duty! Flagrant!' The vein is back, hammering a tattoo in his temple.

'I know,' Howard wheedles, 'but what happened was, you see, Aurelie, Miss McIntyre, discovered a large quantity of alcohol in the toilets, too much for her to carry, and we wanted to store it out of harm's way, so we briefly went to the Geography Room, because that seemed like the safest place . . .'

'And how long were you briefly gone for, would you say?' The Automator's gaze bores into Howard; Howard uplifts his eyes to the ceiling, as if for inspiration: 'Um . . .' He squeezes them tight shut, then half-opens just one. 'Ten minutes?'

The stare has not gone away. 'Ten minutes?'

Cold sweat breaks out under his collar. 'Roughly that, I would say, yes.'

The steely eyes narrow – and then are averted. 'Yes, that's pretty much what Aurelie said – Trudy?'

Trudy leafs through a manila folder: 'That's what I have here – confiscated alcohol from girls' toilet, left to store in Geography Room, gone ten to twelve minutes.'

'Although it sounds like you and Aurelie have overestimated slightly, because Trudy and I timed it and it takes just under four minutes for a person walking at average speed to get from the hall to the Geography Room, and four minutes back is eight minutes,' the Automator comments.

This information, however, and the good fortune of Miss McIntyre's lie corroborating his, are drowned out by the mention of her name. 'She was here? Aurelie – I mean, Miss McIntyre?'

'First thing this morning.' The Automator wags his head solemnly. 'Whole thing has shaken her up pretty badly. She's an investment banker, she's not used to that kind of unbridled depravity.'

Howard descends into a momentary reverie of Aurelie unbridled, bare, on the other side of those twelve tumultuous hours, and wonders, at the same moment that his stomach churns with guilt, just how he can recross them, get back to her.

'Let's call it ten minutes,' the Automator resumes. 'Whatever our doper used, it must have packed a heck of a wallop for the effects to take hold that quickly. A *heck* of a wallop.' He rounds on Howard, who looks back with a gesture of helpless imbecility. 'Well, the boys in the lab will be able to clear that up for us. The bigger question is, who's responsible?' He picks up a paperweight from his desk, roughly the size of a hockey puck and vaguely weapon-like. 'I think we both know the answer to that one. This has Juster's fingerprints all over it.'

'Juster?' Howard wakes abruptly from his Aurelie-reverie. 'You mean Daniel Juster?'

'You're darn right I mean him, Slippy or Snippy or whatever he wants to call himself.'

'But what . . . I mean, what does he have to do with it?'

'Well, damn it, Howard, do I have to draw you a picture? Just look at the facts. One week ago we have this kid, in contravention of all classroom protocol, throwing up in his French lesson. Next thing we know, an ordinary school Hop turns into a mass vomiting spree. The connection's unavoidable.'

Perhaps it is, but Howard's brain is struggling to make it. 'I really don't see Juster drugging the punch, Greg,' he says. 'I just don't think he has it in him.'

'Okay, Howard. To me the vomiting seems incontrovertible. But I'm going to let you play devil's advocate. God knows we don't want Juster's parents dragging us into court either. Try this on for size, then. We've definitely placed Juster at the Hop last night. Father Green remembers him arriving. But when I lined the kids up against the wall, guess who wasn't there, Howard? Guess who'd already made his exit?' He bounces the paperweight up and down on his palm, and continues theatrically, 'But maybe I'm jumping to conclusions. Maybe he just went to bed early. Maybe he came to you and asked for special permission to leave. Did he do that, Howard? You were in charge of the door. Do you remember him asking your special permission to leave?'

'No,' Howard admits.

'So already we've got him breaking one of the house rules, viz. leaving without notifying a supervisor. What's to stop him breaking another? Breaking all of them? It's open and shut, Howard. Open and shut.'

That the Automator has a scapegoat for this debacle is certainly good news for Howard; at the same time, something seems not quite right with this version of events. He struggles to marshal his thoughts against the crashing guilt-hangover that tugs him floorwards like a massive psychic drain – and then he remembers. 'Greg, Carl Cullen tried to get into the Sports Hall last night. He knocked on the main door around 9 p.m. He seemed . . . agitated.'

'Did you let him in?'

'No, it was after the curfew so I turned him away.'

'Then I don't see what he has to do with our situation, Howard, if you didn't let him in.'

'Well, what if he didn't go home? What if he, you know, if he decided to take revenge – sneak in and . . . and do this?'

The Automator stares at the floor for a long time. Trudy gazes at him, her pen poised over the page for the moment he recommences speaking. 'You say you sent Carl away at what time?'

'Around nine.'

'And you left for the Geography Room at what time?'

'Maybe . . . half past nine?'

'So, would he have had time to go home, load up on dope and come back here in that time,' the Automator muses. 'Yes, he would. But that's assuming he knew you'd go off on your little excursion and leave the hall unsupervised, which he didn't. Even if he had the mickey with him from the get-go, would he have hung around outside on the off-chance he'd somehow get in? For a half-hour? In the rain? The boy's wild, but he's not a masochist. No, this smells to me like an inside job. Someone watching you all night, waiting for his opportunity. He doesn't need much time. A few seconds, that's all it takes. The moment you step outside, he makes his move. Maybe even before you step outside. Either way, he makes the drop, then he's out of there, home free.'

'But there's no proof it was Juster,' Howard argues, knowing that it is futile. 'I mean, it could have been anyone in that room, couldn't it?'

'Well, sure, it could have been anyone. It could have been mischievous pixies. It could have been the Man in the Moon. But all the available facts are pointing to this kid Juster.'

'But why –'

'Exactly, Howard! Why? That's what we have to get to the bottom of.' He taps the ballpoint pen against his teeth. 'You get any change out of him when you talked to him?'

'Well . . . uh . . .'

'You *did* talk to him?'

'Of course, yes . . .'

'And? He give anything away? You get any kind of a fix on where he's coming from?'

Howard claws frantically through his memory of his encounter with Skippy, but cannot remember a single thing the boy said; only Miss McIntyre's hand on his arm, her perfume in his nostrils, her teasing smile. 'Well, uh . . . he largely just seemed like a fairly normal young . . .'

'Maybe you should just tell me verbatim what he said to you – Trudy, are you getting this?'

'Yes, Greg.' Trudy's pen hovers expectantly over the pad.

'Hmm . . .' Howard frowns effortfully. 'Well, the thing is, it was less of an actual formal conversation, and more a sort of a . . . letting him know the door was open? So that if in the future he had any problems, he could –'

'*If* he had . . . ?' the Automator splutters. He bangs his palm on the desk, as though to jog himself back into motion. 'Jesus H Christ, Howard, we *know* he has problems! Any kid throws up all over his pals in French class, yes, he has problems! The whole point is that you were supposed to find out what those problems *were*! To avoid exactly the kind of scenario we're looking at now!' He sinks heavily into one of the new swivel-chairs, pressing the peak of his steepled fingers to his forehead, and issues a sigh that sounds like a sheet of flame crisping everything in its path.

'Well, why don't I go back to him?' Howard says hastily. 'I'll talk to him again, and this time I promise I'll find out what's wrong with him.'

'Too late for that,' the Automator mumbles into his hand. Then, spinning in the chair, 'Time to send in the big guns – Trudy, make an appointment for Juster with the guidance counsellor, as soon as he gets back. Father Foley'll get to the bottom of this.' He gets up and goes to the window, his back to Howard, his hand on the beaded cord of the Venetian blind.

'Have you had a chance to, ah, speak to Juster?' Howard asks huskily.

'We did have a very brief chat last night, while you were at your janitorial duties,' the answer comes, dripping with false brightness. 'Found him upstairs brushing his teeth. All innocence. Told me he hadn't been feeling well, so he'd gone out for a walk. The door was open, he said, so he thought it was all right. Didn't know anything about anything.' The light greys as the louvres of the blind close, and brightens as they part again. 'A nice little walk, all on his own, in the middle of winter, dressed like a goddamn hobbit. Kid might as well have given me the finger. The bitch of it is, I've got no one to gainsay him. No one can remember a single thing that happened. Some kind of anterograde amnesia brought on by the mickey, maybe. Or maybe this Slippy of yours got to them first.'

For a long moment there is only the dimming and brightening of light, the blind pulley squeaking in the Automator's hand. And then: 'I might as well tell you that this collective memory loss has probably saved your ass as well.'

Howard starts. Squeak, squeak, goes the pulley. Trudy's attentions are fixed deferentially on the manila pad, as though this part of the conversation is not for her ears. Impassive, the Automator's silhouette fades and resolves. Howard begins to speak but stops, feels his shirt cling clammily to his back.

'You like fish, Howard?' The Acting Principal leaves the window abruptly and crosses the floor to the aquarium.

'Do I *like* them?' Howard stammers.

'Old man used to sit up here half the day, watching the damn fish float around. Never saw the point of them myself. Fundamentally useless creatures.' Crouching down, he snaps his fingers at one of the brilliant shapes that float tranquilly inside the tank. 'Look at that. No idea what's going on. In this office twenty-four seven, doesn't know me from a hole in the wall.' Turning to Howard again: 'You know the difference between humans and fish, Howard?'

'They have gills?'

'That's one difference. But there's another difference, a more important difference. See if you can spot it. Come on, take a look.' Obediently Howard rises from his chair and studies the variously sized fish in their heated limbo. He can hear the Automator breathing behind him. The fish flap their fins, placid and inscrutable.

'I can't see it, Greg,' he says eventually.

'Of course you can't. Teamwork, Howard. That's what the difference is. Fish aren't team players. Look at them. There's no system at work there. They're not even talking to each other. How are they going to get anything done, you may ask? Answer: they're not. What you see right there is fish at the height of their game. I've been watching them for a month now and that's pretty much as far as it goes.'

'Right.' Howard feels like he is being assailed from all sides by an invisible enemy.

'Might ask yourself what place they have in an educational institution. They don't seem to have much to teach us. And by the same token, we don't have much to teach them. Can't educate a fish, Howard. Can't *mould* a fish. Mammals, your dogs, cats, beavers, even mice, they can be trained. They know how to play ball. They're willing to play their part and work towards the greater good. Fish are different. They're intransigent. Loners, solipsists.' He taps on the glass, again to no response; and then he says, 'You screwed up last night, Howard. I don't know how much, maybe I'll never know. But it's opened my eyes.'

Howard flushes. From the desk, he catches Trudy gazing at him with an expression of profound pity and compassion; quickly she reverts to the manila pad.

'I had you pegged for a team player. Now I'm wondering if you aren't more like one of these fish. You'd like to just float around on your own in the water, daydreaming. No law against that, you'll say. True enough. But a fish isn't much use to us here in Seabrook College. At Seabrook College, we're interested in getting things done. We have goals to achieve, goals of academic and sporting excellence. We work together, we think things through. We're mammals, Howard. Mammals, not fish.'

'I'm a mammal, Greg,' Howard hastens to assure him.

'Can't just say you're a mammal, Howard. Being a mammal is about what you *do*. It's reflected in the smallest of your actions. And the feeling I'm getting from you is that you haven't decided either way.' He straightens up, looks Howard in the eye. 'Over the course of this mid-term break I want you to have a good hard think about where you're going. Because either you start acting like a mammal and become part of the team. Or else maybe it's time you found a new aquarium. Do I make myself clear?'

'Yes, Greg.' *Clear* might be the wrong word; but Howard understands that he will walk out of the office with his job intact. A wave of relief rides through him as the spectre of a long, explanatory conversation with Halley recedes, for now, into the distance.

'Okay, get out of here.' The Automator goes to his desk and lifts the sheet of paper with the list of names.

'Good morning, Acting Principal's office,' Trudy says to the phone, and Howard thinks he detects a thankfulness in her voice too.

Brian 'Jeekers' Prendergast is still perched on the edge of the bench outside the office with the same expression of incipient doom. 'Hasn't the Dean spoken to you already?' Howard says.

'He told me to wait,' Jeekers says quaveringly.

Howard bends down, puts his hands on his thighs. 'What happened last night?' he asks in a lowered voice. 'Did you see who got to the punch?'

The boy does not respond: he merely gazes back at him blankly, lips pressed together, as if Howard has uttered a string of nonsensical words.

'It doesn't matter,' Howard says. 'See you next week.' And he clatters away down the stairs.

As soon as you open the door you can tell something's wrong. It looks like just an ordinary room but then you notice smoke coming up from the floor – you jump back just in time as the black tail slices up through the flagstones, and then the Demon comes billowing out of the hole! It rises in a cloud until it's almost taken up the whole room, coiled above you like a shroud of smog over a city, and already everything around you is on fire! Even with the amulet your energy is starting to plummet, you have no idea how to fight it – all you can do is raise your shield, dive forward with the Sword of Songs –

Danny? You in there, pal?

Yeah, come on in.

Dad comes through the door. What're you up to, sport? Oh, you brought the machine back, did you?

Yeah, I didn't want to leave it in school.

What's the game? Is this a new one?

Hopeland.

Hopeland, still? Didn't you get that last Christmas?

It's hard. But I've nearly finished it.

Good for you! But, dinner's ready, so . . .

Oh, okay . . . Skippy hits Pause and gets up from the floor.

In the kitchen pouring a glass of water at the sink. The condensation makes the garden look like it's disappearing in fog. Dad takes two smoking pieces of meat from the grill and puts them on plates. Okay! he says. Chicken à la Dad.

Smells great.

Well – Dad spoons out rice from the rice-cooker, then sauce from a saucepan – I guess we're working on the principle that whatever doesn't kill us makes us stronger. He laughs. Then he stops laughing.

Back at home, with the two of them together all day, the Game Skippy and Dad are playing becomes a lot harder. With it right there in the room with them it would be so easy to let something slip! So what they have done is invent a code. The way you use this code is to replace almost all words with the word *great*. A typical coded conversation might go like this:

So how's the swimming, sport?

Oh, great, it's going great.

That's great! When's the next meet?

It's in Ballinasloe, in two weeks?

That's the semi-final, right?

Yeah, it'll be harder than last time but Coach thinks we've got a great shot.

Did he say that? Wow – great! That's great!

By now they are real pros, no one who was listening in on them would ever think there was anything wrong. Sometimes because they are so good at it Skippy almost even likes the Game. It's like a very precious, very fragile cargo that he and Dad are carrying through the jungle; or it's a house and they're creeping through it like spies late at night. But sometimes it is like the air is made of glass and he has waited so long for it to shatter that he starts wanting it to shatter! He wants to scream and shout so it falls to a million pieces! Does Dad feel that way too? He wonders sometimes, but of course it would be against the rules of the Game to ask him.

He doesn't know how you are supposed to win the Game.

The clock ticks on the wall. Skippy listens to Dad's knife scrape against the plate, the chicken exploding between his teeth. He looks at the scrape-shaped film of brown sauce on the plate. Dad chews and says, How about we give your sister a call?

Okay, Skippy says.

But immediately he worries. Nina is really bad at the Game. There are too many rules, she is too small to understand them, she keeps crying or saying things.

Tonight, after she's talked to Dad, she tells Skippy she wants to talk to Mummy. Hey, what do you call a girl in an ambulance? Skippy says. Ni-na, Ni-na, Ni-na! Normally she thinks this is funny. But tonight she doesn't. I want to talk to Mummy, she says.

You can't, he says.

Why not?

She's asleep, Skippy says, looking at Dad. Dad is gazing at the plug socket by the back door.

Wake her up.

I can't wake her up.

Why not?

You know why not.

I want Mummy.

Skippy is getting angry. Why can she not understand the Game? Why does she think she's outside the rules? Stop being an asshole, he says.

What? Nina says. Beside him, Dad stirs to life.

Asshole, you're an asshole! Skippy shouts.

Nina starts to cry, which makes him even angrier, because even from Aunt Greta's she is ruining the entire Game! But you have got to hand it to Dad, he always stays cool. Shh shh, he says, putting a hand on Skippy's shoulder. Let me have another quick word with her, there, will you, sport? Skippy passes him the handset.

Hi, honey . . . I know, he's, but . . . no, it's not nice, but listen, I forgot to ask you something, did you get the present Mummy sent you? I know, but she's asleep, but did you get it? Oh well, I bet it'll come tomorrow . . . What? I can't tell you, she wants it to be a surprise . . . shh, I know . . . well, you can have fun with Aunt Greta too, can't you?

While Dad is talking, Skippy gives Dogley his dinner. He breaks brown gristly lumps into the bowl. Chomp, chomp, goes Dogley, his head down. Afterwards Dad turns on the football. From the corner of his eye Skippy watches him watching the white dot zip over the green field between the different-coloured men, his face emptied out, his hand plucking emptily at the arm of the armchair, rolling together little balls of fuzz then pulling them free.

At the station the tube of pills fell out of his coat as he was getting into the car. What's this, sport? Oh yeah, they're travel pills Coach gave me. Travel pills? Yeah, um, because coming back after the swim meet that time I felt really crap? Hmm, you don't normally get carsick. Yeah, it was weird. Could have been just the excitement, I suppose. Yeah, probably. Or you swallowed too much water! Yeah!

They burst through the front door in a flurry of bags and laughter, but thinking back on it now, Skippy can't remember what they were laughing about, or if they were laughing at anything. Inside the stairs were everywhere. They angled upwards and around and in upon themselves. Dad stood at the foot of them. Why not go up and tell Mum you're here? Skippy hesitated and examined Dad's face, it was like a face torn out of a magazine. Go on, she's been expecting you all day. Okay. Skippy climbed the thousands of angling stairs, towards the door that waited at the top.

YOU HAVE DEFEATED THE FIRE DEMON, DJED! It's the owl, the one you cut out of the spiderweb in the Mournful Woods! BUT THERE IS NOT A SECOND TO SPARE! WITH EVERY HOUR, MINDELORE GROWS MORE POWERFUL. IN HIS VILE LABORATORY, DEEP UNDERGROUND IN THE SOUTHERN LANDS, HE LABOURS NIGHT AND DAY TO CREATE HIS FOUL MONSTERS. SOON, HE WILL HAVE RAISED SUCH AN ARMY THAT HE WILL BE INVINCIBLE! YOU ARE THE ONLY ONE WHO CAN STOP HIM! YOU ARE OUR LAST HOPE! The owl's head swivels to the left, and when it returns to you its tawny eyes are full of tears. THE REALM IS DYING, DJED. THE EARTH HAS TURNED TO POISON, THE RIVERS AND LAKES TO ICE, THE AIR TO FIRE THAT CHOKES ALL WHO BREATHE IT. THE DOOM WE FACE IS DARKER THAN ANYTHING WE IMAGINED. SOON HOPELAND ITSELF WILL BE NO MORE, AND MINDELORE WILL CROWN HIMSELF KING OF THE NOTHINGNESS THAT REMAINS. SAVE THE PRINCESS, DJED! MAKE HASTE!

Doing push-ups in your room. Posters all around you, footballers, rappers, superheroes, bands. Swimming star Michael Phelps, the youngest man ever to break a world record (aged fifteen years, nine months). The *Star Wars* duvet and all your old toys on the shelves, Lego, Boglins, Zoids. You feel like you're camped out in the room of another boy. You feel like the replacement boy they've got in after something awful happened. You move through the house as if you've been programmed with information about it.

The kitchen radio pops and frazzles every time you cross its path.

The magpies chatter like machine-guns, their claws scrape on the shed's tin roof.

The drain refilled every morning with worn-out grey hairs.

Dad holds the book but never turns the page.

And the door stays closed all day.

You got a sec, Danny? I need to talk to you about something.

Sure thing, Dad.

This came this morning. Dad waves a pink slip of paper in his left hand. It's Skippy's mid-term progress card.

Oh.

Yeah, we need to have a talk about it. I mean, we should probably have a talk anyway, shouldn't we.

They sit down at the table. Dad grips the underside of his chair and turns it diagonally so he's facing Skippy. This close, he seems very big, a bear crammed into a kitchen chair. His breath smells of whiskey. Skippy sits very still and peeks sideways at the card lying next to them on the table. A line of C's and D's, and at the bottom in someone's slapdash grown-up writing, probably the Automator's, *Disappointing – must try harder.*

First of all – is there anything you'd like to say about these grades, Danny?

Well . . . no . . . I mean, they're disappointing.

No, I mean, I'm wondering if there's some reason, like if they gave the tests that time when you were sick?

No. Dad's eyes pour into his. He tries to think of something else to say. I'm sorry, he says. I suppose I'll just have to try harder.

Dad exhales. It's the wrong answer. What I'm wondering is . . . he says. Obviously what I'm wondering is, are you having difficulty concentrating at the moment? Are you finding it hard to focus on this stuff?

Hmm. Skippy makes a carefully-thinking-it-over face. No, not really. No, I wouldn't say so.

You haven't found you've got too much on your mind to . . . ?

No – Skippy sounds like he's surprised by the question. No, nothing like that.

And yet these grades are way down.

Skippy looks at Dogley, telepathically trying to call him over.

You're not on trial here, sport. I'm just trying to find out, you know . . .

Skippy takes a deep breath. Well, maybe it's just taking me a while to settle into senior school. I think I just need to settle in more, and try harder.

Dad stares at him. The sour tang of whiskey, the metallic hum of the refrigerator. That's it?

Mm-hmm, Skippy nods firmly.

Dad sighs and looks off to the left. Danny . . . in certain situations . . . well, let me put it this way, in my own work, personally speaking, I can find it difficult at the moment to, to *care* about what I'm doing. I was wondering if you felt that at all.

Skippy's eyes smart with tears. What is Dad trying to do here? Why is he trying to catch him out? He does not reply, blinks at him to say, *What?*

It's not the grades that bother me, sport – Dad doesn't notice – it's more the thought that you might be feeling like . . . His clasped hands dip between his knees like the head of a dead bird; then in a new voice, he says, I suppose what I'm thinking is, maybe we made a mistake in our original plan. Maybe we didn't foresee quite how – how long it would take for things to pan out. Don't you think it might make more sense if we arranged for some kind of – if I spoke to your Mr Costigan and said to him, Well, here's our situation, just so you're aware.

Dad, what are you doing? What about the Game! Don't you know what happens when you talk about it? Don't you remember what happened last time?

I know you said you didn't want to do that. And obviously I'm going to respect that decision. I'm just wondering if it's something you've thought about since. Just as something that might take the pressure off you a little bit?

Skippy keeps his mouth tight shut, slowly shakes his head.

You're sure? Dad's eyebrow raised, pleading.

Skippy nods, just as slowly.

Dad drags his hands over his face. I just hate to think of you, off at Seabrook . . . I mean . . . we want you to be happy, if you can, Danny, that's what we want.

I am happy, Dad.

Sure. Okay. I know that.

Hold tight to your chair, wait for it to end. The pills in the drawer in your room.

Okay. Dad throws his hands up. I guess we'll just see how it goes, then. He smiles mirthlessly. End of interrogation, he says.

You get up to go. Inside you feel cold, hollow, like a ruined castle with the wind gusting through it *whhhhssssshhhhhhhwhhhhhhhhhhhshhhhhhhhhh.*

Hey – I was thinking of going for a swim tomorrow after work, down to the pool, you interested?

Hmm . . . no, I'm okay, thanks.

You don't need to practise for the race?

No, Coach said it wasn't so important.

Really?

Yeah, actually he said we should take a break from it. I might take Dogley for a walk. Come on, boy. He swings the collar and lead over him and Dogley reluctantly rises from his bed.

Nights are the worst. Outside the fireworks explode like cluster bombs; through the walls the cries are like missiles screaming into your heart. But in the secret compartment of memory where Frisbee Girl is waiting, everything's just like it was. Her hands, her hair, her eyes, her voice, singing her secret song – the moment picks you up and swirls you into it; you lose yourself again in her sideways-8s, and everything real fades away to a dream.

That week of mid-term is the longest of Howard's life. The house has never seemed so small, so confining – like an underground bunker, shared with a ricocheting bullet that zings off the walls night and day, hour after hour. His teeth ache from smiling vacantly; his muscles throb from maintaining his meticulously arranged slouch on the sofa; everyday conversation is like juggling fire, Halley's most basic inquiry – *Are we out of milk?* – setting off a mental pandemonium, every synapse blazing in the panic to construct a reply before the delay becomes obvious. By the second day, he is fantasizing about throwing himself at her feet, confessing everything, simply to bring an end to this exhausting assault on his nerves.

Then he discovers an escape route. Thinking he'd better avoid antagonizing the Automator any further, he goes into the school library Monday morning and borrows a couple of books on Seabrook history as research for his piece for the concert programme. Both are written by the same stylistically unblessed priest, and breathtakingly dull – but while he is reading them Halley leaves him alone. He spends two days blissfully submerged in the mind-numbing minutiae of Seabrook's past; when he is finished he returns to the library and asks the psoriatic brother in charge if he has anything else on the school. The brother does not. For a moment Howard is at sea. Then he has a brainwave. 'How about the First World War?' he says.

There are seventeen books on the First World War. Howard checks out all of them. At home he piles them around him on the living-room table, and reads with an engrossed, not-to-be-disturbed expression; he even keeps a box of candles beside him for when the construction work on the Science Park knocks the power out.

'You're really getting into that stuff,' Halley says, regarding the stacks of books, their stern, catastrophic covers.

'Oh you know, it's for the kids,' he replies abstractedly, and peers into the page to make an imaginary underlining.

For the rest of the week he does nothing but read. Textbooks and yarns, elegies and entertainments, eyewitness accounts and fusty donnish histories, he reads them all; and on every page he sees the same thing – Miss McIntyre's white body stretched out before him, her mouth straining for his, her intoxicated, half-closed eyes.

He aches to talk to her. Her absence, his powerlessness to reach her, are agonizing. One evening he ends up telling Farley what happened just so he can speak her name: even sketching it minimally down the phone line brings the electricity of that night thrilling through him again, with a strange mixture of shame, pride, shame at his pride. But Farley does not seem to share it. Instead he is sombre, as if Howard had announced some fatal illness.

'So what are you going to do?'

'I don't know,' Howard says.

'What about Halley?'

'I don't know.' These are all the questions he has avoided asking himself. Why is Farley asking them? 'I think I'm in love with Aurelie.' Howard realizes this only as he says it.

'You're not, Howard. You barely know her.'

'What difference does that make?'

'It makes all the difference. You've been with Halley for three years. If you mess it up now, I promise you'll regret it.'

'So what do you suggest I do, pretend it never happened? Just bury my feelings away? Is that it?'

'I'm just telling you what you already know, which is that this thing with Aurelie is a fantasy. It's a fantasy, you know it. And now you've had your fun, you should let it go. You haven't told Halley anything, have you?'

'No.'

'Okay, well, keep it that way. In my experience, honesty is

definitely not the best policy with these things. Just sit tight until things are clearer. If she asks, deny everything.'

Howard is angry. How many of Farley's fantasies has he listened to over the years? Chewing Howard's ear off about the new waitress in the deli, the new assistant in the pharmacy, the girl at the Internet café with the incredible jugs – all of them, conquered or (mostly) otherwise, forgotten completely two weeks later. Who is he to sermonize? Who is he to dictate what is and isn't real? To say what Howard is or isn't feeling? Just because he likes having friends who are living the straight life, likes being able to come over to a nice house where he can eat a nice dinner and tell his wild stories, vicariously enjoy the stability and routine for a night without ever having to submit to the slog of it, the endless strictures and limitations –

Later on, however, when the initial sting has abated, he admits to himself that Farley might have a point. Yes, Miss McIntyre is beautiful; yes, what happened in the Geography Room was exhilarating. But did it actually *mean* anything?

He's back on the couch with his books; on the other side of the room, Halley taps at her computer, cigarette smoke gathered at her shoulder, a spectral familiar.

People do crazy things, Aurelie said it herself. They do arbitrary things to test the boundaries, to feel free. But those moments don't have any meaning beyond themselves. They don't have any real connection with who you are, they aren't *life*. Life is when you're not doing something arbitrary to feel free. *This* is life, this living room, the furniture and trappings they have picked out and paid for with slow hours of work, the small treats and fancies their budget has allowed them.

'You look deep in thought,' Halley says from her desk.

'Just straightening something out,' he says.

She gets up. 'I'm going to make a smoothie, do you want one?'

'That'd be great, thanks.'

A life and a place to live it versus a momentary flame of passion. For a grown man, that should hardly be a difficult choice.

248

Confident he's on the right track now, he sets it out mathematically, constructing an elaborate equation in his head in order to prove it to himself beyond any doubt. On one side he places his relationship with Halley, factoring in as much as he can – the loneliness of his life before he met her, the sacrifices she has made for him, their relative happiness together, as well as more abstract concepts like loyalty, honesty, trust, what it means to be a good person. On the other side –

On the other side Miss McIntyre's mouth, her eyes, her nails in his back.

Halley is asking something from the kitchen. 'What?' he calls hoarsely.

'Are you in a blueberry mood, or a pineapple mood?'

'Oh – whatever you think.' His voice, strained, high, adolescent, melds into the turbulent whine of the blender.

Leaned up louchely against the Geography Room door, telling him, *To be bored, that's really a crime.*

Howard has been so bored.

He has been so bored with Howard, and all the accoutrements of being Howard. He does not hold Halley to blame for this; boredom is congenital to cowards, like thin blood is to Russian royalty. But the fact remains that in the Geography Room he had not felt bored. In the Geography Room, lying back in the darkness, he'd felt like he was waking from a long, long sleep.

'Here you go.' Halley hands him a tall cold glass, runs her fingers through his hair on the way back to her computer.

'Oh – thanks . . .' Well, maybe for now the best thing would be to wait. Until he returns to school and finds the lie of the land, maybe he should take Farley's advice. Keep his head below the parapet, and Halley – stealthily, unnoticeably, via a careful weave of mishearings and mistimings – at arm's length; make do for now with secret visits to his memory, replaying his store of Aurelie-moments, imagining their future life together, a smiling haze of uncomplicated rightness. He sips down cold citrusy pulp, picks up his book and sinks into a fantasy in which he walks with her side by side over war-torn earth, through shards of former trees and khaki-shrouded limbs that reach plaintively up out of the ground: he a Tommy covered head-to-toe in mud, she spotless in a cream angora sweater, giving him a pop quiz on his own life he has not studied for, but to which she, fortunately, has all the answers.

Carl in the dark in the shadows.

It's late. He doesn't know how long he has been there.

Behind the gates at the end of the grey tongue of drive is a house, it is her house. There are no cars outside and no lights on but this is a trick because Carl saw a shape moving in the dark inside the window.

Above the gate, a little red dot of light that belongs to the security camera. That's why Carl is standing here crushed up to the wall. The gates are locked and the walls are high with glass on top. The road is narrow and winding and quiet and dark, nothing is moving. Except inside close up everything is jumping! Everything is speeding and screaming at a million miles a second!

In his ear the phone buzzes and a voice tells him he has reached Lori's number. It speaks the number all chopped up like a broken robot, it tells him to leave a message after the tone. The first times that's what he did, he left messages, like WHY WEREN'T YOU AT THE HOP? WHERE ARE YOU NOW? WHY WON'T YOU ANSWER? But then he got bored and now instead he leaves silences. *Hello, you have reached numbernumbernumbernumber, please leave a message after the tone –*

Silence

until the network cuts him off. Then he hits the button and it all happens again. By now he has stopped expecting her to pick up or not pick up, it's almost like it's going on without him, *buzz voice silence buzz voice silence.* But in his head he can see it, the phone ringing in her bedroom, playing the BETH₳ni song, Lori cross-legged on her bed in her pyjama bottoms, in the house all alone, watching it on her desk flashing, then it stops and the little envelope tumbles onto the screen,

YOU HAVE A NEW VOICE MESSAGE,

and she gets up and goes to hear it, and into her ear pours the scary sound of the silent outside going *kchhhhhhhhhhhhhhshhhhhhhhhhhh*, piling up with all the other silences he has sent her, silences floating through the house like cold chunks cut out of the night, she is scared, she is crying, then suddenly she presses the button and this time it is him in her room, staticky, night-shaped, like a bad spirit in a fairy-tale, and with him the night, the cold, the trees, the dark, they're all transported inside, packed into her bedroom, she is screaming *What is happening???!!!* then she is running –

Holding the phone between his chin and his shoulder he takes the tube of pills out of his pocket. He brought them for her but now they are mostly gone. He pours a little pyramid on his fingertip and lifts it up to his nose. It is a message he is sending to himself, he leans his head back and looks up at the cold stars and waits for it to arrive like a bolt of lightning –

Then there is a noise. A message on his phone! It's her, she's been watching him on the CCTV! And now she's going to open the gates!

But it's not from her, it's from Barry.

WER R U U HV 2 CUM 2 EDS RIT NOW

Carl does not want to go to Ed's. He writes back,

WOTS DA STORY?

The reply comes almost as soon as he's sent it:

JUST FUKIN GET HEER NOW

Carl is pissed off, as soon as he goes he knows the gates will open, he sees her creeping on tiptoes over the gravel going, Carl, Carl. Fuck it! Fuck Barry!

But he gets on his bike and flies back towards Seabrook. The lights of the road swirl and beam extra-bright, he gets there in record time! When he goes behind the doughnut shop though, none of the faces that turn to look at him are Barry. First he thinks it's a mistake, like he got the wrong message. Then he realizes he knows these faces. He turns to run but someone's behind him and next thing he knows he's on the ground.

It's the knackers from the park, all four of them. One of them is pinning him down, another is crouched a little way away doing the same thing to Barry. From the ground between the arms and legs he stares across at Carl with eyes full of fear. What is going on?

'Two posh cunts from Seabrook College,' the knacker with the shaved head says in a loud voice, like he's making a speech. 'Two little faggots.' He walks around in a small circle with a can in his hand. The knacker with greasy hair is kneeling on Carl's chest. 'Did you think you could just go on like this for ever? Did you fuckin think we'd just let you go on doin this and we wouldn't mind? You fuckin queers?'

Is he asking Carl? Carl does not understand, he is still trying to understand when Shaved-Head's face suddenly changes from a question to a snarling, like he's taken off a mask and beneath it there's a fire. Carl only catches a glimpse of this, then everything is spinning and stars. His head rings, he feels something wet running down his face.

'What is it?' Shaved-Head shouts. 'Where'd you get it?' His foot lands with a splat in Carl's eye. Carl rolls his head, panting. From the dark the smashed lights of a burned car stare back at him like someone burned and lying on the ground in the weeds and garbage.

Greasy-Hair is searching through Carl's clothes, into the pockets of his trousers and jacket. 'We are going to kill you,' he tells

Carl, softly, like the doctor telling you the needle might sting a little bit. He finds Carl's wallet and throws it to Shaved-Head.

'That's a fuckin start at least,' Shaved-Head says.

'Here we go.' Greasy-Hair has found the tube.

Shaved-Head takes it and opens it. 'This is what you've been selling? What is it? Speed?'

Barry tries to say something but his teeth are chattering too much. Shaved-Head opens the tube and pours a mound onto the back of his hand. He lowers his nose into it and then a moment later he folds his arms into himself in little jerks. 'Whoa, I like *that*! Ah!' He throws his shoulders back, twists his head. 'Fuck, yeah! Where did youse shitheads get hold of this?'

In a little squeaky stammery voice Barry tells him about the pills. He tells him everything, about Morgan, about the girls on diets, about the little kids in junior school and the fireworks.

'Sellin to all the rich bitches,' Shaved-Head says. 'Not a bad little plan. Unfortunately you fucked with the wrong people.' His voice is bright with the drug, it makes you think you are on TV. 'Get the rope,' he says.

Now a knacker with bad teeth comes out of the trees at the edge of the waste ground. In his hand is a blue rope. When he sees it Barry starts shouting. The spotty guy on top of him slaps him, then when Barry doesn't stop he grabs an old newspaper lying on the ground and stuffs Barry's mouth full of it. 'Better do this one first,' he says, and pulls Barry to his feet. Through the newspaper, Barry's still making a noise, a high-pitched gurgling squeal like a drowning pig. Tears are running down his face, and Carl can feel them too, burning in a lump in his throat.

Greasy-Hair hauls him to his feet as Spots drags Barry over to the burned-out car and pulls him up onto the bonnet. 'Don't worry, you'll get your turn,' he says in his doctor voice. 'But first you have to watch your boyfriend die.'

'A suicide pact,' Shaved-Head announces, 'for two little Seabrook queers who can't take it any more. I don't think the cops will be too surprised. They'll just be glad it's two less faggots.'

Spots has made the blue rope into a noose. Now he puts it over Barry's head. Barry is just staring into space, it's like he is watching something horrible happening somewhere far away that none of the others can see yet – but then, as Shaved-Head calls, 'Do it!' and Spots steps behind him he wakes up again – making the noise, his body shaking so hard it looks like he might shake to pieces, his eyes full of panic and tears flinging themselves at Carl and clutching at him, begging him to do something – but what is Carl supposed to do? When all of this was Barry's great idea? Barry who knows all the answers, who thinks he is so smart? Who tricked Carl into coming down here so he could die here too? Suddenly Carl's body floods with anger, and inside although a part of him is going *Oh fuck* another part is thinking *Die* –

'Wait!' Bad-Teeth calls sharply. Spots stops with his hands right at Barry's shoulders. Bad-Teeth runs over and pulls down Barry's pants. Everyone laughs at Barry's wang, shrivelled white and pea-like and squirting floods of yellow piss. They laugh and laugh, the knackers, the trees, the garbage, the black and steel skips behind the Doughnut House, the people inside eating their doughnuts, the boarders in the Tower, the sky overhead, and Carl laughs too, or maybe he cries, it could be he is crying, it's impossible to tell, and now Spots runs forward with his hands stretched out –

And Barry goes tumbling to the ground.

Carl doesn't know what's going on. Then he understands. The rope wasn't tied to anything. The knackers are laughing their heads off. Ha ha, the face on him, a-ha-ha-haaaa . . .

Barry is on his hands and knees. 'Take that thing off him before he fuckin strangles himself,' Shaved-Head says. Bad-Teeth goes over to him and lifts the rope over Barry's head. Barry tries to get up, but gets caught in his trousers and falls flat on his face again. The knackers are rolling around the ground with tears on their cheeks. At last, Shaved-Head stops laughing enough to say, 'Ah here, Deano, give 'em a fuckin can.'

Bad-Teeth takes a couple of cans out of his bag and throws one to Carl and one into the bushes where Barry sits pulling his trousers up and crying. 'You thought you were goin to die!' Spots hoots. After a second Carl starts to see the funny side too. When he hears Carl, Barry comes out of the bushes, now he is laughing as well, a little bit, everyone is laughing, except for Greasy-Hair who is more sort of staring at Carl and Barry and smiling in this wolfy way.

'No hard feelings,' Shaved-Head says. He sticks out his hand to Barry. Barry shakes it and then Carl does. 'We wouldn't kill two good customers like youse,' Shaved Head says. 'Bit fuckin cheeky, though, dealin on someone else's patch.'

'Sorry,' Barry said.

'You were fuckin clever bastards, though, comin up with a nice little earner like that. Shame to let the whole fuckin thing go tits-up.'

Everyone is sitting down now on the circle of black burned ground. Bad-Teeth has skinned up a joint, it's superskunk or something, just the smell is enough to get you destroyed. 'You never sold us this stuff,' Barry says.

'Always keep the best shit for yourself,' Bad-Teeth grins. His mouth is like a car crash.

Then it could be a minute later or it could be an hour. Carl and Barry are both wrecked. The sky is spinning all around them, the ground is sucking them down like it's full of magnets. Bad-Teeth leans on his elbow, chuckling, playing with the dirt. Shaved-Head and Spots lie on their backs like someone tipped them over. Now Barry starts to move. Spinning in front of him he tells Carl he has to go home. 'Hang on –' Carl crawls about to find a direction that leads upwards. The ground is throwing itself around, it's like being on a ship.

'See you lads,' Barry says to the knackers.

'Cheers, amigos,' Spots says. 'Talk to you.'

Carl and Barry lurch over the bumpy ground, tripping over cans and springs and glass, they giggle because it is taking them so long to get anywhere. Then something hard hits them from behind and they fall to the ground.

Hands grab them and turn them on their backs. Greasy-Hair's breath that smells of shit is in their faces and through stars Carl sees Shaved-Head standing over them with his smile gone and a long metal bar in his hand. 'Sorry, lads,' Spots says. 'But we do still have to punish you.' Greasy-Hair rolls up Barry's shirtsleeve over his white arm.

'It's just business,' Shaved-Head says. He swings the bar back over his head.

Beneath the scream the snap of Barry's arm is one short flat crack like breaking a Kit-Kat in two. When Bad-Teeth and Greasy-Hair climb off him he lies there twitching like a fish taken out of its bowl.

Then it's Carl's turn. He tries to push them away, but he's too monged. They pin him down, the bar lifts –

But it doesn't come down. After a bit Carl opens his eyes. The four knackers are all staring at Carl's arm. 'Fuck's sake,' Spots says. 'This cunt's a fuckin mentalist.'

It's November.

The laneway down to the side-gate is slick with fallen leaves, beaten flat and sodden with rain and grit; it's no longer so much fun to have them wedged down your jumper or, indeed, covering your sheets when you turn back the duvet in your dorm. Everything smells of decay, although the frost in the morning hides this nearly till noon, when the watery sun reaches its feeble peak.

The boarders begin trickling back Saturday morning, and on Monday classes resume for all. Initially, the dejection of return is partly offset by the excitement of reunion. A single week in the Outside – that tilt-a-whirl of flux and adventure! – provides more stories than a whole term in this dump where time stands still. People have chugged a *lot* of beers and gotten *really, really* drunk. They have accidentally or deliberately set fire to things. They have visited Disney World, they have been bitten by dogs, they have watched 18-cert movies. There have been tonsillectomies, orthodontal work, sexual awakenings, haircuts. Vaughan Brady has had his ears bandaged after getting his head stuck in railings attempting to reach a five-euro note; Patrick 'Da Knowledge' Noonan comes back from Malta with a mahogany-like tan with which he almost passes for black, much to the dismay of Eoin 'MC Sexecutioner' Flynn, around whom Patrick has taken to making pointed remarks about 'the Man' and 'Whitey'.

With each passing second, though, the school's morbid gravity reasserts its control: the old familiar inertia sets in, and soon encounters with the world outside have become little more than dim dreams, wild jumbles of shapes and colours quickly fading like Patrick Noonan's tan, until by the end of the first day's classes, it's as if the boys have never been away at all.

'It's as if we've never been away, except worse,' Dennis amends, stretched out in the attitude of a corpse on Ruprecht's bed. At the window it's already getting dark; the clocks have gone back, and from now until Christmas the slim supply of sunshine available to them will dwindle daily to a sliver.

'Ha ha! I have got you now, little treasure-stealing leprechaun,' emits Mario, gathered over a tiny, futuristic-looking phone.

'I wish I was dead.' Dennis is in especially bad form after a week in Athlone being dragged to novenas by his stepmother. 'I wonder why I *don't* die. It's not like I have any reason to live.' He settles back and closes his eyes. 'Maybe if I just lie here quietly enough, I can just . . . stop . . . being . . . alive . . .'

'Go and die on your own bed,' Ruprecht mutters, not looking up from his calculations.

'That's it, Blowjob, you're out of my will,' says Dennis's corpse, then sits up abruptly as BETHani comes on the stereo. 'Jesus Christ, Skip, are you playing that damn song again?'

'What's wrong with it?'

'Nothing was wrong with it, the first *four hundred times*.'

'Don't pay any attention to him, Skip,' Geoff says. 'He's just jealous because he's never been in love.'

'I don't mind anyone being in love,' Dennis says. 'I mind them endlessly going on about it when the whole thing's totally *imaginary*.'

'It's not imaginary!' Skippy rejoins pinkly.

'Oh no, of course not, incredibly hot Frisbee Girl grabs you and pulls you out of the Hop and the two of you go running around in the dark and then she kisses you?'

'That's what happened!'

'*She?* Kissed *you?* Like, come on, Skippy.'

'But you *saw* us leave together! You were the one who pushed me into her, don't you remember?'

'No.'

'We were talking to Mario – Mario, remember, you'd struck out with all those girls? They kept telling you they had to take their insulin and running away?'

'Hmm, that does not sound like the kind of thing that would happen.'

'Are you sure you didn't dream it, Skippy?'

Arrrgh – Skippy's been having this same conversation ever since he got back. At first he was sure Dennis was behind it – it has all the hallmarks of one of his practical jokes. But the thing is, it's not just his friends who're playing dumb. *No one* remembers him leaving with Lori; no one remembers even seeing them speaking together. Meanwhile, all trace of the event has been removed: the Sports Hall restored to its normal role (while smelling oddly of disinfectant), the Hallowe'en posters replaced by new ones advertising auditions for the Christmas concert. It's as if the night never happened; and Skippy is left facing the horrific prospect that he did actually dream the entire thing.

'Although if it's a dream that you truly believe in your heart,' Geoff attempts to console him, 'then in a way, you know, it is real?'

'It's not a dream in my heart,' Skippy scowls.

'Whether you dreamed it or not –' Mario emerges temporarily from his phone, which is new '– the key question is, did you get this bitch's digits? This is the mark of success or failure in any romantic encounter.'

'No,' Skippy says miserably.

'Did you say you'd meet her after the holidays?' Geoff asks.

'No.' Skippy plonks abjectly down on the side of the bed.

'Holy shit, Skip, you can't even imagine stuff properly,' Dennis says. 'So what's the plan now, stare at her out of that creepy telescope for the rest of your life?'

'I don't know,' Skippy says glumly. 'I suppose I could wait outside the gates after school until she comes out. Or call over to her house?'

'No and no.' Mario shoots these down straight away. 'You have to keep your cool. You don't want to come across like some crazy stalker.'

'You know, as opposed to the guy who watches her all day through his telescope,' Dennis says.

'How about you become really, really good at something she likes?' Geoff suggests. 'Like, you know she likes frisbee, okay, so how about you train at frisbee until you're one of the world's top frisbee players, and then one day she sees you on TV and she remembers you and she writes you a letter, but you're all like, See you later, bitch, I'm a professional frisbee player now, I've got chicks all over me. But then back in your lonely hotel room one night you start thinking about her, and you realize you still love her, so you write her a letter back, except you write it on a frisbee and you throw it from the top of the wall so it goes in her class-room window and then she comes out and sees you standing on top of the wall and then, you know, you get married?'

Skippy looks doubtful.

'Get the digits,' Mario repeats. 'Then we'll have something to work with.'

'Lori *Wakeham*?'

'Yeah, I was talking to her at the . . .'

'Why would *you* want Lori Wakeham's number?'

'Well, you see, I was talking to her at the Hop, and I just wanted to give her a call and . . .'

'*You* were talking to her?'

'Yeah, I don't know if you remember but actually you were the one who –'

'Hey, Titch, good job on KellyAnn Doheny,' Darren Boyce says, bouncing by.

'Don't know what you're talking about,' Titch says expression-lessly.

'No really, good *job*,' Darren Boyce says, and laughs to himself as he walks off.

'I don't know what you're talking about!' Titch shouts at his retreating form, then slamming his locker door he stamps off towards the exit. Skippy trots after him. He can appreciate he's going out on a limb here and is prepared to abase himself as much as is required.

As they approach the pool table Jason Rycroft detaches himself from it and intercepts them. 'All right, Titch?'

'All right,' Titch returns, a little defensively.

'What are you doing with this bummer?' Jason nods at Skippy.

'Oh, he's fucking driving me mad looking for some bird's phone number.'

'Juster? What's he going to do with a bird, take her to the playground?' Jason turns to Skippy. 'Seriously, Juster, no offence or anything, but I mean have your balls even dropped yet?'

Titch laughs. 'Yeah, Juster, stick to your Nintendo.'

Skippy goes red. In the playground in the rainy night-time park, her fingernail scratching hearts into the old black wood of the swing . . .

'Oh, here, Titch, I have something for you.' Jason Rycroft reaches into his bag, takes something out and puts it into Titch's hand. 'Thought you might need it.' He bounces away, yukking. Titch and Skippy look at the object in Titch's hand. It is a soother.

'Fucking arsehole,' Titch says, flicking it over his shoulder. They stand there a moment, staring after Jason Rycroft. Actually Skippy doesn't know if Titch remembers he's there. At last he says, 'So . . .'

'For fuck's sake, Juster,' Titch explodes, 'don't be a twat all your life, will you not.' With that he storms off, carrying Lori's number with him.

In English class they're doing haiku: *Ruprecht, your fat ass / I am going to kick it so hard / Your nuts fall off* – 'Ha ha, I think you'll find a haiku is supposed to have seventeen syllables?' While Kipper Slattery recites slender poems about wheat-sheaves and cherry trees at the top of the room, Skippy sinks deeper into gloom. From his bedroom in mid-term it had all seemed so simple. They had kissed, that was the important part, surely when you kiss someone everything else just falls into place! But when you get in close there's a thousand tiny barriers in the way, like an army of microscopic terriers chewing at your ankles, too small to see but making it impossible to move . . .

'Wakey-wakey, Skip! Class is over!' Mario standing over his desk.

'Time to go, Skippy,'

Geoff addresses him in haiku form,

> 'Geography next, I like
> Our sexy teacher.'

'He is busy moping about his dream-girl,' Mario says.

'Well, then there's no point us bothering him,' Geoff says.

'No, there is no point me bothering him with her phone number,' Mario says.

'Nope, I wouldn't bother him with that.'

'What?' Skippy says, head jerking up.

'What?' says Mario.

'What did you say about her number?'

'What number? Oh, you mean this number?' Mario is waving a strip of paper. He pulls it out of reach as Skippy makes a grab, then relents and hands it to him. Skippy gazes at it in astonishment. LORI, it says in Mario's flamboyant scrawl, followed by a number – a crystalline shard of her, like a strand of DNA.

'But how . . . ?'

Mario shrugs smugly, a sort of smrug. 'I am Italian,' is all he will say. 'Come on, Geoff, we're going to be late.'

Now the question becomes what to say to her. A text message is deemed preferable to a call: other than that, though, there is little consensus.

'Why don't I just say, Hi Lori, this is Daniel, it was nice to talk to you the other night, if you want to meet up again sometime give me a call.'

'That's fine,' Mario says, 'if you want to send her into a coma. You need something with oomph.'

'How about a haiku?' Geoff says.

'How about, instead of "if you want to meet up again", you say, "if you want me to sex you hard",' Mario says.

It's the end of the school day; they are walking down the laneway to the Doughnut House. In the dusk the world appears pale and exhausted, like a vampire's been drinking from its veins: the thin pink filament of the just-come-on doughnut sign, the white streetlights like dowdy cotton bolls against the grey clouds, the soft hand-like leaves of the trees with the colours leeched away to match the asphalt.

'What have you got so far?' Geoff asks.

Skippy presses a button. '"Hi,"' he says.

'That's all you have after four hours?'

'It's the only thing everyone agrees on.'

Geoff frowns. 'Actually, I'm not all that crazy about "Hi".'

'What's wrong with "Hi"?'

'It just seems like the kind of thing my mum would say.'

'It's the kind of thing everyone says.'

'Have you thought about "Hey"? Don't you think "Hey" might be more kind of rockin'? Or "Yo"?'

Dennis and Mario, meanwhile, have fallen behind to debate the merits and demerits of Mario's new phone. 'The thing you don't understand about this phone is that it's state of the art, which means, this is the best phone you can get.'

'I do understand that, you moron, I'm saying what's the *point* of having a state-of-the-art phone when everyone who's going to call you on it is living six feet away from you?'

'I think what it is, is, you are jealous of my state-of-the-art phone, which has a camera and an MP3 player.'

'Mario, if you can't see why your parents suddenly gave you that gay phone you're even dimmer than I thought. I mean, think about it, they leave you in school for the entire holiday, and then they give you some rinky-dink piece of plastic so they can talk to you without having to see you face-to-face. They couldn't say, "We don't love you" more clearly if they wrote it in skywriting over the rugby pitches.'

'That shows what you know, because my parents do love me.'

'Well, why did they leave you here over mid-term, then?'

'They did not go into it, but they were very specific about it not being because they didn't love me, and I know because I asked them that very question.'

'What did they say? Did they say it would be character-building?'

Mario suddenly takes on a hunted look.

'Face it, Mario, the only reason any of us are here is that our parents don't want a bunch of stinky, no-longer-cute adolescents getting in their hair.'

Skippy turns round. 'Would you say "Hi" or "Hey"? If you were talking to a girl?'

'I would say, "Put on your crash-helmet, hot stuff, because you are about to have the ride of your life!"'

'I would say, "Please ignore my friend, his parents dropped him on his head when he was a baby, over and over, because they do not love him."'

Ed's buzzes with blonde hair and St Brigid's plaid; but Lori's not there, and the table where they sat that night is occupied by two others blithely unaware of its history. At the back of the restaurant, however, they find Ruprecht, surrounded by maths books.

'What have you got so far?' he asks.

'"H,"' Skippy says.

'"H,"' muses Ruprecht. '"H".'

'A haiku would be nice and sort of different,' Geoff says, mostly to himself. 'Lori, your eyes . . . your big green eyes . . .'

'How about asking her a riddle?' Ruprecht says.

'A riddle?'

'Yes, a riddle always grabs the attention. Something about your name, for instance. Instead of "this is Skippy", you could say, "Who am I? Above a rope, or Down Under. Pass over my name, and you will find it." Something like that.'

'What?'

'What the hell is that supposed to mean?'

'Ruprecht, have you ever actually *met* a woman?'

'*Lorelei Wakeham,*' Geoff blurts, '*your sad eyes of emerald are my only stars.*'

Everybody stops dead and stares at Geoff. 'It's a haiku,' he explains.

Ruprecht repeats the words softly to himself:

Lorelei Wakeham
Your sad eyes of emerald
Are my only stars.

'Seventeen syllables,' he pronounces.

'Holy smoke, Geoff, that's really beautiful.'

'Oh, it's just a little something I thought up,' Geoff demurs.

'You see, this, this is what I have meant by oomph,' Mario tells Skippy. 'A haiku like this is the express train to Sexville.'

'Yeah, and Geoff can recite it at your funeral after Carl kills you,' Dennis scowls; but the heady combination of Japanese poetry and chocolate doughnuts sweeps away any misgivings, and Skippy hurries to key in his message before anyone can change his mind.

Ever since the Hop, Ruprecht has been acting strangely. According to Mario, who also stayed in school over mid-term, he spent most of the break in his laboratory, and since term resumed he has scarcely been seen. In the morning and at lunch break he skips the Ref and heads directly for the basement, huffing down the corridor with papers spilling from his pockets and a distrait air; meanwhile in class he keeps putting up his hand to ask convoluted questions no one can follow – haranguing Lurch about *Riemannian space*, pestering Mr Farley about *Planck energy*, in Religion, most startlingly, asking Brother Jonas whether God was God in all universes, or 'just in this universe'.

Loss of appetite, sleeplessness, erratic behaviour – if you didn't know better, you'd almost think Ruprecht, like his room-mate, was in love. You do know better, though, so you conclude it's far more likely to be something to do with this new theory he's been going on about.

Actually, Ruprecht has discovered, the term "M-theory" is something of a misnomer. *Theory* suggests a hypothesis of some sort, a line of inquiry, a set of principles, at the very least a vague idea of what it is, itself, *about*. M-theory offers none of these things. It is pure enigma: a nebulous, shadowy, multi-faceted entity infinitely bigger than what it was originally intended to explain. Confronted with it, the best scientists in the world are as schoolboys – less than schoolboys, *cavemen*, primitives who, foraging with their stone axes in the jungle, stumble upon a spaceship squatting huge and opaque amid the ferns. It swallows entire fields of mathematics like they were nothing at all. The most complicated equations devised by the most brilliant minds operating at the very limit of human capability represent only the most childish gestures at description of its outermost edges, weak flames that reveal the barest inkling of the vastness retiring back into the darkness. For all their labours, the reality of the theory – what it actually *means*, what it *says*, what it is a theory *of* – remains hidden behind the inscrutable M, and while each of them dreams of being the one who will crack it, bring the theory, like King Kong wrapped in chains, into the light, they are prone, late at night, to the chilly thought that rather than illuminating, their efforts are merely feeding it, gorging it with knowledge, which it devours with no sign of satiety.

'So what's the *point* of it?' Dennis takes a dim view both of the theory and of Ruprecht's obsession, which he suspects to be just another layer of self-mystification.

'Well, I suppose the "point" would be a total explanation of reality,' Ruprecht harrumphs. 'I imagine that's what the basic "point" would be.'

'But it's just a load of maths. How's that going to help anybody?'

'There is already too many maths,' Mario chimes in. 'More beaver, less maths, that's what I say.'

'Yes, well, if Newton had said that, we wouldn't have the law of gravity,' Ruprecht says. 'If James Clerk Maxwell had said, "More beaver, less maths," we wouldn't have electricity. Maths and the universe go hand in hand. Formulae worked out in a single copybook with a single pencil can transform the entire world. Look at Einstein. $E=mc^2$.'

'So what?' says Dennis.

'So, if it weren't for "a load of maths", we'd all be living in shacks in fields, tending sheep.'

'Good,' says Dennis.

'Oh, you'd like living in a world without phones or DVDs, would you?'

'Yes, I would.'

'You'd like going to hospital and being operated on without an anaesthetic, in candlelight, by doctors who had no clue what was wrong with you because there were no X-ray machines?'

'Yes, I would.'

'You would?'

'That's right.'

'Well, good.'

'Good.'

'Good.'

The theory is not without its doubters, to be sure, and not all of them are as ill-informed as Dennis.

'Mathematically, yes, it does have a lot of explanatory potential,' Mr Farley says, after yet another Science class has been diverted into a discussion of the possible physics of other universes. 'But that doesn't actually make it *true*. A lot of people have very compelling theories about what happened to Atlantis. There's even a theory that Ireland is the remnant of Atlantis. But unless they could verify it somehow, show you some sort of proof, you wouldn't believe them, would you?'

'No,' Ruprecht admits.

'The fact is that it would take a trillion trillion times more power than our most powerful energy source to find any evidence for M-theory. On those grounds alone, many scientists would say that it simply isn't commensurate with twenty-first-century science. That is, even if it's true, there's not a lot *we* can actually do with it, any more than Galileo could have used, for instance, computer operating code if he'd stumbled across it back in the seventeenth century. So while it's undoubtedly interesting, we shouldn't let it obscure the less glamorous but just as important scientific work there is to do here on planet Earth. Does that sound fair?'

'Yes,' Ruprecht concedes.

No! The more arguments he hears against it, the deeper his adoration grows for this esoteric, unreadable scripture that the crude unthinking world will not take time to understand – the longer he spends in his basement lost in topologies, mapping out the imaginary surfaces that undulate beneath its hyperspatial penumbra, shunning human company except for other faceless devotees in sleepless Internet chatrooms, reciting back and forth those golden shibboleths, string, multiverse, supersymmetry, gravitino, the theory's hundred names . . .

In fact, maybe it is love after all. Why can't we fall in love with a theory? Is it a person we fall in love with, or the idea of a person? So yes, Ruprecht has fallen in love. It was love at first sight, occurring the moment he saw Professor Tamashi present that initial diagram, and it has unfolded exponentially ever since. The question of reason, then, the question of evidence, these are wasted on him. Since when has love ever looked for reasons, or evidence? Why would love bow to the reality of things, when it creates a reality of its own, so much more vivid, wherein everything resonates to the key of the heart?

Once upon a time there was a beautiful young girl named Lorelei who lived on the banks of the river Rhine. She fell in love with a sailor who was going off to sea. 'When I come back I will marry you,' he said, so every day she would go up to the cliffs and watch out for his ship. But it never came. Finally one day she got a letter from him. He said he had married another girl, so Lorelei threw herself off the cliff and into the river. To this day she appears on a rock, singing her song and combing her hair. If you hear the song, you can't escape it, you will sail onto the rocks and she will pull you underwater. If you see her, she is so beautiful that you go insane.

Focus, Daniel, focus! Coach calls from the side.

They are the first to use the pool since the holiday. The surface has been harvested of bluebottles and Band-Aids, it shines like amethyst. In the lanes around Skippy, the machine-like churn of the team, ploughing steadily up and down. But he can't do it. It's like the water is conspiring against him, like he can feel the individual molecules pushing him back. Like something is there, trying to take hold of him.

Come on, Dan, get it together!

He shakes it off, plunges back into the spell of chlorine, imagines himself surging towards a girl kneeling at the top, combing her hair as she waits for him, humming irresistibly, *If I had three wishes I would give away two . . .*

Dawn is just breaking, pinkening the perspex roof, as they climb out for the showers.

So where is the race taking place? Coach asks.

Ballinasloe, Antony 'Air Raid' Taylor says.

And when?

November 15th, Siddartha Niland says, his golden body rippling and glistening.

Wrong and wrong, Coach says. The race is going on this very minute, right here. He taps his head. In your mind, he says. That's where a race is won or lost. If you don't have the right attitude, it doesn't matter how strong or how fit you are. From now until November 15, I want that race to be all you think about. Write it in your diaries, on your calendars, on the insides of your eyelids. Everything else comes second. Even girls. Girls will still be there when the race is over. And you'll do a lot better with them if we win.

Everybody laughs.

Now I've said this before but I'll say it again. Not everybody's going to make the cut. If you made it last time, don't assume you'll be selected this time. If you were left out last time, you could be racing this time. A lot can happen between then and now.

After training Skippy gets sick in the toilets by the Ref.

Later in his room he puts an X on the Garfield calendar. The swimming goggles look down at him from their hook; he feels his whole arm go cold, as if he'd plunged it into a barrel of ice-water.

The knackers did not kill Carl. When they saw what he had done to his arm they did not even break it. So now everything is even and they can all be friends.

Friends?

We have a good thing going with those pills, dude, Barry says. These guys can help us. Give us protection, access to distributors, good deals on other products. All we have to do is cut them a little slice of our profits.

They broke your arm, Carl says.

They had to, Barry said. That's just the way it works. It's just business, that's all.

So now they see the knackers nearly every day. In the park, behind the shopping mall, in Deano's flat. Deano is the one with bad teeth. Shaved-Head, he's the leader, is called Mark. Greasy-Hair = Knoxer, Spots = Ste. Barry laughs and jokes with them like that night never happened, and at school he walks around like he's ten feet tall. He gives shit to fifth-years twice his size and they back off. How do they know Barry has the knackers on his side? It's like they just know.

One night Deano tells them about Mark. See your man? He acts hard but he's really a posh cunt like youse lads. He went to your school then the priests kicked him out for dealing hash. Now he's stuck with us bunch of scumbags. But it's good, see, cos he's got ambitions. He's like you, he says to Barry, always thinkin.

The deal is they hand over a cut of their Ritalin sales to Mark, and once a fortnight they buy other stuff from him for a special price. Their first consignment is a few E's and some coke but mostly the mental weed. Carl and Barry are supposed to sell it but they end up smoking most of it themselves. It fries your brain, it's like on a hot day when the tar on the road melts and your feet get stuck in it or like when you have a shower and the bathroom mirror gets all fogged up, like you'll be talking to someone and then all of a sudden it'll be like half an hour later and instead of fractions the teacher will be going on about exports and it will be a different teacher and you will be in a different room without knowing how you got there.

It's good that they have something new to sell though because there are serious problems with the diet pill market. Some of the junior school parents have got suspicious about how hyperactive their kids have been lately, and started tightening up on the pre-scriptions. Carl and Barry's supply has been cut in half, but it doesn't even matter because the girls aren't buying anyway. Why not? They never stay interested in anything for more than two weeks, Barry says, that's the problem with girls as a customer base. He tries ringing a couple of them up offering them coke but this just seems to freak them out. Now a couple of them buy like one E a week and the rest totally ignore Carl and Barry.

And Lori ignores them too. She does not return any of Carl's phone calls, she's never in the places she used to be. Then her friend Janine tells him Lori left the Hallowe'en Hop with some guy.

What? Carl says.

They are in the church car park. Janine still wants to buy pills. It's dark, the church windows are dark, there are no cars around.

This guy Daniel, Janine says. She looks up at Carl through eyelashes covered in black shit. Carl searches his head for Daniel but he cannot find anything, his head pounds like it is splitting in two.

Well, what did you expect? The girl twirls her hair with a bony hand. You stood her up. You don't do that to a girl like Lori and just expect her to forgive you.

I was stuck in my house, Carl mumbles.

I mean, she's got guys queuing up to go out with her, Janine says.

Go out with her? Carl's mind churns like the propeller of a boat caught in weeds, trying to catch all the little pieces of that night and glue them back together, the messages she sent him saying come and meet me, it was right here in the church car park –

I thought she just wanted to buy pills, he blurts to Janine. She laughs, a film laugh, with her head back, ha-ha-ha. You don't know much about girls, she says. Then she pulls in closer to him so her tits are just touching his arm and her voice drops. I could teach you, she says, playing with the cord of his hoodie. But Carl is still thinking of what she said about Lori and after a second Janine pulls back, stares at him with eyes like a dog you have kicked. Then, She was with him, she says, stabbing the words like a knife. He's been texting her. He sends her poems.

With little shuffling steps, Carl turns away, facing into the dark. The girl dances round in front of him, grabs his hands and cries, Oh Carl, why do you even care what Lori does? She's a child, she doesn't understand what men want. But Carl doesn't move. He is staring at the concrete ground, where the no-faced boy is kissing Lori, going to all the places Carl had been, shoving his hands under her shirt, sticking his fingers into her box, flooding her little white fist with jism . . . Janine steps back. Her hands are still wrapped around his, he can feel her eyes on him like they're in the distance. In a cooler voice she says, Do you want to get her back?

He raises his head. He is so angry, for a second she is Daniel and his arms pump with the message of grabbing him and tearing him up into little pieces. But then it is gone and his arms are empty and Carl is broken.

Janine reaches out, she strokes his hair and then she says, You really screwed up at the Hop, Carl. That's not the only problem, either. Her parents found out she'd been lying to them. All the time she was with you she told them she was with me. Then my mom met her mom at the deli and told her she hadn't been in my house for weeks. She got into major shit. Her daddy likes to know exactly where his little princess is and who she's with at all times. I don't think he'd be too happy about you, daddies don't like you, do they, Carl? He follows the movement of her head, wagging at him like a sad dog. Anyhow, she's basically grounded. So even if she did want to see you, it would be pretty hard. She smoothes back his hair with gentle fingers. Don't be sad. If you want me to, I can talk to her for you. I could at least tell her how sorry you are. Would you like me to do that, Carl?

Carl nods. She puts her arms around him and gives him a comforting hug. Oh Carl, she sighs, like a teacher with a favourite but always-naughty child. Carl has never been that child, he has always been the one they are afraid of. Janine leans back to gaze at him, then she plants a little cheer-up kiss on his cheek. I'll talk to her, she promises. Everything will be all right. Then she chucks his chin. Did you bring my dolly mixtures?

He takes the baggie from his pocket and hands it to her. She unfastens her purse, then says, like they are two people just come out of church standing on the steps talking about the weather, Lori says you and her had an arrangement.

Carl shifts from foot to foot without saying anything.

Oh Carl, she says again, squeezing herself against him. Don't worry, I'm going to take care of you. And bending upwards, she gives him another little kiss, a friendly mom-type kiss on his cheeks, and then one on his nose, then on his chin, his eyes, his neck, until accidentally one lands on his lips, which are open, and then accidentally she does it again, and accidentally they are accidentally locked tight and wet together, his mouth full of hers, there on the steps in the dark, just like in his imagination Lori's mouth is full of the mouth of the faceless Daniel. But soon Carl will find his face, and then he will be sorry.

With posters for the Christmas concert everywhere, Audition Fever has swept the school. At lunch break, after class, the halls are filled with parps, twangs, thumps of varying degrees of musicality, the rec rooms clotted with knots of boys dreaming up routines that range from opera to gangsta to a new form of Wagnerian tropicalia invented by second year's Caetano Diaz, which he has dubbed 'apocalypso'. The Seabrook Christmas concert may be small potatoes in the grand scheme of things, but as any modern student of fame knows, there is no platform so low that it does not make you look slightly bigger than the next guy. Competition is fierce, and the lowest common denominator does not go unplumbed. Among the rehearsing voices, a surprising number can be heard performing more saccharine versions of already toxically gloopy ballads – 'Flying Without Wings', 'I Believe I Can Fly', 'Wind Beneath My Wings' and others, flying-related and not. Credibility is not the issue for these boys that it might have been for previous generations. A lot of contentious arguments have been resolved in the last decade, a lot of old ideas swept away; it is now universally acknowledged that celebrity is the one goal truly worth pursuing. Magazine covers, marketing deals, artificially whitened smiles, waving from behind barriers at the raving anonymous multitude – this is the zenith of a world now uncluttered by spirituality, and anything you do to get there is considered legitimate.

The concert's musical director is Father Constance 'Connie' Laughton, a kindly, epicene man with white hair and a candy-pink complexion whose burning desire to instil a love of classical music in the hearts of his teenage charges, combined with a softly-softly approach to discipline, sees him occupying a regular spot near the top of Dennis's Nervous Breakdown Leaderboard. While he recognizes the populist leanings of the boys, his own tastes are strictly canonical; in particular he is a fan of the French horn, and has already taken Ruprecht aside for a word in his ear regarding perhaps a performance? No orchestra exists in the school at present, after some past event Father Laughton never talks about, but maybe Ruprecht has some chums, the priest suggests, who might like to accompany him. Dennis laughs long and hard when he hears of this plan. 'Pity the poor suckers who get roped into *that*,' he says. 'It's like having the world's biggest kick-me sign stuck to your back.'

Hot ticket for this year's concert are the rock group Shadowfax, who, in Wallace Willis and Louis O'Brien, boast not one but two classically trained guitar wizards: actual girls pay actual money to hear the band's immaculate covers of the Eagles and other giants of adult-orientated rock. Even the Automator is a fan, following the band's performance of Toto's 'Africa' at a benefit for victims of the Ethiopian drought organized by Father Green last summer. Not every aspiring performance is musical, however. Down in a shady corner of the basement, at this very moment, a small crowd is gathered around Trevor Hickey, bent over with his bottom in the air and a lit match in his hand that, with the solemnity of the magician stepping into the cage of swords, he slowly extends backwards . . .

Diablos: the name given to the igniting of, and ignited, farts. Trevor Hickey is the undisputed master of this arcane and perilous art. The stakes could not be higher. Get the timing even slightly wrong and there will be consequences far more serious than singed trousers; the word *backdraught* clamours unspoken at the back of every spectator's mind. Total silence now as, with an almost imperceptible tremble (entirely artificial, 'just part of the show,' as Trevor puts it), his hand brings the match between his legs and – *foom!* a sound like the fabric of the universe being ripped in two, counterpointed by its opposite, a collective intake of breath, as from Trevor's bottom proceeds a magnificent plume of flame – jetting out it's got to be nearly three feet, they tell each other afterwards, a cold and beautiful purple-blue enchantment that for an instant bathes the locker room in unearthly light.

No one knows quite what Trevor Hickey's diet is, or his exercise regime; if you ask him about it, he will simply say that he has a gift, and having witnessed it, you would be hard-pressed to argue, although why God should have given him this gift in particular is less easy to say. But then, strange talents abound in the fourteen-year-old confraternity. As well as Trevor Hickey, 'The Duke of Diablos', you have people like Rory 'Pins' Moran, who on one occasion had fifty-eight pins piercing the epidermis of his left hand; GP O'Sullivan, able to simulate the noises of cans opening, mobile phones bleeping, pneumatic doors, etc., at least as well as the guy in *Police Academy*; Henry Lafayette, who is double-jointed and famously escaped from a box of jockstraps after being locked inside it by Lionel. These boys' abilities are regarded quite as highly by their peers as the more conventional athletic and sporting kinds, as is any claim to physical freakishness, such as waggling ears (Mitchell Gogan), unusually high mucous production (Hector 'Hectoplasm' O'Looney), notable ugliness (Damien Lawlor) and inexplicably slimy, greenish hair (Vince Bailey). Fame in the second year is a surprisingly broad church; among the two-hundred-plus boys, there is scarcely anyone who does not have some ability or idiosyncrasy or weird body condition for which he is celebrated.

As with so many things at this particular point in their lives, though, that situation is changing by the day. School, with its endless emphasis on conformity, careers, the Future, may be partly to blame, but the key to the shift in attitudes is, without a doubt, girls. Until recently the opinion of girls was of little consequence; now – overnight, almost – it is paramount; and girls have quite different, some would go so far as to say deeply conservative, criteria with regard to what constitutes a gift. They do not care how many golf balls you can fit in your mouth; they are unmoved by third nipples; they do not, most of of them, consider mastery of

Diablos to be a feather in your cap – even when you explain to them how dangerous it is, even when you offer to teach them how to do it themselves, an offer you have never extended to any of your classmates, who would actually pay big money for this expertise, or you could even call it *lore* – wait, come back!

As the juggernaut of puberty gathers momentum, quirks and oddities and singularities turn from badges of honour to liabilities to be concealed, and the same realpolitik that moves boys to forsake long-nurtured dreams of, say, becoming a ninja for a more concerted attention to the here and now, forces others, who once were worshipped as gods, to reinvent themselves as ordinary Joe Blows. Rory Moran will put away his pins, Vince Bailey find some product that de-greens his hair; in five years' time, as they prepare to leave school, how many of the crowd who applaud him now while he takes his bows ('I thank you. I thank you') will remember that Trevor Hickey was once known as 'The Duke'?

'Hey, Blowjob, you fat moron,' Dennis charges as Ruprecht emerges blinkingly from his basement. 'You've crossed the line this time, you fuckwad!'

'What?' Ruprecht is mystified.

'Did you tell Father Laughton I played the bassoon?' Dennis's bassoon, a present from his stepmother, is a tightly guarded secret kept permanently underneath his bed.

'Oh, that,' Ruprecht says.

'You idiot, now he wants me to play with you in the crappy Christmas concert.'

'Yes!' Ruprecht's chubby face lights up. 'Won't it be fun?'

'I'll saw my hands off before I appear on stage with you and your Orchestra of Gays!' Dennis bellows. 'Do you hear me? I'll saw my hands off!'

But it is already too late for that: his stepmother has caught wind of his participation via her vast network of religious, and is right behind it. 'Music has wonderful healing power,' she tells him that morning, adding sadly, 'you are such an angry boy.'

Other boys have been more adroit, however, and the priest, faced with a mass vanishing act on the part of the school's musical community, has been forced to scale back his original concept. Instead of a full symphony, the Christmas concert orchestra will now be a quartet, with Ruprecht and Dennis joined by Brian 'Jeekers' Prendergast on viola and Geoff Sproke on triangle. 'It's *quite* unconventional,' Father Laughton, ever the optimist, pronounces. 'It's *terribly* exciting.'

The participation of Jeekers, while doing little for the Quartet's street-cred, comes as no great surprise: Jeekers's parents are obsessed with Ruprecht and with making their son more

Ruprecht-like. It is, in its small way, a tragic story. In any other school, in any other year, Jeekers – academically gifted, diligent to a fault – would have been undisputed top dog. The caprices of fate, however, have consigned him to the same class as Ruprecht, in which Ruprecht, in every exam, in every test, in every Friday just-for-fun quiz, reigns supreme. This drives Jeekers's parents – his mother, a pinch-faced dwarf with the permanent appearance of sucking sulphuric acid through a straw; his father, a wound-up solicitor who makes Pol Pot look like the Fonz – into paroxysms. 'We didn't raise our son to come in second place,' they shriek. 'What's wrong with you? Are you even trying? Don't you *want* to be an actuary?' 'I do, I do,' Jeekers pleads, and so it's back into the study, surrounded by homework timetables, performance-tracking graphs, brain-boosting fish oils and vitamins. His extra-curricular activities, meanwhile, largely revolve around shadowing Ruprecht, doing whatever he's doing, be it the Quartet or Chess Club, in the hope of discovering whatever it is that gives him that *edge*.

The choice of music for the performance has been left to Ruprecht, who has gone for Pachelbel's Canon in D, explaining to Jeekers that the Canon is the piece favoured by Professor Tamashi for his METI broadcasts into space.

'I really like that song,' Geoff says. Then his brow puckers. 'Although it really reminds me of something.'

'But, ah,' Jeekers feels he has to point out, '*we* won't be broadcasting into space. We'll just be playing to our parents.'

'Perhaps,' twinkles Ruprecht. 'But you never know who might be listening in.'

'I'm in hell,' Dennis whispers to himself.

'What's going on with the girl, Skip?' Geoff asks as they make their way back to class after break. 'Has she texted you back yet?'

'Not yet.'

'Hmm.' Geoff strokes his chin. 'Well, I suppose it's only been a couple of days.'

A couple of endless days. He knows she is alive: yesterday morning, he saw her through the telescope, emerging from a silver Saab and tripping, with a shake of her hair, the few steps to the door of St Brigid's. But maybe she lost her phone? Maybe she has no credit? Maybe she never got the message? Maybes surround her in a fog, like Ruprecht's theory that doesn't explain anything, just hangs a question mark over everything it touches; and the phone remains smug and mute in his pocket, like someone with a secret they will not tell.

'Maybe you should send her another haiku,' Niall suggests.

'Send another message and you might as well paint a big L-for-loser right there on your forehead,' Mario says. 'Right now, your strategy is to sit tight and play it cool.'

'Yeah,' Skippy agrees glumly, but then: 'Are you *sure* that was the right number you gave me?'

'Sure I'm sure. I don't make a mistake about something like that.'

'Like you're sure it's *her* number?'

Mario clicks his teeth. 'I'm telling you, that's her number. Go and check for yourself, if you don't believe me.'

'Go and check for myself?' This does not sound right to Skippy. 'What do you mean, go and check for myself?'

'The toilet,' Mario replies blithely. 'In Ed's Doughnut House.'

Skippy stops in his tracks. 'You got her number from a *toilet*?'

'Yes, it is on the door of the middle cubicle.'

At first Skippy is too dumbstruck even to respond.

'Holy smoke, Mario,' Geoff says, 'a toilet door . . . ?'

'What's the problem? It's not like someone's going to put up a fake number. We can go back and look if you want – it is in the middle cubicle beneath a drawing of a joint that is also an ejaculating penis.'

Skippy has now recovered his power of speech, and uses it; Mario retaliates, the others join in, and they become so engrossed in the argument that none of them notices the figure coming towards them out of the crowd – not until the last second when, moving with a facility and speed surprising in someone of his build, he looms up behind Skippy like a shadow, seizes either side of his head and quickly, deftly, dashes it against the wall.

Skippy drops to the ground like a swatted fly, and for several moments he remains there, sprawled beneath the noticeboard, diverting the flow of his schoolmates. Then, with Geoff's help, he drags himself into a sitting position, and gingerly touches his bleeding temple. Dennis watches Carl shoulder his way back through the pullulating hall. 'I suppose that means it must have been the right number,' he says.

That night Halley dreams of old loves; she wakes, flushed and guilty, some hours before dawn. 'Howard?' she calls his name gently, as if somehow he might know. In the velvet darkness her voice sounds thin, careful, concealing. But he does not respond; beside her, the drowsing bulk of his away-turned body rises and falls, placid and oblivious, a gigantic unicellular organism sharing her bed.

She closes her eyes but can't fall back to sleep, and so instead she conjures up again the substance of the dream, a flame of hers from years ago, in a sun-flooded apartment on Mulberry Street. Awake it doesn't take, though; it feels like someone else's life and she like a voyeur, watching from outside.

By the time she's showered, the sun has come up. It has been raining during the night, and the day is drenched and quivering and singing with colour.

'Morning, morning.' Howard bustles into the room with his jacket already on and kisses her on the cheek before opening the refrigerator. He sets the toaster, pours some coffee, and sits down at the table, studying his lesson plan. For the last two weeks he has tried not to look at her; she does not know why. Has she changed somehow? In the mirror her face does not seem different. 'So what's going on today?' he says.

She shrugs. 'Write about technology. How about you?'

'Teach kids history.' Now he looks up, smiles at her, flat and false as a cereal commercial.

'You know what, though, I'm going to need the car this afternoon.'

'Oh yeah?'

'Yeah, I have to go see this Science Fair.'

'At the RDS? Farley's going to be there, you should say hello.'

'I will. But the car. Can I come into school lunchtime and pick it up?'

'Why not just take it now? I can get the bus in.'

'You're sure?'

'Sure I'm sure, makes more sense than you having to – whoops, in that case I'd better skedaddle though –' He looks at his watch and is grabbing a kiss in the next instant: then in the same flurry of movement he has closed the door behind him.

This is the way they live now, like two actors in the final performances of a show no one comes to see any more.

The morning is a quagmire of e-mails and missed calls, voicemails promising more e-mails, more calls. Still, the prospect of an afternoon in the outside world makes it easier to bear. People are always telling Halley how lucky she is to be able to work at home. No commute! No boss in your face! You don't even have to get dressed! She herself used to write up the housebound life, or *fully networked society* as it was called then, as the great promise of the digital revolution. Now here she is, thrilled to be going to a science fair for teenagers because it gives her an excuse to put on make-up. Be careful what you wish for, she supposes.

In Ballsbridge she parks the car and leaves the bright afternoon for the darkness of the exhibition hall. Inside it is murky and frenetic with activity, like a juvenile ant colony. Everywhere she looks, arcane contraptions hum, spark, crackle, splash; animals dutifully nose electrodes and spin wheels; computers encrypt, decrypt, configure. For all the commotion, though, science is palpably of secondary importance to the teenaged exhibitors; between the stalls, stares are being swapped so nakedly lustful that even to pass through them is to feel vaguely violated.

She does the rounds of the exhibits, speaks to their breathless or monosyllabic progenitors, while around her their peers, obviously attending under duress, shuffle by with the hopeless expressions of prisoners on a death march – pasty, raw-boned kids in dreary uniforms, fidgeting, slapping each other, repeating unfunny jokes. Seeing Howard's friend Farley looming in the distance, she makes her way to the Seabrook stalls, where a study of the heat-release system in reptiles has been thrown into jeopardy by a gecko gone AWOL. A couple of boys are crawling around in the space behind the stall in search of it, proffering little pieces of Mars Bar; the other two members of the team appear more concerned with looking cool in front of the Loreto girls with the wind generator on the other side of the aisle. 'I knew we should have brought a reserve gecko.' Beside her, Farley shakes his head. 'That guy's not coming back.'

'How is everything? Gecko aside.'

'Everything's fine. Counting down to Christmas, I suppose, like everybody else.'

She wants to ask him about Howard, try to discover what might be on his mind, what she can do; but she hesitates, and a moment later two boys arrive from another Seabrook exhibit – one swarthy with a daunting single eyebrow, the other with pale, ginger features strafed with acne, both of that slightly dysmorphic cast common to teenage boys, as though their faces have been copied out of a catalogue by someone working in an unfamiliar medium – to tell Farley that someone spilled Coke on their laptop.

'"Someone"?' Farley repeats.

'It just sort of happened,' the ginger boy says.

'Oh God,' Farley sighs, 'sorry, Halley,' as he follows them away.

How strange that Howard spends his whole day with these creatures, she thinks. She finds her energy sapped just from being around them a few moments.

Climbing into the car afterwards – an ancient Bluebird, a compendium of idiosyncrasies held together by rust that represents Howard's only significant investment in life prior to meeting her – she pretends to herself that she doesn't feel bad about going home. She turns on the radio, hums unlisteningly over the chatter of voices, does not resist as her mind slips back to those grand days of irrational exuberance, when hardly a day went by without a new start-up starting up, or an IPO, or some other such glamorous wing-ding, as her old editor called them, for Halley to dress up for; the great days of the Internet Boom, when all the talk was of the future, imagined as a kind of secular, matte-black Rapture, an epoch of convergence and unending bliss that it was widely believed, there at the end of the twentieth century, was just about to arrive, and Halley spent her nights in a little apartment on Mulberry Street –

The dog bounds out in front of her in a flash of golden fur that disappears immediately out of sight. She jams on the brakes, but the car, with a surprisingly heavy, almost industrial sound, has already hit it. Opening the door she scrambles out onto the street – *her* street, with *her* house, and the rest of the day as it should have been, only yards away! – at the same moment that the woman from the house opposite opens hers and runs down the footpath towards her.

'It just appeared out of nowhere,' Halley gabbles, 'it jumped right out in front of the car . . .'

'The garden gate was open,' the woman says, but her attention is on the dog, kneeling to stroke its pink-tinged head. It lies flat on its side, a little distance from the car bumper; its brown eyes smile at Halley as she crouches down beside it. Blood is trickling along the gravel from underneath its head. 'Oh, Polly . . .'

A car has pulled up behind Halley's. Unable to pass, the driver gets out and stands over them. 'Oh, the poor thing . . . did you hit her?'

'She came out of nowhere,' Halley repeats miserably.

'Poor old girl.' The man hunkers down by the two women. The dog, enjoying the attention, looks from one to the other, thumps its tail weakly on the ground. 'She needs to be taken to the vet,' the man says. They begin to discuss how she might best be lifted. If a sheet were slid under her, a kind of hammock? – A shrill scream issues from a short distance away. The woman's little girl is frozen by the garden gate.

'Alice, go inside,' the woman commands.

'Polly!' the girl cries.

'Go in*side*,' her mother repeats, but the girl is dashing pell-mell down the path and by the time she reaches them is already in floods of tears. 'Polly! Polly!' The dog pants and licks its chops, as if to try and calm her.

'Shh, Alice . . . Alice . . .' The woman half-rises as the little girl begins to wail, her entire head turning mauve, becoming one huge mouth. 'Shh . . .' The woman presses the child's head into her body; the small hands fling themselves around her skirt. Gently she leads her back towards the house. 'Come on now . . . it will be okay . . .'

Absently, Halley swirls her fingertips over the drab tarmac while the man phones the DSPCA. Before long the woman from the house re-emerges, a white sheet bundled in her arms. She waits for the man to finish his call and then the three of them lift the dog to the side of the road. There is no longer any need to take it to the vet. They stretch the cover loosely over its body.

'I'm so sorry,' Halley pleads yet again.

'I kept meaning to do something about that gate,' the woman says distractedly. 'I suppose the postman must have left it open.'

The man puts his hand on her elbow and tells her that these things happen. Halley aches for him to say it to her too, but he does not. The three of them exchange phone numbers, as if their drama still has an act to go; 'I live across the street,' Halley tells the woman uselessly. Then she gets back in the car and drives it the stone's throw to her own gate. Once inside, she peeks through the curtains to see the woman, cheeks streaked, still keeping vigil on the corner, by the bedsheet from which the dog's paws protrude, neatly, two by two. The other retriever lies on the grass in the woman's garden, snout poking abjectly through the railings; from an upstairs window the little girl looks out, palms pressed to the glass, wailing soundlessly.

Halley closes the curtains and bunches herself up in a corner. The phone flashes at her from the desk with incoming calls; digital fish swim back and forth across the computer screen. For the first time since she arrived in Ireland, she wishes without reservation she were at home. It feels like her whole life here has been tending towards this point, turning her into someone who runs down a dog.

Not long after, she hears Howard coming in, preceded by a whistle like the theme tune to some balsa-wood sitcom. She sits up on the couch, glares at his unwitting, friendly smile. 'So how was the Fair?' he asks.

'What?'

'The Science Fair?'

The Science Fair! The gecko! The reminder of that distant afternoon and her own part in it – how trivial, how perfectly fucking useless to anyone! – is petrol on the flames of her anger. 'Howard, why didn't you get the car serviced?'

'What?' Howard, slow-witted, lays down his briefcase and overcoat.

'The fucking brakes are fucked, Howard, I've asked you a million times to bring that heap of shit to the garage and you never fucking do it –'

Howard regards her carefully as if she's speaking in tongues. 'Well, I will, if you want me to, I will. What's wrong, did something . . . ?'

She tells him, in an overheated rush, about the dog, the woman, the little girl.

'Oh God . . .' He musses her hair. 'I'm sorry, Halley.' But his sympathy only makes her angrier. Why should he get off scot-free? Yes, she drove the car, but everything else is his fault! His fault!

'What's the use of being sorry? God, Howard, what if it had been the little girl who ran out on the road? What would you say then? Sorry?'

Bowing his head, Howard mumbles contritely.

'Why don't you just *do* what you say you're going to do? You have to *think* of things, Howard, you have responsibilities, you can't just float around your own little world, buried in your war books, dreaming you're fighting the Nazis –'

'The Hun,' Howard says to the floor.

'What?'

'The Nazis are the Second World War. I'm doing the First.'

'Oh, for God's sake – are you even listening to me? Are you even aware you have a life here? Am I just some phantasm who interrupts your reading? You have to fucking commit to things, Howard, you have to wake up to the people around you, who are depending on you! Even though you find it boring, it's still your life!'

She lets him have it, both barrels, all the frustration that's been building up for the last few weeks and longer; Howard listens in silence, shoulders hunched, eyes screwed up as if he's got a stomach pain, and the more she chastises, the more his brow creases into this stymied attitude, somewhere between bafflement and agony, and the more he doubles up, until with a start she wonders if he is actually going to be sick, at which point he sits abruptly on the arm of the armchair and says, almost to himself, 'I can't do this any more.'

'What?' Halley says.

'I'm so sorry,' Howard says in a strangulated voice.

At some preconscious level she must know what's coming, because she already feels like she's been punched in the stomach: there is no air in her lungs, she does not seem able to breathe new air in. Not now, she thinks, not now! But the next thing he is babbling to her about Robert Graves and Hallowe'en, 'Wild Horses' and global warming, a substitute geography teacher who drinks Cosmopolitans – it descends on Halley in a rain, and before she can unpick the sense of it the blood has drained from her face, her fingers buzz with lightness . . .

And a part of her is thinking of feminism! A part of her is thinking of all the women who fought for their rights, and feeling ashamed for letting them down, because as the story of his infidelity unspools, she feels only an agonizing crumbling, a horrible literal disintegration, as though she's turned into slush and cascaded all over the floor; he tells her how he doesn't know how he *feels*, he doesn't know what he *wants* – and all *she* wants is for him to mop her up and gather her together as she was; she wants to plead and beg and cry so that he'll unsay what he's just said, hold her in his arms, tell her that nothing has changed, that everything is all right. But of course that is not what happens.

By the morning after the incident in Our Lady's Hall, Skippy's temple has blossomed into a gruesome purple-red flower. Some bruises you wear like badges of honour: when you got it playing rugby, or quad racing, or falling off something while drunk, no opportunity is lost to show off a good contusion. A bruise inflicted by someone else, however, is a whole other story: it's like a big flashing arrow marking you out as punchable, and before long there'll be boys queuing up to add bruises of their own, as if they'd just been waiting for somebody to show them it could be done. In one morning Skippy's had a week's worth of shit from people – swinging the door shut on him, tripping him up in the corridor, not to mention a punishment essay from Ms Ni Riain, three pages on the Gaelic origins of the name *Seabrook*, for coming late to class. By lunchtime he's too dispirited even to eat; while the others go to the Ref, he skulks off on his own.

'Poor sucker,' Niall says. 'He's got it bad.'

'That bang on the head was the best thing that could have happened to him,' Dennis says, carrying his tray to the table. 'Maybe now he'll realize what a stupid idea all this Frisbee Girl stuff was. And we won't have to listen to that gay BETHani song any more.'

'That song really reminds me of something,' Geoff says with a frown.

'It's a shame though,' says Niall. 'Because he does really like her.'

'Really liking something is an automatic way of making sure you don't get it.' Dennis has just come from Quartet rehearsal – forty-five minutes of sarcastic remarks ('Ah, I think you'll find the piece is in *four-four* time?') and eye-rolling from Ruprecht – and is in an especially bilious mood. 'That's the way it goes in this stupid crappy world.'

'I suppose,' Niall says. 'Though I don't see why.'

'Maybe God made it that way to test us?' Geoff suggests.

'Oh sure, Geoff, and then at the end we all get lollipops,' Dennis scowls.

'Well, the thing is, of course –' Ruprecht raises his head from his copybook like a sagacious hamster '– that the universe is asymmetrical.'

'What? What's that supposed to mean?'

'I mean, what we're looking at here is a system that went from a high degree of symmetry in the moments immediately after the Big Bang – ten dimensions, all matter and energy conjoined – to the quite low degree of symmetry we have now, with some dimensions curled up, disunited physical forces, what have you. Obviously, it's still a little bit symmetrical, we have our laws of physics, relativity, rotational symmetry, and so forth. But when you compare it to some of the other possible topologies that M-theory allows for, our universe does seem quite unbalanced. And patterns that occur on a quantum level carry all the way up.'

Dennis puts down his fork. 'Blowjob, what the hell are you talking about?'

'Exactly the same thing you are. The fundamental structure of the universe means that things consistently fail to balance out. Toast lands butter side down. Intelligent students get wedgies, instead of being respected as the future leaders of their society. You can't get what you want, but someone else, who doesn't want it, has it in spades. Asymmetry. It's everywhere you look.' He hefts his pudgy body around on the bench, scanning the room. 'Over there, for instance. Philip Kilfether.' He points to where Philip Kilfether, Seabrook's Smallest Boy, sits just visible behind his juice carton. 'All Philip Kilfether has ever dreamed of, since he was old enough to talk, is becoming a professional basketball player. But because of his underdeveloped pituitary gland, he's never going to be more than four feet tall.'

They gaze at the tragic sight of Philip Kilfether, who spends hours on the basketball court every day, dashing from one end to the next as the ball whizzes unreachably over his head, and more hours still in his room, decorated wall-to-wall with posters of Magic, Bird, Michael Jordan and other famously tall men, performing stretching exercises in defiance of the medical prognosis. Murmurs of comprehension rise from the company at the table.

'Skippy and this frisbee-playing girl is another obvious example. He likes her. She kisses him. The path of least resistance would seem to be to continue in that vein. But instead, she vanishes and Carl beats him up. It's baffling.'

'Or, how about Caetano,' Geoff chips in. 'He was in love with this girl in Brazil and he spent his entire life-savings on buying her this MP3 player because one day they were watching the Shopping Channel together and she said she'd like an MP3 player and then practically the very next day after he gave it to her she got off with this guy who was fixing her parents' drains in their summerhouse even though she told Caetano this other time that the guy was an idiot and he had these really hairy knuckles and smelled of drains and then when Caetano asked her to give him the MP3 player back she wouldn't?'

'The asymmetry does seem particularly pronounced when girls are involved,' Ruprecht observes.

'Wow, Ruprecht, you really think in another universe girls wouldn't be so asymmetrical?'

'I don't see why not,' Ruprecht says, adjusting his glasses donnishly. 'As I say, patterns occurring on a quantum level are replicated on every scale.'

'That's great, Blowjob,' Dennis rejoins. 'Now all Skippy has to do is find his way into a parallel universe.'

'It is theoretically possible,' Ruprecht says.

'Well, is it theoretically possible you could come up with something that might actually help him?'

'Like what?'

'I don't know, like a death ray to shoot Carl with.'

'Violence never solved anything,' Ruprecht asserts sanctimoniously.

'Violence solves everything, you idiot, look at the history of the world. Any situation they have, they dick around with it for a while, then they bring in violence. That's the whole reason they have scientists, to make violence more violent.'

'It sounds to me as if your grasp of history is of a similar standard to your ability on the bassoon,' Ruprecht snaps.

'Shove it up your hole, Ruprecht, and your lame theory too.' Dennis kicks back balefully in his chair. 'The truth is, Skippy'd still be a loser in a parallel universe. We'd *all* still be losers, even in a universe of tiny girly ants.'

In the hallway some of the swimmers are gathered around the noticeboard. 'Hey, Juster! Have a look at this!' Antony Taylor calls out.

Coach has posted up the team for the meet. Your name's second from the end.

'I can't believe he picked you,' Siddartha Niland says. 'He might as well throw a fucking brick in the water.'

'You'd better not blow this for us, Juster,' Duane Grehan says.

'Why the fuck would he pick you?' Siddartha shakes his head. 'It just doesn't make any sense.'

Upstairs you call Dad to give him the news. 'That's great, buddy!' Dad's voice crackles from far away.

'Do you think you'll be able to come along?'

'I hope so, sport, I really hope so.'

'What does Dr Gulbenkian say?'

'What does he say?'

'Wasn't he coming over?'

'Oh yeah – oh, you know, just the usual. You know him. Listen, D, it's crazy here today, I'd better go. But that's great news, great news. This'll really give us a lift.'

You hang up, you go to the window and look through the telescope. From the back of the door, the dead plastic eyes of the goggles watch you watching.

You don't know why Coach picked you. You've got the worst

times in the whole squad. It's not just that you're slow. Whenever you swim now it's like there's this secret tide waiting there just for you; and while all the other boys power ahead in straight lines to the finish, while Coach claps his hands and shouts them on, it is trying to lead you away, down to some unseen place there under the water, a dark door behind which lies a room that, as you descend towards it, you find you *almost recognize* . . . and like in a dream when you realize it's pivoted into a nightmare, that's when you start freaking out, flailing and thrashing, which only helps the dark magnets pulling you down, till it genuinely seems you're going to drown, there in the shallows of the school pool – only at the last second something will kick back in and you'll fight it off, struggle to the surface and claw for the wall as fast as you can, *Paddy Last again, Daniel*, and behind you it will disappear again, sink back into the innocent blue, waiting for the next time . . .

She's not out there. You abandon the telescope, step back into the room. The X of the meet burns red on the calendar. The pills call to you from the dresser. Deep breaths, Skip. Remember what Coach said. A lot can happen between then and now. A mer-boy enrols at Seabrook and bumps you off the team. You get stuck in a lift, you break your arm. Something worse.

For now though it's back to class, turgid deserts of grammar and rules and facts, the faraway life it is all a preparation for glimpsed through the windows of reading-comprehension texts and business models and vocabulary-boosting role-plays –

'Good morning, I would like *to buy* a new bicycle.'

'Certainly, sir. What kind of bicycle are you looking for? Is it for *everyday use?*'

'I need it to *commute to work*. I am looking for something *durable, portable* and *not too expensive*. Can you *show me your range?*'

– seeming only fractionally less desolate than the preparations themselves, and the malign influence of the bruise still working its evil magic, like an anti-amulet, a bad-luck charm you can't take off . . .

'Oh, Mr Juster . . .'

Calling you back to the doorway of the now-empty classroom. Hanging there across it like a spider in an invisible web. 'Deep in thought, Mr Juster . . . ?'

'Uh, yes, Father.' He keeps *talking* to you.

'Is something troubling you, my son?'

'No, Father.' Trying not to wriggle under his incendiary stare.

'You've been in the wars, though.'

'Uh . . . I ran into a door.'

'Mmm.' The fingers that reach out and touch your pulpy temple are chilly and damp and curiously grainy, like they are on Ash Wednesday, rubbing wet ashes onto your skin. 'That wasn't too clever, was it?'

'No, Father.'

'What are we going to do with you, Mr Juster?'

'I don't know, Father.'

'If you can't negotiate even a simple door.' The priest pauses. A sigh ripples through his knife-like body. 'Well, boys will be boys, I suppose.' The black eyes sparkle. 'Won't they, Mr Juster.'

'Uh . . . yes, Father.'

'They will,' Father Green exhales, as if to himself, 'they will . . .' And he withdraws, like smoke being sucked out a chimney; leaving you to scurry away, wiping the spot where the fingers touched you, the bones that seem to push right through your skin and into your soul . . .

Ruprecht returns from the lab that night to find Skippy sitting with the lights out and the duvet wrapped around him, doing battle with a deathly-white hydra that breathes frost and flails its limbs like blizzards of razors.

'Nasty-looking character,' he says.

'Ice Demon.' Cross-legged on the floor, Skippy tugs the controller left and right, his mouth set in a tight line, his expression one of furious concentration; when Mr Tomms comes down the corridor for lights-out he switches off the machine and gets into bed without saying another word.

Then, just when Ruprecht is sure he is asleep, through the darkness: 'Carl hitting me doesn't necessarily have anything to do with Lori.'

'No?'

'Carl's an asshole. He's always doing that kind of thing. He doesn't need a reason.'

'That's true,' Ruprecht concedes.

There is a pause, then the voice comes back over the gulf of floor between the beds. 'Anyway, how would he even know I'd texted her?'

Springs groan as Ruprecht redistributes himself, folding his hands on his stomach and twiddling his thumbs computatively. 'Well, the surmise would be that your friend had told him . . .'

This followed by another pause, as in a long-distance phone conversation in days of Yore; and then the defiant reply, 'She wouldn't do that.' He turns on his side, towards the wall, and, shortly after, tinny music rises from his headphones, the BETHani song in miniature like a distant field of harmonizing grasshoppers.

Ruprecht, still humming with sugar from a feed of doughnuts

earlier, cannot sleep. He gets up, opens the SETI window, spends a while watching the computer processing the meaningless news the universe brings it; he makes a list of random M words, MOOSE, MARKER, MILK, MINNOW, to see if any unusual connections emerge; he watches the softly rising and falling shape of his friend, cocooned in his nimbus of nanomusic.

He is thinking about asymmetry. This is a world, he is thinking, where you can lie in bed, listening to a song as you dream about someone you love, and your feelings and the music will resonate so powerfully and completely that it seems impossible that the beloved, whoever and wherever he or she might be, should not *know*, should not pick up this signal as it pulsates from your heart, as if you and the music and the love and the whole universe have merged into one force that can be channelled out into the darkness to bring them this message. But in actuality, not only will he or she not know, there is nothing to stop that other person from lying on his or her bed at the exact same moment listening to the exact same song and thinking about *someone else entirely* – from aiming those identical feelings in some completely opposite direction, at some totally other person, who may in turn be lying in the dark thinking of another person still, a fourth, who is thinking of a fifth, and so on, and so on; so that rather than a universe of neatly reciprocating pairs, love and love-returned fluttering through space nicely and symmetrically like so many pairs of butterfly wings, instead we get chains of yearning, which sprawl and meander and culminate in an infinite number of dead ends.

Just as the shape of natural objects like rainbows, snowflakes, crystals and blossoming flowers derives from the symmetrical way that quarks arrange themselves in the atom – a remnant of the universe's lost state of perfect symmetry – so Ruprecht is convinced that the unhappy state of affairs regarding love can be traced right back to the subatomic. If you read up on strings, you will learn that there are two different types, closed and open-ended. The closed strings are O-shaped loops that float about like angels, insouciant of spacetime's demands and playing no part in our reality. It is the open-ended strings, the forlorn, incomplete U-shaped strings, whose desperate ends cling to the sticky stuff of the universe; it is they that become reality's building blocks, its particles, its exchangers of energy, the teeming producers of all that complication. Our universe, one could almost say, is actually *built out of loneliness*; and that foundational loneliness persists upwards to haunt every one of its residents. But might the situation be different in other universes? In a universe where, for instance, *all* of the strings were closed, what would love look like there? And energy? And spacetime? The siren call of the question mark: his thoughts drift laterally, inevitably, away from Skippy and his predicament to grander matters – universes coiled voluptuously in secret dimensions, sheets of pure sparking otherness, crimped topographies cradling forms unsullied even by being dreamed of . . .

A noise summons him back to reality – a tapping, barely audible, at the window. It is a moth, beating a feeble tattoo of yearning for the moon on the other side of the glass: another unrequited love story, Ruprecht thinks. He lifts the sash to let it out, then goes to his copybook and writes down MOON, MOTH. Midway through the second word he stops, and for a long moment he remains motionless, as if stalled over the page; then he hurries back to the window and stares out, as if he could descry there in the dark the quick upward beat of tiny wings . . .

Once a week, more if his schedule permits, Father Green makes the journey from the haughty garrisons of the bourgeoisie into St Patrick's Villas, to visit those parishioners who are too sickly or frail to attend mass. The journey is less than a mile, but the Villas belong to a different world, a world corroded by neglect and stinking of human waste. He climbs flaking stairwells to arrive at graffiti-limned doors; even after he announces himself, a timid eye will size him up and down through a crack before undoing the final chain. They are women, almost exclusively. Mrs Doran, Mrs Coombes, Mrs Gulaston: liver-spotted, blue-rinsed, forgotten, and yet, somehow, still here. Inside will be the television, muted in deference though not switched off; floral wallpaper webbed with damp images of Padre Pio and John Paul II beside pictures in oval frames of long-deceased husbands, of children and children's children now living in Ongar or in Spain or simply too busy for the inconsolable laments of age. He will sit in the kitchen; they bring him tea and he will make himself listen as they tell him of their woes – the electric heater that is not working, the sores on their legs, the neighbourhood's decline. It's all gone to the dogs, Father. It's like a jungle. Worse than a jungle! These kids robbin cars and racin them up and down. Breakin bottles. Shoutin and screamin at all hours. Gurriers they are, on drugs, the lot of them! It's the drugs have been the ruin of this place. It used to be a lovely place, Father, you remember. A lovely place. Now you daren't go out at night. Sure even in broad daylight you're takin your life in your hands. They'd knock you down soon as look at you. They'd be in your flat before you're halfway out the door.

Father Green nods, sips from his cup. In truth, this has never been a lovely place, not for the twenty years he has been coming here. The 'boom' never penetrated; to look out the window, it might be the 1980s still, the height of the heroin plague, the police doing nothing, the politicians doing nothing. The same faces loitering in the forecourt of the boarded-up garage, proud of their intractability, the notoriety of their home. Wearing their failure like a badge of honour, generation after generation, parent and child. Everybody knows what they are doing there; you may call the guards if you want, talk to a bored-sounding young man, and an hour later, if so inclined, the squad car will roll by, and they will disperse until it has gone, or regroup outside the shopping centre, or in the park. But nothing changes, and no one is overly concerned, as long as 'the problem' stays down here, in the slums.

Before he leaves today Father Green stops at the grotto of Our Lady. It used to be that no matter what horrors raged around it this little corner remained immaculate. Now her devotees are too old and frail to maintain it, and the paintwork on the plaster statue has bleached with time, turning her serenity to exhaustion, her gesture of providence to a shrug. Reaching over the railings he fishes out a can, crisp packets, a condom; people eddy around him, glancing indifferently as they go past, as they might at a tramp rooting through a rubbish bin. He hauls himself painfully back over to the street, cradling his armful of filth to his chest, goes in search of a receptacle – when out into his path steps a man –

A *black* man, perhaps forty-five years old, glossy-skinned, muscular, the negative of the listless washed-out natives: inside Father Green a clock winds backwards at supernatural speed, and from the man's yellow-tinged eyes a corresponding recognition seems to leap into being, and he raises his hands, huge, animalistic –

Gently they reach out and take the load from his. Thank you, Father, the voice says. Those familiar plodding vowels. *Tank you, Fodda.*

Of course, Father Green whispers, as the man returns inside with the garbage. Through the doorway, carousels and dusky faces may be glimpsed: a shop, a new shop, it seems.

He is still trembling when he arrives back at the school. At dinner in the priests' residence he is eager to discuss his encounter; he waits for the conversation to turn to the past, as it so often does, that he might casually bring it up. Do you know, he says when the time comes, hearing the words ring high and false in his ears, do you know, making my rounds of St Patrick's Villas today I was struck by the influx of Africans to the neighbourhood. A few seemed to me to be just of the age that I might have taught them on the missions!

And he waits, braced, for what they might say.

I can never understand why in God's name anyone would leave Africa to come here, Father Zmed remarks. Give up all that sunshine to live in a slum.

Land of opportunity, Father Crookes responds. Civilization. Read about it in their schoolbooks, quite natural they'd want to see it for themselves.

It's our fault then, Father Dundon says gloomily.

What I mean to say is – Father Green attempts to steer the conversation back around – do you think it possible that those same children we taught might by pure chance have ended up living in Seabrook? Wouldn't that be . . . wouldn't that be marvellous?

Father Zmed's brilliant diamantine squint searching him out across the table. What is he thinking?

I'd imagine most of 'em would be dead by now, Jerome, Father Crookes says through a mouthful of dessert. Know what the life expectancy is for the average African man?

Father Dundon sighs. I often wonder did we do the right thing at all. Heard a chap on the radio blaming the Church for the spread of AIDS over there. Said the Pope was responsible for the deaths of 22 million people.

Well, that's just –

Of all the silly –

That's twice as many as Hitler, Father Dundon says.

Oh, come – they know this is wrong but they do not know

why; they look to Father Green to refute it. We can't rewrite the word of God, he says obligingly. And disease does not give one licence for immorality. Even in Africa.

Not everyone is like us, though, Father Zmed says to Father Green – fixing on him again with that curiously penetrating gaze, that barely visible smile. Not everyone has the . . . moral strength for abstinence.

Then they must pray for it, Father Green says, and crumples his napkin summarily.

Dead, so. Heart eased, he stays with them at the table till well into the night, trading old war stories, what they'd done, what they'd achieved. Young men faced with an impossible task, a continent, a whole continent subsumed in witchcraft! Natives who'd kneel down to pray with you, then after sunset melt away into the bush, returning at dawn daubed in blood, eyes rolling like lunatics. Every night you'd lie half-awake waiting for the footfall outside your tent – drift off expecting to awake on the altar yourself! Or cooking in a pot! No time for subtleties – only surefire way was to terrify them. His name is Satan. He lives in a place of flames. That they could understand. Pointing white-eyed into the desert. Yes, yes, Hell. Only God can protect you. Reading to them from Dante. Sometimes you'd scare yourself! But it worked, that was the thing! They came to heel! They could learn, they could be lifted out of that squalor! For all its savagery there was hope there! The sheer volume of souls saved, one came home feeling one had done something! Is it any wonder that they themselves retreat there now, into these stories each has heard a hundred times, when the present is nothing but ambiguity and accusation, intent on dismantling everything they believed in?

Perverts, monsters, brainwashers.

Retiring to his room, Father Green stays up for another hour correcting homework. He sits in a small pool of lamplight, reviewing the bright dull portraits of the world – bicycles to be rented, purchases to be made – that the textbook presents for the boys to complete. He works steadily, unhurriedly, and although he knows exactly where Daniel Juster's copy lies in the pile he pretends to himself that he doesn't; when he reaches it, he does not stroke the page, imagining the boy's own hand travelling slowly across it; nor linger over the handwriting, its guileless, meticulous loops and crosses, nor sniff the paper, nor kiss, ever so softly, the bitter ink.

Handwriting. Chalk on slate. Plane trees outside a church, wind rolling in from the desert, laughing carefree children, zig-zagging half-naked, ebony-thewed, through the stern young priest's classes . . . Those children! Irrepressible! You couldn't help but smile – and now, alone in his bed decades later, with the children dead, safely dead, a smile plays again over Father Green's face, carrying him down into sleep, a sleep of flames, a thousand tiny white-hot desert tongues licking and searing and scalding him everywhere, an agony of guilt that is also, dreadfully, an ineffable ecstasy.

Ruprecht is up to something. For two days now he's been feigning illness to get out of class – stuffing his bed with pillows and relocating himself to his lab. But what he's doing down there remains a mystery even to his room-mate; until, late on Friday night, Skippy awakes to find a portly silhouette standing over his bed. 'What are you doing?' he mumbles through the remnants of his dreams.

'I'm on the verge of a historic breakthrough,' the silhouette says.

'Can't it wait till morning?'

Apparently it can't, because Ruprecht continues to hover there, breathing snuffily in the darkness, until Skippy with a groan throws back his covers.

An hour later, he and the others shiver on pieces of styrofoam packaging, still waiting for whatever it is to happen, while Ruprecht, in goggles and some sort of cape, attaches cables to circuit boards and makes adjustments with a soldering iron to what looks like several hundred euros' worth of tinfoil. The basement is ice-cold, and patience is beginning to wear thin.

'Damn it, Blowjob, how much longer is this going to take?'

'Nearly finished,' Ruprecht's answer returning somewhat muffled.

'He keeps saying that,' Mario mutters dourly.

'Ruprecht, it's the middle of the *night*,' Geoff pleads, rubbing his arms.

'And this place is full of spiders,' Skippy adds.

'Just one more minute,' the voice assures them.

'Can you at least tell us what it is?' Niall says.

'It looks sort of like his teleporter,' Geoff observes.

'It's a similar principle,' Ruprecht agrees, emerging momentarily from a forest of cables. 'An Einstein-Rosen bridge, only recalibrated for an eleven-dimensional matrix. Although the aim of the teleporter was merely to create a conduit between two different areas of spacetime, whereas this – this . . .' He pauses mysteriously, then disappears back inside his creation with a spatula.

'It doesn't *look* like a bridge,' Mario says, scrutinizing the tinfoil wigwam.

'I wonder what it's a bridge to,' Geoff ponders huskily.

'*Nowhere*, you clown,' Dennis snaps. 'The only place it's going to take you is up the garden path. God damn it, it's Friday night! Do you realize that out there, right at this very minute, millions of people are having sex? They're having sex, and they're drinking beer, while *we* sit here watching Von Blowjob play with his toys.'

'Mmm, well,' Ruprecht replies on his way to one of the computers, 'I doubt very much that having sex and drinking beer will be of much use to humanity when its entire future hangs in the balance. I doubt that they'll be drinking much beer then, when the whole planet is underwater and life is on the brink of extinction.'

'I feel like I'm extinct already, listening to you,' mutters Dennis.

But it seems the moment of truth is finally at hand, for now Ruprecht steps back from his silver pupa and adjusts his cape. 'Mario?'

'Yo.' Mario waves his camera phone. 'Ready when you are.'

'Excellent.' Ruprecht straightens his cape and clears his throat. 'Well, you're probably wondering why I brought you here. The concept of the multiverse –'

'Cut!' says Mario.

'What?' Ruprecht regards him captiously.

Mario explains that his phone can only record in twenty-second segments.

'That's fine,' Ruprecht says. Narrowing his eyes, he continues his historical speech in twenty-second bursts. 'The concept of the multiverse is not a new one. The idea of parallel worlds goes right back to the Greeks. With M-theory, however, we have our strongest indication yet of what the structure of the multiverse may look like – an eleven-dimensional ocean of Nothing, which we share with entities of various sizes, from points to nine-dimensional hyperuniverses. According to the theory, some of these entities are less than a hair's breadth away from us; that is to say, gentlemen, they are here in the room with us right now.' A tightening of the silence succeeds his words, save for the near-inaudible hiss of hairs standing up on the backs of necks. Steepling his spongy fingers, he fixes each of them in turn, the crepuscular light of the computers glistening on his damp brow. 'The problem is, of course, access. The higher dimensions are wrapped up so tightly that current Earth technology cannot supply anything like the amount of energy required to break through to them, or even to see them. But the other night I had what I can only describe as a revelation.'

He steps over to an easel stencilled ART ROOM! DO NOT REMOVE! and flips back the cover to reveal a star map. 'Allow me to introduce Cygnus X-3.' He levels his pointer at one among an innumerable array of dots and splodges. 'What it is we are not quite sure. Maybe a large, spinning neutron star. Maybe a black hole that is devouring a sun. What we do know is that it emits gigantic quantities of radiation that bombard the Earth's atmosphere daily, at energies ranging from 100 million electron volts to 100 billion billion electron volts. In approximately –' he glances at his watch '– twelve minutes, we're going to have the biggest radiation burst since the summer. On the school clock, a specially adapted receptor is waiting to harness that energy.'

'Like in Back to the Future!' Geoff exclaims.

'From the receptor –' Ruprecht ignoring this '– the radiation will be fed into this Escher loop.' He indicates a heavy-duty cable that snakes over the floor, under the boys' legs and out the door. 'The loop has a radius of approximately a quarter-mile, taking it around the rugby pitches and back. The cosmic rays are cycled around the loop using the Escher free-acceleration process, building up more and more energy until enough has been created for our purposes.

Then it comes back in here, into this Cosmic Energy Compressor. Having achieved optimum capacity, the gravitation chamber in the pod will be activated, allowing us, if all goes well, to create a tiny rift in space. Effectively, what we're doing is borrowing energy from a large, distant black hole to create a small, local and controllable black hole, right here in the basement.' He allows a moment here for awed murmuring, then resumes: 'We know from Einstein's equations that for a black hole to make sense mathematically, there must be a mirror universe on the opposite side. We also know that the infinite gravitation of the hole will instantly crush anything that enters it. However, by aligning it along the *exact trajectory* of the axis, it may be possible, in the moments before the rift repairs itself, to pass an object through the centre of the hole unscathed and into whatever lies on the other side. Tonight this toy robot will be our Columbus.' From a schoolbag he produces a plastic red-and-grey android about ten inches in height.

'Optimus Prime,' Geoff whispers approvingly. 'Leader of the Autobots.'

A low hum emanates from the foil-covered pod. Beside it, the computer screens throw up impenetrable screeds of numbers, like digital incantations, or the ecstatic babblings of some distant reality now very close –

'Hey, Ruprecht – these other universes – will we be able to go there? Like, if your portal works?'

'If the portal works,' Ruprecht says, solemnly handing goggles to each of them, 'it'll be a whole new chapter in the story of humanity.'

'Holy smoke . . .'

'Goodbye, Earth! So long, you piece of crap, except for Italy.'

'Think of it, Skip, there could be millions of parallel Loris out there! Like whole universes full of them?'

'Oh, sure,' Dennis chips in. 'And planets of lingerie models addicted to sex? Galaxies of girls who have built their entire civilizations on the moment the Virgins from Outer Space arrive in their little jumpsuits?'

Ruprecht glances at his watch. 'It's time,' he says. 'Witnesses, don your goggles, please. For your own safety, I must request that you keep your distance. There may be some radiation emitted by the vortex.'

Skippy and the others lower their masks, and even Dennis is not immune to the pregnant tingling that pervades the dingy basement, the undispellable sense that *something is imminent*. Ruprecht inputs some last figures into the computer, then gently lowers Optimus Prime into a kind of metallic crib. And there, for a moment, on his knees by the foil-lined pod, he bides – like Moses's mother, perhaps, with her bulrush basket on the banks of the Nile – gazing reflectively at the robot's painted eyes, thinking that to do anything, epic or mundane, bound for glory or doomed to failure, is in its way to say goodbye to a world; that the greatest victories are therefore never without the shadow of loss; that every path you take, no matter how lofty or effulgent, aches not only with the memory of what you left behind, but with the ghosts of all the untaken paths, now never to be taken, running parallel . . .

Then, rising, he throws the switch.

What seems like a long moment elapses in which nothing happens. Then, just as Dennis is about to emit a caw of triumph, the pod begins to thrum, and very quickly the room fills with heat. Geoff looks at Skippy. Skippy looks at Geoff. Mario gazes intently at the tiny screen on his phone, where the scene is reproduced in miniature as it happens, although there is nothing as yet to actually *see*, there is only this hum, which is getting louder and louder and also with every passing instant less smooth, more of a *judder*, accompanied by disconcerting whines and rattles . . . The heat, too, increases by the second, pulsing from the cable beneath their toes, until rapidly it is almost insufferable, like being in a sauna, or an engine room, or an engine, like being inside an actual engine; foreheads drip with sweat, and Skippy is just beginning to wonder exactly how healthy a state of affairs this is, when he chances to glance over at Ruprecht, nibbling the ends of his fingers, nervously eyeing the humming pod – and has the sudden and extremely disquieting intuition that his friend has *no idea whatsoever* what he is doing – when there is a loud electrical *zap!* and an eyeblink of blinding white light, as if now they're inside a lightbulb, and then absolute darkness.

For an alarming spell the darkness is also a silence, with only the hiss of the Escher cable to assure Skippy he is still in the basement and not himself in a black hole, or dead; then from somewhere over to the right, Ruprecht's voice rises quaveringly: 'Nothing to worry about . . . please remain in your seats . . .'

'You fat idiot!' Mario says invisibly from Skippy's left. 'Are you trying to kill us?'

'Perfectly normal . . . small power outage . . . no need to be alarmed . . .' Noises issue from Ruprecht's portion of the darkness, as of someone picking himself up from the ground. 'I must have . . . the, ah, limiter seems to . . . bear with me for one moment . . .' A narrow shaft of torchlight appears and waves about the room as Ruprecht attempts to get his bearings. 'Very strange.' He clears his throat officiously. 'Yes, I'd imagine what happened is –'

'Ruprecht – look!'

The beam whips around to pick out Skippy's thunderstruck face, and then back in the direction he's pointing in: the open door of the pod, where the ellipse of light hovers for an instant before dropping to the floor as Ruprecht's hand falls slackly to his side.

'He's *gone* . . .' Mario whispers.

Optimus Prime is no longer in the crib.

'Holy shit, guys,' Geoff Sproke breaks in urgently, 'Dennis is gone too!'

'I'm over here,' a faint voice calls from the far side of the room. With his keyring-torch, Ruprecht illuminates a pile of dusty cases and motherboards, from which Dennis comes clambering out.

'How'd you get over there?'

'Some kind of *force* . . .' Dennis says dazedly, hugging his arms to his chest. 'I was sitting watching the pod, and then . . . and then . . .'

'Ruprecht,' Skippy says steadily, 'what just happened?'

'I don't know,' Ruprecht's whisper almost non-existent.

'Where's Optimus Prime?' Geoff asks. 'Did he get vaporized or . . . ?'

Ruprecht, who seems more surprised than anyone, shakes his head. 'If he was vaporized, there'd be traces,' he mumbles, staring into the empty crib.

'Which means . . . ?' Skippy attempts to fill in the blanks.

Ruprecht looks at him, an expression of unadulterated rapture spreading across his face. 'I have no idea,' he says. 'I have no idea – in the world!'

The others – when they have recovered sufficiently to speak – want to call the news stations right away. 'You just teleported a robot into another dimension, Ruprecht! You're going to be on TV!' But Ruprecht insists they verify their findings before they call anybody.

'Come on, Ruprecht, it's not like Optimus is going to re-appear.'

'Yeah, you should be celebrating. You can verify tomorrow.'

Ruprecht smiles benignly and continues about his work. 'First verify. Then celebrate. That's the way we do it.'

He is oddly calm. Apart from a maniacal twitch that pulls sporadically at the ends of his mouth, the vertiginous weirdness of what has just happened, the world-historical *hugeness* of it, seems to have passed him by, or even had a sedative effect on him; he moves around the room with a quiet surety, setting up the equipment for another run, like a man who after long months roaming in an unknown territory has spotted a landmark for home.

'Guys . . .' Since the experiment, Dennis has been hunched over on a piece of styrofoam. 'I don't feel well.'

'You don't *look* well . . .'

Dennis's complexion is pale and clammy, his hands wrapped protectively around his stomach.

'What's wrong with him, Ruprecht?'

'Do you think he got radiation from the rays?'

'It's not impossible.' Ruprecht frowns. 'Although they *shouldn't* do him any harm . . .'

'Maybe you've turned radioactive, Dennis!'

'Holy shit, Dennis – maybe you've got superpowers!'

'I don't feel super,' Dennis says sorrowfully.

314

'You should go and lie down,' Skippy says.

'I don't want to miss the verifying.'

'We'll tell you what happens.'

'Plus, I can film it on my phone, which ironically you said earlier was no use.'

'Okay,' Dennis agrees reluctantly. Hands still clutching his stomach, he limps to the door. But there he pauses. 'Hey, Ruprecht?'

'Hmm?' Ruprecht, bent over his keyboard, quarter-turns.

'I don't know what just happened here. But all those things I said before, about how you were a big fat fake and a liar, and your portal was a piece of crap that couldn't heat a bowl of soup, and you were gay and all scientists were gay?'

'Yes.'

'Well . . . I was wrong. I'm sorry.'

'That's all right,' Ruprecht replies gallantly. With a nod, Dennis makes his sickly way out of the basement. Among the others, this uncharacteristic show of contrition causes a brief flurry of concern, tied to speculation over the nature and desirability of an irradiated or super-Dennis; but it is quickly lost in the excitement as Ruprecht primes the pod, this time with Skippy's wristwatch inside it, and invites them to lower their goggles again.

Verification, however, proves harder than expected. Enough power from the original radiation burst should remain, by Ruprecht's calculations, to facilitate a second teleportation; but while the pod hums as before, the cable overheats and the power surges, the magical apex of the first experiment, that consecrated instant in which Optimus Prime was snatched away, never rearrives.

At breakfast the following morning the mood is greatly changed. 'I just don't *understand* it,' Ruprecht says, staring into space and chomping his cereal disconsolately. 'Why would it work perfectly the first time and then every other time not work at all? It just doesn't make any *sense*.'

To make matters worse, it appears that Mario's phone for

some reason failed to capture the original successful experiment. 'But *we* saw it, Ruprecht. We *saw* it.'

Ruprecht will not be consoled. 'Who's going to believe a bunch of fourteen-year-old schoolboys? They'll say we dreamed it.'

Leaving his toast uneaten, he returns belowstairs to wrangle some more with his creation; as the hours drag by, it seems that even two storeys up in their dorm, Skippy can feel his friend's exasperation, the exuberance of last night bleeding away. *Did* they all just dream it? Was it just some kind of consensual illusion they'd conjured up from sheer boredom, like the others said he'd done with Lori?

Dennis will have none of this. 'That robot left that pod,' he says, 'and that is a fact.'

'Okay, but even if it did work that time, what if he never gets it to work again?'

'Well, Skipford, I'm no scientist, but I can tell you this: if anyone can open up a gateway to a parallel universe, it's Ruprecht.' Dennis is in his pyjamas on Skippy's bed; he seems to have recovered from his dose of radiation-poisoning, and isn't showing signs of paranormal or any other ability, aside from a new-found and somewhat unsettling appreciation of Ruprecht.

'He didn't seem like he thought it was going to work again.'

'That's why he needs us to support him,' Dennis says. 'We might not know much about science, but we can help by believing in him.'

'You believe in him?' Surprised to hear Dennis even use the word, Skippy turns momentarily from the computer.

'Of course,' Dennis says simply.

But Skippy – eyes darting involuntarily, for the hundredth time since lunch, to his unlit phone, and from there through the window to the empty yard of St Brigid's, like a grey showcase for the rain – is not so sure. What if the truth about other worlds is that when they touch yours – through a gateway opening, or a perfect kiss – it's only ever at a single point, for a single moment, before the turning of the Earth drags you away again? What if the world is not just a bare stage where magic sometimes but usually doesn't take place, but rather a force actively opposed to magic – so it doesn't matter whether these other worlds, gateways, kisses, were dreamed or real, because either way you will never be able to get them ba–

Wait –

'Did you find tits?' Dennis clambers up to peer over Skippy's shoulder at the computer. 'What is it – holy shit . . .'

Night falls. In the Junior Rec Room the legendary barbarian warrior Blüdigör Äxehand, a.k.a. Victor Hero, calls a timeout from the fell Mines of Mythia, where he and the other doughty souls of Lucas Rexroth's role-playing group seek the legendary Amulet of Onyx, to take a bathroom break. He proceeds through the door and is passing down the corridor when he is descended on by a large, Lionel-shaped mass.

'Well, well, if it isn't the Prince of Gays, off for his evening poncing.'

'Get off me!' Victor/Blüdigör shrieks, writhing uselessly under Lionel's splayed, block-like knees.

'Out hunting for kisses? How about a kiss from Uncle Lionel. Open wide . . .' A huge gobbet of sputum unspools from Lionel's mouth to quiver just over Victor's lips – Victor, revulsed, increases his thrashings, which only brings the mucus-pendulum swinging closer. And then, soundlessly, the power winks out. Victor takes advantage of the darkness to scramble out from under Lionel, who, rising in pursuit, finds his slaver pasted to his chin – 'Damn it!'

'Damn it!' In the basement, Ruprecht, emerging from his tinfoil radiation-blocker, shines a torch through the smoking air to peer into the crib. But there is Geoff's shoe, exactly where he left it.

'It didn't work?' Geoff, hopping over, isn't entirely devastated to find his shoe still inhabiting this universe. He bends over to retrieve it from the pod. 'Well, it's not the end of the world – I know, why don't we try . . .' His eyes flick around the basement as he squeezes his shoe back on. 'Mario, do you still have your lucky condom?'

'Ha ha, no way are you putting that inside this foolish death-machine.'

'But maybe its luckiness would help the experiment,' Geoff cajoles.

'I am not going to hand over my fail-safe secret weapon to some parallel-me in another universe,' Mario says firmly. 'He can get his own bitches.'

'Okay . . .' Geoff's eye sets to roving once again. 'How about . . .'

'What's the use,' Ruprecht cuts across him desolately.

'What do you mean, what's the use?'

'I mean, it's not going to work. Clearly what happened with Optimus Prime was some sort of fluke. Maybe the result of an external factor we didn't take into account, the position of the moon, the quantity of moisture in the air. It could have been anything.'

'But that doesn't mean you should just *give up* on it . . .'

'Let's just call it a day,' Ruprecht says monotonously, prodding the charred computer keyboard with his foot. Sixteen hours of repeated disappointment have etched themselves into his face, like an acute strain of the grey necrosis of disillusion the others feel creep across them every second of every day, transforming them into adults.

'What about the future of humanity?' Geoff appeals; but Ruprecht has already turned his back and is shuffling geriatrically around the room, shutting down the computers one by one, when the door bursts open and Dennis and Skippy come running in.

'Hold everything!' Dennis exclaims.

Skippy, who's holding some sort of a printout, says that he was searching online for material for this punishment essay Ms Ni Riain gave him, about the Gaelic origins of the name Seabrook, 'and I found this site?'

The site is called *The Druid's Homepage*, and purports to be *A Resource for Bards, Shamen, Mystics of Erin, and all those Seeking the Rituals of the Old Time*. 'It's mostly about Druids and making

potions out of leaves and stuff. But then in the middle of it . . .'
He scans down through the page. '. . . *names can still give clues as to the whereabouts of these sacred sites, even in the modern* – oh yeah, here it is – *while Seabrook's present Gaelic translation of "Siobruth" is a meaningless back-formation from the English, it is possible that Seabrook, now home to a church and well-known school, may have its origins in* Sidhe an Broga, *pronounced 'Shee an Brugga' and meaning 'Fairy House'. This is the name given to the cave-like chambered cairns referred to in the Old Lore as the traditional homes of the Sidhe and the entrances to the 'Other World'. The correct term for these mounds is* tumuli; *they are frequently found, like similar sites such as Stonehenge in England and the Boyne Valley in Meath, at the intersection of ley lines in order to harness the power of the grid of electromagnetic energy that covers the earth. Many experts believe that these tumuli, created to astronomical specifications so precise they are still beyond the reach of our most advanced computers today, were the work of a race of extraterrestrial beings who briefly made their home among us and used them as gateways to travel through and outside the universe . . .'*

'Why are you telling me all this?' Ruprecht says.

'Aliens, Ruprecht!' Dennis chimes in. 'The mounds were built by aliens! And there's one of them somewhere in Seabrook!'

Ruprecht, wiping grease from his hands with a towel, merely grunts.

'You think the mound has something to do with what happened to Optimus?' asks Geoff.

'Think about it for five seconds,' Dennis says. 'Remember what Ms Ni Riain told us, the old Irish legends, you know, about this race of magical beings who lived in the countryside, only most of the time they were invisible? Doesn't that fit what you were saying, Ruprecht, about the higher dimensions, and how even though they're right there we can't see what's happening in them? Don't those old fairy-stories sound like they're describing people, or *something*, who know how to move in and out of the higher dimensions? And these mounds are the gateways they built between our world and theirs, using their extraterrestrial knowledge.'

'Poh, those stories are just stories,' Mario says, 'made up by drunk Irish people from days of Yore.'

'Sure, that's what I thought too, when I first heard them,' Dennis says. 'Like, why would a race of hyper-intelligent extra-terrestrials want to live in Seabrook? But after what happened last night –'

Ruprecht is not even listening any more; he has turned back to his clear-up.

'– and then I remembered what happened to Niall's sister . . .' Dennis continues.

Mario and Geoff look at each other. 'What happened to Niall's sister?'

'You didn't tell me about her,' Skippy says.

'I didn't? What happened down at the gym?' Dennis shakes his head. 'Well, that's the most incredible thing. Niall's sister's a fourth-year in St Brigid's. She's in the drama society, and she's got a big part in the Christmas play this year?'

'What play are they doing?' Geoff asks.

'*Oliver.*'

'*Oliver*, in a girls' school,' Mario says disgustedly. 'That makes like zero sense.'

'Anyhow, she and this other girl have been staying behind after school to do extra rehearsals of their scenes. They use a room down by the gym. St Brigid's is a bit like this place, with a new part and an old part. The old part doesn't get used much any more. There's a Latin room, and a room they use for sewing classes and stuff like that. And there's also this other room that's always kept locked. If you ask the nuns, they'll say it's just an old storeroom, and that it's kept locked because the floor is rotten and it's not safe to walk on. But there are all these stories about it too, like that a girl hanged herself in there, or that one time a nun was cleaning ashes out of the fireplace when she saw the Devil coming down the chimney, so they closed it off?'

The others are giving him their full attention now; even Ruprecht is dismantling machinery more quietly than he had been.

'Okay, so one night a couple of weeks ago – it would have been about the same time as the Hop, I suppose – Niall's sister and her friend are down in their room, rehearsing. They get quite caught up in what they're doing and they end up staying down longer than they planned.'

'This friend, is she hot?' Mario puts in. 'I have seen Niall's sister, thanks but no thanks – however, how about the friend?'

'I haven't met her,' Dennis says. 'It doesn't really affect the story either way.'

'Yes, yes, carry on.'

'Anyway, all of a sudden the two of them notice it's got very cold. Like *icy* cold. So they decide to call it quits for the evening. They start walking back to the main door, when her friend grabs Niall's sister's arm and asks if she can hear something. They stop right there and listen as hard as they can and Niall's sister makes out this very faint music playing. It seems to be coming from behind them. They look at each other. It's after five and they didn't think there was anyone else around. They retrace their steps back down the hall. The music's still really faint, almost too quiet to hear, like it's being played way off in the distance. But there's no doubt where it's coming from. The locked room.'

The silence around the listeners seems to deepen.

'Niall's sister tells her friend to knock on the door. The friend says Niall's sister should do it. Niall's sister dares her, so the friend knocks. No one answers. The music keeps playing –'

'What sort of music?' Geoff asks.

'Beautiful music. Like with harps and stuff.'

'Just like in the Irish story,' Geoff says huskily.

'Anyway, they knock and then they call out, "Hello, is anybody in there?" No reply. Niall's sister reaches out and turns the handle. It's locked, of course. But Niall's sister's friend has keys. The janitor gave her a set so she could lock up the spare room

322

when they'd finished rehearsing. She doesn't want to try them, though. She's afraid, she wants to go and tell one of the nuns. But Niall's sister knows there's no way the nuns will let them hang around to see what's inside the room. This is their one chance. So they start trying the keys in the lock. There are forty keys on the ring. Not one of them fits. They try the last one and then just stare at the door, totally flummoxed. They can still hear the lovely music, in fact it seems to have got louder. Then Niall's sister, without knowing why, reaches out her hand and turns the handle again. And this time the door opens.'

Geoff, Mario and Skippy stare at Dennis moon-eyed, like three raccoons caught in headlights. From a distance, Ruprecht fondles his asthma inhaler impassively.

'The friend says, "Okay, we should definitely go and get someone." But Niall's sister has already pushed the door open. Afterwards she said it was like the music had put her in a trance. There's a big *cre-e-e-eak*. The two of them huddle together and step inside. And guess what they find there?'

'What?' whispers Geoff.

'Nothing,' Dennis says.

'Nothing?'

'Nothing. The room is totally empty.'

'But . . .' Mario utters in a strangulated voice. 'What about the music?'

'They can still hear the music, clear as a bell. And there's also a lovely smell, like a field full of flowers, though it's almost winter, and the room has no windows and is covered in dust and cobwebs. But almost immediately the smell and the music just . . . fade away. And they're standing in an empty room.' Dennis pauses summatively, and then, 'Ever since, Niall's sister's friend's been saying that the music must have come from somewhere else. Like maybe one of the boarders was playing it in her room, and it was carried through an air vent, or down the pipes? But the boarders' dorms are way over on the other side of the school. Niall's sister is certain that *somehow* the music was coming from that room.'

'Whoa,' Geoff says.

'But how is it possible?' Mario says.

'Well, they must have built the room on top of the ancient burial mound,' Geoff replies. 'It's the only logical explanation.'

Ruprecht gets up and paces about the room, gnawing his knuckles.

'We know that St Brigid's was a convent before they opened it as a school.' Dennis is all seriousness now. 'But what was it before that? This Druid guy says in days of Yore everyone worshipped this goddess called the White Goddess, and these mounds and things belonged to her. But when the Church came and spread Christianity across the country, it took over all the magical places for itself. Changed the names, converted the old legends into stories about, you know, God and stuff. Or else covered them over completely. It makes sense. You're a bunch of nuns or monks or whatever, you want everybody in the neighbourhood following orders and doing what you tell them. If there's some mystical fairy fort in the neighbourhood where weird shit keeps happening, you wouldn't want people to know about it. You'd build your convent right on top of it and lock it up so no one could get anywhere near it.'

Ruprecht halts his peregrinations and rounds rather fiercely on Dennis. 'Well, even if it is the long-lost Seabrook fairy fort, even if Niall's sister did hear music – so what? What does any of it have to do with my experiment?'

Geoff fields this one: 'Gee, Ruprecht, you said there might have been some hidden factor influencing the outcome last night . . .'

Ruprecht opens his mouth to reply, but breaks off and turns his back on them, muttering unintelligibly and throwing his hands about like a derelict in an underpass. 'Ley lines, fairies – that isn't science. Who ever heard of an experiment using fairies?'

'It does sound pretty unorthodox,' Dennis admits. 'But didn't you say yourself that a scientist has to open himself up to every possibility, no matter how weird?'

'You did say that, Ruprecht,' Geoff confirms.

'And didn't you say M-theory is weirder than any other theory in the history of science?' Dennis perseveres. 'And hasn't your Professor Tamashi always said that probably the only way we'll master hyperspace in time to save Earth is if a superior civilization comes along and gives us the technology? Well, what if the technology's already here? What if the aliens have been and gone three thousand years ago, but they've left their gateway behind? What if, all this time, the solution to M-theory has been literally right under your nose?'

'Mound does begin with M,' Mario observes thoughtfully.

'Holy smoke, Ruprecht – so does music!'

'All right!' Ruprecht, as his resistance crumbles, flinches in self-disgust. 'Say it *is* possible. Why would this mound – why would it suddenly *stop* influencing the experiment?'

'I don't know. Maybe . . .' Dennis taps at his temple like he's starting an old watch. '. . . maybe its influence fluctuates. Maybe there was a surge at the exact moment of the first experiment, but normally it doesn't reach any further than that little room.'

'So if there were some way to gain access to that room . . .'

For the first time since Optimus Prime disappeared, the pregnant sense of last night, the nearness of something overwhelming, pervades the basement again, filling the corners and slowly building . . .

That's when Skippy's phone beeps with a new message; and each of them realizes, before he even looks at Skippy's dumbstruck face, that he knows who it's from.

The night of the break-up Halley slept on the sofa. She wouldn't take the bed, no matter how he pleaded with her; it was plain she would have preferred to go, if she'd only been able to summon the energy. Howard was surprised at the way she'd capitulated. He had expected screaming, punches, excoriation. Instead, she simply sank onto the couch as if he'd sapped her across the back of the head; she cried longer and harder than all the other times he'd seen her cry put together. And he could not comfort her; he was transformed into some monstrous creature whose touch brings only pain.

The next morning she left. He has not seen her since. He guesses she is staying with one or other of the motley straggle of friends she has assembled in her time here – people from work, Americans she'd met on expat forums, other émigrés and castaways who'd found themselves stranded on the margins of Dublin life. She calls to the house when he's not there to collect her belongings; every time he comes home from work some new small thing is gone, as if he's being burgled in instalments.

The house feels different without her. Though she still has clothes in the wardrobe, though her hairdryer still sits atop the dresser, her razor on the shelf in the shower, the rooms seem bare, denuded; her absence dominates the house – becomes, oxymoronically, a kind of physical presence, shaped and palpable, as though she moved out and this emptiness moved in to take up the space she left. There is a new kind of silence that the stereo turned up all the way can only fill one side of; the air that meets him when he unlocks the door now is clean and clear, smokeless, odourless, breathable.

'I just wish you hadn't gone and told her about Aurelie,' Farley says. 'You could have done it without telling her that.'

'It wouldn't be fair, just giving her half the story.'

'You've burned your bridges now, though. She won't take you back.'

Howard sighs. 'What could I do, Farley? If your hand's in the fire, you know?'

'How's that?'

'Something my dad used to say. If your hand's in the fire, eventually you have to accept that the only solution is to take it out. Aurelie was the catalyst, that's all. It would have happened sooner or later.'

But he's not sure this is true. If he hadn't met Aurelie, maybe it would never have happened; maybe he would never have found the courage to leave Halley; maybe he'd have stayed with her, got married and lived the rest of his life without ever knowing what real love could feel like – how singular, how incandescent, how complete. Aurelie changed everything, and the truth is that when he confessed to Halley, he did it in part for *her* – as a kind of prayer to her, a declaration of faith on which to found a different kind of life.

An attempt, as well, to conjure her back from whatever cloud she'd vanished behind. She never came back after mid-term break; according to the Automator, 'unforeseen circumstances' had forced her to extend her holiday. Every day Howard sees her classes trooping despondently from the Geography Room to the Study Hall, or carrying votive bundles of cardboard and paper to the recycling bins, their faces anxious, hopeful, like Indians doing a rain dance. He knows how they feel. Since mid-term he's existed in a constant state of tension, braced against every moment as the one that might finally restore her. Even out of school, even on his own, shopping in the supermarket, sitting at the traffic lights, he finds himself holding his breath. But the days are a series of ghost pregnancies, delivering nothing.

'Unforeseen circumstances.' He can imagine what – who – that means. Seabrook was supposed to be a career break for her, a transitional phase; she hadn't intended to get mixed up with anyone, especially not someone already mixed up with someone else. Now she's wondering what she's got herself into, and whether there's still time to get herself out. If only he could talk to her! If only he could let her know that this is real to him, more real than anything that has happened before! Or better yet, magically transport the two of them to the time in the future when they've started out on a life together, the chaos and agony of these interim weeks already faded, the blizzard of flyaway moments that is the past replaced by something exhilarating, serene, lit from within . . .

As for Halley, except for Farley he tells no one that she's gone. Remembering what happened to Jim Slattery all those years ago, he's haunted by the thought that somehow the boys will find out. But so far the news appears not to have reached them. In fact, he finds his classes going unusually well. The second-years in particular: thanks to his mid-term reading on the First World War, which having nothing better to do he'd continued after Halley left, Howard finds himself able to speak about his subject from a rare position of authority, and to his surprise, the boys listen. Listen, speak, formulate theories: in the limbo days after mid-term, while he waits for Aurelie to return and his new life to begin, these classes – which have so often resembled trench warfare themselves, a huge amount of labour and bloodshed for a dismally small area of terrain – become something he actually looks forward to.

This weekend is his first as a single man for almost three years. He has neglected to make plans and spends most of it in his house. It feels, at the start, a lot like the times his parents left him home alone as a teenager. He is free to stay up as late as he wants, listen to music as loud as he wants, eat what he wants, drink what he wants, download porn, belch, walk around in his boxer shorts. By seven o'clock he is drunk; by eight, the novelty has worn off and he finds himself slumped over the kitchen table, watching the microwave defrost a frozen spring roll. Then he hears the key turn in the door and Halley walks in.

Both of them freeze, she by the light switch, he at the table. It is a moment quite electrifying in its cold, untempered immediacy – not quite like seeing a ghost, more like discovering, in the face of another, that you have become a ghost yourself.

'I didn't think you'd be here,' Halley says.

'Yeah,' is all Howard can think to say. He wishes he was wearing trousers. 'Can I get you something? Tea?'

He doesn't know quite what tack he should take with her – chastened? Solicitous? Tender? Stoic? The question is moot: 'Someone's waiting,' she says, gesturing towards the road where an indistinct figure sits inside a car. She goes to their bedroom and begins to throw things in a box. He waits in the kitchen for her to finish, which she does in fifteen or twenty minutes – whisking back through the house and bidding him goodnight with all the warmth of a solicitor's letter. Then she is gone, and he is left with the hum of the electricity, to go into the bedroom, if he so desires, and see what she has taken.

He drinks the rest of the beer and goes to bed early, but he can't sleep. The bereaved dog across the road has taken to howling into the small hours of the night, long ululations laden with rage and grief for its lost companion. Howard lies there for an hour or two, listening to the howls and watching the ceiling; then, with a sigh, he throws back the sheets and goes down to the kitchen to sit at the bar with one of his library books (now overdue, and subject to a fine, the borrowing sheet pasted to the flyleaf informs him sternly, of one penny a week).

He's read so many books about the war at this point that he's in danger of becoming a buff; he's even started to develop Ideas. At some point in his reading, he realized the conflict had coalesced into two separate wars. The first, the war of the generals and the dons as well as the dull school textbook, proliferates with causes, strategies, notable battles, and is fought in the moral light of the so-called 'Big Words' – Tradition, Honour, Duty, Patriotism. In the other war, however, the one the soldiers actually experienced, these features are nowhere to be found. In this war, any kind of overarching meaning, even straight enmity between the two sides, seems to dissolve into nothing, and the only constants are chaos, destruction and the sense of being lost in a machinery too huge and powerful to be understood. The very battlefields of this war – so clearly delineated on the arrow-strewn relief maps of the first – are deracinated, volatile, pitching themselves up without warning into the sky, to make landmarks, place names, measurements meaningless. The two disparate accounts remind Howard strangely of what Farley said in the Ferry that night about the differing explanations of the universe – the relativistic and the quantum, or the very large and the very small. The generals during and the dons after it wanted more than anything else for the war to make *sense*, to embody the classical concept of conflict, to look, in short, like a war, just as Einstein tried to fit all of creation into his one perfect geometric scheme; but in the same way that the subatomic particles defied any attempt at explaining them, rebelled towards an evermore violent schemelessness and disorder, so the war, the more its leaders insisted on the contrary, spiralled into incomprehensibility, the more soldiers in their tens and hundreds of thousands were wiped out. From those soldiers' perspective, meanwhile, the war was one sprawling, senseless confusion, a four-year horror story with no discernible point, other than to belie not only the generals' causes and big words but the very idea of a comprehensible and God-sanctioned world – which seems to Howard nicely quantum, if nothing else.

'You could argue that the Great War was, in historical terms, like the Big Bang – a singular event, for which none of our explanations is sufficient, but which at the same time our whole civilization is founded on. The *force* of it blew the century apart. From a strictly ordered regime where everyone knew their place, where everything was arranged in nice harmonious symmetries, the Western world entered a period of great turbulence and discord, what the poet T. S. Eliot called "an immense panorama of futility and anarchy", which, arguably, we are still living in today. At the same time that Einstein was working on the theories that would completely overturn classical ideas of what space and time were, how reality worked, the war was reordering our whole concept of civilization. Empires centuries old disappeared overnight, people lost faith in institutions they had trusted without even thinking about it, like a child trusts its parents. The old world fell and our modern world was born, as a direct result of the war – not so much from the outcome of the fighting, as from the terrible things the soldiers, ordinary men, had seen and endured.

'So what was the war like for that ordinary soldier? To even get to the Front, he would have marched twenty miles a day, carrying equipment weighing anything from forty to a hundred pounds. While in the front line, he might spend an entire day standing up to his armpits in muddy water. He rarely slept for more than two hours at a time, and exhaustion was one of the major sources of trauma during the conflict. In fact, almost fifty per cent of the casualties during the war on the Western Front came not from battle but from the conditions the men were living in. Trench foot. Head lice. Rats. The war was a boom time for rats. Two of them could produce over eight hundred offspring in a single year, so soon there were tens of millions of them, flocking to the corpses . . .'

The boys listen with open mouths. They eat up details like this, the gruesomer the better – but what harm is that? Isn't the main thing that they are actually interested? Although admittedly not everyone sees it that way.

'I'm just wondering if this stuff is going to be in the exam,' Jeekers Prendergast says in his twangy, nervous voice. 'I mean, if it's not covered in the book.' The class groans, but Jeekers holds his ground. 'It's just that, ah, according to your lesson plan, we're supposed to be doing the Easter Rising this week –'

'Yeah, when are we going to do some Irish history?' Jeekers finds an unlikely ally in the form of Muiris de Bhaldraithe, piping up disaffectedly from the back row.

Howard spreads his hands placatingly. 'I promise, we have time for both –' His head snaps round involuntarily at the sound of wheels on the gravel outside: could it be? – but no, it's just Father

Green, returning from one of his errands. He collects himself and returns to the boys. 'We'll get to the Rising in due course,' he says. 'The lesson plan isn't set in stone. And anyway, Muiris, the war is Irish history. Aside from the fact that the Rising came out of the First World War, many Irishmen fought for the Allies, at the Western Front and elsewhere.'

'Uh, not according to the textbook, sir,' Jeekers says, the page of his own carefully laminated copy opened to the box giving the breakdown of war dead.

'Well, the textbook is wrong, in that case,' Howard says.

'Yeah, my great-grandfather fought in the war,' Daniel Juster says.

'There you go,' Howard says to Muiris. 'I'm sure that many of you have relatives who fought in the war, even if you don't know about it. And those who didn't fight were still affected. The war transformed everything. So I think it's worth spending some extra time on it.' Also, though he doesn't say it to Muiris and barely admits it to himself, he feels that keeping himself and the class immersed in the Great War somehow preserves a connection with Miss McIntyre.

After class he finds Ruprecht Van Doren and Geoff Sproke waiting behind.

'Yes, gentlemen?'

There is a brief, tacit interchange between them, as if to decide who should pose the question; and then Ruprecht says carefully, 'We were just wondering if you knew anything about the history of Seabrook – the older part of its history?'

'Like from days of Yore?' Geoff Sproke chips in.

'That depends,' Howard says. 'Whenabouts in Yore are you talking about?'

Ruprecht meditates on this a moment, then, once again with some delicacy, 'When the world was ruled by some kind of goddess?'

'And they built these mounds?' Geoff blurts, before he is silenced by a look from Ruprecht.

'Hmm,' Howard strokes his chin. 'Sounds like pre-Christian times. Not really my field, boys, sorry. But what's this about, anyway?'

'Oh, you know,' Ruprecht says vaguely.

'It just seemed interesting, to find out more about the place our school is built on top of,' Geoff adds, inspired.

'I'll ask around,' Howard says. 'And if I find anything out, I'll let you know.'

'Thanks, Mr Fallon.' They hasten away, deep in discussion. The opacity of the fourteen-year-old mind: Howard smiles to himself and continues on his way.

Opening the door of the staffroom, he is greeted by an unusual hubbub. Teachers are thronged around the middle of the room, all talking at once in an uncharacteristically jubilant way. From the periphery the school secretary, Miss Noakes, turns to Howard. 'He's back!' she says, beaming at him as though under the influence of some wonderful drug. The meaning of this is obscure to Howard, but it gives him a bad feeling. His own smile wilting like a neglected house plant, he squeezes through the knot of bodies to find at its heart, enthroned on the sofa, Finian Ó Dálaigh, the geography teacher.

'Not too hard!' he exclaims comically to the colleagues clapping his shoulder. 'I've still got stitches!' In his hand is a jar containing something roundish and grey and approximately the size of a golf ball, which someone behind him tells Howard is his gallstone.

'Howard!' Ó Dálaigh spots him; he steps forward, hastily reaffixing his smile. 'What do you make of that, Howard?' Ó Dálaigh wiggles the jar under his nose. 'The doctor said it was the biggest one he'd ever seen.'

'Really . . .' Howard coos feebly.

'Yes, and he said the gallstone was pretty big too!' The company laughs indulgently, although this witticism is by now on its fourth or fifth outing.

'Fantastic,' says Howard through clenched teeth and a thickening glaze of unreality. 'So . . . does this mean we'll have you back at work soon? How long a convalescence are you looking at?'

'Convalescence be damned,' Ó Dálaigh declares, thumping his chest. 'I was bored out my tree lying around there at home, watching the grass grow. Doctor says I'm fighting fit. Says he's never seen anything like my powers of recovery. I'm going to convalesce right here, standing on my own two feet. Teaching Geography!' A raucous sally of approval from his colleagues. 'Those little so-and-so's won't know what hit 'em!' Ó Dálaigh, enjoying his moment, adds, to another cheer.

Howard pretends to join in, and when the noise dies down remarks, as if to himself, 'So I suppose that Miss McIntyre won't need to come back after all.'

But the name means nothing to the geography teacher; he shrugs, and then launches into a fresh account of his surgery for a new arrival. As for the others, few of them seem to hear him, and those who do merely blink at Howard distractedly, as if he's mistaken them for his pupils, and started spouting on to them about some phantasmal figure from a textbook.

'Was your grandfather really in the war, Skip?'

'He was my great-grandfather. My mum's grandfather. He got his right hand shot off.'

'Wow –' Dennis performs some internal calculation '– does that mean you have an ancestor who *wasn't* a bender?'

'You know what I am thinking is –' Mario speaks up here '– if you needed to raise an army of zombies, this Western Front would be a good place to go.'

'Mario, what the hell do you want an army of zombies for?'

'*I* don't want an army of zombies, I'm just saying that if you *did*, a good place to go would be the Western Front, because of all the dead people lying around there from the war?'

'No, it wouldn't, you stupid wop, they'd all be missing arms and legs and stuff.'

'Up yours, Hoey, you are the wop, because FYI if you die and then you are reanimated you can attach your limbs back on.'

'That's bollocks.'

'It's not bollocks, everyone knows that.'

'It's total bollocks.'

'Well, they could throw the arms and stuff at you,' Mario continues gamely.

'With what, Mario? They could throw their arms at you with what? With their mouths? With *Il Duce*?'

But now Skippy's phone bleeps and the conversation gives way to a charivari of coos and kissy-noises as Skippy, transformed into one giant goofy grin, reaches for his pocket.

In the end it was all so simple! What happened was, Lori's dad saw her kissing Skippy outside the gates the night of the Hop and he freaked – he thinks she's still too young to be with boys, and he grounded her for two whole weeks, and even confiscated her phone. That's why she hadn't replied to Skippy's poem, and she was sorry because it was so beautiful! And she had missed him so much.

At first Skippy couldn't believe it. When he'd got that first message, sitting in the basement, it was like a wrecking ball had just crashed through the wall and he suddenly found himself looking out into the airy night. But he replied, and she replied to his reply, and to the reply to her reply; and though he was sure every message he sent would be the one that brought the whole magical card-house tumbling back down again, his phone kept buzzing with her responses, each one a little golden hit that travelled straight to his heart, right through and into today, until it's like they've never been apart!

OMG Irish is SOOO BOORRRRIIIINGGGGG like wat is the point

Im in religion its worse

Our techer looks like an overweight vulture

**Ours is like the little one from different strokes
except not so little and not funny**

Gross camamber baget for lunch wot u got

Ricotta its like eatng heatd up walpapr past

Ur so funy!!

In class the phone sits on his lap under the desk, set to silent but lighting up as each message arrives, as if it's just as excited as he is; he tries to remember to keep half an eye on the teacher, because if he gets caught then *his* phone'll be confiscated, which'd be a disaster – but somehow he can't bring himself to worry, the world going on around him seems so far away, a dim flurry of ghosts, warm, noisy, coloured-in ghosts . . .

You won't find the answer staring at your feet. *Mr Juster, je vous en prie.* Wakey-wakey, faggot. Concentrate, Daniel!

But when's he going to see her? To have her so close and still out of reach is almost worse than the torture of not hearing from her at all. Isn't her dad ever going to unground her?

**Im just glad he didnt find out about da drinking +
pils he probly wd hav sent me off to bording skool!!!**

He sounds scary

**Hes not I love him but maybe he thinks all boyz r
like he was wen he was 14!!:)**

Sorry ur rite its my fault ur grounded Im sorry

Dont worry I wont be here 4ever,

she says, although, arrgh, that doesn't feel like much of a consolation right now.

And then midway through Science class, after a minor lull, he gets this:

Ive got an idea DJ -

DJ is what she calls him in texts, as in 'Last Night a DJ Saved My Life' –

- why dont u com visit me in my house!

Somewhere a trillion miles away Mr Farley is telling the class about natural incidents of electricity.

Seriously?

**Why not they sed I cant go out they never sed I cant have
frends over and then they cd c wot ur rly like!!>**

337

Sure, but visit her *house*? With her overprotective dad who hates him? Okay, and then why not go for a picnic on the North Pole? Or swim to Atlantis?

It's not a big deal DJ!!! U can come after skool, u r so sweet they wil love you + theyl stop worryin Just come bring ur frisbee it wil be fun I promis everything wil be fine

He lingers over these last words. *Everything will be fine.* It's been so long since he thought this, since he could even imagine himself thinking it. And now here it is. Everything will be Fine! The Future, the Universe, will be Fine!

Okay so how about Friday?

Fridays miles away I cant wait that long! Why dont you just come up tomorrow!! I think you know where the house is?:)

And he laughs like she is right there to hear him laughing.

'You find something funny about the term "ball lightning", Mr Juster?' Mr Farley asks him.

'Uh . . .' Skippy, yanked back those trillion miles, flails around helplessly. But Mr Farley just smiles, and carries on; and it's like the room is filled with sunlight, too bright to see.

'Greg? Do you have a minute?'

'Why, Howard!' The Automator turns from his window where he's peering out at the yard. 'What are you still doing here?'

'Uh, yes, I had a –'

'Scared to go home, that it?'

'No, actually, I was correcting some, uh –'

'Just pulling your leg, Howard, come on in. Always welcome in these parts. On the pale side there, buddy, you feeling all right?'

'Oh yes, absolutely, I just wanted to ask you about some – oh, I'm sorry, has there been some bad news?'

'News? Oh, you mean this?' The Automator glances down at the black armband adorning his shirtsleeve. 'No, no – well, that is to say, yes, as a matter of fact there has been some news, Howard, and while it's not as bad as it might have been, it's still not what you could call good. Old Man's taken a turn for the worse. Doctors say he could slip off at any minute. In fact, they don't really understand how he's still alive.'

'Oh . . .' Howard bows his head solemnly, trying to think of an appropriate platitude.

'I wouldn't give up on him yet, though. If Desmond Furlong goes down, you can bet it's not going to be without one heck of a fight.' He raises his chin, looks sternly into the middle distance. 'In the jungle there are many animals, Howard. Macaws, parakeets, flamingos, those are just the birds. Then you've got your rhinos, orangutans, tapirs, various kinds of reptile, you name it. But there is only one beast that gets to be called the King of the Jungle, and that beast is the lion. Lion doesn't get where he is by grubbing for ants or swinging from tree to tree. He lives life on his own terms. He sticks to his guns. When he acts, it's with one hundred per cent decisiveness and self-belief. That's why year after year, when the animals get together to crown their king, they always pick the lion. Because it's those values that mark out a leader, not how good you are at sucking sap out of a tree trunk or using sonar to navigate at night. Desmond Furlong was just such a lion.' He pauses. 'What do you think, Howard? Too much?'

Howard, in spite of his best efforts, can only goggle, like a man in a bell jar.

'You're right – Trudy, cut that whole lion part, it's too much.' Trudy assiduously takes a red pen to a printout sitting on her desk. 'But I'll tell you this, Howard, whatever else happens, this Father Desmond Furlong Memorial Concert is going to give the Old Man exactly the send-off he deserves. We're having the auditions day after tomorrow, though we've preselected most of the acts, obviously.'

Howard is confused. 'This is a different concert to the 140th . . . ?'

'No, Howard, one and the same, except that now it's doubly momentous, in that it not only marks a milestone anniversary in the school's history, but also commemorates the passing of one of its leading lights. The Father Desmond Furlong Memorial Concert, it has a ring to it, don't you think? Gives it that extra touch of gravitas.'

'But he isn't actually dead yet,' Howard establishes as delicately as he can.

'No, he's not. No sir, those doctors have another think coming if they believe they've got some shrinking violet on their hands here.'

'So by the time the concert comes round . . . does that not mean he may actually still . . .'

'Well, in that case we'll have all the more reason to celebrate, won't we? Unfortunately, Howard, that is not likely at all, not at all, I'm afraid, according to the latest prognosis. At this point he needs a miracle, poor man. That reminds me, though, how are you getting on with those programme notes? Real surfeit of riches, once you dive into those school records, isn't there?'

'Oh – absolutely,' Howard says, picturing the empty notepad sitting under his library books at home. 'Yes, it's really coming together . . .'

'That's outstanding, Howard, knew I could count on you. Now, you said there was something you wanted to ask me?'

'Oh yes . . . I'm thinking of taking my second-years on a class trip to the museum . . .'

'Oh really?' the Automator turning away again to part the louvres of the blind. 'A class trip, eh?'

'Yes, we're doing the First World War at the moment and for a while now I've been thinking it would be good for the boys to see some of the uniforms and guns and so on. It's not really treated in the textbook, you see, so this would be a way to bring it to life a little, as opposed to being just dead facts on a page . . .'

'It's not treated in the textbook?'

'Not in any depth, no. Hard to believe, I know, but it actually does the whole war in half a page, and it doesn't mention Ireland's involvement at all. A field trip would be a way of engaging the boys on a personal level, to show them what their counterparts of ninety years ago would have experienced – actually, I'm sure there were Seabrook boys who went to the Front, we could ev–'

'Yesyesyes,' the Automator interjects, in what sounds like a distinctly minor tone. 'I have to say, Howard, departures from the textbook always set alarm bells going in my head. These *dead facts on a page*, as you call them, are the same ones that your class are going to have to reproduce in their exam papers next year. Engaging the boys is all well and good, but your job first and foremost is to get those facts off the page and into their brains by any means necessary. Not to start confusing them with a whole slew of new facts.'

'I do feel that this is something they'd find particularly beneficial, Greg –'

'Of course you do, but where does it end? Heck of a lot of facts out there, Howard, heck of a lot of history. You wanted to put all that history in one book, it'd be the size of a warehouse and take you a thousand years to read, by which time of course a thousand more years of history would've elapsed. Until they invent, first of all, a history-supercomputer that can fit the whole thing on a single chip, and then some way of downloading the information directly into your brain, we have to be selective about what areas we're going to concentrate on, you see what I'm driving at here?'

'It would just be a half-day trip,' Howard points out. 'If we left at lunchtime we'd be back here by four o'clock.'

'Things can happen between lunchtime and four o'clock,' the Automator pronounces ominously. 'I can't help remembering what happened the last time I left you alone in charge of a group of second-years. That's not the type of scene I want replicated on the streets of our nation's capital.'

Howard, notwithstanding that he came up with the idea of the field trip purely as a pretext for asking the Automator about Aurelie, feels his choler rise. 'I think you're being a little unfair, Greg,' struggling to keep his tone polite. 'That was a freak incident. These are good boys, and I have a decent rapport with them.'

'Mm-hmm.' Addressing the question to the dusk, 'That Slippy kid's in your second-year class, isn't he?'

'Daniel Juster?'

'That's right – how's he doing these days?'

'Good as gold. I've had no trouble with him whatever.'

'I'll bet,' the Automator says softly, peering through the blind like a predator waiting for his prey to step into his trap.

'I really think you've got the wrong impression of him, Greg. He's a very bright boy. A little shy, that's all.'

'Mm.' The Automator sounds unconvinced. 'Howard, come over here a second, would you? Something I'd like to show you.'

Obediently Howard leaves his chair, and Trudy scoots out of his way so he can join the Acting Principal at the window. Below them, through the narrow aperture of the blind, the twilit yard is deserted save for a sprinkling of cars and, Howard sees now, a single, diminutive figure standing on his own among the shadows. In his grey jumper and slacks he has almost entirely disappeared into the monochrome background, but now, as Howard watches, he pivots his upper body to one side and then, like a spring, uncoils, letting fly something from his hand. It travels only a short distance before wobbling dismally to the ground, where it scrapes to a halt with an ugly skittering noise that Howard realizes has been present on the periphery of his consciousness for some time.

'Know who that is, Howard?'

'Difficult to tell,' Howard says evasively.

'It's Juster, Howard. He's been out there this last half-hour.' They watch the boy trudge over to the object where it has landed, then throw it back in the direction it came. It fares even worse this time, veering off to the right and rolling away into the bushes, to an audible epithet of dismay from the lone figure outside.

'Any idea what he might be doing?'

'Looks like he's playing frisbee.'

'He's playing frisbee *by himself,* Howard. He's playing frisbee by himself, in the dark. You ever played frisbee by yourself in the dark?'

'It does look like he needs the practice.'

'Howard, this may seem like a big joke to you. But damn it, you can't look out that window and tell me that's normal behaviour. Even watching him is giving me the creeps. Now you're telling me you want to let him loose in the city? My God, there's no knowing what kind of stunt he might pull.' He turns back to the window. 'Look at him, Howard. He's up to something. But what? What's going on inside that head?' This provokes a thought – 'Trudy, wasn't Al Foley supposed to be profiling that kid for us? Damn it, how long can it take for a man to have his ears drained?'

'He should be back in the next couple of days, Greg,' Trudy says.

'Well, as soon as he is, I want Juster as a top priority.' He turns round to his underling, staring gloomily at the dusk, and claps him on the shoulder. 'Sorry, Howard. Just can't do it. Still, I appreciate your initiative. Next time maybe we'll be able to come to an

343

arrangement. But in the meantime let's not have any more dis-paragement of the textbook, all right? Textbook's on your side. It's like a map. Stray from the map, take a wrong turn, you're in Injun territory, friend. Those kids'll smell it on you in a second and they will take you out, Howard. They will take you out.' He hits him a hearty giddy-up slap on the arm. 'Now, why don't you get yourself on home? Little lady must be wondering where you are.'

Howard is so demoralized that he almost leaves without ask-ing the very question he came in for. Then in the doorway it returns to him. 'Finian Ó Dálaigh's back,' he says, in a warbling burlesque of nonchalance.

The Automator relinquishes the window, still aglow. 'He sure is. See the size of the stone they took out of him? Doctor said it was the biggest one he'd ever seen. I'll tell you what, though, Fin-ian Ó Dálaigh could have a cannonball in there, still wouldn't keep him away from that blackboard. He's a Seabrook man through and through.'

Howard shakes his head in wordless admiration, then, as if in afterthought, 'So, will Aurelie McIntyre be coming back this side of Christmas, or . . . ?'

'Haven't spoken to her about it yet, Howard, she's still on holi-day to the best of my knowledge. That business at the Hop seems to have shaken her up quite a bit. She asked to extend her break. I agreed. I was just happy she didn't file for trauma.'

'So she's still away?' Howard leaping for this unexpected life-line.

'I believe so, yes. Apparently what happened was that her fiancé sprung a surprise cruise on her. When she called me they'd just pulled into the Seychelles.'

The universe silently crumbles around Howard. 'Her fiancé?' he repeats, barely audible even to himself.

'Yes, he'd popped the question just the night before. Sounds like quite a production. Woman like that, guess you'd better be ready to spend some money.' He chuckles to himself. 'Not that he's

344

short of it, by the sounds of it. You know him, Howard? Clongowes man, played on their Cup team in his day. Working up in Accenture, doing pretty well, year or two younger than yourself?'

'No, I haven't met him,' the dust of Howard's dreams swirling round him, clogging his throat.

'Anyhow, now that Finian's back there's no real need for her here,' the Automator continues somewhere in the distance. 'She might come back, do a couple of hours here and there, extra-curricular stuff, the environment, so forth. More likely she'll go back into banking, that's where I'd put my money. That's where most people put their money, am I right?' He shakes his head. 'Boy oh boy, though. The size of that gallstone. Try teaching with one of those rattling around your spleen, Howard. But he kept soldiering on. I practically had to strap him down to get him to the hospital . . .'

Howard makes his exit from the office with small, agonized steps, as if it is he who has just emerged from Intensive Care, wound still gaping in his side.

'So what are you going to do on your date, Skippy?'

'I don't know . . . maybe play frisbee for a while, before it gets dark? And then watch a DVD or something?'

'That is the wrong answer,' Mario says severely. 'There is only one reason you are going to this house, and that is for full sex with a girl. Do you think the Italian national team of 1982 stopped to play frisbee on their way to winning the World Cup? Do you think Einstein took a break to watch a DVD when he was inventing his famous theory of relatives?'

'I don't know.'

'Well, I will tell you, they didn't. Focus on your objective. Full hardcore sex. Frisbee or whatever can come after that.'

'I can't believe you're going to her house,' Dennis says. 'It just seems wrong somehow.'

'Well, she asked me.'

'I know that, it's just, you know, *you*, and *her* – it just, doesn't it seem wrong somehow?' addressing this to the others. 'Like sort of implausible?'

'Maybe a tiny bit,' Geoff concedes.

'Like, what about Carl?'

'What does Carl have to do with it?'

'Hmm, well, he practically put you in a coma just for sending her some gay Japanese poem. What do you think he'll do if he finds out you've gone to her house? He'll rip your head off.'

'That's true.' Geoff frowns. 'He probably will rip your head off, Skip.'

'He'll rip your head off and piss down your neckhole,' Dennis elaborates. 'And *then* he'll get physical.'

'It's got nothing to do with him,' Skippy says. 'Anyway, how would he even know about it?' At this Dennis, who has spent much of the day asking people whether this whole Skippy and Lori thing doesn't seem really weird, and how it must be a real slap in the face for Carl, clams up abruptly and then goes off to look for Ruprecht.

Ever since his irradiation on the night of the experiment, Dennis has thrown himself into his new-found admiration of and support for Ruprecht with a gusto that those who know him find almost eerie. He fetches Ruprecht doughnuts when they are working late in the lab, he listens to Ruprecht's long rambles about maths – he even toes the line in Quartet rehearsals, playing only the notes he is told to, Ruprecht having edited these down by about half.

He has also played a key role in the attempt to smuggle the pod into the girls' school. This afternoon, Niall's sister came through with the map of St Brigid's, and now the plan – which Ruprecht has codenamed 'Operation Condor', in preference, thanks all the same, to Mario's 'Operation Mound' and Dennis's 'Operation Immaculate Penetration' – shifts into the next gear.

By the looks of it, getting into the girls' school will be only marginally less difficult than accessing the higher dimensions. The main gates close at five, leaving only a pedestrian entrance that leads right by the window of the gatekeeper's lodge, home to an infamously vigilant janitor named Brody and also to Brody's small but bloodthirsty dog, Nipper. Anyone eluding these two will find the front entrance to the school building locked, and the back entrance taking him into the administrative area, comprising the Dean of Boarders' office, the Principal's office, the Secretariat and the Prefects' Lounge – the lion's den, in short.

'The only realistic point of entry,' Dennis says, 'is here, via the fire escape.' He points to the symbol on the map demarcating the iron staircase. 'The window at the top brings you directly into the nuns' quarters. From there, it's a matter of getting from the second storey to the basement on the other side of the school, while avoiding the nuns, booby-traps set to maim trespassers, hockeystick-wielding prefects, and so forth. Then all we have to do is get into the locked room with the burial mound under it, reassemble the pod inside, run a lead back over the wall to hook us up to the Cosmic Energy Compressor, and open the portal, this time making sure we get everything on film. Next stop, the Nobel Prize.'

'No more school for us,' Mario says. 'We will become global celebrities.'

'Well, I will,' Ruprecht amends.

'Do you think it'll work?' Skippy says.

Ruprecht does: since that night in the basement, he's become a total convert to the mysterious power of ancient burial mounds. 'I've been reading up on them on the Internet, and scientifically speaking, there are all sorts of strange phenomena attached to them that have yet to be explained. It's an unconventional approach, I know. But as Professor Tamashi says, "Science is the realm of the formerly impossible."'

'But what happens if the nuns catch you?'

'It's a chance we have to take,' Ruprecht says.

'The Condor flies tomorrow night, Skip,' Dennis says. 'There's still room on our team for one more.'

'Well, even if I wanted to, I couldn't go tomorrow,' Skippy says. 'That's when I'm going to Lori's house.'

Another time Skippy might have been jealous of Dennis and his new role at the centre of Ruprecht's life; tonight, as he lies in bed, he is thinking only of tomorrow – not Dennis, not Carl, not pills or the swim meet or Operation Condor: tomorrow and nothing else. He's so excited he doesn't know how he'll ever get to sleep; but he must do because next thing it's 6 a.m., and he's plunging *pow!* into fresh chlorine.

The lucky boys who made the cut have extra training all this week, a half-hour every morning before the others start; through the perspex roof the sky is still pitch-dark, it could be midnight. From the side of the pool, Coach claps a rhythm, while they race up and down, up and down, an endless journey over the same short distance. Breaststroke, backstroke, butterfly, crawl: Skippy's arms and legs do the movements by themselves, while he floats somewhere inside his body like a passenger. In flashes, through foam, Garret Dennehy and Siddartha Niland appear in the parallel lanes either side, like fragments of reflections, different Skippys in different worlds.

Outside the showers, while the others are washing, the team huddles round, arms folded across slippery cold bodies, listening to Coach with serious grown-up expressions. There's only three days left before the meet!!! He gives them the itinerary and assigns them their buddies for the trip. 'Daniel, you'll partner with Antony as before . . .' 'Ha ha, tough shit, Juster!' 'Better bring some ear-plugs!' Antony 'Air Raid' Taylor, the loudest snorer in the whole school, who cannot be woken till morning once he falls asleep unless you throw a bucket of water over him.

'Okay, hit the showers. And remember, take *care* of yourselves over the next few days. No horseplay. I don't want all that good work going to waste because someone's pulled a muscle wrestling, or stood on a nail.'

On a nail, on glass, on acid, on burning coals, or you walk under scaffolding and a girder drops on top of you, or you get burned in a fire, or you're kidnapped by terrorists? When you think about it there are so many things that could go wrong! But Skippy's not thinking about it, his brain is full of LORI LORI LORI LORI! He can't think of anything else, through swimming, through breakfast, German, Religion, Art, the thought of her making everything beautifully unreal, like the last days of school, when you're walking along the edge of June and though class hasn't ended summer's creeping into everything like spilled orange juice through the pages of your copybook, summer that's stronger than school, Lori that's like a one-girl summer . . .

In English they're doing a poem called 'The Road Not Taken', about this guy Robert Frost in a wood, reading which Mr Slattery becomes unaccountably emotional.

'A life, you see – a life, Frost is saying, is something that must be *chosen*, just like a path through a wood. The tricky thing for us is that we live in an age that seems to present us with a whole raft of choices, a maze of ready-made paths. But if you look more closely, many of them turn out to be simply different versions of the same thing, to buy products, for example, or to believe whatever prefabricated narratives we're offered to believe in, a religion, a country, a football team, a war. The idea of making one's own choices, of for example not believing, not consuming, remain as less travelled as ever . . .'

'Hey! Skip!' Mario hisses, leaning across Geoff to poke Skippy in the arm. 'Have you got a present to bring to your lady?'

'I need to bring a present?'

Mario claps his hand to his forehead. '*Mamma mia*! It is no wonder you Irish remain virgins until you are forty!'

At lunch break they walk up to the shopping mall to get Lori a present. All the money in his wallet buys Skippy the second-smallest box of chocolates. On the way back, Dennis, who has been unusually quiet this lunchtime, speaks up. 'I've been thinking about that Robert Frost poem,' he says. 'I don't think it's about making choices at all.'

'What's it about, so?' Geoff says.

'Anal sex,' Dennis says.

'Anal sex?'

'How'd you figure, Dennis?'

'Well, once you see it, it's pretty obvious. Just look at what he says. He's in a *wood*, right? He sees two *roads* in front of him. He takes the one *less travelled*. What else could it be about?'

'Uh, woods?'

'Going for a walk?'

'Don't you listen in class? Poetry's never about what it says it's about, that's the whole point of it. Obviously Mrs Frost or whoever isn't going to be too happy with him going around telling the world about this time he gave it to her up the bum. So he cleverly disguises it by putting it in a poem which to the untrained eye is just about a boring walk in some gay wood.'

'But, Dennis, do you think Mr Slattery'd be teaching it to us if it was really about anal sex?'

'What does Mr Slattery know?' Dennis scoffs. 'You think he's ever taken his wife up the road less travelled?'

'Poh, when have *you* ever gone up the road less travelled?' Mario challenges.

Dennis strokes his chin. 'Well, there was that magical night with your mother . . . I tried to stop her!' – ducking out of the way as Mario swings at him. 'But she was insatiable! Insatiable!'

Passing back beneath the tattered sycamores, they see a commotion at the entrance to the basement. Boys are milling around, wisps of smoke gusting over their heads. As they approach, Mitchell Gogan detaches himself from the group rubbernecking at the door and arrives breathlessly at their side. 'Hey, Juster –' barely able to contain his glee '– isn't your locker number 181?'

Yes, and it's on fire. Skippy squeezes through the crowd to find flames coursing up the open door, roaring proprietorially in the interior; sparks shoot up to the ceiling and descend again, trailing soot like downed aeroplanes. Boys watch, grinning, their faces dyed a hellish orange; and in the midst of them – staring at him with eyes that in the gothic light are like the windows of an empty house – is Carl. Skippy gapes back in horror, unable to look away. Then from behind him comes a gravelly voice, and Noddy emerges through the bodies, his lumpy troll face flushed red, the fire extinguisher in his hand. 'Ah Jaysus!' he shouts. 'What de fuck's dis?'

He aims the extinguisher and the crowd, with a single howl of delight, leaps backward as foam cascades into the flames. In less than a minute the fire is out; the boys disperse, but Skippy hovers shamefacedly as Noddy pokes through the charred contents, taking care of any embers. 'Dis your locker, is it?' he accosts Skippy. 'D'you have fireworks in dere or lighter fluid or something?'

Skippy shakes his head mutely, gazing into its sodden black heart.

'So how'd dis happen, so?'

Noddy's rancid breath blasts against his nostrils. Through the miasma of smoke he can see Carl watching him, motionless as a waxwork. 'I don't know.'

'*I don't know,*' the janitor mouths, turning back to the devastated locker. 'Well, de whole ting's fuckin banjaxed – here, where're you goin, gimme your name, you . . .'

But Skippy's broken free and reeled away. Next thing he knows he's in his dorm room. The sky in the window is icy-cold; particles of soot cling to the ribbons of the microscopic box of chocolates. Without thinking he finds himself reaching for the pills – then he stops. Dennis, Geoff, Ruprecht and Mario have appeared behind him, arranged in the doorway musicians-of-Bremen-style, regarding him sombrely.

'What?' he says.

'Are you all right, Skip?'

'I'm fine.'

'Was there a lot of stuff in there?'

'It doesn't matter.'

'What are you going to do?'

'What do you mean?'

There is a pause, an exchange of looks, and then Ruprecht: 'Skippy, I think what happened to your locker may not have been an accident.'

'You can't go to Lori's house, Skip!' Geoff blurts. 'Carl will kill you.'

'I'm going to go.' Skippy is adamant. 'Carl's not going to stop me.'

'But, uh, Skip, what if he *does* stop you?'

'He can *try*,' Skippy says defiantly.

'What's that supposed to mean?'

'Maybe it's time someone stopped *him*.' He doesn't even know it's what he's thinking until the words leave his mouth, but as soon as they do, he knows he means it.

'What are you talking about? You don't stand a chance against him!'

'This way you're going to lose the girl, *and* get stomped into the ground.'

'And you've got a race in three days!' Geoff remembers. 'Skippy, how will you be able to race if you're stomped into the ground?'

'Skippy?'

Downstairs, bitter smoke from the cheap wood of the locker still inflects the air, and heads turn and snicker at Skippy as they drift back to class. He ignores them, sweeping the hallway from left to right, until there, in the doorway of the Mechanical Drawing Room, he sees him: the only person Skippy knows whose *back* looks angry . . . Heart beating in his ears like a kettle-drum, with a momentum that seems to come from elsewhere, he moves through the tunnel of air connecting the two of them, and stretches out his hand to tap Carl on the shoulder.

Around them, the corridor comes to a standstill. In the doorway, Carl slowly turns, and his bloodshot eyes fall emptily on Skippy. They show no sign of knowing who he is; they show no sign of anything. It is like staring into an abyss, an infinite, indifferent abyss . . .

Skippy swallows, then in one quick rush charges, 'You set fire to my locker!'

Carl's expression doesn't alter; when at last he speaks it's as if every word is a deadweight that must be hauled up with chains and pulleys from the bottom of his feet. 'What are you going to do about it?' he says.

Apologize! Walk away! Thank him for doing such a thorough job! 'After school,' Skippy says, praying his voice won't break. 'Behind the swimming pool. You and me.'

A low buzz emanates from the encircling crowd. It takes a moment for Carl to react; then slowly his jaw drops and a leaden series of laughs come out. Ha! Ha! Ha! Ha! The hollow laugh of a robot that laughs without knowing why things are funny. Gently he places a hand on Skippy's shoulder and, leaning in to his ear, whispers, 'You faggot, I am going to kill you.'

Within minutes the news is all over school: no way out now, even if he wanted it. The general response seems to be simple mystification.

'*You're* going to fight Carl?'

Skippy nods.

'*You* are?'

Skippy nods again.

'He's going to massacre you,' Titch or Vince Bailey or whoever it is says.

Skippy just about manages a shrug.

'Well, good luck,' they say, and wander off.

All through class, faces keep flicking back to Skippy, scrutinizing him like he's a ten-foot lizard sitting there at the desk; and the day, which had been going so torturously slowly, begins to hurtle, as if time itself were panting to view the fight. Skippy tries to grasp on to the teachers' lessons, if only to slow things down. But it's as if the words themselves know they are not intended for him and pass him by. This must be what it's like being dead, haunting the living, he thinks. Like everything is made of glass, too slippery to hold on to, so that you feel like you're falling just standing still.

Two minutes after the final bell, the first boys arrive at the patch of gravel at the back of the Annexe. Enclosed by the swimming pool on one side, the boiler room and an ever-growing chaos of brambles on the others, it can't be seen from anywhere else in the school; whenever there's a score to be settled, for as long as anyone can remember, this is where it's been done. In no time at all the space is packed, and from the chatter it's clear there is little doubt about the outcome: the crowd's been drawn here not by the promise of a close-fought battle, but by the chance to see some actual bodily harm.

'This is a crazy mania,' Mario says morosely. 'Carl is going to pulverize him. Skippy will be lucky if he ever gets to ogle a woman again.'

'Do you think we should do something?' Niall says.

'Do something?' Dennis repeats. 'Like what?'

'Like, stop him somehow.'

'And just let this Neanderthal waltz off with the great love of his life, is that it?' Like many pessimists, Dennis becomes strangely energized when things are actually at their worst. 'He should sit tight and let himself be bullied and trampled over for another four years, and then some day when he's an accountant married to some mediocre-looking girl the bullies didn't want he can take revenge by giving Carl Incorporated a really exacting audit?'

'But what's the point of a fight he's guaranteed to lose?'

'I don't know what the point is,' Dennis avows. 'But we've been getting pushed around this dump for nine years now and if one person has actually found the guts to do something about it, I'm not about to stop him. Maybe it'll inspire the rest of us to stop being such a bunch of losers. In fact, this is exactly what Robert Frost was writing about in that poem.'

'I thought you said it was about anal sex.'

'Poems can be about more than one thing. You guys can say what you want. I'm with Skippy. He knows what he's doing. You'll see.'

Skippy's locked in a cubicle in the bathroom. In his hand is the tube of pills. He knows he probably shouldn't. But it feels like his head is about to fly away, and maybe just a half would be enough to make the room stop spinning round –

The phone rings. It's her! 'Daniel, are you going to fight Carl?'

How does she know? 'Am I what?' he says, hurriedly stowing the pills in his back pocket.

'Oh my God,' she moans. 'Daniel, are you?'

'It's nothing to do with you,' he says.

'Oh God,' she says again, breathlessly. She sounds even more freaked out than he is, which in spite of everything sets a little ember of warmth aglow in his heart. 'Daniel, Carl's *dangerous*, you don't know what he'll do –'

'Can I ask you a question?' He doesn't want to, but can't stop himself. 'Are you and him . . . are you, uh . . .'

She sighs in a way that's almost a groan. 'Listen, Daniel –' she stops and sighs again; he waits with his entire insides coiled into one impossibly tight spring that is pulling his chin down into his shoulders '– I haven't seen Carl since before the Hop. But he gets ideas into his head. He's wild, Daniel. So stay away from him.'

'Don't worry,' Skippy says, simply and not unheroically.

'Arrgh – I mean it. It's stupid to fight him. You don't *need* to. Do you understand? Just come up to the house like we said, okay? Just stay away from Carl, and come straight up.'

'Okay.'

'Do you promise?'

'I promise,' he says, crossing his fingers, and opens the cubicle door.

Behind the swimming pool, boys continue to cram into the shrinking space. The air is thick with cigarette smoke and invisible messages flying back and forth, leaving barely enough oxygen to breathe; morale in the Juster camp has been dealt a further blow by the discovery that Damien Lawlor has opened a book on the fight and is giving even money on Carl to win in twenty seconds or less, and ten to one on Skippy requiring an ambulance, with the proviso that there has to be an actual ambulance, and he has to be stretchered into it. He meets their disapproval with his well-practised blank look. 'What?' he says.

'That's bollocks, Lawlor.'

'What's Carl ever done for you? He's kicked your ass loads of times, I've seen him.'

'Look,' Damien says, pausing to take five euro from Hal Healy on Carl to KO Skippy in one punch at eleven to two, 'my heart is one hundred per cent, completely behind Skippy. I have a totally unshakeable belief in him. This is a completely separate business venture, run by my head. The two things have nothing to do with each other.' He gazes from one frosty, sceptical face to the next. 'You people need to learn how to compartmentalize,' he tells them.

'What are the odds on Skippy winning?' Geoff demands.

'Skippy winning . . . let me see . . .' Damien pretends to leaf through his book. 'Ah, that would be . . . a hundred to one.'

'I'll take five euro on Skippy to win,' Geoff says firmly.

'Are you sure?' Damien says, surprised.

'Yes,' Geoff replies.

'Me too,' Mario says, proffering a note of his own. 'Five euro on Skippy to win.'

Dennis and Niall follow suit, and so does Ruprecht, albeit somewhat reluctantly, as he has computed the odds himself and come up with a figure astronomically higher. 'Five euro on Skippy to win at a hundred to one,' Damien repeats blithely, handing Ruprecht his chit. 'Best of luck, gentlemen.'

'What's a hundred to one?' None of them sees Skippy coming; out here in the cold and surrounded by older boys he looks paler and scrawnier than ever, and also, although bone-dry, somehow gives the impression of being soaking wet.

'Nothing,' Mario says quickly.

'How do you feel?' Ruprecht asks him.

'Great,' Skippy says, shivering, and wedges his hands in his pockets. 'Where's Carl?'

Carl is not here yet; the mob is getting restless. Five past four becomes ten past becomes a quarter past; a drizzle sets up as the light fades, at the edges of the gathering stray bodies begin to drift away, and Geoff Sproke decides to allow himself to entertain the tiniest hope that Carl will not show – that he is so stoned he forgets about it, or that he is arrested by the police en route for locker arson, or just that he is a neglectful person who is too lazy to come along. In fact, as soon as Geoff opens the door, he finds all kinds of reasons for the fight not to happen, and the small hope skips free and expands until suddenly it is almost a certainty, and Geoff feels a kind of elation, and is just about to poke Skippy, looking so pensive and grey-faced there, and explain to him that he needn't worry because Carl's not coming, meaning victory goes to him by default, so he can go and hang out with Lori and everything will be good and happy for all of them for ever – when there's a collective intake of breath and the hubbub shifts to a single pitch and everybody turns to look in one direction and Geoff's face falls and the hope dwindles instantly and is extinguished.

At first Carl doesn't even seem to notice the crowd – he loiters by the boiler room, finishing a cigarette. Then, flicking away the butt, he lopes towards them. Instantly the bodies around Skippy melt away, and he finds himself at the centre of a perfectly circular clearing, though Mario's still at his ear, jabbering about some one hundred per cent fail-safe and lethal karate move that they do in Italy –

'Italian karate?' Skippy murmurs.

'It's the deadliest form of karate there is,' Mario is saying, and there is more, but Skippy no longer hears him. He is fixed on Carl, who's laughing to himself like he can't believe he's even bothering to do this, and other people are laughing too, because as he comes closer you can see just how huge he is, and how ridiculous is the idea of Skippy trying to fight him, and Skippy blushes at the realization that his grand gesture is in fact a joke, as embarrassing as it will be brutal. Yet at the very same time a voice keeps repeating inside him: every Demon has a weak spot – every Demon has a weak spot – over and over, as if the owl from Hopeland is there on his shoulder – *every* Demon has a weak spot – then Carl takes off his school jumper and rolls up his shirtsleeves, and this voice stops with all the others.

His arm is covered, from the wrist to the elbow, with long, thin cuts. There must be a hundred of them, in different states of freshness – some bright-red, others sour, dull, fragmenting into scabs – winding up his forearm so densely there is hardly any untouched skin left to see, as if he's being woven anew from tiny red threads. Now for the first time he looks at Skippy and though he is still smiling, behind his eyes Skippy can see his brain bucking and fizzing and short-circuiting in the grip of some flashing, clanging force, and suddenly and very vividly he understands that Carl has no brakes or conscience or anything like that and when he said he was going to kill him that's exactly what he meant –

'Okay then.' It's Gary Toolan, of course, ushering any stragglers out of the ring and bringing the two fighters together to shake hands. It's like shaking hands with Death, Skippy can feel the life sucked out of him, and he's just realizing that he's never actually been in a fight before, he doesn't even know what you're supposed to do, the idea of walking over to someone and hitting them seems absurd – when Gary Toolan shouts, 'Fight!' and Carl runs at him, and he ducks out of the way by the skin of his teeth. In an instant the crowd has transformed, becoming a screaming, baying frenzy, like when you throw the switch on a blender, their voices a single bloodthirsty gurgle from which only rare individual words emerge, *kill – smash – fucking – down*, just as the faces are mostly a blur, which is probably a good thing because the two or three that momentarily, inexplicably, pop out at Skippy are contorted into masks of such pure undiluted hatred that if he were to stop and think about it – instead he tries to remember Djed's moves from Hopeland – better than nothing, right? – fighting the Ice Demon, the Fire Demon, doing the forward roll and jab, the spinning kick, the tiger throw – sometimes Skippy practises these in his bedroom when Ruprecht's not around, although never on any enemy more formidable than his pillow – but these go out of his head straight away, as the fists come at him and again he just manages to get out of the way – except he doesn't, Carl's grabbed him, there's a tearing noise as Skippy's jumper rips and Carl's fist pulls back and this is it, this is the end of the fight already –

And then from Carl's pocket comes a merry electronic jingling. Carl stops where he is, fist frozen mid-air. The jingling continues – people laugh, it's that BETHani song, '3Wishes'. Dropping Skippy to the ground, Carl takes out the phone. 'Hello?' he says, and walks away towards the trees.

Ruprecht bumbles forward and wordlessly helps Skippy to his feet, and in a rapidly cooling froth of sweat he waits – fists still clenched, every inch of him trembling, not looking at any of the spectators who ten seconds ago were screaming for his blood – while Carl marches back and forth with the phone beneath the laurels. He speaks in a low voice through gritted teeth; after a moment, with a sour 'All right', he tosses the phone to the ground. This time there is no smile as he stalks back towards them – even the onlookers back away involuntarily, and Skippy discovers he has a whole other register of fear –

'Fight!'

– and instantly they're back in the blender, the whirl of screams, the hate-masks, through which the white-shirted figure of Carl thunders, moving so fast it's like there are a dozen of him, coming at Skippy from every direction, the fists lightning-quick, every time a little closer, whistling through the air bare millimetres away, as Skippy ducks, wriggles, dodges, with every last ounce of energy he has, for what seems like hours but is probably only a handful of seconds –

And then he stumbles, one ankle sliding away from him.

It all seems to happen quite slowly.

Carl raises his two fists like a hammer, high over his head –

Skippy's just standing there, tottering –

and everyone bellows because they know that as soon as he's hit he's toast, and that's when the real fun starts –

As the fists come down he swings out blindly –

he doesn't know whether it's meant as a punch or a block –

but it connects with Carl's jaw:

the impact shoots back through his bones and up his arms; Carl's head snaps sideways –

and he goes down –

and he doesn't get up.

Nothing happens for a long moment; it's as if all sound has been sucked out of the world. And then everyone is cheering! Maniacal, incredulous, ecstatic cheering, as if this is the first time in their lives they have truly cheered – laughing and whooping and jumping up and down, like the Munchkins in *The Wizard of Oz* when Dorothy's house lands on the Witch, the same people who a second ago were roaring at Carl to pull Skippy's guts out. Skippy might have found this odd, but he's too dazed to think about anything, and now he's swamped by his friends.

'A glass jaw,' Niall marvels, 'who'd've thought it?'

'It was the move he did,' Mario explains. 'The Italian karate move, didn't you see it?'

It seems as if the only person not celebrating – other than Damien Lawlor, who is sunk on his heels, whispering ashen-faced to himself, 'I'm *ruined . . .*' – is Skippy himself. Instead he's gazing at the spot of gravel occupied only a moment ago by Carl's fallen body. Where'd he go?

'Legged it,' Niall pronounces.

'He'd *better* leg it,' Ruprecht comments darkly.

'Come on, Skip.' Mario takes him by the arm. 'We should clean you up before you go see your lady. You have a limited amount to work with at the best of times.'

'Make way for the champ!' cries Geoff, clearing a path to the Tower.

And ten minutes later – hair tamed, teeth brushed, irremediably shredded school jumper exchanged for a clean hoodie – Skippy's leaving it again, pedalling Niall's bike uphill towards the gate. The rain has cleared and the clouds given way to a sunset that blushes deep and fiery, lush pinks and warm reds piled on top of each other in a breathy rushed jumble like a heart in love; and as he weaves out weightlessly into the traffic, leaving their final words of advice – 'Full hardcore sex!' 'Just don't puke on her!' – to disappear into the evening, the euphoria blossoms inside him at last, and with every yard travelled, continues, star-like, to grow. The grave canopies of the trees overhead merge with the incoming dusk; the dual carriageway hooshes by him, its tall streetlamps seeming to sing through the twilight; the chain and wheels hum at his feet, the chocolates swing from their bag on the handlebars, as he turns down her road, past the old stone houses with their ivy veils, to arrive at her gates; and there, at the end of the driveway, just as he imagined it, she is – in the lamplight, on the doorstep, laughing like he's just told the greatest joke in the world.

In the beginning he has to keep pinching himself to remind himself this is actually happening: it seems unreal, like one of those Kinder ads where everyone's been dubbed into another language.

'You're here!' she exclaims, holding her arms out to him. Her eye catches on the bruise on his temple as she leans in to kiss him, but she doesn't say anything about it. 'My parents are *dying* to meet you,' she says instead, and taking his hand she leads him inside. They go down a hall full of paintings to an airy kitchen with a huge domed skylight, where a tall, slightly fierce-looking woman in a black dress is chopping courgettes. Skippy wipes his palms on his trousers, ready to shake hands, but Lori breezes right by her, through a glass door: 'Hey, Mom, look who's here!'

The woman stretched out on the divan is the image of Lori: the same magnetic green eyes, the same carbon-black hair. 'Oh my goodness!' she lays down her magazine and swings her bare feet onto the tiles. 'So this is the boy! This is the famous –'

'Daniel,' Lori says.

'Daniel,' Lori's mum repeats. 'Well, you're very welcome to our home, Daniel.'

'Thank you for having me,' Skippy mumbles, and then, remembering, 'I brought some chocolates.' He hands Lori the box, which in the cathedral-like conservatory looks downright microscopic; nevertheless, both women make exactly the same *Ohhhh* sound.

'He's ad*or*able,' Lori's mum pronounces, skating her fingertips over Skippy's cheeks.

'Can we have some OJ?' Lori asks.

'Of course, sweetie,' her mum says, and calls through the door to the other woman, 'Lilya, fetch the kids some juice, would you?'

then kneels down on the floor in front of Skippy so her perfume swims up his nose and it becomes nearly impossible not to look down her top. 'It's nice to finally meet you,' she says in a fake whisper. 'I knew there had to be a boy on the scene. Though Lori'd deny it till the cows came home.'

'*Mom*,' Lori groans.

'You may find it hard to believe, young lady, but I was actually a girl myself once. I know the tricks.'

'Mom, go and do some Pilates or something,' Lori pleads, moving towards the kitchen.

'All right, all right . . .' She resists her daughter for long enough to fix Skippy with an appraising eye and declare again, 'Oh he's just *too* adorable,' before disappearing, laughing, back to her divan.

'Sorry, I should have warned you,' Lori says. 'My mom is like the world's biggest flirt.' She reaches for one of two glasses of Sunny D that have appeared on the counter along with a big plate of chocolate-chip cookies, and shines Skippy a lighthouse-beam smile. 'Come on, I'll give you the tour.'

The house is endless. Every room gives way to another even bigger, each one an Aladdin's cave of screens and sculptures and stereo equipment. Following after Lori, half-listening to her chatter, Skippy feels happy but strange, like a shadow that's won some competition and been invited for one day to be an actual person and not just a fuzzy shape on the ground – 'And this is my room,' she says.

He snaps out of his reverie. Holy shit! It's true! They're in her bedroom! The walls are pink and covered with girl-type posters – two horses nuzzling each other, the Sad Sam dog, a boy-cherub stealing a kiss from a girl-cherub, BEThani in an almost-but-not-completely-see-through swimsuit, and again, in a picture cut out of a magazine, hand in hand with her boyfriend, the guy from Four to the Floor. On the dresser is a photograph of Lori, the beautiful mother and a man who must be Lori's dad, kind of like if GI Joe was made of wood and wore a suit, the three of them looking so perfect together, like the example picture that comes with the frame.

'Let's watch TV!' she says. There's a television in here but she's already going down the stairs to one of the living rooms, where she sits on the sofa about two feet away from him, the cat cradled in her lap and her pop-socked feet dug comfortably under a cushion. *The Simpsons* is on. Skippy wonders if he was supposed to have kissed her upstairs. She didn't act like she was expecting him to. So should he kiss her now? She does seem quite interested in the programme. Bollocks, maybe it's not a date! Maybe they are friends!

'So are you still swimming?' she asks him during the ad break.

He tells her about the swim meet coming up this weekend.

'Wow, that's so exciting,' she says.

'Yeah,' he says, nodding. (Hit by runaway hotdog cart, trip over cat, catch chickenpox, water shortage → all pools empty everywhere.) 'It's the semi-finals?'

'Cool.' She scratches her nose thoughtfully. 'So you didn't quit?'

'Quit?'

'Yeah, when I was talking to you the night of the dance, you said you wanted to quit it.'

'Oh –' *when I was talking to you the night of the dance??!!* '– um, well, it's quite hard work, I suppose. Like, we have to get up at half six to train, and stuff. So it's hard work, that's what I meant.'

'You told me you hated it,' she says.

'I hated it?'

She nods, her eyes fixed on his.

'Yeah . . .' he says vaguely. 'Yeah, sometimes I feel a bit like that.'

'Why would you do something you hate?'

'Well, I suppose my parents are excited about it, so . . .'

'They don't want you to do something you hate, do they?'

'No, but . . .' The Game, even here! It rises up monolithic out of the floor like a staring tombstone: caught in its shadow he trails off, sitting there dumbly, miserably, wishing she'd stop looking at him – then the door opens and the tall man from the photograph comes in.

'Daddy!' Lori cries, and leaps up from the couch.

'There's my princess!' The man puts down his shopping bags so he can lift her up and swing her. 'And who do we have here?' he says, looking at Skippy scrunched up on the couch.

'This is my friend Daniel,' Lori says.

'Aha . . . so this is the man who's been keeping you out till all hours,' her dad says. 'Well, well. Gavin Wakeham.' He lopes round to crush Skippy's hand in his and peer at him interrogatively.

'Daniel's in Seabrook,' Lori tells her dad.

'Is he?' The man brightens at this. 'I'm an old Blue-and-Gold myself! Class of '82. Tell me, Daniel, how's Des Furlong? He back yet?'

'No, he's still sick,' Skippy says. 'Mr Costigan is in charge.'

'Greg Costigan! I was in school with that bastard. What do you make of him, Daniel? Talks a lot of shite, doesn't he? Actually, tell him I said that, will you? Tell him Gavin Wakeham says he talks a lot of shite, will you do that for me?' His big face looks down at Skippy avariciously, like a hungry monster that has discovered a plate of bonbons. Skippy doesn't know what to say. 'Good man, he's true to his school!' Lori's dad guffaws, slapping his back. 'Matter of fact, Greg is a good friend of mine. Still see him for the odd pint up at the Rugby Club. You play yourself, Dan?'

'Daniel's on the swimming team,' Lori says, snuggled under his arm. 'They've got a big race coming up. They're in the semifinals.'

'Is that so? And who's coaching you? It's not still Brother Connolly, is it? Brother Fondle-me, we used to call him.'

'Mr Roche does it now,' Skippy says.

'Ah yes, Tom Roche, of course. Tragic story. You know it?'

'Yes,' Skippy says, but Lori's dad starts telling him anyway. 'Probably the best winger of his generation. Could have walked on to the international team. Walked on to it, if it wasn't for what happened. And now I hear the other fellow's back in Seabrook too, the one who let him take the drop for him, what's his name again . . . ?'

'Daddy, what did you buy?' Lori tugs at his elbow.

Gazing into her upturned face, he brightens again. 'Just some bits and pieces for the gym.'

'*More* stuff for the gym?'

'Just a couple of things.'

'Mom's going to kill you.'

'Aha,' smugly, 'not so, because I've already taken care of that.' He draws a smaller bag out of the larger and shakes it at her.

'And what about me?'

'What about you?'

'It wouldn't be fair if everyone got something except me.'

'Well, I'm sorry, in that case.'

'Let me look in the bag.'

'I think not.'

'Let me look – Daddy!' She lunges for the bag, he hoists it out of her reach, matador-style, and Skippy takes a step backwards as the two of them become one giggling, wrestling mess. The woman from the kitchen appears in the doorway. She pauses there a moment, shooting a brief, expressionless glance at Skippy on the far side of the tussling couple; then, in a vampiric mono-tone, she announces, 'Dinner is served.' Lori's dad and Lori split, gasping and emitting little leftover fragments of laughter.

'Okay, Lilya, thank you,' her dad says. 'There, you little madam, though you don't deserve it . . .'

He tosses Lori a shopping bag with a pair of lips on the side, and she lights up as she takes out a plastic case. 'Oh, thank you, Daddy!'

'Without make-up she looks like the back end of a bus,' her dad winks at Skippy; and then sternly, to Lori, 'But you can only wear it on special occasions, when your mum and I say you can, okay?'

'Yes, Daddy.' She nods earnestly, taking his hand and trotting alongside him into the dining room, with Skippy following behind.

They sit down at the table while the black-clad woman silently lays plates before them. 'Isn't this nice?' Lori's mum says. 'I can't think of the last time we all sat down for a meal together.'

'Daddy's *always* working,' Lori tells Skippy.

'Someone has to pay for all this, don't they?' Lori's dad says, through a mouthful of food. 'You girls seem to think it just drops out of the sky.' Lori and her mum make identical eye-rolling motions. 'So what kind of racket's your dad in, Daniel?'

'Pardon?'

'Your dad, what does he do?'

'Oh – he's an engineer.'

'How about your mum? Is she working too?' Across the table his tanned arms flex as he saws into his chop.

'She's a Montessori teacher. Well, not right now, but . . .'

'That's great. And how are you enjoying school?'

'It's okay,' Skippy says.

'Daniel's one of the smartest boys in his year,' Lori says.

'Good for you,' her dad says. 'So what kind of career do you see yourself in, Daniel?'

Lori's mum, laughing, lays down her fork with a clink on the plate. 'Gavin, give the boy a chance to eat his food!'

'What do you mean?' Lori's dad says. 'We're simply having a conversation, that's all.'

'You're interrogating him. In a minute he'll start burning your feet with cigarettes,' Lori's mum twinkles at Skippy.

'I'm simply trying to find out a little bit about him,' Lori's dad rejoins. 'God forbid I should want to try and find out a little bit about the boy my daughter's been out roaming the streets with for the last month –'

'I wasn't roaming the streets,' Lori says, flushing.

'Well, you weren't watching *Buffy* at Janine's, were you?'

Wait a second – what?

'Leave her alone, Gavin,' her mom reproves.

'I just think it'd be nice to have some *idea* what your own child –'

'We've been through all this – oh, now look.'

Lori's head is bowed, and jerks with sobs.

'Oh sweetheart . . . sweetie, I didn't mean . . .' He extends his hand across the table, lays it in Lori's sparkling black hair. She doesn't respond; a tear splashes down into her half-eaten meal.

'Oh God,' he says heavily. 'Look, I honestly don't see what the fuss is about. Myself and Dan are getting along famously, aren't we, Dan?'

'Yes,' says Skippy. There is a tense silence, filled only by Lori's snuffles. He clears his throat. 'Actually, I think I'd like to design video games. When I grow up?'

'Video games?' Lori's dad says.

'Or else be a scientist, you know like the kind that discover the cures for diseases?'

'What kind of console do you have? Nintendo or Xbox?'

Lori's dad turns out to know quite a lot about video games and they have a good conversation about that. After a little while Lori stops crying, and the black-clad woman brings in a lemon meringue tart on a tray. 'So who's knocking around Seabrook these days?' Lori's dad asks. 'Is Bugsy O'Flynn still there? How about Big Fat Johnson? And Father Green, is he still dragging lads out to the ghetto? Ha ha, I remember carrying boxes around some kip, scared the life out of me. Didn't forget to keep my arse to the wall, though. Old Père Vert.'

'You and that school,' Lori's mother laughs, and as the woman comes in again to clear the dishes, she says to Lori's dad, 'Do you think our daughter could have Daniel back for an hour before she starts her homework?' Lori's dad grins and says, 'I suppose so – okay, scram, you two.'

Lori and Skippy go back into the living room. This time Lori cosies right up next to him on the couch. 'My parents *love* you.' She smiles. Her legs are curled up and her toes wiggling against his hip.

'They're really nice,' he says.

An old film is on the TV, the one about the guy in high school in America who finds out he's a werewolf. Skippy has seen it before but it doesn't matter: his hand is in Lori's and her little finger is absently stroking his little finger and the whole universe is centred in those two little fingers. On the table her phone starts to ring, but she silences it and turns to him again and smiles. After a long time debating whether to put his arm over her shoulder he finally decides that he should, and he is just lifting his elbow onto the top of the couch when the doorbell goes. It makes both of them start. Lori jumps up on the couch to peek out through the curtain, then – does he hear a little gasp? – she runs to the door, shouting, 'I'll get it!' down the hallway.

While she is gone, Skippy tries to focus on the film, where the guy is discovering that when he is a werewolf he is really good at basketball. But although he can't make out the words, he can hear her voice – muffled, urgent-seeming – in the hall, as well as whoever is at the gate, the scrambling of the intercom making him sound ragged, angry . . .

Lori returns to the living room. 'Just someone looking for directions,' she says, wiping her hands on her jeans.

'Oh,' Skippy says.

She sits down next to him again, but this time with her feet on the floor and her body leaning forward, staring at the screen with her mouth tight shut. His hand now rests mournful and unloved on top of his knee. He pretends to himself he doesn't notice the sick feeling in his stomach. 'Do you want to start eating the chocolates?' he asks her.

'Actually, I'm on a diet,' she says.

'Oh.'

'Don't say it to my parents, I haven't told them about it.'

'Okay,' he says, and then, gallantly, 'I don't think you need to go on a diet, though.'

She doesn't seem to hear him; she is staring at the TV, where the werewolf-boy is having an intense conversation with the girl he is in love with.

'Here, you know what you were saying, about quitting the swimming team?' Skippy says.

'What about it?'

'Like, do you think I should? Just quit?'

She arches her back, wriggles her shoulders, first one, then the other, as though the cat is there clinging to her. 'I don't know,' she says. 'I mean, it just sounds so boring.' She turns back to the TV. 'Isn't that the guy who was in that show and then he got that gross disease?'

Skippy doesn't know what's changed but everything has. They watch the rest of the film in silence. Then the door opens and Lori's mum is standing there. 'Homework time, missy.'

Lori looks up at her with a disappointed *aw* face.

'It's a school night,' her mum says. 'I'm sure Daniel has home-work too.'

'Can I just very quickly show Daniel something in my room?'

Her mum smiles. 'All right. But be quick.'

Lori flashes a quick smile at Skippy. 'Okay?' she says. For a moment Skippy just stares at her uncomprehendingly like she's a new letter of the alphabet. Then he remembers himself and mumbles something and follows obediently as she ascends the stairs again and leads him into her room.

This time the night framed in the window is utterly dark, and in the instant before she switches on the light the stars shine in on him deliberately like they're trying to tell him something; then Lori draws the curtains and places herself in front of him. Her eyes are closed and she is standing there like a sleepwalker, her mouth slightly open, her hands slightly lifted. He tries to think of something to say, until the meaning of the closed eyes finally pene-trates. At once it's like some crazy carnival orchestra strikes up inside him, all the instruments playing at the wrong speed in the wrong key, everything whirling and toppling over, while outside him the room's so quiet, not even the wind audible through the double glazing, and Lori so still, her lips parted. He leans into her and her mouth latches on to his, an alien being attaching itself to its host. But he can't stop thinking of the voice in the intercom. Was it the same person that was on the phone? Who she was

370

roaming the streets with? His eyes flick open and see hers, burning green and staring back at him, right up close like planets filling a *Star Trek* sky. Now they shut, her eyebrows furrowing momentarily – he shuts his too. She takes his hand and thrusts it under her shirt. His hand locks on her boob and squeezes, hard? soft? through raspy synthetic material. She makes small squirmy noises, her tongue licks his tongue. Why isn't he happy? Why does it feel different?

A knock at the door. It's already over. Lori walks away briskly to open it. Her mother is there with her hand raised to knock again. 'Sorry, kids. It's eight o'clock.'

'Okay,' Lori says. 'Daniel was just about to go anyway.' She passes under her mum's arm to the landing, and now he is watching her shimmering black crown disappear down the stairs, chatting away to her mother as if nothing had happened at all.

In the kitchen, Lori's dad sets down his Palm Pilot and rises from the table. 'Great to meet you, Dan.' He outstretches his hand. 'Give 'em hell at that swim meet, all right? Show them how we do things in Seabrook College.'

'I will,' Skippy says.

Lori sidles over to him and takes his hand. 'Thanks for coming to see me,' she says.

'Thank you,' Skippy says, meaninglessly.

'Do you want to hang out again sometime?'

'Do you?' He is surprised.

'Sure,' she says, swinging his hand a little back and forth.

'Oh, don't the two of them look sweet!' her mother sighs in a pouty baby voice.

'Maybe we could do something on Friday? I'm not *grounded* any more –' shooting a look at her dad, who pretends to be fixed on his Palm Pilot.

'We could go and see a film?' he says.

'Sure, and then we could go for ice cream,' she says.

'*Too cute!*' Lori's mum exclaims, hands to her cheeks. 'I can't look at you any more, I'll just *die!*'

371

'*Mom,*' Lori blushes, but she can't help grinning down at her shoes. Skippy grins too but does not know why. He feels like he's inside a sitcom, but he can't find where they are on the script. Maybe if he just keeps smiling no one will notice. Maybe nothing was wrong after all – maybe second kisses are always different to the first.

She brings him to the door to say goodbye.

'Thank you so much for coming,' she says again. She is boxed in the yellow light of the doorway like a toy fairy.

'It was fun,' he says. He is outside now, on the flagstones; as he stands there he feels the cold scurry away with the warmth of his body, hungry goblins happening upon an unguarded bakery.

'Well, I'd better go and do my homework,' she says.

'Okay,' Skippy says. 'Bye.'

'Bye.'

The door closes. He gets his bike and turns dazedly towards the darkness. The gates glide slowly open before him, a mouth spitting him out. Then behind him he hears the latch.

'Daniel, wait!' She is running over the flagstones, her bare arms luminous in the dusk. 'Wait,' she says, arriving.

He notices how sometimes her eyes, even when they are open, are closed, like when she was kissing him upstairs; now they are open-open again, urgent.

She composes herself, suppresses her shivers. 'That was really brave, what you did today.'

Skippy semi-shrugs, pretending not to know what she's talking about.

'It was – I mean, I know I told you not to, but still it was so amazing that someone would care enough about me to do that, even when . . .' There is more but it's like she can't say it; instead she just gazes at him, pleadingly, biting her lip, cheeks flushed with cold, as if she wants him to guess what it is, or she thinks he might even know what it is; but Skippy doesn't know, and just looks back at her helplessly. 'Oh,' she moans, like this is something she shouldn't be doing, and then the next thing she is kissing him again, and this time it's like the first time, like they're tumbling down into a dream, warm and sweet with sleep, everything above left behind a million miles away – it's funny how a kiss, which is just two mouths, can feel like this, like for ever, like infinity.

'Okay.' She detaches herself so she can look at him.

'I'll call you about Friday,' he says, not able to keep from smiling but managing at least to stop himself saying *I love you*.

She studies his face before answering, suddenly, for some reason, very solemn. 'Sure,' she says. 'Goodbye, Daniel.' She hurries back inside, and the door clunks shut behind her.

Skippy reels down the driveway and onto the road. He wants to paint her name across the sky. He wants to shout it out to the world at the top of his voice. He makes his way back to Seabrook through the starry night, barely noticing the time go, even though he has to wheel Niall's bike alongside him – he must have ridden over glass or something on the way up here, because when he came out of her house both his tyres had punctures.

In the afterglow of Skippy's victory, the mood in Ruprecht's dorm room, where Team Condor has assembled for its final run-through, is buoyant. As omens go, the fight couldn't have been better; and now the stage seems set for a second contribution to the history books.

The full line-up looks like this: R. Van Doren (Team Commander and Scientific Director), D. Hoey (First Officer) and M. Bianchi (Navigator and Cinematographer) constitute the 'A-unit' that will carry the pod into St Brigid's; G. Sproke has the dual role of i) Janitor Diversion, and ii) Point Man back at Seabrook HQ.

The plan is simple and bold. While the St Brigid's janitor, Brody, is being diverted by Geoff in search of a lost football, planted earlier that evening, the A-unit – having neutralized Brody's dog, Nipper, with dog biscuits – will breach the partition wall via rope-ladder, Geoff keeping them apprised of his and the janitor's exact location by casually singing the theme song to *Bunnington Village*, which apparently is the only song he knows all the words to. Upon successful breach of the main school building, the A-unit will proceed to the Locked Room and unlock the Locked Door using Ruprecht's OpenSesame!™ Skeleton Key, 'Guaranteed 100% Effective on Every Known Form of Lock', as endorsed by Mossad and purchased by Ruprecht on eBay; an electric drill, purloined from Potato-Head Tomms's woodwork class, is to be brought as backup. The pod having been erected in the Locked Room, and the power cable relayed back to the lab via Geoff, a portal into higher-dimensional space will be opened, this time recorded by a functional camera, and international fame and fortune, newspaper headlines to the tune of NEW DAWN USHERED IN BY SCHOOLBOY, last-second rescue of Earth from eco-

logical disaster, golden era of harmony and peace, etc., etc., will
ensue.

'Are there any questions?'

'What about this Ghost Nun?' Mario says.

Ruprecht pooh-poohs the notion. 'There is no Ghost Nun.
That's just some silly story they tell to make the girls behave.'

'Oh,' Mario says, not looking entirely convinced.

The time of the strike has been set for nineteen hundred hours,
when the residents of St Brigid's, staff and students alike, will be in the
dining hall. With twenty minutes to go, everything is in place. The
pod lies on the floor in a tennis bag, attending its hour. Geoff pores
over the instructions for the Cosmic Energy Compressor. Victor
Hero has been primed to sign the team in at Study Hall. Ruprecht
paces about, working on his speech for the camera: '. . . history
books have been written in pencil . . . though we be young, scorn
us not . . . (*awestruck look*) Can it be so? Are we the lucky ones for
whom God has left the door on the latch? (*With growing sense of
rapture*) Into what lambent destiny have we taken the first step?'

And though none says it, this same lambent destiny seems
already to invest the room, to fizz at their pores, as if the Mound,
anticipating their arrival, has sent its emissaries to hurry them on.
Or rather, sent *her* emissaries. Earlier that evening, seeking to fill
the nervous interim as much as for extra information, Geoff had
returned to the Druid's website, and found tucked away there a
poem by Robert Graves, on the subject of the White Goddess
who ruled the Otherworld:

> If strange things happen where she is,
> So that men say that graves open
> And the dead walk, or that futurity
> Becomes a womb and the unborn are shed,
> Such portents are not to be wondered at,
> Being tourbillions in Time made
> By the strong pulling of her bladed mind
> Through that ever-reluctant element.

None of them knew quite what it meant ('what's a tourbillion?') and Ruprecht said it had no immediate relevance to the task at hand; but ever since then, each of them finds himself with a vivid mental impression of the Goddess herself, imprisoned by floorboards and masonry and centuries of coercive unbelief, somewhere underneath their sister school; and experiences this curiously externalized impatience, as of something tugging at their sleeves . . .

Then, with five minutes to Zero Hour, there is a groan from the doorway; they turn to see Dennis propped wretchedly against the jamb. 'I don't know what it is,' he croaked. 'A minute ago I was fine, then suddenly I started feeling really *bad*.'

'What do you mean, "bad"?'

'I don't know . . . Kind of tingly? And energized? It's totally inexplicable.'

'Holy smoke,' Geoff looking round wildly to the others, 'it must be his radiation sickness returning.'

'No, no,' Dennis dismisses this. 'Although now that you mention it, the symptoms are completely identical.'

'Will you be able to do the mission?' Ruprecht wants to know.

'Oh yes, absolutely,' Dennis says, and then collapses.

'What are we going to do?' Geoff says after they have carried him over to the bed.

'We have to get the nurse,' Niall says.

'No nurse,' Ruprecht replies tersely. 'Nurses ask questions.'

'But Ruprecht, he's *sick*.'

'We can't jeopardize the mission. Not now.'

'Maybe you could go instead of him?' Geoff proposes to Niall.

'I have a piano lesson,' Niall mumbles sheepishly.

'What about you, Victor?'

'No way,' Victor says. 'I'm not getting expelled.'

'Looks like we'll have to put it off till another night,' Mario says to Ruprecht.

'We can't put it off till another night,' Ruprecht replies through gritted teeth. 'Tonight's the end of the Cygnus X-3's radiation burst. It *has* to be tonight.'

But a condor can't fly on one wing, everyone knows that. The Operation is in serious trouble, and it must be said that the Team Commander's reaction to the crisis leaves something to be desired: stamping about the room like a giant, bellicose toddler, kicking the wastepaper basket, slippers, anything else that crosses his path, while the rest of the team bow their heads plaintively, something in the manner of humble banana farmers in the midst of a tropical storm. And then fate intervenes, in the form of Mario's room-mate Odysseas Antopopopolous arriving at the door looking to borrow some anti-fungal cream.

Five machinating pairs of eyes fix on him.

'Well, I don't know if it's a fungus,' Odysseas says. 'It might be a reaction to rayon.'

The situation is explained to him in double-quick time. It isn't clear, at the end of it, whether Odysseas has any real idea what he's getting himself into, but after months of listening to Mario's fantasies on the subject, he is keen to see the interior of St Brigid's for himself. The Condor is aloft again! Odysseas, furthermore, has a whole wardrobe of black fencing gear, custom-made for covert operations, which he invites the Team to make use of.

As the hour strikes on the school clock – with Geoff Sproke gone on ahead to buttonhole the security guard – the three others jostle at the door, synchronizing their phones, resembling, in their dusky regalia, not so much condors as fugitive punctuation marks: two brackets and one overfed full stop. 'So long, Victor! So long, Niall! We'll send you a postcard from the next dimension!'

With that they run out the door and down the stairs, and into history.

Five minutes later, as Skippy is sitting down to eat with Lori's family, they are straddled on the partition wall. From somewhere in the darkness beyond, the theme to *Bunnington Village* may be heard, as Geoff thrashes through dock leaves with the St Brigid's gatekeeper. Directly below, staring up intently and wagging its stumpy tail in a decidedly foreboding manner, is a small brown-and-white beagle.

'Maybe it just wants to play,' Odysseas suggests.

'Ha,' Mario says. The dog's eyes gleam at them through the darkness; its long tongue palpitates over smiling rows of teeth.

'*In a glade in a forest,*' Geoff Sproke's voice wafts over faintly, '*where there's magic in the air . . .*'

A cold, rain-laced wind plays over their cheeks.

'This is some plan,' Mario says sarcastically to Ruprecht's ignominious silence. 'Oh yes, clearly the work of a mastermind.'

It appears that at some point during the lead-in to the mission, Operation Condor's Team Commander and Scientific Director ate the biscuits intended for the neutralization of Nipper.

'*Here comes William Bunnington,*' sings Geoff anxiously, '*with his friend Owl – he's the Mayor . . .*'

'*Dog* biscuits! You draw up this big complicated plan, with the bells and the whistles, and then before we even *leave* you *eat* the *dog biscuits!*'

'I couldn't help it,' Ruprecht replies miserably. 'When I'm nervous I get hungry.'

'They were *dog biscuits!*'

'Well, we can't stay up here for ever,' Odysseas says.

'I'm not going down there to get my family jewels chewed off,' Mario states, then scratches his ear. 'This damn rayon, it's making me itchy!'

'*Bunnington Village,*' Geoff, with mounting urgency, '*where the squirrels make Nut Soup . . .*'

'Lad, why in God's name do you keep making that infernal racket?' comes the rough voice of Brody the janitor.

'It helps me concentrate,' they hear Geoff reply. 'When I'm looking for things?'

'Are you sure your ball even came in here?'

'I think so,' Geoff says.

Below, the dog flexes itself in a settling-in sort of way.

'Maybe we should just abort the mission,' Mario says.

'Never!' comes the defiant reply from his left.

'Well, what are we going to do, just stay up here all night?'

Ruprecht does not answer.

'Isn't that a football right there?' they hear the guard say.

'Where?' Geoff's voice says.

'There, right there, you're looking right at it.'

'Oh yes – hmm, I'm not sure that's *my* football . . .'

'Well, it'll do ye –'

'*A bunny place, a funny place . . .*' desperately –

'Ah for Jesus' sake –'

'*. . . an always bright and sunny place, Bunnington will keep a space for you . . .*'

'Stop it! Go home now! I don't want to see you in here again!' The guard starts clapping his hands and calling the dog. The dog, without taking its eye off the top of the wall, barks. 'Hold on, sounds like Nipper's found something . . .'

'Wait!' Geoff implores. 'I have to tell you something! Something of the utmost importance!'

'Well, *commandante*?' Mario inquires acidly. 'May we please go home now?'

But before Ruprecht can reply, Odysseas has peeled off his black sweater, leapt off the wall into the yard and thrown it over the dog. 'Quickly!' he urges the other two, as the sweater charges blindly left and right, emitting muffled barks of ever-growing anger. Mario and Ruprecht land painfully on the wet asphalt, just as the dog's vengeful snout pokes into view. 'Go!' Odysseas exhorts, stepping protectively before them; and they take to their heels and run to the shadow of the school. Snarls and the sound of tearing fabric echo across the empty yard. But there is no time to wonder or grieve, nor is there any way back. The guard's feet thump over the ground, his torch-beam flashing in every direction. Without stopping to think, they scurry around to the back of the school and up the rickety metal staircase, wrestling open the window sash and hurling themselves through it –

It's only as they pick themselves up from the moth-eaten carpet that they realize where they are. *Inside* St Brigid's: inside the grey walls that have stared back at them for so long, teasing them with the mysteries they conceal. Not yet ready to speak or move, every breath seeming like a thousand-decibel explosion, the boys roll their eyes at each other in mute incredulity.

One aspect of the plan has panned out – there doesn't seem to be anybody around. Silently, warily, Ruprecht and Mario tread away from the window, leaving the dark crenellations of Seabrook behind. The deserted hallway is both alien and familiar, like the landscape of a dream. There is a chipped dado rail and a picture of Jesus, dewy-eyed and rosy-cheeked as a boy-band singer; passing into the girls' dorms, they see through the open doors rumpled bedcovers, balled-up foolscap, posters of footballers and pop stars, homework timetables, bottles of spot cream – uncannily like the dorms in Seabrook, except in some unplaceable but totally fundamental way *completely different*.

As they descend the stairs to negotiate the ground floor, this creepy schizoid feeling only grows. Everywhere they look, there are analogues of their own school – classrooms with cramped benches and scrawled blackboards, printouts on the noticeboards, trophy cabinets and art-room posters – almost identical, but at the same time, somehow, not, the discrepancy too subtle for the naked eye and yet omnipresent, as though they've entered a parallel universe before the portal has been opened at all, where instead of atoms everything is composed of some mysterious other entity, quarks of hitherto unseen colours . . . It is quite different from how Mario imagined breaking into a girls' school would be, and the idea that this place has been here, existing, *the whole time he's been around* is one that he finds deeply unsettling.

If Ruprecht is struck by this he shows no sign; he treks on wordlessly, five or six steps in front of Mario, the pod clinking gently in the bag slung over his shoulder. Then, up ahead, they hear footsteps, and Ruprecht yanks Mario into an unoccupied classroom just as two grey-frocked nuns round the corner. In the very back row they crouch beneath the desks, bathed with sweat, Mario's breathing heavy and rushed –

'You're making too much noise!' Ruprecht hisses at him.

'I can't help it!' Mario gesticulates. 'These nuns, they give me the willies . . .'

The nuns have stopped right outside the door. They are talking about a Brazilian priest who is visiting in spring. One nun suggests they take him to Knock. The other says Ballinspittle. A polite argument ensues over the competing merits of the materializations of Our Lady in these two places, one being more accredited, the other more recent, and then – 'Did you hear something?'

Under his desk, Mario gazes in horror at his phone, which has just released two loud, self-satisfied bleeps, and now emits two more. Hysterically, Mario fusses over the buttons, trying to shut it up –

'Could it be mice?' one nun wonders from the corridor.

'Funny sort of mice,' the other says, her tone hardening. '*Coronation Street*'s starting.'

'I'll just have a peep –'

The light comes on: the nun's eyes scan the bare surfaces of the desks. The boys hold their breath, clench every muscle, painfully aware of the fug of sweat and hormones and odours that pump from every pore, waiting for a nostril to twitch in recognition –

'Hmmph.' The light goes off again, and the door closes. 'That didn't sound like a mouse to me, you know.'

'No?'

'Sounded more like a rat.'

'Oh goodness, no . . .'

The voices recede: Mario whips off his balaclava and sucks in lungfuls of air. 'These nuns,' he pants, 'in Italy they are everywhere, everywhere!'

By the time he has calmed down sufficiently to carry on, their window of opportunity is starting to look decidedly narrow. Dinner hour is over at eight, and although the students will be continuing from there to Study Hall, the nuns, of whom it seems Mario has a pathological fear, which Ruprecht thinks is the kind of thing that ought really to have been mentioned prior to entering the convent, will be at liberty and on the loose.

They exit the classroom and hurry along as directed by the map. Nerves are strained now, and the uncanny *familiarity* of their surroundings paradoxically disorientates them, leading them repeatedly down false paths – 'That was the chemistry lab back there, so the gym must be this way!' 'No, because the lab was on the right, by the AV Room.' 'No, it wasn't.' 'Yes, it was – just trust me, it's this way – oh.' 'Oh, this is the gym, is it? This is the gym, that they have disguised as a second, identical AV Room? And they play badminton with the televisions, and hockey with the VCRs? Wow, they must be strong, these girls, to use heavy AV equipment instead of balls –' It starts to seem like the school itself is misdirecting them, reacting hostilely to their presence here – either that, or the corridors simply don't link up in a linear way, don't actually correspond to the map, but instead are obeying some circuitous, rhizomatic feminine principle, the influence of the Mound, maybe . . .

And then, quite by accident, they find themselves in a recognizably older part of the school. Here there are holes in the wainscoting and crumbling walls; even the light seems dimmer, greyer. They hasten along by dilapidated rooms stacked full of chairs, till they arrive at a pair of wooden doors. Very softly, Ruprecht twists the doorknob and peeks inside. Inside there are climbing frames and mini soccer nets: the gym. 'Meaning that *this*,' turning one hundred and eighty degrees to the door across the corridor, 'must be the Locked Room.' He can't keep the quaver out of his voice.

The door, of course, is locked when they try it. Ruprecht sets down his equipment on the floor, produces the OpenSesame!™ Skeleton Key and inserts it in the keyhole. After jiggling it around a moment, he tries the door again. It is still locked. 'Hmm,' Ruprecht says, stroking his chin.

'What's the matter?' Mario asks him. He does not like this corridor. Mechanical noises are emanating from somewhere, and a draught that seems unnaturally cold circles his ankles. Without replying, Ruprecht examines the teeth of the key and replaces it in the keyhole.

'What is it?' Mario repeats, hopping from one foot to the other.

'This is supposed to be able to open any conventional lock,' Ruprecht says, twisting it about.

'It's not working?'

'I can't quite seem to get it to connect . . .'

'We don't have time for this! Try something else!'

'It has a guarantee,' Ruprecht points out.

'Just use the drill and get it over with.'

'The drill will make noise.'

'It'll take two *seconds* with the drill.'

'All right, all right –' He looks at Mario expectantly.

'What?' Mario says.

'Well, give it to me then.'

'I thought you had it.'

'Why would I have it?'

'Because I don't have it . . .' The realization hits them simultaneously; Mario's shoulders slump. 'I thought you said you planned this.'

'I did,' Ruprecht says humbly. 'It's just that I made the plan before I knew what was going to happen.'

It is then that they hear the voice. By its pitch it is clearly a woman's, but any feminine softness has long desiccated away, replaced by an eldritch darkness and attended by what sounds an awful lot like the snipping of spectral shears . . . For a moment they remain frozen to the spot, and then – 'Run,' gurgles Ruprecht. Mario doesn't need telling twice. Scrambling his bag from the ground, he is set to scarper down the corridor when a hand fastens about his arm –

'What are you *doing*?' hisses Ruprecht.

Mario stares at him, nearly apoplectic with terror. 'I'm *running*.'

'It's *coming* from down there,' Ruprecht blinks back at him.

'It's not, it's coming from up *there* . . .'

They pause, almost but not quite clutching each other, with their ears cocked. The hideous dried-out croak is drawing inevitably closer – apparently, whether by some quirk of the architecture, the type of stone in the masonry perhaps or the curious way the corridor bends, from *both directions at once*. The boys gibber at each other helplessly. With every passing instant now the temperature drops precipitously, the grey light wanes; the ghastly voice chants its message, necrotic and Latin, over and again, as though doomed to repeat it, doomed for eternity, a doom that any second now they will be sharing, when the voice's owner comes around that corner, or the other corner, or possibly even both corners, to find them quaking before her –

And then a hand – whose hand neither of them can remember afterwards, but a hand in desperation – reaches for the door, and this time, miraculously, it gives. Without a second thought they hurry through it to crouch on its far side, ears pressed to the wood, as the voice outside, now accompanied by an ugly dragging noise, passes right by them, no more than a couple of inches away (they can't suppress a shudder) . . . and then recedes, or rather ebbs, or rather, actually, dissipates . . .

As soon as it's gone they feel warmer, braver; straightening up, they dust themselves off, scoffing at the idea that either of them thought for a second that whatever was outside was the Ghost Nun: 'I don't even believe in the stupid Ghost Nun.' 'No, me neither.'

It is the smell that returns them to their surroundings, like a finger tapping them on the shoulder. Potent and alien and deep, it suffuses the air to the point, it almost seems, of replacing it; as they inhale, they realize that it has been present in the atmosphere all along, too rarefied to notice until now. Whatever the mysterious feeling of difference is, this is the source, the omphalos.

'We, ah, seem to be in the Locked Room . . .' Ruprecht says at last.

'Yes,' says Mario.

There is silence, silence and darkness. *The dead walk . . . futurity becomes a womb . . .*

'Okay then,' Ruprecht says, with false bravado, 'let's get this show on the road.' He stumps with his pod into the shadows; Mario hastens after, following the clinking from Ruprecht's bag, trying not to think about the legends Niall's sister spoke of – and then he sees it, the blue corpse of a girl suspended from the rafters, dangling there right in front of him!

Luckily he is too shocked to scream. And when he has steadied himself, he realizes that it is not a girl at all, only a school blouse, hanging there weightlessly in space.

Ducking beneath it, he presses on. Even in the darkness the room appears considerably larger than they expected. As their eyes adjust, they make several other unexpected discoveries. It is not, for instance, bare.

'Show me that map again,' Ruprecht says. Bringing it right up to his face, he studies it carefully. 'Hmm,' he says.

This is unquestionably the place. And yet, instead of cobwebs and cracked floorboards, there are clothes horses, washing machines, jumbo-sized boxes of detergent. 'More of a laundry than a classroom,' Ruprecht muses to himself. Perhaps an abandoned laundry? And yet the tracksuit tops with the St Brigid's crest, the skirts and jumpers, some damp, some dry, heaped in baskets or strung on criss-cross lines, none of these looks especially old –

He studies the map again. 'You don't hear any music, do you?' he asks Mario. 'Like supernatural music?'

Mario doesn't reply. With another *Hmm*, a kind of verbalized frown, Ruprecht forges on through the thick foliage of wet fabric. No evidence of a looming Otherworld presents itself; reaching the back of the room, his only new discovery is three huge sacks filled to the brim with girls' unmentionables, waiting to be washed. This puts the tin hat on it, as far as Ruprecht is concerned –

'There's no Mound in here!' he exclaims. 'Just piles and piles of schoolgirls' underwear!'

A sound from outside. Someone's coming! These voices are unambiguously modern, vital, somewhat raucous, the kind that might shout matily to one another over the judder of laundry –

'We have to get out of here!' Ruprecht says. 'Quick, the window!'

He pries open the bolt and shoves up the sash, and is on the point of wriggling through when he realizes he is on his own.

'Mario!'

Team Condor's cinematographer and navigator is rooted to the spot, slack-mouthed and staring, as if in a trance.

'Mario!' Ruprecht cries. 'What's wrong with you! Mario!'

The voices outside stop abruptly. But still Mario does not respond. A huge, happy smile spreads slowly across his face, like the man who has found the back door to the Promised Land; then, uttering a single, incomprehensible noise, like *bleer* or *meep*, he breaks loose of Ruprecht and dives headlong into the pile of knickers –

Skippy's back in his room. The others are still out on their operation; he makes it in here without talking to anyone. He knows what he has to do now, he doesn't want to waste any more time. He closes the door and switches off all the lights except for the lamp on his desk. He takes a blank sheet of paper from the stack in Ruprecht's printer, and sits down.

The goggles stare down from the door. The swimming trophy gleams with little fragments of remembering. Driving through Thurles on the creaky old bus. The day like elastic, stretched tighter and tighter till the moment of the race when all of time snaps. In the bleachers the blank space where Mum and Dad aren't. The green underwater hotel, the room where you can't sleep, the numbers that count down in gold to the door –

Hurry, Skippy, hurry! You have to do it now!

It's like he can see the door opening again.

Come on, come on!

Slowly opening, the streams of future wrapping around him and pulling him forward into it –

No! He picks up his pen. He writes, *Dear Coach*.

Ruprecht has not returned by lights-out. The next morning, however, when Skippy opens his eyes, he is there – lying on the duvet in his underpants, staring at the ceiling as if it has done him some grievous wrong.

'How did your mission go?' Skippy asks.

'Not well.' Bits of what appears to be foliage litter his hair.

'Did you visit any higher dimensions?'

'No.'

'Did you find the Mound?'

'No.'

Skippy gets the feeling he isn't that eager to talk about it, and drops the subject. At breakfast, however, Dennis is less forbearing.

'I don't understand,' he says with an expression of concern. 'Didn't you follow the map?'

Ruprecht, gazing blackly into his breakfast, says nothing.

'Hmm, maybe you should have asked one of the nuns,' Dennis remarks contemplatively. 'Did you ask them, Ruprecht? Did you ask the nuns to show you their mound?'

Ruprecht's eyes narrow, but he remains silent; then the door opens and Mario enters the Ref. Seeing Ruprecht at the table, he halts. 'Oh,' he says, and hovers there, as if uncertain how to proceed. Still without speaking, Ruprecht gives him a long hostile stare. Then he rises, leaving his meal half-eaten, and departs the room.

Once he is gone, Mario is able to shed some light on Ruprecht's Stygian mood. It appears that after being 'sidetracked' in some manner that Mario doesn't go into, the two of them were surprised in the St Brigid's laundry room and narrowly escaped capture, only to spend two hours in a tree hiding from the janitor's dog. (Odysseas, it turned out, was already in the tree following an earlier incident, and presented to the infirmary this morning with hypothermia and mauling.)

'No one actually saw you though?'

'No. But we had to leave behind the pod.'

Ruprecht's fury now becomes quite understandable. To have pan-dimensional travel in the palm of your hand, and then leave it in a girls' school laundry room – 'Holy smoke, Mario, you don't think the nuns will work out how to use it, and claim the Nobel Prize for themselves?'

'That's just the kind of thing they would do, those sneaky nuns,' Mario says bitterly.

'What were you doing in the laundry room, anyway?' Skippy asks.

'Following the map,' Mario says. 'That's where it said the Mound was.'

'How strange,' Dennis says, shaking his head. 'Could it be Niall's sister made a mistake? I suppose we'll never know.'

'Ruprecht can build another pod though, right? I mean it was mostly just tinfoil.'

'The problem is that he has no blueprint. From the original design he keeps making changes, but these he does not write down. So it is impossible to replicate exactly.'

Later that day, Ruprecht approaches Skippy. His expression is feverish. 'I've devised a foolproof plan to get my pod back from St Brigid's,' he says. 'I call it "Operation Falcon".'

Skippy looks dubious.

'This is your chance to get in on the ground floor!'

'No way, Ruprecht, not after how that last one went.'

'That was Operation Condor. This is Operation Falcon. It's a totally different operation.'

'Sorry.'

Ruprecht trudges off to canvass the others.

Bad as he feels for his room-mate, Skippy can't deny that he personally is having a great day. He woke that morning with the memory of the night before waiting for him, like a gold coin hidden under his pillow, and whenever he thinks about it, which is every few seconds, he is overtaken by a big daffy smile.

'You kissed her again, didn't you?' Dennis is finding Skippy's uncharacteristic happiness disconcerting and even somewhat offensive.

'Whoa, Skip –' Geoff is awestruck '– that means she's your girlfriend. Holy shit – you have a *girlfriend*!'

And then at lunch break he leaves Maths class and walks directly into Carl.

For some reason, after the fight yesterday all thought of him disappeared from Skippy's mind; he hadn't considered what would happen when their paths inevitably crossed again. From the way the boys around him instantly come to a halt, though, from the way the air of the hall quickens, he realizes they've been waiting for this moment all morning. There is nothing more he can do now than brace himself for the blow – the sucker punch, the sly kick to the ankles, the swift knee groinwards –

But Carl seems not even to see him; instead he drifts on by like an old, grizzled shark hulking through particoloured schools of minnows, oblivious to the catcalls and heehaws aimed at his receding bulk.

In today's History class, Howard the Coward – who looks like he hasn't slept much lately, or washed, or shaved – wants to talk about *betrayal*. 'That's what the war was really about. The betrayal of the poor by the rich, the weak by the strong, above all the young by the old. "If any question why we died / Tell them, because our fathers lied" – that's how Rudyard Kipling put it. Young men were told all kinds of stories in order to get them to go and fight. Not just by their fathers, of course. By their teachers, the government, the press. Everybody lied about the reasons for war and the true nature of the war. Serve your country. Serve the King. Serve Ireland. Do it in the name of honour, in the name of courage, for little Belgium. On the other side of the water, young German men were being told the same thing. When they got to the Front, they were betrayed again, by incompetent generals who sent wave after wave of them into machine-gun fire, by the newspapers who instead of telling the true story of the war churned out this brave-Tommies-death-or-glory stuff, making it seem like a great big adventure, encouraging even more young men to enlist. After the war, the betrayal continued. The jobs the soldiers had been promised would be kept for them had mysteriously disappeared. They could be heroes and wear medals, but no one wanted "war-damaged goods". Graves's friend Siegfried Sassoon called the war "a dirty trick which had been played on me and my generation" . . .'

'Did he seem a little off-balance to you?' Mario asks afterwards.

'One of these days he's going to come in with uniforms for us and we're all going to march off to the Somme,' Dennis says, and taking out his ledger moves Howard five places up the Nervous

Breakdown Leaderboad, so that he's just behind Brother Jonas and Miss Timony.

'Betrayal,' Ruprecht muses to himself, while letting his gaze linger over Dennis.

'What's that?'

'Oh, nothing,' Ruprecht says airily. 'I just like saying the word. Betrayal. Betrayal.'

'What's your problem, asshat?'

'Betrayal,' Ruprecht muses. 'Has kind of a ring to it, doesn't it? Betrayal.'

'Get bent, Blowjob, don't try and blame me for losing your gay pod.'

'Guys, come on,' Geoff pleads. 'The audition's in two hours.'

It is, and by four o'clock, what looks like a kind of musical zoo has gathered outside the door of the Sports Hall. Folk and rock groups, choirs and quartets, dancers both tap- and break-; here, warbling up and down his scales, is Tiernan Marsh, the fourth-year wheeled out at all official events to share his angelic tenor, although he's better known among the student population for his propensity to eat his own scabs; here Roland O'Neil, bass wizard of Funkulus, quivers slightly in his tight pink leggings under the baleful stare of John Manlor, hirsute lead singer of MANLOR, definitely the most impressive act the school has in terms of side-burns; here Titch Fitzpatrick, running over his MC routine for the hundredth time, affects not to notice the unmistakeable smirk on the face of his rival for the slot, Gary Toolan, nor to hear Gary Toolan's not quite *sotto* enough remarks, such as 'What's he going to do, change nappies on stage?'

Just ahead of the Van Doren Quartet in the line is Trevor Hickey, aka 'The Duke', who with no visible means of making music is staring into space, mumbling a speech to himself: '. . . *since the dawn of time . . . our oldest and most indefatigable foe . . .*'

Geoff keeps catching snatches of this, and curiosity eventually reels him in. 'Uh, Trevor, where's your instrument?'

'*Shock and amaze* – oh, I'm not giving a musical performance.'

'Not musical . . . ?' Geoff repeats, and then the penny drops. 'Here, you're not going to do *Diablos*, are you?'

'Mmm-hmm.'

Geoff gazes at him with a mixture of awe and concern. 'It's just,' he says, after a moment, 'you know, the Automator's in there.'

'Mmm-hmm.' Trevor's ceaseless shifting from foot to foot is only partly to do with nerves; he has eaten five cans of beans on either side of going to bed in order to build up a plentiful supply of trapped wind, or as he calls it, 'The Power'.

'I'm just wondering, you know, whether the Christmas concert might not be more of a family-type show?'

'Your family don't fart?' Trevor turns on him.

'Well, they mostly wouldn't set them on fire –'

'That's the beauty of what I do, you see,' Trevor interjects, eyes a-glimmer, already lost in his own myth. 'Turning tedious bodily functions into a magical encounter with the elements – it's what the whole world dreams of . . .'

Beside him, Brian 'Jeekers' Prendergast listens to this green with anxiety. Thanks to this ridiculous business with the pods and the mounds, the Quartet is severely under-rehearsed; as if that weren't enough, it seems the old friction between Ruprecht and Dennis has broken out again, worse than ever. Ruprecht has told Jeekers not to worry, that the piece is so easy it can't possibly go wrong – but he isn't the one who'll have to face Jeekers's parents if they don't get into the concert.

'Next!' The door swings open and Gaspard Delacroix, creator and sole performer of *The Little Sparrow: Gaspard Delacroix Sings the Songs of Edith Piaf*, flounces out, tugging off his fright-wig and muttering about *philistines*. Patrick 'Da Knowledge' Noonan and Eoin 'MC Sexecutioner' Flynn exchange a single nervous glance; then, with a deep breath, they put on their showbiz faces and troop inside.

The gym is totally empty, save for a single classroom-type desk set right in the middle of the floor, behind which sit the Automator and Father Laughton, the concert's musical director;

Trudy, the Acting Principal's wife, stands to one side with her clip-board.

The boys mount the stage, gold chains clinking, and spend the next few moments slouching back and forth, mumbling mysteriously to themselves. Then, to an enormous, naked drumbeat that explodes from Sexecutioner's ghettoblaster to rock the entire hall, they begin to bounce around the boards, making inscrutable hand signals, their vast trousers flapping about them like sails, and Knowledge grabs the mike: 'I got X-ray EYES, but she's wearin lead PANTS, so I got to get her BOOTY wi–'

'Next!' The judgement issues summarily from the review panel before Sexecutioner has even a chance to drop his first *motherfucker*. For a moment, the boys remain rooted to the spot in ungangsta-like attitudes of woundedness, mocked by the drumbeat that is still thumping around them; then, unplugging the ghettoblaster, they clamber down and make the walk of shame to the exit.

'What in God's name was that?' the Automator says as soon as they have left.

Trudy peers down at her clipboard. '"Original material."'

'Our old friend original material,' the Automator says grimly. 'I've had some plumbing mishaps that sounded a little like those guys.'

'It did have a certain rough-hewn vitality,' Father Laughton moderates.

'I've said it before, Padre, this concert's not about rough-hewn. It's not about "doing your best". I want *professionalism*. I want *pizazz*. I want this concert to put the Seabrook name out there, tell the world what we're all about.'

'Education?'

'Quality, damn it. A brand right at the top of the upper end of the market. God knows that's not going to be easy. I've given serious thought to bussing in other kids, talented kids, just so we don't have to drop the curtain after half an hour –'

'I'm not sure that would be quite in the, ah, spirit,' mutters Father Laughton.

'Just a thought, Padre, just a thought. Speaking of which, though, had a couple of other ideas I wanted to run by you. First one: thought we might stick Brother Jonas in there somewhere – you know, representing Africa, various peoples the Paracletes have helped over there, bright future they can have if everyone rows in, sort of thing.'

'Mmm, mmm,' Father Laughton's bowed head turning from cherry-pink to a florid magenta.

'Maybe wear traditional dress, say a few words of gratitude in his tribe's language. I want to remind people of this school's long and continuing history of charitable work.'

'Is the, ah, is the money from the concert going to Africa?'

'Well, we haven't decided exactly how it's going to be allocated. That 1865 wing isn't going to rebuild itself. But anyway that's one idea. The other one's this: Father, what comes to mind when you hear this word?' The Automator pauses dramatically, then with a shimmer of fingers pronounces, 'DVD.'

Father Laughton blinks. 'DVD?'

'Memorial concert's all about remembering, right? What better way to remember than with a special-edition commemorative DVD? Let me break it down for you. You put on an event like this, you're going to get parents coming along with their cameras wanting to film it. Psychology of the twenty-first-century crowd: people like to capture the spectacle, own it. Call it a side-effect of late capitalism, call it an attempt to stave off the ineffable transience of life. Point is, at these precious moments they all want to get little Junior down on tape. So what I'm thinking here is, we beat them to the punch. We film the entire thing, and so instead of a shaky hand-held recording complete with Aunt Nelly coughing and rustling sweets beside him, Junior's dad can have a professionally edited, digitally enhanced DVD, his to own for ev– yes, yes, carry on.' This last is addressed to Trevor Hickey, who has been hovering on the stage with a glazed expression these past few minutes, and now hurriedly begins his speech: 'Ladies and gentlemen, the feat of daredevilry you are about to

see will shock and amaze you. Fire, man's oldest and most indefatigable foe . . .'

'I've made a few inquiries, couple of old boys working in the
business, they're telling me we can get the discs printed for about
fifty cents a pop. Packaging, probably work something out there
too. Main outlay's going to be the recording – lighting, camera
hire, sound desk, labour. But whatever we spend, we'll make back
ten times over. Think about it, DVD like that, it's the perfect
Christmas gift. Every uncle and grandmother and third cousin
twice removed'll be getting a copy of it.'

'The Ancient Greek philosopher Heraclitus believed that the
universe was made of fire,' Trevor says.

'And they'll be glad to, because not only will they be getting
white-knuckle rock'n'roll by classically trained musicians, French
horn playing of the very highest calibre, a patriotic ballad in our
national language, Irish, and more, all on the same unique historic
bill, but with the proceeds they'll also be investing in Seabrook's
future – actually, that's pretty good, make a note of that, Trudy, *a
piece of history, an investment in the fut*– Jesus God, what the hell is
that kid doing? What the hell are you doing, God damn it!'

Trevor Hickey's startled face emerges from behind the eclipse
of his rump, which is facing the hall with a match poised at its
business end. Showmanship deserting him, he begins to babble
out his speech again: 'Ladies and gentlemen, the feat of daredevilry you're about to witness will shock and amaze you –'

'The hell it will –' In what seems a single bound the Automator
is on stage, seizing Trevor Hickey bodily and hauling him down
the steps. 'My office, nine o'clock tomorrow morning,' he bellows after him as he hurls the boy out the door. 'If you need
someone to light a fire under your arse, then by golly you've
found your man. A week's detention, let's see how that shocks
and amazes you.'

Brick-coloured, dusting his hands, he returns to the table. 'See,
this is the kind of thing we're up against. Is that the way we want
to commemorate Des Furlong? Is that the way we thank the man

for forty-two *years* serving the Holy Paraclete Fathers? With some joker lighting his farts on stage?'

'No,' Father Laughton remonstrates, 'no, of course not –'

'You're darn right it's not.' The Automator, simmering, reinstates himself at the desk. 'This is going to be a night of quality musical entertainment if I have to sing every damn song myself. Now, who's next? Ah!' He brightens as the Van Doren Quartet troop through the door. 'What is it they're playing again, Father?'

'Pachelbel's Canon in D,' Father Laughton says, adding, after a moment of internal debate, 'You might recognize it from the current advertisement for the Citroën Osprey.'

The Automator nods. 'Quality,' he comments, settling back in his seat.

The Quartet seems a little unsettled at first: some kind of interchange appears to be ongoing between French horn and bassoon, and the viola is looking positively unwell. But a note from the triangle brings them to order, and Ruprecht – after telling the bassoon quite audibly, 'Play quietly' – leads the foursome into the soothing circulations of the Canon. As it unspools, the slow descending harmony repeating and elaborating, a beatific peace invests Father Laughton's pink, pointy face, and beside him, perhaps unconsciously, the Automator murmurs, 'Citroën Osprey . . . mile for mile, that's one of the top-performing cars in its class.'

THE AMULET . . . IT SAVED ME.

Djed on the riverbank, kneeling by the rushes. Below, the princess's eyes glow up at him from the water's surface, the river passing beneath her translucent image, making her ripple and dazzle. The tiny harp of the amulet, with the power to turn a demon's flames into warm pacific chords of music, dangles between them, over his knees, twisting lullaby-slow like a leaf in the memory of a strong wind.

YOUR HEART IS WHAT SAVED YOU, DJED.

Her words are carried to the surface in bubbles, one word held in each, rising in sequence to recompose her sentence. She's projecting herself from the demonic prison where she is frozen in ice – she has just enough magic left to do that. Within the pale image of her face his reflection is just visible, as if they are turning into each other.

It's night. On the horizon, a half-day's ride away, the shadow of the castle has gone from the mountainside. After you kill the Fire Demon the walls fall and the whole valley blooms, not just with flowers and ferns and grass and trees but mice, bats, worms, frogs, swans and ducks, deer and horses, appearing from the corner of your eye, all in a moment, in a silver brake of light where the cloud has ebbed and the moon fights through.

YOU ARE COMING TO THE END OF YOUR QUEST, DJED! THERE IS ONLY ONE FOE LEFT TO FIGHT! Her eyes shimmer with the river, quicken then dwindle like shooting stars. BUT IT WILL BE THE HARDEST BATTLE OF ALL. I WISH THAT I COULD BE BY YOUR SIDE FOR IT. She raises her face entreatingly. BUT DJED . . . A HEART IS A DOOR INTO ANOTHER WORLD, AND ONCE YOU OPEN IT, IT IS NEVER TRULY CLOSED. SO ALTHOUGH YOU MAY NOT SEE ME . . . I'M ALWAYS THERE WITH YOU.

And somehow her hologram comes to life here, the frail image detaching itself from the surface of the water, the pale hand rising outward to touch his cheek . . .

Wait, to touch *his* cheek?

Aftershock jolts through him where he sits on the dorm-room floor, sparking icily down his arms to pulse in his fingertips.

What just happened?

GOODBYE, DJED. GOOD LUCK. The princess is already serenely back on the water, surveying him from her swirl of floating golden hair. He gathers himself as best he can, closes his mouth, grips the controller once more; her long sad eyes hold his a moment; then slowly she dissolves, into the darkness.

The very next moment there is a knock at the door. Head spinning, Skippy goes to answer it.

Coach is standing there, filling the doorway.

Daniel, he says. Just wanted a quick word.

His face is not angry, it does not have any expression. In his hand is a piece of white folded paper.

Can I come in?

From the Rec Room the pock, pock of the table-tennis table and a rerun of *Saved by the Bell* on TV. Then the door closes with Coach on the inside.

He is too big for the room, it looks wrong. His head revolves slowly to take in the beds, the desks, the books, the computer. Through his eyes everything must look small and breakable, toy things in a child's game.

You weren't at training this morning, Coach says.

Skippy looks at the floor.

You can't afford to be missing sessions this close to the meet, Daniel. We only have two more days to prepare. Were you not feeling well? Was that it? Were you sick?

Floor floor floor floor.

Coach's body creaks and rearranges. I got this today, Daniel. The sound of paper unfolding, like the blade of a guillotine coming down.

Dear Mr Roche, I regret to tell you that because of personal reasons I will no longer be able to come to swimming training or to go to meets. I apologize for any inconvenience, yours sincerely, Daniel Juster.

The paper folds closed again. Coach's fingers press and re-press it along the seams, back and forth.

Did you write this letter, Daniel?

I'm not angry at you. Frankly I'm more confused than anything. But did you write it?

Okay, unless you say otherwise right now I'm going to assume you wrote this letter.

Okay. Well, at least we've established that much. Now the question becomes why. Why, Daniel? After so much preparation, after all that *work*? With only three days to go till the race? Why would you do this to your team-mates? Why would you do it to yourself? I mean the sheer –

Sorry, I'm sorry. I promise, I'm not angry, I just, you can understand, can't you, how frustrating it is for me, for one of my best athletes to drop out at the last minute without so much as an explanation?

Footsteps patter up the hall outside; Coach turns and waits till they go by. Then he sees the X on the calendar. That cross there, that's to mark the day of the meet?

When you wrote that up there, you were intending to come to the meet. That wasn't so long ago. Okay, what we need to establish is what happened between then and now for you to want to write this letter.

I need an explanation, Daniel. If this is your decision I'll respect that, but you have to give me some kind of explanation. You owe me that much, at least.

These 'personal reasons' you mention, can you tell me what they are?

It's me, Daniel, it's Coach. I'm your friend, remember. You can talk to me.

What's on your mind, fella? Are you finding the training

too much, is that it? Is it too much pressure on top of your studies?

Are the other boys bullying you? Siddartha and Garret?

Is something wrong at home?

Is it your mum?

Daniel, if there is something seriously the matter then I think you should tell me. Bottling things up inside won't do you any good. I'm worried about you.

Is it me?

Daniel, I have to tell you that I'm getting pretty sick of this silent treatment. I'm getting pretty, pretty flipping sick of it.

Are you even listening to me?

Is it something that happened in Thurles?

Is that what it is?

What happened there, Daniel?

What is it you think happened?

The seconds go by, you think how can they just keep going by, but they do, and you are still here, the two of you in this tiny room, second by second by second –

The phone yips and vibrates on the table.

Leave that!

‹‹LORI CALLING››

Put it down. Coach's face bone-white.

Skippy puts the phone down.

Daniel – flexing and unflexing his fingers – if you don't want to talk I can't make you. But I think you're making a serious mistake here, a mistake that you will come to regret. So here's what I propose we do. I propose that we rip up this letter –

Rip, rip, rip, the long triangles flutter to the floor.

– and we just carry on where we left off. You come to training tomorrow, you race in the meet on Saturday as we've planned for months, and after that, when we've a bit of breathing space, then we can hash out any difficulties you might have.

What do you say to that, Daniel?

Can I take that silence as a yes?

Painfully bending his knees so he can squat down and look up to you: Look, buddy, I don't know what's going on in your head. I guess it must be pretty serious if it's making you do this. But whatever happens, I hope you'll still feel able to – I hope you know you can confide in me, anything you might find . . . hard to tell someone else.

Blink, blink –

Okay. Coach's head sinks a moment then rises as his body rises upwards. Okay.

The door closes behind him. Trillions of particles fizz up into Skippy's head, his shirt clings to his back ice-cold and soaking as if he'd just been swimming in the Arctic – as if he'd swum a thousand miles, every muscle utterly empty. The pills beneath the pillow, obsolete, on the wall Ruprecht's moon map, a million places to visit. And then:

Lori?

Hey, DJ, I was just calling you.

I know, sorry, I had to talk to one of my teachers. What are you doing?

Just hanging out. In the background the happy sound of Lori's house, TV voices, warm rooms with open doors. It's Daniel, he hears her say to someone. My dad says you should come over again next week, she says, returning to the mouthpiece. He's got more boring stories from his schooldays for you. What you doing there?

Nothing. Oh, but here, guess what, I quit the swim team.

You did? When?

Today. Just now.

Oh, yay! Oh, Daniel, I'm so happy. It didn't seem like you were having any fun.

I wasn't. I just needed someone to tell me.

I'm glad I could tell you.

I'm glad you could too.

So do you still want to meet up Friday? she says.

Definitely!

Great!

Bay of Rainbows Bay of Love Bay of Harmony! He has already forgotten all about Coach, he is way away on the moon! Lake of Happiness Lake of Hope Lake of Joy – he closes his eyes, he bounds weightlessly over the silver night –

The boys have finally given up on Miss McIntyre returning. Coke cans and paper are tossed in the bin with everything else; hairspray and deodorant are deployed with abandon; the Chinese government builds what it wants, untroubled by the pupils of Seabrook College.

If only Howard could move on so easily. Instead he is tormented by her day and night – purring at him from the moonlit deck of an ocean cruiser, through a garland of muscular arms; winking at him from a four-poster bed, where she lies entwined with her faceless fiancé. Sometimes his jealousy comes dressed up as outrage – how could she lie to him like that? How could she lie to *herself* like that? – and alone in the dark he will clench his fists, inveighing against her on the deck of her imaginary ship; other times he aches for her so badly he is scarcely able to bear it.

But simultaneously he's beset by memories. Independently of him, his mind has started filling in the Halley-shaped blanks. He'll be reading in the kitchen in the small hours, and realize that he is waiting for her to come through the door – can almost see her, in her pyjamas, rubbing her eyes and asking him what he's doing, forgetting to listen to the answer as she gets sucked into an investigation of the contents of the fridge. At the cooker scrambling eggs; crossing the living room to straddle him as he watches TV; lost in some corporate website with a cigarette and a dogged expression; brushing her teeth in the mirror while he shaves – soon the house is haunted by a thousand different ghosts of her, with a million infinitesimal details in attendance, things he'd never noticed himself noticing. They don't come with an agenda, or an emotional soundtrack; they don't pluck at his heartstrings, or elicit any reaction that he can identify definitively as love, or loss; they are simply *there*, profusely and exhaustingly *there*.

Farley says the whole thing reminds him of a joke.

'That's great, Farley. That's exactly what I need.'

'I can't help what it reminds me of, can I? Now do you want to hear it or not?'

Howard makes a gesture of resignation.

'Okay then. Man walks into a bar, and sees a guy sitting two stools down has the smallest head he's ever seen. Body's perfectly normal, but his head is no bigger than a cue ball. He tries not to stare but after a few minutes he can't stand it any longer so he goes down to the guy and says, "Look, I'm sorry if this seems rude, but would you mind telling me what happened to your head?" The tiny-headed guy in this little tinny high-pitched voice tells him that many years ago, back in the Second World War, he'd served in the Navy. "My ship got torpedoed and every one of my shipmates drowned," he says. "I should've drowned too, only as I sank to the bottom I felt hands around me, pulling me upwards. When I came to, I was lying on a rock in the middle of the ocean, being given mouth-to-mouth by a beautiful mermaid. I realized she'd saved my life and I asked her how I could repay her. She said she didn't want anything. 'There must be something I can do for you,' I said. 'No,' she said, but she was so moved by my gratitude that she decided to give me three wishes. Well, all I really wanted was to be back home, out of the damn war. I told her and she snapped her fingers and next thing you know we're just off the shore, and I can see my own house waiting for me. 'What next?' she said. 'You've done so much for me, it's hard to ask for anything more,' I said. 'But maybe some cash, just enough to tide me over?' She snapped her fingers and suddenly my pockets were spilling over with money. 'Done,' she says, 'you will never want again. And for your third wish?' Well, I thought long and hard," says the soldier, "as I floated there beside her. Finally I said, 'I don't want to seem forward. But not only have you saved my life, brought me home from the

405

war, and made me rich beyond my wildest dreams – you're the most beautiful creature I've ever laid eyes on. I know you're going to return to the ocean, and I'm going back to the land, and we're never going to see each other again. But before that happens, what I would like more than anything else in the world is just once to make love to you. That's my third and final wish.' The mermaid looked sad. 'I'm afraid that is the one wish I cannot grant,' she said, 'for I am a mermaid, and you are a man, and to know each other carnally is impossible.' 'Really?' I said. She nodded regretfully. I thought about it for a moment. 'Okay,' I said, 'how about a little head?''''

A few seconds elapse before Howard realizes he's finished. 'That's it?' he demands. 'So I'm like the idiot with the tiny head, is that it?'

'It *reminded* me, that's all,' Farley protests. 'Because, you know, be careful what you wish for.'

'I didn't wish for this, did I? I didn't wish for Aurelie McIntyre to have a fiancé and hang me out to dry, why the fuck would I wish for that?'

'I don't know, Howard. Why would you?'

Now the door opens and Howard slouches down behind his newspaper as Tom hefts himself in. Every November, when the anniversary of the accident in the quarry comes round, a gloom descends over the coach; this year, more than ever before, it seems Howard can sense his rage mounting, cracks appearing in the noble sportsmanlike façade, until it's as if he is inside Tom's mind, sharing that furious urge to launch his wrecked body at Howard and beat him until Howard is as mangled as he is. Sometimes he wishes he'd do it, get it over with.

'How's Tom?' Farley hails him.

The coach grunts as he passes the sofa, heads for his pigeon-hole.

'Something on your mind?' Farley asks innocently, as Howard's stomach does somersaults.

'Busy day,' Tom returns unwillingly. 'Trying to finalize the arrangements for the swimming trip. Ten boys, nearest hotel only has four rooms.'

'Pile 'em all into bed with you,' Farley suggests. 'Keep you all warm on these cold winter nights.'

'That's hilarious,' Tom says tonelessly. 'That's very, very funny.' Envelopes tucked into his back pocket, he limps out through the door again.

'Some day,' Howard says, lowering the paper again, 'that guy is going to snap. And I'm the one he's going to snap *at*.'

'Howard, I swear to God, you've got an imagination like Stephen King,' Farley says.

'Then why has he been looking at me all week like for two pins he'd disembowel me?'

'Because you're a paranoid man with too much time on your hands. Too much time and a tiny, tiny little head.'

On Thursday morning the programme for the concert goes up on the noticeboard. The Van Doren Quartet are there, to Jeekers's inordinate relief; he peels away, wiping the sweat from his brow.

'Did we get in?' Eoin 'MC Sexecutioner' Flynn asks anxiously, stuck at the back of the crowd examining the board.

Patrick 'Da Knowledge' Noonan scans the list again, then, scowling, turns away. 'No.'

'We didn't?' Eoin is shocked.

'What did you expect, man?' Patrick throws up his hands at him. 'Take a look at the programme, it's wall-to-wall Whitey!'

'Hey, Skip, what's that chit with your name on it?'

'What's what?' Even standing on tiptoes, Skippy still can't see the board.

'Hold on . . .' Geoff reaches over the collected heads and passes back to Skippy a miniature white envelope with the school crest on it.

'I'm being sent for Guidance Counselling.' Skippy studies the card. 'With Father Foley.'

At the name, hands are cupped and brought to ears. 'Father Who?' 'What's that?' 'Speak up there, young man!'

'Why are they sending me for Counselling?'

'They've found you out, Skippy,' Dennis taunts, wiggling his fingers in his face. 'They *know*.'

'Could be they suspect about Condor,' Ruprecht frowns. 'Skippy, if anyone asks, I was with you all night, helping you with your maths. Keep calm. They can't prove anything.'

Can't they? All through German class his worry mounts. Have they found out about him and Lori? Maybe they don't like people having girlfriends? He sends her a text just to say hi, but she doesn't reply.

'*Nicht* makes a verb negative,' the teacher says. '*Ich brauche nicht*, I do not need. *Ich liebe nicht*, I do not love. Let's look at the textbook. *Was hast du heute nicht gekauft, Uwe? Ich habe ein Schnitzel für meine Mutter nicht gekauft*. What did you not buy today, Uwe? I did not buy a Schnitzel for my mother.'

'I've got a Schnitzel for his mother.'

'Mario, your Schnitzel wouldn't feed a mouse.'

I do not go I do not eat I do not see I do not hear

He raises his hand, presents the chit to be excused.

Father Ignatius Foley sits with a pen braced horizontally between his index fingertips, contemplating the youth bunched on the other side of his desk. After protracted and unpleasant ear surgery, he has returned from convalescence to find a stack of emergency cases awaiting his attention, and this lad is top of the heap. A pale fellow of slight build, he looks like butter wouldn't melt in his mouth; in his file, however, you will find Attitudinal Problems, Inattention, Disruptive Tendencies, Vomiting in Class and Playing Frisbee Alone. Trouble comes in every shape and size – when you've been counselling youngsters for as long as Ignatius Foley, you'll know that.

'Do you know why you're here, boy?' Father Foley gives him the full benefit of his stentorian baritone voice. The boy shrinks a bit, stares at his thumbs, mumbles something. Father Foley's eyes narrow. He knows all right. There's a wiliness beneath that guileless countenance, the look of someone who'll try and wriggle around the rules. Well, he won't find much wriggle room in here.

But first the folded hands, the kindly, avuncular smile. Put him at his ease. 'Don't be alarmed, Daniel. No one's "out to get you". Your Acting Principal has simply noticed a dip in your grades recently, and asked me to take a look to see if I can help.' Father Foley rises from his chair. 'Now, why don't you tell me in your own words why you think your grades have gone down.'

As the boy launches into the usual prevaricatory flim-flam, Father Foley, slowly circumnavigating the room, peers into the file again. The case is somewhat unusual; this boy does not seem one of the baffled imbeciles that typically washes up in his office. His marks are excellent, or rather were excellent until quite recently – you could almost pinpoint the day they began their steep decline. Father Foley's got a hunch, and when you've been in this business for as long as he has, you learn to trust your hunches.

'Drugs!' Spinning around, he jabs a finger in the boy's face, who, caught off guard, jumps in his seat.

'I want you to look at me,' Father Foley commands, 'and tell me if you've encountered any of the following substances.' The boy nods timorously. Father Foley reads from the Department of Education leaflet. 'Cannabis, also known as ganja, hash, hash joints.' He peers at the boy. Nothing. 'Marijuana, grass, weed, mary-jane.' No. 'Speed, whiz, Billy Whiz, crank. Ketamin, Special K.' What in God's name is Special K doing here? 'Cocaine, coke, Charlie, snort, blow. Heroin, horse, shit, junk, China White, the White Lady.'

If there were something there, Father Foley would find it, be it merely a twitch, a blink, a bead of sweat that gave the game away. This boy has no reaction to any of the drugs on the checklist. Still, Father Foley has the distinct sense that he is withholding something. But what?

Returning to his desk, casting about the room for inspiration, he lights on a framed picture from his missionary days – his younger self on an airstrip in the desert, intrepid, golden-locked, with his arm around a black whose name he forgets. That plane in the background Father Foley had actually flown, the pilot letting him take the joystick as they soared over the mountains with their vital consignment of Bibles. He smiles fondly at his handsome avatar; and then his eyes shift from the picture to the cotton buds next to it and his smile fades as he is swamped by unpleasant memories of the last two weeks, being poked and prodded by little Oriental nurses, yapping to each other in whatever it was – poke, poke! do they think everybody's ears are the same? Can they not appreciate that some men have unusually complicated ear structures?

But then his eyes flick back to the plane. Flying. This business of the lone frisbee-playing. It had left Father Foley with a bad taste in his mouth when he first encountered it in the report; now he thinks he knows why. Coughing gruffly: 'Tell me, Daniel . . . have you begun to . . . *feel* anything lately?'

He sees the boy's lips, after a moment of deliberation, begin to move. Did he say thoughts? It sounded like he said something about thoughts. Well, well. The pieces begin to fall into place. The disappeared ambition, the blank stare, the sociopathic attitude, the constant twitching – Puberty, we meet again.

'Daniel,' he begins, 'you have entered that stage of life when you leave childish things behind and enter manhood. This can be a bewildering experience, what with changes in your body, hair appearing in unexpected places, growth spurts, and so forth. Adult sexuality, while one of the most precious gifts bestowed upon us by our Maker, brings with it great responsibility. For when abused, it can plunge a man into mortal danger. I am speaking of impure acts.

'These acts may present themselves at first quite innocently. Something to fill an idle moment, perhaps introduced to you by a friend. But believe you me, there is nothing innocent about them. It is a slippery slope, a slippery slope indeed. I have seen good, upstanding men brought to their knees by these disgusting activities. Not merely falling grades. I am speaking of shame, disgrace, exile. Decent families' names blackened for generations. Most deadly of all, the risk to your immortal soul.'

From the boy's saucer-eyed stare, Father Foley knows he is on the right track.

'Fortunately, God, in his wisdom, has supplied us with the means to avoid these deadly traps of the spirit, in the form of the wonderful gift of sport. *Mens sana in corpore sano*, as the Romans had it. You don't build an empire like the Roman Empire without knowing a thing or two. Of course, they wouldn't have known about rugby, but I think we can assume that if the sport *had* been invented then, they would have been playing it night and day. It's amazing how many of life's problems simply disappear after a rousing game of rugby.' He steeples his fingers, gazes at the boy benignly. 'You don't play rugby, do you, Daniel,' he says. The boy shakes his head. Textbook case, absolutely tex– wait, he's saying something. Good God, child, you'll never get anywhere speaking into your chest like that. What is it? 'Winning? Well, yes, here in Seabrook we've had our fair share of trophies. But I like to say, it's not the win– what? *Women*? That's absolutely the last thing you should be thinking about, take my advice and just stay away –'

That isn't it either, though. The boy is gesticulating and gurning, he is barking out the same word again and ag– oh, wait, *swimming*, that's what it is. He's on the swimming team. No – more dumbshow and protestation – no, he *isn't* on the swimming team.

'Well, which is it, lad, for goodness' sake?'

At the top of his voice the boy announces that he has *quit* the swimming team.

'You *quit* it?' Father Foley repeats. This fellow takes the biscuit! When did anyone ever get anywhere by quitting, pray? Did the Romans quit, halfway through their empire? Did Our Lord quit, on his way up Calvary with the Cross? Clearly it is time that someone took a firm hand with this young man. 'Well, the first thing we need to do is unquit you,' he says, and raising his voice over the anticipated caterwaul of protest, 'no buts! It's time that we stopped this rot.'

Well! If the boy doesn't jump right out of his chair and start *shouting* at Father Foley! A long stream of speech, by the looks of it not short on emotion, bellowed at the very top of his lungs. In all his days as a professional educator, Father Foley has never seen the like! But by golly, he knows how to shout too! He's not going to be hectored in his own office! Getting to his feet he yells over him, 'It's for your own good! It's for your own good, so sit down this instant and stop . . . stop . . . crying.' Because a positive flood is now coursing down the boy's cheeks and flying onto the desk and carpet! 'Sit down, sit down!'

At last the boy obeys, still leaking tears. Dear, dear, is this the pass they have come to? One might expect this kind of display over in St Brigid's, but from a Seabrook man? Father Foley swivels his chair, massaging his temples, intermittently peeping over in the hope that the boy has stopped.

'Daniel, let me be perfectly blunt,' he says, when the worst of it appears to be past. 'The Acting Principal has some serious reservations regarding your future at this school. The fact is that not every boy is cut out for Seabrook, and it benefits neither school nor student to persist with a relationship that is simply not meant to be.' This shuts him up all right: the very tears seem to freeze on his cheeks. 'Now, before making a decision, dragging parents into it and whatnot, the Acting Principal has asked for my thoughts on the matter. My report to him will have a bearing on any decision he makes.' The sonorous weight of those words – *report, bearing, decision*, adult words, the words of a man of responsibility – please him, and he continues with a renewed sense of purpose. 'It seems to me that you have a lot of promise, if these marks are anything to go by. I feel that if you can conquer these demons of yours, you may yet have something to contribute to Seabrook life. However, I cannot in good conscience recommend you unless I see some evidence that you are at least attempting to get back on track.'

He picks up the pen again, twiddling it through his fingers as the boy recommences his silent crying. 'This business of leaving the swimming team – I can't say it speaks in your favour. At the same time, I am not sure that as a sport swimming gives quite the dose of team spirit that you need. Also, the chlorinated water, I have found, plays havoc with the ears. If you are determined to swim so be it, but my preference would be that you give rugby another try. Have a think about it over the weekend and we can discuss it on Monday. Perhaps I will have a word with Mr Roche and see what he thinks. In the meantime, we need to show your Acting Principal that you're willing to make an effort. I know

Father Green is looking for volunteers for his hampers.' In fact Jerome is so starved for volunteers that he's been making noises in the Residence about the priests joining in! 'I suggest you speak to him without delay. Spending some time with the less fortunate may bring home to you just how good you have it here in Seabrook.'

The boy considers this while staring at his shoes. Then, raising his head, he looks for what seems like a long time at the priest with reddened eyes; and then he says – what is it he says? Father Foley can't quite make it out. But the sense is clear.

'You're welcome,' Father Foley says.

The boy remains a moment stiffly where he is; then leaves his chair, and the office, closing the door noiselessly behind him.

Noiselessly: it takes a moment for this to intrude on Father Foley's thoughts. That door used to make the most infuriating squeal. He was constantly after that shirker of a janitor to come and oil the hinges. Now he rises from his desk and potters over to it. Open: close. Open: close. Not a peep. Hmm. He must have attended to it while Father Foley was away having his treatment. Open: close.

Returning to his seat, Father Foley folds his hands behind his head, leans back and spends a number of minutes surveying in satisfaction the silenced door.

'Volunteering?' Alone with him in the classroom the priest seems to buzz with some antic energy – as though, while he stands there quite still, he has four phantom limbs flailing invisibly around him, a spectral spider.

'Yes, Father.'

'Well, of course I'm always happy to have a fresh pair of hands – yes, indeed . . .' The tinkling politeness belied by the black burning eyes, like smouldering holes in space. 'Many hands make light work, don't they . . .'

Skippy hovers without replying, like a prisoner awaiting his sentence.

'Excellent, excellent . . . well, I'm planning a run this weekend, as it happens, so why don't you come to the office, let me see, after school tomorrow, shall we say at 4:30?'

After school tomorrow is when he's meeting Lori!

But packing hampers can't take all night, can it?

Anyway, what choice does he have.

'Yes, Father.'

He turns to go, but is called back. 'Is everything all right, Mr Juster?'

'Yes, Father.'

'You look like you have been . . . crying.'

'No, Father.'

'No?' The skewering eyes. 'Well then.' His hand lifts to ruffle Skippy's hair, the dead fingers like a mummy's or something stuffed. 'Carry on, Mr Juster, carry on.'

He bustles back to the blackboard; Skippy leaves him humming to himself, scrubbing at the ghostly traces of French verbs and nouns as if they were stains on his soul.

After lunch in the Ref they go to Ed's with Ruprecht. He has found no volunteers for Operation Falcon, and is resigned to recovering the pod on his own.

'Will you go in the fire escape like last time?'

Ruprecht shakes his head. 'Too risky,' he says, with a mouth full of doughnut. 'The pod could be anywhere by now. What I need is a cover story that'll not only get me inside, but also let me walk around without arousing suspicion.'

Brows are furrowed. 'Why don't you pretend you're an exterminator?' Geoff suggests. 'Tell the nuns you're an exterminator on the trail of a mouse. That way you could go around the whole school, and you'd be by yourself because the nuns'd be scared of mice.'

'Isn't he on the small side for being an exterminator?' Niall points out.

'He could be a midget exterminator,' Geoff says.

'Where am I going to find a midget exterminator costume?' Ruprecht says.

Geoff concedes that this might prove difficult.

'How about a midget TV repairman?' Mario suggests.

'Or a midget plumber?'

'I'd like to get away from the whole midget thing,' Ruprecht says.

'The answer is obvious: vibrator salesman,' Mario says. 'Not only will the nuns let you in, but I bet you sell your whole stock.'

'Hey, Skip, what did Cloth-Ears want to talk to you about?' Dennis says.

'Nothing. Careers stuff. It was pretty pointless.'

'Oh, you're so lying,' Dennis says.

Skippy looks up with a start.

Dennis leans over the table, flickering his fingers in a web. 'He wants to take you away from Father Green, doesn't he? He wants you all to himself . . .'

'Ha ha,' Skippy says, but he gets up to go.

On the way back to school he tries calling her again. He pretends to himself it's to tell her about the hampers. But really he just wants to hear her voice. Something has started to feel *wrong*: it's like being in a car that's gradually going faster and faster, and though to everyone around it still looks totally normal, you know that the brakes have been cut. She doesn't answer; he leaves a message on her voicemail, asking her to call him back.

Overnight a new cold sets in, the kind that permeates your bones while you sleep and, once arrived, will not leave again till spring. Armadas of leaves set sail with every fresh gust of wind; fingers are blue on the straps of bags and satchels; and the school-doors in the distance appear, uncharacteristically, as a blessed haven, to be hastened towards.

'No training today?' Ruprecht asks, surprised to find Skippy only getting up now. No, no training – no getting up before dawn, no stripping off in an icy-cold changing room, no punishing your body till every muscle aches before you've even had breakfast. Instead there is an extra hour of dreams, and you arrive at the Ref still cloudy with sleep to –

'Hey, Juster, what's the fucking story?' Siddartha comes rushing up with Duane Grehan in tow.

'What story?' Skippy like he doesn't already know.

'You missed fucking training again.' Beneath his freckles Siddartha is pink with anger. 'The race is *tomorrow*, shithead, why weren't you at training?'

Skippy doesn't say anything, just hangs in the breeze that seems to have sprung up around him in the corridor, austere and silent.

'This is total fucking bullshit,' Siddartha seethes. 'Coach never should have picked you. You're his little bum-chum, that's the only reason.' From behind him, Duane gazes at Skippy with expressionless eyes. 'Asshole,' says Siddartha, by way of a parting shot.

'You didn't go to training?' Geoff says, when the other two are gone.

'I didn't feel like it,' Skippy says vaguely.

'Oh,' Geoff says, and doesn't say anything else.

*

In the shopping mall at lunch break a huge silver-needled Christmas tree has been installed, making the people rising and descending on the escalators around it look like tiny decoration-angels in anoraks and polar fleeces.

'Where are you going with your *girlfriend* tonight, Skip?'

'I'm not sure – maybe to the cinema? She's going to call me.'

'Cinema is good,' Mario says approvingly. 'I have been on many dates in the cinema – but I have not seen very many films!'

'Because I was having sex,' he adds a moment later, in case the others haven't understood. 'In the cinema.'

Yesterday she never called back. In the Study Hall carved into the desk a new graffiti: CARL CAME IN THE GIRLS HAND BEFORE SHE EVEN TUCHED HIS PENIS.

But now, as if to squash these doubts, Skippy's pocket starts to bleep. It must be her! He hurries out the door of the video-game shop and fumbles open his phone. No, it's just Dad. 'Hi, Dad.' He tries to keep the disappointment out of his voice.

'Hi, D. Just thought I'd give you a call, see how you were set up for the big race tomorrow.'

'Oh, right.'

'How do you feel? Are you excited?'

'Yeah, I suppose.'

'You don't sound it.'

Skippy shrugs, then realizes Dad can't see it, and instead says, 'No, I am.'

'Okay,' Dad says. In the background Skippy can hear the printer whirr and telephones ringing. There is a long strange pause: Dad takes a deep breath in through his nose. 'Listen, Danny,' he says. 'We had a phone call last night.'

'Oh yeah?' He stiffens, turns a little to the fluted wall.

'Yeah, from Mr Roche, your swimming coach.'

Skippy stops dead.

'Yeah,' Dad muses, like he's thinking over a crossword clue, but you can hear his voice stretched taut like it's on a rack. 'He told me you'd quit the team.'

Frozen by the wall next to the kitchen spoils shop.

'Danny?'

'Yeah.'

'I was pretty surprised to hear that, I have to say. I mean, I know how much you were looking forward to this race.'

'Oh, well . . .'

'Oh well what?'

'I've been getting a bit tired of it lately.'

'You have?'

'Yeah.'

'Of swimming?'

'Yeah.'

They circle each other through an imaginary space that is not mall or office: in Skippy's head it is a clearing in a winter forest, with sun clinging to the trunks of bare trees.

'Well, that comes as a surprise,' Dad says slowly. 'Because you've always loved to swim, ever since you were a tiny tot.'

Pan-pipe 'Away in a Manger' descends like nerve-gas from the speakers above. All of a sudden Skippy feels a great weight tugging on him, tugging on the whole mall, pulling it downward towards a single point.

'Your coach was surprised too. He says you're a natural. Phenomenal natural ability, that's how he put it.'

Dad pauses but Skippy doesn't say anything. He knows what is coming and there is no way to stop it. Around him the walls of the mall begin to tremble.

'He wondered if it might be him, if he'd been too hard on you in training. Well, I told him you'd never said anything like that to me.'

Screws twist from their sockets, girders creak.

'He said you'd mentioned personal reasons.'

Everything is vibrating, like the shopping mall is one big tuning fork.

'Danny, I told him about your mum.'

Skippy closes his eyes.

'I had to, Danny. I had to.'

Windows exploding, huge reefs of masonry descending from above, the walls of the mall tumbling in on themselves.

The Game blown all over the road.

'I know we had our pact and everything. But I've often wondered whether I'd done right by you there, sport. I mean, in a school there are people, there's a framework in place to help you deal with exactly these kinds of things. I should've told you – I don't know, I just . . .' Dad's hands dropping hopelessly to his sides, the two of them, Skippy and Dad, falling to the ground, shot in the head. 'I feel like I've let you down, son. And I'm sorry. I'm so sorry, Danny.'

A glazed Christmas-coloured distance away, Mario in the door of the game shop, making an *Is it her?* face at Skippy. Skippy yanks his face into the shape of a smile and waves him back.

'Anyway – well, your Mr Roche was quite taken aback by that, obviously. But he said it explained a lot, in terms of your attitude lately. He said it was clear you'd been under a lot of strain. But he also said – and I agree with him – that the very worst thing to do would be to let that strain stop you from doing the thing you love.'

Skippy just nods. Disbelief all that is keeping him upright: the blood that whomps through his head, as stars whiz back and forth through the mall, through the bodies of the shoppers, which fade into negatives behind the bright streaks.

'He says – he seems to me like a good man, a really decent man, he was a very promising rugby player, did you know that? Anyway, he – he knows all about missing chances, that's how he put it to me. And whatever about chances and potential and all that – swimming's what you love, Dan. It's what you've always loved. God, I was telling him how we'd put you in the pool when you were only a year old, and you'd steam about like a, like a dolphin!' Dad laughs to himself. Then he stops. 'I know you're worried about Mum, sport. Maybe it's impossible to carry on a normal life while this is going on. But you know how much she wanted to come to the race tomorrow, you know how hard she'd been working to get herself strong enough to see you. If she thought for one second that you'd had to stop because of her, that after all this preparation you'd quit because of her . . . well, that would break her heart, sport, it really would.'

Oh Jesus.

'I'm not putting any pressure on you. Whatever decision you make I'll support that, and your coach will too. He's not going to mention this to anyone in the school, he won't talk to you about it either unless you want to. But he wanted you to know that if you did change your mind, if you did, there's still a space for you on the bus.'

'You're not going to come.' Knowing the answer in advance.

'We can't, Danno. I know I promised we would, and I feel terrible. But Dr Gulbenkian's saying it might be unwise. Just at the minute he says he couldn't advise it. And I don't . . . I don't want to be away from the house right now. I'm sorry, sport, I really am. But you don't need me to have fun, right?'

'Was that her? Was it Lori?' they ask when he comes back into the shop.

He shakes his head. 'Just my dad wanting to wish me luck for tomorrow.'

'Champs don't need luck!' Geoff Sproke declares.

Soon they are leaving, zagging down the escalators. A man in a top hat and white gloves reluctantly gives them sample chocolates from a silver platter. At the sliding doors, carollers are gathered, swaying arm-in-arm and singing 'Winter Wonderland'.

'Help fight cancer!' One of their number, a young man in glasses and a green anorak, thrusts a bucket under Skippy's nose; then, 'Sorry,' he says, and takes it away again.

Back at school, the bad feeling grows and grows. The pills call to you from under the pillow. Speeding out of control, Skip? The brakes are right here! Wouldn't you like to be Danielbot again? Cool as a cucumber?

You try Lori's phone but it goes straight through to voicemail.

'Has she called you yet, Skippy?'

'Not yet.'

'Oh, well, maybe she's out of credit.'

'Here we go again,' Dennis says tartly.

'What's that supposed to mean?'

Dennis keeps mum, looks out the window.

'She's going to call,' you say.

His schedule so falls as to leave Father Green's Fridays free of classes after two o'clock; typically, he will spend this time in his office, attending to various administrative duties that arise from his charitable work. This afternoon has been passed on the phone to the biscuit factory, trying to confirm a donation for this year's Christmas hampers. The company has always given generously in the past; now, however, the man with whom Father Green is used to dealing has moved on, and his replacement – younger, bored-sounding – insists that charitable donations come under PR, which has been 'outsourced' to another company. So Father Green calls this other company, where he speaks to a woman who does not understand what he wants. Is it T-shirts? TV coverage? Celebrity endorsements? It is simply a donation of biscuits to be delivered to households in poor areas, Father Green tells her. Oh no, that would be a decision for the biscuit company itself, she tells him, and, after tapping at her keyboard, she gives him the name of the man he spoke to earlier.

He hangs up the phone, checks his watch. Twenty past three. Classes will be over soon.

Jerome.

Switching on the kettle, he sits down to open a drawer of correspondence.

I can hear your heartbeat, Jerome. When is the last time it beat this fast?

Old ladies' handwriting, pitifully frail. Reaching across the desk for his reading glasses.

In Africa?

The kettle has boiled. He pours the water into a cup, places the bag in the water, watches the umber clouds billow forth.

He knows your desire, Jerome. He trembles whenever you look at him. So uncommonly beautiful, so desperate for love.

Spooning out the bag, pouring a little milk, just a splash, from the small carton.

You will show him how to pack the hampers, how each object must be arranged. He will kneel here, working quietly while you read through the accounts. Then, absently, you start to stroke his hair. He makes no protest or complaint. Instead his head slowly comes to rest against your thigh, you see his eyelashes flutter closed – then you fuck him in his little rosebud, over this desk, you fuck him!

The cup overturning, tea pooling on the varnish, devouring the letters of his parishioners –

Ha ha ha ha!

And the air is filled by that burning wind, that roiling stew of carnality: animal sweat, the fetor of unwashed loins, white eyes rolling at you while black arms hammer languorously at the walls of the church, that tiny outpost of decency, so laughably flimsy in the relentless heat –

How you missed it, Jerome. The voice, that Old Familiar, so close now its words and his own thoughts are almost indistinguishable. *Why deny what is in your heart! Why deny yourself life?*

The heat! He feels it now, again, as if he were in Hell already! Waves of it, beating in through the metal walls of his hut, all night long, dreams and desert melted into one overpowering carousel, sweat soaking the bedclothes and he with the cold blade to his flesh, tears in his eyes as he implored God for the strength to do it, to rid himself once and for all of this ever-flourishing root of wickedness, this lightning rod for all that is unholy –

But you did not.

He did not – could not!

Because you knew the truth.

He could only flee Africa, batten the door on those memories, those flames of desire and their quenching! And every day since he has heard it rattling!

Open it, Jerome.

Has he not prayed for it to be silent? Has he not prayed to be cleansed? Has he not begged God to show him the light, to lead him to goodness? And yet there is only desire, temptation, the Devil, gleaming at him from every grain of sand, calling from every pair of plump, incarnadine lips, and Christ not once, not the faintest glow of a presence, not the vaguest adumbration in a dream, not once in nearly seventy years!

You knew that there was no one watching.

How is a man to win that battle? Where is he to find the strength?

The hour arrives, Jerome. This is my last gift to you. Once more, to feel a body touching yours. Love. And after that, perhaps, peace.

In the corridor he hears a bell, doors opening, a thousand youthful footsteps rushing free.

Trudging back down the hall towards the priest's office, every Loriless step like getting cut up into shreds. You take out your phone. It gazes back at you blank and placid. You imagine being with her and telling her what Dad said, maybe telling her everything, her saying kind things, wise things. It's just a swim meet, Daniel, no biggie. Hey D, don't worry, everything's going to be fine. You imagine her being with you, a bandage over a wound.

WHERE ARE YOU?

You write the text and then delete it, you've already left two voicemails, there are rules about these things, you don't want to seem desperate. But you are desperate! And the unsent message bounces around inside you agonizingly,

WHERE ARE YOU WHERE ARE YOU?

like a scalding ping-pong ball. You descend the steps into the basement, past Ruprecht's laboratory. Silence from the priest's door. Then, weirdly, as if just for a second you had X-ray vision, it's like you see him waiting on the other side, a praying mantis poised there motionless. You unlock your phone again. Fuck it anyway! Type in the message and send it,

WHERE ARE YOU?

You knock on the door.

'Come in,' the voice returns.

You enter to find Father Green sitting at his desk, a china cup poised primly at his lips and a small black missal between his fingers. 'Ah yes, Daniel, very good,' he says. 'Close the door, would you? It's just the two of us today.'

Pock, pock, pock: if ping-pong's your game, Friday night in the Junior Rec Room is where the action's at its hottest. The table tocks like a clock gone crazy, as reigning champion Odysseas Antopopopolous, in spite of a badly bitten ankle, continues to vanquish all comers.

The weekend exodus of boarders has long since trickled to a halt; of the remnants, some rush in and out of dorm rooms, spraying aftershave haphazardly and hustling each other out into the evening; others have found alternative means of entertainment.

'Hey, Geoff, here's you this morning, brushing your teeth.'

'Hey, look, there I am!'

'Hey, Victor, here's Barton Trelawney punching you in the head, remember?'

'Oh yeah!'

Mario, perched on a bench, is going through the video library on his phone. 'Geoff, here you are again, taking stuff out of your locker. Hey, Dennis, here's you telling me to stop filming you.'

'God damn it, don't you have any porn on that thing?'

At that moment the door opens and Ruprecht enters the Rec Room, wearing school blazer, cufflinks and generally sparkling from head to toe.

'Hey, looking good, Blowjob!'

'Where are you going, Ruprecht? Are you going to ask the nuns out on a date?'

Diffusing a redundant cloud of hairspray over his wiffle, Ruprecht explains the latest variation of Operation Falcon, viz., to go over disguised as himself, Ruprecht Van Doren, explain to the nuns that his science project, i.e. the pod, was thrown over the wall by bullies, and ask if he can please have it back.

'Not bad,' Dennis considers. 'That sounds like it could actually work.'

'The danger is that they might have seen me escaping through the laundry window,' Ruprecht says. 'But it's a chance I have to take.' He examines himself in the mirror over the water fountain.

'Gaylords,' Darren Boyce fires at the group on his way to the bathroom. As he's passing out the door, Skippy passes in; that is to say, suddenly he is there, in the doorway, though attended by such a palpable sense of *weight* it's hard to imagine him actually moving anywhere, as if he's subject to some private gravity that makes it impossible to raise his limbs. In his hand, meaninglessly, is a frisbee.

'Yo, Skipford, how was hamper-packing?'

'Didn't let Father Green bum you, did you?'

'Hope you at least made him buy you dinner first!'

Skippy drags himself over the threshold without reply.

'Hey, what's with the frisbee, Skip?'

'What happened to your date?'

'She just called.' Footsteps slooching zombie-like over the linoleum. 'She can't come out, she's sick.'

'Sick? What's wrong with her?'

A shrug. 'She's got a cough.'

'Crap.'

'That sucks.'

'Maybe you could go up to her house and see her?'

'She didn't sound like she wanted me to.'

'Poh, girls never tell you the truth about what they want you to do,' Mario states. 'That is lesson number one in dealing with girls. You should go up there right now and give her a big fat kiss.'

'Even if you can't kiss her, you could still feel her boobs?' Victor Hero suggests.

'Victor's right,' Mario concurs. 'I'm no doctor, but I don't think anybody ever got sick from feeling a girl's boobs.'

'You're more likely to get sick from *not* feeling a girl's boobs,' Victor remarks, a little wistfully.

'Though if you don't feel like it,' Geoff says, as Skippy does

427

not seem much cheered by this, 'you could just stay here? Why don't you put your name down for table tennis?'

'Or join me in a game of Russian roulette,' Dennis offers. 'I play it with five bullets?'

'Or hey –' Mario opening his phone again '– check this out, Skip, it's Geoff brushing his teeth, see? And there's a seagull on the rugby pitch . . . and the rugby pitch on its own, without the seagull . . . and here's you coming through the door, remember that?'

'Mario, for God's sake, that was three minutes ago, of course he remembers.'

'Yes, but he has not seen the film of it.'

'Benders,' says Darren Boyce, on his way back from the bathroom.

Close your eyes and the sky is full of burning planes. The night is caused by _____, it grinds its teeth, it scrapes its arms. The air feels like girl's hair, the moon is an eye rolled back in its head, here is a nice lollipop for you bitch how do you like that you thought you were so great now you better do what I tell you

That's not what you say, Carl. Janine's voice in his head, explaining the Plan to him. *Say what I tell you to say. Then she'll do whatever you want*

the O like a pink mouth wide open clamped round you tight as a hand sweet and sore at the same time like cuts on your arm the grey roof like craters of the moon the sky whooshing and wobbling like it's just snorted a big line do you like that you slut do you like the taste how many pills do you want for that

What do you want her to do? You want her to suck your dick?

Like this?

[   ]

Oh my god

The Plan works she meets him wrapped up in a hoodie and scarf I can't let Daniel see me *It's been so long tell her* It's been so long *and then You look so beautiful* You look so beautiful she takes your hand her finger traces over the cuts like a tongue Why do you do that Because I am bored you think but instead you say Because I missed you she starts crying

Then tell her I love you

Like this

I love you

last night in Janine's granny's greenhouse Is this part of the Plan? a secret part he didn't care

I love you, Carl, I love you

doggystyle in dirt and plants and empty mini-bottles of gin with Vaseline to stop it hurting It still hurts Well here is something that will hurt more BAM that is what she deserves she puked gin into her granny's plants afterwards you switched the heaters off so the flowers will die

I love you, you say

Oh Carl!

The Plan works like a dream the zip comes down

I love you too

Ha ha you slut the taste in your mouth is your friend's asshole you win the prize it's on its way – you don't say that

around you the night freezing melting

the gook's slanty eyes at the end of a long black gun

the O so bright the whole sky burning with napalm

everything smells like petrol and with the sawn-off no with a flamethrower you take out the gook he falls through the door with a burned-off face and then up to the school letting rip in the assembly bodies tumbling eyes crying blood everybody teachers Nurse Barry Mark Lori Daniel no wait I have a special plan for you she doesn't know shooting her in the face with the BIGGEST GUN IN THE WORLD –

mmmf Lori's head pops up from between your legs making a choking noise and she twists about reaching around for her bag dribbling globs of jizz onto your jeans that are Diesel she has a Kleenex in her hand is she just going to spit it out? your left hand zips out and grabs her jaw she wriggles about going mmmf

mmmf till finally you hear the gulps and you see her throat go up and down and release her back into the seat to wipe her eyes, sobbing, why did you do that?

Your head so heavy and sleepy now

Why do you have to be such an asshole?

and then she sees the phone in your hand, and freezes, and her green red eyes go wide, What the fuck are you doing?

Nothing, you don't even look at her

and suddenly like a wildcat she's lunging over you and screaming at the top of her voice and scrabbling and scraping trying to reach it even though it's too late ha ha and you push her back and away shouting at her at the top of your voice shut up bitch shut the fuck up ho

'Hey, someone sent me a video-message!' Mario exclaims, springing out of his seat. 'Ha ha, up yours, Hoey, someone's sent me a video-message! I told you this phone wasn't a waste of money!'

'Who's it from, Mario?'

'ID withheld,' Mario reads. 'Whoever it is, though, he's got the good stuff. Check this out.' Four heads gather eagerly around the phone, knocking together like clunky moons.

'Oh-ho-ho! This is a bit more like it!'

'What is it? I can't see.'

'Yeah, move over, Victor . . . holy shit, hey Skip, take a look at this.'

The picture is fuzzy and dark, but there at the centre, in a vortex of shadow, a pale, pixellated face may be seen attached to an anonymous penis.

'Ho, this bitch is really chugging it back.'

'That's my kind of woman,' Geoff says approvingly.

'Isn't that your mom, Mario?'

'Fuck you, Hoey.'

'Fuck *you*, you can't see anything properly on your stupid phone.'

'Well, don't look then, and the rest of us will enjoy this porn.'

'She's *hot* . . . like it's hard to tell, but I'd say she's hot.'

'Shut up, he's about to – here it comes . . . oh yes! Take it, bitch!'

The money shot, cheers mixed with disappointment: 'Why didn't he do it on her face?' 'Some of it went on her face.' 'Yeah, but I'd totally do all of it on her face.' 'Oh sure, when you're a hundred years old and you finally crack open your penny jar and you go down to some skank on a street corner, is that it?'

'Play it again, Mario.' The crowd around the phone now swollen to take in everyone in the room, shouting encouragement as the grainy face, no bigger than a fingernail, tentatively sets to work again.

'Hey –' someone – Lucas Rexroth – extends a finger '– what's that there in the background?'

'Where?'

'There, right there in the corner, see? That ring thing?'

'I don't know, a sign or something?'

'It looks sort of like . . .'

But here comes the messy denouement again, and the boys cheer like they're at a Senior Cup match and Seabrook has just scored a try.

It was eleven years ago tonight that Guido LaManche, Hawaiian-shirted pariah of Seabrook's graduating class, came into Ed's Doughnut House and advanced his proposal.

'They call it the "Bungee Jump",' he said. 'They've been doing it in Australia for years.'

'Why?' Farley asked.

'What do you mean, why?'

'Why would you want to throw yourself off a cliff with elastic tied around you?'

The Doughnut House had opened just a few weeks before; the lights made Guido's olive skin shine, as he turned to Tom and his entourage at the next table – Steve Reece, Paul Morgan, and a trio of soft-haired St Brigid's girls who looked like they'd just been taken out of their packaging – with a scoffing, palms-up gesture. 'Because it's exciting, that's why. So that when you're a grey-haired old fart drooling into your soup, you'll have at least one thing to remind you that you were alive. Seriously, you've never felt a rush like this. It's like sex to the power of a thousand – that's a good thing, by the way,' he glosses for Farley's table, winning a laugh from the jocks.

'It sounds dangerous,' one of the cashmere-clad girls said dubiously.

'You're damn right it's dangerous. What's more dangerous than jumping off a thousand-foot drop? But at the same time, it's one hundred per cent totally safe, because of the elastic rope and the harness, see? I've personally tested it out fifty times, and it's absolutely foolproof. Although perhaps it's not for the ladies.' He directed another sly, theatrical glance at where Farley sits with Howard and Bill O'Malley. 'Or all of the gents.'

Guido LaManche, though he'd failed every exam he ever sat, was a bona fide genius when it came to the psychology of the adolescent male: even when you knew he was playing you, it was nearly impossible to resist. 'Well, where is it, so?' Farley said, bringing his Coke down on the table with a thunk. 'Why don't you show it to us, instead of just sitting here talking about it?'

At this Guido became demure, folding his hands like a chaplain. 'If anyone thinks he is ready for the ultimate challenge, I will bring him to it personally right now. All I ask for in return is a small contribution towards expenses – say, twenty pounds a head?'

'Twenty *pounds*?' someone spat incredulously. But Farley was already on his feet.

Howard grabbed his arm: 'What are you doing?'

'I want to see this thing,' Farley replied.

'Are you mad?'

'It's not like there's anything else going on. We're just going to sit here all night and, let's face it, not talk to any girls. Anyway, you guys don't have to come.' Turning away, he fished around in his pockets till he found a twenty-pound note. 'I'm in,' he said, slapping it into Guido's palm.

'All right!' Guido said. 'At least there is one brave man here tonight.'

Tom, Steve Reece and the others looked at each other in consternation.

'Don't go *now*?' a blonde voice pleaded. 'It's like the North *Pole* out there.'

But the shame of being out-faced by a nerd was too great; already coats were being put on, scarves wound around necks, and the next thing Howard knew he was wedged into the back of Tom's Audi with two of the blonde girls, cruising down the dual carriageway after Guido's moped.

In spite of his reservations, he couldn't suppress a wave of excitement. Earlier in the week, Tom had scored four tries in the Paraclete Cup match against St Stephen's; Howard's own father, who rarely showed interest in any aspect of the world not preceded by a pound sign, had come home raving about this 'boy wonder' everyone was talking about, and his prospects of ending Seabrook's five-year dry spell in the Cup Final next month. Even sitting half-asleep in a dingy classroom, Tom exuded prowess, vitality, the sense that something was about to happen; he moved in broad, bold strokes, sweeping through the complications and dithering that for most people constituted life. Howard thought of him as a kind of anti-Howard, a bolt of lightning to Howard's ever-dissipating fog. And now Howard was in his car!

He would have been happy simply to stay here for the rest of the night; it was warm, and his thigh was welded hip to knee to the blonde girl next to him – her name, he thought, was Tarquin, and she was, or had been, Tom's girlfriend. But after ten minutes the red eye of the moped turned off the dual carriageway, and down a series of darkened, narrowing roads; then it passed through a gateway and now puttered to a halt in an unlit car park surrounded by storm-blown trees. Dismounting, Guido, rendered silver by the headlights of the cars, removed his helmet and with a little comb began arranging his hair into its customary nest of swirls.

'Everybody ready?' he inquired chirpily when the second car had pulled up and everyone had disembarked. Farley was acting nonchalant, smoking one of Steve Reece's cigarettes. Howard tried to picture him hurling himself off a cliff. Maybe he could still be talked out of it if it was done right. Years of careful self-attendance had taught Howard that there was a back door to most situations, through which the prudent man could slip discreetly.

'It's fucking *freezing*,' a caramel blonde from the other car said, wedging her hands under her armpits.

'Where *are* we, anyway?' Tarquin asked, looking around disgustedly at the accoutrements of Nature.

'Killiney Hill,' Bill O'Malley told her.

'Come on.' Guido had already half-disappeared into the shadowy band of trees. Cursing, the party followed after him.

In the distance, on the crest of the hill, the silhouette of the obelisk protruded like the nib of a fountain pen, inscribing a clouded signature on the tenebrous contract of the night sky, a secret pact between world and darkness. When he was younger, Howard used to hear stories about Satanists coming up here to perform black masses. Tonight he couldn't hear much more than the wind, and the damp crunch of twigs under his feet.

They reached a fork and pursued the coast northwards, out of the park and into the compact wilderness around it. To the right the sea foamed blackly beneath a static, ominous overhang of cloud. The track climbed steeply upwards until the trees fell away to grass and rocks and heather.

'Dalkey Quarry,' Guido announced, raising his voice over the wind. 'A sheer vertical drop of about three hundred and fifty feet. It's not the Grand Canyon, but believe me, you'll find it plenty high enough.'

En masse, they peered over the edge. The rockface dropped swiftly into shadows, long before it reached the ground.

'You *cannot* be serious,' the platinum blonde said.

'I told you, it's one hundred per cent safe!' Guido interjected irritably, huffing as he hauled a metal harness from under a brake of gorse. 'I've jumped in it myself like twenty times.'

'You told us in the pub you'd tested it fifty times,' Tarquin said icily.

Guido rolled his eyes. 'I wasn't there *counting it*, Jesus Christ. It was a lot of times, okay? Just trust me.'

She stared at him, arms folded, for a long moment, while Guido pretended to be engrossed in untangling the rope; then she tottered away to Tom, who'd been listening to this exchange with a mirthful expression as he smoked a cigarette and looked back over the lights of the Southside, the exclusive postcodes sparkling back from the seafront – his world, Howard thought.

'I'm just worried you're going to do something crazy,' she wheedled, stroking his chin beseechingly.

'It's just a bit of fun,' Tom said. 'Chill out.'

'Heads up, Tommo!' Something glinted through the air: a hip

435

flask, tossed over by Paul Morgan. Tom took a swig, gasped, threw it on to Steve Reece.

'Well, I'm not hanging around to watch you kill yourselves,' Tarquin, displeased, decided. 'I'm going back down to wait in the car.'

'Me too,' the platinum blonde said.

'Fine!' Guido shouted, kneeling by a tree trunk with the rope. 'Go!'

'Wait!' The caramel blonde tripping after them as they marched off down the path.

Farley stood at the edge of the quarry, contemplating the abyss with an indecipherable expression. Peeping over the brink again, it seemed to Howard the drop had grown even steeper. 'Are you absolutely sure you want to do this?'

'Hey, Farley, heads up!' called Steve Reece. Farley looked round just in time to clasp the flask to his stomach. He gazed at it blankly a moment, weighing it in his hand. Then, opening it up, he pulled from it until he was overcome by coughing. 'Give some to those guys too,' Steve Reece instructed.

Gasping, Farley handed the flask to Howard. 'I just think it would be fun,' he said, in a whiskey falsetto.

'We'll do it too,' Bill said heavily. Howard's throat had seized up from the alcohol: all he could do was nod his head.

They trooped over to where the others were waiting for Guido to complete his preparations. Metallic objects clinked in his hands. 'Nearly ready . . .'

'What are you doing?' Tom called amusedly over his shoulder. Howard turned to see the outline of the girls bunched at the end of the path.

'We don't want to walk through the woods on our own,' the squeak came back. 'We're just going to wait here.'

Tom let out a belly-laugh. 'Birds,' he said, flashing his teeth at Howard.

'Yeah,' he returned shakily.

'All set.' Guido, holding in his hands what looked like a straitjacket attached to an orange rope, rose to his feet, to dutiful whoops of excitement from the huddle of boys, which the wind seemed to swallow before they had even left their mouths. 'Before we continue, I will be needing your contributions, please, gentlemen.' The famously serpentine eyes darting from one face to the next. 'Twenty pounds each.'

Checking their wallets, Bill and Howard realized that they didn't have enough money. For an instant, Howard saw a lifeline. Then Tom stepped in, offering to cover him. Steve Reece did likewise for Bill. 'Thanks,' Howard mumbled. 'We can settle up later in the week.'

'Don't worry about it,' Tom said.

The notes disappeared into Guido's back pocket. 'Okay.' In his voice Howard thought he heard the trace of a quaver. 'Who's going first?'

No one said anything. Howard occupied himself with gazing down into the drop, much in the same way he'd examine his fingernails when the teacher put a question to the class, until it started making him nauseous and he had to step back. Guido shifted from foot to foot.

'What's the matter? I'm telling you, this is a hundred per cent safe. They've been doing it in Australia for years. But no problem, if you're too afraid, you can go and wait with the girls.'

Still no one responded. The sea crashed; nightbirds cried; the wind hollered mockingly.

'Jesus Christ!' Guido exclaimed. 'What's the problem? Are you all faggots?'

'Fuck it –' Tom stepped forward and grabbed the harness. At exactly the same moment, however, Steve Reece had the same idea, and now a new and vociferous argument broke out over who would go first.

Finally it was decided that the fairest solution would be to draw lots for the privilege.

Taking an expensive-looking pen from his jacket, Tom wrote out their six names on a flyer for an Indian restaurant. Even in his careless handwriting the list had the look of something fraught with destiny; no one spoke as he passed it to Guido, who tore it into strips, curled the strips into balls and dropped them into his helmet. Closing his eyes, he reached in and plucked a single ball back out. Each of the boys arranged his face into an attitude of yawning indifference. Guido untangled the strip of paper and extended his palm so that everyone could see it.

HOWARD

'Great,' Howard said tightly.

Guido picked up the jingling harness.

'Good luck,' Bill O'Malley said. Farley nodded dumbly, staring at Howard with an almost parodic expression of guilt.

The others punched his shoulder and said in terse voices, 'Good man, Fallon, fair fucks.'

In a daze, Howard raised his arms and the harness was strapped around him. Beside him Guido issued last-minute instructions: '. . . elasticated . . . last second . . . adrenalin . . .' But he was aware only of his numb fingers and the frenetic clamour of his heart, the wind charging about below like a wounded beast, and the bleak, stony faces of the other boys, uncomfortably resembling the front row of mourners at his funeral . . .

'Don't worry.' Guido intervened in his field of vision again. 'Nothing can possibly go wrong.'

Howard nodded and, in the manner of a man who has just stepped out of the deep freeze, lumbered up to the brink.

The chasm at his toes yawned and seethed, a single undifferentiated blackness that bore no relation to anything earthly, but rather resembled some terrifyingly literalized condition poised just beyond the edge of human apprehension –

'Ready . . .' Guido at his shoulder.

– resembled, it hit him in a flash, his own future –

'And . . . go!'

Howard did not move.

438

'What's the problem?' Guido asked.

'Nothing, I just need a second to . . .' He bent his knees, a caricature of a diver.

'You want a little push?' Guido advanced. Involuntarily Howard sidestepped away from him, raising a hand in defence. 'What?' Guido appealed. 'Are you going to jump or not?'

'Okay, okay . . .' Howard went back to the brink, shut his eyes, clenched his teeth.

The wind in the trees, on the rocks, like a siren's song.

'What's going on?' The girl's voice sounded like it was coming from the other side of the world.

'Fallon won't jump,' Steve Reece said. 'Come on, Fallon, for fuck's sake, I'm freezing my bollocks off.'

'Yeah, Fallon, come on.'

'He doesn't have to jump if he doesn't want to,' he heard Farley say.

'For fuck's *sake*,' Steve Reece repeated heavily – and then a hand dragged him back from the precipice.

'*I'll* go. Jesus Christ.' Tom was unstrapping the harness; Howard let him, gulping in air like he'd just been hauled out of the sea, then, freed, stumbled away on jelly legs to collapse on a tussock of grass a safe distance away, still too disoriented to be ashamed.

'Jesus Christ, Fallon,' Paul Morgan said. 'You fucking pussy.'

'Howard the Coward,' Tom said, shrugging on the harness.

'Howard the Coward!' Steve Reece laughed delightedly.

In the distance he heard the girls' laughter like the chirr of woodland animals, and he blazed with disgrace, feeling like he'd been at long last unmasked, outed, shown for what he really was.

'Is *anybody* going to jump tonight?' Guido was playing up the incident as a personal affront. 'Maybe I should just take you home now?'

'Chill the fuck out, LaManche.' Tom had buckled the harness belt and now stepped forward to survey the void. 'Everything's ready?' Guido assented. 'Right,' Tom said crisply, and hurled himself over the edge.

The others leaned out to witness his descent, his brawny body in a matter of seconds dwindling to a little toy as it dropped through space, straight down, not twisting or turning, and hit the ground with a flat thud.

For a moment no one reacted: they simply remained craned over the chasm, looking down at the tiny prostrate dot of colour motionless at the bottom. Then Guido mouthed, 'Oh, shit.' And from their position over by the edge of the trees, one of the girls began to scream.

Eleven years later, two hours after his last class, Howard is still haunting the school. First he attends a meeting about the upcoming Father Desmond Furlong Memorial Concert, to which he contributes mostly by way of nods or ambiguous throat-clearing noises; then he installs himself in the staffroom where, taking advantage of the silence, he corrects a class's worth of essays on the Land Acts, appending meticulous individual critiques and advice for future projects. He has moved on to potential questions for the fourth-year Christmas exam when the cleaner starts hoovering pointedly under his feet; accepting defeat, he slinks for the door.

It's Friday, and Farley has been sending regular texts from the Ferry, which Howard has ignored; Tom is bound to be there, and tonight of all nights he would prefer to avoid him. When he reaches his car, however, he realizes that even the prospect of being beaten to a pulp is more appealing than another night in his lonely house. Perhaps he can hide out in a corner without being seen? It's worth a shot: pocketing his keys, he turns in the direction of the pub.

The time is after six, and most of his colleagues are, in their own parlance, 'well-oiled'. To Howard's dismay, Farley is talking to Tom, conspicuously flushed and laughing too loud. He salutes them curtly and heads for the snug, where a little crowd has gathered around Finian Ó Dálaigh, the restored geography teacher, who's in the middle of a diatribe about the bastards in the Department of Education: 'Those bastards do nothing but sit around in their fine government buildings playing battleships, I'd like to see them supervise four hundred maniacs running around a gravel yard . . .'

'H-bomb.' Farley materializes at his elbow. 'Why didn't you come over?'

'You were talking to . . .' Howard nods clandestinely over his glass at Tom, waiting at the bar with his back to them.

'So?' Farley says. 'He's not going to bite you, is he?'

Howard stares at him. 'How do you know? Don't you realize what day it is?'

'Friday?'

'It's the *anniversary*, you clown, the anniversary of the accident. Eleven years.'

'Oh, for –' Farley swats his hand at the idea. 'Howard, I swear, no one in the world is aware of that except you. Forget about it, for God's sake. You've got enough to worry about.' He drains his glass and sets it down on a nearby ledge. 'Aha, perfect timing,' as Tom appears beside them and hands him a drink.

'Sorry, Howard,' he says, 'are you all right for a pint?'

'I'm still on this one,' Howard mutters.

'It's nearly gone – excuse me.' Tom grabs the lounge girl and orders another beer. This is the first drink he has ever bought for him; Howard raises his eyebrows in bewilderment. Farley shrugs back at him. Well, perhaps he is right, Howard thinks, perhaps it is only himself who keeps clutching on to the past, who's been obsessively watching the calendar. Tom is certainly in better form tonight than he has been lately – relaxed and jovial, if not what you could call sober. It's Howard who remains stiff and diffident, unable to settle; he can't help feeling thankful when Jim Slattery ambles up.

'Found myself thinking of you the other day, doing "Dulce et Decorum Est" with the fourth-years. You remember it, I'm sure, Wilfred Owen . . . ?' He tilts his head back oracularly: '*Dim, through the misty panes and thick green light / As under a green sea, I saw him drowning* . . . Gives Graves a run for his money there, eh? Drowning on dry land. Such a striking image. Mustard gas,' he explains to the others. 'What did for Hitler in the First World War, though it didn't kill the scut.'

'Ah,' says Farley.

442

'Dedicated it to a teacher, as a matter of fact, Owen did. Woman called Jessie Pope wrote this jingoistic doggerel, prodding youngsters to go off and get themselves shot to pieces. "Who's for the Game?", other such rubbish.' He sighs over his ginger ale. 'No wonder boys learned to stop listening to their teachers.'

'It'd never happen now,' Howard agrees mordantly.

'That reminds me. You were saying something the other day about one of your boys turning up an ancestor who'd fought in the war. It struck me that that could make a very interesting project for them – discovering their own forebears' actions during the war, I mean.'

'Yeah,' Howard says non-committally.

'Need a fair bit of spadework, of course, if they wanted to unearth anything significant, war record wasn't popular in Ireland, as you know yourself. But this is probably the first generation that would even be able to research it – so you'd be breaking new ground in all kinds of ways.'

'That would certainly be interesting,' Howard says. And it probably would; but over the last few days, in his double loneliness, he's found it hard to muster enthusiasm about anything, even the classes he was enjoying so much.

'Well, just a thought,' the older man says. 'I'm sure you have plenty to be going on with yourself.' He checks his watch. 'Hell's bells – I'd better be getting home, or it'll be the firing squad for me. Good luck, Howard.' Tapping the handle of his satchel at the other two: 'Till Monday, gentlemen.'

Howard turns lugubriously back to Farley and Tom, who are immersed in a discussion about the junior swimming team's prospects in the meet in Ballinasloe tomorrow. Tom is getting drunker by the minute, gesturing so expansively that at one point he knocks the glass clean out of Peter Fletcher's hand behind him, although somehow it doesn't break and Tom continues his monologue without even noticing, as Fletcher decamps stoically to the bar. Howard decides to follow suit, not wanting to be left with Tom if Farley should get called away.

He forges through the glistening Friday faces, the circular, alcohol-infused conversations. It's not just Tom; since Halley left, all these exchanges, the countless minor social transactions that make up the fabric of the day, have come to seem impossibly difficult. He keeps saying the wrong thing, taking people up wrong; it's as if the world has been fractionally recalibrated, leaving him chronically misaligned. In this kind of form, maybe his empty house would be better after all. He buys drinks for Farley and Tom and extricates himself from the proceedings with the excuse that he is driving, although at two drinks he's already well over the limit.

Outside the crowded pub the night is clear, and walking back through the school he feels more himself again. The dark frost-spangled pitches, overhung by the laurel trees, glister all around him, and the silhouette of the Tower looms up over the null expanse of the yard as though rearing out of the past. He opens the car door and spends a moment in the austere radiance of the moonlit campus, before turning the key in the ignition.

And then all of a sudden there's a kid in front of his car. He appears out of nowhere to flare up phosphorescent in the head-lights – Howard swerves frantically, misses him by an inch, jolts up the kerb and onto the manicured lawn surrounding the priests' residence, where he sits tilted in the cold interior, blood hissing in his ears, unsure what just happened. Then, switching off the engine, he climbs out of the car. To his disbelief – to his fury – the boy is continuing blithely down the avenue.

'Hey!'

The figure turns.

'Yes, you! Get back here!'

Reluctantly the boy makes his way back. As he draws nearer, a white slip of face discloses itself. 'Juster?' Howard says incredulously. 'Jesus Christ, Juster, what the hell were you doing? I nearly drove right into you.'

The boy looks at him uncertainly, then at the car mounted on the grass, like he's being asked to solve a puzzle.

'I missed knocking you down by *this much*,' Howard shouts, demonstrating with finger and thumb. 'Are you trying to get killed?'

'Sorry,' the boy says mechanically.

Howard clenches his teeth, trapping an expletive. 'If I'd hit you, you really would have been sorry. Where the hell are you coming from, anyway? Why aren't you in Study Hall?'

'It's Friday,' the boy says, in that maddening monotone.

'Have you got permission to be out?' Howard says, and then sees that in his hand the boy is holding, surreally, a white frisbee. 'And what are you doing with that?'

The boy looks blank, then follows Howard's finger to the plastic disc in his own hand, apparently surprised to find it there. 'Oh – uh, I was going to play frisbee.'

'Who with?'

'Um . . .' The boy scours the asphalt, bringing a hand to his head. 'Just me.'

'Just you,' Howard repeats sardonically. Greg was right, there is something seriously awry with this boy. Someone needs to tell him a few home truths. 'Nothing strikes you as odd about playing frisbee in the dark, on your own?'

The boy does not reply.

'Don't you understand –' Howard feeling his temper beginning to fray '– that there's a right way and a wrong way of doing things? You exist in a society, in the society of this school, you're not an island who can just, you know, do what he wants. Although I'll tell you what, if you want to be an island, if you want to be some isolated weirdo out on the margins of things, you're right on course. Just keep going as you're going, mister, and before long people will be crossing the street to avoid you. Is that what you want?'

The boy still does not speak, merely huddles into himself, continuing to stare at the ground as if he can see his reflection in the tarmac; his breathing, however, has taken on the snuffling quality that presages tears. Howard rolls his eyes. Say a word to these kids and they just dissolve. It's impossible, impossible. Suddenly

445

he feels emptied out, as if all the exhaustion of the rollercoaster week has hit him in a single wave.

'All right, Juster,' he surrenders. 'Get inside. Have a good weekend. And for God's sake, if you're going to play frisbee, find another human being to play with. Seriously, you're giving people the willies.' He returns to his car, opens the door. Juster, however, stays where he is, head bowed, passing the disc through his fingers like a vaudevillian's hat. Howard feels a twinge of guilt. Was he too hard on him? Half in and half out of the car, he casts about in his mind for some neutral remark to take his leave with. 'And good luck with your swim meet tomorrow! How are you set for it? Confident?'

The boy mumbles something Howard does not hear.

'Attaboy,' Howard says. 'Well, see you Monday!'

Nodding agreement with himself, in the absence of any reaction from Juster, he climbs into his car.

At the gate he checks his mirror. It seems at first that the boy has gone; but then he sees the frisbee, a dim double of the moon, hovering a couple of feet from the ground, in the same spot Howard left him. He purses his lips. These kids, they want you to live their whole lives for them. Teach me! Entertain me! Solve my problems! Sooner or later you have to step back. There's only so much a teacher can do. Good thing he got those brakes fixed, though. A dead student, that's all he needs.

Ed's Doughnut House is always half-empty on a Friday night, when anybody with a life and a fake ID heads somewhere that serves alcohol. But KellyAnn is going to *die* if she doesn't get a Double-Chocolate Wonderwheel. So here they are.

'It's like I totally crave them all the time,' she says, licking chocolate off her fingers. 'I can't explain it, it's like this weird *craving*?' After allowing a moment for suggestions that do not arrive, KellyAnn makes the connection for herself. 'It must be because I'm pregnant,' she says thoughtfully.

Janine rolls her eyes.

'Oh my God, these are *so . . . gorgeous*,' KellyAnn pronounces, through a mouthful of caramel gunk. 'Are you sure you don't want one?'

'I *want* to get out of here,' Janine says. 'This place is like Loser HQ.'

'Okay,' KellyAnn says. She has noticed that Janine is a little snippy this evening? But she's not going to make a big thing out of it. 'So where's Lori tonight?' she says, sucking her thumbs clean.

'Beats me,' Janine shrugs.

'Is she seeing that boy Daniel?'

'I have no idea,' Janine declares theatrically.

KellyAnn unwraps another doughnut. 'He sounds really sweet – are you sure you don't want one?'

'I'm not hungry.'

'I'm *always* hungry these days. I'm going to be the size of a *house!*' She chortles to herself, then remembers, 'Yeah, Titch knows him. He doesn't sound like Lori's *type* exactly? Like he's slightly a dweeb? But he sounds nice. And anyone's going to be better than that psycho Carl. Like, *oh* my God. He's totally going to wind up on like *America's Most Wanted*.'

Janine's eyes narrow and bore into her, and her voice is like a knife: 'This is Ireland, KellyAnn. Not America.'

'Yeah, but you know what I mean.' KellyAnn reaches for a napkin and wipes her fingers one by one. 'Like, I don't understand how she could even be attracted to someone like that, who's on drugs and hangs around with scumbags from the flats and *cuts* his own *arm*? I mean, hello? Probably not Mr Right?'

Janine doesn't answer, grinds the waxy doughnut paper into a little tiny ball.

'My mom says girls who like those kinds of boys have problems with their self-esteem,' KellyAnn says. 'But why would Lori have problems with her self-esteem? Every boy in South Dublin is completely in love with her.'

Now Janine mashes the paper through the slit cut for a straw in the lid of her empty beaker.

'Like, she's so beautiful,' KellyAnn continues. 'She could have any guy she wants.'

Janine doesn't say anything to this either.

'Anyway, I'm glad she's found someone she can be happy with. Now all we have to do is find a nice boy for you!'

'Don't bother,' Janine says.

'Oh, Janine, don't give up!' KellyAnn reaches over to stroke her arm. 'I know there's someone out there for you!'

'That's what I'm afraid of.' Janine turns at the sound of the door opening, then quickly turns back again as four more shaggy-haired losers come in through it. 'Men are such assholes,' she says.

'Titch isn't an asshole,' KellyAnn says emphatically. 'He cares about me.'

'They're all the same,' Janine comments sweetly. 'Now, can we please get out of here? And maybe go somewhere something might actually *happen*?'

Now you're deep in the forest, searching for the final Demon's castle. The sun is going down, the tree trunks glow pale silver, wrapped root-upwards with spiderweb. You left your horse down in the valley, there was no way to take it along. Where will it go? Someone kind will take it in and afterwards you can come and collect it.

Afterwards.

When you came back from Lori's, Ruprecht was still out on his mission. You put the frisbee in the wardrobe and got the tube of pills from under the mattress. Through the dorm window the sky is the same dead black as the empty schoolyard, as if they've tar-macked over it, and on the desk, like a yellow leaf, the note you found stuck to the door: BUS LEAVES FOR BALLINASLOE 8 A.M. SEE YOU THERE! ☺

No one knows much about the Third Demon, even on the Internet it's hard to find any information. You've crossed the Realm three times hunting for this Castle. You leave the woods for the wetlands now, in blazing moonlight heading north. You run until there's no further you can go and you hit the border of the Realm, the invisible wall where though the grass and water continue into the distance your legs move without taking you anywhere. Okay, try going west instead.

According to one solution of M-theory our universe is a HYPER-SPHERE, which is to say it's shaped like a bubble. That means that if you were to run as far as you could go, i.e. for fifteen trillion light years, which is the size of the universe, you would eventu-ally end up right back where you started. So how would you end up somewhere else? Ah, well, from *inside* the bubble, that is to say hyperspace, you could go wherever you wanted. Like back in

449

time? Backwards, forwards, any point in space, not to mention the other universes, an infinity of them maybe. So how do you get into the bubble? Well, that's where it gets tricky. Because we're too big and heavy for the dimensions? You could put it like that.

Djed running and running, west and west, through the pre-dawn gloom. Now you come to a fork in the path you don't remember being there before. Both ways look identical, lined with trees and mist. You pick one at random and start walking. Before long you notice the mist getting thicker, soon it has spread to cover everything, leaving only ghosts of trees, ghosts of a path. Still, if you keep going the same direction you're bound to get somewhere eventually. So you keep going.

Sleep pulls at your eyelids. The clock ticks, pushing you closer and closer to tomorrow.

BUS LEAVES FOR BALLINASLOE 8 A.M.

Flu epidemic, ebola, plague. Bus explosion, revolution, dinosaur skeletons in the museum coming to life and wreaking havoc. Alien invasion. Death.

SEE YOU THERE! ☺

The mist goes on and on. As you walk things come up out of your thoughts, frazzles of memories swirling around you and binding together, gathering like ghosts out of the dark. The swim meet, the last one, in Thurles. Grown-ups squeezed into plastic bleachers: country parents in frilly blouses and jumpers with diamond patterns, Seabrook parents in sunglasses, jewellery, fake tan. The other teams had bogger accents and broad shoulders, in the changing rooms they called you 'townie ponces', you were huddled in a corner not talking, with your goggles you looked like scared insects. Then Coach pulled you in together. You can do it, guys! They're already afraid of you! Because you're better than them! Then the whistle blew.

On and on, deeper into the mist.

As soon as you hit the water you stopped being scared. Water is the same everywhere! Your body moved without even thinking, you realized all the times before in training were just shadows of this time and the realness made you fly. The cheers from the bleachers were crashes of sound like the breaths of a monster that hit you whenever you came up for air. Your arms burned, they ploughed and dug like you were travelling right through the Earth. You didn't know what was happening around you, just kept hurling yourself forward till your fingers touched the wall. Then you saw Coach jump up with his fist in the air.

The metal trophy Made in Korea in the fat fingers of the judge. Coach's blue shirt black from carrying you on his shoulders. The space in the crowd where Mum and Dad would have been, that's where you kept looking. She can't come to the phone right now, sport. Okay, Dad, maybe later. A black hole is a region where the rules break down, where we don't know why what happens happens. Likewise, the word 'cancer' does not designate a specific disease, instead you should think of it as the name we give to a huge hole in our knowledge, a blank space on the map so to speak.

Who wants hamburgers?!! McDonald's in Thurles tasted different to home. Then back to the hotel, it was green like mint ice cream that had been left in the rain for years and years. In the next bed Antony Taylor fell asleep straight away. The others were in Siddartha's room watching *Dunston Checks In*. Is she awake now? She's just gone to bed, sport. But she's so proud of you, Danny, she wanted me to tell you.

You lay there in the dark. Antony's snoring was like a cement mixer. You just wanted to talk to her! You just wanted them to tell you what was happening! And then your leg felt like it was twisting up inside, you couldn't lie still. It was twisting you right up out of the bed! You got up, you hopped around. Then you opened the door, the wallpaper in the hotel was green too, it looked like you were underwater, the gold numbers on the doors counting down, you raised your hand to knock – and then –

How long have you been walking in this mist?!! It's got so thick that everything else has been blotted out, all you can see is this endless pearly-grey sea. Crap, maybe when you came to that fork in the path you should've gone the other direction. Now there is no path. You turn round, head back the way you came but it does not seem to make any difference. East, south-east, south. Nothing but mist. You start to wonder if maybe the game has crashed, leaving you stuck in some corner at the edge of the map, and you're just leaning forward to press the reset button on the console when you catch sight of something, a way off in the distance.

At first it hardly looks like anything – just a speck, almost too small to see. But the speck quickly grows into a dot, and the dot into a tiny patch of dark-grey against the background of silvery fog. As you hurry towards it you realize that whatever-it-is is also making its way towards you. Thud, thud, goes your heart. Your hands on the controller are slippery with sweat. You know it's the Demon, even from this distance, you can tell from the way the hairs on your arm stand up, the room thumps with your heartbeats, the night-colours drain and pulse in rhythm. And now it steps at last out of the mist.

Reality lurches left then right.

Because you know its face.

You rub your eyes. You pinch your arm, glance around you. The room is still here; you are still cross-legged on the floor, your floor. Behind you, Ruprecht's SETI scan bleeps quietly to itself. In the window, the usual stars and the far-off sound of Casey Ellington chasing Cormac Ryan around the car park with a shaken-up can of Dr Pepper.

But when you look back at the screen nothing has changed. On one side, Djed, with his golden hair, his Sword of Songs, the princess's amulet. On the other –

On the other is Coach.

He looks just like he always looks, in his hoodie with the Seabrook crest, a whistle on a string around his neck. His body listing slightly to one side, his hands hanging empty at his sides. He looks back out at you.

You don't know what to do. Is this supposed to be happening? Is this still the game? You laugh, because it's so ridiculous. But there's no one there to hear your laugh. You wish Coach would

452

stop looking at you, out of the screen. But he doesn't stop. And now he says, 'Swim meet.'

Your whole body jolts. The walls of the room churn round like a fairground ride.

Maybe you imagined it. But then he speaks again. 'Swim meet,' he says.

Is this really happening?

'Swim meet.'

'Coach?' you say to the screen.

But he just says it again, 'Swim meet,' and again, louder, 'swim meet.'

'Stop!' you shout back.

Now he's coming towards you. 'Swim meet.'

'This is impossible, you're in a game –'

'SWIM MEET.'

You pick up the controller where you've dropped it at your feet. Maybe you can just run past him? But without appearing to move he blocks your way. You try another direction. There he is again, standing in front of you. It's getting harder and harder to think. Mist rolls around the two of you, like a ring of ghosts watching a schoolyard fight. And now he advances towards you – *you*-you, like he's going to come through the screen. 'SWIM MEET,' he says.

You let out a cry, lunge at him with the sword. You slash at his arms and neck. The blows have no effect, he keeps coming forward. 'SWIM MEET.'

You run backwards, take out the bow and release four arrows into his chest. They stick out, shafts wobbling, as he advances towards the screen. 'SWIM MEET.'

'Shut UP!' You take out the Axe of Invincibility and run towards him, you hack at him, hew at his face and body. You cast spells, Fire Storm, Reversal, Banishment.

'SWIM MEET SWIM MEET SWIM MEET.'

Now you start to cry. 'Shut up?' you plead.

'SWIM MEET,' he says.

You yelp. You kick the monitor.

'SWIM MEET.'

You go for the console but something has gone wrong because it won't switch off, you flick the button back and forth but nothing happens and now Coach's face is right up against the screen going over and over and over

SWIM MEET SWIM MEET SWIM MEET SWIM MEET

and there is a sound like a door opening and you reel back from the screen as like it's been summoned it appears there right in front of you, the Door, its gold number, and you see yourself walking inside

into a hotel bedroom

Hey there, Daniel, what's up? He's rising from the chair, on the dresser the pills and a glass of wrong-tasting Coke, and you know what's going to happen but it's like you're locked into the movements, like you're watching yourself –

You just relax there, don't worry about a thing, he says, his hand reaches out for you

Yes, you remember now don't you

Into your hair gritty with chlorine

while Mum lies on her back with tubes going into her

And your soul slides down a slippery slope your body is black-magic encased in ice never again to escape or change or grow

And tomorrow it will happen all over again.

BUS LEAVES FOR BALLINASLOE 8 A.M. SEE YOU THERE! ☺

Do you understand now, Skippy? You cannot run any longer. You've come fifteen trillion light years to the very place you started from. That's the shape of the universe, that's called the Way It Is, it's a door that pulls you like a black hole into the future: and everything that promises to take you away from it, a girl, a game, a portal, these are no more than stray gleams and sparkles of light, shining at you from somewhere you will never be able to go.

On the monitor the Third Demon turns expressionlessly and walks back into the mist.

Now you're lying with your head on the carpet. Somewhere

above you a clock ticks. Your body feels like lead, it feels like you're already dead. But then you notice something.

On the game-over screen, from his mist-shrouded body, you see Djed's soul fluttering upwards. Up and up it goes, a dancing ball of light, till it's reached the title screen, to bob around the princess where she waits in her glittering cage of ice. Around and around her it dances. And suddenly you think:

His *soul*.

You sit up.

A soul doesn't weigh anything, it doesn't have a size.

On the screen the princess's eyes twinkle at you.

The dimensions are there at every point, too small to be perceived by clunky human bodies. But if you were just a soul –

That's when you see them! As if a veil's been pulled away, suddenly you see the air is full of little doors! All around the room, they're floating there everywhere, and when you scramble up to peep through them, you can see what's on the other side! Each one leads to a different time and place! Through this one you see you and Ruprecht, in the basement, working on the Invisibility Gun –

And here's the Hallowe'en Hop, when the things she said on her doorstep tonight do not exist yet, and you're realizing that Lori is the exact shape of what's been missing from your arms –

Here's tomorrow morning, 8 a.m., the sulky sky denim-blue, shivering boys with otter-like morning eyes, Siddartha and Garret and Antony Taylor, climbing one by one up the steps of the bus, fighting each other for the back seat, as Coach checks his watch, his clipboard, his watch again, studies the school door, which does not open –

(Faster, Skippy! a voice, the princess's voice, urges you, as the room swims, the particles break apart, the strings unweave like an old school jumper)

And here's summer, years ago, before any of this started, and Mum's in the back garden giving Dogley his first bath, he's still a pup, he doesn't know what water is, suds are flying everywhere, he yaps and wriggles, nipping at anyone in reach, and Mum goes,

If you just hold him so I can scrub his – when he squeezes out of her arms and shoots up in the air like a bar of soap, then landing on the grass turns and barks at you, shaking off the water so it flies all over you, and Mum laughs so hard she has to lie down on the grass, her hair is gold, her tummy round with Nina, the rainbow bubbles bob over the garden like perfect brand-new universes, the sound of her laughter is like music, it is music, and it guides you towards the door, against the rushing tide of time, swimming with all your strength, up and up –

'What are you *doing*?'

You open your eyes. Ruprecht towers over you with a baffled expression.

'Must've fallen asleep . . .' You haul your head off the carpet. 'I was playing the game,' you say, gesturing at the monitor. But it's not switched on. You drag yourself onto the bed and sit up.

'What's this?' Ruprecht has picked up an empty amber tube from the floor.

'Nothing,' you say, 'just getting rid of some stuff.' Sleep sizzles into your thoughts like radio static. The little doors have disappeared. 'Did you get your pod back?'

Ruprecht looks grimly out the window. 'That damn dog,' he says. A growl issues from his stomach. 'You don't have any food, do you?'

'No,' you say. Was it all a dream then? Disappointment burns within you, beads in your eyes, almost too much to bear.

'Hmm.' Ruprecht checks his watch. 'Ed's is still open . . .'

He turns away to count coins from his penny jar. You're looking at SEE YOU THERE! ☺ just trying not to cry. And then you realize you're floating six inches off the ground.

Holy shit! What's going on? Ruprecht has his back to you, he's saying something about making a new pod, meanwhile you are slowly rising up towards the ceiling! You try not to laugh – it's like invisible hands have slipped under your feet and are lifting you, higher and higher –

Ruprecht turns round. Instantly you're back on the floor.

456

'What happened to Frisbee Girl?' he says. He can't see them, but quarks and electrons are shooting through the air, sparking from his body like a million miniature multicoloured lightning bolts.

You shrug. 'Some other time.'

'Oh.' Another ferocious rumble issues from his stomach. 'I don't seem to have enough change,' he says.

'I'll pay for both of us,' you say. 'We can have a race.'

'A race?'

'Why not?' Your atoms are pulling upwards again. Every second you feel yourself lighter and lighter! *Say if we started going back in time tonight, could we keep going back for as long as we wanted?*

Ruprecht does one of his scoffing laughs. 'My dear Skippy, no one's beaten me in fifteen consecutive races. And those times I wasn't even hungry.'

'Well . . .' You zip up your coat. Through the window the neon doughnut sign shines in at you, the door of doors, the gateway to everything beyond, today and yesterday and the day before, all the times and people you have ever loved. 'Maybe it's my lucky day,' you say.

III

Ghostland

For where there are Irish there's memory undying,
And when we forget, it is Ireland no more!

Rudyard Kipling

'SERVICE: Smile; Efficiency; Reliability; Volunteering product information; Instant attention to new customers; Courtesy; Excellence.

'Smile. The Smile is your personal storefront. It is the first point of contact between the Customer and the Café-restaurant, and so should be as carefully maintained as the espresso machine or the counter display.

'Efficiency. Ed's Doughnut House is dedicated to offering the Customer the two Q's: Quality, Quickly . . .'

The boy isn't even pretending to listen; he is chewing gum, which is banned on the very first page of the Employee Manual, and gazing off at the upper reaches of the kitchen walls, which Lynsey notes are discoloured by grease. She keeps going anyway, and the more he sighs and shrugs the slower she gets, just to remind him who's in charge.

'These are the absolute basics,' she concludes. 'Any Level One employee is expected to know them off by heart, before he or she even begins to think about Level Two. Now, let's proceed to the espresso machine. Why don't you make me a skinny mochaccino.'

Off he goes, slouch slouch scowl scowl, as if she'd just asked him for a pint of blood.

In ordinary circumstances, someone like Zhang would not have even a snowball's chance of making Level Two. But of course these aren't ordinary circumstances. We need to tread carefully here, Lynsey, Senan told her. This business has caused enough trouble for us already. An employee claiming trauma is the last thing we want. Have a chat with him, take his pulse. If he seems disgruntled maybe a promotion would sweeten him up a bit.

Well, Lynsey's not sure how she feels about *that*. Okay, fair enough, Zhang's been through a traumatic experience, she doesn't deny that. Having someone die on your shift, that's pretty unlucky. At the same time, he hasn't actually put in for a promotion, and Tragedy or not, in her opinion it'd be totally unfair on Ruby and every other Level One worker if Zhang got promoted and they didn't. Because, like, when is he *not* disgruntled? He's *always* like that. But Senan's Regional Manager, so what he says goes – plus, he's hinted there could be a promotion in store for Lynsey too if they ever manage to get this mess sorted out. And why wouldn't there be? The stuff she's had to do in the last week has been way outside of her job description! Management calling her from London every day for updates, the Food Safety people sniffing around, though the worst has got to be the newspapers – they will just not let up, those people. Someone once said there's no such thing as bad publicity, well, in the Café-restaurant business there is!!! Unless you think that people are going to queue up to eat in a place someone's *died*!!! So Lynsey's been running around like a blue-arsed fly, barely getting a wink of sleep, doing her best to take the calls and field the questions, and as Senan said, just make it absolutely clear, as delicately as she can, obviously, given the circumstances, and with all due respect to the family, that the death of the boy in question, while tragic, was NOT caused by or resulting from or in any way related to any Ed's Doughnut House product, in fact the police said he actually hadn't eaten anything at all in the Café-restaurant, unlike his little porky friend who'd eaten about twenty-five doughnuts. She must have used the words 'tragedy' and 'unrelated' five million times this week – her dad is keeping a scrapbook with all her newspaper and magazine appearances, ten all told, although four spelled her name wrong and one said she was *thirty*!!! *Excuse me???* And of course who gets his own headline except Spa-face – ZHANG: HEROIC EFFORTS. She supposes he was quite heroic doing the Heimlich manoeuvre and stuff, even though the kid Daniel didn't actually choke, but still it seems a bit unfair on Ruby and the other staff members, like suggesting they're *not* heroic just because

462

they come in and do their job every day, when in fact if it wasn't for everyday people like that the world would just grind to a halt and the economy would be ruined.

Also, this is the worst mochaccino she has ever tasted in her entire life.

The Principal of Seabrook College came in to speak to her too, a couple of days after it happened. He was a tall, dynamic man, in his late thirties maybe? Basically he was doing the same thing she was, trying to protect the school's image and explain that while it was a tragedy it was just this one crazy kid, and not anyone else's *fault*. Having said that – he put his hand on her arm – on behalf of the school I want to apologize for any distress this might have caused you or your employees. He shook his head. I've been teaching for nearly twenty years, he said, and I'm at a loss to understand this.

Lynsey doesn't understand it either. He's *fourteen*, and he takes an overdose just because his girlfriend dumped him? Jesus, like, relax! That's life! People get dumped! If Lynsey had killed herself over every fucking self-absorbed arsehole who'd dumped her, she'd . . . well, she'd be pretty dead at this stage. Anyway he should've known it would happen sooner or later, that girl was way out of his league, it's obvious from the photographs – no shortage of those, needless to say, *Ravishing* this and *Tragic Beauty* that and *Teen Heartbreaker* the other, not to mention *Gorgeous Juliet in Real-life Romeo and Juliet Story*, which, hello, a) that would only make sense if her name was Juliet but it's not it's Lori, and b) if the person had ever seen *Romeo + Juliet* they would know that is nothing like what happened in the Café-restaurant.

Though at the same time . . . you can't deny it's romantic, writing her name with his last breath. Like in a way that girl is so lucky – most women won't ever experience anything even close to as romantic as that. She wonders what he was like. Daniel Juster. She imagines the annoying Seabrook boys that crowd in here at lunchtime, and him standing apart, different, sort of quiet and wistful and melancholy . . . Life is so sad, and love is so unfair.

She wonders if Zhang has a girl he's in love with back in China. Maybe he's saving up to go home and marry her. Maybe he misses her and that's why he's so grouchy. She temporarily feels sorry for him and she marks him as twelve out of twenty on the Product Information section even though he has actually scored a zero.

'Zhang, let's talk about the other night. How are you feeling? Are you feeling all right?'

He looks back at her blankly.

'I mean, after what happened. With that boy?' Hallo, Earth to employee! Remember, he took about five hundred painkillers? Died just over there by the jukebox? You were holding him at the time? 'We're just wondering if you're experiencing any after-effects. Trouble sleeping, flashbacks, anything like that? Perhaps you're finding it difficult to fulfil your work duties, maybe you need some time off?'

He draws a rasping breath, pulls his head back. 'You wan' cuh' ma owas?'

God, he's so obnoxious. She releases a light, fluttering laugh. 'No, we don't want to cut your hours. We just want to make sure that, although the company holds no responsibility for the events of last week, you don't feel yourself adversely affected such that continuing to carry out your responsibilities here as per your contract might now or at some future date result in anxiety, depression or similar conditions. Also that you're satisfied that the company has made available to you such time and resources as you might need in the course of making a full recovery.'

Suspicion gives way to the blank look again. Lynsey takes a card from her personal organizer. 'If you do feel the need to talk to someone, this is the counselling service available to all company employees. It's a special low-cost line.'

He flips the card between his fingers. It's hard to be sure he's taking any of this in. But it doesn't *look* like he's planning on milking them over the Tragic Event. She can go back and tell Senan to relax, and the relief and pleasure she imagines flooding to Senan's face at this inspires an unexpected wave of sympathy and gratitude for Zhang. She promises him a prompt response on his appraisal, and as she leaves she is thinking that even if it hasn't occurred to him to sue them (God, if it'd been an Irish guy behind the counter that night! €€€!) she may bump him up to Level Two anyway. It's only twenty euro extra a month, after all.

Halfway to the door she pauses, imagining she can see a trace of strawberry syrup still there on the floor tiles, and she disappears into a little daydream about Senan writing her name there – but instead of dying getting up, and staring deep into her, Lynsey's, eyes, and unscrewing his wedding ring and tossing it over his shoulder . . . They'd have a house in Ballsbridge near the park, and another in Connemara by the sea, and three little boys who Senan would drive into Seabrook College every morning. But she wouldn't let them come in here. Once you find out what's in those doughnuts they're actually really disgusting.

The intervening days between the 'Tragic Event', as it's become known, and the funeral mass in Seabrook parish church are a dreamlike mixture of chaos and odd, affectless serenity, like watching a riot on television with the sound turned down. Classes are suspended, and in the ensuing vacuum reality too seems on hold, the boundaries and precepts that ordinarily govern the schoolday, that had seemed until now like fundamental laws of the universe, simply no longer there: the ringing of the bell at three-quarter-hour intervals just a meaningless sound, the corridors full of people wandering around like drones in some computer simulation.

As if to compound the weirdness, parents keep bursting through the double-doors at every hour and charging up the stairs to besiege the Acting Principal. From their expressions, blending the implacable determination of the irate customer with a touching, infant-like helplessness, one might think these parents, many of whose sons are not even in the same year as Daniel Juster, to be more upset than anyone else. And maybe they are; maybe for them, Howard thinks, Seabrook College really is a bulwark of tradition, stability, constancy, all of the things it says in the brochure, and so in spite, no doubt, of their best intentions, they can't help viewing the Tragic Event, the suicide of this boy they do not know, as a hostile act, a kind of vandalism, a swear-word wantonly scratched into the sleek black paint of their lives. 'Why would he do such a thing?' they ask, over and over, wringing their hands; and the Automator tells them the same thing he tells the newspapermen and -women that appear at the school gates, outside the doors, skulking down Our Lady's Hall – that the school is conducting a full investigation, that he will not rest until an explanation is found, but that the number one priority for all of them now must be the care and reassurance of the boys.

On the day of the service, the school chapel being deemed too small for the purpose, the entire year of two hundred boys, accompanied by Howard and five other teachers, makes its way crocodile-fashion down the perimeter path and out the gates to Seabrook village. Ordinarily, this type of operation would be a logistical nightmare; today they march the mile to the parish church with barely a sound. The boys' faces have the same pasty, just-scrubbed, vaguely otter-like look they have when they've just got out of bed, and they flinch as they cross the church threshold – as if the coffin were not sitting there inertly between the aisles but hanging over them like a rod of untold power, a splinter of something supermassive and implacable that's come spinning down like that inscrutable black slab in 2001 from somewhere dread and ulterior to call time on their flimsy Wendy-house lives.

Just before the mass begins a contingent of girls from St Brigid's is led in by a nun. Heads turn and a restrained but audible murmur of displeasure indicates that the girl at the heart of the affair is among them. Howard identifies her from the newspaper pictures – though slighter than she looked there, and younger, hardly more than a child, delicate features rhythmically appearing and disappearing behind a veil of black hair. The story going around is that Juster, improbable as it seems, had some kind of romantic entanglement with this girl, which on the fateful night, less improbably, came to an end. She certainly has a face custommade for heartbreak; still, Howard struggles to reconcile this melodrama with the nondescript boy who sat in the middle row of his History class.

The organ sounds and the boys rise in unison: Tiernan Marsh leads the choir into the hymn that opens all Seabrook College ceremonies, 'Here I Am, Lord'. While they sing, Howard surreptitiously scans the rows of young faces, staring deliberately ahead, muscles tensed against any expression of emotion; the hymn is so beautiful, though, and the choir's voice so sweet, that even as he

467

watches, the fault-lines spread, eyes redden, heads drop. At the end of one bench he sees tears coursing down Tom Roche's cheeks; it is shocking, like seeing your dad cry. Turning away he finds himself looking right into Father Green's eyes. He bows his head hastily, and they sit again.

Father Foley says mass with his lips too close to the microphone; the loudspeakers pop with every plosive, making the boys wince. 'How telling it is,' he says in his sermon, shaking his illustrious golden-locked head, 'that Daniel's short life should come to its end in a restaurant devoted to doughnuts. For in some ways, is our modern way of life not comparable to one of these doughnuts? "Junk food" that satisfies only temporarily, that offers a "quick fix", but has, at the centre of it, a hole? Is that not, indeed, the shape of any society that has lost touch with God? At Seabrook College we strive to fill this hole with tradition, with spiritual education, with healthy outdoor activity and with love. Today, the report card that our Holy Father has given us tells us that we must try harder. Daniel is united with Him now. But for the other boys, and for ourselves too, we must learn to be more watchful, more vigilant, against the forces of darkness, in the many alluring guises those forces have learned to hide themselves . . .'

A photographer is waiting on the steps after the service. As the doors open he springs into position, but before he can snap a single shot, Tom Roche has charged over to accost him. The man half-rises, hands wheeling, arguing his case; Tom does not listen, keeps jostling him backwards till the photographer loses his footing and stumbles down the steps. The Automator places a discreet hand on Tom's shoulder, but the man is already on his way, complaining bitterly about censorship.

After the cemetery, there is a reception in the school. The St Brigid's girls are whisked away by their guardians, but many of the second-years come back for weak tea and drooping, plasticky ham-and-cheese sandwiches, served from a trestle table in Our Lady's Hall. The slim man in the dark suit talking to one of the priests is

Juster's father; he looks exhausted, wrung-out, like he's spent the last seven days in a spin-cycle. His wife is washed up against him, clinging lifelessly to his arm like seaweed, with no pretence of listening to the priest's small talk. Howard searches about for Farley, wondering how long he has to wait before he can politely leave. Then: 'Ah, Howard, there you are,' a voice says at his ear. 'Someone I'd like you to meet.' Before he can protest or escape, the Automator has steered him right up to the bereaved parents.

They greet the stuttering interloper without pleasure; on hearing his name, however, Juster's father's face quite changes – opens, in a curiously literal way, making him seem younger, recalling his son. 'The history teacher,' he says.

'That's right.' Howard is not sure how to pitch his smile.

'Daniel used to talk about your class. You're doing the First World War at the moment.'

'Yes, yes,' Howard burbles gratefully, seizing on it as if for a lifebelt but then unable to find the words to advance the conversation.

'He was telling me about it just the other day. As a matter of fact he had a great-grandfather who fought in the war, on my wife's side – isn't that right, honey?'

Juster's mother's lips briefly approximate a smile; then she pinches her husband's sleeve and he leans over so she can bring a cupped hand to his ear. He nods and, extending the smile and bowing to Howard and the others, she withdraws and makes her way down the hall. 'My wife is very sick,' he says, almost in passing; then, in a more meditative tone, 'Yes, his name was Molloy, William Henry Molloy. He served in Gallipoli, though, not on the Western Front. I think Sinead still has some bits and pieces belonging to him somewhere in the house. Would they be of interest to you? I could dig them out for you, if you like.'

'Oh, well, I wouldn't want you to go to any trouble . . .'

'No trouble, no trouble . . .' The man drifts off, tracing a thumbnail along his lower lip, then, resurfacing, says quite conversationally, 'He didn't want me to tell anyone about his mum – I don't suppose he mentioned her to you, did he?' He flashes ringed eyes at Howard, who takes a moment to realize that they are talking about Juster again. Stiffly, he shakes his head.

'Kids are so secretive at that age – I don't need to tell you that, I'm sure.' The man smiles softly at Howard. 'Do you have children yourself?'

'Not yet,' Howard says, visited as he speaks by an image of his empty house, the floor covered with pizza boxes and unfinished games of sudoku.

'They have definite opinions on how things should be done.' He smiles the weird faraway smile again. 'I shouldn't have listened to him, of course, I realize that now. I should have told someone to keep an eye on him. He needn't have known. I was just so distracted. You know, an illness like that becomes such a marathon, the endless waiting for test results, for the next round of treatment. And at the back of my mind I suppose I was thinking the same thing he was, that if we all just sat tight maybe the whole thing would disappear. I didn't think about the pressure it was putting him under, coping with it all alone. Now it's too late.'

He trails off, lifts the spoon to stir his tea, replaces it without raising the cup to his lips, while Howard flails about for some words of consolation. 'But Mr Costigan tells me –' it is the other man who speaks first, addressing Howard with a resolute air '– that you talked to Daniel on a couple of occasions. I wanted to thank you for that. I'm glad he knew there was somewhere he could go.'

'You're welcome.' The words whistle faintly through Howard's lips, like his mouth has been shot full of novocaine; he reaches out to shake the hand the man extends, as inside he feels his body turn to ashes. Then, gratefully, he steps aside, as Tom approaches to pay his respects, his handsome, lean-jawed face heavy with compassion.

Juster's mother is waiting in the car outside, and it is not long before her husband, thanking the faculty again, leaves to join her. Shortly afterwards the caterers begin to stow the dirty crockery.

The crowd has dissipated, and the remnant that continues to

the Ferry is made up of teachers alone. The mood they bring in with them is broody and mean, and drinking at three o'clock the worst thing for it. In an hour everyone is tipsy and unstable. The women, most of whom are mothers, dab at tears; emergent sunlight streams through the window and blares from the hideous floral carpet, combining with the beer to make Howard's head ache. He wants to go home but is locked into a corner by Farley, who's drinking double whiskeys and has embarked on a long, bitter diatribe that has no real subject but keeps coming back to Father Foley's sermon. 'He's supposed to be a man of God, and he gets up there and spouts this stupid, vacuous – I mean, did he think for a second about how people might feel?'

'I didn't think it was that bad,' Howard says blandly. 'I mean, no worse than you'd expect.'

'For God's sake, life is like a *doughnut*? Has the poor kid not undergone enough without being dragged in to star as a metaphor for modern society?'

'Well, he did have a point,' Howard says. 'I agree it may not have been tasteful . . .'

'Juster didn't die from eating a doughnut, Howard. He died from a fucking giant overdose of painkillers.'

'I know that, but the stuff about junk food, and the world we're handing down to these kids . . .'

'I'm not denying that for one second. It's a shitty fucking world, no question, and right from the off these kids are in the crosshairs, being told to buy this, buy that, lose weight, dress like a hooker, get bigger muscles – by grown men, Howard, it's grown men and women doing this, I mean the cynicism of it is unbelievable, but my point is, my point –' he stalls, head veering in vague circles like an errant compass needle '– that fool, that silly old man, and the Automator and all of them, they carry on like it's *outside*, all the bad stuff is outside, and we're this embattled force protecting them from it, when it's us too, Howard, when we're filling them with our own brand of bullshit, about tradition and whatever, setting them up to take their places at the top of the shitheap like this is some noble thing, when it's all just money, and who they *are* is incidental, they're just the means of allowing Seabrook to keep being fucking Seabrook –'

'I don't see what this has got to do with Juster,' Howard says quietly, aware of how loud Farley has got.

'No one cares, Howard, that's what it's got to do with him! If someone had been looking out for that kid this wouldn't have happened, I guarantee you – I *guarantee* you,' over Howard's mumbled protests, 'but no one was, because no one cares, instead we just pay lip-service to caring, like we pay lip-service to charity and all those Christian values we supposedly stand for while we're slumped in front of our incredibly high-resolution plasma TVs, or we're driving off to our holiday homes in our SUVs. Like, don't you think it's a fucking joke, calling that a Christian life? Do you think fucking Jesus would have driven around in an SUV?'

'Here,' Tom interjects roughly. They look up: he is glaring at them intently through reddened, bleary eyes; a rash of sweat glistens across his forehead.

'What?' Farley says, pointedly.

'I don't know what you're shiteing on about,' Tom says, 'but leave Jesus out of it.'

'Why?'

'Just do it, is why. Show some respect.'

'*Show some respect* is just another way of telling people to keep their mouths shut,' Farley says.

'Okay, keep your mouth shut.'

'See, that's exactly the kind of thing I mean,' Farley ripostes, the whole room looking at him now, 'we spend all our time congratulating ourselves on what a great school we are, we go into class every day and fill the kids' heads up with crap, but you try to say anything about what the world's actually genuinely like and someone'll tell you to keep your mouth shut and show some respect –'

'You know what your problem is, Farley?' Tom raises his voice.

'I don't know, Tom –' Farley raising his own right back '– what's my problem? Enlighten me.'

'Your problem is you're a knocker. You're a typical fucking Irish knocker. While decent people are putting their heads down and getting on with the job and doing the best that they can, you hop about like a little bird, picking away at everything, chipping away at everyone's morale, because you're too spineless and selfish to try and make a difference –'

'You're totally right, Tom, you're absolutely right, I am spineless, I am a spineless selfish useless person, and I don't do anything to try and make a difference, but you know what, neither do you, and neither does anyone in this fucking place beyond the bare minimum, instead we just look after ourselves and the people like us, because we know that otherwise things might actually *change* –'

'Take it easy,' Howard tells him, and when this has no effect, appeals to Tom, 'He's had a lot to drink.'

'Fuck off, Fallon, you're worse than he is.'

'Things might change,' Farley repeats, standing now with his arms outstretched, 'we might even have to let *strangers* into our little treehouse. Poor people! Foreign people! How would you like that, Tom? How would you like to see your precious school full of knackers and refugees?'

'At least it'd be better than faggots like you,' Tom rejoins.

'Boys, please,' pleads Miss McSorley.

'Oh right, I'm a faggot now, am I?' Farley inquires.

'Come on now, lads,' Slattery weighs in. 'This isn't the time or the place.'

'I think *you're* the faggot,' Farley says.

'Say that once more and I'll knock you down,' Tom promises.

'I think you're an arse-crazy homo, you're a flaming mincing fudgepacking queen, and all you think of from one end of the day to the next is boys in their pretty little swimming togs –'

Tom lunges at Farley but several men intervene to hold him back and his punch fails to connect. It seems to waken Farley, however; he stares at Tom, his mouth open in surprise.

473

'Come on, let's get out of here.' Howard tugs at his arm.

While Tom wrestles with his captors, he hustles Farley out of the pub. The street outside is wintry and monochrome. Above, a blood-red sun flares through the clouds, like a last live coal uncovered among the cinderwork of the dying seasons. When they are a safe distance away, he turns on him. 'What the fuck are you doing? What was the point of that?'

'I don't know, Howard.' Farley looks off bleakly at the sea. 'It's just, they're just kids, you know? And the people who're supposed to be looking after them, and teaching them about maturity and responsibility, we're worse than they are.'

Howard pushes him away, grinds his teeth. They walk down to the main road, where after five minutes Howard manages to pluck a taxi from the traffic. He declines Farley's invitation to come back to his apartment and drink more.

At home there are no messages on his answering machine. He picks up Graves and numbly turns the pages. *We no longer saw the war as one between trade-rivals: its continuance seemed merely a sacrifice of the idealistic younger generation to the stupidity and self-protective alarm of the elder.*

If someone had been looking out for that kid this wouldn't have happened.

According to the papers, Howard was the last adult to see Daniel Juster alive. Alive, in the rear-view mirror, merging with the dusk, as if he stood on the threshold right at that moment, a dark door Howard couldn't perceive. But how was he supposed to know? And even if he had known, what was he supposed to have done? Bring him home with him? Ditch his car and go and play with him, in the freezing cold car park? That would somehow have made everything all right? Throwing around a frisbee like he was fourteen years old? When was the last time he even played frisbee?

But then thinking about it he realizes he remembers the last time quite clearly; and with a disarming vividness finds himself not so much in the grip of a memory as slipped back to that very time, to the shape and feel of being fourteen – the taste of apple-flavoured bubblegum in his mouth, the humiliation of a spot on his chin, the unending turmoil of that endless struggle to stay afloat in a roiling sea of emotions, and the thousands of hours spent out on the gravel, determined to master an utterly valueless skill – the frisbee, the yoyo, the Hacky Sack, the Boomering – in the unshakeable belief that in this lay his salvation. Half of him battling to become visible, the other half just wanting to disappear. God, how had he ever endured it?

A knock at the front door. Howard has lost track of time, but knows that it's late: hoping against hope – Halley! – he springs out of his chair to turn the latch. He ducks just in time to dodge the fist that comes flying out of the darkness.

And in the village the wind sets the lids of the wheelie bins chomping at nothing, and in the cinema Hulk bounces and swings his fists, and in the video-game shop the Christmas games are in, and in Ed's there's a special offer, two boxes of doughnuts for the price of one, someone says it's because of what happened but someone else says no, actually they're doing it in all the branches. It doesn't matter where you go though, nowhere feels big enough to contain you, even if you're right in the middle of the mall it still somehow seems too shallow, like when you were younger and you tried to make your Transformers visit your Lego town, and they were just out of scale, it didn't work – it's like that, or maybe it isn't, because you also feel really tinily small, you feel like a lump in somebody's throat, or actually who cares what you feel, and everywhere you go you encounter other grey-clad boys from your year, looming up like hateful reflections – Gary Too-lan, John Keating, Maurice Wall, Vincent Bailey and all of the others that are the pinnacle of the evolution that began so many years ago with that one depressed fish that if you met him now you'd tell him to stay in the sea – there they are, pale-faced but smirking, sleeves rolled up, and though it's sad, it's sadder than a three-legged dog, it's also flat, it makes you angry, so when someone says Skippy was a homo you're almost glad because you can fight them, and they're glad too, so you fight, until someone gets his jumper ripped or the security guard chases you out of the mall, and you've already been kicked out of the other mall, and it's too cold to go to the park, and you think it must be almost time to go to bed but it's not, it's only just time for dinner, which is car-tyre with phlegm sauce and which you leave mostly uneaten, and privately you're thinking Skippy is a homo too, you're thinking, Fuck you Skippy, though you're also thinking, Hey, where's Skippy? or Skippy, did you borrow my – and then you think, Oh fuck, and everything shakes around the edges again and you have to hold on tight to your lucky condom or your Tupac keyring or your actual live shotgun bullet, or if you don't have one of those things, wedge your hands deeper in your pockets or throw a stone at a seagull or shout after a knacker in the village how his mother was in excellent form last night and run for it, and dream of being Hulk, or a Transformer in a Lego town going *smash! bash! crash!* stomping the whole city to the ground, incinerating the little yellow-headed Lego people with your laser eyes till the smiles melt right off their faces.

And in the schoolyard the lisp of a last fallen leaf skating around the tarmac is the only sound, everywhere else is totally silent, even when people are talking, it's like someone's thrown a switch and reversed the polarity of everything so that being alive now is like being dead, like zombies, grey bodies shuffling loose-limbed through the perpetual gloaming, or like universes, same difference, matter or energy adrift in nothingness, descending, like veils, through the darkness. Classes rebegin but it doesn't make any difference, there is still that empty seat, and in Maths class, calling the roll, Lurch goes, 'Daniel Ju– oh no, of course not,' and *scratches his name out*, right there in front of you. Farts go unpunished, clear jinx situations unheeded, Pokémon cards unswapped; the Junior Rec Room is deserted, the table-tennis table folded up and tidied into a corner, the pool balls lined up in their perspex womb, the television, unprecedentedly, switched off. You don't talk about It, and you don't talk about not talking about It, and soon the not-talking-about-It has become something real and tangible existing among you, a hideous replacement-Skippy like an evil twin, a dark blastula that presses evermore insistently against your lives. The dormitory corridor presents only closed doors, behind which are closed faces, secreted beneath headphones or locked into mute dialogues with illuminated screens. Geoff hasn't done his zombie voice after the night in the Ref it escaped without thinking, *My roast beef needs more GRAVEy,* and sounded different from how it had before – louder than he meant it to be, and not funny, and even sort of frightening, like it knew something you didn't.

And then one morning you go to your locker and find a note there from Ruprecht, calling you to an urgent meeting in his room, and even though it's probably bullshit you find yourself climbing the Tower stairs to his dorm.

The others are there already, scrunched up on Ruprecht's bed because no one wants to sit on Skippy's, even though his duvet is gone as well as his other stuff. Ruprecht looks feverish and drawn. Ever since that night, in the middle of all this weird nothingness, he's been rushing about back and forth from his laboratory, one pen in his mouth and another behind his ear, stacks of paper and star maps and set squares bundled in his arms. He waits for everyone to sit down, and then he unscrolls a chart with a familiar shape drawn on it.

'The Van Doren Portal, Mark Two,' he says. 'Let me say at the outset that the science of this is far from being stable. This operation, if it works at all, will be highly dangerous. But by rebuilding the pod, and recalibrating it to a monotemporal matrix, I have calculated that it might just be possible to travel backwards to a nodal point in time, e.g. the Hallowe'en Hop, and bring Skippy, as he was then, forward to the present. If we adjust the figures of the original teleportation for a temporal "drag" of –'

'Aaaaugh!' cries Dennis.

Everyone turns to look at him. He is ice-pale, breathing rapidly, and directing at Ruprecht a stare of unaccountable vehemence.

'What?' Ruprecht says.

'Are you serious?' Dennis says.

'I know it sounds far-fetched, but there is a small but real chance we could use the pod to rescue Skippy. In effect we're doing the same thing we did with Optimus Prime, only with minor tweaks in order to –'

'Aaaaugh!' Dennis goes again.

Ruprecht looks nonplussed; Dennis, in a single strange and complicated motion, throws his arms over his head as if shielding it from a bomb-blast, or as if it itself is about to explode, and then, springing up, marches out of the room. The others look around in bemusement, but before anyone has a chance to say anything, Dennis has marched back in and thrusts something into Ruprecht's hands. 'Here!' he shouts. 'Special delivery from the eleventh dimension!'

'Optimus . . . ?' Ruprecht turns the plastic robot over in wonderment; then his gaze jabs upwards to Dennis. 'But . . . how? I mean . . . where was he?'

'In my laundry basket, underneath some Y-fronts,' Dennis recites.

Ruprecht is baffled. 'Some kind of wormhole . . . ?'

Dennis slaps a hand to his face, leaving a bright red mark. 'Oh my god – I put him there, Ruprecht! I put him there!'

'You . . .' Ruprecht trails off, his mouth becoming an anxious *O*, like a baby that has lost its soother.

'Don't you understand what I'm saying to you? Your pod *doesn't work*! It *doesn't work*! *I* took the robot! Your invention didn't do anything! Your inventions never do anything!'

'But –' Ruprecht increasingly distressed '– the Mound? And the music?'

'I *made that up*, moron! I made it all up! I thought it would be funny! And it was! It was really, really funny!'

The others wince sympathetically; Ruprecht very slowly doubles over, an expression of intense concentration on his face, as if he's drunk weedkiller and is making a study of the effects. The sight of this makes Dennis only more ruthless.

'You know what your problem is, Blowjob? You're sure you're right. You're so sure you're right, you'd believe anything. You remind me of my crazy God-bothering stepmother. All day long she casts her little spells, Jesus this, Virgin that, Sacred whatever, say nine of these, sprinkle some of this on that, hey presto. She's so busy that she doesn't even notice that none of the things she prays for ever actually happens. She doesn't *care* whether they happen, because all she wants really is something to let her walk around with her head in the clouds. And you're no different, except with you it's maths instead of prayers, and gay universes, and oh yes, in case we forget, the aliens who are going to come down and build us a spaceship before the Earth goes pop!'

On the bed, Ruprecht stares vacantly into space, his body drawn in around him.

'Skippy's dead, Blowjob! He's dead, and you can't bring him back! Not you, not every bent scientist in every laboratory in the world!' Breathing heavily, Dennis pauses, then turns his dreadful gaze on the others. 'You bummers need to get it through your heads that this is *real*. None of the stupid bullshit we do to distract ourselves is going to *help* any more. Spiderman isn't going to help. Eminem isn't going to help. Some fucking gay lame tinfoil time machine isn't going to help. All that stuff is over, don't you see? He's dead! He's dead, and he's going to stay dead for ever!'

'Stop saying that!' Ruprecht gasps.

'Dead,' chants Dennis, 'deado, deadsville, deadorama, dead-ington –'

'I mean it!'

'Dead-dead-dead,' to the tune of 'La Marseillaise', 'dead-de-de *dead*-dead-dead, dead-de –'

Ruprecht rises from the bed and, inflating himself like one of those Japanese pufferfish, to surprisingly alarming effect, hurls himself at Dennis. The latter throws a punch that lams directly into Ruprecht's midriff, but his fist simply gets lost in the folds of Ruprecht's flab; a split-second expression of horror crosses his face before he is bowled over and disappears underneath his antagonist, who proceeds to bounce on top of him like a malevolent Buddha.

'Stop, stop!' Geoff cries. 'Come on, you're hurting him!'

It takes all four of them to haul Ruprecht away. Dragging himself up from the floor, Dennis dusts himself down and, with white cheeks, levels a maledictive finger: 'Skippy's dead, Blowjob. Even if your stupid plans ever worked, it'd still be too late. So stop getting everybody's hopes up for nothing.' With that he hobbles out of the room.

As soon as he's gone, the others cluster around Ruprecht to sympathize and reassure: 'Don't listen to him, Ruprecht,' 'Tell us the rest of your plan, Ruprecht.'

But Ruprecht won't say anything, and after a while, one by one, they drift away.

When they have gone, Ruprecht lies for a long time on his duvet, Optimus Prime, leader of the Autobots, held loosely in his hands. On the other side of the room, the empty bed, its sheets turned down, crisp and hospital-white, roars at him like a locomotive.

The sun has set long ago, and the only light in the room now comes from the computer screen, where SETI diligently chomps through the barrage of unintelligible noise that hits the Earth every second, searching for anything that might resemble a pattern. For some minutes Ruprecht watches from his bed as the bars file across the screen and drop off the far side. Then he rises, and shuts the computer down.

The School Board sits in conclave for almost three hours before Brother Jonas knocks on the door of his fourth-year class and summons Howard to the Acting Principal's office.

Tom's is the only face not to turn his way when he enters. As well as Father Green, the Automator and Father Boland, the school president – one of those sleek, silver-haired, ageless men who manage to connote prestige and power without ever having expressed a single memorable thought – there are two men Howard does not know. One is a priest, small and gaunt, with a foxy, Jesuitical cast of features and a mobile jaw that works constantly, as though chewing some indigestible foodstuff; the other, an innocuous balding man in rimless glasses, perhaps forty. Brother Jonas hovers by the door; Trudy, the only woman in the room, brandishes her pen and minute-pad expectantly.

'Well, before anything else, let's make sure we're all reading from the same page here,' the Automator announces heavily. 'Howard, do you have anything you want to add, subtract or modify, with regard to the statement you made this morning?'

Seven pairs of eyes bore into him. 'No,' Howard says.

'Because these are very serious allegations you're making,' the Automator warns.

'They aren't allegations, Greg. I passed on to you exactly what Tom . . . what was said to me by Mr Roche last night.'

This meets with a cold silence; the silver-haired president permits himself a slight shake of the head. Howard flushes. 'Are you suggesting I shouldn't have passed it on? Are you suggesting I should have listened to him confess a crime and then clapped him on the shoulder and sent him home right as rain, is that it?'

'No one's suggesting anything, Howard,' the Automator snaps.

'Let's all try to keep a professional attitude here.' Eyes closed, he massages his temples a moment, then says, 'Okay. Let's go over this one more time. Trudy?'

Rising from her chair, Trudy arranges her papers and reads, in a clear, neutral voice, Howard's account of his adventure of last night: how at some time between eleven and twelve he had opened the door to find Mr Roche there in an agitated state; how Mr Roche told him, after he'd brought him in and made him tea, that the night of the junior swimming team's meet in Thurles, Daniel Juster had come to his hotel room suffering from pains in his leg; how after Mr Roche had treated him manually for cramps the boy became upset and told him that his mother, who had been supposed to attend the meet, was extremely ill; how Juster had grown more and more distressed until Mr Roche made the decision to give him a sedative in the form of painkillers that he carried to treat his spine injury. Shortly afterwards the boy lost consciousness from the effects of the painkillers, at which point Mr Roche sexually molested him.

'"Apart from a panic attack on the bus back to Seabrook the following day, for which he gave him another sedative, Mr Roche told me that the boy showed no signs of being aware of what had happened. But then last Wednesday, three days before the junior team's semi-final meet in Ballinasloe, Juster wrote him a letter telling him he was leaving the swimming team. Mr Roche grew alarmed. He contacted Juster's father and persuaded him to discourage the boy from quitting. Juster's mother's health was precarious and he knew the boy was afraid of doing or saying anything that might upset her. His father called Juster and at that point the boy agreed to go along to the meet. Shortly afterwards, however, he overdosed on painkillers."' Trudy, as she concludes, cannot resist raising her lowered eyes for a swift left-right sweep, with the satisfaction of a pupil who has performed her lesson well.

'You're happy with that?' the Automator puts to Howard.

'I'm not *happy* with it . . .' Howard mutters. The Automator switches to his neighbour. 'Tom?'

Tom says nothing; a tear slides like a raindrop down his stony cheek. There is a collective sighing and creak of chairs. The little foxy man takes a fob from his pocket, fogs the glass with his breath and buffs it with his cuff, aspirating, 'Dear, dear, dear.'

The Automator folds his brow in his hand. Emerging blinking, he says, 'Jesus Christ, Tom, were you planning to do it again? Were you bringing him down there to do it again?'

'No!' Tom blurts. 'No.' He does not look up. 'I wanted to show him that it was all right. That was why I wanted him to go. If this time it was all right . . . it might be as if . . . the last time never . . .' He dissolves into sobs. 'I didn't mean for this to happen,' he gurgles. 'I loved that boy. I love all my boys.'

The Automator considers this impassively, his mouth a tight line. Then, turning to the table at large, he says, 'Well, look, we need to decide what the hell we're going to do here.' There is a general susurrus of papers and trouser legs. 'I'm not a man of the cloth, I don't have a direct line to God, so it could be I'm all wrong about this. But what I'm thinking is that there is not much to be gained by taking it to the next level.'

'By the next level, you mean turning it over to the police?' Father Green clarifies in his arch manner. At the word, Tom lets out a moan and reburies his face in his hands.

'That's exactly what I mean, Father. The plain fact of it is, the boy is dead. There is nothing we can do to change that. If we could turn back time, we would. But we can't. And at the risk of sounding cynical, I think we have to ask ourselves now how it would serve any of us, and I include in that the boy's family, to bring the police into this. The benefits, as I see them, are pretty few. On the other hand, the cost, to the school as well as to his family, would be enormous.'

Howard starts. 'Wait, are you proposing we just brush this under the carpet?'

'Damn it, Howard, just listen to me for five seconds, can't you? There's more to think of here than just some abstract notion of justice. This kind of thing can *ruin* a school. I've seen it happen.

Even as it is I've got four sets of parents threatening to pull out their kids. This comes out and they'll leave in their droves. Every boy who's ever stubbed his toe here'll be filing a lawsuit. As for the media, they'll have a field day. They've been waiting a lifetime for something like this. We'll be lucky if we're left with so much as a blackboard by the end of it. So before you get up on your high horse, you tell me, Howard, who gains, exactly, from dragging this whole thing into the open? Juster's parents? You think this is going to help them at all? His sick mother? Or the boys, think it'll be good for them?'

Howard does not reply, just scowls.

'When these matters arose in the past–' the foxy, delicate priest, when he speaks, has exactly the voice that Howard would have guessed: high and feminine, dry and friable as tissue-paper '– we always found it more satisfactory to handle them in private.'

'I agree with Father Casey here,' the Automator says. 'It seems to me that the best way to deal with this is internally, through our own existing disciplinary channels.'

'As we started, so shall we go on, is that it?' Father Green addresses the dapper little man, who only laughs mirthlessly and places a hand on his companion's knee.

'Ah, Jerome, if it were up to you who of us would not be clapped in irons?'

Something grotesque about his laughter sets off a trigger inside Howard; while the conversation flows back and forth around him, he stumbles unhearing through it, nauseous and dizzy as if he's been drugged, until he sees his own hand rising in front of him and hears his voice say, 'Wait, wait . . . a boy is dead. Juster is *dead*. It doesn't matter what the school has to gain or not gain. We can't let –' absurdly, he turns to Tom here '– no offence, Tom – but we can't just let this . . . go.'

The silver-haired president starts making noises about reviews and hearings and sanctions, but the Automator hushes him with a hand: 'Howard –'

'He's right,' Father Green interjects.

'Excuse me, Father, he's not right – Howard, no one's saying we're letting this go. No one's saying we should forget about Juster. But if Tom goes to trial it'll be a kangaroo court and you know it. They'll send him down without a second thought even though the facts are in actuality far from clear –'

'The facts are perfectly clear, Greg, he made a full confession.'

'I mean the facts, the circumstances of Daniel Juster's death. We don't know what was going through that kid's mind, we'll never know. Who of us can say for certain that these events that took place involving Tom were finally and definitively what pushed him over the edge? We know that he had other things bothering him. His sick mother, for instance, and this girl, this business with the girl.'

'Yes, but –'

'And the fact of the matter is that these pills that Tom allegedly gave him, there's a question mark over whether he had any awareness at all of what happened, so setting aside the rights and the wrongs of it, can we genuinely –'

'Jesus, Greg, he took him into his room and drugged him and abused him, how can you even –'

'You settle down there!' the Automator cuts him off. 'Settle down, mister. Here at Seabrook, we judge a man by the sum of his actions, the *sum*. In this case we have a man with an unparalleled dedication to this school and to the boys of this school. Does one error of judgement, however grievous, does that cancel out at a stroke all the good he's done? The good of that care?'

'An error of judgement?' Howard says, dumbfounded.

'That's right, any one of us –'

'An *error* of *judgement*?'

'That's what I said, damn it,' the Automator bellows, flaring brick-red. 'You had one of your own, or don't you remember? Three and a half million pounds down the swanny in under a minute – under a *minute*! When you came here you were the laughing stock of the City of London! Unemployable! But who took you in? Who took you in when no one else would? This school, that's who, because we look after our own! That's what *care* means!'

'How the hell –' Howard on his feet '– does losing money compare with physically drugging and abusing –'

'I'll tell you how!' the Automator rising too to tower above him. 'You take a look at this man, Howard! Before you start laying blame, you take a good look at him! This man was a hero! This man was going to be one of the all-time sporting greats of his country! Instead, he's a cripple, in constant physical pain, because of you! Because of your cowardice! You talk about justice. If there were any justice, you would have been at the bottom of that quarry, not him!' This silences Howard all right. Beside the Acting Principal, the president nods ruefully. 'Any other man, that kind of blow he might have retreated into his shell for ever. Not Tom Roche. Instead he has devoted himself to the education of these boys. I would even argue – you won't like it, but I would even argue that it's his very devotion that has led him to make this terrible mistake. But that's beside the point, which is, when he tried to do the right thing, when he came to *you* of all people and confessed – when otherwise, no one would ever have found out – you just want to have him strung up! Well, let me tell you, you're up to your neck in this too!'

'*Me?*'

'I sent you to talk to Juster. This is a troubled boy, I said, go and talk to him, and you came back with diddly-squat!'

'Was I supposed to hold a gun to his head? Was I supposed to hold a gun to his head, and say, Okay, Juster, start talking –'

'Daniel,' Tom mumbles.

'What's that?' The Automator snaps round.

'He preferred to be called Daniel,' Tom, tilted forward awkwardly in his chair like a classical sculpture in transit, repeats through a patina of tears and mucus.

The men lapse into a simmering silence.

'The question is, how difficult would it be to keep the matter internal?' the foxy priest remarks eventually. 'From what I hear, the boy's father doesn't seem the type to cause trouble.'

'Is he one of ours?' the jowly president inquires blandly.

'Class of '84,' the Automator says. 'Went in for tennis mostly. Pretty decent team back then. Yes, he's got enough on his plate with the wife's cancer, I'd say.'

'Nevertheless, it might be to our benefit to be seen pursuing some definite line of inquiry,' the foxy priest counsels.

'Well, he was upset about this girl,' the president says. 'Isn't that the perfect alibi right there?'

'I don't want to encourage this Romeo and Juliet claptrap,' the Automator says. 'Otherwise they'll all be at it like lemmings.'

'The mother might be the angle to take, then,' the foxy priest says.

'That'd be my preference. Mum's dying, boy can't take it, game over. Press haven't found out about her yet. We can throw them a few hints, at this end amp up the counselling service, maybe.' He makes a note on a pad. 'Well, gentlemen, I think we're all agreed that the best thing is to sit tight. If Desmond Furlong were here, I'm sure he'd say the same.' The board members around the table nod donkey-like, with the exception of Father Green, whose head is cocked at a contemplative angle, as if he's savouring the fragrance of a spring meadow, and the unknown bald man, who catches the Automator's eye.

'Oh yes, that's right . . .' He rummages among the papers on his desk and locates a slim sheaf of three or four pages. He holds it out to Howard. 'This is Vyvyan Wycherley, Howard, old classmate of mine. He and Father Casey here have drawn this up for you to sign.'

'What is it?'

'It's your new contract. I'm pleased to offer you a position as Seabrook's first-ever school archivist. Runs concurrently with your existing teaching duties. Money's not enormous, but tidy enough all the same. Work the hours you want, whatever particular areas take your fancy . . .'

Howard flicks dumbly through the pages – job description, salary, and then, near the back, his eye catches on a short paragraph –

'It's a confidentiality clause. No doubt you'll be familiar with these from your days in the City. In signing, you consent by law not to disclose sensitive information pertaining to school affairs, including what we have discussed here today.'

Howard gapes back at him stupidly. 'Are you serious?'

'Merely a precaution, Howard, making sure we've got all our angles covered. No need to rush into it right away. Take it home with you, think it over. If you want to turn it down, do the honorable thing, I can't stop you. I'm sure you'll find a position elsewhere easily enough. Gather there are vacancies in St Anthony's at the moment. Teacher got stabbed there just last week.'

'I can't believe you're doing this to me, Greg,' Howard says softly.

'Like I say, Howard, it's up to you. Here at Seabrook we take care of each other. Play by the rules, listen to your captain, and we'll always find a place on the team for you. But if you can't stick by your school when it has a bad bounce of the ball, why should it stick by you?'

With numb fingers, Howard leafs again through the pages of dense, recondite text till he arrives at the last, where he sees his own name, with a line above it for his signature, and the date already added. He can feel the surreptitious and lowered gazes on him, pressing against him like bodies in a crowded elevator.

In the closeness Father Green's voice rings out like a bell, in a merry sing-song: 'And will *God* be apprised of what has taken place?'

An irritated mutter passes around the table. The priest re-phrases his question. 'I am merely asking, as a matter of protocol, whether on the Last Day, when God demands of us our sins, our confidentiality agreement requires that we keep silent then too?'

'With all due respect, Father –' the Automator visibly annoyed '– now is not the time.'

'You are quite right, of course,' Father Green agrees. 'I daresay we shall have plenty of opportunity to consider it, when we are condemned to eternal hellfire.'

The quick-eyed, foxy priest turns to him exasperated. 'Why must you always be so *medieval*?'

'Because this is *sin*!' The priest's bony hand pounds on the table so that the teacups in their saucers and the plastic biros jump, and a raging eye roves over the table to fix each of them in turn. 'It is *sin*,' he repeats, 'a most egregious sin against an innocent child! We may hide it from ourselves with our nice talk of the good of the many. But we cannot hide it from the Lord God!'

For the rest of the day, while school continues at some invisible remove, Howard wanders alone in a clammy, evil fog. Farley asks if he wants to go for a drink after work, and Howard can barely look him in the eye. With every moment he feels the secret worming deeper into him, making itself at home, like some monstrous parasite.

When these matters arose in the past: the words spoken so casually, a parent explaining the change of seasons to a child. Is this what he's been living in all along? Old stories rise up from the depths of his mind – the straying hands of this priest, the sadistic tendencies of another, doors that were kept locked, eyes that lingered for too long in the changing room. Stories, though; stories were all he'd ever taken them for, idle gossip made up to pass the time, like everything in Seabrook. Because otherwise how could those men still be walking around? Wearing Pentecostal doves in their lapels? Surely at that level of hypocrisy God or whoever would be compelled to swing into action! Now it's as if a panel has been slid back and he's glimpsed the secret machinery of the world, the grown-up world, in which matters arise – hotel doors are pushed open, pills are dropped into glasses of Coke, bodies are laid bare, while outside life goes on oblivious – and are dispatched again, by small cadres of men in rooms, the priests in their conclave, the Automator and his legal team, it doesn't really make any difference. A little white lie for the common good. That's how we keep it on the road.

His last period is free; today he doesn't feel like staying around, so he gathers his things and makes his way out. At home he unsheathes the contract from its envelope and lays it on the table, from where it seems to glow at him, polar-white.

Halley's phone rings out three times before she answers it. When she does it's a shock to hear her voice – outside his own head, independent of his memory. He realizes he's imagined her suspended in some atemporal state; only now does it hit him that in the moment before his call, and all the moments before that for the last weeks, she's been doing other things, living through days that he knows nothing about, just as before he met her there were thousands more days as real to her as the hand before her face that he will never have an inkling of, in which he never figured even as an idea.

'Howard?'

'Yes.' He hasn't planned out what he was going to say. 'It's been a while,' he manages finally. 'How are you? How have you been?'

'I'm fine.'

'Are you still staying with Cat? Is it okay?'

'It's fine.'

'And work, how's that going, it's all . . . ?'

'Work's fine. What do you want, Howard?'

'I just wanted to see how you were.'

'Well, I'm fine,' she says. The ensuing silence has the conclusive air of a raised guillotine.

'Me too,' Howard says miserably. 'Although I don't know if you heard, we've had some trouble at the school, this boy, he was in my History class . . .'

'I heard.' The ice in her voice melts, if only fractionally. 'I'm sorry.'

'Thanks.' He has an impulse to tell her everything, about Coach, the Board meeting, the confidentiality clause. But at the last second he recoils, not sure it'll do him any favours at this point to show her the contaminated world he's living in. Instead he blurts out, 'I made a mistake. That's what I called to say. I've been a fool. I've done such terrible things. I hurt you. I'm sorry, Halley, I'm so sorry.'

A single word, 'Okay,' like a barren atoll in the oceanic silence.

'Well, I mean, what do you think?'

'What do I think?'

'Can you forgive me?' Spoken out loud the question sounds laughably misjudged, as if he'd started quoting *Casablanca* at her. Halley doesn't laugh, though. 'What about your other woman?' she says in an indifferent, uninflected voice. 'Have you checked this with her?'

'Oh,' he waves his hand dismissively, as if the past were a smoky image that could be dispelled at a stroke. 'That's over. It wasn't anything. It wasn't real.'

She doesn't reply. Pacing distractedly back and forth over the room, he says, 'I want to try again, Halley. I've been thinking – we could get out of here. Start over somewhere else. Back to the States even, we could get married, and move back to the States. To New York. Or wherever you wanted to go.'

In fact this is a plan he has thought of only now – but as he speaks it sounds so perfect! A new, committed life, somewhere far away from Seabrook! In one fell swoop all their problems would be solved!

But when she answers, although a measure of affection has returned to it, her voice sounds sorrowful and weary. 'When your hand's in the fire, right?'

'What?'

She sighs. 'You're always looking for ways out of things, Howard. Escape routes out of your own life. That's why you liked me, because I wasn't from here, and I seemed to offer something new. When I stopped being new, you slept with that woman, whoever she was. Now because you don't have me I look like a way out again. You have something to aim for, you have a quest to get me back. But don't you see, if you did get me back the quest would be over and you'd be bored again.'

'I wouldn't,' he says.

'How do you know that?'

'Because it'll be different, because I *feel* different.'

'It can't just be feelings. How can I trust my life to a feeling?'

'What else is there?'

'There has to be something,' she says. He can't think of anything to say to this, and while he is searching about, she speaks again. 'The point is that life isn't a quest, Howard. And it's not the kind of fire you can take your hand out of. You need to accept that, and start dealing with it.'

The hostility has dropped from her voice now and her tone is the plaintive mixture of urgency and pity of someone trying to save a self-destructive friend. Howard waits for a moment after she has finished talking and then says softly, 'And what about us?'

The hum of the empty phone line is like a knife twisting between his ribs.

'I don't know, Howard,' she says at last, in a small sad voice. 'I need time. I need a little bit of time to work out where I'm going. I'll call you in a little while, okay?'

'Okay.'

'Okay. Take care, Howard. Bye.' The line clicks dead.

The day after the Board meeting, Father Green fails to arrive for his morning classes. The official word is that he's been taken ill, but this is confuted almost instantly by a sighting of the priest lugging boxes down Our Lady's Hall, hale and hearty, or as hale and hearty as he ever is. He doesn't turn up for his afternoon classes either, and then the news emerges – from no particular source, it's just *there*, floating in the ether – that he has retired from teaching to concentrate on his charity work.

This is greeted with incredulity. The priest's loathing of the French language, and indeed of his students, has never been too closely disguised; still, most expected that he would keep teaching until he died, if only in order to spite them, and perhaps himself too (of those, more than a few privately believed he would never actually die). But now, just like that, he's gone, and right in the middle of term-time; although of course he's still there, carrying in deliveries for his hampers, carrying out hampers to his car, making runs to St Patrick's Villas and the bleak housing estates to the north and west of the city.

All very strange and sudden; and then someone remembers that on the day Skippy died he'd been in Father Green's office packing hampers, and they put two and two together.

'What do you mean?'

'Well, duh, what do you think? After a million years' teaching he's just quit overnight, with no one to replace him? There's no way they'd let him do that unless some serious shit was going down.'

'Yeah, and remember it was like that actual *day*, and there was no one there except Skippy and Cujo . . .'

'Holy shit . . .'

'But wait, come on, if he did do it, they'd hardly just let him get away with it, would they?'

A moment's thought elicits the realization that this is *exactly* the kind of thing They would do. The more the boys think about it, the more they see Father Green making his rounds, with his eternal air of impassive rectitude, of existing on some higher spiritual plane in which they feature as free-roaming coagulations of dirt, the more the rumour crystallizes into certainty.

'This is bollocks,' Geoff Sproke, fists clenched, avows for the umpteenth time. 'This is total fucking bollocks.'

It is total bollocks; but who's going to do anything about it? Geoff, who cried at the end of *Free Willy 2*? Niall, always cast as the heroine in school plays? Bob Shambles, with his collection of naturally occurring hexagons? Victor Hero, probably the least aptly named boy in history?

No, not them, and not Ruprecht either. Ruprecht's mouth is usually full of doughnut these days, and even in those rare moments when he is not eating, he has little to say. He does not scribble equations on scraps of paper; he does not check the computer for signals from outer space; the upstretched Ruprecht arm, a landmark for so many teachers, disappears from the classroom horizon, and when Lurch gets stuck solving a problem, he merely watches, chewing his gum impassively as the maths teacher gets more agitated and the jumble of wrong numbers sprawls gradually over the entire board. It's the same when someone calls him a shithead or kicks his arse or punches him in the back of the head; he will stumble but not fall down, and, righting himself, continue on his way without so much as turning round.

The rest of the gang might well have found these developments worrying, and possibly even done something about it: the thing is, though, there does not seem to be a gang any more. Without anything actually being said, they have relocated themselves to opposite sides of the classroom; after lunch, bolted as quickly as its noxiousness will allow, Mario now plays football in the yard, while Dennis and Niall have taken up smoking cigarettes with Larry Bambkin and Eamon Sweenery by the lake in Seabrook Park, and Geoff has succumbed at last to the lure of Lucas Rexroth's role-playing group, and spends his lunch hour exploring the dread Mines of Mythia in the guise of Mejisto the Elf. When their paths do cross, in the corridor or the Study Hall or the Rec Room, they feel embarrassed without quite knowing why; the not-knowing makes them feel more embarrassed still, and resentful of the other for making them feel this way, and so before long they go from avoiding to actively persecuting each other – flicking ears, mocking peccadilloes, spilling to third parties secrets entrusted in happier times, e.g. Dennis in the Ref the other evening, 'Hey, everyone, know what Geoff's afraid of? Jelly!', brandishing a gelatinous bowl at him as Geoff squeaks and cringes. 'What's the matter, Geoff? Too *wobbly* for you?', till Geoff, pushed past the brink, blurts out, 'Dennis's stepmum isn't his stepmum, she's his real mum, he just pretends she isn't because he hates her!' Stunned silence from Dennis, giggles and jeers from Mitchell Gogan and the others at his table, though ultimately they don't care either way.

It's as if Skippy had been one of those insignificant-looking pins that it turns out holds the whole machine together; or maybe it's that each of them is secretly blaming the others for saying or doing something that brought this whole thing down on them, or not saying or not doing something that might have stopped it. Whatever the reason, the less they see of each other, the better, and Ruprecht, who was always more Skippy's friend than theirs anyway, is allowed to continue on his downward spiral without interruption.

But not without parallel. Someone else is exhibiting very similar symptoms, although the two of them being at opposite ends of the academic register, nobody seems to have noticed. Carl's catatonia, of course, is merely the latest phase in a long process of disconnection; unlike Ruprecht's, furthermore, it is shot through with a constant stream of tics and twitches – darting eyes, glances over his shoulder, jumping at shadows. But in their walk, the two are identical: they drag their heavy bodies through the corridors like wax effigies, not to say dead men.

For all that, some shade of normality seems to have been restored in the school. Classes resume, tests are given, games played; the story fades from the news, and Skippy from the forefront of memory, to be visited only in obscure asides of conversation as a fatal example of getting it wrong: 'It's like Tupac said, G – money before bitches.' 'Word up.'

'Life goes on, Howard,' the Automator says. 'We all carry a piece of Juster with us in our hearts, and we always will. But you have to keep moving forward. That's what life's all about. And that's what these boys are doing. I have to say I'm proud of them.' He turns to the younger man. 'I'm proud of you too, Howard. You made a tough decision there. Took real maturity and strength of character. But I knew you had it in you.'

The night before, Howard signed the contract. He is not quite sure why – a definitive act of self-sabotage? A final, comprehensive extinguishing of his hopes? He doesn't care to investigate too closely. Instead, he makes the rounds of his new life, taking a perverse pleasure in the guilt that aches in his jaw like a rotten tooth from one end of the day to the next. Sitting in the staffroom, he envies the other teachers their inane small talk, their old jokes, their gripes and whinges, as a world that is lost to him. He envies Father Green too, and as he leaves on his missions, Howard sometimes has urges to hop into the car with him, to Help Out, do something good. But in their wordless encounters on the corridor the priest's contempt is all-conquering.

As for Tom Roche, Howard can barely turn round these days without bumping into him. It has been decided that he should be moved elsewhere, away from Ireland, just to be on the safe side; but while the Board seeks out a suitable position, he will continue to take classes and to coach the swimming team as though nothing had happened. And he does so, quite convincingly; and that too, Howard thinks, must take maturity and strength of character.

Lori is coping with Personal Tragedy. At school she doesn't make a big thing out of it – instead she acts like the same old Lori, she smiles and laughs just like always and it's only if you're really paying attention that you'll notice she's a tiny bit quieter, a tiny bit paler, and sometimes she'll look away, out the window, and a sort of sadness will cross her face? But Mom and Dad are really worried about her. They keep leaving little presents in her bedroom for when she gets home, and then on Saturday Mom said they were going on a Girlie Day Out – just the three of them, Mom, Lori and the credit card! They got their hair done and had facials and went to Brown Thomas and bought shoes, it was so much fun! But then when they were in the café Lori's mom put her hand on Lori's and said, Oh honey, and Lori saw tears coming down from behind her sunglasses and she started crying too and the two of them hugged and cried, all the other women in the café must have thought they were crazy!

He was a very sweet boy but he had problems, Mom said when they had finished crying. Your dad was talking to the Seabrook Principal, who is a very good friend of his, and he said unfortunately this was a boy with a lot of problems. There are people like that in the world and what you have to accept is that you can only help them up to a point, and after that there's nothing more you can do. And – Mom started to sniff again – baby, I know it seems impossible now, but some day your heart will heal and you'll be able to love someone new?

And for a second Lori felt a warm mochaccino glow rising up from her stomach but then Mom said that Dad wanted her to see a child psychologist and the feeling turned sickly cold. A child psychologist poking around in her brain, wanting to find everything out? Telling Mom and Dad what really happened? For a second Lori thought she was going to puke right there on the table, but then Mom said, But I told him I didn't think it was necessary because you've been coping very well on your own, all things considered. You've been so brave, she said, I'm so proud of you, and then she started talking about the woman from the modelling agency who called up after seeing the pictures of Lori in the paper and wanted her to come in. We should really get you a new outfit, Mom said, and also maybe go to the dentist and have your teeth whitened, you only get one chance with these people.

Mostly the teachers and nuns and girls in her year have been really nice to her, but of course, like BETH⟨a⟩nꙇ says, wherever there is someone who is getting attention or enjoying success you will find haters and people who try to bring them down with negativity, e.g. like yesterday when she overheard Mirabelle Zaoum saying, Oh God, all it takes to be a big star in this school is for some loser to write your name on a *floor*. Janine says, You can't let them get to you, Lori, and she made Lori a card that read, *Never frown even when ur sad, coz u never know whose falling in love with ur smile!* And it's true! So as she goes through the school doors into the buzzing swarming nest of blue-uniformed girls it's with a big smile for everyone, ☺☺☺!

Janine's the only person she reveals her true feelings to. If you don't know her Janine can seem like a bitch, but underneath it all she has the giantest heart. She wanted so much to help Carl and Lori get back together, it wasn't her fault the Plan didn't work out, and ever since what happened she has been the best best friend anyone could ever ask for. Lori would be so happy if Janine could find someone to love – underneath her tough exterior that's all she really wants! And she looks amazing these days, like she's totally lost that little you wouldn't call it a spare tyre but anyhow it's mostly totally gone? Still, Lori's glad to have her to herself until everything gets back to normal.

Today at lunchtime they go up to the mall. Denise and Janine

500

are talking about KellyAnn, she is totally wrecking everybody's head talking about her stupid baby, you'd think she'd be embarrassed about it but instead she can't shut up and she keeps putting on this wise old woman voice like speaking in this *slllooooooowwwwww soooooffffffft* way, like she knows something you don't just because she got drunk and let that gimp Titch Fitzpatrick get her up the duff.

I wouldn't mind so much except she keeps trying to give me like relationship advice? Denise says.

Me too, Janine says, I'm like, KellyAnn, you've totally ruined your life, the day I need advice from you just put a bag over my head and shoot me.

What do you think will happen when Sister Benedict finds out? Do you think she'll be expelled?

I don't know, Janine says, but if KellyAnn had any cop at all she'd be saving her money for a little holiday.

Lori is shocked. You mean go for an abortion?

There's no way she'll get an abortion, Denise says.

What else is she going to do with it?

Well, maybe Titch will help her take care of it?

Janine laughs. Have you ever met Titch's mother? She's like Godzilla in drag. There's no way she's going to let her precious Tom-Tom's life go down the tubes just because some slutty Brigid's girl couldn't keep her knickers on.

I heard she just gave him a BJ, Denise says.

You can't get pregnant from a BJ, Janine says.

I know this girl whose sister's friend gave this boy a BJ and then she got pregnant even though she was a virgin.

Did she spit it out? Janine asks.

I don't know, Denise says.

And it's so weird, one moment Lori's listening to her friends and the next she's on the ground and the shops on the mezzanine are whirling around her head like bluebirds in those old cartoons when the coyote gets whacked with an anvil or something.

Oh my God, oh my God, Denise flaps above her like a skinny

bird. Janine is crouched down beside her. Oh sweetie! A security guard appears and looks down with dark-brown hair and a kind stupid face. Is she OK? he asks in a voice like Lilya's. She's fine, Janine says, she just needs some air. He moves in closer. She's *fine*, Janine snaps and the guy cringes away like a dog you've thrown a stone at. Sweetie, she murmurs again and hugs her and for a moment Lori can hide in the warm friendly darkness, the Janine-smell she knows so well. But then everything comes down on her again, the day the night the Plan, she knew it wouldn't work the moment she called him, the moment Daniel answered the phone she knew it was a bad idea, lying to him like that felt wrong, it made her angry, and he kept asking her questions – What's wrong? How long have you had it? Do you have a temperature? – so she had to lie more and more when she just wanted him to go, and she felt so awful but she is a terrible person because then the second Carl appeared she forgot about Daniel completely, everything that usually made up Lori like memories and things she liked was instantly washed away and it was just her and Carl walking through the park, he looked so sad I missed you he said it was the first time he'd ever said anything like that she started to cry and then when he held her to cry and laugh at the same time I missed you too and that was just the beginning because then next he started to talk like really talk in a way he never did before like about how he didn't think she cared about him he thought she was in love with Daniel How could he think that when he knew about Janine's Plan but he did he thought she didn't love him not like I love you he said oh my God but I do love you I love you I love you but he didn't think she did because she wouldn't have sex that doesn't have anything to do with it she said but he wouldn't believe her that's why she did it the doughnut shop roof was sore against her knees the doughnut was like a giant halo round his head he kept saying I love you she felt like she was drunk with happiness his thing tasted strange but not terrible but it was weird the way it moved in her mouth like it was alive a little blind creature she liked the feel of his hands in her hair but then he shot the stuff and he wouldn't let her take it out and it was going down her throat it kept coming not letting her breathe it was like she was drowning and then she saw what he was doing oh my God why Carl why she couldn't get the phone from him he was shouting she broke free and jumped down from the roof she twisted her ankle and had to run all the way home on it she was crying and when Mom asked her why she had to say Amy Doran's cat got run over and when Mom tried to hug her she wouldn't let her because she was worried she might smell the stuff she couldn't get the taste out of her mouth she could feel it on the back of her teeth all slimy she used up a whole bottle of mouthwash it didn't do any good and the next thing Mom calls her down from her room and Daniel is there holding a frisbee why did he bring a frisbee in winter he always did everything weird like that like texting her poems that don't even rhyme but anyway he's looking at her all white with big round eyes and she knows that he's seen the video and maybe she could have just pretended nothing happened he would have believed her but before he can even say anything before she even knows what she's doing she starts screaming at him, screaming at the top of her lungs Get out, get out, fuck off, what's your problem, I never ever ever want to see you again, screaming and screaming the most horrible things that came into her head loud as she could till Dad came out and put his arms around her and told him it was probably best if he went and he was looking back at her dad like he didn't know where he was and she turned round and ran up to her room and next thing Kelly-Ann is calling her crying from the doughnut shop and then there are police cars outside her house and I am so sorry, I am so sorry, Daniel I am so so sorry! But she still knew in the middle of everything she wasn't going to tell them about Carl.

And now Zora Carpathian is calling her the Death Girl and all over the school someone keeps writing LORI L'S DANIEL 4 EVER it must be Tara Gately, she copies everything Lori does, she has all of her things, bangles, hairbands, BETHani badge on the strap of her schoolbag, she's probably never even kissed anybody herself well if she wants to be her so much Lori wishes she could just let her, say to her okay you can be Lori and see how you like it and I'll be nobody I'll just be some air in the sky up where nobody can breathe it but then what would she do about CarlCarlCarlCarl

They are back in the toilets in school. Janine is wiping Lori's eyes and cheeks. Denise and Aifric Quinlavan are smoking cigarettes and talking about boys. Would you do it if you really liked him?

I wouldn't ever like someone who would want me to do something like that.

They all want to do it, Aifric says, they see it on the Internet and then they want you to do it. You should see the stuff my brother has on his computer, it's totally vile.

Like what sort of stuff?

Like, you know, men spraying their, you know, on girls' faces? Like their semen?

Ewww, that's so gross!

Or sticking their thing up your arse.

There's no way I'm ever doing that, Denise says. Like why would anyone want to do that?

You can't get pregnant, Janine says. If they shag you up the arse it means you can't get pregnant.

How romantic, Denise says.

It's like going to the toilet in reverse, Aifric says. It's fucking sick, I don't care.

He tried to talk to Lori at the graveyard but she ran away from him. She blocked his calls from her mobile and he hangs up whenever Dad picks up the house phone. At night she can feel him outside in the dark under the trees looking up at her window, and a part of her wants to go out to him in spite of everything. But Janine says, Stay away from him. She says he tried to talk to her too, after school one day. What did he say? I didn't listen I just blanked him. And you should too, Lori. There's something wrong with that guy, I'm serious.

And it's true, what kind of psycho would do something like that? When he knew about the Plan, when she'd explained that it wasn't real! But inside she knows why he did it, it was because he was jealous of her and Daniel. If only he hadn't been jealous, if only he'd believed she just loved him! (Though then she thinks of Daniel's hand on her breast . . .) And she thinks of him hanging around with all those weirdo knackers selling drugs, they give her the creeps, and of his horrible dad who had sex with a girl in sixth year and his mom wandering around the house stinking of drink and chain-smoking and listening to Lionel Richie, and Carl says he doesn't care if they split up but that's why he's acting weird even for him, it's got to be, and she knows what he really needs is someone to care for him?

Janine says, He's a bad guy, Lori, I mean it. There's something missing from him. He's dangerous.

You don't know him like I do, Lori says.

Janine thinks for a minute. Maybe not, she says. But I can still tell.

And she's right, Lori knows it, he's bad, he's all fucked up, you can see it in the marks on his arms, and if her dad ever had a clue that a guy like him had gone near her she'd be sent off to boarding school in a split second because you can tell he's never going to be all right or good, and he swears and he's always in a bad mood and all he ever talked about was wanting to have sex with her like does he even really care about her but then she thinks of his teeth that are just the right amount of crooked and she thinks of his body crushing hers like a door into a world of mmmm and stuff she had never thought about before not really and now she can't stop lying in bed and her mom came in I was thinking of you I had my eyes closed oh my god I've never done that before and when you press against a body did you think it could get so hot like your skin's in flames and everything underneath like a volcano and even when you're not touching me it's like you are it's like I can see the secret fire beneath everything even if we're just standing outside McDonald's or on the roof of Ed's that time you were setting the paper planes alight and throwing them at the guy down on the ground I'd drunk a can my head was spinning I never laughed so much and then I stopped laughing and I lay my head down and looked at you and the black sky and I loved you and the air was full of burning full of sparks coming off the fiery planes full of candybursts of sugarflames of honey-fire of dreamruindisobey, I am never going home . . .

You were a million miles away, Mom says.

Thinking of your TV career, Dad says with a grin. Here is the news: Lori Wakeham is going to be famous!

It's just a screen test, Daddy, she says, they might say no.

There's no way they'll say no. Look at you, you were born to be on television! I'll tell you a secret – I always knew you were going to make it big.

Oh stop, Mom laughs, you're embarrassing her!

Seriously, the day you were born, I looked at you and I thought, This girl's got it. Star potential. Dad sits back and rests his hands behind his head. Something good may yet come out of all this, he says contentedly. And you deserve it too, after all you've been through.

She is back in her house. Mom and Dad are all excited because during the day the woman from the modelling agency called again, and a different woman from a different modelling agency, and a PRODUCER from a TV company who thinks she might be perfect for a new kids' programme they're making. Maybe Dad is right, maybe everything will work out after all. But tonight she just can't concentrate on it.

She's got this weird feeling in her stomach.

Dad is talking about some big deal going down at work, secret plans to take over another company.

'Mouth closed when we eat, darling,' Mom says. 'No one's going to let you on TV with a mouthful of chewed food.'

'Sorry,' Lori says.

It's different to earlier. Then she just felt empty. This is a definite *tingling*, like something is *alive* down there.

Lilya comes in and clears the plates. Mom tells Dad about a new kind of tan you can have injected into your skin. 'Maybe we should get Lori a salon session before her screen test . . . ?'

And now worry beats into her head, she feels it strike her temples and cheeks with each fresh wave of blood and she bows her head so Mom and Dad won't see. (*What if the stuff leaks through her stomach into her womb?*) (Don't be a spa, it doesn't work that way, you know it doesn't!) (But what if it *does?*) (But Janine said it couldn't happen just from a BJ.) (But Denise said it could.)

Oh fuck. Another crash of worry, now she feels sick and there are tears in her eyes and the Taste in her mouth and the tingling in her stomach gets stronger. Why is she only thinking of this now? Why didn't she think of it before, you can get that magic pill that Janine got that time she was with Oliver Crotty?

'It's a kids' show, they're not going to want her waltzing in like she's just arrived from St Tropez,' Dad is saying. 'They want the natural look. That's what Lori's got. Natural, fresh-faced, innocent.'

'But I'm telling you, this is how they all look these days,' Mom says. 'What if she goes for the screen test and all the other girls have tans?'

Lori is trying to remember the sex talk they had in school and what they said about getting pregnant. But all she can remember are the diagrams of the Reproductive Organs, all that equipment secretly packed in there, coiled up on itself like a bomb in a suitcase, *waiting*, and those freaky horrible words, *womb, uterine, fallopian*, that sounded like the names of aliens not her own insides . . .

'Well, let's let her decide for herself,' Mom says. 'Darling?'

'What?' Lori says.

'If you had the choice, would you rather be a model or a TV presenter? Modelling's classier, I think.'

'But TV has more exposure,' Dad points out.

'I don't know.' It's all Lori can do to mumble.

'I think it's a waste of a girl with Lori's looks to just plonk her on the television,' Mom says.

In the average ejaculation there are roughly 350 million sperms, that is another thing she remembers. 350 *million*! It's like an army, it's like a whole *country* marching through her insides – taking her over, searching for the egg – and suddenly it's like she can *see* them, in the great hollow cavern of her stomach, white slithery terrorists hiding in the shadows, waiting till nightfall to creep into other parts of her body, their tadpole-tails flickering almost too fast to see – oh God, stop or I'm going to –

And then Lilya comes in and sets a bowl down in front of Lori.

'What in God's name is this?' she hears Dad ask from a long way away.

'It's tapioca pudding,' Mom tells him. 'Remember I was telling you, about retro desserts?'

'Retro is right, I haven't eaten this in twenty years.' Dad digs his spoon into the white-grey mess and lifts it to his mouth.

'It's a bit runny . . .'

'May I be excused?' Lori says.

As soon as she's left the room she starts to run. She makes it to the bathroom just in time. Hanging over the toilet bowl she hears Sister Benedict's voice ring through her head, saying, *'Though God can do all things, He cannot raise a virgin after she has fallen'* – she sees the nuns ringed around her, staring at her big belly, they are shaking their heads and whispering *slut* to each other . . .

And Mom not saying slut but thinking it, and Dad not saying anything just going red and then walking downstairs to the gym and doing bench presses for three hours, and the woman from the TV production company saying, I'm terribly sorry, NO SLUTS. But she's not a slut, she just wanted to make him like her, she just didn't want him to think she was frigid or a lesbian! Her stomach is so sore, the muscles there are crying out, and she is crying too, the tears dripping down into the bowl like kids coming down a waterslide, and after she's finished she can still feel the things in her stomach! They're still there! And in the distance the intercom goes and she hears Mom and someone else

508

go mumble mumble mumble and then Mom's voice rings out, Lorelei!

Oh my God, who is it? She looks in the mirror, she is hideous, her eyes are all red and her cheeks too and her hair is straggly and there is snot everywhere – Lori! Mom calls again. Oh no, is it the producer? This is definitely God punishing her, though if he punishes her this way maybe he won't make her pregnant – Just a second, she calls down, and scrubs her face in the sink so it looks like she's just been washing not crying and blows her nose which some sick has got into and then puts on some lip gloss and goes downstairs.

But it's not the producer or the woman from the agency. Instead it's an extremely fat boy in a Seabrook uniform. Unless she's imagining it, he's giving her a really evil stare. In a cold *Falcon Crest*–type voice she says, Yes?

I have a message for you, goes the fat boy, and in that instant Lori feels her heart stop dead and freeze up like a ghost has wrapped its hands around it, even before the fat boy goes on, From Skippy. She looks down at Mom hoping she'll say, I'm sorry, dear, we're having dinner. But Mom has already gone back into the dining room.

Come upstairs, she says to him in a low voice.

Some fat people though not actually attractive can look cuddly or jolly. That's not the kind of fat he is. As he climbs towards her he gasps for air. The stairs groan under his feet and when he reaches the top he has sweat on his forehead.

She leads him into her bedroom, where he peers around at everything like he's never been in a girl's room before, which is quite likely. Were you one of Daniel's friends? she asks, slipping off her scrunchie and swinging out her lustrous black hair. I was his room-mate in school, he says, studying the pictures on her wall, the horses, BETHani and her boyfriend. It was so terrible, what happened to him, she says devoutly. He does not say anything to this, just releases a kind of a hiss, like steam from a pressure cooker. Suddenly she feels sick again. She wishes he would go. What was the message he wanted you to give to me?

He wanted me to tell you he loved you, the fat boy says. He says it levelly, icily, like a teacher telling you that you'll never amount to anything. It was his last wish, the fat boy says.

I know that, she says.

Now he's dead, the boy says.

Lori flushes. She doesn't like that word being said in her room. She considers asking him to leave but another part of her is advising her to tread carefully, be diplomatic.

The boy has sunk into a chair and flops there motionlessly, staring at the floor. There is a black anger radiating from him.

Was there anything else? she says coldly, the way her mother speaks to shop assistants.

The boy doesn't respond. He keeps clenching and unclenching his fat fists. Then in a low mean voice he says, It was you in that video.

Lori flinches. What? she says.

It was you on the doughnut shop roof. You and Carl.

I don't know what you're talking about, Lori says in a steely voice.

You pretended to love him, the boy goes on, so you and Carl could play this trick. And now he's dead.

SHE DOES NOT LIKE THAT WORD BEING SAID, she does not like it, and in a flash she knows that Carl is outside and all she has to do is cry out and then the fat boy would know all about dead. But instead she says, Nothing you are saying makes any sense to me.

With that the fat boy erupts, his moon-like face screws into a horrible mask of hate, and he shouts, You lied to him! You kissed him, you made him think you cared about him, you used him!

That isn't true! Lori finds her whole body is shaking, maybe vibrating in time with the fat boy, who is wobbling like a jelly made out of explosives, his face a big swollen blackcurrant. But then he becomes quite still. He stares into her eyes and he whispers, You are an evil person. You are a person who pretends to love people so you can control them. But you don't care about anyone except yourself.

Lori wants to shout That isn't true! again but she can't because she is wondering if it is true and for a second the guilt-wave knocks her backwards. But then another wave rises up in her to meet it – a wave of anger, anger at Daniel for doing this to her, for making her feel this way, for weighing her down with death and making her carry it around with her for ever when she barely knew him! She barely knew him! And now jumping up she shouts back at the fat boy who has come into her house to do this to her, Daniel didn't even know me! I saw him three times in my entire life! I didn't ask him to write my name on the floor! I didn't ask him to do any of that! Sparks are shooting from her, she is so sick of boys and all the things they want from her, endlessly endlessly wanting and pulling and draining her away – he didn't know me, I didn't know him. I didn't know about his life, I didn't know his mom was sick –

The toad's little squinty eyes open in surprise. His mom? he says.

You didn't know that? Lori's dad had told her, he'd heard it from his friend the Seabrook Principal. But it looks like it's news to toad boy. She's dying, she says, how can you not know that? Weren't you supposed to be his friend?

The toad boy looks at a loss.

How about the swimming team, did he tell you about that?

The swimming team?

How he wanted to quit but he couldn't?

The toad boy frowns. Lori laughs, this is just too funny. Wow, some friend, she says. Do you actually know anything about him at all?

The toad doesn't reply, he is totally confused because he's come to punish her and take revenge on her and put the blame on her for what's happened but now he's finding out it might not be so simple as the video, it might be that some other things were bothering Daniel too that someone else might have been able to help him with, e.g. him fatso his so-called friend. You can see it sinking in, he falls back into the armchair with a look of shock crossing his face, but instead of wanting to make him feel better and say, Hey it's OK, we're in this together, and share the pain they're both feeling between them instead she finds now the tables have turned she wants to finish him, she wants to pay him back for what he's done, for making her feel evil and love-less, for making her feel rotten and black inside, when if he knew the first thing about her he'd know that she's a lovely sweet per-son that everyone likes, and that Love is all she cares about and all she thinks about all day long, FYI Mr fat slob, Mr disgusting monster, Mr giant repulsive toad who nobody will ever want to kiss even if they're blind, she wishes he was dead cold in a grave somewhere too, she would love to put him there, she would love to really hurt him, she would love to go over to him and scratch his face, scratch and scratch and dig and dig until there's nothing left no face just red like a plate of spaghetti Bolognese after you've eaten all the spaghetti off it and she even gets up and takes a step towards him and emerging out of his reverie she sees his eyes widen in terror –

Everything OK in here? Mom's face in the door.

Yes, thank you, Mom. The face that Lori presents back to her is sweet and composed.

Would your friend like some OJ? Or some Pepsi? Mom won-ders.

No thank you, Mrs Wakeham, toad-thing says.

Actually he was just about to leave, Lori adds.

On cue, the fat boy rises from his chair. Mom nods and closes the door again. Lori and the fat boy stare at each other. He is trembling, in his eyes there is despair and not-understanding as far back as she can see. Goodbye, she says. He goes to the door and down the stairs. She hears him open the front door and shut it. Crossing over the landing she pushes back the curtain so she can see him in the driveway. He is standing there in the light of the security lamp, clutching his head as if he's experiencing a tre-mendous pain. Maybe it's the same pain that's in her stomach. He stays there so long without moving that the security lamp switches off. She pulls the curtain closed in one quick motion and sinks onto the bed and cries until the duvet is soaked.

I did love him, she croaks through snot and tears to Lala the teddy bear, and as she says it she knows it's true, and she knows that Carl knew it too even before she did and that's why he did what he did. And she realizes that love doesn't go in straight lines, it doesn't care about right or wrong or about being a good person or even about making you happy; and she sees, like in a vision, that life and the future are going to be way more complicated than she ever expected, impossibly, unbearably complicated and difficult. In that same moment she feels herself grow older, like she's finished a level in a video game and moved on invisibly to the next stage; it's a tiredness that takes over her body, a tiredness like nothing before, like she's swallowed a ton weight . . .

And so she's glad when her phone buzzes with a new message and she can stop thinking about it. When she checks, she finds that in fact she's got messages from lots of people in the last hour – from Janine, from Denise, from KellyAnn, Shannan, Richard Dunstable (Seabrook), Graham Canning (St Mary's) and Leo Coates (Gonzaga); she reads them one by one, replies, replies to the replies, time slipping by, phone buzzing, messages wrapping around her like a cocoon, protecting her from the thought of the toad-boy, of what is in her stomach, of everything else.

Obviously the text from Shannan she deletes without even reading. Lori and Janine have been ignoring Shannan ever since Lori found out Shannan told Kimberley Cross that Janine hates Lloyd Dalton even though she knows Kimberley's boyfriend and Lloyd Dalton are best friends. It's as she's sending the message to the trash that she gets her idea. When something annoying or stupid or evil or all three like Shannan is in your life, the best thing to do is treat it like it doesn't exist. So, that's what she should do with the invaders in her stomach too! While they are living inside it, she will cut her stomach out of her life, just like she and Janine and Denise have cut out Shannan. She will act like it's not there until she's sure the problem has been solved.

513

She knows her body will not like this. Her body wants to eat food, it wants to grow and make itself stronger. Even now her stomach is mewling with hunger, not knowing that it's in control of the enemy. But she has the answer to this too, in fact the answer has been here all along – tucked away inside her favourite bear, a baggie of at least one hundred pills, enough to last her for a couple of weeks at least. She reaches for Lala, finds the secret tear underneath his left arm. She'll start now with one pill or maybe two. Soon she'll have everything back under control.

Something is following Carl.

In the beginning he just feels it, in the classroom, in Texaco, outside Lori's house. It's watching him but it doesn't let him see it, he turns round and it's gone. He asks Barry if he's noticed anything.

'Like what?' Barry says.

'Just like someone following us around.'

'Shit, you mean like the pigs?'

But Carl doesn't mean the pigs. He doesn't know what he means. But just because he doesn't know what it is doesn't stop it from watching him, even in places where it's impossible to watch him, in Deano's flat or in his own room, or in his dreams where he starts to feel it too, the same pair of eyes that track him invisibly when he's awake, there silently in the dream-space. For a long time though he doesn't see it, it's just a feeling, so he smokes more and more of the superskunk and tries to bury it under the feeling of nothing.

And then one night he is with Janine. They are in the greenhouse talking about what to do about the Plan, which is over because Carl ruined it. He doesn't remember why he did it. It was a very good plan, the way that Janine explained it. We trick Lori's mom and dad so they think she is going out with Skippy, but really she is going to meet you. They won't know about you. Skippy won't know about you. The only people that know about you will be the three of us. Lori will have to be with Skippy a little bit sometimes for the Plan to work. But it won't mean anything. And the two of you can be together, Janine said, my love, and she ran her tongue over Carl's neck. And Carl understood. Lori would be with Skippy sometimes, but it wouldn't mean anything, the same way it didn't mean anything when he was with Janine. It was just a trick to

515

fool her parents, so she could say, I'm going to meet Skippy, and then she would go to meet Carl. He understood, he could see it was an excellent plan. But then at the last minute, when it was actually happening, he realized he didn't understand. Most of him did but he couldn't explain it to the part that didn't. And he worried about whether the boy Skippy understood. That's why he sent the film from the roof of Ed's, so that everyone would know what was going on, everyone would know that Lori was his. But you see that was not part of the Plan. So what happened then was, instead of bringing him and Lori together, he has actually split them apart, and now he is in Janine's granny's greenhouse and everything is different. She is telling him Lori will not see him, will not talk to him. She is crying. He is breaking her granny's flowerpots. She is begging him to stop. She is telling him that it will blow over, that Lori will come around, that she will talk to her. She is saying you can't blame yourself for this, Carl! She keeps scrambling up his leg to try and kiss him, and he keeps pushing her back but then she gets close enough that he sees something. I love you, she says, but he doesn't hear her, he is staring deep into her eyes.

The dead boy is staring back out at him.

Carl always thought it was him. Now he knows for certain.

After that Dead Boy becomes braver, he will appear not just in eyes and dreams but like a hologram beside Carl, or behind him, or in front of him, there and gone, a split second at a time. No one else can see him, only Carl. 'See what?' they say. 'A person.' 'Yeah right, haven't you ever heard the saying, don't get high on your own supply?' and then they laugh. And right in the middle of them Dead Boy will be standing, staring at Carl with his big empty eyes.

Carl tries to get used to him and ignore him. Then he tries to fight him, to hit him kick him stab him, one day in school when he sees him standing in the window he throws a chair at him he screams at him in his bedroom, Stay away from me, but nothing works, just Mom appears at the door with messy hair asking if he wants a sleeping pill.

It gets hard to concentrate on things. Mark gives him jobs to do and he can't find the money afterwards. Did he forget to take it? Did he leave it somewhere? You better get it from somewhere, dude, Barry says, otherwise he's going to freak. So Carl ends up replacing it himself. After a while he starts running out of replacement money. But Mom's written her ATM pin at the back of her address book.

Get it together, Barry says. You snooze you lose in this game, bro.

Barry is jealous because Carl has been suspended for a week because of throwing the chair. But being suspended is not that great. Most of the time he just goes to Deano's gaff. Deano lives in the flats behind the shopping mall with his mom, only he calls her Ma, she looks like his granny and most of the time she stays in the kitchen drinking cups of tea and pretending not to know what they're doing. Outside, everything smells like piss. The blokes are all scobes in tracksuits and the birds are mingers with ponytails and earrings as big as their heads, they laugh at Carl and call him a Seabrook bum boy and a poshie. But no one ever tries to mess with him because they know Deano has a sawn-off in a sports bag under his bed. He sits there with the others watching *Ren and Stimpy* and smoking and Dead Boy flicks in and out and Carl's heart screams Lori Lori Lori Lori until the grass blots it out.

So where does all this shit come from? Barry says one night.

What? Mark says.

All this stuff we smoke and we sell, where does it come from?

A stork brings it, Deano says.

We buy it off the fuckin Mafia, Ste says.

Really? Barry goes.

No, you thick cunt, Ste says. Barry goes red.

What do you fuckin care where it comes from, Knoxer says. Are you on fuckin work experience or something?

Work experience! Deano says, laughing so hard snot comes out of his nose.

Knoxer is a cunt with greasy hair. Gee, Ren, says Stimpy, he is holding out a plate of sick.

It comes from different places, Mark says. They make the pills mostly in Holland. Coke, that's all from South America. And heroin, that comes from poppies that these ragheads grow in Afghanistan.

From poppies? Like – poppies?

Yeah, then it comes up here from Spain, through Africa.

This is like fuckin Geography class, Knoxer says. I'm goin for a shite.

The &(*DEAD BOY→% revolves around the @@):/ DEAD BOY *¥入.

But where do *you* get it? Barry says. Deano looks at Mark. Mark shrugs.

We get it from a *mysterious Druid*, Deano says, in a spooky voice. Barry looks at Mark.

This bloke that calls himself the Druid, Mark says.

Fuck off, Barry says.

I'm serious, Mark says.

Seriously, Deano says, that's what he's called.

Why?

It's what he calls himself. He's a nutjob. You'd get on with him, he says to Carl.

What's a Druid, Carl says.

When do we get to meet him? Barry says.

What do you want to meet him for, Deano says.

It just seems like we should meet him, Barry says. If we're part of the gang.

The gang, Ste says, with a chuckle.

Trust me, you're not missin anything, Deano says. Bats cunt. Off his rocker. Gives me the fuckin willies.

Well, can we come next time? Barry says. When are you going to meet him next?

Mark doesn't say anything, neither does Deano.

Saturday, Ste goes from the couch.

What? says Barry.

We're going to see him on Saturday, Mark says. Outside the door the toilet flushes. There's some stuff coming in.

Can we come? Barry says.

Youse can take my place if you want, Deano says. You wouldn't hear me complainin.

Barry's eyes glow like he's in *Reservoir Dogs*. Ren's eyes pop out and explode.

Hur-hur-hur, goes Ste. You're like Ren, and this dozy fucker's like your man Stimpy, he says to Barry.

Carl's phone calls to him through the wall of fog surrounding his mind. Where is it? It's right in front of you. Janine is talking, Come and meet me, she says, it's important. He rolls his eyes but gets up. Through the door in the hall, Knoxer has his hand in Carl's jacket where it hangs by the stairs. When he sees Carl he takes it out and smiles and pats Carl's cheek. Then he goes into the living room with the others. A moment later Carl is standing there with a churn of anger in his stomach but no idea why it's there so he just leaves.

Janine is waiting in the church car park. They can't go to the greenhouse any more, her granny called the police after it got wrecked. Don't worry, she thinks it was Romanians, Janine says. Carl doesn't care what she thinks. He hates Janine but she is the only way he has left to get messages to Lori. Every day he tells her something to tell her and she comes back with nothing. But there must be something he can say that would make her talk to him! There must be something!

Today Lori collapsed in class, Janine tells him.

They are behind the trees, watching the rain.

She hasn't been eating, she says. For days. Today in English she had to stand up to read something and she just keeled over. The doctor came in and she had to go to hospital.

She puts her hand on his hand. If she could open the door marked Janine in Carl's soul, she would find a wall of black puke that would pour out and drown her. I think she's been obsessing about Daniel, she says.

Carl doesn't say anything. He doesn't take Janine's head and smash it against the wall. You see, if she wanted to Janine could tell Lori about what he's been doing with her, and that would be the absolute total end of everything. So he has to keep seeing Janine to stop her from telling Lori he's seeing Janine! It's like a riddle! It's like a cage with invisible bars! She stares at him spastically. Dead Boy flashes up in her eyes, he is laughing at Carl.

I need some more vitamins, she says,

He takes a little baggie out of his pocket. They're for free, he mumbles.

I want to pay you, she says. She kisses him on the cheek, it's like being pressed into wet ground.

Don't worry, she tells him, sliding her hands under his shirt, this is strictly business. She sucks at his neck like quicksand, she rubs his trousers. He looks away at the rain and the fallen leaves. She cries out, Stop thinking about her, Carl!

And she kisses him desperately like a starving animal and Carl kisses her back to stop her talking and puts his hand into her pants to close her eyes, his fingers slip-sliding into her, deeper deeper deeper, like they think that that way is a way back to Lori.

He had gone there for an explanation. Ruprecht has always believed in explanations; he has always seen the universe as a series of questions posed to its inhabitants, with the answers waiting like prizes for the boy lucky and diligent enough to find them. To believe in explanations is good, because it means you may believe also that beneath the chaotic, mindless jumble of everything, beneath the horrible disjunction you feel at every moment between you and all you are not, there dwells in the universe a secret harmony, a coherence and rightness like a balanced equation that's out of reach for now but some day will reveal itself in its entirety. He knew the horror of what had happened could not be undone. Still, an explanation might fix it in time, seal it in, silence it. He imagined her breaking down and confessing, like people did on TV, spilling out answers like tears, he sitting in judgement until he finally understood.

But that is not what happened. Instead, like a theory that promises everything and delivers nothing, that spreads like a virus to nullify what you thought you already knew, she had left him only with questions, terrible questions. Why didn't he tell Ruprecht about his mum? Why did he want to quit the swimming team? In Ruprecht's dreams every night now he is back in the Doughnut House – back amid the shouts, the lights, people crying, doughnuts scattering the floor, and Skippy, rapidly becoming a figure from the past, sprawled drowning on the tiles beneath him, while the sea beats away in the distance, unheard under the traffic, a dark blue line lost in the greater darkness of the night – Why? Ruprecht yells at him in these dreams. Why, why, why? But Skippy doesn't answer, he is going, going, slipping away through his fingers, even while Ruprecht is holding him, even though he holds on as tight as he can.

The days that follow see an exponential increase in Ruprecht's doughnut intake. He eats them constantly, at every hour of the day and night, as though in an endless race with some invisible, inexorable competitor. The other boys find this creepy, given what's happened, but for Ruprecht it's like the more he eats, the less they mean, and the less they mean, the more of them it seems he can eat, as if they are genuinely becoming zeros that take up no space, crowding into his stomach, a bellyful of nothings. His skin becomes pocked with angry-looking hives, and he is no longer able to do up the top button of his trousers – Dennis jokes that it's a good thing he didn't go ahead with that new portal idea or he might have got stuck halfway into a parallel universe, but Niall, for once, doesn't laugh.

In the classroom he ceases to be a moribund non-participant, but although his hand goes up all the time, the answers he gives are never the right ones. Eight colours in a rainbow? The capital of Sweden is Oslo? Erosion, a process of gradual wearing away, from the Greek word *eros* meaning love? No one has ever witnessed Ruprecht getting a question wrong before; there is, initially, a certain level of Schadenfreude at this lapse in perfection, even among his teachers. But from straightforward wrongness it soon degenerates into something much more unsettling. A hydrogen atom has two *dads*, the main export of Russia is *C sharp*, Jesus instructs us to *diffract sunlight*; every time the teacher asks a question, often before they've finished asking, there is Ruprecht with some dizzyingly untrue response, and when they ignore him, he shouts things out, completing their sentences for them, turning whole lessons into gibberish, snowdrifts of nonsense so deep and bewildering the teachers often have no choice but to abandon the class and start again from the very beginning. They give him the benefit of the doubt, hoping he'll snap out of it; but time goes by and Ruprecht's behaviour only gets worse, his grades lower, his homework more obscene, until finally, feeling as if they are banishing their firstborn, they start asking him to leave the classroom. Soon he's spending the greater part of his day out on the corridor, or in Study Hall – or in the infirmary getting an icepack on his nose, because the forces of darkness do not like this new rebellious Ruprecht either, do not welcome his deviation from his ordained role in the hierarchy. The messages posted on his back become more virulent, and the blows intensify too, slaps becoming punches, shin-kicks heading groinward; every time he takes a piss someone will push him into the urinal. Ruprecht carries on like none of it is happening.

'Please stop,' Geoff Sproke begs him.

'Stop what?' Ruprecht asks blandly.

'Just . . . just be yourself again?'

Ruprecht merely blinks like he doesn't know what Geoff means. And he is not the only one. The whole of the second year is undergoing some dark psychic metamorphosis whereby each of them is less and less himself. Test results are plummeting, indiscipline soars – boys talking among themselves, turning their backs, telling the teachers if they object to fuck off, fuck themselves, get fucked. Every day brings some new outrage. Neville Nelligan, previously unassuming middle-of-the-roader, asks Ms Ni Riain how she'd like to smoke his cock. Kevin Wong pulls a punch on Mr Fletcher in Science class. Barton Trelawney kills Odysseas Antopopopolous's pet hamster, Achilles, by lifting it out of its cage and squeezing it into pulp with his bare hands. Bus stops are vandalized, chippers defaced with flung punnets of curry sauce. One morning Carl Cullen gets up in the middle of his Remedial Maths class, lifts his chair and puts it right through the classroom window.

For a time the Automator explains away the growing anomie as a process of 'resettling'. But soon the malaise begins to spread through the school. When the senior rugby team are defeated in the first round of the Paraclete Cup by traditional whipping boys Whitecastle Wood, the Acting Principal finds himself under the cosh. The senior team *is* Seabrook; this humiliation seems to articulate something deeply amiss at the very heart of the school. There are whisperings among parents and the higher echelons of the alumni organization; those priests who do not approve of the Automator's plans for modernization, who have grave doubts about the very idea of a lay principal, become more vocal about their misgivings – especially since the word from the hospital is that Father Furlong is out of danger and on the road to recovery.

'Des Furlong's not coming back, they can get that through their heads for a start. Man's heart's like a puff-pastry, how do they think he'd be up to running a school?' A whole new vein has appeared in recent days to throb in the Automator's forehead. 'I've got teachers moaning at me because they can't control their classes, I've got parents whining down the phone because their kids flunk a test, I've got the rugby coach telling me the team's got no morale, everyone expects me to have the answer, I feel – God damn it, I feel like I'm carrying this place on my own! On my own!'

'Tea?' a low voice at his elbow causes Howard to start. He keeps forgetting Brother Jonas is there: he has an eerie capacity to melt into the background. Trudy is on sick-leave; the absence of her feminizing touch heightens the militaristic feel of the Acting Principal's office.

The Automator turns to Howard with his newly characteristic expression, a blend of brow-beating and entreaty. 'I want your professional opinion, Howard. What the hell is wrong with these kids?'

'I don't know, Greg.'

'Well, Jesus, give me something. You're out there on the ground. You must have some idea what's bugging them.'

Howard draws a long breath. 'The only reason I can think of is Juster. This all started after Juster's . . . after what happened. Maybe they're reacting to it somehow.'

The Automator dismisses this summarily. 'With all due respect, Howard, what the hell's Juster got to do with the senior Cup team? He wasn't even a blip on their radar! Why in God's name should they care what happened to him?'

Howard stares with loathing at the Automator's gleaming white collar. This is not the first of these impromptu meetings; apparently the contract he signed had a hidden rider, making him the Automator's confidant and confessor. He takes another calming breath, gathers his words. 'Well, I don't know, Greg. I don't know why they should care.'

'I mean it's not as if – you haven't *told* anyone what we discussed up here, have you?' His eyes narrow on Howard, a hunter drawing a bead.

'I haven't said anything,' Howard says.

'Well then!' the Automator ejaculates, as though the object of the exercise were to make Howard look a dunce. 'You're on the wrong track, Howard. This has nothing to do with Juster. These kids have short memories, they've moved on.'

The Automator is right of course: the boys don't know what happened, they have no reason to be reacting. And yet it seems to Howard that while the full facts of the Juster episode may have remained within these four walls, the *spirit* of those facts did not; instead it escaped to roil like poison gas down the stairs and through the corridors, slowly infiltrating every corner, every mind. It makes no rational sense, he knows; still, he can taste it in the classroom every morning, the same darkness he encountered that day in the office.

He knows better than to offer this to the Automator. Instead he says, 'There's a rumour going around that Father Green . . . that he had some involvement in the boy's death.'

The Automator sets his mouth, half-turns away. 'I'm aware of that,' he says.

'In which case what it must look like is that we're sitting here allowing –'

'Damn it, Howard, I said I'm aware of it!' He goes to the aquarium, to which three new fish have been added – 'Seabrook Specials' the Automator calls them, big blue-and-gold fellows imported from Japan. 'Jerome Green didn't do us any favours, quitting out of the blue like that. I know what it looks like. But obviously I can't say anything without making it worse. And I can't get rid of Jerome, no matter how much I might like to.'

'Maybe it would help if the school could be seen to be more mindful of Juster's . . . of his death.'

'Mindful?' the Automator repeats, as if Howard has broken into Swahili.

'Just show, you know, that we care about it. That we're not just sweeping it under the carpet.'

'*Ob*viously we care, Howard. That's obvious to anyone. What are you saying, we should all go into the forest in our boxer shorts and sit in a circle and cry? We should build a monument to Juster in the quadrangle, is that it? Jesus Christ, it's not enough that this kid ruins what should have been a milestone year? That he sends our 140th Anniversary Concert down the crapper? Now we all have to stay depressed till June?'

Howard reflects his gaze primly. 'It's perhaps a question of ethos,' he pronounces deadpan.

The Automator glares at him then turns away to shuffle some papers on his desk. 'That's all well and good, Howard, but I've got a school to run. We need to find some way to boost morale, get the show back on the . . .' He tails off; a new light flickers at the back of his eyes. 'Wait a second. Wait just one second.'

That afternoon, at a special assembly for second-years, the Automator announces that the 140th Anniversary Concert – in limbo after the recent tragedy – will go ahead after all. As a mark of respect, however, and in a spirit of commemoration, a percentage of the proceeds from the event will now be going towards the refurbishment of Daniel Juster's beloved swimming pool.

'It was really Howard's idea,' the Automator explains afterwards. 'And you know it makes sense whatever way you look at it.' On the one hand, it gives the boys a chance to do something for their friend; on the other, it gets the concert up and running again, and also lends it that extra touch of gravitas, which it can definitely use now that it appears Father Furlong is going to pull through, in fact in some ways they were quite fortunate to have had Juster in the wings, so to speak, not to be crass about it but you take his meaning. The Automator's hope is that the revamped concert will revitalize the moribund student body. 'Give them something to get excited about. Take their minds off all this gloom.'

It seems to Howard that it will take a lot more than a Christmas concert to rouse the boys out of their present despond; he is surely not the only one hoping that Greg has bitten off more than he can chew. But the Acting Principal has a plan. He spends the day after the announcement sequestered in his office, making phone calls; the day after that, at a second special assembly, he delivers the news that RTÉ has agreed to broadcast live radio coverage of the event.

'Historic occasion like that in the country's most prestigious school, why wouldn't they want to broadcast us?' the Automator jokes afterwards, as his staff congratulate him on this coup. 'Course, it didn't hurt to have a couple of alums out there in Montrose, ready to twist the right arms.'

It appears the Automator knows the boys better than Howard gave him credit for. News of the concert – or, more specifically, the live radio coverage of it – creates a buzz on the corridors that hasn't been heard for months. Any grievances the boys had are forgotten, the air of introversion and menace dissipates as quickly and mysteriously as it arrived; even students with no stake in the event (an ever-dwindling number, as the Automator invents a phalanx of new positions in Concert PR (stuffing envelopes) and Concert Tech Assist (sweeping the floor of the Sports Hall)) get caught up in the excitement. 'A rising tide lifts all boats, Howard,' the Automator comments approvingly. 'That's simple economics.' The halls resound once more with rehearsing instruments, and it begins to look like 'the Show', as the Automator has taken to calling it, will not only turn the school's *annus horribilis* around, but silence the Acting Principal's enemies for good.

And then, with eight days remaining until the curtain rises, the concert's musical director, Father Connie Laughton, arrives at the Automator's door in tears.

A dainty man of a nervous disposition, Father Laughton detests discord above all things. He always climbs down before seriously disagreeing with anyone; he can't dismiss the most disruptive student from his class without feeling sorry twenty seconds later and racing down the corridor to summon him back. As a result, his music appreciation courses are notoriously anarchic – in fact they make anarchy look like a slow day at the library – and yet, at the same time, they are marked by a kind of goodwill, and the priest always seems happy there, in the midst of the melee, humming along to a Field larghetto or a Chopin mazurka while paper planes, pencil cases, books and larger objects fly through the air around him.

Discord, though: that he cannot abide.

As musical director of Seabrook events for a number of years, Father Laughton is by now largely immune to bad playing. But what he was subjected to at this morning's Quartet rehearsal – the egregious timbre, the proliferation of atonalities, the disregard for even the rudiments of timing – this was something else, this was something, it seemed to his ears, *deliberate*, a calculated and mindful assault on music itself; just to recall it now sets the teacup trembling in his hand. And when he realized that the perpetrator was none other than Ruprecht Van Doren! Ruprecht, his star student! Ruprecht, the one boy who actually seemed to *understand* music as he did, to recognize in its symmetry and plentitude a unique interpolation of perfection in our inconstant world! Well! Knowing the boy had had some difficulties lately, he withheld from comment as long as he could, but eventually – he was sorry, but he could not bear it, he simply could not bear it. He asked Ruprecht quite politely if he would mind sticking to the score as Pachelbel had written it.

'And what did he say?'

'He told me –' the priest crimsons at the memory '– he told me to *sit on it*.'

'He told you to *sit on it*? Those were his exact words?'

'I'm afraid so.' Father Laughton dabs at his forehead fretfully. 'I don't see how I can – I can't *work* with someone with that attitude, I simply can't.'

'Of course, Father, I quite understand,' the Automator concurs. 'Don't you worry about it, I'll take it in hand.'

The Automator has been aware, of course, of the staffroom chatter regarding the former favourite's sudden decline. Until now, though, he has stayed his hand. Van Doren's projected performance in next year's state exams is calculated to lift the year's average by four per cent; he, or his genius, must be allowed a certain leeway.

He invites Ruprecht to his office later that day and over tea and biscuits reminds him just how important the Quartet's recital is to the concert. He reflects on the concert itself, a uniquely prestigious and historic event which is, let us not forget, to be broadcast live on national radio. He attempts bribery, offering to allow Ruprecht to keep his dorm room to himself, and then threats, ruminating on the positive effects it might have on one of the more troubled students, e.g. Lionel, to be roomed with one of the very gifted, e.g. Ruprecht. Finally he loses his temper and yells at him for five minutes straight. This meets with the same response as every other tactic.

'He wouldn't even *speak*! Kid sits there like a, like a blancmange –' The Automator slumps, huffing and puffing over his desk, much as Dr Jekyll might have while metamorphosing into his fiendish alter ego.

Howard adjusts his collar. 'Can't they just play without him?'

'It's a quartet, for God's sake, who ever heard of a quartet with only three musicians? And Van Doren's the only one with any talent. Send out the other three as a trio – you'd be better off pumping the audience with sarin gas! Or just whacking them on the ears with a lump hammer!' He kicks over his wastebasket, sending paper and apple cores across the floor; Brother Jonas scuttles from a corner instantly, like a domesticated spider, to tidy them up. 'We need Van Doren, Howard. He's what this whole concert is about – high-quality, timeless entertainment. And damn it –' the bloodthirsty eye staring sightlessly at Brother Jonas, who is winkling stray staples from the fibrous turquoise carpet '– I'm damned if I'm going to let some little blimp defy me on a whim. No sir – if he wants a war, I'll give him a war.'

The following lunchtime, the three uneponymous members of the Van Doren Quartet make a pilgrimage to Ruprecht's room. No one answers their knock, and the door opens only grudgingly, the way blocked by doughnut boxes, Pepsi bottles, soiled underwear. Inside they find Ruprecht, on the first day of a three-day internal suspension, lying on his bed with his eyes closed. By the wardrobe the French horn slumps at a drunken angle, the bell full to the rim with Snickers wrappers. On the floor his next-door neighbour, Edward 'Hutch' Hutchinson, sits glued to Ruprecht's computer screen, watching an enormous purple dildo being plunged and re-plunged into a carefully depilated vulva.

'The thing is,' Geoff Sproke begins, then breaks off: every time he turns his head he is confronted with a giant close-up shot of a clitoris, it's very distracting. He coughs deliberately, repositions himself, and tries again. 'I suppose what we're thinking is, we've all put a lot of work into this thing, and it seems like a shame to let it go to waste, you know?'

Ruprecht does not know, indeed makes no sign of having heard them. Geoff shakes his head, and turns his gaze to Jeekers, who steps somewhat diffidently to the fore.

Jeekers finds himself with something of a conflict of interests here. On the one hand, yes, Geoff is right, he has worked hard for this concert, and he feels that throwing away an opportunity to shine in public – his parents have already bought tickets for not only themselves but a wide spectrum of relatives – instead of merely on bi-monthly report cards is profligate in the extreme. On the other, this strange torpor afflicting Ruprecht has been very good to Jeekers. After what seemed a lifetime labouring in Ruprecht's expansive shadow – spending hours over-preparing for every test, hoping for just one minuscule victory, appreciable only to him, only to be trounced, effortlessly, time and time again – Jeekers is now, officially, Best Boy in the Year, and it tastes every bit as sweet as he expected. The praise of the Acting Principal, scribbled on the back of his bi-monthly report card; the envious stares of Victor Hero and Kevin 'What's' Wong; the proud voice of Dad, crying out over the dinner table, 'More carrots! More carrots for the Best Boy!' – much as he likes Ruprecht, he does not know that he is ready to give these up just yet.

And so, instead of marshalling the skills he has honed in Debating Club, appealing to Ruprecht's love of the Arts, reminding him of the duty people like Jeekers and Ruprecht have to uphold and preserve these finer things from the troglodytes surrounding them – instead of this, after some procrastinatory throat-clearing, he just says, 'All of us have parents coming to the concert, and they're going to be pretty cross if we're not playing. I know you're an orphan, but try to think how it feels for us, having our parents getting cross with us just because you don't want to play.' With that he steps back, and shrugs happily at Geoff, leaving Ruprecht's catatonia unstirred.

Geoff, in desperation, fixes an eye on Dennis.

'What?' Dennis says.

'Can't you say something to him?'

'Why should I say anything to him? I don't even want to be in this lame concert. As far as I'm concerned, he's doing me a favour.'

'It's not just about the concert, though, it's . . .' Geoff falters, sincerity being to Dennis what salt is to slugs. 'Like, maybe if you said sorry to him, that might help.'

'Sorry?' Dennis is incredulous. 'For what?'

'For the whole Optimus Prime thing. And all the stuff you said?'

'I was trying to help him,' Dennis argues. 'I was trying to help him stop being such an asshole.'

Geoff's mouth sets in a tight line. 'Well, why did you come up here then?'

Dennis shrugs. He isn't sure why he came up here. To see Ruprecht in squalor, with the shell of his genius stripped away, and the grotesque soft squirming larva of his true self revealed to all? To have everything Dennis said over the years gloriously confirmed, viz., that everything good is fatally flawed, that life is inherently evil, that for those reasons there is no point trying or caring or hoping? Something along those lines, anyway.

Geoff keeps staring at him; Dennis shrugs again, and leaves the dorm.

In the Rec Room he sits down by himself, smirking to show how unguilty he is feeling. For a little while he watches the table tennis, then turns to the window. As he looks out something enters the car park below. It is a van, a dark brown van, and on it is written in gold lettering:

VAN DOREN DRAINAGE

∞ SEPTIC TANK'S EMPTIED
∞ TOILET'S UNBLOCKED
∞ LEAK'S FIXED

FOR ALL YOUR PLUMBING NEEDS NO JOB TOO SMALL!

The van pulls up alongside the flowerbeds, and a small unprepossessing man in an ill-fitting suit and a voluminous woman with a floral hat – both of them somehow familiar – emerge from either side. Dennis watches as they bustle over to the school doors. A slow, wolfish smile spreads over his chops. 'Well, well,' he says to himself. 'Look who's back from the Amazon.'

Making the right impression, as Father Foley never tires of telling the boys, is half the battle in any situation. You might have straight A's in your Leaving Cert, but walk into the prospective employer's office with scuffed shoes or an inappropriate tie and you've as good as flushed your chances down the toilet. That is why, even though he had previously washed it only last night, Father Foley, understanding the gravity and delicacy of this particular case, took the trouble of washing his hair again this morning, and spent the quarter-hour prior to the interview arranging it until he judged it exactly right.

Contrast this effort with the young man on the other side of the desk. Here we have a lad who clearly does not care a jot about impressions. His posture is slovenly, he is grossly overweight and, to top it off, he will not speak! Not one word! Father Foley struggled for several minutes to 'get through' to him; now he addresses his comments solely to the parents, leaving the boy out of it. See how he likes it.

'There are five stages of bereavement,' he tells them. 'Denial, Anger, Bargaining, Depression and Acceptance.' He has just been reading about this on the Internet, it's actually very interesting. 'Obviously young Ruprecht here is presently going through the Anger stage. Now, that is perfectly natural, indeed it is a vital part of the grieving process. Nevertheless, we are getting to a point at which Ruprecht's grief is having a negative effect on the orderly running of the school. So what the Acting Principal and I are hoping is that if we all put our heads together, we might be able to find some way of getting Ruprecht to the Acceptance stage sooner rather than later, so to speak, or at least to one of the other, less disruptive stages that would enable him to participate constructively in normal school activities, such as the 140th Anniversary Concert.'

The boy's father, a man of few words, nods sombrely. The woman in the hat claps her hands very quietly and mouths, 'A concert!'

Father Foley is pleased to give her some details about the event. Some of the priests tend to look down on the whole thing, but from his studies in psychology Father Foley knows the importance of letting the lads express themselves. Indeed, in his younger days, wasn't a certain Father Ignatius Foley known to strap on the guitar and strum out a few 'hits' for the entertainment of long-term and terminally sick children in hospital? The way those youngsters had looked at him! He was quite the 'pop star'!

'And the touching thing,' he continues, 'is that a portion of the proceeds have been dedicated to refurbishing the swimming pool, in memory of the unfortunate boy, Daniel Juster.'

The boy's mother, who some might call quite an attractive person, coos at this approvingly. Father Foley returns an avuncular smile. 'It seemed to us to be the most appropriate way of marking the event,' he says. 'Here at Seabrook we don't believe in brushing things under the carpet. It is a way for us, for the boys and the faculty alike, to say, Daniel, you will always have a place in our hearts, in spite of, that is to say, the, ah, circumstances of your passing.'

Sweeping a loose strand of golden hair back over his brow, he turns to Ruprecht, who is staring back at him with undisguised hatred. Can he really be her son? Perhaps she is a second wife, she does seem considerably younger – but no, only a mother could dote on a repellent being like this. 'There are two words I should like you to keep in mind during this difficult time, Ruprecht. The first of them is "love". You are lucky to be loved by many people. By your father and your –' he can't resist it '– very charming mother' (a twinkling, effervescent little smile!) 'by your Acting Principal, by myself and the rest of the faculty, and by your many friends here in Seabrook College. And most of all, by God. God loves you, Ruprecht. God loves all of His Creation, down to the very lowliest, and He never takes His eyes from you, even when you think you are alone in the world. Daniel is, hopefully, with Him in Heaven now, and he is happy there, happy in God's love. So let us not be selfish. Let us not let our grief interfere with the good, honest work of our peers. Yes, we have suffered a tremendous loss. But let us mourn Daniel's passing in the correct way, the loving way, such as by participating in the upcoming Christmas concert, and making it a really special occasion he would be proud of.'

The boy's mother is rapt – so, indeed, is the father. Father Foley is rather pleased with this little homily himself. 'The second word, or actually two words,' he says, 'is, or are, "team sports". In the days of the Roman Empire . . .'

Afterwards, he waits outside the Automator's office while his parents have a private interview inside. Darren Boyce and Jason Rycroft come along and stand across the hallway, just staring at him. When his parents come out he walks them down to the van. They would like to stay longer, but Father is terribly busy. In the car park, Mother cups Ruprecht's face in her hands. 'Dearest Ruprecht, we love you very much. Promise me you will remember that one thing, that whatever happens, Mama and Papa will always love you.'

'Let's have no more of this silliness, Ruprecht,' Father says. He wipes his mouth with a paper tissue.

Ruprecht returns to his room alone. On his pillow has been laid, neatly, a toilet brush. He removes it and lies down.

Mother loves Ruprecht. Lori loves Skippy. God loves everybody. To hear people talk, you would think no one ever did anything but love each other. But when you look for it, when you search out this love everyone is always talking about, it is nowhere to be found; and when someone looks for love from you, you find you are not able to give it, you are not able to hold the trust and dreams they want you to hold, any more than you could cradle water in your arms. Proposition: love, if it exists at all, does so primarily as an *organizing myth*, of a similar nature to God. Or: love is analogous to gravity, as postulated in recent theories, that is to say, what we experience faintly, sporadically, as love is in actuality the distant emanation of another world, the faraway glow of a love-universe that by the time it gets to us has almost no warmth left.

When he gets up he spends an hour kicking and stamping on his French horn so he will not have to play it again. Music, maths, these are things that no longer make any sense to him. They are too perfect, they do not belong here. He does not know how he ever believed this universe could be a symphony played on super-strings, when it sounds like shit, played on shit.

With the revelation of his true origins the last vestiges of

Ruprecht's dignity are torn away. Wherever he goes now, a wave of plumbing-related ridicule pursues him; his head is forced so often down the U-bends of Seabrook commodes – 'It's a gateway to another dimension, Ruprecht!' (flush) – that it never fully dries. The worse it gets, the worse it gets, because in school your enemy is anyone you can't fight off, so the more enemies you have, the more you'll find queuing up to join the fun. Ruprecht lumbers through it like some elephantine Golem. He does not cry out when someone flicks his ear with a rubber band or slices his arse with a ruler or jabs it with a compass point or mushes wet tissue in his ears or spits on his back or leaves a dump in his shoe. He does not complain when Noddy boards up the door of his laboratory; he does not protest when he is given detention after several of his non-water-resistant possessions are found blocking one of the dorm toilets; he does not show any signs of caring when his room is festooned yet again with toilet roll. Instead he merely withdraws further into himself – into the ever-expanding cellulite fortress he buttresses daily with doughnuts and a new Ed's milkshake called SweetDreamz, which contains no milk and more calories, somehow, than pure sugar.

'I'm just concerned that the school's attitude might come across as somewhat confrontational . . .'

'Van Doren's the one who's being confrontational, Howard. Firm but fair, that's what we're being. Am I right, Brother?' A svelte ebony nod from the sentinel in the corner.

'But the boys – there does seem to be some evidence that the boys may be ganging up on him.'

'The boys know the rules, Howard, and if they're caught breaking the rules they'll be punished for it. At the same time, they've all put a lot of time and effort into this concert, and if one person is spoiling it for everyone on a whim, then I can understand why they'd be angry. And I can understand that they need to express that anger.'

'Yes, but . . .'

'No one's bigger than this school, Howard.' The Automator's attaché case snaps closed like the jaws of a crocodile. 'Van Doren's going to find that out sooner or later. I just hope for his sake that it's sooner.'

And so Howard merely looks on, as by the day the glutinous orb of Van Doren's face grows wider, paler, converging on a dinner-plate blankness, his yearning to take him aside – to comfort him, simply to speak to him – cancelled out by an equally agonizing guilt. For what could Howard possibly say to him that wouldn't be a barefaced lie? And if he told him the truth, how would that help him?

So he says nothing, instead goes in the opposite direction, bury-ing himself in his history books just as Van Doren cocoons him-self in hydrogenated fats. He delivers his lessons mechanically, not caring whether the boys are listening or not, quietly loathing them for being so predictably what they are, young, self-absorbed, insensate; he waits for the bell just as they do, so that he can dive once more into the trenches of the past, the endless accounts of men sent to their deaths in their tens of thousands, like so many towers of coloured chips pushed by fat hands across the green baize of the casino table – stories that seem, in their regimented wastage, their relentless, pointless destruction, more than ever to *make sense*, to present an archetype of which the schoolday in its asperity and boredom is the dim, fuddled shadow. Womanless worlds.

Outside, meanwhile, the winter turns sadistic, cold rain flaying him whenever he steps through the door; he wakes each morning with a mouth full of gravel, like he's just coming off a three-day bender. He remembers Halley's magical camera, which can turn anywhere into California. Every night he hopes that she will call, but she does not.

And then one day a package arrives for him at the school. Inside is a letter, written in a neat, crimped hand. It is from Daniel Juster's mother.

My husband tells me that Daniel's class is studying the Great War and
I thought your boys might find this of interest. It belonged to my
grandfather, William Henry Molloy. After leaving Seabrook he fought
at Gallipoli with the Royal Dublin Fusiliers. He never spoke about his
experiences, and he kept the uniform hidden in a box at the top of a
wardrobe where he thought none of us would find it. Daniel was too
young to remember his great-grandfather, nevertheless he was very
excited to learn about his participation in the war and would have
enjoyed sharing this with his class.

Inside, carefully wrapped in tissue paper, is a khaki military uniform. Howard holds it up to the light of the staffroom windows.
The rough cloth is spotlessly clean, and smells gently musty; he
passes it through his hands like bolts of pure time.

'What you got there, Howard?' Finian Ó Dálaigh asks him.

'Nothing, nothing . . .' Howard flashes him a cursory smile,
refolds the uniform and stows it rapidly in his locker.

Later, when they have the room to themselves, he shows it to
Jim Slattery. The older man studies the coarse fabric intently, as if
the story of the campaign were inscribed there in the twill. 'Sev-
enth Battalion,' he says. 'There's a story. You haven't come across
them before? "D" Company? Gallipoli? Suvla Bay?'

Howard is vaguely aware of Gallipoli as an infamous disaster
in which thousands of Australians were killed, but no more than
that. 'It wasn't just the ANZACs,' Slattery tells him. 'I have some
books, if you're interested.'

That evening – having been granted a special dispensation from
his wife – Slattery meets Howard in the snug of the Ferry, and proceeds to relate the tragic history of 'D' Company, from their assembly in Dublin at the outbreak of the war to their near-annihilation
on an obscure mountain on the Gallipoli peninsula. Howard, without knowing quite why, has brought Molloy's uniform in his bag,
and as the story unreels he becomes increasingly aware of it as a
presence, an olive-drab ghost attending their conversation.

'They were volunteers, among the first, who joined up from

rugby clubs around the country. Most were professionals, who'd gone to well-known schools, Seabrook included, and worked now as businessmen, bankers, solicitors, clerks. They actually became quite famous in Ireland, even before they went off to fight, because they could have been officers if they'd wanted, but they preferred to stick with their friends. They were known as the "Dublin Pals", and the day they set sail for England huge crowds turned out to watch them march through the city.

'Now, they'd joined up expecting to be sent to the Western Front, and it wasn't until their ship sailed that they discovered they were en route to Turkey instead. Churchill had this plan to force a passage through the Dardanelles, create a new supply route to Russia and draw the Germans away from the Front. The previous attempt to land, at Gallipoli, had been a total catastrophe. They'd tried a Trojan horse trick – packed up a division in an old collier that was to run right up onto the beach and catch the Turks by surprise. But the Turks were waiting, with machine-guns. Supposedly the whole bay turned red with blood. This time round, the commanding officers were so paranoid that they kept their plan completely to themselves – to the point that nobody else knew what they were supposed to be doing. "D" Company and the rest of the Dublins were landed in the wrong place, with no maps and no orders. Temperatures were in the hundreds, the Turks had poisoned the wells, it was raining shrapnel. They waited there on the beach while their general tried to work out what to do . . .'

On the dismal story goes. From this distance, the bloody ending seems inevitable, and the Pals' adventure – voluntarily leaving good jobs, easy lives, wives and children, in pursuit of some tally-ho vision of honour and glory – painfully naive; as if they'd imagined the war to be no more than an extension of their clashes on the rugby pitch, the heightened danger merely guaranteeing the glory there to be won.

'But the worst of it was what happened afterwards,' Slattery says, turning his glass about on the table. 'I mean, they came home and were forgotten about. Not just forgotten about, banished from history. After the Rising, the War of Independence, suddenly they found they were traitors. The struggles they endured, the horror, the hardships, all for nothing. That must have been a real knife in the back.' He looks over at Howard. 'Hard to believe that something that big could simply be buried away like that, as if it had never happened. But it can, that's the tragedy of it. There's a terrible cost, but it can.'

'Yeah,' Howard says, feeling his cheeks flame.

'Although things do change, I suppose . . .' The old man runs his hands over the cloth of the uniform again. 'Anyway, it'll be a great story for your boys.'

Howard makes an indistinct sound. As a matter of fact, he has already decided that he will not tell the boys about the uniform. It would mean nothing to them; there is nothing to be gained from exposing it to their indifference. Slattery is surprised to hear this – even, Howard thinks, a little offended. 'I thought they'd enjoyed studying the war . . . ?'

Howard had thought so too; but recent events have brought home to him just how greatly he'd misjudged them. Every day he watches them yammer to each other about the revived concert, swarm obliviously around the empty seat in the centre of the room, the events of – what, three weeks ago? long vanished from their memories, and eventually he understands that they simply do not have the capacity to relate to the past, their own or anyone else's. They live in a continuous sugar-rushed present, in which remembering is a chore left to computers, like tidying your room is a chore left for the Third World maid. If the war briefly caught their imagination, it was only as another arena of violence and gore, no different from their DVDs and video games, the movie clips of car accidents and mutilations that they swap like football stickers. He doesn't blame them for it, the mistake was his.

The old man swirls the ice in his drink. 'I wouldn't write them off just yet, Howard. In my experience, when you can show them something tangible, bring them out of the classroom so to speak, it can have quite an amazing effect. Even a recalcitrant class, they can really surprise you.'

'They've already surprised me,' Howard says curtly, and then, 'I just don't think this is something they care about, Jim. I don't know what they care about, frankly. Apart from maybe getting on TV.'

'Well, you have to teach them to care, don't you?' Slattery says. 'That's what it's all about.'

Howard does not respond to this, other than to wonder how the old man can have stayed so sentimental for so long. Does he simply not see the boys, is that it? Does he not hear what they say?

He takes Slattery's books with him; when he gets home, he checks the photograph of Molloy in the company history against a team picture in one of the old school annuals he's been going through for his programme notes. There he is, grinning from the centre row, carefully lacquered hair giving him a brawny, equine look, the same man that appears in the portraits of the Pals, as if he had simply hopped from one book to the other, ready to charge the Turkish trenches on Chocolate Hill just as he charged Port Quentin in Lansdowne Road. How could he have known what lay ahead of him? Catastrophic defeat, pointless obliteration, disappearance from history, that's not the fate you expect for a Seabrook boy –

Thinking this brings back Juster again, that empty seat in the classroom like a tile missing from a mosaic. He studies the photograph in the book again. Is he imagining it, or can he see a family resemblance there, between Molloy and his great-grandson? Over the generations the set mouth has grown uncertain, reticent, the blue eyes dazed, as if the genes themselves had never recovered from the disintegration of Suvla Bay and its aftermath, as if some infinitesimal but vital part had got lost in the churn of time. And yet it seems that Daniel Juster, or the man he might have become, is *there*, gazing out of the soldier's face like a reflection on glass; and gazing back in the candlelit living room, Howard finds the hairs on his arms and neck stand up. The uniform floats on its hanger; alone in the candlelit room Howard is suffused by a curious sense of *convergence*, as if he's been appointed as one terminal of a mysterious circuit.

Maybe Slattery was right, is what he's thinking. Maybe this is what the boys need to wake them up; maybe this is a way of bringing Daniel back into the classroom, and forcing them to see him. Two ghosts, briefly rescued from oblivion; a small act of reclamation, a chance to make amends.

Next morning he goes in early to get to the photocopier; he's in the staffroom, collating pictures of pre-war rugby teams, when the Automator comes in. Crossing swiftly to the armchair where Tom sits reading the sports section of the *Irish Times*, 'Quick word?' he says.

Tom looks up blankly. 'Sure, Greg, do you want to go . . . ?' He motions at the door.

'Actually, perhaps you won't mind me sharing this with the others,' the Automator replies, taking from his jacket an envelope emblazoned with the Paraclete crest. It is from the Congregation's headquarters in Rome; the letter inside, which the Automator reads aloud, announces that Tom has been selected to teach in Mary Immaculate School, Mauritius. Tom lets out a whoop; the Automator, laughing, claps him on the back.

It takes a moment for Howard to understand that what he is witnessing is an act, put on for the benefit of the onlookers. He is struck by how convincing they are – Tom flushed and starry-eyed, the Automator with a paternal arm over his shoulder, nothing veiled or calculating detectable in their expressions. It's as if, for them, their lie has already replaced the truth; and now, while he watches, that lie crystallizes outwards, inscribes itself in reality with the help of his unwitting peers, as they crowd around to pump Tom's hand.

'So you're *leaving* us . . .'

'Yeah, it was a hard decision, but . . .'

'I'd say it nearly killed you. Mauritius, no less!'

'You won't have to put up with this shite over there.' 'Ricky' Ross, the economics teacher, gestures humorously at the lugubrious Irish weather outside.

'No, though it has its own problems, of course . . .'

'And what about us? How will Seabrook go on without you?'

'What about the *Ferry*? They'll have to close down!'

'We didn't even know you were thinking of leaving.' Misses Birchall and McSorley are quite overcome. 'You never told us, you bold boy.'

'Yeah, well, it was all a bit out of the blue. Greg told me this position had come up, and I decided to go for it. Seabrook's where my heart is, obviously, but, you know . . .'

'Tom felt like they needed him more over there,' the Automator contributes judiciously. 'They haven't got it easy, those poor kids.'

'Will you be teaching or coaching?' Pat Farrell asks.

'A bit of teaching, English and whatever else they'll let me near. But mostly I'll be training the rugby team. They've a decent enough programme out there – is it Father McGowran set it up, Greg?'

'That's right, Tom. Father Mike's been doing some really Trojan work, getting that school into shape. But he can't do it all on his own. And God knows he can't kick a rugby ball to save his life!'

They laugh. Then delicately, Ó Dálaigh, 'So, back on the rugby pitch, eh?'

'In a manner of speaking.'

'Been a while, all the same.'

'It's time,' Tom says, and gives them that disarming, lopsided smile. 'Got to face up to the past eventually, don't you?'

'You do. You do.' This sentiment pleases his congratulators. Howard feels like his head is about to explode: he makes for the door, but gets entangled in the crowd and finds himself redirected towards Tom. Up close, the coach seems taller than before, virile, vital, as if his ruptured spine had miraculously healed itself; his blameless eyes fall serenely on Howard, who by comparison feels like a ghost, can almost hear his bones rattle as he shakes Tom's hand. 'Congratulations,' he says mechanically.

'Thanks, Howard. Thanks.' In that heartfelt, manly grasp,

Howard is suddenly overcome by nausea. He springs away to the toilet and throws up weak tea.

Walking down to the Annexe later on, he is buttonholed by Farley. 'Heard the news?' Farley asks, matching step with him.

'About Tom, you mean?'

'He's got the right idea,' Farley says. 'I've been thinking about doing something like that lately.'

Howard feels like a piece of driftwood afloat on some tempestuous sea of irony. 'Go to Mauritius?'

'Go somewhere they might actually need me. Somewhere I could make a difference. I don't think I'd have to travel that far.'

Howard has been avoiding Farley lately, but from a distance he's seen a change come over his friend, a morbid, directionless anger. 'They need you here, Farley. Everyone needs a good teacher, rich or poor.'

'These kids don't,' Farley says. 'Why would they? They're set up for life, and they know it.'

'It's not their fault their parents have money.'

'Of course it's not their fault. Nothing is anybody's fault,' Farley replies, deadpan. 'It's not just the boys, Howard. It's this whole place, the hypocrisy of it.'

As if on cue, Father Green sails by – affecting not to see them, keeping his gaze fixed on some imaginary point over their heads, like a missionary posted to the last days of Sodom, determined to ignore the temporal murk.

'Walking around as if nothing ever happened,' Farley says darkly. 'It's sick.'

'We don't know that he had anything to do with it.'

'We can join the dots, can't we?'

Someone keeps writing PEDO in Tipp-Ex on the priest's office door. Every morning Noddy scrapes it off, and then by lunchtime it's back again.

'The sooner this school gets the fucking priests out of the picture, the better,' Farley says. 'Greg may be a cretin and a fascist, but at least he doesn't pretend to be anything else. He doesn't act like he's got some superior moral insight. Just good old-fashioned greed.'

'Father Green's done a lot of good things,' Howard says weakly. 'If you're talking about making a difference. He's probably the only one in the whole school who actually has.'

'A power trip, that's all that is. Junkies and down-and-outs are the only people he can still feel superior to. Though it's better he's hanging around them than the kids.' He emits a curt, bitter laugh, then stops and shakes his head. 'It's not right, Howard. It's just not right.'

In his classroom Howard leans heavily on the lectern as the students slouch in. Ruprecht is next to last, making his bloated way like an ailing dowager. He waits for them to settle as much as they're going to, then gathers himself together. 'I have something special to show you today,' he says. There is a general snigger. He takes the uniform from the bag.

'This belonged to an Irish soldier who actually fought in the First World War,' he says. 'His name was William Molloy and he attended this very school – in fact he was Juster's, he was Daniel Juster's great-grandfather.' The name feels wrong, alien in his mouth, and it produces no effect on the boys; they look on disinterestedly, as they might at an uninspired street-performer while waiting for their bus.

'He would have volunteered in 1914, as Lord Kitchener . . .'

A tittering can be heard at the back of the room; something amusing is evidently occurring outside the window. Howard breaks off, turns to see Carl Cullen stumbling across the car park towards the school.

'He's forgotten he's suspended,' someone remarks gleefully. 'It's the second time this week.'

'He's off his head,' someone else observes.

Even from this distance, Carl's eyes are visibly scrambled, and in his stagger Howard, for one freezing instant, foresees something awful . . . but he isn't wearing a jacket, nor has he a bag, so it's difficult to see where he might conceal a firearm; anyway, Howard tells himself, that kind of thing only happens in America, not here, at least not yet . . . Now a teacher emerges from the school to intercept him. 'Slattery,' someone says.

'Maybe he wants to score some E's.'

Howard watches the old man grip the boy by the shoulders, lean into his slack face, speak to him softly and briefly, then spin him 180 degrees and send him on his way.

'Good thing the Automator didn't see him,' Vince Bailey says. 'He'd get another week's suspension.'

'Oh yeah, I'm sure Carl really cares about being suspended,' Conor O'Malley mocks.

'Oh right, I forgot you're his best friend, that knows everything about him.'

'Fuck yourself, shithead.'

'All right, all right.' Howard raps on the lectern. 'We've got work to do here. Now let's see what this uniform can tell us.'

He holds it up, as if it had some Grail-like power to penetrate the fog of the day. But in the morning light, in the intermittent, corrosive adolescent gaze, the uniform no longer appears to tell them very much. It no longer feels charged with history, nor with anything else, save for the smell of mothballs; and when Howard tries to recall that epiphany of last night, the catharsis he was going to bring about in them – he sees only that little scene in the staffroom: the joy on Tom's face as he is handed his escape route; the affection and pride, real, genuine affection and pride on the Automator's; the staff gathering round to pass on their congratulations, Howard himself shaking the coach's hand.

Somebody twangs a rubber band with his teeth, somebody yawns.

Why should they care about the doings of 'D' Company? Why should they believe a single thing he tells them, or anything they're told within the walls of this school? They know how it goes, they know how it works in places like this – even if they don't know they know.

548

'Jesus Christ,' he says.

The boys look back at him desultorily, and suddenly Howard feels like he's suffocating, like there is nothing breathable left in the room. 'Okay,' he says. 'Everybody go and get your coats. We're getting out of here.'

Nothing happens. Howard claps his hands. 'Come on, I mean it. Let's get moving.' He doesn't know what he means; he only knows that he can't stay in this room a moment longer. Now the general apathy gives way to a nascent stirring of interest, as the boys realize that, whatever has happened to him, he is serious about this. Bags are lifted, books hastily put away before he can change his mind.

Jeekers raises his hand. 'Are we going on a class trip, sir?'

'Sure,' Howard says. 'Exactly.'

'But don't we need permission from our parents?'

'We'll clear it with them afterwards. If anyone doesn't want to come, that's fine. You can proceed to the Study Hall for the remainder of the class.'

'So long, loser.' Simon Mooney twists Jeekers's ear on his way to the door. The thin boy wavers; then, clambering out from behind his desk, he grabs his bag and hurries after the others.

It takes mere seconds for the boys to reappear from the locker room with their coats. Bringing a finger to his lips – 'Let's be sure not to disturb the other classes' – Howard leads them up Our Lady's Hall, past the oratory and the Study Hall, towards the daylight framed in the double-doors – and then they are outside, clipping down the winding avenue between the rugby pitches and chestnut trees.

He walks them down to the station and they take a train into the city. He still hasn't decided where they're going, but as they pass Lansdowne Road, the site of internationals and schools rugby finals, 'Seabrook's second home', he finds himself telling the boys how within weeks of the outbreak of war, Juster's great-grandfather and hundreds of other professional men were going to the stadium every night after work for military training, among them many who would join 'D' Company. Disembarking, he leads them up Pearse Street, around College Green, along Dame Street, the same route, he tells them, the 'Pals' had taken on their triumphant leave-taking of the city.

Cutting through Temple Bar toward the river, they pass the cinema outside which Howard met Halley for the first time: this nugget of history he does not pass on to the boys. He remembers walking with her down to the riverside, but it's only as they are crossing Ha'penny Bridge – the elderly construction seeming to sway beneath their impatient feet, the quays of the city stretching away on either side – that he remembers the museum was where she had been headed that day too, was where he had promised to take her, but never did, instead falling in love with her, leading her away into the backstreets of his life. Now he's finally on his way there, but with twenty-six hormonal teenage boys instead of her. Nice job, Howard.

The boys climb the hill through the gates of the museum grounds. Gerry Coveney and Kevin Wong shout, 'Echo!' at the walls of the vast courtyard. Here and there, groups of tourists make their way over the cobblestones: huge Americans like sides of beef, prim Japanese ladies in black, all with cameras dangling at the ready from their necks. By the entrance, a horde of children from primary school are clustered around a besieged-looking man in a red sweater. 'Now a museum,' he is telling them, 'is a place with lots of objects from the past. By studying these objects, we find out about things that happened long ago . . .'

The children nod seriously. They can't be much older than six or seven; everything to them is long ago. From a safe distance their teacher looks on with a mixture of fondness and gratitude for a moment's peace.

Howard brings the boys inside and approaches the man at the reception desk. 'I wanted to take my class for a look around . . .'

'We can probably arrange a tour, if you like,' the receptionist says. 'Is there a particular area you're interested in?'

'We're studying the First World War,' Howard says.

The receptionist's face clouds. 'I'm sorry,' he says, 'we don't really have anything about the war at the moment.'

Behind Howard, the man in the red sweater, with a hounded look, leads the children into the bowels of the museum. 'Objects! Objects!' they cry deliriously as they go.

'Anything at all?' Howard says, when the noise has passed. 'Uniforms from the Irish regiments? Rifles, bayonets, medals, maps?'

'I'm sorry,' the man repeats sheepishly. 'It's not something there's much demand for at the moment. Though we're hoping to feature it in a forthcoming exhibition?'

'Forthcoming when?'

The receptionist calculates. 'Three years?' Seeing Howard's face fall, he says, 'You might take them to the Memorial Gardens in Islandbridge. It's really just a park. But I'm afraid that's about all there is.'

Howard thanks him and steps back outside, the class billowing behind him like a murmurous cloak; on the cobblestones they congregate around him expectantly. 'Sorry,' he says. 'It's my fault, I should have called ahead. I'm sorry.'

He knows they are only disappointed because they fear this means the end of their outing. Still, as they hang there in the weak, cloud-filtered light, shuffling a little, waiting for him to tell them what to do, they appear different to their everyday school selves – younger, less cynical, lighter even, as if Seabrook were a weight that they carried, and set free of it they might just float off into the air . . .

Traffic pants on the quays in a shimmer of monoxides. The park does not sound terribly inspiring; Howard is debating whether to cut his losses when his phone rings. It's Farley. 'Where the hell are you, Howard?'

'In town,' Howard says. 'On a class trip.'

'A class *trip*? What, without telling anybody?'

'It was sort of a spur-of-the-moment thing,' Howard replies, keeping his voice carefully neutral.

'Greg is going ballistic, Howard, we just about talked him out of calling the guards. For God's sake, have you gone mad? I mean, what are you doing?'

'I don't know,' Howard says, after a moment's consideration.

Farley releases a strangulated sigh. 'Look, if you want to have even a chance of keeping your job, you'd better get back here right away. Greg is climbing the walls, I've never seen him this angry.'

'Oh,' Howard says.

'In fact maybe you should talk to him now – hold on, I'm going to put you on to him and you can –'

Howard hangs up the phone and switches it off. 'Okay,' he says. 'Let's go and find these Memorial Gardens.'

The boys brighten visibly, and set off ahead of him up the street.

He has read about the gardens but never visited them. Island-bridge is an out-of-the-way and not especially inviting part of the city. Bleached posters for last year's music acts account for most of the colour to be seen; down-at-heel pubs front mazy streets where at the turn of the last century thousands of local prosti-tutes attended to the needs of British soldiers stationed in the barracks that now houses the museum. It may no longer be the biggest red-light zone in Europe, but it couldn't be accused of gentrification; as they turn towards the river, the grime becomes thicker, the flats more dilapidated. The boys are fascinated. 'Sir, is this the ghetto?' 'Quiet.' 'Do people buy drugs here?' 'Shh.' 'Are those people on drugs?' 'Do you want to go back to school? Is that what you want?' 'Sorry.' Their faith in him is at once touching and alarming – their trust that they are safe simply because he's with them, as if an adult presence warded off all possible threat, emanated an unbreachable forcefield.

The gate to the Memorial Gardens is at the end of a laneway, between a scrap merchant's and a mental institution. They file through one by one; Howard does not know whether to be cheered or not when they find the park deserted.

'How come nobody's here?' Mario asks.

'Maybe they heard you were coming, Mario.'

'Yeah, Mario, they heard the biggest bummer in Dublin was on his way and they all ran inside?'

'You're the bummer, asshole.'

'Quiet, all of you,' Howard snaps.

From here, aside from its eerie emptiness, the Memorial Gardens looks like any other park. The grassy lawn stretches off into the distance, rising on its left to a hill; the wind ruffles the water of the river to the right, and whispers through the leafless trees lining the avenue. The only edifice in sight is a small stone gazebo. They walk down and crowd into it. Inside a stanza from a Rupert Brooke poem is inscribed in the floor:

> We have found safety with all things undying,
> The winds, and morning, tears of men and mirth,
> The deep night, and birds singing, and clouds flying,
> And sleep, and freedom, and the autumnal earth . . .

'Look –' Henry Lafayette points up the hill. A tall stone cross can now be seen, looming over the crest. They climb towards it, talking less now; fanning out over the grass, they appear to Howard younger again, as if they are going backwards in time.

At the top of the hill they find themselves in a long garden, encircled by trees and ivy-clad colonnades. Water trickles into the basins of two identical fountains, winter roses grow in the borders. The surrounding city can no longer be seen: they might be in the garden of a country manor, were it not for the towering cross, and, about a hundred feet in front of it, a white stone sarcophagus.

'*Their name liveth on forevermore*,' Dewey Fortune reads from its side.

'Whose name?'

'The Irish soldiers', you spa.'

'They got that wrong,' Muiris says.

Lucas Rexroth shivers. 'This place is spooky.'

This provokes a chorus of ghostly *woohooos*; but Lucas is right.

The chilly air that shrinks their voices, the wet grass and lonesomeness, the strange disconnection from the world around, the inexplicable sense of having *interrupted something . . .* they give the garden the character of an afterworld – the kind of place you can imagine waking up in, stretched out on the grass, immediately after some horrific collision. The damp air swirls around them; gradually, the boys' chatter peters out, and they shuffle about uncomfortably until each of them is facing Howard. For a moment he waits, reluctant to dispel the curious chanting silence. Then: 'Okay,' he says. 'The Dublin Pals.' And he begins to tell them what Slattery told him about 'D' Company – how they had joined up together from the school rugby clubs, how, while Robert Graves shivered and fought off rats in a ditch in France, they were dispatched to the furnace of the Dardanelles. 'They were landed on beaches along the Gallipoli peninsula – hundreds of them, packed into a tiny space, waiting to be told what to do. Days went by, dysentery, enteritis, fever broke out, shrapnel was going off overhead the whole time, wounded and dead men were being carried through on stretchers, huge swarms of flies buzzed from corpses into the mouths of the living so it was almost impossible to sleep or eat.

'Finally the order came through for an attack on Kiretch Tepe Sirt, a long ridge overlooking the bay. The men set out in unbearable heat that only got worse as the day went on. They hadn't been given enough water and the Turks had poisoned the wells. They hadn't been given enough ammo either and they soon ran out of that too. Near the top of the ridge they found themselves pinned down by Turkish guns. They sent for reinforcements but none came. It got so hot the gorse caught fire, and they had to listen to their own wounded being burned alive.

'They spent the night trapped on the mountain, being picked off one by one. When they ran out of bullets, they threw stones. One Pal, Private Wilkin, started catching Turkish grenades and throwing them back – he did this five times before the sixth grenade exploded in his hand. At last, after hours of watching their friends being slaughtered, the men – Seabrook men, Clongowes men, St Michael's men and others, who a week before had never been out of the country, most of them, let alone experienced enemy fire – mounted a bayonet charge on the Turkish guns. During this charge, Juster's great-grandfather, William Molloy, got shot in the hand and had to crawl back to his own lines. He was one of the lucky ones. Half the Pals were lost that night.

'After that episode the Allies changed their plans. The division packed up and the remnants of the Pals were split up and transferred to Salonika. As their ship sailed away, as they left their friends behind them on the cliffs and hillsides, the men vowed that their sacrifice, what had happened there, would not be forgotten. But as we've seen, it was forgotten. Or rather, it was deliberately erased. It seems pretty hard luck, after enduring so many terrible hardships and pointless deaths. But that's what happened. The years went by and the Pals became casualties again, this time of history.'

He stows his notebook in his bag and looks up at the boys looking back at him, dotted around the viridian sward in clumps of three and four, like rain-jacketed statues.

'It's hard for us, living in peacetime, to imagine the mindset of the people who lived through the war. So many men had been killed, one in every six who served, and there was barely anyone who wasn't touched by loss in some way. Fathers, mothers, brothers, sisters, wives. Friends. This was a world overwhelmed by grief, and the ways that that grief manifested could be quite extreme. In France, for example, there was a plague of graverobbing. Poor families spent every penny they had on locating their sons' bodies and bringing them home from the Front. In Britain there was a huge outbreak of spiritualism. Fathers and mothers held séances to speak with their dead sons. Very respectable, normally quite rational people got involved. There was even the case of the celebrated scientist, a pioneer in electromagnetic waves, who believed he could use them to build a bridge between our world and the next, "tune in" to the world of the dead.'

He halts momentarily, thrown by Ruprecht Van Doren, who is

goggling at him as if he's choking on something. 'Above all, though,' he fumbles for his thread, 'people coped with their grief by *remembering*. They wore poppies in honour of their loved ones. They erected statues and built cenotaphs. And all over Europe, in villages, towns and cities, they opened memorial gardens like this one. This particular garden was different to all the others, though. Can anyone tell me why?' He gazes evenly from face to pallid face. 'This garden was never actually opened. It wasn't begun until the thirties, and it wasn't completed until the very end of the century. For the decades in between it was let run wild. People grazed their horses here, dealers used it to sell drugs. It was the memorial garden that no one remembered. And it represented most Irish people's attitude to the war, which was to bury it.

'The fact is that, after the Easter Rising and the War of Independence, the Irishmen who'd fought in the Great War didn't fit the new way the country imagined itself. If the British were our sworn enemies, why had two hundred thousand Irishmen gone off to fight alongside them? If our history was the struggle to escape from British oppression, what were we doing helping Britain out, fighting and dying on her behalf? The existence of these soldiers seemed to argue against this new thing called Ireland. And so, first of all, they were turned into traitors. Then, in a quite systematic way, they were forgotten.'

The boys listen palely, the lucent grass-green of the empty park shimmering around them.

'It's a good example of how history works,' Howard says. 'We tend to think of it as something solid and unchanging, appearing out of nowhere etched in stone like the Ten Commandments. But history, in the end, is only another kind of story, and stories are different from the truth. The truth is messy and chaotic and all over the place. Often it just doesn't make sense. Stories make things make sense, but the way they do that is to leave out anything that doesn't fit. And often that is quite a lot.

'The men of "D" Company, like the other men who fought, found this out the hard way. They were told all kinds of stories to get them to join up, stories about duty and morality and defending freedom. Most of all, they were told what a great adventure it would be. When they arrived they discovered that none of these stories was true. Instead they had been lied to and plunged into the most brutal and barbarous mess in the world's history to that point. And the history that was told of that mess was as dishonest as the stories that helped create it.

'When they left Dublin in 1914, with crowds cheering them on, the Pals must have thought that the very least they could hope for was to be remembered. Then again, after so much betrayal, maybe the ones that were left alive afterwards weren't all that surprised it went the other way. And maybe they were wise enough not to let it get to them. They had joined up as friends, and when they got out to the Front, when the grand words evaporated, that bond between them remained. That they stayed friends, that they looked out for each other, most agreed, was what kept them from cracking up altogether. And in the end was the only thing, was the one true thing, that was genuinely worth fighting for.'

He smiles summatively at the boys; they gaze mutely back at him, in their grey uniforms for all the world like an incorporeal platoon, materialized out of the winter clouds to scour the bare park for someone who has not forgotten them.

That night, for the first time in months, the construction work has stopped. The silence is so pristine as to be almost uncanny: Howard feels a light-headedness as he opens his books.

The boys had been quiet on their way back to the station. At first he was afraid he had depressed them, but as the train led them out of the city back along the coast, they emerged from their private reveries with questions:

'So, like, Seabrook students back then, would all of them have been fighting in the war?'

'Well, like you they had parents who were paying a lot of money for their education. So I'd guess that most would have graduated before they joined up. But plenty volunteered after that, I'm sure.'

'And did they get shot?'

'In some cases, I imagine.'

'Wow, I wonder if their ghosts haunt the school.'

'Duh, their ghosts haunt the battlefield, you spasmo.'

'Oh sorry, I forgot to consult the world-renowned ghost expert, who knows everything about where ghosts go to haunt people.'

'If you were interested –' Howard intervening gently '– I'm sure you could find out who joined up and what happened to them.'

'How?'

'Why don't I look into it, and we can talk about it next class.'

He had shepherded them to Seabrook's double-doors and then done a swift volte-face, not yet ready to confront his fate – imagining, as he walked to his car, a hooked finger tugging down a louvre of Venetian blind in an upstairs window . . . Tonight, though, spirits lifted by the boys' interest, he wonders if the situation is as bleak as all that. Isn't it possible that, with the right spin, the story of William Molloy might snag the Automator too? A tale of Seabrook spirit elaborated onto the world stage; a former great, let slip by history, rediscovered by his schoolmates of a century later – wouldn't that be perfect material for, say, a 140th anniversary celebration? Perfect enough for the Acting Principal to overlook Howard's unorthodox (brilliantly unorthodox?) methodology, and allow him to continue, with his formerly recalcitrant class, his groundbreaking work?

The car park the following morning is crowded with company cars. Today is the first day of the annual milk round, in which representatives of various strands of Big Business – Seabrook fathers and old boys, for the most part – come in and speak one-to-one with final-year students. It was just such an interview, a decade earlier, that had set Howard on the road to London. He can still see Ryan Connolly's dad leaned back in his chair, expanding at length on the futures market and the fortunes to be made there, while on the other side of the table the young Howard thought deeply about Ryan Connolly's car, Ryan Connolly's enormous house with swimming pool, the exotic-sounding holidays to Disney World, St Tropez, Antibes, which Ryan Connolly and Ryan Connolly's dad and Ryan Connolly's incredibly hot mum went on every year.

He's in the staffroom, boiling the kettle for tea, when he realizes that Brother Jonas has materialized beside him. 'You gave me a fright,' he jokes, clutching his chest. The little man does not return his smile, merely gazes at Howard a moment with those infinitely deep, melting-chocolate eyes. Then he chants, in his soft musical voice, 'Greg would like to see you now.' With that, like a spirit guide, he glides away, not looking back to see if Howard is following.

A group of sixth-years loiter by the entrance to the Senior Rec Room, where tables and chairs have been set out for the milk round interviews. They are wearing suits – the school encourages a professional approach to the proceedings – of the same tastefully muted tones as the expensive marques in the car park. The change of wardrobe emboldens them; they lean against the door jamb, pronouncing on various topics with careless waves of the hand, the future that has been laid out for them at last being revealed. Howard nods cursorily as he passes them, and they nod back, looking him up and down, perhaps noticing for the first time the less than fresh cut of his own attire.

Howard enters the office to find the Automator behind his desk, staring intensely at a framed photograph of his boys. Following Howard in and closing the door, Brother Jonas installs himself in the corner, from which he shimmers discreetly like a piece of corporate art. The aquarium bubbles gently.

'You wanted to see me, Greg?' Howard says at last.

'I wouldn't say that, Howard. No, that's not how I'd put it at all.' The Automator sets down the photograph, runs a hand over his haggard face. 'Howard, do you know how many messages I had waiting for me when I came in this morning? Take a guess.'

Howard is starting to experience a familiar sinking feeling. 'I don't know, Greg. Eight?'

'Eight.' The Automator smiles ruefully. 'Eight. I wish it were eight. Eight we might have been able to deal with. The answer is twenty-nine. Twenty-nine messages, all of them pertaining to your little exodus. None of them, just so we're clear, telling me what an excellent idea it was.'

The school bell rings for the beginning of class: Howard twitches automatically at the door – 'It's taken care of,' the Automator says leadenly. He rolls his chair back from the desk and in the same dull voice says, 'Tell me, Howard – it's not going to make any difference, of course, but just for my own enlightenment – tell me what you thought you were doing, taking your class off the premises without permission?'

'I wanted to bring them to the museum, Greg. I know it was unorthodox, but I really felt they'd benefit. And they did genuinely seem to get a lot out of it.'

'I don't doubt that,' the Automator says. 'Teacher wigs out, pulls them out of class to wander around the city for the day, I'm sure they had a gay old time. But you see I'm trying to run a school here, Howard. I'm trying to run a school, not a circus.' Howard realizes the Acting Principal's hands are trembling. Suddenly he is very thankful for the brother's presence.

'Greg, I really am sorry I didn't tell you. It was a snap decision and in retrospect I suppose I may have made the wrong call. But in order to complete this module we've been working on, I honestly believed that the class needed to see some actual historical evidence.'

'Oh, is that so?' The Automator folds his hands on his stomach. 'That's very interesting, Howard, because what I'm hearing is that you didn't see any actual historical evidence. What I'm hearing is that you took them to a park in the middle of Junkieville, where you proceeded to tell them about some dismal massacre from a hundred years ago that does not feature on the Junior Cert History course. Is that correct?'

'Yes, but – but the thing is, Greg, they really understood it. I mean they really connected with it?'

'Why the hell would we want them to connect with it?' the Automator exclaims, vein in his temple throbbing double-time. 'Why would any parent in his right mind want the teacher of his children bringing them to an inner-city graveyard to tell them horror stories? Any more than he'd want him telling them that history is . . . is –' he seizes a page from the desk '– "an immense panorama of futility and anarchy". Did you use those words, Howard? Were those your words?'

'I think it was T. S. Eli–'

'I don't care if it was Ronald McDonald! Do you think parents pay ten grand a year so their kids can learn about futility and anarchy? Take a look at the curriculum. Do you see futility and anarchy on it anywhere? Do you?'

Before Howard can reply, the Automator has steamrolled on. 'I've been doing a little historical investigation of my own,' he says, producing a ring-binder crammed with slight, fastidious handwriting – whose? 'See what other interesting things the boys have been learning in your class, such as . . . oh yes, here's a good one, "If any question why we died, Tell them, because our fathers lied." That's great, Howard! Our fathers lied! I don't see any problem with that, do you? I can't see any issues of, of authority or discipline arising out of that one, no. Our fathers lied, why not? And our mothers are prostitutes? And here's how to crack the lock on the drinks cabinet? And then we have Mr Graves –' He brandishes a copy of *Goodbye to All That* – a carefully laminated copy. Howard closes his eyes. Jeekers. 'Are you aware that in the first part of this book, the author details a homosexual affair he has with a boy in his boarding school? Do you think that's the kind of material that a teacher should be presenting to impressionable young men in a Christian school? Or do you think that because Father Furlong isn't in charge, the rules no longer apply? Is that how you see it, Howard? Everybody's swinging, anything goes?' He's on his feet now, face an apocalyptic red. 'And meanwhile you've fallen about a million miles behind your own class plan! My God, Howard, I thought we'd been through this! I thought I told you, no more war! Teach what's in the damn book!'

'And what if there's nothing in the book?' Howard, beginning to lose his temper, raises his voice.

'What?' the Automator shouts back, as if they're standing at either end of a wind tunnel.

'What if there's nothing in the book, what if the book is *empty*?'

'Empty, Howard?' He's got the history book here too, he picks it up and riffles through the pages. 'Doesn't look empty to me. Looks like it's full of history. Full of it.'

'Don't we have a responsibility to give both sides of the story? To make some gesture towards the truth?'

'You have a responsibility to teach what you're paid to teach! I don't care if it's the history of tic-tac-toe, if it's on the curriculum you go in there and you teach it, and you teach it in such a way that there's an outside chance a tiny fragment of it will remain alive in those boys' brains, so that they can dredge it up and repeat it in the state exams!'

'I see, so it doesn't matter if I'm perpetuating lies, then. It doesn't matter that your curriculum leaves out forty thousand dead men, including alumni of this very school. That to you is an acceptable version of history, and a cover-up is an appropriate thing to teach the boys –'

'A cover-up?' the Automator repeats incredulously, spittle flying from his mouth. 'A cover-up?'

'A cover-up, yes, something that, even though it was ninety years ago, still no one wants to talk about –'

'Jesus Christ, Howard.' The Automator runs his hand through his hair. 'This isn't some kind of giant conspiracy! Parents aren't ringing me up because they're worried you're getting close to the truth! They're ringing me up because some crackpot teacher popped a gasket and ran off with their children! That's what people think about, Howard! Reality! Don't you understand that? Why aren't my son's grades better? Will I get my new kitchen in beech or stripped pine? How's the Algarve for golf this time of year? This – this is the *past*, Howard. The First World War, the Easter Rising, a bunch of maniacs shooting and speechifying and waving flags, it's the past! And no one cares about it! The reason they don't talk about it is that they don't care!'

'You have to teach them to care,' Howard murmurs, remembering.

'Teach them to care?' the Automator repeats, as if stupefied. 'Teach them to – wait, do you think this is some kind of a *Dead Poets Society* situation we're in here, is that it? You think that this is some kind of a *Dead Poets*, where we're the evil tyrannical school, and you're, ah – damn it, the man, he was Mork, and he dressed up as the nanny –'

'Robin Williams?'

'Correct, that you're Robin Williams? Is that it, Howard? Because if that's it, let me just ask you something – whose interests are you serving, spending six weeks on something that's covered here in the textbook in a single page? Is it really for the boys? Or is it for yourself?'

Burning as he is with righteous anger, this question catches Howard off guard.

.'Maybe you're right,' the Automator continues, 'maybe the book does leave a chunk of stuff out. And maybe in the future someone will dig it up, and make a TV documentary, and there'll be exhibitions and pull-out newspaper supplements and people all over the country will be talking about it. But when they're finished talking, Howard, then they'll go back to their kitchens or their golfing holidays or whatever they were doing before. The "truth", as you put it, won't change a goddamn thing. You're no dummy, though, you know that. This history business is neither here nor there. No, you're taking some sort of revenge for the Juster business, that's what this is. You're coming in here and attempting to derail regular Seabrook life, you're trying to pollute my boys' minds and warp their sensibilities because of guilt at what you've done. What *you've* done, Howard, you signed that contract, no one held a gun to your head. Well, let me tell you a couple of things, mister. Let me tell you a couple of facts that are true. Fact one, you will fail. You will fail, Howard. Maybe you think that because you know what you know, you've got us over a barrel. You think you can bring Seabrook down. But that is not the case, because if you knew anything about history you would know that this school is not a school that loses, and no matter what you try we will not lose against you. You can go to the police, you can breach your contract, you can betray your fellow teacher, you can do all that, Howard, and bring scandal down on this school, but we will survive. We will survive, we will weather the storm, because we are a team, a team with values and beliefs, which is united by those values and beliefs and is strong because of them.

'And that takes me to fact two, Howard, which is, this school is good. No, it is not perfect, because we live in a world in which nothing is perfect. But this school, if you want a history lesson, has educated generations of Irish children, produced not just doctors, lawyers, businessmen, the men who make the backbone of our society, but also missionaries, aid workers, philanthropists.

This school has a great tradition, furthermore, an ongoing tradition of reaching out to the poor and the downtrodden, of this country and of Africa. Who are you to come in here and undermine that? Who are you to come in, understanding nothing, nothing, of how anything works, and try to sabotage the running of this school? A failure, a coward like you? A man who is like a child, who is so enfeebled by his own pathetic fears that he has never, he will never stand up for anything? He will never have the courage to do anything for anyone?'

He sits back, trembling, in his chair, picks up the photograph of his boys again, as if seeking to convince himself there is still good in the world. 'I'm suspending you with pay until further notice. I need to speak to the school's solicitor before we take any definitive action, but I would strongly advise you to keep away from Seabrook College until then. Katherine Moore's going to take your classes in the meantime.' He looks up dully. 'Get out of here, Howard. Go home to your wife that loves you.'

Howard rises stolidly and moves for the door without saying goodbye. But something arrests his attention, and he stops. Three bloated blue and gold fish are lazily circumnavigating an otherwise denuded aquarium. 'What?' he says. 'What happened to the other ones?'

Brother Jonas, who has been poised silently in the corner throughout the conversation, now releases a laugh – a surprisingly profane sound, like air squealing from a balloon. 'A long way from Japan!' he says. 'A long way with no lunch!'

He laughs again; the sound is still ringing in his ears as Howard passes on to the staffroom to clear out his locker.

Geoff, Ruprecht and Jeekers are trailing wordlessly down the corridor on the way to Science when Dennis steps out from behind a pillar.

'Not so fast, there, losers,' he says.

'What do *you* want?' Geoff replies.

'I want my five euro.' Dennis waves a chaotic-looking ledger at him. 'From you, and you, and from fatty here.' He rocks back on his heels expectantly. Niall, reeking of cigarette smoke, leers at them from over his shoulder.

'I don't owe you anything, asshat,' Geoff says.

'Oh you don't, don't you?' Dennis says airily. 'The small matter of the Nervous Breakdown Leaderboard doesn't ring any bells?'

'What?'

'Allow me to refresh your memory,' Dennis says, opening the ledger with a flourish. 'Here we are . . . Geoff Sproke, ninth September, sum of five euro on Brother Jonas to crack up first. Jeekers Prendergast, September eleven, unlucky for some, predicts Lurch, five euro. Ruprecht Von Blowjob, same date, five euro on Kipper Slattery – bad choice, Blowjob, the old ones never go under, not when their pension's in sight. Anyhow, you all lose, so cough up.'

'What are you talking about?'

'Howard the Coward,' Dennis snaps, gesturing exasperatedly back down the stairs. 'He's lost it. He's the first to go. None of you guessed him. So now it's time to pay up.'

'What do you mean, he's lost it?'

'His mind, you idiot. Why do you think he wasn't in class today?'

'I don't know, maybe he's out sick?'

566

'He's not out sick, his car's in the car park. They're not letting him teach because he's gone mad.'

'He didn't seem mad to me,' Geoff objects.

'Uh, kidnapping us from school to bring us to a museum with nothing in it? Then making us stand around in a freezing park listening to a load of stuff that isn't even in the book?'

'So what?'

'So, what more do you want, him to skateboard through the Annexe in his mother's wedding dress? Give me five euro.'

Geoff and the others continue to resist, but then Simon Mooney comes along and asks if they've heard that Howard the Coward's got the boot.

'This morning, the Automator hauled him up to the office first thing. Jason Rycroft heard Bitchface Moore saying it to Felcher.'

'Holy shit,' says Geoff. Jeekers, on hearing this news, looks deeply unhappy and guilty, even more so than usual.

'I rest my case,' Dennis says.

'What case?' Simon Mooney wants to know.

'Glad you asked me that, Moonbuggy, because I believe you owe me the sum of five euro. As for you, gentlemen, will that be cash or cash?'

'Get bent,' Geoff says defiantly, and makes to move on. Dennis lunges after him.

'Give me my money!' he demands.

'No way!' Geoff yells back, and there is a crackle of that pure enmity that can only exist between former friends.

'Give me it,' Dennis repeats warningly.

'You're just going to spend it on cigarettes!'

'So? You're just going to spend it on polyhedral dice for role-playing, or should I say, role-*gaying*.'

'At least role-playing doesn't give you cancer!' Geoff shouts, tugging his arm free of Dennis's pincer-grip.

'Role-playing is worse than cancer!' Dennis shouts back, and it seems like the dispute is going to devolve yet again into blows, when from the window Simon Mooney cries out, 'Oh my God!'

They turn to see him gazing out dumbstruck. 'It's *her* . . .' he croons. Quarrel temporarily suspended, they flock to his side. Simon's right, it *is* her; and for a single sighing moment, the boys are reunited in memories of a better time.

'Remember the day she wore that blue top, and you could sort of see her nipples?'

'Remember how she used to suck the top of her pen?'

'I wonder what she's doing here?'

'Do you think she's coming back?'

'Hey look, it's Howard . . .'

'He's talking to her!'

'Maybe he's going to run away with her,' Geoff surmises. 'Maybe he told the Automator to sit on it and now she's come to pick him up and they're going off to live on like a desert island.'

'Fat chance,' Dennis says.

'He used to have the horn for her,' Geoff points out.

'Newsflash, Geoff, having the horn for someone does not mean they're going to get jiggy with you. Haven't you heard? There's an asymmetry in the universe.' This last accompanied by a snide sidelong glance at Ruprecht, who does not react.

'I don't care,' Geoff says. 'Come on, Howard! Run away with her!'

Consumed by the urge to make a speedy exit, Howard walks right by without seeing her. Typical perversity of fate: it's probably the first time in the last six weeks he hasn't been thinking of her, hasn't been half-hoping she might appear. He is maladroitly attempting to balance a stack of books while fishing his car key from his pocket, when he hears her voice behind him, cool as the breeze: 'Well, well, so we meet again.'

She looks, if it's possible, even more beautiful than before – although maybe it's not possible, maybe it's just that that level of beauty is too bright to be fully retained in the memory, any more than you can photograph the sun – dressed in a man's white shirt in which her perfection appears so simply and ineffably that it seems to present an answer to any question or doubt anyone might ever have had about anything, so quietly overwhelming that Howard forgets he hates her, instead is suffused with joy, thankfulness, relief, at least until he realizes that the man's white shirt probably belongs to her fiancé.

'Been a while,' she says, evidently unphased by his failure to reply.

'What are you doing here?' No sooner has he said it than the dreadful thought occurs to him that the Automator has drafted her in to replace him, invoking so many layers of irony he thinks his brain might short-circuit; but she tells him that she's come to speak to the sixth-years about careers in investment banking, and also to have a word with Greg about the school's portfolio. She pushes back a tress of golden hair. 'How have you been, Howard?'

How has he *been*? Can she seriously be asking him that, after taking a hatchet to his life? Apparently she can. Her ocean-blue eyes await him with limitless concern; backlit by the sun, the contours of her face seem to glow, as though she is turning into light. And Howard can't actually see a ring on her finger. Could it be that Fate isn't quite done with him? Has she reappeared just in time to ride away with him into the sunset, or to present herself as a sunset for him to ride away into? Could it be that by some miracle *everything might still turn out all right*?

'I've been better,' he says gruffly. 'We've had a time of it here lately. You heard about Daniel Juster?'

'God, yes, it was horrible.' Lowering her voice she says, 'That awful *priest* . . . what are they going to do?'

'Nothing,' he says, shrivelling interiorly at the question. 'They decided not to do anything.'

She considers this. 'Probably wise,' she says judiciously.

'How about you? Anything new?'

'Oh, you know . . .' Her eyes dance over the brutal brick façade of the Annexe. 'Nothing, really. Working. It's okay. A little boring. It's nice to be back here. I forgot how much I enjoyed playing teacher.'

'Ever tempted to come back?' he says, leaving a double-meaning there should she choose to pick it up.

She laughs melodiously. 'Oh, I don't think so. I'm not like you, Howard, I don't have a vocation for it.'

'The boys liked you.'

'They liked staring at my tits,' she says. 'That's not the same thing.'

'I liked you.'

'Mmm.' She shields her eyes with her hand, turns her gaze onto the car park, the wintery trees. 'Hard to believe it's almost Christmas already. Time just *goes*, doesn't it? Faster and faster. Next thing you know we'll all be in a nursing home.'

Howard is getting increasingly frustrated with this conversation. Are they just going to keep going like this, being nice and charming and polite? 'You know,' he says, 'we never got a chance to talk.'

'Talk?'

'I meant to get your number, after . . .' He trails off; she gazes keenly into one eye, then the other, as if he's raving. 'I left my girlfriend,' he blurts.

'Oh, Howard. I'm so sorry. She sounded so nice.'

'Jesus Christ . . .' He turns his back on her momentarily so he can gnash his teeth, clench and unclench his fists. 'Are you really doing this? Do you really expect me just to forget everything?'

'Forget what?'

'Oh, so you do, so you are, okay.'

'I don't understand what it is you want me to say.'

'I want you to act like what happened between us happened!' Howard shouts.

She does not reply, merely purses her lips, as if studying an untrustworthy fuel gauge on a long trip.

'How could you have a fiancé? What kind of person *does* that?' He is still carrying the pile of books from his locker; he deposits them on top of the car, where they totter and spill over the roof. 'I mean, was anything you said true? Did you feel anything for me at all? Have you even read Robert Graves?'

She doesn't respond; the angrier he gets, the more serene she becomes, which makes him angrier still.

'Is this just what you do? Go around making people fall in love with you, and then dropping them, like it doesn't mean anything? Like nothing leads to anything else? Like it's all just there to pass the time, me, and those kids in your Geography class you got all het up about recycling and global warming, I mean do you *care* about any of it? About your job, even? Your *fiancé*? Do you actually care about anything, or is it all just one big game to you?'

She remains silent, and then impulsively, or with the appearance of impulsivity, she says, 'We're not all like you, Howard. Life isn't black and white for everybody.'

'What are you talking about?'

'I mean, not everybody has the ability you have. The ability to care. You're lucky, you don't even realize it but you are.'

'So let me care about you! If I'm so good at it, why won't you let me do it, instead of running away?'

'I don't mean me. I mean the children.'

'The children?'

'The boys. They like you. They listen to what you say. Don't deny it, I've seen it.'

What the fuck? 'Are you talking about *teaching*?' Howard is flabbergasted. 'What has that got to do with anything?'

'I'm saying, not everybody gets to do something good. Those kids will grow up to be better people from being in your class. That makes you lucky.'

'Oh wow, I never thought of it that way,' Howard says. 'Now I feel so much better.'

'You should,' she says. 'I'd better go. Goodbye, Howard. I hope everything works out for you.'

'Wait, wait –' his head is spinning as if he'd downed a bottle of vodka; laughing, he seizes the strap of her bag '– wait, just tell me one thing – what you said at the Hop, remember how you told me that at your own mixer, when you were a kid, no one would dance with you? That was a lie, wasn't it? Just confirm that for me, that it was just another lie?'

She shoots him a cold ugly look and pulls the strap free of his hand. 'Have you been listening to a single word I've said?'

'I'm sorry,' Howard says brightly. 'Goodbye, so. Good luck with the sixth-years. I'm sure they'll be very interested to hear about your work, and all the nice things you can get for making rich old men that little bit richer.'

She steps free of him, holds his gaze a moment. 'A lot richer,' she says expressionlessly. 'They pay me to make them a lot richer.' With that she turns and walks away, into the school. Howard watches her go, possessed by a strange, hating euphoria; then, as he moves for his car, he chances to look up, and sees, from an upper window of the building, a handful of his second-year class – Mooney, Hoey, Sproke, Van Doren – gazing forlornly down at him, and his brief sense of victory is instantly and thoroughly replaced by a crushing sense of failure. He waves at them limply, and gets into his car without waiting to see if they wave back.

But the past isn't done with him yet. Howard's sitting in front of the TV news that night – already on his fourth beer, a fringe benefit of not having a job to go to tomorrow – when he realizes he's staring at an image of his own house. It appears with its neighbours, a series of gently sloping triangles silhouetted on the crest of the hill, behind the brassy bouffant of a reporter.

He starts; then, with an eerie sense of impending revelation, of a kind that perhaps haunts all inhabitants of the television age, he leans forward and turns up the sound.

The story is about the new Science Park. It seems that, while digging the foundations, engineers unearthed some kind of prehistoric fortress. On the orders of the development company, however, they kept schtum and continued with their work, and apparently the whole thing would have been bulldozed if a disgruntled Turkish labourer, denied his overtime for the fourth week running, hadn't blown the whistle. 'Archaeologists are calling it a "find of incalculable value",' the reporter says. 'We put these allegations to the project's Publicity Director, Guido LaManche.'

'No,' Howard says, out loud.

But it is he: Guido LaManche, bestower of wedgies, infamous farter, doughnut-eating champion, pioneer of the bungee jump in Ireland – here he is now in a well-tailored suit, telling the reporter that as far as he can see these commentators are generating much heat but very little light.

'"A find of incalculable value,"' the reporter reminds him.

Guido permits himself a gentle, slightly flirtatious chuckle. The years have been good to him; he is slimmer and fitter, and speaks with the confidence and surety of the world-shaper. 'Well, Ciara, the truth is that in a country like Ireland, you can't build a sandcastle without making a find of incalculable value. If we were to ring-fence every single historic this or that we discovered, there would literally be nowhere left for anyone to live.'

'So you're saying it should be bulldozed,' the reporter says.

'I'm saying we need to ask ourselves where our priorities lie. Because what we are trying to build here isn't just a Science Park. It's the economic future of our country. It's jobs and security for our children and our children's children. Do we really want to put a ruin from three thousand years ago ahead of our children's future?'

'And what about those who say that this "ruin" gives us a unique insight into the origins of our culture?'

'Well, let me turn that question around. If the position was reversed, do you think the people of three thousand years ago would have stopped building their fortress so they could preserve the ruin of our Science Park? Of course not. They wanted to move forward. The whole reason we have the civilization we have to-day – the only reason you and I are standing here – is that people kept moving forward instead of looking backward. Everybody in the past *wanted* to be a part of the future, just as today everybody in the Third World wants to be a part of the First. And if they had a choice, they would swap places with us in a second!'

'Moving forward!' Howard claps his hands like he's cheering on a racehorse; at which point the power cuts out, leaving him with his beer in the dark.

Moving forward. After the bungee jump, Guido had relocated to a private school in Barbados, never to be seen again. It hadn't made much difference: in the eyes of the school, Howard was really the one to blame. Cowardice, that was the unforgiveable sin for a Seabrook boy. Most people were kind enough not to say it to his face, but he knew it with every breath he took, and he has lived with it every day and night since.

But Guido did not live with it. Guido moved forward. He wasn't about to let one fleeting episode determine the whole trajectory of his life thereafter. For Guido the past, like a Third World country, was merely another resource to be exploited and abandoned when the time comes; and that is why civilization is built by men like him and the Automator, and not men like Howard, who have never quite worked out which stories are disposable, and which, if any, you're actually supposed to believe.

He's still laughing – or is he crying? – when the phone rings. It takes him a while to locate it in the chaotic darkness, but the ringer is persistent. Answering, he is addressed by a gruff male voice that cannot quite conceal its youth. 'Mr Fallon?'

'Who is this?'

A cautious pause ensues, and then, 'It's Ruprecht. Ruprecht Van Doren.'

'Ruprecht?' Howard gets an unsettling worlds-collide sensation. 'How did you get this number?'

There is a scuffling sound, as of rodents tussling in the undergrowth, and then, 'I need to talk to you.'

'Now?'

'It's important. Can I come over?'

Dazedly Howard casts an eye over the chiaroscuro dereliction of the house. 'No . . . no, I don't think that would be appropriate.'

'Well, how about Ed's? Ed's in half an hour?'

'Ed's?'

'Beside the school. It's important, half an hour okay?' The boy hangs up. Howard stands there a moment in mystification, dial tone burring in his ear. Then the significance of the venue strikes him, and with it the realization that there is only one possible reason Ruprecht should urgently want to see him. Somehow he has come to suspect the coach.

He pulls on a jacket as he dashes outside. The night has grown teeth, and the cold binds with the anticipation in his stomach to banish the fug of cheap beer. What has Ruprecht found out, and how? An overheard conversation? Did he hack into the school network? Or maybe Juster left a note that's only surfaced now? He climbs into the car, and as the distance between him and the answer diminishes, exhilaration courses over him like the freezing

575

air that gusts through the vents. He bursts breathless through the doors of the Doughnut House.

The diner is almost empty; Ruprecht sits alone at a two-person table with a box of doughnuts and two polystyrene beakers. 'I didn't know what flavours you liked –' He gestures at the box of doughnuts. 'So I got a mix. And I didn't know what kind of drink you like, so I got Sprite.'

'Sprite is perfect,' Howard says. 'Thank you.' He takes a seat and looks around the room. He has not been in here for years. It is little changed: generic Americana on the walls, glossy backlit photographs of pastries and croissants above the counter, air with an anonymous odour you can't quite put your finger on – the smell of fluorescent lights, maybe, or of polystyrene beakers, or whatever the mysterious arid liquid is that they are selling as coffee. He remembers the excitement in school when it had first opened. An international chain, right here in Seabrook! Back then, when Ireland was a global backwater, this had seemed nothing short of a wonderful kindness, like a mission opening a school in the jungle; flocking into its bland homogenous interior, designed by committee and replicated the world over, he and his friends had felt proudly apart from the parent-dominated city immediately outside, aligned instead with something almost mythic, something that transcended the limits of time and space to be a kind of everyplace, an everyplace belonging to the young.

'I'm sorry you got fired,' Ruprecht says to him.

Howard flushes. 'Well, I haven't actually been, ah, it's more of a sabbatical . . .'

'Was it for taking us to the park?'

Without knowing why this embarrasses him so, he affects not to have heard. 'Quiet tonight,' he says, smiling glassily.

'People don't really come here any more,' Ruprecht replies in a monotone.

Howard wants to ask him why *he* still comes here, he of all people; but instead he says, 'It's good to see you, Ruprecht. I've been meaning to have a word with you.'

Ruprecht says nothing, watches his eyes. Howard finds his mouth has gone dry, slurps from his Sprite. 'On the phone you said there was something important you needed to talk about.'

Ruprecht nods. 'I just wanted to know something for this project I'm doing,' he says, keeping his voice carefully neutral.

'What kind of project?'

'Sort of a communications project.'

He catches Ruprecht's eye just as something surfaces to peek out at him; then it bolts back into the impenetrable recesses of the boy's mind. 'Well, that's good,' he says. 'That you're doing a project. Because it seems like you've been a bit under the weather lately. You know, you haven't been taking as much interest in class as you used to.'

Ruprecht does not respond to this, traces invisible ideograms with the end of his straw on the tabletop.

'Since what, ah, what happened to Daniel,' Howard expands. 'I mean, it seems like it affected you a great deal.'

The boy continues to devote his full attention to his straw pictures, but his cheeks crimson and his face assumes an expression of misery.

Howard looks over his shoulder. The only other customers are a foreign couple, pored over a map; behind the till, a bored-looking Asian is emptying coins from plastic baggies.

'Sometimes in these matters,' he says, 'what you really need is closure. To understand what's happened, tie up any loose ends that might exist. Often that, tying up the loose ends, that's what will help you to move on.' He clears his throat. 'And if tying those loose ends seems difficult, or even dangerous, you should know that there are people who are ready to help you. Who will coach you through it. Do you understand me?'

Ruprecht's eyes flash up-from-under at him, seeking to puzzle him out.

Howard waits, on tenterhooks. Then at last, 'Is that, is tying the loose ends, what you wanted to talk to me about?'

The boy takes a deep breath. 'You mentioned a scientist,' he says hoarsely. 'When we were in the park, you mentioned a scientist, a pioneer in electromagnetic waves.'

For a moment Howard is at sea. What is he talking about? Is this some sort of code?

'You said he had worked out how to communicate –' Ruprecht brings his voice down to a whisper '– *with the dead.*' His eyes glimmer with desperation; and finally Howard understands. Ruprecht has no clue about Coach or any kind of wrongdoing; he has no plan to bring anyone to justice; all that remains locked up in Howard's own head. The disappointment is crushing – so much so that for an instant he teeters on the verge of telling the boy himself, telling him everything. But does he really want to be the one who visits the repulsion and cynicism of that world on Ruprecht's? Instead, to sweeten the bitterness, he picks up a doughnut and takes a bite. It is surprisingly good.

'That's right,' he says. 'His name was Oliver Lodge. At the time he was one of the most famous scientists in the world. He'd made all sorts of groundbreaking discoveries involving magnetism, electricity, radio waves, and in his later years he attempted to use these, as you say, to communicate with the spirit world. There was a lot of that going on at the end of the Victorian era – séances, fairies, psychic photography, and so on. Maybe it was a reaction to the society of the day, which was very materialistic and technology-obsessed – quite like ours, actually. It made the scientists of the period very angry, especially because the spiritualists were claiming to use science, specifically new inventions like cameras, gramophones and radios, to contact the spirit world. So a group of scientists, including Lodge, got together to study supernatural phenomena with the aim of exposing the whole thing as the fraud it was.

'But then war broke out, and Lodge's son Raymond was killed in battle. The next thing, Lodge was caught up in the very stuff he was supposed to be disproving. He claimed he had communicated with his dead son – in fact, he wrote a book, part of which was supposedly dictated to him by the boy, from beyond the grave.

According to this book, which became a huge bestseller, the other world, the afterlife – Summerland was the name his son gave it – was only a hair's breadth away from the world familiar to you and me. But it existed in a different dimension, so you couldn't see it.'

'But *he* could see it?'

'Well, no. He had a housemaid who was a medium. Everything came through her. But from his own work in physics, and Raymond's descriptions of the other world, Lodge believed he was on the point of proving conclusively that there was life after death. The key was this fourth dimension, this extra dimension right next to ours but separated from us by an invisible veil. Lodge thought that the new electromagnetic waves he'd discovered could pass through this veil.'

'How?' Ruprecht's eyes pinned on him in as lynx-like a fashion as is possible for a chronically overweight fourteen-year-old.

'Well, there was an idea at the time that space was filled by an invisible material called ether. Scientists didn't understand how these waves they'd discovered, light waves, radio waves and so forth, could travel through a vacuum. There must be something that carried them. So they came up with ether. Ether was what allowed light to travel from the sun to the Earth. Ether connected everything to everything else. The spiritualists proposed that it didn't stop at matter either. It joined our souls to our bodies, it linked the worlds of the living and the dead.'

'Ether.' Ruprecht nods to himself.

'Right. Lodge thought that if electromagnetic waves could traverse this ether, then communication with the dead was not only scientifically plausible but within the grasp of the technology of the time. In Raymond's accounts of Summerland, the dead soldiers reported being able to hear very faint emanations from the world of the living – music, especially, certain pieces of music came through the veil. So in his book Lodge outlines the first principles of how this communication would work.'

'And what happened?' Ruprecht has leaned so far across the table that he appears to be floating above his seat; Howard, beginning to feel uncomfortable, attempts to inch his chair back only to find it welded to the floor. 'Nothing happened,' he says.

'Nothing?' Ruprecht doesn't understand.

'Well, it failed, obviously, I mean it was wrong, it was all wrong. Because there was no ether. There was no mysterious substance joining everything to everything else. Lodge became a laughing stock, his reputation was ruined.'

'But . . .' Ruprecht is scanning the table in disbelief, like an investor being told his entire portfolio has gone south. 'But how could it not work?'

Howard does not quite understand what is going on here, why Ruprecht should be taking this so personally. 'I think it's important to remember the context in which Lodge was working,' he says carefully. 'Yes, he was a great scientist. But he was also a man who had just lost his son. Other champions of spiritualism were in the same position – Sir Arthur Conan Doyle, for instance, had also lost a son in the war. The people who bought Lodge's book, the ones who conducted séances themselves, the soldiers in the trenches who saw the ghosts of their friends – these were all people in mourning. This was a world that had literally gone crazy with grief. At the same time, it was an age when science and technology promised they could deliver all the answers. Suddenly you could talk to somebody on the other side of the world – why shouldn't you be able to talk to the dead?'

Ruprecht is hanging on his words, glassy-eyed, with bated breath. 'But the point was, you couldn't,' Howard says, and repeats it, 'you couldn't,' to bolster himself against the hostility with which this information is received – a stare that is pitched somewhere between crestfallen and mutinous.

'But he says in his experiments he did talk to dead people,' the boy says.

'Yes, but that might be best understood as a manifestation of –'

'Like just because no one believed him doesn't mean it wasn't true.'

'Well . . .' Howard doesn't know quite how to respond.

'Lots of things that are true people think they aren't,' Ruprecht's voice, while remaining at the same pitch and volume, intensifies in some impalpable way, causing the foreign couple to look up from their map. 'And lots of things that aren't true they tell us they are.'

'Maybe so, but that doesn't mean –'

'How do you *know* he was wrong? How do you know the soldiers and people just hallucinated everything they saw? How do you know?'

He delivers all this with such vehemence, doughy head turning an angry pink, like some vengeful jellyfish, that Howard prefers not to contradict him; instead he just nods ambivalently, gazing at the half-melted ice cubes at the base of his polystyrene cup. The tourists leave their table and go outside.

'Let me tell you about another famous man of that time,' Howard says at last. 'Rudyard Kipling, the writer. He wrote *The Jungle Book*, among other things – you've seen the film, I'm sure, you know, Baloo? *Do-be-do, I want to be like you . . .*'

Ruprecht looks at him in bafflement.

'Well, anyway. When the war broke out, Kipling's only son, John, wanted to join up. Because he was only sixteen, Kipling had to pull some strings to get him into the service. The commander of the Irish Guards was a friend of his, and through him Kipling got his son a commission. John went off to train and a year later he was sent to the Western Front. About forty minutes into his first battle he disappeared and was never seen again.

'Kipling was heartbroken. He sunk into a black, black depression. Things got so bad that although he'd always denounced séances as hocus-pocus he was on the point of trying them, in the hope of contacting his son. But then he was approached by the colonel of the Irish Guards. Every regiment had a record of their experiences in the war, and the colonel asked Kipling if he would write theirs.

'Now Kipling was as British as they come. Cut him and he bled orange, as they say. He thought the Catholic Irish were no better than animals. But because it was his son's regiment, he, probably the most famous writer in the world at the time, agreed to write the regimental history. Not only that, but he made the decision to write about the men – not the officers, not the great battles, not any broader themes of the war. He used the regimental diaries and the personal accounts of the Irish soldiers. And as he did he was overwhelmed by their courage, their loyalty and their decency.

'The book took him five and a half years to complete. He found it extremely difficult. But afterwards he said it was his greatest work. He'd had a chance to commemorate the bravery of these men, and to keep the memory of his son alive. A man called Brodsky once said, "If there is any substitute for love, it is memory." Kipling couldn't bring John back. But he could remember him. And in that way his son lived on.'

This parable doesn't produce quite the effect he intended; in fact, he is not sure that Ruprecht, tracing Sprite-spirals on the table with a straw, is even listening. The youth behind the counter looks at his watch and begins to dismantle the coffee machine; an electric fan whirrs, like the smooth sound of time passing inexorably from underneath them. And then, not looking up, Ruprecht mumbles, 'What if you can't remember?'

'What?' Howard rouses from his interior exertions.

'I'm forgetting what he looks like,' the boy says huskily.

'Who? You mean Daniel?'

'Every day more little pieces are gone. I'll try and remember something and I won't be able. It just gets worse and worse. And I can't stop it.' His voice cracks; he looks up imploringly, his face a mess of tears. 'I can't stop it!' he repeats; then, right in front of Howard, he punches himself in the head with his fists, hard as he is able, then again, and again, shouting over and over, 'I can't stop it! I can't stop it!'

From behind the counter the Asian boy looks on aghast; Howard finds himself staring back at him helplessly, as if he might know what to do, before realizing it is up to him. 'Ruprecht! Ruprecht!' he calls, and thrusts his hands into the whirl of fists, like two sticks into the spokes of a bicycle wheel, until he manages to get a grip on the boy's arms and immobilize them. Ruprecht's shuddering gradually subsides into peace, punctuated by sharp, wheezing intakes of breath. He reaches into his pocket for his asthma inhaler and tugs on it sharply.

'Are you okay?' Howard says.

Ruprecht nods, his head damasked with embarrassment even more deeply than before. Fat tears drip onto the table. Howard feels sick to the stomach. Still, to fill the unbearable silence, he forces himself to say, 'You know, Ruprecht . . . what you're feeling is perfectly normal. When a loss occurs –'

'I have to go,' Ruprecht says, sliding himself out of the plastic chair.

'Wait!' Howard stands as well. 'What about your project, do you want me to send you some books, or . . .'

But Ruprecht's already at the threshold, his thin *Thank you, bye* truncated by the swinging shut of the swing-door, and Howard is left shrivelled under the electric lights and the cool, evaluating gaze of the impassive Asian youth as he tamps out coffee grounds into the garbage.

It is night. Janine is lying on the street. Carl is standing over her.

I had to tell her, Carly, I had to.

It's hard to understand what Janine is saying. In the windows of the houses the curtains are closed. In Lori's window the light is not on any more, and she's not in the car when it jumps through the gate.

I did it for us, Janine says. She gets to her knees, she hugs his legs, she shrivels her body against Carl's side like a leech. She's gone, Carl, it's over! Why can't you just forget her?

She will not tell him where the hospital is and the car drives too fast for Carl to follow it on his bike.

Here – Janine's voice goes black and she reaches into her pocket – if you won't believe me, see for yourself. I took a picture of her. Go on, look, that's who you're in love with.

The face twisted up like a piece of chewing gum.

No!

So he throws her phone as hard as he can and leaves her crawling around someone's garden crying, Wait ring me ring me so I can find it.

Now he's at home trying to watch TV. I wouldn't wipe my arse with a Daewoo, Clarkson is saying. On the bed the new All-Blacks jersey. Downstairs Mom goes, Because you can't! And Dad going, Last time I looked this was my fucking house! I'M TRYING TO WATCH TV, shouts Carl. Clarkson says, Dead Boy. Carl's head snaps back to the screen. Give me something with a bit of oomph, Clarkson says. A shiver goes up Carl's arm, tingling in every scar.

That's when the phone rings. Barry. It's happening, he says.

What? Carl says.

Night after tomorrow. The connection, dude. They're taking us with them to meet the Druid.

Carl's brain reaches back into the endless black dark of his memory.

Do you know what this means? Barry is saying. It means we're in. We're made men.

And then in the phone but not Barry's voice: He will be waiting for you, Carl.

He jerks up on his bed. What did you say?

Then Barry again like nothing has happened: This is so big-time, dude. Like seriously, do you know what this means?

But Carl does not know what it means.

At night is when it happens the worst: he'll wake up and feel it, like actually be able to feel it, another constellation of moments disappeared out of his memory. Where *exactly* did Skippy sit that day in the Ref? What was it he always took out of his burger, the pickle or the onion? What was the name of the dog he had before Dogley? So many things to remember! And though Ruprecht tried his best to hold them in place – lying in bed, reciting them to himself, avoiding talking or listening to people, to keep new images, new memories, from pushing out the old ones – still he forgot and at last he realized that the forgetting was never going to stop, that no matter what he did the moments would keep trickling away, like blood from a wound that could never heal, until all of them were gone. That realization was almost worse than anything that had come before. It made him so angry! He churned, he seethed, he boiled with anger – at himself, at Skippy, at the whole world! – and in his fury, he vowed to forget every-thing once and for all, get it over with. But it turned out he couldn't do that either, all he could do was become angrier and angrier on the inside, while on the outside he grew evermore fat and pale and dead.

When they went to the park he hadn't thought about science in a long time. He hadn't turned on his computer in weeks, he didn't even use that part of his brain any more, because what good had it done, M-theory, Professor Tamashi, any of it? Wasn't Dennis right, wasn't it just a giant Rubik's cube for Ruprecht to while away the hours with, arranging its blocks and colours safe in the knowledge that it could never actually be solved? And yet when Howard mentioned the scientist it was as if he, Sir Oliver Lodge as he turned out to be called, had reached

585

across the decades and tapped him on the shoulder. And ever since, no matter how much Ruprecht wanted him to go away, he'd remained there. Tapping.

He should have known better than to expect a teacher to shed any light on it though. What do teachers know about what is true? Look at all the falsehoods they teach every day! The maps in Geography that make Africa look small and Europe and the U.S. really big, the books of Euclidean geometry that say everything's made of straight lines when nothing in the real world is made of straight lines, all that stuff about how good it is to be meek, and how if you're meek and follow the rules everything will turn out great? When it obviously won't? So when Ruprecht returns to his room from the Doughnut House he tries a different source. And on the Internet he finds quite a different story from the one Howard told him.

In this account, Victorian science was a long way from the materialistic, conservative affair the teacher described; and Lodge's experiments, far from being the manifestations of a demented mind, were only one element of a concerted scientific effort to undo the final mystery of life after death. Other participants included Alexander Graham Bell, with his telephone, Thomas Edison, creator of the Spirit Finder, John Logie Baird, inventor of television (to whom Edison's ghost appeared in a séance), William Crookes, Nikola Tesla, Guglielmo Marconi – in fact, when you looked at it, almost all twenty-first-century communication technology originated in scientific attempts to speak to the dead.

And for a time, at the start of the last century, they seemed genuinely to be on the brink of something. The succession of discoveries one after the other – Hertz, Maxwell, Faraday, Lodge, Einstein with his undulating space, Schwarzschild with his *dark star* as it was called at first, and then *black hole*, a hole in the actual universe – and simultaneously, the rise of the table-turners and the clairvoyants and the spirit-photographers, the battery of knocks on walls that had no human source . . . At that time as never before it seemed the whole of reality warped and rippled, as if with the shape of invisible fingers endeavouring to push through the skin of what was, the ghosts of words, spoken by long-lost voices, becoming almost audible in the new hiss and new static . . .

Then it all stopped. The trail went cold. Was there just too much death to cope with, was that it? After devoting itself for two world wars to perfecting new methods of annihilation, did science no longer want to hear what the annihilated might have to say? Whatever the reason, scientists turned away from the spectral, confined their attentions to this side of the veil. They built computers to establish a new reign of logic; they created polymers shapeable to every transient human wish; the hidden dimensions, and the efforts to find them, were carefully forgotten – well of course they were forgotten, fool, because Lodge was wrong, all of them were wrong, there is no ether, there is no magical connector joining the higher dimensions to our own, there is no door, there is no bridge! And you're banging your head against a brick wall! Uttering a cry not unlike a goat's bleat, hurling away his unused but heavily chewed pencil, Ruprecht thrusts himself away from his desk, fragments of truth pinging around inside his head like a malevolent multiball in an insomniac pinball machine. Night swims around him, the school's dim chorus of snores. He sets off for the toilet, as much for a change of scenery as anything else.

In a less preoccupied state the telltale whiff of smoke escaping from underneath the door might have diverted him to the toilets downstairs. But he pushes on in oblivious, only to find himself face-to-face with Lionel – sprawled languorously on a commode, inhaling deeply on a cigarette, unperturbed by or possibly even relishing the stench of piss he imbibes with every drag, like a malign Black Prince in his stinking marble court, waiting for some unfortunate to appear on whom he can take out his boredom.

'Well, well,' Lionel greets him cheerily. He flicks his cigarette into the urinal. 'Well, well, well.'

The pleasing absence of authority figures means that Lionel

can take his time; furthermore, he has the run of six separate cubicles, so he isn't hampered by that pesky wait for the cistern to refill. The only curb on what could be the Ultimate Bogwash is Ruprecht's considerable weight, which Lionel has to haul from one toilet to another. This he does manfully, however, and Ruprecht soon resembles a just-born baby – teary, purple-headed, tiny eyes blinking desperate and unseeing, mouth howling at the savagery of the world it has been introduced to. 'What's that?' Lionel bends down to Ruprecht, who is gasping something. 'Your asthma inhaler? Hmm, I don't see it, maybe it's down here . . .'

Plunged below the waterline again, Ruprecht feels his lungs and throat close up with an air of finality; and now the cataract of stale water and supermarket bleach slowly fades out, yielding to something starless and black that reaches for Ruprecht with glomming hands, squeezing its inky fingers around his heart, his lungs, squeezing and squeezing . . .

And then in the distance – as if arising out of this blackness – he hears something. A moment later, the pressure at the back of his neck disappears, and there is the sound of footsteps receding at speed. With the last of his energy, Ruprecht hauls his head out of the toilet bowl and he slumps, panting, against the cubicle door. A tuneless whistle echoes down the corridor: Mr Tomms, on a rare late-night patrol. Ruprecht listens to it louden and grow faint. And then it hits him.

Music.

Thursday: two days until the curtain rises on the 140th Anniversary Concert. A palpable elation infuses the school; down in the fell Mines of Mythia, however, it's business as usual. Of late, the lusty band – Blüdigör Äxehand (V. Hero), Thothonathothon the Mighty (B. Shambles) and Barg the Dwarf (H. Lafayette) – have been joined on the trail of the legendary Amulet of Onyx by a swashbuckling new companion, Mejisto the Elf (G. Sproke), bearer of the storied Shield of Styx, which will carry its owner across the most raging of torrents. Today the dauntless fellowship has just unlocked the mysterious Casque of Quartz, but within find a nasty surprise – a brace of Hellworms, hungry for flesh, who seize on hapless Mejisto the Elf!

'Who's the elf again?'

'*You* are,' four exasperated voices chorus.

'Oh right.'

Thothonathothon, Blüdigör and Barg valiantly come to the aid of their hapless elven friend, dispatching the Hellworms with blows from their halberd (2d6 HP damage), broadsword (1d10) and flinten pike (3d4). But another shock awaits our courageous fellowship – an underground river, too furious to be crossed by ordinary means, with the drawbridge raised on the other side!

'Wow, how are we going to cross this?' Mejisto the Elf wonders.

'It is too furious to be crossed by ordinary means,' Valdor the Dungeonmaster (L. Rexroth) repeats.

'Wow,' Mejisto says again, shaking his head.

'By *ordinary* means,' Valdor says. Looks are exchanged among the other members of the band.

'Hmm,' Mejisto says.

Barg the Dwarf passes a hand over his face and rubs his temples.

'The shield!' Blüdigör Äxehand exclaims at last, in the hope of getting at least ten feet further along in their quest before lunch break is over. 'The Shield of Styx! That's the whole point of it, is it carries you over every kind of a torrent!'

'Oh great,' Mejisto says. 'Who's got that then?'

It's beginning to look like the inseparable comrades may actually be on the verge of, if not separating, then saying things they might regret – when the door flies open and Ruprecht Van Doren bursts in. It is a long time since Geoff has seen Ruprecht burst anywhere, but he finds he is not completely surprised: some small, amulet-like part of him always knew that one day his overweight friend would come crashing through this door or another, with the maniacal sheen glistening on his brow that indicates that Something is Up. At the same time, who would have guessed that his first words would be, 'We need to find Dennis, *fast*!'?

On the way to the park, Ruprecht explains his new plan. The maniacal sheen did not deceive: this is big, *extremely* big, with many complicated scientific elements that Geoff loses track of almost immediately. But he is too excited to care, because it is so much like old times; and descending the hill to the lake where Dennis and his smoker friends stand smoking, he feels a big yellow glow of anticipation fizzing up inside him like a Vitamin C tablet in a glass of water.

Dennis, though, is not all that pleased to see them. 'What do you want?' he says.

'Listen to this, Dennis. Ruprecht's got an amazing plan!'

'Well, I don't want to hear it,' Dennis says, fumbling a fresh cigarette from his packet and jabbing it in his mouth.

'But you're a part of it! The whole quartet is in it!'

'I don't care!' Dennis shouts. 'Leave me alone! Can't you see I'm smoking?'

'I think we may be able to get a message to Skippy,' Ruprecht says.

Dennis turns ghostly-pale and lowers his lighter. 'What?' he says.

'Music,' Ruprecht explains. 'There's a certain amount of evidence that music of various kinds is audible in the higher dimensions –'

'He's going to use the Van Doren Wave Oscillator, Dennis!'

'No,' Dennis interrupts, more loudly, 'I mean, what – the fuck?'

Ruprecht, checked, glances over to Geoff uncertainly.

'Skippy's *dead*, Ruprecht,' the words appearing in a rush of sepulchral white smoke. 'Haven't we been over this?'

Ruprecht begins to explain about the historical precedent, but Dennis cuts him off: 'What the hell is wrong with you?' he says, pursed lips the only part of him not trembling. 'Skippy's gone, why can't you leave him be?'

'But Dennis,' Geoff intervenes, 'see, he's in the hidden dimensions, remember, like those fairy-tales in Irish class?'

'Geoff, do you really understand what he's talking about?'

Dennis turns to him. 'I mean, really, do you have even a vague idea?'

'No,' Geoff admits.

'Well, I'll tell you,' Dennis says. 'It's bollocks.'

'But you haven't even heard it yet.'

'I don't need to hear it. All he's ever told us is bollocks. The castle on the Rhine, the private tutor flown in from Oxford, the magic portal. Fairy-tales, you said it yourself.' He drops his cigarette and crushes it under his foot.

Ruprecht, forlorn, unblinking, says, 'This could actually work.'

Dennis laughs. 'You're lying, and you don't even know it! You can't even tell what's true and what's a lie any more!'

'No, this is true. I know it. But it has to be tomorrow night. The concert is our only chance.'

'Fuck you, Von Blowjob. Find some other chump for your gay plan.' And turning on his heel, Dennis marches back towards Niall and the other smokers.

Geoff covers his face with his hands.

'Please,' Ruprecht says.

Dennis turns round. 'You asshole, what is it you even want to say to Skippy? What do you have to say that you couldn't have said before, if you hadn't been too busy trying to prove what a great scientist you were?'

Ruprecht's whole body slumps, his second chin slipping down into his third and fourth.

For a long moment Dennis holds his gaze; then, 'Forget you,' he says, and strides away.

Ruprecht watches him go with an expression of agony, as if Dennis too were passing beyond the veil; his lips tremble with words he cannot quite bring himself to say – and then at last, in a bark like a gunshot, he exclaims, 'I didn't have a private tutor.'

Dennis stops.

Ruprecht is standing there in a daze, as if he's not sure where the words have come from. But then reluctantly, 'I didn't have a private tutor,' he repeats. 'You're right, I made that up. I went to boarding school in Roscommon. My parents moved me to Seabrook after I . . . I . . .' He takes a deep breath. 'One day after swimming I got an erection in the showers.'

The sea comes to them in gusts, barrages of white noise like great cargos of emptiness crashing onto the shore.

'It just happened,' Ruprecht concludes dismally. He bows his head, stranded in the grass like some spent atoll.

Dennis is still turned away. For a long time he does not speak; but then, Geoff sees his shoulders begin to shake. A moment later, over the wind and the waves, the first chuckles escape him. 'A boner in the showers . . .' He throws his head back and guffaws. 'A boner in the showers . . .' He laughs for a long time; he laughs and laughs until he is doubled over, until tears stream down his cheeks. Then he stops, and straightens, and regards Ruprecht closely, Ruprecht's pleading eyes like shiny buttons in his doughy gingerbread face. 'You poor fuck,' he says at last. 'You poor fat fuck.'

That afternoon the news is all over the school that Ruprecht Van Doren and his quartet have been restored to the concert programme. Master of Ceremonies Titch Fitzpatrick actually saw it happen, having been in the Jubilee Hall rehearsing his material when Ruprecht and the others walked in. Contrary to some reports, there were no tears, or explanations, or even an apology, hardly; Ruprecht just said they were ready to play again, if there was still a place for them. Still a place? Connie was all over him like a spray-tan. It was like that story in the Bible where the bloke comes back from wherever and they have a huge feast even though the bloke's a bit of a waster.

Don't get him wrong, Titch is a huge fan of Ruprecht's Frenchhorn playing. But after everything that's happened, you have to wonder about the wisdom of letting him just waltz back in like that. Not to get on his high horse or anything, but in Titch's opinion Ruprecht hasn't displayed the kind of attitude that this 140th Anniversary Concert is all about. More importantly, how can the Quartet possibly be ready in time? The concert is on *tomorrow*! Tomorrow!

No point mentioning these reservations to Connie, he's skipping around the place like he's fallen in love. That's why Titch has taken it upon himself, in his capacity as Master of Ceremonies, to have a little sneak preview of the Quartet's performance. And guess what, the noise coming from behind that rehearsal room door does *not* sound like classical music. Or, some of it does? But those parts keep getting drowned out by other parts that sound like the Death Star exploding. And even as he watches, concealed within an alcove, Mario and Niall stagger by, hefting a) a computer and b) some sort of satellite dish . . . ?

The whole thing is fishier than a mermaid's twat. Titch decides to take the matter directly to the top, i.e. Mr Costigan.

'Actually quite busy here, Fitzpatrick –'

'Yes, sir, but it's important.' He explains his misgivings about the Quartet's readmittance, and the strange noises he heard outside the rehearsal room –

'Death Star? Fitzpatrick, what in God's name are you –' Then the phone goes. 'Costigan – well, well, Jack Flaherty, you old son of a gun! How are ya, big guy? How's everything in petrochemicals? A little bird told me you guys were running out . . . ha ha, of course not, listen here, we're throwing a little shindig over here Saturday . . .' The chair swivels away. Titch stands there jilted a moment before becoming aware that Brother Jonas is staring at him from the other side of the room.

'What is troubling you, my child?' he says, in his soft muggy African voice.

Titch takes one look at the little black man, and another at the Acting Principal, gabbing away with his feet on the desk. He smiles. 'Nothing, Brother, it's not important.' Then he leaves the office. If they want to ignore their own Master of Ceremonies, they deserve everything they get.

It was Jeekers, not Dennis, whom Geoff thought they would have the hardest time getting back on board; privately he wondered if Ruprecht might be better off not mentioning the whole séance-experiment end of things, Jeekers generally being quite strait-laced and not such a séance-experiment sort of fellow, especially with his parents looking on. But to Geoff's surprise, Jeekers agreed straight away, to all of it – actually he even seemed glad about the clandestine element, as if he had been waiting for just such a secret enterprise to burrow himself away in. That doesn't mean the rehearsals are plain sailing.

'It just doesn't *sound* right.'

The three subordinate members of the Van Doren Quartet lower their instruments for the nth time with pained expressions.

'It sounds like it's always sounded. What do you *want* it to sound like?'

That's just it: Ruprecht doesn't know. He stares blearily at his notes. Symbols mathematical and musical chitter back at him meaninglessly, like glyphic fleas hopping about the page. They have been in here for what seems like years, playing Pachelbel over and over and over, until they can hear it even when they have stopped; so that when Geoff starts in again about how he wishes he could work out what the hell it reminded him of, Dennis gives him short shrift: 'You idiot, it reminds you of *itself*. It reminds you of the nine squillion times you've heard it before.'

'I don't think that's it.'

'Trust me.'

'All right.' Ruprecht taps his baton on the Oscillator. 'Let's try it again.'

They try it again. In Geoff's opinion – which he will accept as triangle-player is not worth all *that* much, certainly not as much as Jeekers's or Dennis's – they sound pretty good, especially considering their fortnight-long hiatus, and that Ruprecht's French horn looks like it was run over by a truck. The sweet-sad notes slide circling slowly around them, *derr . . . derr . . . derr . . . derr . . . bom . . . bom* – darn it, Dennis is wrong, it's not *itself* it reminds him of! But what the hell is it? It's driving him mad – oh wait, here's his triangle part – (*ping*).

'Stop, stop –' Ruprecht, who has been playing with an ear cocked and his brow so parodically furrowed his forehead resembles a concertina, holds up his hand.

'What?' Dennis beginning to fray at the edges. 'What is it this time?'

'It's like there's something *missing*,' Ruprecht says wretchedly, seizing at his hair.

The room is a latticework of sidelong glances. Time is running out.

Derr . . . derr . . . derr . . . derr . . . Geoff thinks.

'Maybe,' Jeekers says slowly, 'we should just play it the old way.'

Bom . . . bom . . . bom . . . BOM . . .

'Because *we'll* still know it's for Skippy, and, you know, there's going to be a presentation –'

'It's BETHani!' Geoff exclaims. Everyone turns to look at him. 'Oh, sorry. I just realized what Pachelthing reminds me of. That BETHani song? You know, the one Skippy used to play? After he went to see the girl? If you listen to it, it's actually the same tune. Sorry,' he says again, as from every direction stares bore into him, and then, 'what?'

Friday night in the Residence. The Residence is what everyone calls it, they act like it's this exclusive hotel? But inside it's like being trapped in the world's most boring horror movie, a house full of zombies with grey faces and huge hollow eyes that track you as you come down the stairs and stare at you as you search through the magazine rack for a magazine you haven't read yet, and when they move they move like people who aren't really alive, shuffling over the flowery carpet at like zero miles per hour with their arms hanging like old string at their sides and their Prada jeans flapping around their stick-waists and worst of all their horrible disgusting breath like something is rotting inside them. That's why most of the time Lori stays in her room, except when she has to go to You-time or Group. She lies on her bed, holding Lala to her chest. The tears just come by themselves, she is not sad.

Her room actually is a bit like a hotel room, there are fresh-cut flowers and flounces on the bedspread, and though there is no TV you can write in the journal they give you to record your thoughts or sit by the window and look through the bars at the garden. Some girls – it is all girls – have been here for months or even longer. Most of them are sicker than Lori, still they laugh when Lori tells them she won't be staying. Some are from the years above or below her at school, some she recognizes from the mall or mass, or they will turn out to be someone's sister or ex–best friend. There's one girl who Lori was in ballet class with years ago, she used to be so beautiful, like a beautiful dancing flower. Now she looks like some vampire drank all her blood and threw her away. For a little while Lori felt sorry for her and made an effort to talk to her, then she found out the girl was telling everyone that Lori came into her room at night and tried to touch her.

The Residence you see is basically exactly the same as school, bitchiness and cliques, all the girls in a secret race to be the thinnest. In Group they fight with each other to get Dr Pollard's attention, sucking their fingers, swinging their legs back and forth, weighing each other up (ha ha) out of the corner of their eye while he shites on about esteem, it's pathetic, it's freaky, like watching skeletons trying to be erotic, you can practically hear their bodies rattle, in her journal she writes *macarbra*. Dr Pollard is a total dweeb, he wears lame Christmas-type jumpers every single day and you can tell the only reason he knows about self-esteem is because he learned it out of a book, still they drool over him like he's the last piece of chocolate cake which they will vomit up afterwards anyway. Group is really the only time Lori misses being beautiful. She would love to show these skanks how it's done, wrap Dr Pollard around her finger and then get up and walk right out of there, at the door she'd turn and blow him a kiss, Dream on, loser!

Yesterday the woman from the modelling agency called Mom and told her not to worry, they could reschedule the interview for when Lori was feeling better. This kind of thing happens all the time, she said, the important thing is to intervene before any lasting damage is done to the complexion. Mom told her this then she threw her arms around her. Oh Lori, get better! Don't throw away the chances I never had! Lori hates to upset her, she would almost get better just to go to the interview and make Mom happy again. But the weird thing is, she doesn't care any more if she doesn't become a model. She doesn't even remember wanting to be a model! So many things seem like they happened to another person, someone almost too fuzzy to see.

She has been here nearly two weeks now. Most of the time it's okay, but sometimes in the middle of the night there are sirens, the sound so loud and swooping it makes her sit up cold in her bed, and then next morning when you wake up someone is gone. You hear the nurses say, Poor thing she's at death's door, and you imagine the Door black as black. But it's all about how you think of things, like okay the Door is scary but the word *siren* makes her think of singing girls, so when she gets scared about her Plan and going through the Door she imagines that's what they are, singing girls who come and take you by the hand and bring you away from here. And that makes her happy again, because she knows soon they will come for her (it could even be tonight!).

Tell me about Daniel, Lori. Dr Pollard sits on a revolving chair, she sits on a beanbag. There are no bars on his window. Outside it's raining, how come the rain doesn't rise up and turn into a sea and smash through the glass? Some kind of spray is in Dr Pollard's hair to puff it out and make it look like he's not going bald.

It was shortly after his death that you began to experience these self-destructive urges? And you became addicted to diet pills?

She rolls her eyes because of how boring it is to have to explain this all over again. She has explained like a million times already, it didn't have anything to do with Daniel, she started taking the pills because she thought she might be pregnant. But then she'd found out she wasn't pregnant, and everything was getting back to normal – better than normal, she was going to be a top model, she went dancing with Janine in LA Nites and kissed a boy, a sixth year, he was on the Terenure Senior Cup Team! She was looking to the future, she would have stopped taking the pills if she'd even thought about it for a second –

So why didn't you?

Why didn't I what?

Why didn't you stop taking the pills?

She sighs, she wriggles in her seat, rolls her eyes again, how are you supposed to explain this stuff? It wasn't anything. It was just she started noticing things.

Like what?

Annoying things. Stupid stuff. It's totally stupid, there's no point even talking about it.

Give me an example.

Oh whatever, like the way Mom kept buying her clothes for the interview with the modelling agency, like every day practically she'd go out and buy a new outfit, even though they'd both decided the one she had was perfect. Or if it wasn't an outfit it was something else, pumps eyeshadow clutch purse mules, try these on Lori, try them with that, then try that with this, oh how about these with those? She wanted Lori to make an impression, that was all, it just started getting a bit annoying, and meanwhile Dad had ordered new separates for his den and also new gym equipment for the gym, except the extension was still being done so they were all heaped up in the hallway in cardboard boxes, great big piles that bulged like Dad's new muscles, and as well though she knew it was starting to bother her Lori kept buying things too, in the mall on Saturdays with the money Mom gave her to cheer herself up, make-up and magazines and bangles and knickers and tops and these things that just appeared in bags in her hands and suddenly it was like the house was filling up with stuff, more and more every day, more and more and more, moreandmoreandmoreandmore, moremoremoremoremoremoremoremoremoremoremoremore-moremoremore like millions of teeming sperms, heaping and piling and crowding until she began to imagine one day it would come bursting through her door and pin her against the wall! and the only thing she could do was keep taking the pills because they could make little spaces for her, open up new spaces that she could slip into to breathe? it was like she had to keep shrinking herself just so there'd be enough space for her?

That's good, Lori, that's very good.

It's why Lori's room here is practically empty, she made them take out a lot of the furniture, and most of the flowers and presents she gets from people she asks the nurses to keep downstairs. From home there is only Lala on her pillow and her BETHani scrapbook, and when Dad comes to visit she often pretends she's asleep, turning her face to the window while he sits there flicking through a men's health magazine, unconsciously flexing and bulging.

You know, Lori – Dr Pollard revolves his chair – the feelings you describe are far from unusual. When a person is in a vulnerable state of mind, the simple facts of day-to-day life can indeed seem overwhelming. And not eating is a common reaction to that sensation of being overwhelmed. We may think of food as the physical link tying us to the world. By refusing it, we attempt to disengage ourselves and our bodies from what we feel are the destructive intrusions of that world. But paradoxically, that act of self-assertion can be deeply harmful.

He crosses his legs so she can see his disgusting hairy white shins. She wishes Mr Scott the French teacher was counselling her. She imagines him by her bedside reading French poetry to her, explaining the vocab and the imagery – *elle est debout sur mes paupières, et ses cheveux sont dans les miens* . . .

The achievement of maturity, psychologically speaking, might be said to be the realization and acceptance that we simply cannot live independently from the world, and so we must learn to live within it, with whatever compromises that might entail.

. . . and he wouldn't ask her questions, and because he didn't ask she would tell him, what it's like to be a person who is a ruin, who has done the worst thing she can ever imagine doing, whose life has become a series of lies that she lives trapped in between like a ghost, and all she wants is to be gone gone gone –

Shh shh, he would say, and he'd put his arms around her. And just hold her? And he would not have gross hairy shins.

She knows Dr Pollard only wants to help but it would be so much easier if he left her alone! She wishes she could explain that she *doesn't feel bad*? Like she knows what she's doing, it sounds weird she knows but it's like the thinner she gets, the better she feels – like she's on a mountain that's growing out of the ground, carrying her higher and higher into the clouds, away from all the hands that might try and grab hold of her. She doesn't mind when the girls come to visit her and can't hide their disgust or their satisfaction at the way she looks now, and when Janine arrives for her big confession scene to tell Lori about her and Carl, Lori is not even angry. She watches Janine bawl and rub her fists in her eyes, sobbing, *We couldn't help it, Lori, we're in love*, like you would watch like an insect or something gross like that flipped over on its back or caught in a drain. She doesn't get angry, she doesn't tell Janine Carl still texts her even though she can imagine herself saying it and enjoying how much it hurts Janine. Because Carl feels like a long long time ago, she can't understand now how she ever wanted him or anyone to touch her. And Janine too, these are all things that she's leaving behind. Every day she is more free, *free of herself* or what people thought she was. And soon she will be totally free, as free as the air.

Inside Lala are the pills she bought from Carl with her kisses. Now they will be kisses to herself, kisses to say, I love you, Lori. Who else would kiss her, with the taste of death on her breath all the time? The real taste underneath everything and now she can taste it all the time. But soon she will never have to taste anything again. The Plan is ready – the new Plan, *her* Plan – the singing girls on their way. They will come singing, *Lori, Lori* on the wind, and she will dance away, graceful as a ballerina – hey, can she hear them now? Is there someone calling her name? Someone right under her window? But when she pulls back the curtain, the figure she sees below is not a girl. And he is definitely not thin.

Howard is amazed how quickly he loses track of things without the clanging school bell to chop his day into forty-minute portions. Darkness seems to fall shortly after he's got out of bed; he finds himself increasingly dependent on the TV for any sense of reality, and whenever there is a power cut he experiences, in that first second of darkness before his eyesight adjusts, a terror that it is he, in fact, who has been switched off.

Yesterday Finian Ó Dálaigh had appeared at his door with a card signed by the whole Seabrook faculty. At first Howard thought it was for him, a gesture of support. It wasn't, of course; it was for Tom Roche. There was going to be a presentation during the concert, an award for his years of dedicated service to Seabrook. 'I didn't think you should be left out,' Ó Dálaigh said considerately. 'Thank you,' Howard said. He wrote his name on a blank space in the interior; after some deliberation, he left it at that.

A presentation for his years of dedicated service to Seabrook. Today, on the way home from the supermarket with a bootful of discount beer, Howard stopped his car outside the police station. He sat there for five full minutes, in the cold. Then he pulled out again and drove home.

He starts drinking early, and as the fatal hour of the concert approaches, combines it with a half-hearted sally against the creeping entropy that has been taking over the house. He doesn't get far; before long, he's hunkered on the floor with a boxful of Halley-memorabilia – photographs, cinema stubs, museum plans from foreign cities, all spread out in front of him. This has been happening a lot lately. The feebler his grip on the present, the more vivid the past – which for so long he has let disappear behind him, a frothing wake swallowed in the cold endless ocean of a world's lived lives – seems to become; this sense is only amplified when the power goes and he has to light a candle to supplement the waning daylight. He doesn't mind – on the contrary, he feels like he could happily spend the rest of his life here, revisiting city-breaks, holidays, friends' parties. He only wishes he had Halley with him, so he could say, *Hey, look at this one, do you remember such and such?* And hear her reply, *Yes, yes, that's how it was.*

And then at the back of a cupboard he finds the camera – the magical summer camera, the one she was reviewing a couple of months ago. With a sense of exhilaration, knowing that it contains actual moving images of her, he switches it on; and moments later, there she is, that day in the kitchen, with a cigarette in her hand and the light falling across her. His heart leaps, watching her shimmer at him from the screen; and then sinks, as the little scene disintegrates, inexplicably and inexorably, into a fight. He plays the clip again with numb fingers, watching their conversation unravel, listening to her tell him to forget it, to put that thing away. Even on the tiny screen the sadness etched into her face is unmistakeable. You did that, Howard.

Everything clangs like bells inside his head. He switches off the camera and sets it down. He scoops up the photographs and stubs and tickets, but the box slips from his grip and the contents, all those days so carefully misremembered, scatter across the floor like orphans escaped from an ogre's cellar. He lets out a roar, he bends again to pick them up, but this time manages to scorch his elbow on the candle. Fuck it! Fuck! Grinding his teeth in rage, he flattens his hand and thrusts it palm-down into the flame. He holds it there for as long as he is able, and then for a little while more, until all thoughts have been seared from his head, and then still more. Tears run down his cheeks, lightning bolts flash beneath his eyelids. The pain is astonishing, like a new world underneath this one, raw and vivid and shivering. The air fills with the smell of cooking meat. Finally, with a cry, he pulls his hand away and staggers to the bathroom.

His whole hand is inert; it feels like an alien substance, a lump of fire or of pure pain grafted onto the end of his arm. When he runs cold water over it, it's like his whole body has been hit by something – like a knight lanced in a joust, or two waves clashing, matter and antimatter. One forgets quite how painful pain is, how literal and unironic. He stands there sobbing, the water drilling into his flesh, the agony shrill in his ear like an alarm. His mind, however, suspended above the scene, is suddenly crystal-clear.

The car park has been decked out with blue-and-gold fairy lights – nice touch, Trudy's idea. From the top of the steps to the Sports Hall, Acting Principal Greg Costigan watches the guests arrive, proceeding from their cars in dinner jackets and long elegant gowns, the yard's schoolday soundtrack of high-pitched expletives replaced with a stately, dignified murmur. They can see him too, framed in the glowing threshold of the Hall, waiting to greet them like, he supposes, the captain, the captain of a ship. The good ship *Seabrook*.

Looking out on all this magnificence and decorum, the word that comes unavoidably to mind is *vindicated*. Greg would be the first to admit it has not exactly been plain sailing here in the SS *Seabrook* these last few months. The Juster episode, discipline issues, poor rugby performances – in uncertain times like these, most men in his position would have been inclined to keep their heads down, weather the storm, not attempt a high-profile, high-risk venture like this. But Greg is not the kind of Acting Principal who shrinks from adversity. A bold gesture was what was needed to stop the rot – something big and showy and extravagant, to rally the shareholders and generally boost confidence. Because a school, as well as being like a ship, is also like a market, and when the market is confident it doesn't actually matter what small technical hitches might be going on behind the scenes.

And, thus far at least, that decision has been one hundred per cent borne out and vindicated. An atmosphere of excellence, the kind that cannot be bought, pervades the hall tonight. Sprinkled in among the parents – it's a full house, by the way, bearing out and vindicating his decision re ticket pricing – is a sort of Best of Seabrook, some of the leading lights of the last thirty years:

sportsmen, captains of industry, media personalities, basically the cream of Irish society. A hell of a turnout, and a testimony to that special bond Seabrook creates – as Greg explains to Frank Hart, class of '68, scrum-half for Ireland 1971–78, now in property development and a millionaire several times over. 'Doesn't matter whether you graduated five years ago or fifty-five. You'll always be part of the family. In today's modern world, that's a rare and precious thing.'

'Father Furlong coming tonight?' Hart inquires.

'I wish, Frank, I wish. Because in a way this night is for him, a tribute to him and his predecessors and the great gift of education they have given to so many generations of Irish boys. Unfortunately, he's not yet well enough to leave the hospital, which is a real shame.'

'Leaves the stage clear for you, though,' quips Hart.

Greg laughs artificially. 'Those would be some hard shoes to fill,' he says.

Of course, Frank Hart is totally right; this 140th Anniversary Concert marks the changing of the guard. Surely by now even the Paracletes must recognize their time is up. You can't get away with hiding behind a crucifix these days: whoever steps into Desmond Furlong's small and somewhat effeminate shoes will have to be able to reckon with the realities of twenty-first-century life. Could Desmond Furlong have organized a 140th Anniversary Concert to be broadcast live to the whole country? Let alone faced down a potential scandal that might have destroyed the entire school? Somehow Greg thinks sitting in a traditional African chair watching fish swim around might not have been quite enough this time. And the Paracletes know it.

So this is in some ways a sad occasion – he segues in his imagination into a kind of acceptance speech, delivered to a hall much the size of this one, similarly filled with notables – marking as it does the passing of an era. But in other ways it is a joyful one: because it proves that although the Paracletes may be gone, for all intents and purposes, their values will live on. Maybe the men upholding them will wear a suit and tie instead of a dog collar; maybe they will carry a laptop instead of a Bible, and maybe 'common business model', not 'God', will be the name of the bridge they use to bring communities together. But although appearances may change, the values themselves remain the same – the Seabrook values of faith, decency, various others.

Yes indeed, as he surveys the scene – the towering sound system, the radio engineer at work behind the desk, the first (of two) cameramen panning over the audience, the majestic banners and pennants (actually sourced outside the school at the last minute, the Art Department's offerings having been disappointingly slipshod – frayed hems, uneven lettering, misspelling of 'Christ' as 'Chrit', etc.), the audience members perusing with interest the gold-trimmed, white-and-blue envelopes left on their seats, which contain exciting news of a forthcoming Seabrook-affiliated credit card – Greg is thinking that tonight will have done him no harm at all, no harm at all. Now he only has to keep his eyes peeled and make sure nothing goes –

'Ha ha, look what the cat dragged in –' In an instant Greg has slipped through the crowd to pounce on the rumpled figure arguing with the ticket-checker on the door. 'Howard, fantastic to see you, what can I do for you?'

Howard blinks up at him, mouth ajar. 'Uh, yeah, I wanted to come and see the show . . . ?'

'He doesn't have a ticket,' the boy on the door says sullenly.

'Oh, gee, that's a real shame, because – Jesus Christ, Howard, what the hell happened to your hand?' The erstwhile history teacher's hand is swathed in about a quarter-mile of not very clean bandage. He starts babbling something about an accident incurred while cooking a Chinese stir-fry, addressing himself to Greg's midriff.

'Have you taken it to a doctor?' the Acting Principal interrupts.

'Well, no, not yet,' Howard says, still avoiding eye contact. He's up to something, Greg thinks. You spend your day with teenage boys, you learn to detect the signs of a plot pretty quickly.

'Looks like it needs medical attention. If I were you, I'd take it to a doctor, pronto.'

'Yes, but . . .' Howard mumbles, 'but I didn't want to miss the show.'

Greg makes a gesture of frustration with his fist. 'Well, darn it, Howard, that's a real shame, because the thing is we're totally sold out.'

Howard gapes at him helplessly. Waves of booze radiate from him. 'You couldn't . . . I mean . . .'

There's no way Greg would let him anywhere near this concert even if he didn't look like he'd spent the last three days drunk in a ditch. 'I'd love to, Howard –' he puts his arm around Howard's shoulder and steers him out of the way of the real guests, who are beginning to whisper and point '– I truly would, but we're already turning people away here.'

'It's just –' Greg can practically hear the motors in the man's clogged brain '– just after, you know, working on the programme, I sort of, I feel a sort of a personal . . . personal wish to . . .'

'I thoroughly understand that, Howard. I thoroughly understand that.' Brother Jonas has appeared at his elbow; Greg nods at him meaningfully. 'Tell you what, why don't we get you some nice fresh air outside, and we can talk about it there?'

'Okay,' Howard says dismally, then checks himself. 'Or actually, I wonder if I could have a quick word with Tom?'

'With Tom?' Greg smiles solicitously. 'Now what would you have to say to Tom?'

'Just wanted to wish him luck? For the future?'

'That's very kind of you, Howard, and I'll be happy to pass that message on. We're just about to start here though, so I think it would be better if –'

'Okay, but . . . maybe just a quick . . .'

'No, I don't think that would be a good –'

'I can see him right over – Tom! T– aagh!'

'Howard? You all right, Howard?'

'I – ah – uh –'

'Just take a second to get your breathing back – that's it, nice fresh air . . .'

'Anything wrong there, Greg?' calls Oliver Taggart, class of '82, from the steps of the Hall.

'Ha ha, Olly, you old son of a gun – no, just a little, a little stage fright, that's all . . .'

With Brother Jonas's help, Greg encourages Howard a little further into the bushy shadows of the Quad. 'Sorry, buddy, just caught you a little awkwardly, must have accidentally brushed against that hand . . .' Howard pants and burbles to himself. The man's clearly having some kind of meltdown. Could be a good thing. Maybe he'll go the whole hog, give up teaching and spare Greg a major headache. Damn hard to actually fire somebody these days. 'How you doing there, feeling better? Tell you what, Howard. I'm sorry you can't catch it live, but in view of your contribution, I'm going to send you a complimentary DVD of the concert, on the house, what do you say to that?'

Howard gurgles dispiritedly.

'Attaboy. You take yourself home now and have a nice rest. Brother Jonas will see you to the gate. Enjoy your time off.'

Whatever he had planned, Howard now admits defeat and stumbles off into the night, the brother following a few steps behind. Greg keeps smiling and waving till he's safely out of sight. Then he tells Gary Toolan on the door to alert him *immediately* should Howard reappear. What a headcase. Darn it, if there were any justice in the world it would be Howard being sent off to Timbuktu, not Tom Roche.

The upshot of this anyhow is that he misses all but the very end of Tiernan Marsh's overture. But it goes down a bomb. The MC for the night comes on, Titch Fitzpatrick, a kid with a great attitude and charm by the bucketload, and introduces the next act – it's Shadowfax, doing Pink Floyd's 'Another Brick in the Wall'. Lost in the strutting, spiky rhythms, Greg soon forgets about the unpleasant business with Howard. *We don't need no edu-cation* . . . Might surprise his pupils to learn that Greg had his own band once upon a time. Called themselves the Ugly Rumours, used to cover this very song. *Hey! Teacher! Leave them kids alone!* And now he's Acting Principal of a school! Life's funny that way.

Checking his programme (featuring a brief essay, 'A Good Bounce of the Ball: 140 years of Seabrook Life', by Gregory L. Costigan), he sees the Quartet's up next, doing the Citroën ad. He seeks out Connie Laughton with his eye, and finds him hovering anticipatorily by the edge of the stage, conductor's baton tucked under his arm. Good to have Van Doren back on-message, for Connie's sake as much as anyone's. And the audience'll lap this up, just you watch. It really is a heck of a line-up. Maybe he should charge an extra fiver for those DVDs.

Titch Fitzpatrick vacates the stage, and Greg smiles expectantly. But as the Quartet emerge, his smile quickly fades to a frown. What the hell's happened to Van Doren's horn? And why are the four of them covered in *tinfoil*?

Mom is cleaning the kitchen. She has been cleaning it for hours, down on her knees in her dressing gown. The bucket of stuff smells like it could get you high. I'm going out Carl says. Mom doesn't hear him.

Barry is waiting at Ed's when he gets there, walking up and down like a dog that's been tied up. A second later the car pulls up and the door swings open.

Inside everybody's eyes are red from hash smoke. They're all laughing and slagging each other like usual but underneath you can feel other things swirl around like sharks. Carl sits in the boot because there's no room. He watches the Saturday-night streets outside, chippers, billboards, traffic lights, like a huge hand slowly closing around them.

Across Deano's knees the sports bag from under the bed.

In his head a black field, hands rising out of the grass.

Where is the place? Barry says.

Not far, Mark says.

Everybody chewing the inside of their mouths. To distract them Deano asks, if they could have any bird, who would be their number one. I'll go first. Angelina Jolie, hands fuckin down. Mark says Scarlett. Knoxer says BETHanl. Uh, is she legal yet? Deano goes. If she's old enough to bleed, goes Knoxer. Barry says Beyoncé. But she's black! Ste says and everyone laughs.

What about you, head? Deano says.

Carl wants to say Lori just to say her name. But he doesn't want to say it in this car. It's like she's sand now, magic sand, he has only a little left, and if he takes it out here it will be blown away.

Well?

LORILORILORI, goes his brain. He feels like crying. Beyoncé as well, he says.

Knoxer grunts, Fuck's sake.

Stephen? Deano says to Ste. Ste is quiet for a long time. Then he says, Helen of Troy.

What?

Who the fuck is Helen of Troy?

She was Greek, Ste says. They had a war about her. Vietnam? Carl says. No, you spa, Ste says, like a thousand years ago, in Greece.

That's stupid, Deano says.

Why is it stupid?

Because, you don't even know what she looked like.

They had a fuckin *war* over her. Obviously she must have been pretty fuckin hot.

Yeah, but it has to be someone *alive*, Deano says.

Why? Ste says.

Because how are you goin to ride her if she's fuckin dead?

For fuck's sake – Ste is getting pissed off – it's a *game*, you cunt. It doesn't matter who we fuckin pick. You think Angelina fuckin Jolie's going to ride you just cos you picked her? If Angelina Jolie was right here in this fuckin car I bet you a million quid she'd ride fuckin Looney Tunes here before she rode you.

Deano shuts his mouth tight and looks out the window.

I'm just sayin, Ste says, if you want to pick the hottest bird, like, you've got your Beyoncés and your Angelinas and all them, but the little old lady shufflin off to fuckin bingo night, fifty years ago she could have been sexier than all of them. She could've been the sexiest bird of all time. And *then*, on top of that, there's all the birds that are dead. Like in history, there must have been millions of amazing rides. But we'll never even know what they looked like.

What the fuck are you on about, you gimp? Knoxer says.

I dunno, Ste says. It just seems sort of unfair.

Maybe some day someone will invent a time machine and you can go back and ride all the dead birds, Deano says.

Youse lads are fuckin *strange*, Knoxer says. Then the car stops and everyone goes quiet.

We're he-ere, Mark says in a *Poltergeist* voice.

They are on an ordinary-looking road lined with ordinary-looking houses. Right in front of the car, though, in the middle of the normal houses, are these gates. They remind Carl of Lori's gates but they're not in Foxrock, he doesn't know where they are. A wall too tall to climb runs from the gates away behind the houses.

For a minute they sit there in the car, like they're waiting for something, but Carl doesn't know what. I can't do this without a blast, Mark says at last and reaches over Ste's leg for the glove compartment. Inside there's a package wrapped in brown paper and a film canister filled with coke. Mark takes a big snort then gives it to Ste, then Deano and Knoxer have some. But Knoxer gives it back to Ste without Carl or Barry having any. He doesn't look at them, he acts like for a minute he's forgotten they're there. Okay, Mark says. He gets out of the car and goes to the intercom. Carl can't hear what he says. He gets back in the car. They don't talk, coke frazzles electric through the air. The gates swing open. Mark drives through. The gates close again behind them. He pulls the car up outside a little house that doesn't look like there's anyone in it. The others all get out, someone opens the boot. There are no lights, the air has gone dark blue and everyone has turned into shadows. This is fucking weird. A second ago, just on the other side of that wall, they were in the city. Now it's like they're in the country. Come on, Mark says with the package in his hand and he disappears instantly into the dark like he's fallen down a hole.

The ground sinks under Carl's feet. They're in a bog or something. He has to hurry not to lose the others, he can't see his own hand in front of his face and something is there, something is moving, thudding towards them, Deano reaches into the sports bag –

Horses. They come close enough so he can see the outlines of their pointy ears. Then they stop, and wait there, breath snuffing down their noses. They watch them go past, like they know something. They know who's waiting for Carl.

Suddenly it's freezing cold. The others are under the trees, there is the sound of rushing water. Their faces appear as he gets closer like ghosts in a graveyard. Do they know too? A slimy log stretches across a stream. Deano is smiling. Ladies first, he says. Carl goes over the log on his hands and knees.

Where is this cunt? he hears Knoxer say.

He said he'd light a fire for us, Mark says.

They're talking about the Druid, Carl! They don't know about Dead Boy, they're not bringing you to him!

Now they're in a forest, branches keep springing back into Carl's face.

But what if Dead Boy is inside their heads too, pushing their thoughts with his see-through hands? What if none of this is even real? Maybe Carl is in a nightmare, maybe he smoked loads of hash and is sleeping. Wake up, Carl! Wake up wake up!

But then, like a spark from a lighter, he sees a tiny orange flame somewhere in the dark. Look! he shouts. Not waiting for the others he stumbles towards it, ignoring the branches in his face and the brambles that drag at his ankles, until the woods open into a field, and the spark turns into a bonfire.

Two men are standing in front of the fire. One has long hair and a beard that tangles down his chest. He's wearing a cloak with suns and moons on it, and he's leaning on the handle of a huge sword. The other man is short, cross-eyed, a bit mental-looking, he has one hand tucked inside his leather jacket.

I went out to the hazel wood, the tall man with the beard says, *because a fire was in my head* . . .

All right? Mark and the others arrive at the bonfire.

Never better, the man says. I see you've brought some friends along? He tips his head at Carl and Barry.

They're just two young lads have been helping us out, Mark says. They wanted to come along.

Why not, why not, the Druid nods along. The more the merrier. Do come warm yourselves. He waves his hand and they step towards the fire. And then there is a flash, a flash of air, not the kind you can see. Now the Druid's sword is stretched out with the point pressed into Deano's throat.

For a moment nobody moves, like the whole world is balanced on the tip of the sword. Then the cross-eyed man leans in and whips the sports bag out of Deano's hand.

We'll take care of this for now, the Druid says. The cross-eyed man pulls the shotgun out of the bag, splits it open over his knee and rattles out the shells. The Druid lowers the sword. Deano sags like he's deflating. Now friends, the Druid says. Business before pleasure. Let us adjourn to my office.

He turns and walks up the hill. They follow after him with the cross-eyed man behind. No one has said a word since the Druid swung his sword. Fear crackles in the clouds, in the long grass, the lights of the city rise up around like they have come to watch something happen. And now a shape appears at the top of the hill, a rocky black shape that stares out like a skull.

Which of you scholars can tell me what this is? the Druid says cheerfully.

None of them says anything and then Barry says in a voice like he's hypnotized, A dolmen.

Very good. The Druid is pleased. One of the oldest forms of burial chamber. Also known as a Portal Tomb, as it is a doorway to the land of death. Note the distinctive tripartite structure, for the three aspects of the Goddess. He looks from one face to the next. In ancient times it is here that offerings were left for the unseen ones, he says.

Nothing happens for a moment. Then Mark jerks to life. He takes the package from under his belt and holds it out to the Druid. But the cross-eyed man grabs it instead. He rips open the paper and counts the money, muttering. The Druid leans on his sword and watches him with a little smile, like someone watching children playing. When he is finished the cross-eyed man lifts his head. He nods to the Druid. The Druid walks up to the dolmen and stretches his arm into the dark between the ground-rocks and the slab lying across them. His hand comes out holding a bag.

He throws it to Mark. Mark opens it. Inside are smaller bags of white powder, other bags of pills, a brick of hash in clingfilm, it's just like on TV. All to your satisfaction? the Druid says.

Yeah, brilliant, Mark says. Thanks very much. He looks at Knoxer, at Ste. Ste jerks his head in the direction of the car. Well, Mark says.

The Druid has his head tilted back, looking up at the sky. But you're not leaving already? he says.

Let's go let's go let's go, Carl is thinking, they are all thinking, Mark too but he doesn't know what to do.

Come, the Druid says. It is so rare that we see our friends. Let us sit by the fire.

At the bottom of the hill the bonfire has burned low. The cross-eyed man picks up a jerry-can and pours petrol on it. Flames jump out, the Druid laughs. Sit, sit, he says, laughing. They sit in a ring around it like children. Ste is trying to make Mark look at him but he won't. The Druid takes a pipe from his cloak and lights it and passes it around. In the firelight you can see he is not that old, he is less old than Carl's dad.

Once this whole country was a stronghold of the Goddess, he says. Magical sites lie all around here. The modern jackals do not see it, of course, they'd concrete over this very hill if you gave them half a chance. But to anyone with ears . . . He pulls his shoulders in. The sword lies on the ground beside him, pointing into the fire like a gold tongue drinking. You can *hear* them, he hisses. The dead.

Carl gets the pipe. The smoke tastes weird, maybe it's because they're out here in the fields and trees. He is trying not to hear the dead, he is trying not to think of the black space between the rocks of the dolmen where the Druid put his hand.

Hence my little enterprise, the Druid says. I was chosen by the Goddess to protect this hill from the defilers.

So how old would you say it is then? Mark says, because the Druid is staring at him. Like, the dolmen?

The Druid goes quiet like he's thinking back to when he built it. Perhaps . . . three thousand years?

Beside Carl, Deano bursts into giggles. He tries to stop but they just get worse. He laughs and laughs, high hyena yelps, till he's on his side. Then when he can speak he says, Sorry . . . just reminded me of this cunt . . . wantin to ride a fuckin skeleton . . . He explodes into giggles again.

The Druid stares at Deano without smiling. It's just a game we were playing on the way up here, Mark explains. If you could pick one woman, you know, to be with. Ste picked Helen of Troy.

Helen of fuckin Troy . . . gasps Deano. The dozy prick.

Ste looks even more pissed off, like he's just about keeping himself from saying something.

The Druid just stares. Helen of Troy, he says.

Barry hands Carl the pipe again. His eyes are like the black skies of a lost place. But above his head the stars are like millions of eyes. Carl pretends he doesn't feel them watching, he looks into the fire instead. *Q. But in the fire there are hands reaching up trying to get out!!!! A. Don't look in the fire either!!!!* He sucks on the pipe, trying to build up the wall of fog that hides him from the dead! But this time the smoke instead of hiding him is leading him deeper in!

Helen who was Helle, the Druid says, was none other than Persephone, the Goddess of Death and Resurrection. It is she this whole land belonged to, it is her Door atop this hill.

Ste lets out a sigh, looks at his watch.

In Erin of old she was Brigit, the exalted one, the fiery arrow. In Wales she was the Ninefold Muse Ceridwen. She is Ashtaroth, Venus, Hecate, and a thousand others. She is the Goddess who underlies all things, the supreme object of desire whom no man may resist and no man may possess without being destroyed, who ruled us all before her throne was stolen from her.

And suddenly Carl knows why Dead Boy brought him here. He is going to take Carl back with him, through the Door! He wants to scream, he wants to get up and run. But there is a spell on him making him weigh a million tons. It's the hill, already pulling him into it, it's the hands in the fire holding him down. Soon he will hear the Door open, then the shadows will come!

Stolen by the Church, the Druid says, by little priests in cells, scribbling out their Bibles, loving only gold and power! Thieves and paedophiles, who presided over a perversion! But she will be avenged! She will burn them all in her holy fire!

Ste jumps to his feet. I'm freezin me hole off listenin to this shite! he shouts. See youse in the car! He turns to go back down the hill – but now the little man gets up too, he puts his hand in his jacket –

Then Barry slumps forward. After a moment, gently but swiftly, the tips of his hair catch on the bonfire and light into little flames, like birthday candles. He lets out a loud snore. Everybody starts laughing, even Ste, even the little cross-eyed man.

'I think someone's had his fill,' the Druid says.

'Can't say I fuckin blame him,' Deano says. 'This weed is fuckin lethal.'

'It's not weed, lad.' The Druid laughs a big chesty laugh. 'It's heroin.' He laughs some more, and they all do too, laughing and laughing, everyone is laughing!

But Carl feels so, so sad.

And then the screaming starts.

'I'm just wondering if it's going to be entirely safe . . .' Jeekers in the wings.

'I don't imagine anyone will get *hurt*,' Ruprecht says. 'Though there may be some structural damage.'

'Oh my God,' Jeekers whimpers to himself. But it's too late – Titch is already introducing them; and now they are walking out onto the stage. The lights are so bright, and so hot! Yet even through them it seems he can feel the icy gaze of his parents, the avid gleam of their eyes as they wait to grade him out of ten in this new field of endeavour; and although he cannot see them, and in spite of what he is about to do, he works up a watery smile and directs it into the great darkness.

Two days ago, Jeekers was eating lunch in the yard on his own, just as he does every day, when Ruprecht sat down beside him and told him he wanted to get the Quartet back together. Jeekers was surprised to hear this, after everything that had happened. But then Ruprecht explained *why*. He wanted to use the Quartet to get a message to Skippy. I know it sounds unorthodox, he said, but the fact is that there's a sound scientific principle behind it – here he reeled off a list of nineteenth-century names who had apparently tried a similar thing. Where they went wrong, he said, was in thinking of us, our four-dimensional spacetime, as *here*, and the other dimensions as *there*, which meant they needed some kind of magical substance to bridge the gap in between. But in fact, you don't need any such substance – or rather, according to M-theory, ordinary matter is *also itself the magical substance*! He paused here, looking at Jeekers with eyes that blazed like Catherine wheels.

Strings, he said. If they ripple one way they make stuff, and if they ripple another way they make light, or nuclear energy, or gravity. But in each case they perform these ripples in *eleven dimensions*. Each string is like a chorus line with a stage curtain falling down the middle of it, so that one part is in our world, and the other is in the higher dimensions. The same string that makes up one quark of one atom of the handle of your tennis racket could at the same moment be revolving in an entirely other universe. So if *every* string goes beyond the veil, might it not be possible to somehow pass a message along the string from our side so it reaches the other side?

Like two tin cans tied together? Jeekers said.

Exactly! Ruprecht said. Once you see it, the concept is quite simple. It merely becomes a question of *how*. That's where the Quartet comes in.

In Lodge's book, he explained, the soldiers in Summerland, which was what they called the Otherworld, reported that they could hear certain musical performances from the Albert Hall. What they were hearing were radio broadcasts. Evidently certain combinations of sonic architecture and radio frequency have this 'amphibious' quality that enables them to travel over to the higher dimensions. My theory is that some kind of sympathetic resonance must be involved. The tricky thing then is to find these amphibious frequencies. In the past they used human mediums, who sniffed them out by a process of intuition. However, with a simple recalibration of the Van Doren Wave Oscillator, we can alleviate all need for a medium by translating our sonic 'message' into *every possible frequency* – one of which has, of necessity, to be the one audible to the dead . . .

Listening to him elaborate on his plan, Jeekers recognized that Ruprecht had finally lost the plot. His experiments had always been a little zany for Jeekers's taste; still, in the past he could appreciate that they did have some exhilarating, if fleeting, points of correspondence with reality. This, though – this was delusion, nothing more.

So why – why, why, why! – had he said yes? It's not that he hasn't felt sorry for Ruprecht over these last few weeks, and of course he feels terrible about what happened to Skippy. But when he thinks of how much trouble they're going to get into – and right in front of their parents! It's all right for Dennis and Geoff, they don't have academic records to protect. But Jeekers is putting his whole future in jeopardy! Why?

Yet even as he asks it he knows the reasons why. He is doing it precisely because it is pointless and foolish and out of character. He is doing it because it is the kind of thing he would never, ever do, because the kind of thing he *does* do – following the rules, working hard, being Good like a boy ordered from a catalogue – has lately come to seem quite empty. It might have something to do too with Dad getting Mr Fallon fired, even when Jeekers begged him not to; or maybe the creeping realization that it was the Best Boy that Dad loved, not Jeekers, and that if he was kidnapped, and the Best Boy left in his place, Dad would not be sad.

Anyway, here he is. And as he looks across the stage – at the other three primed over their instruments, Geoff's triangle lilting ever so slightly back and forth, like a leaf in anticipation of a breeze; Dennis's smirk just visible at the mouthpiece to his bassoon; Ruprecht breathing very slowly, focus fixed on the back of the auditorium, on his lap the mangled horn that Jeekers still can't look at without setting off an interior pandemonium of alarm; and then at Father Laughton, poor unsuspecting Father Laughton, as he raises his baton – the weird thing is, even though he knows Ruprecht is wrong and there is no chance of this working, still, at this precise moment in time – beneath the bright lights, shaking with nerves, surrounded by parents and priests in the Sports Hall on a Saturday night – reality *does feel distinctly unreal*, and what seemed unreal, conversely, feels a lot closer than before . . .

And the music, when it begins, sounds so beautiful. Pachelbel's familiar melody, worn threadbare by endless TV commercials for cars, life assurance, luxury soap, by street-performers in black-tie, mugging for tourists in high summer, by any number of attempts to invoke Old-World Elegance, accompanied by haughty waiters bearing trayfuls of tiny cubes of cheese – tonight it seems to its audience entirely new, to the point of an almost painful fragility.

What is it that makes it so imploring and so sweet, so disconcertingly (for the older members of the audience who have come tonight expecting merely to be pleasantly bored and now find themselves with lumps in their throats) *personal*? Something to do with the horn that large boy in the silver suit is playing, perhaps, a new-fangled instrument that looks like it must have been run over by a truck, but produces a sound that's like nothing you've ever heard – a hoarse, forlorn sound that just makes you want to . . .

And then the voice comes in, and you can actually see a shiver run through the decorous crowd. Because there is no singer on the stage, and given that Pachelbel's Canon does not have a vocal part, listeners could be forgiven for mistaking it for a ghost's, some spirit of the hall roused by the music's beauty and unable to resist joining in, especially as the voice – a girl's – has an irresistibly haunting quality, spare, spectral, carved down to its bare bones . . . But then one by one the audience members spot beneath the mike stand over to the right, ah, an ordinary mobile phone. But who is she? And what's she singing?

> You fizz me up like Diet Pepsi
> You make me shake like epilepsy
> You held my hand all summer long
> But summer's over and you're gone

Holy smokes – it's BETHani! A new murmur of excitement, as younger spectators crane their necks to hiss in the ears of parents, aunts, uncles – it's '3Wishes', the song she wrote after she broke up with Nick from Four to the Floor, when there were all those pictures of her at her mum's wearing skanky clothes and actually looking quite fat – some people said that was all just part of the publicity, but how could you think that if you listened to the words?

> I miss the bus and the walk's so long
> I got split ends and my homework's wrong

> There's a hole in my sneaker and gum on my seat
> And the world don't turn and my heart don't beat

– which the girl who's singing now fills with such longing, such loneliness, only amplified by the crackling of the phone, that even parents who view BETHani with suspicion or disapproval (often coloured, in the case of the dads, by a shameful fascination) find themselves swept up by its sentiments – sentiments that, separated from their r'n'b arrangement and grafted onto this melancholy spiralling music three hundred years old, reveal themselves as both heart-rending and also somehow comforting – because their sadness is a sadness everyone can recognize, a sadness that is binding and homelike.

> And the sun don't shine and the rain don't rain
> And the dogs don't bark and the lights don't change
> And the night don't fall and the birds don't sing
> And your door don't open and my phone don't ring

So that as the chorus comes around once more, you can hear young voices emerge from the darkness, singing along:

> I wish you were beside me just so I could let you know
> I wish you were beside me I would never let you go
> If I had three wishes I would give away two,
> Cos I only need one, cos I only want you

– so that for these few moments it actually seems that Ruprecht could be right, that everything, or at least the small corner of everything that is the Seabrook Sports Hall, is resonating to the same chord, the same feeling, the one that over a lifetime you learn a million ways to camouflage but never quite to banish – the feeling of living in a world of apartness, of distances you cannot overcome; it's almost as if the strange out-of-nowhere voice is the universe itself, some hidden aspect of it that rises momentarily over the motorway-roar of space and time to console you, to remind you that although you can't overcome the distances, you can still sing the song – out into the darkness, over the separating voids, towards a fleeting moment of harmony . . .

And then – just as manly hands throughout the Hall move clandestinely to brush away rogue tears – something happens. At first it's hard to detect what it is, other than that it's *wrong*, very wrong. Heads recoil involuntarily; a spasm of distress flickers across Father Laughton's cheek, as at some transcendental toothache.

It's the song – it appears to have somehow *bifurcated*; that is to say, it continues on as it was, but also and at the same time in a different key. The result is viscerally, nails-across-a-blackboard ugly, but the musicians do not seem to have noticed, and continue not to notice as the song does it again, so that there are now *three* versions playing at once, in different keys – and then another, and another, like parallel-universe Canons somehow gathered into the same auditorium, getting louder all the while. Wildly you look to either side of you, wondering if you're going mad, because this surely is what madness must sound like. Everywhere you see hands pressed to ears, faces shrivelled up like snails retreating into their shells. Now as the layers mount on top of one another, some supra-song begins to loom above them, a song of all possible songs, something not so much heard as felt, like the awful oppressive atmospheric weight preceding a storm or other impending catastrophe. The volume soars; still Ruprecht et al. play on impassively. The engineer at the sound-desk regards his levels in horror; and now the Automator staggers out from the wings and into the waves of ineluctable noise, which has now achieved the status of *unthinkable, impossible*, no longer remotely discernible as a song; he lurches over the stage, like a man in a hurricane, only to be assailed, just as he reaches Ruprecht, by a peal of sonic energy that is like nothing on Earth –

★

Howard had driven to Seabrook at full tilt – his hand, bound clumsily in a huge swollen mitten of linen bandage, screaming every time he had to change gears or apply the brake, making him scream along with it – without knowing quite what he would do when he got there. The vague plan he had in his mind, of unmasking the coach in front of a gasping audience, followed by a Hollywood-style punch-up, Howard and Tom *mano a mano*, had, he knew, some serious holes (how could he fight with an injured hand? How could he fight a *disabled man*?); still, for the moment he preferred to leave these to one side, instead racing ahead to the aftermath, in which he arrived at Halley's door, bruised and bloody from his encounter, but – as she would recognize instantly – inwardly restored. She would quieten his burbled apologies with a finger to the lips; she would smile that smile he had missed so much – so bright and strong, like a kinder, warmer cousin of light – and take him by his good hand inside to her bed.

All these fantasies had been summarily squashed by the Automator. Ever since, Howard has been in the Ferry, trying to stoke up the remnants of his anger – 'He *hit* me! The fucker actually *hit* me' – sufficiently that he can . . . that he can what? Take the coach behind the swimming pool and teach him a lesson, like they were both fourteen years old? And then everything would be peachy, the world restored? Too late: reality has indelibly set in again. So he abandons his plans and just drinks. The pain in his hand provides an excellent excuse. It is excruciating, and has extended itself to colonize his entire body; everything pounds at him, like clumsy fingers on a piano – the laughter and grumbling of the other drinkers, the beauty of the beautiful lounge girl, the hideous carpet, the miasma of body odour . . . and now a familiar hound's-tooth jacket.

'Ah, Howard, wasn't expecting to find you here . . .' Jim Slattery pulls up a stool, motions to the lounge girl. 'Mind if I . . . ?'

Howard makes an indifferent gesture with his good hand.

'Didn't make it to the concert?'

'Sold out.'

'Yes, indeed, even those of us with tickets – that is to say, there was a group of late arrivals from KPMG, Greg asked me if I wouldn't mind . . . Didn't bother me, of course, especially if it gives me the chance of a snifter without herself being any the wiser – cheers.' The clink of glass causes Howard to wince, and the wince to set off a chain of small agonies. 'Good lord – what happened to your hand?'

'Caught it in a mousetrap,' is the tight reply.

'Oh,' Slattery says equanimously. He sips at his drink, swirls it around his mouth. 'I heard you'd been in the wars lately. That is to say, not just with the mice.'

'Rodents of one kind or another,' Howard says; then reflecting, he adds glumly, 'mostly brought it on myself, though.'

'Oh well. Things will come round, I'm sure.' Howard merely grunts at this; the older man clears his throat and changes the subject. 'You know, I came across something the other day that made me think of you. An essay by Robert Graves. "Mammon and the Black Goddess".'

'Ah, Graves.' Howard, who feels that the poet has something to answer for in his present situation, smiles sardonically. 'Whatever happened to old Graves?'

'Well, I daresay you know most of the story – married after the war, moved to Wales, tried to live the domestic life. Didn't last long, as you can imagine. He got himself mixed up with a poetess, an American named Laura Riding, and took off with her to Mallorca, where they set up shop with her as his muse. She was as mad as a hatter, by all accounts. Ran away with an Irishman, named Phibbs if I recall.'

'Some muse,' Howard remarks bitterly.

'As a matter of fact that fitted Graves's conception of things pretty neatly. The muse is an embodiment of the White Goddess, you see. If she settles down with you and starts a home, then she loses her powers. Becomes merely a woman, so to speak. Which means no more poetry, which in Graves's eyes was almost as bad as death. If she deserts you, on the other hand, then you find another muse to inspire you, and the whole circus starts all over again.'

'Makes you wonder why you'd even bother,' Howard says.

'There must have been an element of self-punishment to it, I think. Graves had always suffered tremendous guilt over his part in the war, the men he'd killed and seen killed. And then, you see, his son died – his son David was killed in Burma, in the Second World War. Graves had encouraged him to sign up, and helped him to get into the Royal Welch Fusiliers, his old regiment. It was directly after the death of his son that he started writing about the White Goddess, all this business about suffering and sacrifice in the name of poetry. Trying to make sense of it all, in his own barmy way.'

Howard says nothing, recalls Kipling and Ruprecht Van Doren.

'But that's what was interesting about this essay,' Slattery says. 'Near the end of his life Graves met a Sufi mystic, who told him about another goddess, a Black Goddess. Mother Night, the Greeks called her. This Black Goddess existed beyond the White. Instead of desire and destruction, she represented wisdom and love – not romantic love, but real love, as you might say, reciprocating, enduring love. Of those who devoted their lives to the White Goddess, and this endless cycle of ravagement and restoration, a very few, if they managed to survive it, would eventually pass through her to the Black Goddess.'

'Good for them,' Howard says. 'And what about everybody else? All the mugs who don't manage to transcend or whatever?'

Slattery's face crumples into a smile. 'Graves said that the best thing to do was to develop a strong sense of humour.'

'A sense of humour,' Howard repeats.

'Life makes fools of us all sooner or later. But keep your sense of humour and you'll at least be able to take your humiliations with some measure of grace. In the end, you know, it's our own expectations that crush us.' He raises his glass, sending ice cubes tumbling about his upper lip, and drains it. 'I suppose I should be getting along, before my own goddess starts to wonder. Goodbye, Howard. Keep in touch. I hope I'll see you before too long.'

Just as the door closes behind Slattery, the lights go out in the pub, and the sudden darkness is filled by a dim but quite unearthly noise – at once eerie and, somehow, mechanical . . . but it lasts for only a few seconds, and then power is restored, and all returns to normal. The drinkers settle back into their chat; Howard, with no one to talk to, contents himself with nursing his drink and watching the lounge girl as she crosses and recrosses the floor, tray in hand – another muse-in-waiting, another goddess who would transform everything, whose beauty you could surely never get tired of . . .

Muses, goddesses, it sounds so preposterous, but wasn't that how Halley had appeared to him in the beginning? A fragment of pure otherness, a radiance who burned through the stale facts of his life like a flame through an old picture? She told him stories of her home and he heard something transcendental; he looked at her and he saw another world – America! – a magic soil where dreams, like seeds, would alight and instantly take root – far away from this tiny island where you never lost your old nickname, where people couldn't help sliding into the positions left by their fathers and mothers, the same ones at the top, middle and bottom all the time, the same names in the school yearbook.

And she, no doubt, had done the same with him. She had looked at him and seen Ireland, or whatever she thought that was; she had seen history, paganism, romantic landscapes, poetry, and not a man who needed help to love. From the beginning, each was for the other first and foremost a flesh-and-blood representative of a different life, a passport into a fresh new future; what had happened since then was nothing more or less cruel than the real person seeping through the illusion – not a gateway to anything, just somebody like you, fumbling their way through the day.

A sense of humour, he thinks. A sense of humour. If only someone had told him before.

Two hours after the chaos that closed the Seabrook College 140th Anniversary Concert – when it seemed that nothing could ever be quiet again – and the school is calm once more, although anyone who was present at the Quartet's performance is still experiencing it as a ringing in his ears, and over the next few days a lot of people will be talking IN CAPITAL LETTERS. Everyone else has gone to bed; Geoff, Dennis and Mario are sitting on the slatted benches of the unlit Rec Room.

'What did he say?' Mario asks. 'Are you going to be expelled?'

'Probably,' Dennis says.

'We have to go and see him first thing on Monday,' Geoff says. 'He said he needed time to think before he decided what our punishment should be?'

'Shit-o-rama,' Mario says. 'This is a high price to pay for a foolish experiment that did not work.'

'Totally worth it,' Dennis says. 'Best thing Von Boner's done in his whole useless overweight life.'

In terms of the comprehensive destruction of a night's entertainment, Ruprecht's experiment was an unqualified success. The multifrequencied Pachelbel loop, building and building so unendurably, was merely a starter, noise-wise. Just as the Automator took the stage, the Van Doren Wave Oscillator crashed. Instantly, the Sports Hall was filled with a jangle of indescribable static: keening, popping, crackling, hissing, tweeting, belching, roaring, gurgling, a bedlam of utterly alien sounds unleashed at such a volume as to be palpable physical presences, a menagerie of impossible beasts marauding through our reality, disembodied, robotic voices interspersed among them, like a demented mechanical Pentecost . . .

Too much for this audience; they fled for the doors. Hats were lost in the jostle, spectacles crushed, women knocked to the ground; they ran until they reached the entrance to the car park, where, a safe distance away, they turned back to view the still-ululating Hall, as though expecting it to implode or lift off into the sky. It did not; instead, after a couple of moments, the noise came to a sudden halt, as the sound-desk shorted out and with it the school power supply, at which point a large minority of them stormed back in again to track down the Automator and ask him *what the hell kind of bloody game he was playing at.*

'I'm damned if I'm paying you ten thousand a year to turn my son into a *terrorist* –'

'This never would have happened in Father Furlong's day!'

It took nearly an hour of placating, assuaging and mollifying before the Automator could return to his office, where the Quartet had been confined. When he did, he made little effort to disguise his fury. He railed; he roared; he pounded the desk, sending photographs and paperweights flying. There was a new tone in his voice tonight. Before he'd treated them as he treated all the boys – like insects, flimsy and inconsequential. Tonight he spoke to them like enemies.

Ruprecht got the worst of it. Ruprecht, a deviant who had brought his parents nothing but shame; Ruprecht, whose brilliance covered a deep-rooted degeneracy of which this farrago was merely the latest example. You know what I'm talking about, Van Doren. The Acting Principal stared across the desk at him, like a ravenous animal through the bars of its cage. A lot of things have become clear to me now, he said, a lot of things.

The others were all crying; but Ruprecht just stood there, head bowed, while words fell on him like axes to the chest.

I'll be honest with you, boys, the Automator concluded. For various legal reasons expulsion can be difficult to arrange these days. It's not impossible you'll get away with a long suspension. And in a way I hope you do. Because it means I will have the next four and a half years to make your lives hell. I will make them a living hell. You assholes.

'Mamma Mia,' Mario says now.

'He can say what he wants,' Dennis retorts. 'We're part of Seabrook history now. I mean, people are going to be talking about this for *decades*.' The moon has peeped out from behind a cloud, and he is seized with a creeping euphoria. 'The look on my mum's face! Oh, Von Boner, you are a genius after all!' A thought occurs to him. 'Hey, maybe if I get expelled I could write his biography. What do you think? *Bummer on the Loose: The Ruprecht Van Doren Story.*'

'Where *is* Ruprecht, anyway?' asks Mario. 'He's not in his room.'

'He seemed pretty down,' Geoff remarks cautiously.

'Well, what did he expect?' Dennis says. 'Skippy's going to appear in a big ball of light and give us all high fives?'

'I did not say to Ruprecht before, but if I am in Heaven getting it on with a sexy angel, there is no way I am coming back to attend some gay school concert,' Mario says, then with a yawn rises from the bench. 'Anyhow, I have heard enough bollocks for one evening. For the record, I hope you are not expelled. I would miss you guys, though this does not make me a homosexual.'

''Night, Mario.'

'Yeah, whatever.' The door wheezes shut behind him. For a time, the remaining two sit in silence, each occupied with his own thoughts; Geoff turned to the window, as if the faint silvering cast by the unveiled moon might reveal everything absent to be right out there in the yard . . . Then, after taking a moment, perhaps to summon up courage, he says casually to Dennis, 'You don't think it worked?'

'What?'

'Ruprecht's experiment, you don't think it worked?'

'Of course not.'

'Not even a little bit?'

'How could it possibly have worked?'

'I don't know,' Geoff says, and then, 'it's just that when all that noise started . . . I thought I heard a voice that sounded like Skippy's.'

'Are you talking about the German truck driver?'

'Didn't he sound a lot like Skippy?'

'Okay, explain to me why Skippy would be talking in German, about trucks.'

'I suppose,' Geoff admits.

'Geoff, you should know by now that none of Ruprecht's ideas ever works. And this one was off the wall even by his standards.'

'Right,' Geoff says. His face falls a little; then rouses, as he is struck by something. 'Hey though – if you didn't ever think it would work, how come you agreed to do it?'

Dennis considers this, and then at last, 'I would say malice.'

'Malice?'

'Like the Automator said. Malice, wanting to spoil the concert for everybody, that sort of thing.'

'Oh.' Geoff allows a polite interval to elapse while he affects to take this on board. In the moonlight he has been seized by a tingle of euphoria – the same sensation Dennis had earlier, reflecting on the concert, only Geoff's is from a different source. Then, attempting to muffle his delight, he says, 'I know the real reason you did it.'

'Oh, you do?' Dennis all caustic surprise. 'Enlighten me, please.'

'You did it because you wanted all of us to be together again. You knew it wouldn't work, and you knew we'd get in trouble, but you also knew that what Skippy would want, if he was here, is for us all still to be friends? And this was the only way to do it. And even though it didn't work, it did sort of work, because when we're all together, it's like Skippy's there too, because each of us has his own little jigsaw piece of him he remembers, and when you fit them all together, and you make the whole picture, then it's like he comes to life.'

Dennis remains silent, then issues a long, slow tocking with his tongue. 'Geoff, how long have you known me? Is that really the kind of thing you think I'd think? Because if it is I'm very disappointed.'

'Mmm, yeah, I knew you'd say that too.'

'I'm going to bed,' Dennis says peremptorily. 'I don't have to sit here and listen to my character being assassinated.'

He gets up; then he stops, sniffing the air. 'Did you just cut one?' he says.

'No.'

Dennis sniffs the air again. 'That is *rough*. You need to stop eating those urinal cakes, Geoff.'

With that he's gone, and now Geoff's alone in the Rec Room. But he doesn't *feel* alone, not nearly as alone as you can feel sometimes, when the room is full of people playing table tennis and copying homework and throwing wet tissues at each other: in the wake of Ruprecht's song, everything seems unusually placid, contented, still; and you can sit, just another object, not so colourful as the pool table nor so lightful as the Coke machine, and think of what Skippy might say if he were here, and what you, Geoff, might say back to him; until a yawn comes over you, and you rise and pad back out to get your toothbrush and go to bed – so tired all of a sudden you don't notice the evermore acrid tint to the air, nor the first wisps of malign black smoke as they creep up the stairs.

It sounded like when you set an animal on fire. Then all around him were black bodies rising out of the grass. They rose up, they were screaming, only Carl could hear them.

Then he was on the street outside his house. He didn't know how he got there. The noise was gone, THEY were gone, but the night kept getting darker and darker. He blinked to push it back but then it came crashing in again. Lights did not make any difference. The rain in the pocks of the path joined up to make words he could not say, words made of secret letters. Every word was a shell that held an empty universe.

The key was in the door. There was mud on his trousers.

Carl's life had become a series of scenes featuring Carl. They joined up for a second like words made of rain in the pocks of a path then came apart again. Everything was like an answer that was on the tip of your tongue. Coats. Tiny flowers of the wallpaper.

He could not remember how things join up!

The bodies, the shadows, a thousand, a million, going, WE ARE THE DEAD. So loud, the horrible sound! The Druid staring at Carl with his mouth open. Then in a glow Dead Boy at their front.

That's when Carl ran, he ran all the way back home.

The living room smelled like chemicals. *I love the smell of napalm in the morning.* Light shot at you from everywhere! Gleam gleam went the wood and glass, the TV, the rowing machine, the gin bottle. Through the dark. On the couch Mom lay. From the doorway it looked like a fairy-tale with a princess fallen asleep in an enchanted garden. The curtain was open, the streetlight shone on her bare legs. Carl reached down and very gently, like he was plucking a flower, took the burned-down cigarette from between her fingers. He carried it to the fireplace and put it there.

In the kitchen he poured water into a glass. He held up the glass and looked into it. In the glass the room: the cream walls, the grey refrigerator, the cookery books with famous TV chefs on the never-opened covers, all shivery and blurred. He drank and felt the room wobbling icy-cold in his stomach. Now when you open your eyes there will be nothing there.

Carl!

He opened his eyes. He was in the living room. Mom rose silver out of her sleeping body and floated above it. She watched Carl but did not speak. The moon was full, they had turned it into a streetlight. She looked down sad like something terrible was going to happen. But it was not she who said Carl's name.

Standing right next to Carl was Dead Boy.

Oh fuck!

Now when you stared at him he did not disappear any more. That was what happened on the hill, that was why Carl was screaming. You screamed and screamed, FUCK OFF and I'M SORRY, he just hovered, he just smiled. Now he was here in Carl's house, there was nowhere left to run.

He is dead. I've been wanting to talk to you, he said.

He can talk?!

First you had to smoke the poppies first, then I can talk to you.

???

The poppies are made of In the war they grew out of the bodies From the LAND OF DEATH People spat on them So They moved underground To give them ANTEROGRADE AMNESIA so When you smoke them Now you can see us

Do you live in the dolmen? Carl said.

Dead Boy nodded. It is very cold, he said.

Yes that is what THEY said, now he remembered We are cold We are sad.

I am cold too, he said.

I know, Carl, said Dead Boy.

Then he realized: Dead Boy is his friend! He wanted to help him! That was why he'd been appearing!

Carl's eyes were full of tears. Lori won't talk to me, he told Dead Boy. It's like I'm dead too.

Dead Boy nodded.

I love her, Carl said. How can I get her to talk to me again?

You have to show her that we're friends now.

But how?

You have to help me finish the quest, Dead Boy whispered.

Everything went dark like the room was filled with [black paint] [millions of crows].

Carl was afraid. The quest?

You have to kill the final Demon. Now it was just Dead Boy's eyes like two big moons.

It's the priest, Carl. It's the peterphile. He's the one who killed me.

He is? Carl said.

Dead Boy nodded slowly.

Something was not right about this but Carl shook it away.

Everything glowed.

You have to show her.

The holy fire, Mom said above the couch. Her hand was a flame.

And Carl knew what he had to do.

Father Green had intended to attend tonight's concert, if only out of a childish wish to irritate Greg. But at the very last minute he had been called out to administer the last rites to an ailing woman on the other side of the city. He drove for an hour only to find she had made a miraculous recovery. Father Green had no option but to concede the point to his rival. Well played, sir! When he returned everyone had gone. The halls are empty as he makes his way down to his basement office, where he will sit and watch the hands of the clock.

No work, Jerome? That's not like you! Getting old at last?

It has been like this since the boy died. He does not work, he does not sleep. You know he sees him still, in his office, dutifully folding cardboard sheets into boxes, taping shut the flaps, oblivious to the silent battle raging only a few feet away, the carnal ravenings of an old man. Even now, approaching Our Lady's Hall, Father Green thinks he hears footsteps behind him; and he cannot stop himself from a shiver of hope as he turns round. But of course there is nothing.

At the top of the hall, he stops by the crib – as yet only half-occupied: no Infant, no Kings, only the oxen and donkeys to keep watch over the Holy Parents as they kneel in the straw. Before it, the offerings for the hampers. He bends to examine the labels. Mascarpone cheese, semi-sundried tomatoes, lychees. Donations are down this year. The idea of giving food, of taking actual food from your larder and putting it in another's, must seem tiresomely Victorian in this ethereal age of numbers flying through the air. Poverty far too literal for these abstracted people.

That is not the reason, Jerome. The reason is you.

Yes. Father Green is aware of the rumours surrounding him.

He sees the graffiti on his door; he hears the whispers, detects the snubs in the corridor, the staffroom, the vestry even. All in all it has pained him surprisingly little: the blessing of being an unsociable man. Except that now it has taken away what power he had to do good. For how can a criminal tug at anyone's conscience? Who will give to a monster? He himself becomes the excuse not to think of those wretched slums, those addled lives. Irony upon irony! One always underestimates the capacity of life to diminish one.

So why do you stay?

He asks himself the same question as he descends the steps to the office. Why stay? He has given Greg his scapegoat. Scandal is averted, the swimming coach may make his escape unblemished, the school continue as a shining beacon of the bourgeoisie. What they *need* of him now is to go. Go, that they may curse his name and forget this ever happened. And he *wants* to go. He has done enough for Seabrook. Why stay, to be calumnied? To be painted with the sins of another?

It's obvious, Jerome. You wish the sin had been yours. That's why you will not tell the truth, that's why you will not leave. Instead you must stay here and be punished. Yet you committed no crime.

Only because I was afraid.

Ah, Jerome. Come, it is over. The boy is in the ground, with nothing to touch his lips but the worms. You have done him no wrong. Why must you torture yourself?

Why?

For Africa? For what happened forty years ago? Who remembers, Jerome? Those little boys? Most likely they are dead too. So who then? God? But what God do you believe in any more?

The priest sits at his desk, leafs through the paperwork unseeingly.

You would rather punish yourself than accept the alternative, is that not so, Jerome.

That noise outside again. Footsteps?

None of this matters. That is what you will not accept. None of it

639

has mattered, nothing you did, the good, the bad. And nothing matters now.

Definitely something out there. A smell too, acrid. He rises, crosses the floor.

But you, you would rather burn than think this. You would rather hellfire, than look at the world and see the truth. See nothing.

Tears, or the ache of tears that will not come. He opens the door. As the red flame leaps for him he staggers backwards. Shock at first, but then a glimmer of joy.

Hellfire!

Howard stumbles out into December. The night, once it has slipped its fingers beneath his insulation of alcohol, is exceptionally cold, with a sour, chemical note to the air. He walks back in the direction of the school car park, deferring until he gets there the knowledge that he is unfit to drive and has not enough money for a taxi. His conscience taunts him with memories of the many times Halley rescued him from comparable situations, driving across the whole city sometimes to pick him up, and he falls morosely into his fantasy of earlier on – calling at her door, attractively bloodied from his encounter with Tom Roche, to be swept up into her arms. Somehow he doesn't think turning up unbruised, sacked and drunk will have quite the same effect.

The moon tonight is full, and bright enough that he notices it disappear when he turns in the gate. He looks up, and sees an enormous black cloud printed over the school. It is of an unusual solidity, and low enough to partially obscure the Tower. The very next moment, all the lights in the upper floors come on; and now – he finds himself braced for it – the frenetic shrilling of the alarm clamours into the sleeping yard. Breaking into a run, he hurries down the avenue, through the car park, the dense black cloud growing over his head all the while, until, passing the Sports Hall, he arrives in the Quad.

The never-opened doors at the top of Our Lady's Hall have been flung open, and boys are pouring out like pyjama'd ants from a disturbed nest, coils of black smoke snaking out with them at ankle height and slithering opportunistically into the night. Already the heat is palpable, a tropical warmth on his cheek. Bright amorphous hands beat at the leaded glass of the windows, and from within comes a rapturous roar of destruction, mingled with crashes and breaking. Howard locates Brian Tomms by the doors, hollering at the exiting boys to line up in order of their dorms. 'What's going on?' he yells over the alarm.

'Fire.' Tomms does not appear surprised to see Howard. 'Seems to've started in the basement. We've put in a call to the fire brigade, but it'll probably have eaten up the Tower by the time they get here.' He speaks in calm, clipped tones, a general surveying his battlefield. 'Looks deliberate to me.'

'Can I do anything?'

'We've got most of the boys out. These are just the last few.'

As he speaks the crocodile line begins to peter out and Tomms descends the steps to oversee the prefects as they do the head-count. The boys, dim-eyed, tuft-haired, wait in orderly two-by-two rows. A few are filming the event with their phones – the white shapes behind the glass like furious dancing ghosts – but most merely look on vacantly, as though attending a special mid-night assembly, lending the scene a weird peace.

Then it is broken by a commotion at the doors. Two fifth-years struggle to contain a handful of smaller boys, who are apparently attempting to run back into the school. Tomms runs over to help the prefects, and as they are jostled out into the Quad, Howard identifies the breakaways as Geoff Sproke, Dennis Hoey and Mario Bianchi from his second-year History class. The tears on their cheeks, in the unearthly light, give their faces the appear-ance of melting wax. 'He's still in there!' blurts Geoff Sproke from behind the chain of arms. 'He's not!' Tomms shouts him down. 'He's not, we checked!' As he speaks, a plume of fire shoots over the roof, bathing the onlookers in a freakish orange glow. 'Ruprecht! Ruprecht!' the boy's friends cry, throwing themselves once more against their captors. The sound is pitiful and thin against the flames, like kittens crying for their mother. With a sinking heart, Howard reels around and stumbles towards the doors. Heat blasts his face; beneath its bandages, his hand sings ecstatically, as if recognizing its own.

Burning, Our Lady's Hall has become something alive, something new and terrible. Flames race over the walls, seizing and devouring, and the dull matrix of the school beneath them – the chipped timber, the shabby plasterwork, the doorways, the desks, the statue of the Virgin – seems already to have retreated from the world, half-turned to shadow. Looking on, Howard feels like a dinosaur watching the first meteors fall; like he's witnessing an evolutionary leap, the arrival of an insuperable future. He imagines Greg's tropical fish boiling in their tank.

Tomms appears by his side at the threshold. Howard looks back at him in a daze. 'We have to do something.'

'There's no one in there,' Tomms says. 'We checked all the dorms.'

'Then where's Van Doren?'

Tomms does not reply. 'Could he be in the basement?' Howard says, thinking aloud.

'If he's in the basement, it's already too late. But why would he be down there?'

No reason, of course; and yet, looking into the phantasmagoria of clashing light, Howard has a terrible sense of something left undone. And then, 'What was that?'

'What?'

'Didn't you hear that? It sounded like . . . music.'

'I didn't hear anything,' Tomms says. His nostrils twitch, detecting the alcohol on the other teacher's breath. 'Come on, Howard, we need to get everyone clear.'

'I was sure I heard music,' Howard repeats distractedly.

'How would there be music?' Tomms asks. 'Come on, there's nothing more we can do.' He may not be an expert on history like Fallon, he may not have grand conversations about the First World War in the staffroom with Jim Slattery, but he knows plenty about fires – how they work, how hot they get, when you can be a hero and when you can't. 'Nothing,' he repeats confidently.

But before he can stop him Howard's disappeared into the burning school.

Desks are burning. Chairs are burning. Blackboards are burning. Crosses are burning. Maps of the world, set squares, rugby photographs. Everything you hate is on fire. So why are you crying?

Once upon a time Carl came in a window in the utility room. He had come to kill the Demon. The school was dark but after only a few moments the priest came walking down the hall. Carl followed him to his office. When the priest went in and closed the door, Carl poured petrol over it and up and down the basement. Then he set it on fire.

He waited in the fire just to be sure. The priest opened the door and stared around at the flames. Then he saw Carl, and he nodded like he'd been expecting him. He came out his door, Carl dodged back, but the priest went the other direction, a little way down the hall, and broke the glass of the fire alarm. Then he went back into his office and sat down in his chair. The bell rang, boys came running everywhere and teachers and prefects. Carl went to hide.

That was a hundred years ago, they've all gone now. Ever since, Carl has been walking in the smoke. It burns his eyes, it's dark as night, and every turn he makes just leads him further in. He thought when he killed the Demon something would happen! Lori would appear, Dead Boy would bring him to her! But there is nothing, only smoke. He walks, the flames make him think of the night he first met her, he was a dragon with flames coming from his mouth, burning Morgan Bellamy's small girly feet –

He stops.

Because he has just realized.

Flames from his mouth.

He's the one who killed me.

The Demon is not the priest.

The Demon is him.

He looks down at his hands. They are huge scaly claws. When he touches his face it's like rock.

He is the Demon. He is the one that has to die for the game to be over.

Now he knows, that is why he is crying.

The smoke is everywhere black like the world's been scribbled out. There's no way out of here. He's alone in the black fire. He feels so sad! But the smoke is so soft, it rolls around him like a blanket. So he lies down.

In the distance of his hand his phone rings. It is the World to tell him it's time to die. But that's okay, he is remembering other things. He is remembering that first night, when Lori rolled up to him and swept over him like a bright white wave. Even after everything he still has that night, and as the smoke piles up over him, becoming a Door that slowly opens, he holds it tight in his Demon's hand.

And when it sings to him – so far away, wrapped up in his fingers! – he imagines even after everything it is her voice, a song calling him, calling and calling him, to where she is waiting, into sleep.

But no one answers. She hangs up, goes to the window.

Outside there is a strange red light to the sky, and sirens are whirling over the trees and houses – Lori can't see though where they are or which way they're coming. The pills are laid out on her dresser, she sits down in the window sill and she waits.

An hour ago Ruprecht came to see her. That's two nights running he's come, if it was anyone else she would think he had a crush. He has this key that can open any door, e.g. the door at the back of the garden, he appears under her window and throws pebbles at the glass just like in *Romeo + Juliet* (except with Jabba the Hutt as Romeo and Skeletor as Juliet, ha ha). Nurse Dingle has been on both these nights, so Lori could go outside:

'I just want to get some fresh air?'

'Okay, sweetheart, but don't get cold!'

'I won't!' smiley-smile and she slowly walked down to the pergola where he was waiting for her.

When she looked at the window last night and saw him staring back, her heart felt like it had turned into a lump of ice there in her chest. She didn't know what he could want, except to scream at her again maybe, she didn't know why she agreed to go outside. She went down the stairs like she was in a dream, a dream where you're finally being sent to the guillotine, she walked over the grass with her whole body shaking. He was waiting for her among the December roses. She thought he might hit her, but he just stood and stared. He'd gotten fatter since the night in her room – much fatter, she was shocked. And he was shocked too, looking back at her, though he tried not to show it.

For a moment neither of them said anything. She watched the feelings battling in his face, she watched him attempt to smother the hate or cover it over at least. When he spoke at last his words were cold and emotionless. He told her he wanted her to sing with his quartet in the Seabrook Christmas concert.

That was not what she expected. She didn't know what to make of it. The first thing that came into her head was that it must be a set-up for some kind of revenge, like in that film where they pour blood on the girl?

We need a singer, he said, Skippy told me you could sing. Can you?

She didn't say anything.

We're trying to send him a message, he said, send Skippy a message.

Skippy's dead, she said automatically and instantly she got that horrible picture of kissing him in her room only his skin has gone green and his mouth is full of clay.

I know, he said, still we're trying to do it.

She didn't know what he meant, did he mean like a Ouija board? It sounded weird, and also Ruprecht didn't look well, he looked like he had a fever.

How? she said.

He started talking about strings. Apparently there are these really small strings that everything is made of. Once the strings were part of a much bigger universe, where everything was all joined together. But then it broke in two. One half of it became our universe, which got bigger and bigger and spread out faster and faster and made suns and planets including planet Earth. The other half did the opposite, it shrank until it was extremely tiny, tinier than you could ever conceive of. Now the miniature universe is hidden inside this one, except it's too small to see or touch. But the strings still join them both together and Ruprecht believed he could use them to conduct this song through to Daniel.

You think he's in the miniature universe?

There is a certain amount of scientific evidence, he said.

Science has always been Lori's least favourite class and she did not fully understand what he was talking about here. It sounded like

647

he was talking about Heaven, and in her mind she had a picture from one of Mom's art CD-ROMs of everyone looking up at the sky which had been part sort of torn away and light was coming through the hole and angels stood there with Jesus who was holding a flag. She had never imagined Daniel being in Heaven, she never thought of him being anywhere really, because whenever she did think of him her throat bunched up and she had the clay vision.

You don't have to understand, Ruprecht said. You just have to sing.

His eyes blinked and begged behind their thick glasses. She thought of how desperate you would have to be to come to someone you hated and ask them to do something this weird.

How can I sing? she said. I can't leave here.

We have a plan for that. But will you do it?

I don't know, she said, I don't know. Once she had always wanted to be a singer, but it was so late now for anything like that, she was so tired, her body ached like a heap of old bones, like a game of Jenga that had been going on for ever and now just wanted to fall down. Then she asked Ruprecht what song he was going to do.

BETH𝔞nI, Ruprecht said. '3Wishes'.

And for a split second it was like everything in the garden lit up, *FOOM!* as if secretly there was a thousand-watt bulb hanging in the clouds and someone had turned it on. Because '3Wishes' was the song she'd sung that night to Daniel, on the way home from the Hop, and how many dreams had she had where she was back in that night singing it to him?

And so next morning – the morning of today, though it feels so long ago! – she took an extra-long shower and practised scales and training exercises she'd learned from the Internet, and she listened to '3Wishes' a trillion times even though the words were burned into her heart long ago. Then after Group 'dinner' she came upstairs and locked her door, and even though she wasn't leaving her room she did her make-up and hair and put on the dress Mom got her for the interview.

Then she took the pills from Lala's tummy and laid them out with the pills the nurse had given her on the dresser for when she was finished, because as soon as she'd heard Ruprecht say it, she knew the song was a sign – a sign that the Plan was ready, that tonight the sirens would come for her.

It was weird how the idea of singing in front of people, even just down a phone, was actually more frightening than being dead. Eight o'clock came like something falling out of the sky, getting huger and huger until it was all there was. She tried to get sick but there was nothing in her to get sick with. She bit her nails and listened to the tinny crackle of applause, Titch Fitzpatrick introducing the acts, other singers in her phone. Then at last Ruprecht's voice came in her ear. We're going on.

She could hardly hear the music but she sang as well as she could, just hoping. She sang walking around barefoot on her carpet and then she stood at the window and sang it looking out at the trees and stars and houses. The metronome tocked in the corner of her room – Ruprecht had set it the night before – she closed her eyes and imagined she was BETHani; then she imagined she was herself, walking back from the Hop with rain in her hair and Daniel beside her. She imagined the song was bringing that night to life around them, and if she kept singing it right, they would be able to walk right back into today . . . Then there was that freaky noise and the line went dead and she was standing on her own in a silent room.

She thought Ruprecht might call afterwards but he didn't. Still, she supposed that didn't matter now. She was feeling a strange floaty feeling – not like when you don't eat and you're going to faint, more like when she was little and she'd walk around the garden holding out a mirror and pretend she was tumbling upwards into the treetops and the sky. She stopped the metronome and sat down on the bed for a while, not even thinking. Then she got up and went over to the dresser where the pills were. She was wondering what to do when the pebble came rattling against the glass. Ruprecht! She ran to the door and tripped down the stairs – Don't get cold, Lori! I won't – and out into the garden.

But when she went behind the pergola and saw the expression on Ruprecht's face she got a surprise. His eyes were emptied out and his enormous fatness seemed somehow even heavier than before. It was like they had switched places from the previous night, like now she was feeling lighter but he had sunk deep into himself. In a low flat voice he said to her, It didn't work.

What didn't work?

The experiment. The song.

Oh, she said, though she didn't quite understand, how can a song not work?

The Wave Oscillator crashed. The feedback blew the speakers and shorted out the sound-desk. We only did thirty per cent of the cycle. The message didn't go through.

Oh, she said again. And then, I'm sorry.

It wasn't your fault, he said. But I thought you'd want to know.

Thank you, she said. It was then she noticed the rucksack on his back. Are you going somewhere, she said.

I'm leaving, he said.

Leaving? He had a box of doughnuts in his hand too. Where are you going?

I'm not sure, he said. Probably Stanford, they're doing some really interesting work on strings there. He told her this in a flat heavy voice, as if they could be clubbing seals or baking brownies and it wouldn't make much difference to him.

Are you leaving because the experiment failed?

He shrugged. There doesn't seem any particular reason to stay.

What about your friends?

He shrugged again, and smiled a nuclear-winter smile; and with a shudder Lori realized that here was someone on the verge of something terrible – that whatever he might say about Stanford or anywhere else, his plan was the plan of someone starved of hope, who saw the future merely as an EXIT sign leading into a black void. She knew because this was how she saw it too, and she knew it was all because of Daniel, because of that gap in Ruprecht's world which he had left there. But what was Ruprecht doing *here*? What did he expect her to do about it? Hunched beside his bloated body in the cold dark suddenly she felt exhausted, as though the weight of him was dragging her downwards; a nauseating gust of oniony sweat wafted to her from his body and with a violence that surprised her she wished he would go! Bother someone else! Leave her to her plan, the pills that had been arranged on her nightstand to spell LORELEI, that would take her away away away from the world and its endless problems.

Ruprecht must have sensed this, because he stood up and said, I should probably get moving.

Okay, she said.

But he didn't go. Instead he hovered, and the wind, the empty wind, blew around them, around his mass of blubber and her toothpick-skeleton; it reminded her of what he'd said about the two universes, one expanding like it would never stop, the other shrinking and shrinking into itself – both of them running from some horror of the past, two halves of something that used to be whole now running, without thinking, without seeing, away from each other and into death. And she realized that there was no someone else. For some reason she did not understand, Ruprecht had come to her tonight; and she was the last person he would come to. She was all that kept him tethered to the Earth. If she let go of him, if she went through the dark door swung open before her, he too would disappear for ever from the world.

From upstairs the pills called out to her!

And in the distance the sirens, the singing girls, crying, Lori Lori!

But she gritted her teeth and squared her bony shoulders and as he moved for the back gate she called out sharply, Ruprecht!

From the doorway Nurse Dingle's musical voice, Lori!

In a minute, she yelled back.

Then to Ruprecht, I don't think you should go to Stanford. Not now.

He blinked back at her expressionlessly. But what could she tell him? What reasons could *she* give for not going? Look at her, what could she possibly tell anyone about anything?

I know it seems like there's nothing left here for you, she said slowly. But maybe there is, and you just can't see it?

Blink, blink, went Ruprecht. God, this was so hard! When she was beautiful this kind of thing was so much easier, all she had to do was look at a boy and he'd be doing cartwheels down the street! But those days were gone, and she found she had no idea how you would get inside the fortress of another person.

It's like . . . Arrgh, come on, Lori, she searched around in her brain for something not useless and black, but all she could think of was something they'd done in French class once about this poet, which she didn't know if it had anything to do with what they were talking about now. Still, it was all she had so she said it. His name was Paul Éluard, and he said this thing once: *There is another world, but it is in this one.*

Ruprecht looked baffled.

It's about how – she could feel herself going red, she squeezed her eyes tight shut, trying to remember what Mr Scott had told them – like, how people are always *going* somewhere? Like everybody's always trying to be *not where they are*? Like they want to be in Stanford, or in Tuscany, or in Heaven, or in a bigger house on a fancier street? Or they want to be different, like thinner or smarter or richer or with cooler friends (or dead, she did not say). They're so busy trying to find their way somewhere else they don't see the world they're actually in. So this guy's saying, instead of searching for ways out of our lives, what we should be searching for are ways *in*. Because if you really look at the world, it's like . . . it's like . . .

What the fuck was she talking about, he must think she's such a spa.

It's like, you know, inside every stove there's a fire. Well, inside every grass blade there's a grass blade, that's just like burning up with being a grass blade. And inside every tree, there's a tree, and inside every person there's a person, and inside this world that seems so boring and ordinary, if you look hard enough, there's a totally amazing magical beautiful world. And anything you would want to know, or anything you would want to happen, all the answers are right there where you are right now. In your life. She opened her eyes. Do you know what I mean?

Like strings? he said.

Well, no, not really, she said uncertainly, but then she thought about it and changed her mind. No, actually, totally like strings. Because you told me they're everywhere, right? They're all around us, it's not like they're just in Stanford.

Ruprecht nodded slowly.

So you could study them right here, couldn't you?

He began to say something about lab facilities, but she cut him off, because she had just had an idea. Like maybe all you need is someone to help you, she said. Like Daniel did.

He did not reply to this, gazed at her from deep within hamster cheeks.

Maybe *I* could help you, she said, or rather the idea said, though inside her head a voice shrieked, *What are you saying?* Like I don't know anything about science, she said, ignoring it. Or strings or other dimensions. But I could get stuff from the shops for you? I could get my dad to drive you places? Or just, when you're busy with an experiment I could bring you lunch? I mean, I'm not going to be in this place for ever.

You want to go back out there? exclaimed the voice. *To that?* But again she ignored it, watched Ruprecht's eyes watching hers. Why don't you stay, Ruprecht, she said. For a little while more, at least.

He pressed his lips together; then he bowed his head as if he had arrived somewhere after a very long journey.

The wind shook the leaves and everything in the garden.

After she let him out the back gate, she stood there for a moment, under the splashing ivy. She was thinking about that French class. It was months ago, but now she thought about it,

653

she found she remembered nearly everything – the cream sweater Mr Scott wore, his hair just beginning to need to be cut, the taste of chewing gum in her mouth, fluffy clouds chasing through the trees, the hairs on Dora Lafferty's neck in front of her, the classroom smell of lipstick and old runners. She remembered telling herself to remember what Paul Éluard said, because it seemed important. But things like the world-inside-this-one are too big to hold in your head by yourself. You need someone to remind you, or else, you need someone you can tell, and you have to keep telling each other, over and over, throughout your whole life. And as you tell them, the things are slowly binding you together, like tiny invisible strings, or like a frisbee that's thrown back and forth, or like words written on the floor in syrup. TELL LORI. TELL RUPRECHT.

Maybe instead of strings it's stories things are made of, an infinite number of tiny vibrating stories; once upon a time they all were part of one big giant superstory, except it got broken up into a jillion different pieces, that's why no story on its own makes any sense, and so what you have to do in a life is try and weave it back together, my story into your story, our stories into all the other people's we know, until you've got something that to God or whoever might look like a letter or even a whole word . . .

Then she walked back towards the house. Suddenly there was mist everywhere, a silver mist, like the Earth was breathing magic breaths; she walked very slowly, with her eyes closed, like a sleepwalker, and as she did she imagined she could feel invisible veils drift over the fine hairs of her arm, break across her face and hands, fragile as a breath or more fragile; she walked and dreamed that she was passing through all these veils and travelling deeper and deeper into . . . into the night? into where she already was?

Ruprecht left his doughnuts behind. Now the box sits beside her on the window sill. She scoops the pills up from the dresser and replaces them in Lala's tummy. Outside, the sirens go whirling off in another direction, leaving only the sky stretched over the houses, the lonely beautiful universe, a sad song played on a broken instrument. She wonders if Skippy did hear them tonight. Ruprecht told her that even though you can't see strings, scientists believed the theory was true because it was the most beautiful explanation. So, Skippy heard their song, that would be the beautiful explanation, wouldn't it? For tonight?

She picks up her phone and tries Carl again. She doesn't know what she will say when he answers. Maybe just, *Hey, what you doing?* Or, *Look at all the mist outside, I love it when it's misty!* She listens to the dial-tone, she imagines the phone ringing in the place that is his life, the music rising through the air to touch his ears. Opening the box, she takes out a doughnut. It looks like chocolate. She takes a bite.

IV

Afterland

A chairde,

I write this, my first Christmas Bulletin to you, with both a great sense of privilege and a deep sadness. Privilege, at taking on the mantle of Principal worn by so many illustrious men, most lately Father Desmond Furlong; sadness at the tragedies that have afflicted Seabrook College in the last two months.

Approaching as we do the end of the year, the temptation is to keep one's gaze fixed on the future, and draw a veil over the events which have already caused us such great sorrow. However, it has never been the way here at Seabrook College to shy away from problems or to flee the past; and although Seabrook's 140th year has not been an easy one, I think that we, as a school and a community, can take heart from the spirit in which we rose to its challenges.

That spirit was never more clearly demonstrated than during the events of 8 December. We know from our history books as well as our trophy cabinet that Seabrook has long been a nursing ground for heroes; that that terrible night was not more terrible still was due to the courage of three more. By now you have heard these stories many times, but you will forgive me if I take a moment, on behalf of the school and on behalf of you the parents, to remember once more the bravery of Brian Tomms, woodwork teacher and Dean of Boarders, in evacuating the Tower so promptly, and of Howard Fallon, history teacher, in rescuing from the premises a boy who had been trapped there. You will be pleased to learn that Howard's doctor in Seabrook Clinic (Milton Ruleman, Class of '78) is very happy with his progress and predicts a full recovery. We look forward to

Howard 'togging out' for us in the classroom again very soon. The boy in question is also, I am happy to say, on the mend.

Jerome Green's courage was apparent to all who knew him. He devoted his life to helping the weakest members of society, both in Africa and in his native land. His unstinting energy, his unflinching morality, his refusal to brook compromise, marked him out as a man in many ways too good for these times. It is fitting that his last act should have been to raise the alarm, and in this darkest of hours we may take some solace in the thought that this is how he might have wanted to go – in the service of his beloved Seabrook, the good shepherd protecting his flock. *Ní bheidh a leithéidse ann arís.*

Police are still looking into the causes of the fire, but it is believed to have been started by a similar electrical fault to the one that interrupted the Christmas concert. There has been much understandable concern among parents at the speed with which the flames spread in an area where students were housed. It goes without saying that these anxieties have been voiced at the very highest levels of the school. My personal feeling is that now is not the time for laying blame. Instead, we must set our minds to the future. For some time now, plans have been circulating to replace the 1865 building with a new, modern wing, and there is no longer any excuse for delay. Until that work is completed, classes for second- and third-years will take place in prefabs that have been very kindly donated by friends of the school; the boarding school will, as you have been notified, remain closed.

You will have seen reports in the media that the Holy Paraclete Fathers will shortly be turning over the day-to-day running of the school to a private management company. Contrary to these reports, this is a change that has been in train for a long time and is totally unrelated to recent events. More details will be made available in the coming months. At present it suffices to say that the management company will be headed by myself and a board of directors from the Seabrook alumni community, with